Jean-Luc & Anna Lise

A Novel of the Napoleonic Wars

A. G. Cullen

Jean-Luc & Anna Lise
A Novel of the Napoleonic Wars

First Edition: 2021

ISBN: 9781524316631
ISBN eBook: 9781524316792

© of the text:
  A. G. Cullen

© Layout, design and production of this edition: 2021 EBL Books

For Kathleen

Europe – 1812

Acknowledgements

First and last, my wife, Kathleen who reviewed my first draft, and many later drafts. This novel would not exist without her help.

The manuscript benefited enormously from my writing group, who endured reviewing and editing each chapter, sometimes multiple times. I'd like to thank Karla Von Huben, James Chesky, Jim Rogers, Sharon Harris, Georgeie Reynolds, Jessie McClure, Penny Simpson, Andi Crockford, and Kumiko Olson. Their honest assessments, while sometimes overwhelming, enabled me to make *Jean-Luc & Anna Lise* a much-improved book.

Aaron Redfern of the firm *Historical Editorial* provided copyediting services. He performed a thorough review, catching errors, and checking appropriateness of language to the time-period.

The Alsace

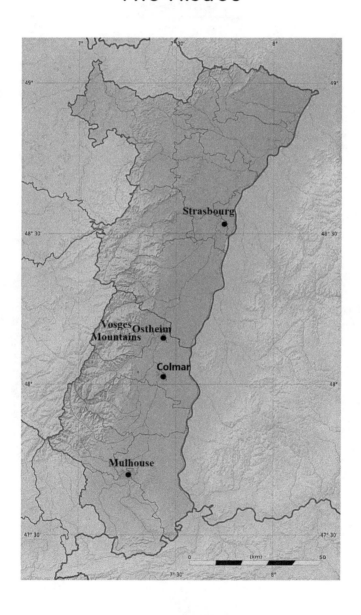

Table of Contents

One

Innocence Lost – Late Spring, 1795

A hard tug on my fishing pole jolts me from my slumber. Another tug. "Adrien, wake up," I whisper as I tense, waiting to jerk the pole with the next tug. But there's no need, as the pole nearly flies from my hands. I give Adrien a kick and hold on tight. "It must be a big one," I shout.

Now fully awake, Adrien grabs his net and wades into the river. "Jean-Luc, start walking your line back. I'm ready," he says excitedly. Slowly, I inch my way up the riverbank, struggling to maintain control over whatever is on the other end of my line. "I see it," my friend shouts. "It's a huge salmon! Move back a little more while I try to get behind him!"

I sense the giant fish's panic as it lashes one way, then the other. It's almost impossible to hold onto my pole. "I'm holding steady against a tree," I shout. "Am I far enough away yet?"

"Yes," Adrien cries. "... I'm waiting for it ... it's going to jump! Hold steady ... hold steady ... got it!"

Dropping my fishing pole, I rush to Adrien's side to admire my catch. Adrien knocks its head with a rock. The fish continues to flail and nearly gets away. Adrien hits it again. The fish flicks its tail one last time, then lies motionless.

After tossing our lines back into the water, we both slump to the ground, momentarily exhausted. We let the afternoon sun give us its warmth while the cool breeze coming across the water tempers the heat.

"I hope I catch one too," says Adrien. "*Vati* needs fresh fish for his butcher shop. He can't seem to get enough meat. He says the revolution is causing so many problems." He pauses. "Listen," he says in a low tone. "Do you hear that?"

I climb up onto the bridge and stretch myself up to see farther.

"What is it, Jean-Luc? What do you see?" The groans and creaks become louder. Then there it is: a man driving a wagon loaded with something that towers above him. I scurry down to my friend, wide-eyed.

"It's a wagon carrying something big. Quick, get the fishing equipment, and I'll grab our fish." We hide the fish and our equipment behind nearby bushes and creep up to a viewing spot hidden under the bridge. The horses drawing the wagon plod nearer, and the wagon wheels protest each turn as if in pain. "What is that?" I whisper anxiously to Adrien.

The wagon bed is filled with a large, odd-looking monstrosity that I've never seen before. Two tall beams, more than twice the height of a grown man, sprout from a heavy-looking wooden base. Another beam tops these two. Dropping from this top beam is a rope on a pulley, attached at the bottom to a slab of wood. A glint of metal peeks out near the middle of the bottom slab.

A skinny, tall young man is driving, sitting erect and staring straight ahead. "Look," whispers Adrien, "he's wearing striped pantaloons like the ones Monsieur Renard wears. My *vati* doesn't like Monsieur Renard. He says mean things about Germans and

Catholics. When he leaves our butcher shop, I've heard *Vati* swear under his breath, 'damned Jacobin', whatever that means."

The man quietly hums a tune as he drives past. I can't make it out, but it sounds very somber. He repeats the haunting tune over and over, sending a chill down my spine. Tied to the back is a tired-looking horse, trudging forward as the wagon rattles along. We peek around the side of the bridge and stare at the contraption until it is out of sight.

"What do you think that was?" I ask, feeling a tightening in my stomach. "I've heard people at our inn talk about terrible things in Paris. They use a machine to punish people who oppose the new republic. They say it slices off their heads with a single stroke. Do you think that was one of those things?"

"Maybe," Adrien replies slowly. "Customers in the butcher shop talk about awful happenings in the capital too. We're lucky we haven't seen them here and that Paris is so far away. Maybe the new leader sent this man and his wagon. Is it coming for someone in Colmar?" Adrien shrinks back down into the brush, recoiling from what this thing may be.

Seeing his fear gives me chills.

"We'll see if he's in Colmar when we go back home tonight," I say. "But first, let's catch another salmon."

Over the next few hours, thoughts about the strange man and his cargo slip away. We get lucky and snare two more fish. I smile at Adrien. "Our fathers will be pleased."

When we're not wrestling with giant salmon, we pass the time playing dominoes. After I beat Adrien for the fourth time, he flings the wooden tiles into the air. "Why do you always win?" he says sullenly. "Tomorrow, we play pick-up sticks. I can beat you at that."

Fine, I think to myself. *I'll let him win tomorrow. My gift for his ninth birthday.*

The edge of the sun begins to touch the hills, and we collect our gear and fish for the trudge home. The fish are heavy, slowing our progress.

Coming up to our village, we hear shouts coming from the central square. We quicken our steps to see what's happening. Crowds of people fill the square, extending all the way up to the far end bordered by the River Lauch. St. Mathew's, the Lutheran church, sits on the north side, and St. Marten's, the Catholic church, lies up the street from our inn on the south side. The crowd is especially thick on the cobbles in front of St. Marten's.

"Look," says Adrien. "That's the wagon!"

We approach carefully. Adrien's father spots us and summons in German to come to him quickly. My papa joins us as well. The two of them look worried.

After we reach the safety of our fathers' presence, I recognize the man who was driving the wagon. He's standing on it and shouting at the crowd, gesturing wildly. Flanking him is a contingent of armed men.

Standing before this man is our village priest, stooped over and on his knees, his hands clasped in prayer. His body rocks back and forth. One of the armed men stands next to him.

Adrien elbows me and points. "It *is* one of those new machines that slices off heads! Why is it in our village, and why is Father Benedict kneeling in front of it?"

The man on the wagon is speaking loudly and tersely. "We must no longer fear the power of the church. The priests have enslaved you—much like the noblemen, but worse. They use the fear of God to bend you to their will. No more! The revolution will protect you. Colmar is far from Paris, but we in the Committee of Public Safety learned that this priest ignored our directives. I've been sent to deal with him."

The crowd grows agitated. A few people are shaking angry fists toward this man, but most wear faces filled with apprehension or puzzlement. No one seems to know what is going on. I, too, am puzzled. Father Benedict is loved by everyone in the village. He is kind and generous to everyone, no matter their religion. Why is this man so angry with him?

A contemptuous grin crosses the driver's face. "Many of you appear to condone his actions. Perhaps this is from fear of the church's power?" He turns to his men. "Seize the priest and bring him up here."

People in the crowd turn to each other as they shrink back, away from the guillotine. Not far from our vantage point at the edge of the square, near our families' shops, we hear a few cheering in support. Among those cheering is Monsieur Renard.

The armed men grab Father Benedict. He struggles against his captors. "May God strike you down for your blasphemy!" he shouts defiantly. They drag him into the wagon, kneel him before the machine, and force his neck into the head cradle, locking it in place.

The driver looks around with his arms outstretched, moving his cold, grinning gaze from side to side. "Nothing is coming to strike me down, priest. I'm afraid yours are the ways of evil, not mine."

The crowd finally begins to shout horrified protests against what they know is about to happen. Turning toward Father Benedict, the man looks at him with contempt, then whips his arm down. I hear a swooshing noise, a snapping crunch, and Father Benedict's head falls into a basket. The man takes hold of Father Benedict's hair, lifting his head for all to see. Blood gushes from his torso, flowing down through the wagon's floorboards.

A gasp ripples across the crowd. Many people scream in horror. Several collapse to the ground. Then there is utter silence.

I'm too stunned to move. Adrien's hand slips into mine. We stare at each other in disbelief and terror. The man speaks again.

"Those of you who continue to cling to the church, remember this sight. Burn it into your soul!" Peering over the crowd and measuring the effect of his words and actions, he continues his rant. "Hear me. The power of the Catholic Church is finished! I'll be leaving men here to oversee church property distribution. Do not interfere with their task."

Adrien turns from the scene and bends over, emptying his stomach. Though I am nearly compelled to do the same, I turn to my friend and clasp his shoulder to comfort him.

A crashing noise startles us both. A large stone rolls onto the ground behind me. Looking up toward where the stone came from, I notice a large dent in the door of the Bauck butcher shop. Papa grabs me and rushes us both toward my family's inn. Herr Bauck puts one of his beefy arms around Adrien and runs for his shop. Glancing over my shoulder, I see Monsieur Renard reaching for another stone, his face twisted in hate.

Papa and I are almost to the door when we hear the sound of a horse galloping on the cobbled street. We stop and turn. In the distance, a white plume bobs from the top of a Hussar's tall shako cap. It's a single rider in a dark green soldier's uniform.

"It's Jean! It's my son, Jean!" exclaims Monsieur Rapp, our janitor, who's standing near the front door of our inn with a broom in his hands.

"Yes," Papa says with relief. "It is Jean."

The horseman brandishes his sword as he gallops up to the wagon with the guillotine. The horse rears, and Jean brings him to a halt. The tense, stunned crowd reacts with cheers upon Jean's arrival.

"What's the meaning of this?" demands Lieutenant Rapp. His eyes land on the headless priest, then rise slowly to study the men around the wagon. They shrink with fear from the sight of a mounted, armed soldier, but the man standing on the wagon stares coolly at Jean. He stretches to full height, and a sneer crosses his face. "Hussar, be careful what you say, or you too may be stretching your neck under this blade."

I glance toward Jean's father. He fidgets with his broom while staring anxiously at his son. We know Jean is not at full strength, having recently suffered sabre cuts to his head and arm in the battle at Ligenfield. He has been stationed nearby in Ostheim to convalesce, not fight.

The man on the wagon continues defiantly. "I've been sent by Robespierre himself and given full authority to enforce the will of the Committee. The revolution will succeed, and those who oppose us must be silenced."

"You fool," shouts Jean. "Have you not heard? Robespierre is dead. He and two of his brothers have been guillotined. His third brother committed suicide. The Committee no longer has power."

The crowd shouts their approval of this news, shaking their fists toward the wagon. *Will this man be stopped and punished?* They surge forward, some grabbing rocks from the ground.

A look of alarm crosses the wagon driver's face. He raises his hands in an attempt to silence the crowd. "It does not matter that Robespierre is dead. The revolution continues! My work becomes even more important!"

These words have no effect. The crowd continues to press him, their shouts of anger becoming louder. "How dare you kill our village priest! You must pay for this sacrilege!" Jean looks alarmed and he backs his horse away from the wagon.

The wagon driver's eyes widen. He jumps to a spot behind his armed contingent. Although the crowd is unarmed, there's little this small contingent can do to stop them, and I watch as they start scrambling away from the wagon toward the edge of the square.

A small group of villagers, led by Monsieur Renard, move up to the man and his companions. Forming a protective wall against the crowd, they whisk the group to the edge of the square, where they've brought horses. The man from the wagon and his companions mount up and hastily retreat from the scene. As they gallop away, he turns and gives Jean a last hateful look.

Meanwhile, the townspeople, regardless of whether they are Catholic or Lutheran, surge toward the wagon, shouting angrily. A few retrieve Father Benedict's body and the basket with his head. Jean uses his horse to open a path to the church, where the priest's remains are taken.

I shrink into my papa's body, and we edge into the doorway of our inn as the crowd becomes frenzied in their desire to erase this evil from their town.

Cries of "Burn it!" in both French and German echo across the square. The crowd rocks the wagon until the guillotine topples. Then they turn the wagon onto the fallen death machine. Dry straw appears from nowhere and is stuffed all around the wagon's edges. In moments, the straw is lit with torches and fire engulfs the murderous contraption.

The fire seems to quiet the crowd. They stand and stare at it, as do Papa and me. Father Benedict has been murdered needlessly, and the townspeople have avenged him by destroying the killing machine. I can't shake my feelings of horror and dismay. Why has this happened to Colmar?

The fire quickly consumes the dry timbers of the wagon and guillotine. The crowd disperses except for the town's church elder, Damien, who is poking into the embers. He finally pulls the guillotine blade out and cools it off with a bucket of water. He ties a rope to the blade through the pulley rope's hole and starts to drag it away. "Damien," Papa calls out. "Do you need help? Where are you taking it?"

"I can handle it," Damien replies. "I want to take this loathsome blade and entomb it for eternity at the bottom of Father Benedict's grave. His soul will watch and keep it from ever being used again."

"A good spot for that vile thing," Papa replies.

Papa looks down at me. He puts his hand on my shoulder. "Come, Jean-Luc. This ugliness is over." He sees that I'm still clutching the sack holding the fish. "You and Adrien had great success today. How many fish did you catch?"

I look at the sack, remembering the joy Adrien and I felt with each fish we hooked. "Three salmon, Papa." I look up to his warm, smiling face, and I'm able to smile back. "We almost had two more, but they jumped off the hook before we could net them."

"Take the fish to the kitchen and tell Mademoiselle LeClair that we will be having salmon tonight. In fact, tell her we will be having guests as well." Papa looks around. "Where is Monsieur Rapp?"

"Here, sir," he responds from the inn's doorway.

"Find your son and invite him to eat and stay with us here at the inn. He can use the room next to yours. Tell him we're grateful for his intervention."

Despite all that's happened, I'm excited about seeing Lieutenant Rapp, whom I've always called Uncle Jean.

"I'm sure Jean-Luc wants to hear about his adventures in the army," Papa says, "and I'm most interested to learn about this new general who has been promoted to be 'General of the Army of the West.' Many say he will save France and the revolution."

"Yes, sir, I'll be most happy to do that."

Papa turns back to me. "After you take the fish to the kitchen, go to the Bauck family and invite them for dinner. We must be with friends after events like these."

"Yes, Papa."

"When you return, cut salmon fillets for everyone and get some sauerkraut from the cellar."

Papa's eyes gleam with anticipation, as sauerkraut with salmon is his favorite dish.

"I think we still have a pot of baeckeoffe stew simmering that we can serve as our first course. And we have almond cake for dessert. Oh, and while you're at the Baucks', pick up some foie gras for our appetizer. I'll prepare the cream sauce for the fish after attending to our inn guests."

I dash toward the Bauck butcher shop, remembering to take one of the fish for Herr Bauck to sell. Adrien will be as excited as me about seeing Uncle Jean, who has been like an older brother to us. We always hang on his every word, and he has taken us to Ostheim barracks to see the Shagyas, the most beautiful horses I know. Then my reverie is broken when I take sight of the glowing remains of the wagon and its awful cargo. *Maybe Uncle Jean can explain what happened here.*

Two

Anna Lise Is Born – Late Spring, 1795

The Bauck butcher shop is near to our inn. Despite the events of the day, it's still open. Herr Bauck is serving a customer when he sees me enter. "Adrien is in the back if you want to go through," he says.

"All right. Here is the salmon Adrien caught. It's a big one."

Herr Bauck examines the fish I hand him. "A fine catch! I know of several customers who will want fillets. Thank you."

"Papa also wants to invite your family for dinner tonight. We're expecting Monsieur Rapp and his son Jean as well."

"Thank God Jean came when he did. Who knows who else that madman planned to guillotine." Herr Bauck puts the salmon on his cutting bench. "I need to see how *mein frau* feels. The new baby will come soon. Ah! Here's Adrien. One moment while I check with her."

Herr Bauck leaves to go to the living area. Adrien still looks pale. "Do you think those people wanted to kill more Catholics after killing Father Benedict? Monsieur Renard was helping them," Adrien says.

"They're gone, Adrien, and can't hurt you or your family anymore. You saw how the town rallied against them. They won't dare come back."

"I hope you're right. Did I hear you ask my *vati* about coming to dinner? Uncle Jean will be there?"

Herr Bauck returns. "*Mein frau* assures me the baby will wait for at least another day. Yes, please tell your father we most happily accept his invitation, and I look forward to seeing the Rapps as well. It will be good to be with friends on this night."

"I'll tell him. He also wants me to buy some foie gras—enough for seven."

Herr Bauck reaches for his foie gras platter and trowels out the proper amount, wraps it, and hands it to me. As I pay him, he says, "Tell your father we will be there at nine o'clock and will bring Riesling."

"Would you like to come and help me?" I ask Adrien. "There's a lot that needs to be prepared. First I'm going to clean and fillet the salmon we caught."

Adrien's face brightens, and together we scurry from the shop. Back at the inn, we go to the kitchen and find Mademoiselle LeClair preparing food. She motions to where she put the salmon.

"I'll clean the fish and cut it in half. You can fillet one of the halves," I say to Adrien. "The fish is more than large enough for all of us, don't you think?"

Adrien agrees and begins looking for a fillet knife.

"Mademoiselle LeClair, do you want me to save the head for soup?" I ask.

She nods. "I'll put it in the baeckeoffe stew I have simmering." I chop off the head and hand it to her. She promptly drops it into the stew, giving it a good stir.

Adrien and I soon have eight large fillets. The extra is for Jean, who we know eats heartily.

"I'm going to the cellar to scoop out sauerkraut," I say. "Can you slice and toast some bread for the foie gras?"

It feels good working like this. Looking toward Adrien, I see his face has color now.

Papa comes in and smiles, looking pleased with our progress. "Our friends will be here soon. I'll make the cream sauce for the fish. Jean-Luc, start heating the sauerkraut. Adrien, make sure the table is properly set."

Turning toward a flustered Mademoiselle LeClair, he says, "We'll get out of your way as soon as I finish my white sauce." He quickly combines the ingredients, bringing the liquid up to a low boil. "Finished," Papa says. "Mademoiselle LeClair, the kitchen is yours."

At that moment, there's a knock on the front door, and Papa turns to us. "Bring out the foie gras and toast, and pour the wine. I'll get the door."

From the dining room, I hear Papa greet our first guests. Frau Bauck comes in, moving slowly and deliberately. I bow and kiss her hand while Adrien pulls out a chair and helps her sit. Uncle Jean and his father come a few minutes later, Uncle Jean resplendent in his uniform. When he takes off his shako, I notice the dressings on his scalp from the sabre wounds. After greeting both Herr and Frau Bauck, he comes over to me and Adrien, giving us a bear hug. "It's so good to be home among family and friends," he booms. "I'm sorry it's under such unfortunate conditions and deeply regret I was too late to save Father Benedict. At least those vermin are gone and that wicked machine destroyed."

He releases Adrien and me. "You two keep growing! You need to spend time with me up in Ostheim while I'm home and learn to ride a Shagya. They're the most magnificent horses in all the world! If I hadn't been on a Shagya, the Austrian sabre would've sliced open my neck instead of ruining my shako and glancing off my scalp."

"I'm so happy to see you, Uncle Jean," I say. "I've missed your visits and your stories. How long can you stay?"

Uncle Jean falls silent. Rousing himself, he says, "Let's join Frau Bauck at the table." We all sit and feast on the foie gras and drink our wine.

Papa also asks Uncle Jean how long he'll be staying. A troubled look crosses his face. Looking around at all of us, he says in a lowered voice, "I'm not sure how long. My wounds are slow to heal, and I can't escape the visions of all the death on those battlefields."

He bows his head, and we all go quiet. "I'm thinking about retiring from the army. I love my comrades, and the travels to foreign lands are exhilarating, but the battles are not the romantic endeavors you hear about as a child. The slaughter is overwhelming. I can't get the faces of those I've killed out of my mind."

Uncle Jean lets out a sigh, then continues. "Uncle Graff has been telling me to stay in the army. He says that this new commander, General Bonaparte, is a true leader, admired by all who serve with him. General Desaix, a close friend of his, serves under General Bonaparte. General Desaix has a need for an aide-de-camp, and Uncle Graff thinks I should transfer to his command."

He looks up, giving a strained smile. "But please, forgive me. This dinner is not about my uncertainties. Tell me all that has happened in Colmar since I was last here." He turns to Adrien's mother. "Frau Bauck, I had not heard you are with child. Perhaps you will be blessed with a daughter. Another boy in addition to Adrien and Jean-Luc would be too much!"

Everyone laughs. Frau Bauck says, "I must confess I do hope for a baby girl. Herr Bauck and I will call her Anna Lise, should we be so blessed. That was my *mutti's* name." She winces, but she keeps smiling.

"A lovely one," Uncle Jean says. "And you can have Adrien help take care of her, as I know you've much to do in your shop." Uncle Jean smiles and turns to Papa. "Monsieur Calliet, you must have Jean-Luc help Adrien as well. One thing I've learned in the army is that family and comrades are what keep us alive."

"Can you share news of the revolution?" asks Papa. "We hear so little in Colmar. The appearance of that man with the traveling guillotine shocked us all. Father Benedict's death is such a tragedy. We all loved him—Catholics, Lutherans, everyone. Is it true the Robespierre brothers are dead and the Jacobins are no longer in control?"

My ears perk. Maybe Uncle Jean will say something that will help me understand what happened.

"Jacobins, non-Jacobins, they all cause trouble," Uncle Jean says, "though the Jacobins are the worst. They are so extreme, wanting to wipe out everything associated with the monarchy and the Catholic Church. Yes, they're out of power, but the revolution is rudderless. It needs a leader."

We sip our wine and dunk chunks of bread into our baeckeoffe stew that Mademoiselle LeClair has served as we talk.

"Do you think Bonaparte can become this leader?" Herr Bauck asks.

"I don't know, but if we don't find a strong commander soon, the revolution will fail and the royalists will take back power."

"Perhaps you should take your uncle's advice and become aide-de-camp to General Desaix," Papa says. "You wouldn't be in battles directly, and it would give you a chance to know this General Bonaparte."

Uncle Jean glances around, seeing everyone's concern. "Maybe you're right. I need to think about it more." He turns to his father. "Papa, we can talk about it tomorrow."

Mademoiselle LeClair brings out our second course. The aroma from the sauce mingles with the scent from the sauerkraut, making me eager to attack the salmon sandwiched between them.

Papa stands, raising his glass of Riesling. "I'm pleased to have all of you here, but the circumstances that have brought us together are somber. Come, join me in a toast!"

We all stand, holding out our glasses. "To Father Benedict!" Papa says.

"To Father Benedict!" we all respond, clinking our glasses.

We sit and quietly begin eating. I reflect on the scene with Father Benedict and the guillotine, puzzled by how such a terrible thing could happen.

The silence is broken by Herr Bauck. "This is delightful! Monsieur Calliet, your white sauce is a work of art, as always, accenting the fish and sauerkraut perfectly."

After another bite, Herr Bauck says, "Colmar is a fine town, filled, for the most part, with people like all of you. But there's a segment, led by Monsieur Renard, who would prefer to drive us out. You saw today how they rescued those with the guillotine. Monsieur Renard probably asked his Jacobin friends in Paris to send that man and his machine."

Herr Bauck takes another helping of fish. "We're from Prussia and we're Catholic, and those are two groups the Jacobins particularly hate. What if they get stronger? Will they march on my butcher shop and destroy it, possibly killing me and my family? Was that guillotine meant for us as well as Father Benedict?" He glances at his wife. "We are about to have another child, and I need to think of our safety. My brother and his family are still in Prussia. They encourage us to leave Colmar and return home or possibly go to Russia."

"Russia?" Papa says. "Why would you go to that frozen country so far away from everyone you know?"

"The tsar is offering bonus money for Germans to emigrate. They have empty farmlands to fill, and they need shopkeepers in their cities. Moscow has a thriving German quarter. My cousin has already taken his family there. We want to stay here, but *mein frau* and I must think of our options."

I look at Adrien. "You might be leaving?" I whisper to him. "Did you know this?"

"I've heard talk about my cousin going to Moscow, but I never heard we might leave."

Frau Bauck moans. She hunches over and holds her stomach.

"*Mutti!*" Adrien says in alarm.

Herr Bauck frowns deeply. "It's the baby. The time has come." He looks toward my father. "I don't think I can get her home. Is there a place here we can take her?"

"Yes, Jean-Luc's room," Papa says. "It's the closest. Here, let me help you."

He turns toward me. "Jean-Luc, tell Mademoiselle LeClair what's happening and have her boil some water. Then go get some clean cloths from the laundry. Adrien," he continues, "find the midwife. Tell her Frau Bauck's baby is coming."

Adrien and I dash away while the men help Frau Bauck toward my room.

I help Mademoiselle LeClair carry hot water and cloths. Frau Bauck is lying on blankets by the hearth, moaning in pain. Mademoiselle LeClair rushes in, takes a quick look at Frau Bauck, then shoos me and all the men from the room.

The door closes. Herr Bauck paces. "Where's the midwife?" he says. "My frau is in pain!"

Adrien returns in about thirty minutes with the madame sage-femme following him. He carries the midwife's birthing stool. Herr Bauck is frantic. "Why have you taken so long?"

"I was finishing another delivery," the madame sage-femme replies, giving Herr Bauck a look of irritation. "I'm here now. Take me to her."

Mademoiselle LeClair hears the commotion and opens the door to my room. "Over here," she says. "Frau Bauck is in much pain and is bleeding." The madame sage-femme enters the room, closing the door behind her, leaving all of us to wait in the parlor.

Herr Bauck rubs the back of his neck as he paces the room. "Bleeding? What does that mean?"

Papa tries to calm him. "There is always blood when giving birth. I'm sure everything is going well." Papa pours Herr Bauck a glass of cognac. "Here."

Herr Bauck downs his glass in one swallow. "*Mein frau* lost a child just two summers ago while giving birth. Father Benedict baptized her before she died, but now Father Benedict is gone. What will I do if my child or *mein frau* dies?"

He leans his head back, trying to control his emotions. "Monsieur Calliet, you lost your wife when Jean-Luc was born. It could happen to mine!"

Realizing what he said, he looks at me and Papa, regret in his eyes. "Forgive me! I was cruel to say that."

Herr Bauck's words do pain me. When I watch Frau Bauck with Adrien, I understand how it feels not to have a mother. I glance at Adrien. He looks scared but gives me a sad nod.

The tall case clock marks each passing moment with its *tick* ... *tock*. An hour passes, then four. The men sit quietly in their armchairs, sipping their cognac and staring at the closed door to my room. We can hear Frau Bauck's cries of pain, and I see this distresses Adrien.

I'm tired and want to sleep, but where? My room is taken. Adrien sits next to me, and he doesn't seem to know what to do either. "Let's go to the inn's office and play pick-up sticks," I tell him. "It will help pass the time."

The case clock tolls twelve. "Adrien, it's midnight. Happy birthday!"

"Thanks," he replies as I give him a hug.

"It will be the baby's birthday too," I add. "Do you think your mother is right and it will be a girl?"

"I'm sure she's had a long talk with God over this," he says, smiling. "When my *mutti* says she knows something, she's always been right. Yes, I will have a sister, and her name will be Anna Lise." A worried look crosses his face. "But why is it taking so long?"

I give my friend a reassuring look. "I'm sure everything is fine. Let's go play the game."

As we head toward the door to the office, an idea comes to me. "I'll meet you in the office after I go and get something."

"What is it?"

"It's something for your new sister. I won't be long."

I go into Papa's room and find the cabinet holding the keepsakes he saves for me from my mother. I search through the items and finally find what I want, a gold necklace with a small gold cross. Papa says Mama always wore it.

I gently hold it in my palm, admiring its delicacy. I know Mama would want me to give it to someone I'll be close to. I'm closer to Adrien than anyone else, and I'm sure I'll be close to Anna Lise as well.

I close my hand over the necklace and go to the office. Adrien has pulled out the pick-up sticks game and is ready to play. "What did you get, Jean-Luc?"

I open my hand, and the light from the lantern reflects off the gold. "It was my mother's."

Adrien holds it carefully. "It's beautiful! You want to give it to the new baby? But what if it's a boy?"

"As you said, your mother is never wrong. Keep it for her until she gets older."

The necklace calms Adrien's nerves, and we play several games of pick-up sticks. He wins them all.

Six hours have passed since Frau Bauck first began feeling pain. Adrien and I have returned to the parlor and are resting, nearly asleep on the sofa, when we hear a baby cry. Everyone gets to their feet as the madame sage-femme opens the door and loudly announces, "It's a girl!"

Herr Bauck struggles to speak. "A girl? She is doing well?"

"Yes. Come in and meet your daughter."

"And my frau, she is fine?"

The madame sage-femme stiffens, sadness in her face. "She lost a lot of blood, but I'm sure she will recover. Come, see your wife and daughter."

Three

Twelfth Night – Winter, 1800 to 1801

During the winter, Adrien and I go to Ostheim to help care for the army's horses. A Shagya nickers and nods as I rub her down. "Good girl," I say. "You'll like it here. We'll treat you and your companions like queens. Where did you come from? The soldiers wouldn't say when they brought you in."

"Beautiful, isn't she, Jean-Luc?" says a familiar voice behind me. Turning around, I'm startled to see Uncle Jean. "The Austrians have done a fine job creating this breed, the perfect blend of fast Arabians with the big and strong Hungarian horses. The ideal horse for our Chasseurs and Hussars."

"Uncle Jean, or I should say Colonel Rapp, what are you doing here?"

Adrien comes in with two more Shagya mares. "Uncle Jean!" he shouts. "I thought you were in Paris."

Uncle Jean smiles. "Boys, look at you, nearly grown men now. So much has happened since I saw you six years ago in Colmar. I'm glad to see you took up my offer to spend time here in Ostheim."

"Did you bring these new horses?" I ask.

"Yes, but let's talk over dinner."

We hurry alongside him to the officers' mess, excited to be invited to this exclusive dining area.

After getting our food, we find a corner table. "Where do I start?" muses Uncle Jean. "After seeing you in Colmar, I became aide-de-camp to General Desaix. He was a great man and taught me a lot. When he died in Italy last year, I ..."

He trails off, staring into space, his eyes glassy.

Adrien glances at me, uncertain. "Uncle Jean? Are you all right?" I ask.

He smiles slightly, recovering, and then says, "General Bonaparte made me *his* aide-de-camp. I've never been so surprised in my life. I find him to be a remarkable man."

He tears a piece of bread and dips it into a platter of olive oil and vinegar, then continues. "General Bonaparte's military genius is undeniable. He's saved France many times. All the monarchies, but especially Great Britain, Austria, and Russia, fear the ideals from our revolution will spread and lead to their downfall. They fear us with good reason."

Uncle Jean's face is flush with excitement. "General Bonaparte is the rudder we've lacked these past years. His emissaries have spoken with the Pope about improving relations with the Catholic Church. In Spain, he halted the Inquisition, and now Jews are welcome in France. He believes in freedom for everyone. When we fight in Italy, the German states, or Austria, we're greeted with open arms by the common people. They see in Napoleon a chance to improve their lives."

Uncle Jean takes a drink of his wine. "But wait," he says. "I'm rambling. I'm sure you would rather hear about how I got the new Shagyas."

"We want to hear it all—General Bonaparte and the horses," I say.

"All right then, the horses. When I became General Bonaparte's aide-de-camp, he complimented the horses ridden by the Hussars from the Ostheim barracks and asked if more regiments could have such fine animals. I told him the Austrians had developed the Shagya breed only recently and that we had secured a few in Ostheim. I explained that we have been breeding our own herd, but many more mares are needed."

"Did General Bonaparte help you get the Shagyas?" I ask.

"Yes. He said the Austrians were balking at the peace terms agreed to in Italy and he was sending General Moreau into Austria to settle the matter. He told me to take a company of men and raid an Austrian Shagya stud farm while they were focused on General Moreau." Uncle Jean shakes his head, laughing. "And that's what we did! We were very successful!"

"Your raid brought us about fifty fine mares," I exclaim. "Adrien and I will be very busy taking care of these new arrivals."

Uncle Jean takes a sip of his soup, still looking exhilarated. "How often have you boys been coming to Ostheim?"

"This is our second year," Adrien replies. "November and the first part of December are slow at the butcher shop and the inn. We come up after All Souls' Day and return Christmas Eve."

"So, you'll only be here for a few more days. I'll help you and the others at the stud farm tomorrow, but I need to see my father in Colmar before returning to Paris. The last letter you wrote for him mentioned he was not feeling well?"

"His joints hurt and he's not able to move his fingers easily," I respond. "Your father's mind is sharp, but his mobility is restricted. Papa is simplifying his chores to help out."

"I'll thank your father when I see him. It's unfortunate I cannot stay through Christmas and Twelfth Night. General

Bonaparte will want my report on our Shagya raid, and I'm to accompany him and his family to the opera on Christmas Eve."

* * *

Adrien and I ride into Colmar late in the afternoon of Christmas Eve. As we pass in front of the Bauck butcher shop, a traditional German Christmas tree with glowing candles shimmers through the window along with Anna Lise's bright, happy face. She watches as we take our horses to the stable and prepare them for the night.

"Did you see her?" I ask Adrien when we finally head toward the butcher shop.

He doesn't get to answer before the door bursts open and Anna Lise races toward us, shouting, *"Frohe Weihnachten, Adrien und Jean-Luc!"* She stretches her six-year-old arms as wide as they can go, giving us both a hug.

"And merry Christmas Eve to you as well, Anna Lise," I say, kissing her forehead.

Taking our hands, she leads us through the shop to the home in the back. Papa and Monsieur Rapp are sitting by the fire with Adrien's parents, drinking *glühwein*. "Merry Christmas," I say. "Has Uncle Jean already left for Paris?"

Frau Bauck pours mugs of *glühwein* for Adrien and me, which we gratefully accept. The warm wine and spices thaw my chilled body.

"Unfortunately, he could only stay one night," Monsieur Rapp replies. "Tonight, he's with General Bonaparte and his family." He shakes his head. "How far he's come since being the strong-willed child who refused to become a pastor."

He smiles as he talks about his son. We talk about his exploits, especially those in Egypt, but also about Adrien's and my time at the Ostheim barracks, and recent events in Colmar. Adrien and I sit on the rug before the fireplace, enjoying its warmth. Anna Lise nestles between us.

The hour is getting late, and Papa, Monsieur Rapp, and I get up to take our leave. "I understand you've a visiting priest from Prussia celebrating midnight mass," Papa says to Herr Bauck.

"Yes, we do," Herr Bauck replies. "He's from our old village and knows my family well." Herr Bauck looks a little troubled. "More of our old neighbors are leaving for Russia," he says. "The tsar's offer is generous, and more importantly, there's peace in Russia."

"I hope you're not tempted," Papa replies. "You would be missed. Adrien and Anna Lise are like my own children."

Herr Bauck nods, but I see his doubt.

We wish the Bauck family a good night and take our leave.

* * *

The days leading up to Twelfth Night pass quickly. Business continues to be slow, giving Adrien, myself, and Anna Lise time to be together.

Anna Lise is most dear to the two of us. Frau Bauck became dangerously ill after giving birth. A doctor from Strasbourg was summoned, and he said she had childbed fever. The only cure he knew was to bleed her. Despite the treatment, Frau Bauck remained bedridden, taking nearly a year to regain full strength. She relied heavily on Adrien to take care of Anna Lise, and I helped as much as I could. She is such a joy that both of us have continued to look after her whenever we can.

On the day of Twelfth Night, travelers from Paris staying at our inn report on an assassination attempt against General Bonaparte. They excitedly tell us that while Napoleon, his family, and their entourage, including Colonel Rapp, were on their way to a Christmas Eve opera, a wagon filled with gunpowder exploded nearby, killing several bystanders. Panic ensued, but fortunately, General Bonaparte and his companions were only badly shaken. Royalists and Catholics were said to be behind the plot.

Later, in the afternoon, I hear shouts coming from up the street and look out the window. A small crowd is forming in front of the Catholic church.

Going outside, I hear, 'Death to royalists! Death to Catholics." Looking closely, I see several known local Jacobins, led by Monsieur Renard.

They begin marching along the square toward our inn, still shouting and shaking their fists. The Baucks join me. 'Are they coming for us?" Herr Bauck says in a whisper. Frau Bauck, looking fearful, takes Anna Lise inside.

Father Mathew pushes his way through the crowd to the front of the Jacobins, pleading for them to stop. Our Lutheran pastor joins Father Mathew. The two of them engage in a heated exchange with Monsieur Renard. Neighbors come out and stand with their clergy.

'How dare you disturb Twelfth Night!" they shout. 'Begone! Leave us in peace!"

The crowd swells, causing Monsieur Renard and his followers to back away. Cheers erupt, then Father Mathew and Pastor Mercier lead the crowd in singing 'Silent Night' in French.

I cannot help but join in.

Douce nuit, sainte nuit!
Dans les cieux! L'astre luit.
Le mystère annoncé s'accomplit
Cet enfant sur la paille endormi,

C'est l'amour infini!
C'est l'amour infini!

Papa and Monsieur Rapp, along with Frau Bauck and Anna Lise, come outside and join in the singing. Anna Lise holds Adrien's hand and mine. With each line we sing, everyone's expression softens.

I look down at Anna Lise and smile.

"We'll see you soon for Twelfth Night dinner," Papa says to the Bauck family as we head back toward the inn. "Mademoiselle LeClair is preparing a wonderful meal and has baked the Epiphany galette cake." Herr Bauck nods, a smile returning to his face.

The Baucks arrive, and Mademoiselle LeClair gives everyone a mug of warm *glühwein*. Monsieur Rapp, whom we think of as family, is also with us. "Dinner will be soon," Mademoiselle LeClair says as she slips back into the kitchen.

Adrien pulls me aside. "Do you remember the necklace of your mother's you gave me when Anna Lise was born? You wanted to save it for Anna Lise until she was older. I have it with me, and I think we should give it to her tonight as her Twelfth Night present. She's old enough now, don't you think?"

Adrien hands it to me, and I admire it, much like I did when Anna Lise was born. "Yes," I say. "She is old enough to cherish it. Come, let's wrap it in some colored paper and put it in the stack of presents."

Mademoiselle LeClair brings out the first course, escargot along with foie gras and toasted bread. It is wonderful.

We toast to the holidays and friends with champagne. Soon we're served our main course, chicken cassoulet, a Twelfth Night favorite of my family. Mademoiselle LeClair presents the dish: a large, bubbling vat of beans and meat, covered in a crust so dark it is almost black. She cracks open the top layer to reveal the beans swimming in a broth filled with tender chicken and sausage slices.

We seem to eat our dinner more quickly than usual, perhaps in anticipation of tonight's highlight: the serving of the galette cake with its hidden dried bean that will identify the "king" or "queen" of the evening.

Mademoiselle LeClair clears our table. Anna Lise is especially excited about eating her piece of galette, hoping hers will have the dried bean and she'll be queen for the night.

The galette is brought out and slices cut for each of us. Next to the cake lies a small wooden crown, painted golden yellow. We each start eating carefully, not wanting to bite too hard. About half of everyone's cake is eaten, and still nothing. Suddenly, Anna Lise cries out. "I have the bean! I have the bean!" She proudly holds up her cake-encrusted prize.

"So you have," Herr Bauck exclaims. "Adrien, please crown our queen of the evening."

Adrien stoops to one knee in front of Anna Lise, places the crown on her sweet head, and says, "I crown thee Queen Anna Lise of Twelfth Night! What is your bidding, my queen?"

Anna Lise smiles broadly, gazing at each of us. She climbs to stand on her chair and, in her best French, says, "Monsieur Adrien and Monsieur Jean-Luc, pass out the gifts."

There is a present for each of us and two for Queen Anna Lise.

"I command you all to open your gifts," she says. We remove the paper wrappings under her watchful eye.

Satisfied that we've each opened our gifts and sufficiently praised what we have received, she sits down and examines her two presents. "Why do I have two?" she asks. "Everyone else only has one."

"The one in colored paper is a special gift from Jean-Luc and me," Adrien says. "Because you're our queen."

'I'll save yours till last," she regally states.

Fumbling to open her first present, she finds a rag doll, which she clutches tightly, smiling. She sets aside the ragdoll and looks at the two of us quizzically. "What have you given me?" She takes off the string around the paper and slowly unrolls it, revealing its golden contents.

Papa's face brightens. He smiles at Anna Lise, overjoyed to see her with his wife's most precious possession.

Anna Lise's face beams as she holds the necklace in front of her, admiring it closely. She places it around her neck and rushes over to embrace us.

"Now I can be queen forever!"

Four

Leaving Home – Late Spring, 1804

The sun settles into the bosom of the Vosges Mountains, casting shadows across the meadows that reach down to the River Ill. The Shagya herd has grown substantially over the years, and Adrien and I help groom and train them in this idyllic setting. They are high spirited, difficult to control, and their strength boundless. Tonight, we lead our stallions back to the stables after a long day of training. Sweat glistens on Adrien's face in the fading sunlight.

"Hervé, settle down," I say to my favorite stallion as he whinnies loudly. "You'll get your feed as soon as I finish your rubdown." I turn to Adrien. "Tomorrow is your eighteenth birthday. Have you decided about joining the army yet?"

"I need to talk to *Vati* about it when I get home. Your papa said you could join when you turn eighteen, right?"

"Only because Uncle Jean said he'll help me join the Hussars, maybe even be part of the Imperial Guard. I'm sure he can give your father the same assurances."

"Maybe, but *Vati* says, 'Remember, we're Prussians.' He thinks I act too French, forgetting my roots and ignoring that there are those in Colmar who hate us." Adrien shakes his head in dismay. "He also wants me to spend more time in the butcher shop. I don't want to be a butcher. I love France; I'm a Frenchman. I want to serve my country and join the army."

"There you go, Hervé. All done."

The stallion snorts and nudges me toward the store of fresh feed. "All right! All right! Here." I fork fresh hay into Hervé's stall, and soon he's chewing contently.

"I can't imagine the two of us being separated, and the sight of you as a butcher is hard to picture. I've put some hay into Basile's stall. Are you done rubbing him down?"

"Yes," Adrien sighs, bringing him over. "If *Vati* has his way, this will be my last time with Basile."

* * *

The glow of the bright summer dawn sweeps through our barrack's window, finding Adrien and me packing the last of our gear. Now that we're older, we spend most of our time in Ostheim, only visiting Colmar for short periods. Since tomorrow is Adrien's eighteenth birthday and Anna Lise's ninth, we are heading home to celebrate. We grab our saddlebags and head for the stables. "It's fine birthday weather, my friend," I say. "Let's say goodbye to our Shagyas before we leave."

Both Hervé and Basile give snorts of greeting as we enter the stables. "I'll miss you, Hervé," I say, patting his nose.

He nickers softly.

"Ah, the Rapp boys," says the barrack's quartermaster, calling us by the nickname the soldiers here have derisively given us because of our friendship with Uncle Jean, who is now General Rapp. "I understand you're off to Colmar."

Adrien and I both give the quartermaster a mock glare, knowing he is only jesting.

"It's your birthday, Bauck, isn't it?" he asks.

"Yes. Jean-Luc and I are saying goodbye to Hervé and Basile."

"Why don't you ride them to Colmar instead of the other horses? No one here has the skill to ride those two Shagyas. Take them. They need the exercise."

Smiling in appreciation, we thank the quartermaster as we leave.

"Won't we look dashing?" says Adrien. "The only thing missing is a fine Hussar uniform to wear. Come, race me to the bridge."

Off we gallop. Hervé takes a nose lead on Basile. "Let's fly, Basile!" Adrien yells. "We can't let Jean-Luc win."

Basile begins to catch up with Hervé. I hold back from giving him a kick, letting Basile come closer. He inches nearer, pulling ahead as we reach the finish.

"I knew we would win," a triumphant Adrien exclaims.

"A lucky break!" I say, grinning, glad to have given Adrien this win on his birthday.

We bring our horses to a walking gait as the midmorning sun heralds the start of a hot day. Heat waves are beginning to shimmer off the fields of grape vines lining the road. Ahead, a green line of trees snakes its way through the vineyards.

"Those oak trees along the River Ill will give us shade soon," Adrien says as he wipes sweat away from his forehead.

The road now edges close to the river, and one side is shaded from the morning sun by towering, ancient oaks. A cool breeze wafts across the water. We fall silent, enjoying the tranquil surroundings.

Some time passes before we come to the bridge that leads into Colmar. "Do you remember us hiding under here the day the guillotine wagon rolled by?" I ask.

"How could I forget? I never want to see one again."

"Colmar is close now. Let's gallop into town, check in with our families, and find Anna Lise. You did remember her present, didn't you?"

Adrien gives me a cross look. "Of course I have her present. Did you remember yours?"

I laugh and give Hervé a kick. Off we fly.

Our horses' hooves clatter on the cobblestone streets of Colmar. Coming into view is the blonde, pigtailed head of a young girl poking out the door of the butcher shop. "*Mutti, Vati*, it's Adrien and Jean-Luc!" I hear her shout.

Adrien secures his horse, and while I'm tying mine to the rail, Anna Lise leaps into her brother's arms. "I've been waiting all day for you. Happy birthday!"

"And to you as well, my little urchin."

Still being held by her brother, she turns toward me, wrapping her arms around my neck. "Jean-Luc, I missed you so much."

Adrien's parents and my papa come out to greet us. "Happy birthday, my son," a beaming Herr Bauck says. "We've much to talk about now that you're eighteen."

Frau Bauck pulls him to her chest. "Welcome home." She too sounds happy, but a look of concern passes between her and her husband.

"It's so good to be here," says Adrien as he lets Anna Lise down and glances across his gathered family. "Yes, *Vati*, we do have much to discuss, but that can wait. Right now, Jean-Luc and I are taking Anna Lise to the river to have a birthday picnic."

"Of course. It's a grand day for both of you," Herr Bauck replies.

I see Papa examining our horses. Hervé snorts as Papa runs his hand down his flanks. "A fine stallion you are riding, my son. Is this one of your Shagyas?"

"These are the two Shagyas Adrien and I train." I pat the neck of my gray dappled horse. "This one is Hervé, and this iron-gray one is Adrien's favorite, Basile. Uncle Jean says we can keep them once we join the Hussars." A momentary grimace crosses Herr Bauck's face.

Frau Bauck goes into the shop and returns with a basket filled with cheeses, sausages, and bread. "Here's some wine for you and Jean-Luc," she says, handing Adrien two bottles as I take the basket. "Only let Anna Lise have one glass. I've put a bottle of water for her in the basket."

"Thank you, *Mutti*," Adrien says. He stoops down to Anna Lise. "Little one, do you want to join us for a birthday picnic?"

"Can we ride on your Shagya? He's so pretty. His name is Basile?"

"Yes," Adrien replies, smiling. "Jean-Luc, you take the basket and wine. Anna Lise, you ride with me."

He mounts his horse, swings Anna Lise up to ride in front of him, and nods to his father. "Yes, *Vati*, we'll talk later."

We find a spot near a tall beech tree by the water. The shade and slight breeze off the river give relief from the heat. I lay out our food on a blanket while Anna Lise and Adrien leap into the water, clothes and all. "Jean-Luc, join us," Anna Lise shouts. She splashes water on me and I leap toward her, but miss, falling into the river and going under. The water's coldness makes me gasp for breath when I break the surface, and I find both Adrien and Anna Lise splashing more water on me.

"I surrender," I cry, raising my hands.

We spend the next hour playing water tag and swimming, lost in the pleasure of deep friendship.

"I'm getting hungry," Adrien says as he drags his sister ashore. We settle on the blanket, and I pour us each some wine. Raising my glass, I say, "To my closest friends, happy birthday." We clink our glasses in a toast.

"I've missed home, and especially my little sister," says Adrien as he pops a sausage in his mouth.

"*Vati* says you won't be going away anymore," Anna Lise says. "He tells everyone that you'll be working in the butcher shop now that you're eighteen."

Adrien looks troubled. "*Vati* and I have much to talk about, my sweet. But today is your birthday, and we're here to celebrate. Jean-Luc and I have each brought you a present."

"It's your birthday too," Anna Lise replies. She reaches into her satchel and brings out a package. She pushes it into Adrien's hands. "*Vati* helped me with it."

Adrien unwraps the present. It's a rolled piece of leather. He unrolls it, laying it out on the blanket. "It's a butcher's apron," says Anna Lise. "*Vati* says you'll need it. I hope you like it."

Adrien looks at the apron. His gaze remains on the gift for several moments, but when he raises his head, he smiles at his sister. "Anna Lise, this is the most perfect gift you could have gotten me. Thank you. I will cherish it." Adrien glances toward me, still smiling, but I can feel his pain.

"Now for our presents to you," Adrien says. "Here's mine. *Mutti* tells me you help her in the kitchen a great deal." Anna Lise unwraps the package. It's a lace apron.

"So pretty," she says. "I'll wear it always." She jumps up, twirls, and kisses her brother. "It's like your present, isn't it?"

"Very much the same, little one."

"Here's mine," I say. "Not so pretty as Adrien's, but I hope it will help you remember us when we're away."

Anna Lise carefully unwraps my present: a two-inch-tall figurine. "It's a Shagya, like your Hervé," she cries. "It's perfect. How did you make it?"

"A cherry tree fell near the barracks, and I cut out a chunk for carving. It took me several tries before I finally finished it. I kept breaking off a leg."

"I'll keep it close. When I'm missing you, I will hold it and know you're thinking of me." Anna Lise touches her necklace from my mother and holds the carved horse closely. She gives me a troubled look. "Are you going away?"

"Yes, I'll be leaving for Ostheim tomorrow and will be joining the Hussars in a couple of weeks, after my birthday. It may be some time before I return to Colmar."

Anna Lise's expression changes immediately. Tears well in her eyes. "You can't go. You've always been here." She reaches out to her brother, wrapping her arms around his neck. "You're not leaving too, are you? *Vati* says you'll be in the butcher shop."

Adrien looks at me sadly, then turns to Anna Lise. "I must still talk to *Vati*, but yes, I too may be leaving, going with Jean-Luc."

"*Vati* will be angry," she says, clutching Adrien even more tightly. "*Mutti* has fixed a special birthday dinner for us. Don't talk to *Vati* until later."

We take the long way home by walking along the trails hugging the river. Adrien and I tell Anna Lise stories about her growing up. We don't hurry. No one wants our bubble of happiness to burst just yet.

Dinner is a masterpiece. Frau Bauck has cooked a traditional German dinner of sauerkraut with sausage, boiled potatoes, red cabbage, and a delightful dessert of muskazine. The almond-flavored pastry is one of my favorites.

The long summer day is drawing to an end with the sun setting over the mountains. Papa and I thank the Bauck family for their hospitality and wish them a good night. I embrace Adrien, again telling him happy birthday.

"Thank you, my friend," he says with a wry smile.

"Come here, my sweetness," I say to Anna Lise.

She comes over and kisses me on my forehead. "You will still be here tomorrow morning, won't you?"

"Yes. I won't leave without seeing you first."

As we go, I hear Frau Bauck say, "Anna Lise, help me clear the table and clean the dishes. *Vati* and Adrien need to talk." I glance over to Adrien, who gives me a determined look.

* * *

The next morning, I make ready to return to Ostheim. "Papa, I'm going down to the stable to get Hervé, then I'll go check with Adrien to see if he is coming with me. I won't be long."

"I'll have some breakfast ready for you," he replies.

Though the sun has only just risen, the air feels warm, promising another hot day.

"Hervé, are you ready to go back to Ostheim?" I say as I put his saddle on. Then I glance around the stable. "Where's Basile?" Panicked, I mutter to Hervé, "He can't have been stolen, can he? Did Adrien take him?"

Pulling Hervé along, I rush toward the Bauck shop. The door opens, and out come Frau Bauck and Anna Lise, their eyes red.

"Adrien has gone," says Frau Bauck. "He and his *vati* argued most of the night. He has already left for Ostheim, intending to join the Hussars with you. Please, you must watch over him."

Anna Lise, with tears in her eyes, says, "Protect my brother. *Vati* won't stay mad." She comes and hands me two small lockets. "*Mutti* had these. I've cut locks of my hair and put some in each to bring you and my brother good luck."

I place both around my neck and tuck them under my shirt. "Thank you, Anna Lise. Don't worry, we'll be back to see everyone again." I turn to my father, who has come outside. "Papa, I'm sorry I can't stay for breakfast, but I must find Adrien."

I mount Hervé and give him a kick. We gallop down the cobblestones toward the road to Ostheim, the echo from the pounding hooves adding to the somber mood. I turn and wave, hoping it's not my last vision of those I love.

Coming up to the bridge over the River Ill, I find Adrien waiting. Dismounting, I go and embrace my friend.

"Jean-Luc, I'm so glad to see you," Adrien says, looking uneasy. "I'm sure you heard I had words with *Vati*."

"Yes, Anna Lise and your mother told me."

"Did you see my *vati*?"

"No, he didn't come out when I was leaving."

"He became enraged when I told him I would be joining the Hussars. He says I'm betraying our people and my family." Adrien drops his head. "He also said he no longer had a son and that I would never be welcomed in his home."

"I'm sorry, Adrien. It must be very hard for him, but he loves you too much to turn you away for very long."

I reach for one of the necklaces I'm wearing. "Here, Anna Lise made both of us lockets with a cutting of her hair—for good luck and remembrance."

Adrien clasps the locket and kisses it.

"This may be all I ever have of my family."

Five

The Campaigns Begin
– Summer, 1805

Excitedly, I cinch my leather belt by a notch. ""This is incredible, isn't it, Adrien? The emperor is going to do it. Invade Great Britain. The best part is, we'll be with him!"

'René," I shout excitedly across the room. 'You ready to march in the morning? Is your knapsack packed?" I grab mine, dumping its contents across my bunk: 'Flint," I mutter, as I sort through the contents. 'Pocket knife, mess kit, pipe, extra shoe soles, socks, shirt, trousers, jacket, brushes, comb, razor, pen and ink, blanket. Everything is here." I repack, carefully putting each item into the knapsack. 'Are you set, Adrien? We don't want to be at the back of the march, stuck in the dust cloud tomorrow."

'Can't find my mess kit. Where is the blasted thing?"

I watch as he paws through the pile on his bed. Adrien drops to his knees and sweeps his hand under his bunk. 'Thank God, here it is."

Though bemused, I refrain from commenting. Instead, I say, 'How long do you think it takes to reach Boulogne?"

Adrien looks up as he continues checking the contents of his knapsack. "My guess? About five days. Didn't the quartermaster say there are already one hundred and fifty thousand men in Boulogne and more coming all the time?"

"One hundred and fifty thousand? I can hardly imagine seeing that many people. The beach must be covered."

"You can see the English coast from the shoreline. I'll bet *les goddams* are shaking in their boots, watching us."

"Yes, but the damn British navy still has our ports blocked. Our allies the Spanish should help. Together, we can get through the stupid blockades and clear the channel for the invasion. What do you think the emperor has planned?"

Adrien doesn't reply. He is still sorting through his gear, tossing things left and right. "My gloves! Where are my gloves? Now I can't find my gloves." Looking panicked, he asks, "Do you have an extra pair?"

"For God's sake, Adrien, calm down. Look down at your feet. They fell off your bed with all your mad scrambles. Quartermaster Beaulac would be disappointed in you. He's drilled us about how we need to keep our gear properly stowed."

Adrien glares at me. "I only misplaced my gloves," he growls.

"And your mess kit," I reply. "It's a good thing you have everything now. It's going to be cold and wet in Great Britain this winter."

I shake my head, wondering if Adrien is ready for the hard life of a soldier.

Looking past Adrien, I spot my new uniform, hanging on the far wall. It's beautiful, and I feel important wearing the green coat, the red britches, and the shiny black boots, all topped by a shako with a red plume. Everyone who sees these colors will know we are with the Seventh Regiment of Hussars.

The past six months of training have been arduous: the drills demanding, the hours long, and no leave time granted. I often need to boost Adrien's confidence. He remains distressed about his father and constantly questions whether he did the right thing by joining the army. But now the training is over, and best of all, we've both received orders to join the Seventh Regiment of Hussars, Uncle Jean's old command. They are already in Boulogne, and we'll join up with them once we get there.

"I hope we see Uncle Jean," I say to Adrien. "He's going to be so proud of us. Maybe our regiment will be stationed near him during the invasion. How long do you think it will take for us to conquer the island? A year or two?"

"Years?" Adrien exclaims. "Do you think we'll be fighting for years? I don't fancy staying in the army that long. I want to serve my country, but I want to get home as soon as I can. Jean-Luc, let's just earn some glory in battle and return home as heroes." He sounds so alarmed that my head jerks up.

Adrien walks over to the window and gazes out toward the river. "Maybe being a butcher isn't so bad," he says. "Maybe once I've proven myself in battle, *vati* will be proud of me and be glad I've come home."

He shakes his head as he turns from the window, looking sad and upset. I know the quarrel with his father weighs on him. We've been away from Colmar for many months now. No leave was given for Christmas or Twelfth Night, but we were promised we'd get to go home for a short time once training was complete.

These new orders change all that.

"Come on, Adrien, it will be all right," I say. "We'll see new places, experience new things. Things that could never happen in Colmar."

Adrien sighs, and I listen as he tries to reassure himself. "Maybe so. Once we conquer the bloody British, the wars will come to an end. No one is as tough as them. The others will crumble once they're beaten. We'll be home again in no time.

I don't relish the prospect of ever fighting the Prussians. *Vati* could never forgive that."

"It's getting late," I say. "Let's try and get some sleep." But sleep won't come. We talk deep into the night about the battles we will fight and the glories we'll gain, as if we know of what we speak.

* * *

Pain shoots through my shoulder as I hit the ground, rousing me. Looking up through the lantern light hovering over my face, I make out the forms of Henri and Bernard. Nearby, I hear Adrien grunt. The sound of a heavy thud echoes from the floor near his bed. "Come on, Rapp boys, time to be real soldiers," they say, sneering and laughing. "Take our gear down to the stables to our horses, and don't be late with your own equipment. The colonel is known to strike laggards with his riding crop, especially green recruits. We wouldn't want that to happen, would we?"

I clench my fists and move toward these two loudmouths, tired of their mockeries and angry that they are pushing us around even on this important morning. There is a pull on my arm, stopping me. It's Adrien. "No problem, we'll take your gear to the stable," he says. Can this be Adrien saying this?

I glower at him, wondering why he stopped me, but he nods his head toward the equipment and starts picking it up. I look at him for a few moments in disbelief, then glower back toward the now laughing bullies. My fists say *strike*, but for some reason I trust Adrien's instinct and instead stoop down and help him with their things.

"Why did you stop me, and why are we taking their gear?" I demand as we move toward the stable. "We can handle those two."

'Until those two fighting us turns to twenty more joining in. Being a Prussian in a French town, you learn such things. We may be grand Hussars, but we're at the bottom—green recruits. Until we prove ourselves, we mean nothing to them. Come on, I don't relish being lashed by a riding crop," he says through clenched teeth.

The delay caused by our taking Henri's and Bernard's gear to the stables has left us in the rear of the march, just where we don't want to be. "Thank God for this cool breeze," I say. "Now, if the dust would just settle as well. Good thing we're riding and not marching. We're at least a little above the dust the infantry kicks up."

The road ascends into the heights of the Vosges Mountains. Trees tower on both sides. The forest shifts from elm to pine the higher we climb. Looking ahead, I catch glimpses of the high peaks, some still with snow near their tops, even now in August. The land is wild, with no villages or farms, only forest for as far as the eye can see. This is the farthest I have ever been from Colmar, and I can't help marveling at everything, taking it all in.

"We'll be stopping for the night higher up in the mountains," I say to Adrien. "It should be cool tonight for sleep, away from the Ostheim heat."

Adrien is searching about, not looking at the surroundings. "What are you doing?"

"Trying to find Henri and Bernard."

I, too, peer around. "There they are, just ahead of us in the column."

"Our friends look tired," smirks Adrien. "I don't think they'll be giving us any trouble tonight."

Two days pass. The cool of the Vosges has given way to the heat of the lowlands. My excitement wanes with the monotony of the long march.

My mind wanders dully for hours on end. Unexpectedly, I am roused by a distant sound. Perking up, I look toward Adrien, who appears to be dozing in his saddle. I move toward him and give him a kick. "Do you hear that in the distance?"

Adrien gives me an annoyed look, then strains his ears to listen. "Yes," he says excitedly. "Those are bells ringing. Do you think they come from the cathedral in Rheims? Making Rheims is our goal for today's march."

"I hope so," I reply. "If it is, we're making good time. We could be camped by late afternoon. Maybe we'll be given leave to explore the city. A town like Rheims should have many fine taverns."

As we arrive at the outskirts of the city, people line the road, cheering and waving. The cathedral bells peal their welcome. Shouts of *"Bienvenue, victoire"* and *"Mort les Anglais"* fill the air. An old man runs up to me, pushing a bottle of wine into my hands, saying *"Dieu te garde."*

The tolling bells grow louder as we march into the city, and soon the spires of the cathedral come into view. *"Mon Dieu!* Have you ever seen anything so huge, so magnificent?" I ask Adrien, amazed by what I see. "The towers are soaring into the sky, humbling those of us confined to the ground."

Adrien, too, appears to be taken aback by the sight of this stunning structure. "I can't believe such a building can exist," he says, making the sign of the cross. "How does it stay up? It's so beautiful!"

We enter a large square, just below the spires of the mighty cathedral, where we are to make camp. Others in our battalion strain their necks, looking high up into the spires and admiring their magnificence.

The colonel informs us that he is giving us leave for the night. The higher-ranking soldiers get to leave first, and no doubt they're swooping into the taverns and monopolizing all the wine, ale, and women.

Adrien and I are among the last to leave, and we enter a tavern near the cathedral square. It's filled with soldiers and curious townsfolk. The locals seem awestruck by our presence and appearance. The uniforms do look splendid, and they seem to embolden us all.

A familiar but unwanted voice fills my ears. "Rapp boys! Too bad there aren't enough women to go around," Bernard sneers, holding a girl in each arm. Sitting with him is Henri, who looks too drunk to comprehend reality. "Take some wine and ale, and dream about what it will be like when you are true soldiers." He laughs and kisses each woman.

Quick to anger, I move toward the fool. Adrien stops me again.

"Remember, we're still at the bottom," he says, pulling me by the arm toward an empty table. "A bottle of Alsatian Gewürztraminer," he tells the waiter.

Adrien tugs me down into a chair. I give him a stare, then turn to the waiter. "We need at least two, if not more." We drink late into the night, ignoring those around us.

As is my custom, I drink a cup of water after every couple of glasses of wine, but Adrien does not. "Come, Adrien, it's time to go." He stares at me through bleary eyes, stumbling as he gets to his feet.

I drag him from the tavern. The cathedral square, where our camp lies, is nearby. Adrien stops, grabs my neck, and looks me in the eye. His speech slurred, he says, "Why is *Vati* so angry at me? He knew I took little interest in being a butcher." Adrien fingers his locket from Anna Lise. "Why has he forbidden me to see *Mutti* and Anna Lise? I've lost my whole family ..." He stumbles, and I catch him.

Settling Adrien onto his sleeping blankets, I watch as he drifts off. His words trouble me. I press my shirt over the locket from

Anna Lise and think, *I also may never see Anna Lise again. She's like my sister.* The wine sharpens my melancholy.

* * *

Morning comes, and I hear a ruckus in the courtyard outside the cathedral. Crawling from my blanket, I see a patrol of Hussars in deep conversation with our colonel. Horns sound, calling us to muster. I leave Adrien behind and go to the foot of the cathedral stairs.

"Plans have changed, my comrades," our colonel says. "We've received word that the Austrians have declared war on our empire, joining the English and Russians. The Russians are moving their armies to join forces with the Austrians. We must stop them. The emperor is marching from Boulogne, gathering all his troops to go back and attack the Austrians."

Murmuring erupts among our ranks. "We're turning around?" "Is the army in danger?" Some look panicked. Everyone appears confused.

Our colonel raises his arm for silence. "You men belong to many different regiments. We were marching to Boulogne so that you could join them. They now are moving toward us and should be coming through Rheims later today. You will join your regiments as they pass through. Until then, prepare your gear and wait for them to arrive."

Coming back to our tent, I look at my hung-over friend. He hasn't taken any of this in, so I repeat the news. "Adrien," I say urgently. "We're returning to Ostheim and not invading Great Britain. We're going to attack Austria." He mumbles something incoherent in return, lying back down and pulling his blanket over himself.

I find this news unsettling and confusing and, for the first time, wonder if the British can be beaten. Perhaps this will be a very long war after all. I look toward my slumbering friend. *I mustn't let Adrien know my fears.*

By early afternoon, we hear bugles announcing the first contingent of soldiers arriving from Boulogne. It's the emperor himself! He's astride his famous Arabian horse, Marengo, surrounded by the Hussars of his Imperial Guard. Though he is only wearing a Hussar's uniform himself, his strong deportment immediately marks him as our leader. He waves toward the troops in the courtyard as he proceeds along the road toward Strasbourg. Uncle Jean is among those accompanying the emperor. I jump on my Shagya and ride out to meet him.

"Jean-Luc," he says upon sighting me, "It's so good to see you! I see you're now a Hussar. Is Adrien with you?"

"He's at the encampment. What's this about invading Austria rather than Great Britain?" I ask, anxiously skipping all pleasantries.

"When the emperor learned that the Austrians had declared war, his focus shifted to this new, immediate danger. We must engage the Austrians before they combine forces with the Russians. I'm sorry, but I must go. You and Adrien take care. There will be great battles soon." With a swift turn of his steed, Uncle Jean rejoins the contingent accompanying the emperor.

I return to our camp and find Adrien rousing from his stupor. "Never let me drink like that again," he says, looking pale, but at least alive. We pack our gear, and by early afternoon, the main body of troops begins to pass through Rheims.

I see our green and red regimental colors. "Let's report in," I tell Adrien.

We find the quartermaster and present our orders. "New recruits," he says as he examines our papers. "And local boys from Colmar. You must be acquainted with General Rapp, our former colonel."

"Yes," I reply, "he's an old family friend. Where are we going?"

"The army is going to assemble along the Rhine, south of Strasbourg. Our regiment is heading to our home barracks in Ostheim. The emperor will determine when we cross the Rhine and where we'll go."

Adrien looks heartened with the news of our returning to Ostheim. "Do you think we could take leave and see our families once we reach the barracks?"

"No," the quartermaster answers firmly. "We don't know when the emperor will make his decision to attack. We need to be at the ready to receive his orders."

I'm dispirited by this news, and Adrien is frankly morose. We join the regiment dejectedly and proceed toward Ostheim.

It takes three days to reach the barracks, and when we arrive, we find there's not enough room to house the entire regiment. Along with many others, Adrien and I are forced to camp along the banks of the River Ill.

From our knapsacks, we each retrieve our tent halves, tent stakes, and twine. Our tent halves can be used to make small individual tents, but using them as halves gives each of us more room. The night is warm, with a low-hanging full moon emerging over the eastern horizon. Crickets chirp and frogs croak as the sun sets and the men settle into their campsites.

Adrien is very quiet, deep in thought. Finishing our camp setup, he turns to me. "Do you think I can sneak away once it's dark and ride to Colmar? I would be back before sunrise."

I'm alarmed at this idea. "You could be shot as a deserter! It's not worth the risk. Don't even think of it."

Adrien contemplates that. "I can't leave for war on the hard terms I have with *Vati*. I must see him. I won't be caught."

As dark deepens, Adrien prepares to leave, despite my frantic warnings. "I'm going to take Basile for a walk," he says. "Once I'm out of sight of everyone, I'll be off. Wish me luck."

I can't sleep, worrying about Adrien. As the skies to the east start to turn pink, the clomping of a walking horse approaches. "Adrien, is that you?" I whisper in the semi-dark of the approaching morning.

"Yes," he replies in a somber tone. He dismounts and joins me by the fire. He says nothing. He just takes a stick and pokes at the embers.

I'm so relieved to see him that I can hardly speak. "Are you all right? Did you see your family?"

"I saw them," he replies. "*Vati* looked at me with scorn, telling me I was not welcome. I told him I will be leaving for battle soon. I said we must come to an accord. All he did was glare back. 'You made your choice,' he said. 'Now be gone. You are no longer my son.'

"I was dumbfounded. I couldn't speak or move. *Mutti* was in tears, telling *Vati*, 'He's our son! He'll always be our son! You must forgive him!' But *Vati* was unyielding."

Adrien jabs at the fire, sending sparks high into the air.

"Anna Lise was weeping. She ran to me, wrapping her arms about my neck. *Vati* took her shoulders, trying to wrench away her grip.

"I held onto her, sobbing. 'My precious Anna Lise,' I told her. 'Are you to be taken from me as well?'

"'No,' she shouted. 'I won't let go.' But *Vati* wrestled her away, putting her into *Mutti's* arms. '*Mein Bruder*,' she cried. 'You'll always be *mein Bruder*! Tell Jean-Luc he must look after you for me.'

"I could bear it no more, and left. Your papa saw it all, but would not interfere in our family matter. He waved goodbye to me as I mounted Basile.

"Riding away, I could hear *Mutti* lamenting and Anna Lise shouting. Their voices faded, leaving me alone with my thoughts. What am I to do, Jean-Luc?"

Muted sobbing overcame my friend, his body shaking. "What am I to do? ... What am I to do?"

I put my arm around Adrien's shoulders. "It will be all right. Your *Mutti* and Anna Lise will talk reason into him." I pull him into me tightly. "... It will be all right."

Adrien leans into me, regaining his composure. "I'll prove my worth in battle and be recognized for my bravery," he says fiercely. "Then *Vati* will be proud of my deeds. He'll see. He'll see."

He takes his stick and again pokes at the fire. The sparking embers rise into the sky.

Turning toward me, he gives a pinched smile and says with finality, "Yes, he'll become proud of me, Jean-Luc." Then, after a moment, he adds, "Has there been word yet about when the invasion begins?"

"Yes. Messengers have been going from campfire to campfire saying we're moving out at dawn tomorrow. We're to make our final preparations today, then move toward the bridges across the Rhine near Strasbourg in the morning."

Adrien shakes his head. "It appears our first battles will come very soon, my friend."

Six

On to Austria – Fall and Winter, 1805

The emerging sunlight glistens off the River Ill, illuminating the feverish bustle of hundreds of men breaking camp and preparing their mounts for this morning's march. "Adrien, pull up those stakes," I say anxiously. "We need to stow our tent halves. We don't want to be late for the assembly."

I glance over to Adrien to see if he's recovered from his father's words. His face is flushed as he tries to pack his gear. "Jean-Luc, what goes where?"

"You can't load your knapsack like that," I say. "Each thing goes into a certain place. Here, let me help you."

Gear is strewn across his blanket. "First thing in are your extra shoe soles, then your extra clothes and blanket on top. Your pocket knife and other small things go into these side pockets. See how mine is done?"

"Thanks," he says, shaking his head. *"Vati* shook me up, but I am all right." Now smiling, he adds, "I'm a soldier, and we have the enemy to fight."

We finish packing and saddle our horses. Adrien is humming a marching tune. "Beautiful day, isn't it?" he says. "Reminds me of those summer days when we went fishing as kids."

"We don't have time to reminisce. Come on, riders are already crowding in for the assembly."

"You ride over and save us a spot," Adrien says. "We still have another half hour, and I see Quartermaster Beaulac standing outside the stable. I'm going to find out if he can tell me anything."

"Don't take long," I say, feeling happy about Adrien's good mood but irritated he's not coming with me.

I settle into the crowd, trying to take everything in. *So many men. Such excitement.* There's some jostling among the horses. "Easy, Hervé, we'll be leaving soon," I say, patting his neck as the regiment waits for our commander, Colonel Marx, to address us.

"Move aside, Rapp boy. Make room for your superior," Henri's all too familiar voice booms. His horse jostles against Hervé, who doesn't take kindly to the shove and nips at the other steed. Henri's stallion rises to the challenge, whinnying loudly and biting back.

"Where's your Prussian sidekick? The one who keeps you out of trouble," Henri asks.

"What does it matter?" I retort. "I'm not moving for the likes of you."

Our horses continue to jostle. Henri is not backing down.

An older voice abruptly breaks into the scene. "What's the problem? Aren't we all here for the same reason? To listen to what Colonel Marx has to say? There's plenty of room for all of us."

I look to where the voice comes and see an old veteran, a *vielle moustache,* mounted on a magnificent Arabian. He sits tall and straight in his saddle, sporting a gray-speckled mustache and beard. His epaulettes signify his rank as captain.

"A thousand pardons, sir," Henri blurts. "This green recruit is being insolent, and I'm trying to teach him respect."

The captain stares at Henri for several moments. His Arabian snorts.

"Corporal. How many battles have you fought? I think none, judging from your pristine uniform and poor manners. In war, we all depend on each other to survive. We put our trust equally in our generals and all our fellow soldiers. We are comrades, and we trust each other with our very lives, regardless of rank."

Henri's face flushes. He bows and says, "Again, a thousand pardons, sir. Please, take my place. A friend is motioning for me to join him." Henri backs his horse away and trots off.

The captain moves his steed up to mine. "I am Paul Bouchet of Strasbourg, my young friend. That is a fine Shagya you ride. Did that corporal call you a Rapp boy? Does that refer to General Rapp?"

"Yes," I say, uncertain how to respond to this man who is far above me in rank. "The general is a family friend from Colmar. His father works for mine and helped me and my friend Adrien join the Hussars. We call him Uncle Jean."

"A good and honorable friend to have. I met General Rapp in my first campaign at Marengo. He was the aide-de-camp to General Desaix, who died there. Rapp and Desaix arrived at the battle just as the Austrians were beginning to overtake us. He rallied the troops and personally led three companies, including mine, straight into the enemy's center."

I look at Captain Bouchet in amazement. Uncle Jean has told Adrien and me many times of this scene when General Desaix died. He credits his life to a group of young infantrymen who rallied to his side after Desaix's death.

The captain continues. "Jean Rapp was cleaving Austrians on all sides, protecting Desaix, but he couldn't stop the musket ball that brought the general down. Several of my green comrades rushed up to aide-de-camp Rapp along with me, helping him protect Desaix's body. I don't know who saved whose life, but many Austrians died trying to kill us."

I reach over and shake the captain's hand. "It's an honor to meet you. Uncle Jean has told me this story many times."

"What is your name, Private? Perhaps you have been assigned to my company."

"Jean-Luc, sir. Jean-Luc Calliet." I nod toward an approaching rider. "Coming to join us is my friend, Adrien Bauck."

Captain Bouchet takes a leather-bound journal from his saddlebag and opens it. "Let's see. Ah, here is the list of privates. Yes, you are both in my company. Who was the corporal you were having the discussion with? Henri, was it?"

"Yes, sir. His name is Henri. His friend Bernard is usually with him. I don't know their last names."

"Well, I do have a Henri Allard and a Bernard Paquin listed," Captain Bouchet replies. He looks up, his steel-blue eyes piercing. "Private Calliet. What I expect from my men is courage and obedience, but above all, I want trust and respect from everyone. This will include Corporals Allard and Paquin."

"Yes, sir," I reply.

Adrien joins us just as a hush comes over the gathering. Colonel Marx strides out onto the barrack's porch, stops, and gazes out over the sea of uplifted faces. "A grand day to start a campaign," he booms. "Word has been sent that the bridges in Strasbourg are overwhelmed with the huge onslaught of our soldiers and equipment. We are directed to go south and cross the Rhine at the old bridge that leads to Freiburg. Let's move out while the day is still young." Hurrahs erupt from the gathered soldiers, and we begin our march toward the bridge.

"Adrien, let me introduce you to Captain Bouchet. He commands our regiment."

Adrien snaps a smart salute. "An honor, sir."

"Captain Bouchet knows Uncle Jean," I tell him. "Do you remember Uncle Jean's story about the Battle of Marengo and how after General Desaix was killed, he and a group of young infantrymen were able to hold off an Austrian charge? Captain Bouchet was one of those soldiers!"

Adrien again snaps a salute. "A very great honor, sir."

We settle into a walking gait and fall silent. To my surprise, Captain Bouchet stays with us. At first, I'm uncomfortable in his presence, but he puts us at ease as we chat about Uncle Jean. The weather is perfect—warm but not hot, with a cool breeze. We pass in and out of oak and ash forests, catching glimpses of the Rhine to our left.

Up ahead is a fork in the road. "That road veering to the right leads to Colmar," I say.

"I grew up just a few leagues away in Strasbourg, but I've never been to Colmar," Captain Bouchet remarks. "I understand the town is most beautiful."

"Many people say it's like a little Venice. The Lauch River flows through town, and we use it like a canal, taking boats from house to house. Yes, it's most beautiful."

"There," Adrien says. "To the right. You can just see the peak of our church steeple."

Adrien's eyes linger on this small speck of Colmar. A pensive expression crosses his face. "It would have been a thrill to have the army march through Colmar. So close. When do you think we will see home again, Jean-Luc?"

"I hope it won't be too long," I reply as I too stare at the steeple.

Captain Bouchet sees we are already homesick. "It may be many months, possibly years before we can come home," he says.

I turn to the captain. "Possibly years?"

"Home becomes a distant, precious memory for a soldier," he says. "The military life is hard. What we do and what we see in battle can be overwhelming. The death. The blood. The savagery. The memories of home help salve these visions. For me, it's memories of Strasbourg, of my boyhood, and my parents. I have no siblings and my parents have passed. I just have memories now."

Adrien and I exchange glances but say nothing, surprised by his revelations. Another hour passes, and the bridge over the Rhine comes into view. *Can it hold an entire army?* I wonder.

Far ahead, columns of soldiers begin to cross the span. Even from this distance, I can hear the structure moan and creak. As we near, Captain Bouchet starts to whistle. It's a catchy tune, but not one I'm familiar with.

I try to copy the melody, but my whistling ability is unexceptional.

"What tune is that?" Adrien asks.

"A song all soldiers must know," Captain Bouchet says. "When going into battle, we rouse our spirits by thundering its lyrics. It's a simple tune with silly words. It's called *The Song of the Onion*. Let me teach it to you."

As our horses clamber onto the bridge, Captain Bouchet begins singing with a rousing vigor. Others around us eye the captain as smiles cross their faces. Its clear most of them know the song.

> *I love onion fried with oil,*
> *I love the onion when it's good,*
> *I love onion fried with oil,*

I love onion, I love onion.

Let's charge, comrades, let's charge, comrades,
Let's charge, let's charge, let's charge.
Let's charge, comrades, let's charge, comrades,
Let's charge, let's charge, let's charge.

By the time he starts the second verse, he is joined by everyone in the regiment.

One onion fried with oil,
One onion, we change into a lion,
One onion fried with oil,
One onion, we change into a lion.

The song reverberates up and down the ranks. Some soldiers sing off key, but all boom out the lyrics. Our pace even begins to pick up as the horses respond to the energy and enthusiasm.

More verses follow, each louder than the last. A broad smile etches Captain Bouchet's face. "Yes," he says. "Our comrades are ready for battle."

The words are absurd, but the song seems to unite the men. How many times will I be singing or hearing this tune in the future?

We set up camp just past the bridge across the Rhine. There are over a thousand of us in the regiment. Our company of one hundred and forty men camps in a cluster surrounding the captain's tent. We are not far from the road, just at the edge of a forest. Nearby is a vineyard filled with workers, seemingly oblivious to the mass of soldiers near them. The harvest season has just begun, and they are busy cutting the ripe clusters of grapes.

"Be sure to keep this area near my tent clear and a pathway open toward the road," the captain says. "There will be a wagon joining us soon."

While we prepare our meal, the men of our company, my new comrades, mingle as we get acquainted. They are from all parts of France, and a few are from the German states.

The sound of wagons rattling up the road from the bridge catches our attention. "Who are they?" I ask. Two wagons veer off the road near us, one moving toward the camp nearby. "Is that one with a woman and boy heading toward us?" I am incredulous. "What are they doing here? The boy looks no older than ten."

The veterans among our company laugh. "All of those wagons are the army's *cantiniéres*," Captain Bouchet says. "They sell food and drink and sometimes wash our clothes. The army could not survive without them. Our company's *cantiniéres* are in the wagon approaching. The woman is Colette, and that is her son, Claude. Her husband, Gerald, died recently. He had been my comrade since Marengo. She was his *cantiniére*. After his death, she asked if she could be our *cantiniére*, and I agreed."

Captain Bouchet waves toward the approaching wagon. "Colette, Claude, I am happy to see you! Welcome!"

The wagon grinds to a halt. "Thank God you're camped near the road and your company colors so clearly visible. I was afraid I would not find you," she says, clearly relieved to see Captain Bouchet. "These are your men? A fine-looking group. Claude, open up the side of the wagon so that the men can see what we have."

Claude pulls the lever that lets down the side of the wagon, displaying their wares. I take a quick glance across what is presented. My eye catches sight of something familiar. "Adrien,"

I exclaim excitedly. 'Look at these sausages. They are like how your father makes them. Could they be from your shop?"

Colette overhears our conversation. 'I bought these from the butcher in Colmar as I drove through."

'My family's shop! How wonderful," cries Adrien. 'How did my father look? Did you see my mother or sister? How much for some of these sausages?"

Colette gives Adrien a look. 'Your father appears well. Very businesslike. After I left the shop and was boarding my wagon, a young blonde girl came up to me. 'Are you going to see the soldiers?' she asked. 'If you see my brother—his name is Adrien Bauck—or his close friend, Jean-Luc Calliet, could you deliver this foie gras? Tell them Anna Lise loves them and wishes they were home.'

'You are this Adrien Bauck? And you," she adds, turning toward me, 'are Jean-Luc Calliet?"

We nod. Colette brings out the crock of foie gras and gives it to us. 'She was very sad, this little girl. You must mean very much to her. I'm glad my son and I will be your *cantiniéres*."

My new comrades excitedly inspect the offerings. It's a treat having food and drink beyond our army rations.

Madame Colette climbs up onto the seat of the wagon. 'Everyone, if I can have your attention. If there is an item you particularly want and you don't see it displayed, please tell me, and I will write down your request. As I stop to shop in the villages and farms, I will see if I can get those items for you."

Many of the men clamber forward. 'I would like some chevre." 'Find me some éclairs!" 'A good bottle of brandy would be heaven."

After our long day, I settle near the fire and look up to see the moon. It is nothing more than a small sliver. The sky grows darker, each passing moment bringing a deeper layer of blue painted on the last. Stars pinprick the growing darkness. Crickets chirp, interspersed with croaking frogs in a euphony of sound. Lying here, I find it hard to fathom that we are at war, with many of us marching toward our death.

Captain Bouchet sits near his campfire, talking to Colette. Claude is resting his head on his mother's lap as she gently strokes his hair.

I can hear parts of their conversation. "Are you companioned with Madeleine again in your daily search for supplies?" Captain Bouchet asks.

"Yes. Did you know she's pregnant again? Hard enough being a *cantiniére* with six children. But she can't bear being away from her husband. He taught her how to use a sword. I think I will have her teach me."

Captain Bouchet smiles and tosses the remnant of his drink into the fire. "Good night, Colette. Let's get some sleep. The coming days will be hard."

Seven

First Engagement –
Fall and Winter, 1805

Though we are feeling on edge, our march deep into Baden proves uneventful. Scouting parties report no signs of the Austrians, although we hear rumors they have armies massed in Ulm, biding time until the Russians join them. Our regiment should be passing just south of Ulm in a few days, and I can feel disquiet gripping our whole company. Near the campfire, men are bickering about who sits where, complaining about the food, and generally growling at each other. One of the corporals shoves a private away from a spot he wants. Fists nearly fly, but rank wins out.

As darkness falls, we prepare our dinners. "I'm going to cook the sausages we bought from Madame Colette," Adrien says. "A taste of home will do us good." The night turns cool as we savor our food, huddling ever closer to the fire. "Look there, between the trees—a shooting star. And there's another," Adrien says. "Perhaps a good omen." We both gaze up into the sky. The dazzling display soothes my nerves.

Quiet spreads among the men clustered by their fires. Captain Bouchet walks into our midst, looking about and calling for everyone's attention. "We cross into Württemberg tomorrow," he tells us. "The Austrians are near, and we must be even more vigilant." He tacks a note on Colette's wagon. "Here's the list of who rides in the scouting parties in the morning."

Neither Adrien nor I have ever been in a scouting party. We anxiously scan the list. "There!" cries Adrien. "We're in the party that leaves at first light. Sergeant Yount will be leading."

Our excitement deflates as we examine the list of names. "Damn. Both Henri and Bernard are in our group. With only six in our party, we won't be able to avoid them."

Adrien and I chat most of the night, smoking our pipes and leaning against our knapsacks near the campfire. We can't sleep with the excitement of our first patrol and the possibility of engaging the enemy. I finally doze for what seems like moments before feeling a sharp kick and hearing a familiar, sarcastic voice. "Come on, Rapp boy. Rise and shine. Get your Prussian friend. Sergeant Yount is nearly ready to leave."

Too excited to care about his usual rudeness, I rouse Adrien. "It's time to go." He immediately jumps up, and in no time, we have our gear packed and stowed. We mount our horses, joining the others. I smile anxiously at Adrien. "This is finally it!"

Sergeant Yount surveys his assembled patrol, shaking his head. "I know this is the first patrol for most of you. Stay close to each other, obey my orders, and remember to always look out for your comrades. No Austrians have been sighted yet, but my bones say they're near."

We start off at a gallop, but once clear of the camps and troops, we slow to a trot. "This road takes us to Tuttlingen, about twenty-five leagues from Ulm," says Sergeant Yount. "I believe we'll encounter Austrian patrols near there. Remember, we want to take prisoners if we can."

I pull at my sabre to ensure it comes easily from its scabbard. The sound of sliding steel comforts me. Inspecting my pistols, I reassure myself they are loaded.

A sound like an angry bee rushes by my ear, then another. I futilely slap at my neck before hearing the report of guns. Hervé skitters to the right, and Adrien's horse dances away from me. "An Austrian patrol," roars our sergeant. "Take cover by those oaks over there!" He points.

We gallop toward the trees, then whirl to meet the enemy. Seven Austrians attack with sabres drawn. "Send a pistol volley, then attack," bellows our sergeant. I take my shot, but to no effect. "Damn!" I exclaim as I draw my other pistol and let go another shot. Another miss.

One Austrian is closing in on me. I draw my sabre and charge. The Austrian's blade crashes into mine. I knock it upward, then feel a sting on my forehead and blood running down my right cheek. Bringing Hervé to a jolting stop, I wheel back toward my assailant, who's doing the same. Again, our blades clash. This time, an underhand twist of my sabre cuts into his sword arm. He drops his blade with a howl of pain, eyes me in shock, then dashes off in retreat.

Wiping blood from my face, I ready myself for more attackers. I spot two closing in and know I can't battle both at once. I veer sharply and strike blades with one of them. I continue to engage while his comrade circles around toward my other side.

"Jean-Luc, push left," Adrien shouts. I make the move as the second Austrian's sabre cuts past my ear. With frenzied determination, I fight on, hoping Adrien is taking care of the other. A third sabre joins my struggle. *The other Austrian?*

I pull my sword back and drive my blade deep into my enemy's chest. Yanking out my sword, I turn to meet the other potential combatant and am greatly relieved to see Adrien.

"Well done, Jean-Luc!" Adrien shouts as he looks down at the two Austrians lying dead beside us.

Quickly scanning the scene, I see three of our comrades on my left engaged with two Austrians, but on my right, Henri fights for his life against two of the enemy. "Adrien," I yell, pointing my sabre toward Henri. I give Hervé a kick and surge ahead. Adrien follows close behind. I cut one enemy across the thigh. He falls. The other, seeing the changing odds, retreats.

Hervé's feet are tangled between a fallen horse and rider, and I'm unable to give immediate pursuit. With a piercing whoop, Adrien takes off after him. I look for more Austrians, but there are none.

Whose horse is this? The saddle has French markings. The fallen horse scrambles to its feet, leaving its rider motionless on the ground. Shocked, I recognize the lifeless form of Bernard.

Looking toward Henri, I see his face is ashen.

Dismounting, he cradles his dead friend, gently rocking him in his arms.

I dismount as well and join Henri, wrapping my arm about his shoulder. Henri gives a muffled sob. "He saved me. I didn't know an Austrian was coming at me from the back ... he blocked his way ... now he's dead."

I squeeze Henri's shoulders and gaze around the skirmish site. So much blood, so much anguish in such a short time. Not a place to feel pride or the swelling of patriotism, only grief.

Adrien gallops back, leading a horse carrying the Austrian who tried to escape. Adrien looks triumphant for a moment, but turns somber when he sees Bernard. "Henri, I'm so sorry."

Sergeant Yount joins us. "Unfortunate we lost young Paquin," he says gruffly, rubbing his hand over his face. "We can't stay here.

The Austrians who fled are undoubtedly reporting our presence and may return at any moment. We will take care of Private Paquin once we get back to camp and make our report."

I look up toward Sergeant Yount. His words seem callous, but perhaps necessary.

"Secure Paquin's body to his horse," the sergeant says. "Calliet, help that wounded Austrian onto his horse and tie him to his saddle. Bauck, is your prisoner properly restrained? We must be quick."

I help Henri hoist Bernard's corpse onto the horse, being careful to handle his remains gently. He is no saddlebag to flop carelessly over the horse's back.

With difficulty, Henri regains his composure, then mounts his steed and takes the reins of his friend's horse. I help the wounded Austrian onto his horse and remount Hervé. Henri sidles his horse up to mine, firmly grabs my shoulder, and gives it a strong shake. "Jean-Luc, thank you."

I give him a small smile. "We're comrades, right?"

Glancing at my prisoner, I see a lad no older than me, his face ashen. In German, I ask, "Can you ride, or do I need to tie you to your saddle?"

He gazes at me with panicked eyes. "My leg. I can't feel my leg."

Blood flows from an open wound, soaking his blue pants leg. Jumping from my horse, I bind the Austrian's leg tightly, stemming the red flow. "Come on, Jean-Luc," Adrien yells impatiently. "We don't have time to waste ministering to the enemy. Don't forget, he would kill you without a second thought. Look at my prisoner. He's attending to his wound with no help from me."

Adrien's face is flushed. *Doesn't he feel the horror?* I help my prisoner onto his horse and tie him to his saddle.

We move out quickly. 'Wasn't that glorious, Jean-Luc?' Adrien exclaims. 'Here, on our first patrol, we both killed and wounded our enemies. And you saved Henri! We'll be heroes in no time."

I say nothing, turning instead to my prisoner. 'We've a physician who can look at your wound once we return to camp."

A weak smile crosses his face as he clutches his saddle horn tightly.

'We have no time to lose, comrades," barks Sergeant Yount. 'A fine effort! We must get these prisoners to Colonel Marx at once."

We ride about twenty minutes before I look back and see my prisoner slumped over. He slides from his horse, thumping onto the ground, an unmoving heap.

I rein in my horse and turn back toward the motionless Austrian. Sergeant Yount sees my actions and brings everyone to a halt, then circles back toward the unmoving form on the ground. 'He's gone," he declares. 'Calliet, bring his horse along."

I grab his horse's reins, spare one last glance at him, then gallop with the others toward camp.

Arriving at camp, we find the battalion rousing to begin today's march. 'Bauck, follow me with your prisoner," the sergeant says. 'We must find Colonel Marx. The rest of you, return to our company."

Looking pleased, Adrien rides off with his prisoner and Sergeant Yount. He gives me a nod, which I return, but I can't help but think of the two Austrians I killed ... and of Bernard's death. I feel empty.

'Let's be off," a somber-looking Henri says, and we ride to our bivouac.

Our company is moving out. Everyone is in a rush, breaking down tents and stowing their gear. Captain Bouchet shouts orders from his stallion. "Prepare to move out. The Austrians have been spotted nearby."

The captain catches sight of us, his eyes taking in the situation. "Corporal Allard, where's Sergeant Yount and Private Bauck? Whose body is that tied to the horse you're leading?"

"They are escorting a prisoner to Colonel Marx, sir," Henri says dejectedly. "The body is Bernard's, Corporal Paquin's."

Captain Bouchet's face softens. "I'm sorry your friend was killed, but as you can see, we need to leave soon. You and Private Calliet must quickly bury Corporal Paquin while we finish our preparations. Private Calliet, tie the Austrian horse to the back of Madame Colette's wagon."

I take the horse and give it to Claude, who secures it to the wagon. Madame Colette looks at me sadly, then tells Claude, "Come along, son. We must return to the main road and buy food and supplies. These men will be hungry tonight."

Henri gently takes Bernard's body from the horse. He lays his friend out on the ground and grabs his shovel. Without words, I join him, and we dig Bernard's grave. Henri lifts the shoulders while I grab his feet. We lower the body into the opening and quickly seal Bernard Paquin into the everlasting dirt from which we all come.

Both Henri and I have been absorbed in this ritual, but Captain Bouchet's shouts bring us back to reality. "Let's move," he commands brusquely. "The Austrians are making a break toward the south. We must push them back to Ulm."

Thoughts of Bernard and the dead Austrians are replaced by the fervor of the moment. Both excitement and fear sweep through me. We race by the infantry and artillery, which move toward attacking positions for the upcoming battle. We are to protect their right flank from any attacks from Austrian cavalry.

"Over there!" roars Captain Bouchet, pointing with his sabre to the crest of a nearby hill, covered with about two hundred riders. "A company of Austrian cavalry."

Coming up on our left is Captain Kintelberger and his company of Hussars. The two captains briefly confer. Returning, Captain Bouchet says, "We're to attack on the right and Captain Kintelberger's company on the left."

Our contingents rush toward the Austrians. The thunder from our four hundred charging horses is deafening. Outnumbered two to one, the Austrians abandon their position, retreating madly down the other side of the hill.

We take the location and crest the hill to see arrayed before us a full regiment of about five thousand Austrians, preparing for battle. Cannon are being placed in position and infantry squares formed. Their soldiers spot us and prepare to defend themselves. The Austrian cavalry we pushed off the hill take a position at the front of the infantry.

I gasp for breath, stunned by the number of men facing us. I look to find Adrien for support, but he is not with us. Instead, I focus on Captain Bouchet.

"We'll be all right, Hervé," I say, patting his neck, trying to calm myself.

Captain Bouchet raises his sabre. "Charge!"

I become part of the surge, pouring down the hill, bellowing at the top of my lungs. No thought of life or death enters my mind. I relentlessly urge Hervé forward, my sabre at ready. Like earlier in the day, the bee-like sounds of musket balls zip past my ears. Then the sound of screaming artillery shells cleaves the air. I look toward Captain Bouchet, who stares up into the sky, appearing stunned. Then, nothing.

* * *

My ears are ringing, and my body feels like it's covered by lead weights. It's difficult to think. Lying on my back, I rub my hand across my face and find blood. Where am I?

There's a nudge on my shoulder. Reaching out, I touch a warm snout. It bumps me again. Through blurry vision, I make out the outline of a horse. "Hervé?" He whinnies at my touch.

"Where is everyone?" The ground quakes as I struggle to get to my knees. Bodies of men and horses are strewn everywhere. Craters dot the surroundings, and shattered artillery is scattered among the carnage. An explosion erupts nearby. *I need to get out of here!*

Something touches my back. I jerk around. "Private Calliet," a sad but gentle voice says. It's Captain Bouchet, and alongside him, Henri and two others from our company. His face is drawn. "We charged into our own artillery barrage," he says. "We lost many men."

Henri takes my arm firmly and helps me to my feet. I feel wobbly, and my head is pounding.

"Mount your horse, Private. We must search the field for any other survivors," the captain orders. "You and Corporal Allard move to the north while we go east." Pointing to the hill we charged from, he adds, "Meet us on that hilltop at high sun."

I mount Hervé shakily. "You're lucky, Calliet," Henri says. "That shell landed very near you. Let's see if we can find any other lucky comrades."

Our horses step carefully through the carnage. The smell of gunpowder and burned flesh pervades the air, embedding in my nostrils. We plod slowly, looking at each body. Whenever we find a body that is whole, we check to see if there is life. All we find is death.

As we head to the top of the hill to meet our comrades, Henri and I exchange bleak glances. We both know we could have been here among these dead.

Strangely, my mind flies to Bernard. "I'm so sorry Bernard was killed," I hear myself say in what seems like a disconnected voice.

Henri smiles weakly. "Let's hope your Prussian friend had a better day than we had here."

Eight

Vienna – Winter, 1805

I gape at the sights as we march into the city. "Vienna! Have you ever seen a more beautiful place, Adrien?" I ask. "Look—over there, perched above the river. I think that's the summer palace. It looks to be nearly half a league wide."

The morning sun glints off the River Wien, striking the palace windows. Against the backdrop of the snow covering the palace grounds, it rises like a jewel. The river gurgles softly as our company, led by Captain Bouchet, rides in double file along the broad boulevard that hugs the river's bank. The snow muffles the sounds of our horses' hooves.

Soon we are passing through the old town walls into the city center. Scattered civilians hustle away as we approach. The façades of grand houses greet us around each twist in the road. We come to an open area bisected by the river. "Over there, to the north—that must be the Hofburg, the imperial palace," I say to no one in particular. "And over there, what is that? And that?" Craning my neck to see everything, I nearly fall off Hervé.

"Adrien, do you think this is what Paris is like? Certainly not Colmar, or even Strasbourg."

"These are just extravagances of a people gone soft," Adrien scoffs. "You'd never see anything like this in Prussia. Maybe you would in Paris. The Prussian palace in Berlin is no larger than some of these homes. Paris, like this place, became soft and rich before the revolution. The Austrians gave this city away to us without even a shot fired. They deserve no respect, and their palaces should be burned."

How does Adrien know anything about palaces in Berlin? Until we joined the army, the biggest town we had ever seen was Colmar. Prussian bravado?

Captain Bouchet raises his arm, signaling us to stop. He points toward an expanse of park bordering the Wien. "We will camp here. Once you set camp, leave is granted until midday tomorrow."

"The only wandering I'm going to do is to that tavern," says Adrien, pointing to one next to the park. "Maybe meet some Austrian women, eh, Jean-Luc?"

It is still only mid-afternoon by the time we set our camp and start toward the tavern. "Don't you want to see the city, Adrien? It's seems wondrous. The Hofburg is not far, and I've heard the emperor has his quarters there."

"I only want my fill of wine and a pretty barmaid," Adrien retorts.

I shake my head and reluctantly agree to go to the tavern. I turn toward Henri. "You're joining us, right?"

Adrien gives me a quick glance of disapproval, but says, "Of course, Henri, you must join us. We are all comrades, right?"

Henri looks at Adrien and his smirking face, but turns toward me. "Thanks, Jean-Luc, I would like to join you. We need to celebrate your promotions."

Entering the tavern, we see soldiers everywhere. Shouts of *"Vive l'empereur"* ring about the tavern hall. The men are boisterous, and wine and beer flow freely. The three of us sit with our company comrades, enjoying this time away from the tedious life of our encampments. There must be two hundred or more soldiers crowding around the many tables. I recognize company colors from other units in our battalion. Around a small table in the far corner, there appear to be some Austrian civilians, keeping a low profile.

'I don't intend to sleep in my tent tonight, do you, Jean-Luc?" says Adrien as he reaches out, unsuccessfully trying to grab a barmaid who has learned all the tricks for avoiding unwelcomed advances by customers. 'I plan to lie in one of the rooms above the tavern tonight in a soft bed with no timetable to follow except to be back at camp by midday tomorrow."

I nod in agreement. 'We should reserve a room before the others think of it and they are all gone." Before I can stand to go and see the tavern owner, an arm takes hold of me. It's Captain Bouchet's, and he gives me a stern look indicating I need to stay sitting.

The captain stumbles a little as he gets to his feet, holding his glass of wine high, tapping it with a spoon to get attention. 'Comrades, comrades, let us toast our grand emperor whose brilliance has defeated the Austrians with little loss of life!" Cheers of 'Vive l'empereur" erupt from all of us as we stand to toast Napoleon. Bouchet waves his arms, indicating we should sit. Still standing, he drains his glass and fumbles to fill it again from the flagon sitting on the table.

The captain loses his balance a bit in the effort, and his face becomes grave. 'Ulm was a great victory ... but we did lose many comrades."

Looking around, his focus falls on me and Henri. He begins to speak again, but now with a quiver in his voice. "Two of you know why we lost nearly two hundred men in the battle near Tuttlingen. Now I need ... must ... share with you the reason we lost those comrades. It was me!" He wavers, barely able to stand. Total silence fills the room. His voice breaks. "I gave the order to charge into the Austrian lines. I should have known that our artillery might open fire soon. The blood of those men stains my hands, and I can't rub it off."

Captain Bouchet collapses into his chair, wraps his arms about his head, and weeps. There is a stunned silence. Time stands still for what seems an eternity. The only sound is that of the captain sobbing.

Henri looks at me, then stands. His eyes scan the faces of all the men about the room. He looks down toward his feet, then back up. After another moment, he begins to speak in a strong, clear voice. "What Captain Bouchet has said is fact when seen with the clearness of hindsight. But we live the military life. What does that mean? It's the simple clarity of living in the moment. Each of us, even the emperor, has made mistakes when viewed in hindsight. In battle, the stakes are high. Life or death. Victory or defeat. Who is to say that the Austrian artillery would not have begun firing on our lines if they had not been distracted by our charge? We mourn our fallen comrades, and the memory of seeing their shattered bodies is seared into my mind. I do not blame Captain Bouchet. I will continue to follow him without question, because we both live the military life." Henri lifts his flagon of ale in salute to Captain Bouchet, drains it, then slams it on the table.

Again, moments of silence pass, and then, in the far corner of the tavern, someone shouts, "Hear, hear." More shouts of "Hear, hear," erupt, then all of the tavern breaks into singing "La Marseillaise."

I look at Henri, smile, and nod. *Yes! I must remember, I am living the military life. Death is inevitable. The horrors of battle as well. I can grieve for those who die, especially those I kill, and shudder at the barbarity, but I must remember, I am living the military life. How else am I to survive?*

A commotion from outside breaks the revelry. We hear the sound of approaching horses and shouts from the crowds lining the street. I peer out the door. "What are those?" My eyes widen in disbelief and I turn to Adrien, who shakes his head in amazement.

"Is that General Rapp leading those odd-looking troops?" I ask.

"Yes," Henri replies. "Those are the Mamelukes. The emperor brought them from Egypt. They are known to be fierce warriors."

"Uncle Jean," I shout, waving my arms. He spots me and says something to one of the Mamelukes, then comes to see us.

"Jean-Luc, Adrien, an unexpected surprise!" Dismounting, he grasps my shoulders, then Adrien's. He surveys our uniforms. "So, you have been promoted, and quickly. You must have done well in battle."

I smile in acknowledgement, adding little, but Adrien is gushing with excitement. "Uncle Jean," he says, "it was amazing. Both Jean-Luc and I killed some Austrians, and we captured some as well. We got information from those prisoners that pinpointed where the Austrian army was, and we destroyed them. It was glorious! So tense, so exciting! Father will be proud of me."

Uncle Jean gives pause as he notes our different reactions. "I heard a company of our Hussars got caught in our cannonade," he says, eyeing me.

A more subdued Adrien responds. "Yes, it was our company. Most of our men were killed. Jean-Luc was there. Thank God he survived."

I look up and see Uncle Jean's sympathetic eyes. He gives me a slight nod. Changing the conversation, he asks, "What do you think of the Mamelukes? Magnificent, aren't they? In Egypt, they proved to be most formidable. The emperor was so impressed, he convinced a contingent of them to come to France and be part of the Imperial Guard. I've been commanded by the emperor to lead them against the Russians. The Russians are close by, did you know? Our time in Vienna will be short."

Adrien and I exchange a glance over this news. We didn't know.

Looking outside, I watch the Mamelukes pass by, sporting white turbans that surround red hats as well as puffed red trousers, loose-fitting green shirts, and blue vests. On each saddle is a leather holster decorated in brass with a crescent and star. Protruding from each holster, I see a sword hilt and pistol stocks. They must strike terror in opposing troops, much like the Russian Cossacks do with their tall fleece hats crowned in red, their bushy beards, and their long spears.

"Uncle Jean," Adrien says, "I would give anything to accompany you and the Mamelukes against the Russians. What a battle it would be with them against the Cossacks."

"As would I," I add after a moment.

Uncle Jean ponders these words. "If your captain approves, you and Jean-Luc could be temporarily assigned."

Adrien looks toward me, excited. "Yes," he says. "We would be delighted at the chance. We will ask our Captain Bouchet."

"Bouchet, you say? Perhaps the same Bouchet who came to my aid at Marengo? I owe him and his comrades my life! Please, take me to him."

"Uncle Jean," I say, "our captain is blaming himself for the men killed under his command at Tuttlingen. He has had far too much to drink. Perhaps tomorrow would be better."

"Even more important that I see him," Uncle Jean says. "Take me to the captain."

We enter the tavern. "Wait," I say. "I will let the captain know you're here."

I go to the table and tell him General Rapp would like to talk to him. "The general?" Captain Bouchet looks toward the door and immediately struggles to stand at attention, swaying a little.

"It *is* you, Bouchet," Uncle Jean exclaims. "My nephews have been assigned to your command? How lucky for them!"

The captain snaps a salute, but the general embraces him. "Captain, please sit. I can't tell you how often I've thought of those moments at Marengo. I haven't much time, but I do have a request."

The two converse for several minutes before rising and embracing once more. A smile returns to Captain Bouchet's face. He and the general stride over to where Adrien and I stand.

"The general has asked if the two of you could join him and the Mamelukes for the upcoming campaign against the Russians," says Captain Bouchet. "I said only if Henri is included as well. An opportunity such as this comes once a lifetime. What do you say?"

The three of us look at each other and exclaim, "Of course!"

"Unfortunately, your leave will need to be cut short. The general tells me he and the Mamelukes will be leaving in the morning. The emperor has ordered them to go north and reconnoiter a good position to set up his headquarters. The Russians are moving in quickly, and the surviving Austrian forces are joining them. The tsar himself is leading their troops."

"Good. Then it's agreed," says Uncle Jean. "Have another drink, then gather your gear and join us on the parade grounds at the Hofburg. You should have no trouble finding it. Everyone will know where the Mamelukes are."

The three of us waste little time. We finish what we have in our glasses and tell our comrades farewell. "This is only temporary," I say to them. "We should be joining you again after our mission."

Captain Bouchet walks with us back to our encampment. 'Such an opportunity you three have been given!" he says, slapping us on the shoulders. 'Since Marengo, I've always wanted to serve under the general's command. Henri, thank you for your speech. I needed that. We say we live the military life, but doubts creep in. The horrors accumulate sometimes. Each of you, hold your heads high and remember to watch out for your comrades."

We prepare to leave quickly. Turning toward Captain Bouchet, we snap a salute, then mount our horses.

"The palace is over there, less than a league away," says Captain Bouchet as he points to the impressive structure we saw when we arrived. 'Follow this boulevard to the east, around that bend up there. It will lead you directly to the palace parade grounds." We wave farewell.

A cold breeze catches our backs as our horses walk down the wide boulevard. The dirtied remnants of an earlier snow line each side of our passage. The boulevard is deserted. I'm sure that in normal times, the road teems with people. The breeze coursing through the gnarled branches of the ancient trees lining the avenue seems to be singing to us—sometimes with a low moan of dread, and other times with the high pitch of excitement and anticipation. I admit, I feel both.

Rounding the corner, we see the massive façade of the imperial palace, its presence imposing. Campfires dot the parade grounds. 'Let's try those over there," I say, pointing to a grouping of campfires off to the side.

'Are you looking for the Mamelukes?" a voice tinged with an unusual accent calls out from the darkness.

Emerging from the shadows astride a handsome Arabian stallion is a tall, olive-skinned man with a white turban. His right hand grips the hilt of a curved blade, sheathed and hanging by his side.

"I am Baiber. The general sent me to meet his three young friends who will be joining our squadron in our move north. Is one of you Corporal Calliet?"

"Yes, I am Corporal Calliet, and these are Corporals Bauck and Allard. I'm honored to meet you."

I reach out my hand in greeting, but Baiber has already turned, bringing his stallion to a trot, leading us toward the campfires.

Coming to the camp, we slow to a walking gait. Everyone wears a white turban. None look up; they stay busy sharpening their curved swords and checking their pistols.

"The general's tent is there," says Baiber. "He is expecting you."

Baiber turns from us, going back toward the Mameluke fires. A private stands guard outside the general's tent. Dismounting, we approach him. "General Rapp is expecting us," I say. "I am—"

The tent flap flies open and General Rapp emerges. "Jean-Luc! Adrien! Thanks for getting here so quickly! And this is your friend, Corporal Allard, right? Come in, come in. Have something to eat. We leave early in the morning." As we eat some sausages and bread, Uncle Jean tells us of the Mamelukes.

"While in Egypt, we encountered bands of fierce warriors fighting for the Ottomans. Our superior weaponry proved to be the decisive factor in our engagements, but the emperor was impressed by their bravery and skill. We captured many in our siege of Acre and offered them the opportunity to join us. Many did, returning with us to France. I organized a company of them in Marseilles after they first arrived."

Uncle Jean continues. "For this campaign, the emperor asked me to again lead their squadron. You've met Baiber. He doesn't say much, but I rely heavily on his leadership. He and all the Mamelukes can be trusted with our lives. In fact, Baiber's brother, Raza, is one of the emperor's bodyguards."

Our conversation doesn't last long. As we finish eating, Uncle Jean says, "You must make your camp and check your gear. First light will see us riding the road toward Brunn. The town is only twelve leagues away, but it may be a very dangerous twelve leagues. The Russians are moving south quickly, and we must secure Brunn as a headquarters before they arrive."

* * *

I brush the crystalline dusting of snow from my saddle as I mount Hervé. The half-light of early morning reveals a mantle of new snow. Some flakes still fall as we proceed down the boulevard lined with sleeping troops. As we leave, lights in the palace glow, and I imagine the emperor is awake, preparing for the upcoming battle with the Russians. Leading our regiment at a slow walk on his Shagya is Uncle Jean. Somehow, being with him makes me feel safe, the demons of war suppressed for the moment by his strong presence.

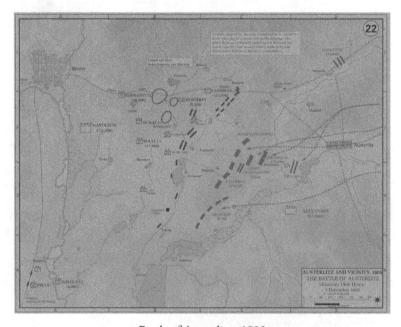

Battle of Austerlitz - 1805

Nine

Austerlitz – Winter, 1805

The sun crests the hills to the east as dawn breaks. "Thank God! Maybe we can warm up, eh, Henri, Adrien?" I say, looking up to the sky. "Having no campfire last night chilled me to the bone. How I miss the warmth of the tavern from the other night."

Adrien glances at our squadron companions, the Mamelukes. "They don't seem bothered by the cold."

I look over, and my eyes meet Baiber's. He gives me a slight bow.

Henri, Adrien, and I, our bodies stiff from the cold, go through the motions of having breakfast and making ready for the day. We mount our horses and continue our journey from Vienna to Brunn. I'm riding near the front of the battalion, just ahead of the Mamelukes. The steamy puffs of my breath join those of my comrades, creating a cloud of glinting ice crystals, twinkling in the rising sun. The forests beyond the fields to our right cast murky shadows across the snow.

I slow Hervé's gait, pulling up near to Baiber.

"No campfire may mean your life," he says as I come alongside. "The enemy is close, and they would spot it."

"You're right."

We ride for a while. "Does it get this cold in Egypt?" I ask.

Baiber glances toward me. "Sometimes it is a little cold. But from childhood, we learn warrior discipline, accepting conditions as they come, so it doesn't bother me. I was born in the mountains of Armenia, and I do remember as a child, before being taken by raiders and sold to be a Mameluke, that it was very cold in the winters, much like here."

"Sold? You are a slave?"

"Are you not a slave yourself? Can you leave if you want? Disobey an order? How is that not being a slave?" Baiber replies.

I'm taken aback. Am I just like a slave? Required to do whatever my superiors say, no matter how dangerous?

Baiber continues. "When I was younger, I was freed by my patron after completing my Mameluke training."

"Did you go back to Armenia?"

"No. My life had become that of a Mameluke. My comrades were those I had grown up and trained with, and my patron helped us all. He gave us work and money. When he was threatened by the French invasion, he called for our help, and we all fought for him. When he was defeated and killed, your emperor became my new patron."

"You were a prisoner. Why do you call the emperor your patron?"

Baiber looks at me. "We Mamelukes are trained to serve. Your emperor honorably conquered the one I obeyed, and in doing so, he gained my loyal service."

"I'm sorry, my friend, but I don't understand how you could change loyalty."

Baiber rides for a few moments without speaking, then says, "My fealty is to Allah, but Allah does not reveal his plans for us. He only shows us different paths. I believe Allah wished for me to serve your emperor. I give him my life and loyalty, just as you do."

I nod as we continue to advance. *Baiber speaks true. My role as a soldier is to give my emperor unquestioning loyalty and, if necessary, my life. Do I really wish to have this life? This military life?*

"Baiber, come forward," General Rapp calls. Our squadron halts as Baiber rides up to join the general. I ride up as well and see we've come to an intersection. A road from the west joins our road, which heads north toward Brunn.

"Wagon tracks. Two wagons, and one, maybe two horses," says Baiber, pointing to the scars in the snow. "Heading north."

"Probably farmers, but they could be Austrian stragglers trying to meet up with the Russians," the general replies. "Take two men and go see." Without hesitation, Baiber chooses two Mamelukes and they gallop toward Brunn.

Snow-covered fields line both sides of the road, and crop stubble pokes through the crusted white. Dotted rodent paths snake in and out of the stubble. A fox dashes across one end of the field into a nearby wood. Outside of the wagon tracks, no signs of human activity are visible.

General Rapp looks toward me. "Corporal Calliet, you and Moushian follow this road coming from the west. Go for about a league to see if there are any other wagons or stragglers. We'll continue north toward Brunn."

Each of the Mamelukes is known by his surname; no rank designations are given.

Moushian's eyes meet mine. He gives a nod, and off we go, side by side. The snow is nearly a foot deep but offers our horses little resistance. Before long, our squadron disappears from our sight and the fields give way to a dense conifer forest.

Slowing our horses to a walk, both of us peer deeply into the woods. As we come to the crest of a hill, the landscape again opens into fields. Moushian grabs my arm and points to a curl of smoke coming from the side of the road ahead. Suddenly, the now-familiar sound of an angry bee zips by my ear, followed by the percussion from a musket being fired. The two of us draw our swords and charge at full gallop toward the sound.

A wagon comes into view, and beside it, a woman with a drawn sabre in one hand and a musket in the other. Several children scramble to hide behind the wagon wheels. A boy who looks to be about ten stands next to the woman, holding a musket pointing in our direction.

"Stop! Stop!" I scream at Moushian, hoping he understands French. I cut in front of him as he pulls his horse to a stop. The woman lowers her sabre. She pushes down the barrel of the boy's musket.

"Do you know what these people are?" Moushian asks in broken French.

"Yes, I believe they are *cantiniéres*. They are part of the army."

Seeing that it appears safe, we sheath our swords and trot our horses toward the wagon.

"A thousand pardons," the woman at the wagon declares. "I am Madeleine Kintelberger, *cantiniére* to Captain Joseph Kintelberger. Your comrade's uniform frightened me. I have never seen one like it before. I thought it must be Russian. I'm sorry we fired at you."

I look over this motley group: six children, ranging from about two years old through about ten, and a pregnant Madame Kintelberger. "I've heard of you. You are a friend of our *cantiniére*, Madame Colette, who serves Captain Bouchet."

"Yes, I know her," says Madame Kintelberger. "She's a good friend. We often travel together. She and another *cantiniére* are scouting ahead right now for good places to purchase things. Once I catch up to her, we're planning to go up to Brunn. Is the army heading that way?"

"Madame," I say firmly. "I cannot say where the army is going. What I can tell you is that you are in very dangerous territory. Going to Brunn unescorted will not be allowed. You and your *cantiniére* friends must either go toward Vienna or stay at the crossroads from which I came. It's safest that way. Perhaps your husband's company will be going by there soon."

The boy with the musket cautiously sidles up to Moushian and stares at him. "Where are you from? Why is your uniform so strange?" he asks.

Moushian smiles, having heard these questions before. "Far across the inland sea," he replies. "A place very hot and dry. This is what warriors wear at my home."

I resume. "Madame, I must insist you break camp and come with us back to the crossroads. The other *cantiniéres* should be there as well. We have no time to waste."

We help Madame Kintelberger pack up camp, and we're soon on our way back to the crossroad. The wagon slows our progress, and I fear Cossacks may be nearby. Moushian and I ride on either side of the wagon.

"Are there more like your friend with the turban?" asks Madame Kintelberger.

"Yes, a full battalion, led by General Rapp."

"General Rapp, you say? You must be on a very important mission for a general of his stature to lead a battalion!" says Madame Kintelberger.

"These are dangerous times," I reply, looking straight ahead. "The emperor has his reasons."

We get back to the intersection by midday. The temperature is warming, and light, puffy clouds scatter across the sky. I spot two wagons settled close to a campfire. Horses are nibbling on fresh hay scattered on the snow.

Baiber gallops up to greet us. *"Alhumdulilah.* We've been expecting you. The tracks we saw this morning were from those two *cantiniéres* over there." Looking over the wagon we are escorting, he adds, "You, too, have found a *cantiniére?*"

"One that nearly killed us," I reply wryly. "Madame Kintelberger, this is General Rapp's attaché, Baiber."

Baiber nods toward her, taking stock of Madame Kintelberger and her children. "We have no such women and children doing this in my country. Women must tend our fields and businesses while we're away. They would slow our armies down."

"And we would have no decent food or clean clothes if we had no *cantiniéres,*" I reply. "Our soldiers would be doomed without them."

"Come," says Baiber. "The general wants us to return quickly. The battalion is nearing Brunn."

We escort Madame Kintelberger's wagon to the others, and Madame Colette and the other *cantiniéres* come greet us. "Is that you, Jean-Luc?" asks Madame Colette, staring at me. "Where is Captain Bouchet? Why aren't you with his company?"

I explain that Captain Bouchet is in Vienna but should be coming this way soon. "I will be joining him again," I add.

"Come, we must go." Baiber interrupts us, urging us to end our conversation. "Come!"

Leaving the *cantiniéres* behind, we ride for several hours toward Brunn. We begin to see more and more farmhouses just off the road, smoke spiraling from their chimneys, but no sign of people working outside their homes. We overtake several wagons, driven by what appear to be local peasants, who give us wary glances as we ride by.

Coming over a rise, we see the village of Brunn in the distance, and up ahead is our battalion. We catch up to our comrades, and the general comes our way. "Good, you've returned. I trust you had no difficulties to the west?" he asks Baiber, though he glances toward me and Moushian.

"Just another *cantiniére*," Baiber replies.

"Baiber, come with me." General Rapp rides with Baiber up a hill. The setting sun illuminates the landscape, and I see the general pointing in different directions as Baiber nods his head.

After a short while, they return, and General Rapp addresses us. "There are no signs of the Russians or any Austrian soldiers. The villagers know we're here. I don't see any unusual activity by them, but we can't be too careful. We will be splitting into four companies and camping at key spots surrounding the village to observe. In the morning, we will take possession of Brunn."

Another night to freeze with no campfire? I look around for Adrien and Henri and see they are on the far side of the battalion.

"Corporal Calliet," the general continues. "You and Moushian go report to the emperor that Brunn appears clear of the enemy. We'll send a message in the morning to confirm after we take the village."

Moushian and I begin the long journey to Vienna. *Perhaps we'll be warmed by a campfire after all when we get there.*

* * *

I have some free time to catch up with my journal and find a spot to write on a low rise overlooking a field, which is continually filling with troops coming up from Vienna. The emperor is now headquartered in Brunn. Anticipation of a major engagement grows. Yesterday, I was among the guard accompanying the emperor as he reviewed potential sites for the upcoming battle.

An area known as the Pratzen Plateau was of particular interest to him. It lies several hundred feet above the Litava River valley, near the village of Austerlitz, with a sharp drop to the north, several lakes to the south, the Rokytnice River to the west, and a plain perfect for cavalry movement just north of it. 'Study this ground well," he told his generals. 'It will be the field of battle."

Nearly seventy thousand men are now stationed on this plateau. The Russians and Austrians are massed just north of us. Scouts estimate their numbers to be over one hundred thousand. Henri, Adrien, and I are still attached to the Mameluke battalion and are sharpening our sabres and cleaning our pistols around our campsite. Henri appears deep in thought as he prepares his weapons. Adrien can't hold still. He polishes for a while, then jumps up, pacing about and swinging his sword before settling again.

'Jean-Luc, this will be the battle for us to gain glory!" I hear Adrien say as I put away my journal. 'No need to worry about their greater troop strength—that just means more for us to kill! Our emperor will outmaneuver them at every step."

Henri glances up and shakes his head, then resumes polishing his sabre.

'You're right, Adrien," I reply dully. 'I imagine the tsar and the Austrian emperor are rubbing their hands, thinking they will finally destroy our army and our emperor. That's not going to happen. We'll win, I'm certain, but there will be a price. I don't relish what tomorrow will bring."

Anxiety and sadness well up inside me.

Adrien chuckles, sliding his blade with vigor down his whetstone. 'You always were the serious one, Jean-Luc!"

I look toward the Mameluke campsites. In contrast to the bustle of the French soldiers, the Mamelukes have already finished preparing their weapons and are either grooming and feeding their horses or simply resting by their fires. My anxiety builds as the day grows long. I walk over to talk with Baiber, who is grooming his horse. "A beautiful stallion," I say. "Did you bring him from Egypt?"

"Yes. Arum and I have watched over each other for many years. I bring him purpose, and he gives me the means to attain what Allah intends for me. With Arum's help, I defend and fight for my patron. Today, the day before battle, we give the other comfort, helping to prepare for our fate."

Baiber continues caring for Arum, absorbed by the movement of each brushstroke. I take my leave and go to attend Hervé.

Hervé snorts as if asking, *Where have you been?*

"I'm here, my good friend," I say, as I give him a handful of oats and begin brushing his sides. "We will watch over one another tomorrow."

* * *

Our entire encampment wakes before sunrise. We quickly eat some bread, break our camp, and pack our horses. Last night, the emperor himself traveled to each bivouac site, personally encouraging us. We lit torches and cheered him as he passed. Shouts of "Vive l'empereur" rang out loudly—so loud that I'm sure our enemies heard it as well. Adrien reminded me that the battle would take place on the first anniversary of Napoleon's coronation.

Henri, Adrien, and I are stationed with the Mameluke battalion near the emperor as reserve forces, waiting to be called if the battle should turn against us. A fog envelops the plateau, making it hard to see. Not far in front of us stands the Pratzen Heights, currently held by the Russians.

As the sun begins to rise, enemy artillery fire can be heard crashing into our right flank. By eight in the morning, scouts begin reporting updates to the emperor. We are close enough to understand the changing situation. The first reports say our right flank fell back before finally making a stand and stopping the enemy. Newer updates say the enemy is committing more forces to this right flank, hoping to overwhelm it.

I feel my heart pumping. "Adrien, this doesn't sound good. Are we losing the battle?"

"Look at the emperor," he replies. "He doesn't look upset." As if suddenly privy to the emperor's plans, Adrien says, "He's creating a trap."

I strain to see the emperor. Adrien is right. He doesn't look panicked as he talks to his generals; he is animatedly pointing toward the Pratzen Heights. Is he planning to attack?

"Look, General Soult is leaving the emperor and moving to the head of his regiment," I say. "What's that I hear?"

The sound clarifies into words and a melody. I've heard this before, when we crossed the Rhine at the beginning of the campaign.

> *I love onion fried with oil,*
> *I love the onion when it's good,*
> *I love onion fried with oil,*
> *I love onion, I love onion.*
> *Let's charge, comrades, let's charge, comrades,*
> *Let's charge, let's charge, let's charge …*

"Yes! The onion song! Yes, they are marching into battle!"

The fog lifts as the battalion moves up the heights. Higher and higher they go, at first meeting no resistance. "The Russians have been taken by surprise," I exclaim, but that doesn't last long.

The Russians surge forward, pushing us back with musket fire and bayonets. The first French attack wave is repulsed, but the second breaks through. Within an hour, the Heights appear secured.

Hervé is getting restless. He pounds his left front hoof. We've been waiting in reserve for hours.

"Look up there, to the right," shouts Henri. "The Russians are counterattacking and pushing us back down the hill!"

Aghast, I see that our forces are being overwhelmed. I glance toward the emperor. He is pointing to the Russian advance and talking to General Rapp. The general salutes, reins his horse around, and rides our way.

With sabre drawn, General Rapp sweeps to the front of our corps. "Hurry!" he yells. "We must rescue our comrades!"

We gallop headlong toward the Russian advance. I hear whizzing about my ears and see many of my comrades fall. Hervé and I sweep forward with nothing on our minds but the faces of the ever-nearing Russians, their cavalry leading the attack into our lines.

We smash into their charging horsemen. The sound of metal-on-metal rings through the air. I slash at the enemy, but my blows are parried away. Over and over I swing. My blade slices into one soldier's neck. His blood gushes fountainlike, covering my uniform as he falls from his horse. Another quickly takes his place. On I push.

Up a ravine to my left, I spot a *cantiniére* wagon under attack by Cossacks and push my way in that direction. A child races from the side, another from the other direction. They cower behind a woman as she swings her sabre. I get a better look. It's Madame Kintelberger and her family with her husband by her side.

A cannon ball strikes her husband, taking away the left side of his chest. Another rips off Madame Kintelberger's arm. She fights on, but the Cossacks don't appear to want to kill her—but why? Above the din of battle, I hear the screams of her children. Madame Kintelberger strikes at the lances with her sword, but to no affect.

My attention snaps back to my own struggles. Russians are flowing down the hill, led by a high Russian nobleman. The yellow plume of his pompous hat flows above his head in a sea of blue uniforms. They swallow the forces before them like an encroaching tide. Behind me, I see reinforcements coming to our aid.

I scream my relief, then turn back to the wagon, but I'm too late. Madame Kintelberger and her family are gone. The Cossacks attacking her are gone as well.

Three Russian infantrymen are upon me. Their eyes gleam as they approach. One of them shrieks as he rushes forward. Hervé is speared by a lance. We start to tumble to the ground as I feel a spear pierce my chest. The last thing I hear is a shout from Adrien. 'Jean-Luc—"

Ten

Peace – Winter, 1805

The smell of gunpowder permeates my senses. Opening my eyes, I can make out only blurry images. Voices are far away. *What is it they're saying? Are they talking to me?* I try to lift myself, but collapse. Rolling my head to the side, I see a wagon next to me. *Did we save Madame Kintelberger? No, that can't be, the Cossacks took her. What's that rumbling noise? Where is Hervé? I felt him fall.*

Again, distant voices. Too faint to hear. *My uniform, is it being cut away? Where's my sword? Is a Russian stripping me of my uniform? I've got to stop him.*

"Jean-Luc! Jean-Luc!" I finally realize someone is saying my name over and over. The voices are becoming clearer.

"Jean-Luc! Can you hear me? It's me, Adrien, and Henri is with me as well. The hospital wagon is here."

Painfully, my eyes turn toward the sound of his voice. I'm lying in the snow. I see a red eddy darkening its whiteness, widening as it arcs away from my body.

"Adrien? Is that you?" I say hoarsely, panic stricken. "Where am I? Have we been taken by the Russians? There were so many of them."

"You're still on the battlefield," Adrien says. "The Russians have been routed. You're safe, but you took a heavy gash. Baron Larrey is stitching your wound closed."

Soldiers on horseback gallop by. *Where are they going? Do they have Hervé?* "Where is Hervé?" I cry out.

Moments of silence. A hand gently touches my shoulder. It's Adrien. "I'm sorry, Jean-Luc. Hervé fell in the battle. He's gone." He's speaking so softly I barely hear him.

Tears swell in my eyes. "Hervé ... Hervé." I cannot say anything more. My world is black. We were to protect each other. I've failed. "Is he near?" I try to peer around, but feel firm hands holding onto me.

"A few feet away," says Henri. "The lance struck him in the heart. He died immediately."

"I must see him," I gasp, distraught. Again, I try to move, but cannot. "Am I all right?" Panicking, I start flailing my arms and try to touch my legs. "No amputation? I have all my limbs?" I say with a quiver. "I would rather die than be without a limb."

"You are whole, Corporal," says the baron. "And very lucky. The Russian lance drove clear through you, but as far as I can see, it missed all your organs."

Turning toward Adrien and Henri, the baron continues. "I've stitched the stab wound closed and also poured vodka onto it. Don't know if it will help, but I have seen fewer cases of infection when I do.

"You are in for a long recovery, Corporal, but you should be fine. Lucky I was nearby to stop the bleeding quickly. I was attending General Rapp when your comrades told me of your fate. The general seems to know you and insisted I leave him and come attend you."

"Uncle Jean—he's wounded?" I cry, panic rising again.

"Nothing more than his usual. A scalp laceration here, several nicks to his arms and legs. Very bloody, but not serious.

"The charge you and the Mamelukes made helped turn the battle. Your Uncle Jean personally captured Prince Repnine and nearly caught Grand Duke Constantine, the tsar's brother. He was quite the sight presenting the prince to the emperor. The emperor commented on his amazing ability to attract wounds, to which the general retorted, 'It's not surprising I am always wounded, as we are always fighting.'" The baron smiles at the memory.

I try to laugh, but can only give a feeble smile and a cough. Listening to the baron has taken my last ounce of strength. I'm relieved to know I still have my arms and legs, but losing Hervé grieves me deeply. Sleep. I must sleep. My eyelids are like weights.

The jostling of the wagon breaks my sleep. Looking around, I find it is filled with wounded. On my left, I'm horrified to see that a soldier is missing his arm as well as part of his shoulder. *Must have been a cannonball,* I think grimly. Across from me, another has no legs beneath his knees. There is blood everywhere. The soldier to my right doesn't appear injured, but he keeps rocking his body back and forth with his arms tightly folded across his chest, talking gibberish.

What hell am I in? So many broken bodies and broken minds. All for the glory of France? The emperor? They can keep their military life. I want no more of it!

"Ach," I say as I reach to hold my wound. *This jostling hurts so much.*

Someone up front leans back and tells us, "The hospital is near. The wagon trip won't be much longer."

Trying to take my mind away from the pain, I peer out through the back flap of the wagon. Snow is falling, and daylight is fading.

Injured soldiers are limping their way toward the hospital, clearing a path for the ambulance as we drive by.

"Damn!" I cry out in agony as the wagon jolts sharply. I grit my teeth, only thinking of my pain. It won't stop. Then I see the others around me and try to think of them.

* * *

Distant voices keep coming and going. *It's so cold*. I pull my blanket closer and huddle tightly. It doesn't help. *Why am I sweating when I feel so chilled? Am I outside?* My eyes crack open. Mucus, creased along my eyelids, tries to pull them shut again, but finally they open wide. No, I'm not outside. I'm in a room with other beds, occupied by wounded soldiers. *The smell! What is that awful smell?*

Someone is walking by. I reach out to grab him, but can barely move my arm. "Please," I croak. "Water. Do you have water?"

The man stops. "Corporal Calliet?" I recognize the voice, but don't remember from where. "I'm Baron Larrey. I stitched your wound closed on the battlefield. Here, let me help you with some water. Careful. You're very weak."

I never dreamed water could taste so good. "Where am I? What is that smell?"

"At the hospital in Brunn. You've been with fever for several days. Unfortunately, the smell must be endured. Many here have dysentery and infection." His hand touches my forehead. "Good, your fever appears to have broken. Let's check your wound. I needed to cauterize it yesterday." The doctor begins cutting away my bandages. "Yes, very good. No new infection. You are one of the lucky ones."

I clench my teeth as the doctor places new bandages about my chest.

114

"You've missed your comrades. They were here earlier, but they're probably at a tavern now, celebrating the truce signed with the Russians and Austrians. The war is over."

"Over?" I say. "No more battles?" I lay my head back in relief. *Maybe this madness is finally over.*

"General Rapp is stopping by my surgery soon so that I can check his wounds," says the baron. "I'll tell him you're awake and out of danger."

The war is over! I can hardly believe this news. Maybe I can go home and be done with the army. Maybe Adrien can too.

* * *

Uncle Jean's voice booms across the room. "Jean-Luc, Baron Larrey tells me you are on the road to recovery. Such good news!"

I smile weakly up at the approaching figure. "I hope you are as well, Uncle Jean?"

The general moves toward me to give me an embrace, but pulls up short, remembering my bandages. "Yes, I'm fine. Just some nicks. Here, I brought you a new uniform. Your old one was ruined, and besides, it didn't show your proper rank." He pulls out a freshly tailored uniform with sergeant stripes.

I smile weakly. "Thank you, Uncle Jean. Do you think I will need it now that the war is over?"

The general looks into my eyes. He knows this tone of voice, this look I give. He knows how the battle terrified me. He pulls up a stool and sits, putting the new uniform on the floor. "Jean-Luc. Do you remember when you were a boy and the traveling guillotine came to Colmar?"

I nod, twisting uncomfortably to look at him.

"I was in Ostheim to convalesce from my battle wounds. You were but nine, but you were among us when I confessed to my father that I was considering retiring from the Hussars. I loved my comrades, but the battles ... the battles held such horror."

Uncle Jean pauses and looks down, then back toward me.

"I was sure I could not endure another battle and would have retired if not for a personal plea from General Desaix. I told the general about my feelings and how I wasn't sure I could fight again. He told me that the army needs to remember its humanity, and it could only do so with soldiers like me. The general finally convinced me to stay. From then on, I embraced the military life."

I start to speak. "Uncle Jean, I don't think I can do this any longer. I—"

"Jean-Luc, it's too soon to decide. Take time to convalesce. When you're able to travel, I'll arrange to have you sent to Colmar. Stay with your father. Have little Anna Lise dote on you, as she always does. I'll come visit in a few months. I fear our wars will never end and we will need men like you. But it will be your decision.

"I almost forgot. Baiber wanted me to give you something and to say he's proud to have you as a fellow Mameluke."

Uncle Jean hands me a package wrapped in silk. Inside, I find a leather scabbard sheath adorned with a star and crescent moon. Beneath the star and moon is a locket of hair from the tail of a horse. I recognize the color and grip it tightly, tears welling.

"Hervé served you well," says Uncle Jean.

I hear steps approaching behind me. Leaning back, I see Adrien's smiling face and Henri right next to him.

Uncle Jean rises and pats my shoulder. "In about a week, a carriage or sledge will come to take you to Colmar." He turns toward Adrien and Henri. "Look at you in your new uniforms! I am proud of you. Your father will be pleased, Adrien, when he hears the news of your bravery and our victory at Austerlitz. I must go. There are many preparations to make before we start our deployment back toward Paris tomorrow."

Henri and Adrien give Uncle Jean a salute as he returns to his meeting with Baron Larrey.

"It's good to see your fever is gone, Jean-Luc," Henri says earnestly. "Adrien and I have been so worried about you."

"You're going to Colmar?" Adrien exclaims. "How I wish I could go. I miss Anna Lise and my mother. Maybe now *Vati* will talk to me again. Did you hear a truce has been signed with the Russians and Austrians? I wonder who we will fight next."

"Hopefully no one," I reply. "Though the English are still a thorn. Did you hear? They defeated our fleet at a place called Trafalgar."

"See those wounded being guarded on the far side of the room?" asks Henri. "They're Russians. Some of the survivors from their retreat across the frozen lakes to our south. The emperor saw that they were trying to escape and had our artillery fire upon them to break the ice in the lakes. It worked—hundreds of the Russians drowned. A horrible death." I can tell Henri is troubled by our emperor's action.

"Wasn't that a brilliant move?" Adrien says. "Henri is right. Hundreds of Russians died. I'm not sure why we are treating their wounded. We should have left them to their fate and let their own army try to save them."

I lean my head back onto my bunk, both in disbelief at this military move by our emperor and from exhaustion. I may be getting better, but right now I want to sleep again.

"Jean-Luc, you need rest. We've got much to do before we leave tomorrow," says Henri, seeing my exhaustion.

"Yes, we must go," adds Adrien. "Please give Anna Lise a kiss for me and tell her I hope to visit home soon. And please talk to

Vati. Let me know how he is. Now that we have peace, maybe I'll be able to take leave soon."

"I will. Adrien, I may ..." But I don't finish my sentence. Uncle Jean is right. It is too soon to decide if I will leave the army. I know Adrien doesn't want to leave.

Instead, I say, "I'm glad to see you both. I'm sorry for being so tired, but I don't think I can stay awake much longer. Adrien, I'll write you. Henri, I'll see you again soon."

They both pat my shoulder, awkwardly wishing me a speedy recovery. Adrien picks up my new uniform from the floor and drapes it across the stool, brushing off some dust.

I cannot help but feel a growing sadness as I look at the new uniform.

Eleven

Home – Winter, 1805

The trip to Colmar will take several days, but the journey home will be much more comfortable than the one that brought me here to the hospital.

Baron Larrey has come out onto the front porch. 'Sergeant, I hope all is satisfactory? The sledge that the general has arranged is comfortable?"

'Yes, it's much roomier than any other sleigh I've ridden in. Please let General Rapp know how much I appreciate this."

'Of course," he replies as he has a private place a wicker basket on the seat beside me. 'Here's some food. It's going to be a long journey."

I'm bundled tightly with blankets, both to keep warm and to minimize the effects of any bumps we will be hitting with the sledge.

'A beautiful day, isn't it?" I say to the private who is helping me settle into the back seat of the sledge. My driver is already sitting on the front bench, ready for the journey to begin.

The sun has just risen, revealing a new cover of shimmering snow. A light breeze jostles the snow into crystalline wisps that dance across the nearby field.

Looking up at Baron Larrey and the building behind him, I can't help but reflect on how happy I am to be leaving this cesspool of misery.

"Here, sir, some hot bricks for your feet," says another private as he positions the bricks he has hauled from the kitchen fires in a wheelbarrow to a blanket under my feet. "Is that good, sir?" he asks while wrapping the blanket up around my knees to hold the warmth of the bricks.

"Very much. Thank you!"

The driver flicks his reins, and the sledge lurches forward down the drive that leads to the Ulm road. I look back at the hospital, giving the baron a wave, glad to be leaving this cruel cavern filled with dying men and the smell of rotting flesh. I fervently hope never to see such a place again, but my heart says that won't be true. I hope this peace holds.

"A good day for travel, sir," says my driver. Indeed, the trees along the road seem to twinkle with their mantle of snow in the mid-December sunshine. Crows caw overhead, seemingly wishing me goodbye.

"A glorious day," I reply, my voice reflecting my relief.

Out of habit, I check to see if my sabre is at the ready and my pistols are loaded with dry powder. My fingers gently touch the lock of Hervé's hair held in place on the leather sheath that holds my scabbard. *Hervé, how I miss you. I promise I will go to Ostheim and remember those days when we were first together. I will visit with the Shagyas and tell them of our friendship and your courage.* A wistful smile creases my face as I think of my lost friend.

I haven't sent word to Papa that I will be home soon. I want to surprise him, but also don't want anyone making a fuss over my arrival. I've heard there have been celebrations across France with the news of our victory at Austerlitz. Returning soldiers have been given heroes' celebrations.

None of that for me! I just want to be with my family and anticipate the day when I will give my final decision about leaving the army. I desperately want to leave and can't think of any reason to stay, but will honor Uncle Jean's request to delay this decision until we talk again.

The hospital disappears from view, and the road leads into the forest. Our sledge is the first to lay tracks on the fresh snow. The clip-clop of the horse lures me into quiet contemplation. *Home! I'm going home!* I look ahead, feeling nothing but joy.

The thoughts of peace at returning to my old life are overwhelming. Maybe I can settle down, have a family, and help run our family inn. The food! I can't wait for good food again. I'll go down to the bridge where Adrien and I fished as children and catch a salmon. Mademoiselle LeClair can prepare salmon fillets on a bed of sauerkraut, smothered with father's white sauce. I remember that the best sauerkraut comes from the Baucks' butcher shop. *Ah, Adrien. What does life hold for you? What will your vati say when I talk to him?*

My mind wanders aimlessly for the remainder of the day— childhood memories filling it one moment, then thoughts about what lies ahead for me filling the next. Perhaps I can get to know Mademoiselle Mayer better. She must be sixteen by now. I'll talk to Anna Lise. I've seen her with Anna Lise many times. The Mayer family are also Prussian and good friends with her family.

My driver glances back at me. 'Sir, your face. You look so happy. You are thinking good thoughts?"

"Yes. I'm thinking of home!"

* * *

It's our third day of travel. The snowing has stopped, and we ride along under overcast skies. "We're coming into Ulm, sir," my sledge driver says. "General Rapp told me to stay at the hotel next to the Rathaus. We should be there shortly." As we pass through the streets, people see my uniform and bow respectfully. Bavaria and Württemberg are friends of France, and the people of Ulm are particularly grateful that the emperor did not attack and destroy the city, but rather negotiated the Austrian army's surrender without a fight.

My thoughts trail to the Battle of Tuttlingen, just to the south of here. I killed my first man there and survived the cannon barrage from our own guns. The repugnant memory of all those mangled bodies floods back.

"We should make Colmar tomorrow," my driver says, "if the weather holds."

The trip has been wearing, and I'm grateful to retire to my bed after our evening meal. I fall asleep as soon as I pull up the covers, not moving until my driver rouses me in the morning.

"God has granted us fortune," my driver says happily. "The air is cold, glazing the snow into a lacquered speedway, and any new snow is holding off as well."

Indeed, the sledge races down the road. Last night's sleep and my growing excitement have made me talkative. Chatting with my driver, I learn about his life, home, and family.

Emerging from the forest, we come to vineyards and fields. "Look over there," my driver shouts. "The bridge over the Rhine. Colmar is not far!"

The sight of the distant bridge brings tears to my eyes. I look to the left and recognize the spot where we made our first encampment. I remember so many things from that first night ... getting to know new comrades, seeing the odd wagon with a woman and boy driving into our camp, the excitement Adrien and I felt after meeting our *cantiniéres* and learning Madame Colette had gifts for us from Anna Lise, our obsession with cleaning our sabres, and so much more.

The bridge grows closer. I imagine I hear the muffled sound of a marching tune. What is it they're singing?

> *I love onion fried with oil*
> *I love the onion when it's good ...*
> *Captain Bouchet, is that you?*

But there is no one. The sound fades from my mind.

The bridge creaks as we drive the sledge up onto its deck. Sheets of ice line the riverbank, but the main channel is roiling with high water.

We have made good time today. The spires of the Colmar church come into view as the December sun dips low. Soon, our horse pulls the sledge into the village. People look up and stare, but no one recognizes me.

I lean forward in my seat, taking in the sights, exhilaration building. 'Driver, do you see that sign ahead for the inn, next to the butcher shop? That's home! Pull up to the inn entrance. We can care for our horse in a moment. First, I must see my papa!"

'Of course, sir. You needn't worry about our horse. I will tend to him at the stable. It's time to see your family again."

The sledge pulls up to the inn entrance. My driver helps me out, and we make our way inside. No one is about, but I hear Papa's voice. The jingle of the bell from the front door has caught his attention. 'I'll be right with you," he says.

My driver returns to the sledge, retrieves our belongings, and enters again just as my father comes into the front room. The noise from my driver entering catches his attention, and he starts to address him. He hasn't noticed me yet. I interrupt. 'Papa, I'm home."

He turns toward me. I see a look of shock and then joy cross his face. Tears well in both our eyes. "Jean-Luc, can this truly be you, my son?" he cries, as we move to an embrace. "General Rapp wrote that you had been wounded and were recovering in a hospital. I could only pray for your recovery. How can you be here?"

Tears stream down my face, and my voice is choked. "It's true," I reply. "My injury was severe, and I need more time to heal. Uncle Jean thought it would be best for me to convalesce here. I'm so happy to be home. I wanted to surprise you."

We embrace over and over, grasping one another's shoulders joyfully. "Let me get Mademoiselle LeClair and Monsieur Rapp," my father says as he heads toward the back room.

My driver has disappeared, likely taking care of our horse and sledge. I look around. *The place hasn't changed.* I walk about the room, fingering the furniture and remembering the times I've spent here, feeling comforted. The tall case clock in the corner strikes five. Looking outside, I see the town square and remember back to that day when the guillotine was in town. Uncle Jean helped stop that travesty while he too was recovering from wounds. I strain my neck to the right, and the front door of the Bauck butcher shop comes into view. Talking to Herr Bauck about Adrien will not be easy.

"Jean-Luc! Jean-Luc! You're actually here! I thought you'd never come home," says Mademoiselle LeClair as she grabs me by the neck and kisses me. Her face then becomes stern. "You should have told us you were coming! All we knew was that you were badly wounded. Shame on you!" Her scolding does not last as she wraps her arms about me again.

Standing off to the side is Monsieur Rapp, Uncle Jean's father. I go to him and kiss each of his cheeks, then shake his hand. "It was an honor to serve with your son. Truly a great man. He was my commander at Austerlitz, and his quick action of sending the doctor to where I fell on the battlefield saved my life. He also arranged for my passage home."

Monsieur Rapp beams with pride. He often receives kind words regarding his son, but to hear it from me, essentially a family member, means much to him.

The jingle from the front door bell pauses our homecoming greetings. It is my driver returning from the stables. "Everyone," I say. "This is Pierre. He drove my sledge from the hospital, and we have become good friends." Pierre is given a hearty greeting by all.

Mademoiselle LeClair chimes in. "You must be exhausted from your trip. Let me prepare some food so that you can get some sleep soon."

Just then, the door to the inn bursts open, and a whirl of blonde energy rushes toward me and grabs hold. "Jean-Luc, it is you! I knew it must be when I saw the sledge being taken to the stable and heard the voices coming through the door."

"Easy, Anna Lise, easy. Don't hold on so tightly. I still have bandages."

"Oh! Have I hurt you?" She says in a panic as she backs away.

"No, no, I'm fine, but I don't know if I could have survived much longer under your squeeze," I say, smiling. "Let me look at you. Have you grown so much in the time I've been gone? And gotten so pretty?"

Anna Lise glows from the compliments and grabs me again, though not as tightly.

"Monsieur Rapp has told us Adrien is fine and that he fought very bravely at Austerlitz. Is he all right?" she asks. "I think *Vati* is softening toward him. You will need to talk with him. Did you and Adrien get the present of foie gras I sent with a *cantiniére* who stopped at our shop last summer? What a strange thing, riding along with the army, getting them food and drink."

"Slow down, Anna Lise. I will be here for several weeks. You needn't ask me everything at once. Yes, Adrien is fine, and yes, he fought very bravely both at Tuttlingen and Austerlitz. Did you know he is a sergeant now? He's with the main army, stationed outside of Paris. I saw him just before he left."

Papa steps forward and rubs Anna Lise's head. "Little one, give Jean-Luc some time to settle in." He turns to Mademoiselle LeClair. "Could we invite the Bauck family and some other friends over for dinner tomorrow?"

"Of course," Mademoiselle LeClair replies. "We have sufficient supplies to create a grand welcome-home dinner." She turns toward me. "Jean-Luc, what would you like for the main course?"

"I must confess," I say, "that I dreamed of having salmon fillets on a bed of sauerkraut, smothered with Papa's white sauce, while riding in the sledge. But salmon is not in season."

"We have smoked salmon," Mademoiselle LeClair replies. "I'll make smoked salmon on a bed of sauerkraut. Anna Lise, go home and extend our invitation for dinner tomorrow to honor Jean-Luc's return home. Also, tell your father we would like to get a bucket of his finest sauerkraut."

I smile down at the little girl who is still clinging to me. "We can talk tomorrow, Anna Lise. Go and tell your family about tomorrow. Bring over the sauerkraut early, and I can tell you about Vienna and the castles I saw. Most importantly, I will tell you about your brother, and also about the fabulous Mamelukes!"

"Mamelukes? What are they?" she asks, looking up at me.

"I'll tell you tomorrow. Now go. I need to talk to Papa and Monsieur Rapp, and then I must sleep."

Anna Lise quickly disappears out the door. Pierre, whom I almost forgot about amid the flurry of Anna Lise's attention, says, "I have some experience as a cook. I will go and help Mademoiselle LeClair prepare the meal. You can talk with your father."

"Thank you, Pierre," I reply.

I turn toward Papa and Monsieur Rapp. 'Let's have some cognac by the fire while Mademoiselle LeClair and Pierre make our meal. I have much to tell you."

I see that Papa notes the serious look on my face. He places a new log on the smoldering fire. It jumps to life. Monsieur Rapp lights two oil lamps to ward off the advancing darkness. The three of us retire to the comfortable armchairs sitting near the now crackling fire. Papa hands me my cognac as I settle into the familiar, worn wood of my chair. I look about the room, noting each corner and crevice with a feeling of satisfaction. Yes, I am home!

Looking to Papa, I smile. He seems to have aged since I've been gone. The little hair he has left has turned gray. His shoulders now seem to stoop ever so slightly. He is still fit, but age is catching up. Monsieur Rapp looks positively elderly. He walks with a bend in his back, and he has scraggily wisps of white hair and few remaining teeth. He still looks capable of performing his janitorial duties, but I'm sure he has slowed. Papa would never turn him out.

I take a sip of the cognac. I savor its rich texture and the flavor of nutmeg and cinnamon for several moments before swallowing. I haven't had the pleasure of drinking a fine cognac in some time.

'Papa, I'm not sure where to begin. I've experienced so much since joining the army. Good comradery, but also horrific sights and experiences. Monsieur Rapp, I've told your son about my thoughts and fears, but no one else. He understands, as I hope the two of you will."

We talk up until dinner is served and again afterward, late into the night. I tell them of my first skirmish and killing two Austrians, then my near-death at Tuttlingen. Papa's face goes pale as I speak. Monsieur Rapp looks as though he's heard these stories before. I finally tell them about Austerlitz. 'Papa, I don't think I can be a soldier anymore, but I promised Uncle Jean I would wait until I talk to him again before deciding."

Twelve

Near Death - Winter, 1805

Pain jerks me awake in the early morning hours. I'm alone as the first light of day slides through my window. The hearth in my room is smoldering, giving little heat. I feel a chill and pull the blankets close, then reach down to my bandages. *Is that dampness I feel? Has the long journey in the sledge jostled open my wound?*

My mind races back to the hospital and those poor souls whose wounds became infected. They endured terrible pain, and few survived. *I must get help, but how?* My ears perk at the sound of Monsieur Rapp relighting the fires in the guest rooms. I try to scream for help, but my throat is constricted. Panicked, I look around for something I can use to make noise.

The only object nearby is my side table. I reach for it, but the wound in my chest protests with a shooting pain. Groaning, I grasp the edge of the table and push it over. It crashes to the floor. Did anyone hear me? I strain to listen, fearing that the noise was not loud enough. I'm relieved to hear footsteps coming rapidly down the hallway.

Monsieur Rapp rushes into my room. "Jean-Luc, are you all right?" He takes one look at me, then turns and shouts down the hall. "Monsieur Calliet, come quickly! Jean-Luc needs our help!" He turns again toward me, his face lined with worry as he moves swiftly to my side, placing one hand on my forehead and the other down across my bandages. "Your forehead is warm and your bandages are damp. There must be infection, and we must clean your wound at once."

Papa enters the room, still in his bedclothes. "What is it? What's wrong?" I can hear fear in his voice.

"His wound has reopened, and he's with fever," Monsieur Rapp says. "We must undo the bandages and clean it out at once. I saw this happen to my Jean when he came home wounded. We have no time to spare."

"I'll be fine, Papa," I say with little conviction. I'm trying to reassure him, but my pain and Monsieur Rapp's immediate worry disquiet me terribly.

"Go get Frau Bauck," commands Monsieur Rapp. "She helped me with Jean's wounds."

Papa shoots me a look of encouragement, gives my hand a quick squeeze, and then rushes out the door.

Mademoiselle LeClair scurries into the room, but before she can say anything, Monsieur Rapp interrupts. "Fetch me some boiling water and clean cloths for new wrappings."

I see fear in Mademoiselle LeClair's eyes, but she says nothing and leaves the room. There's chatter in the hallway. Some guests have been roused by the commotion. "Just an overturned table," Mademoiselle LeClair says. "No need to worry. Go back to sleep."

Monsieur Rapp stokes the hearth with fresh wood and brings the fire back to life. I'm overwhelmed with gratitude at how he has taken control of the situation. "Thank you," I say.

He looks at me, seeing my worry. "You'll be fine, Jean-Luc. My son went through the same thing, and he recovered. With Frau Bauck's help, we'll get you back on your feet."

Frau Bauck bursts through the door, her robust figure seeming to fill the room. With her, carrying bundles of cloth and a bucket of cold water, is Anna Lise. "Is the hot water coming?" Frau Bauck asks urgently. Monsieur Rapp nods.

"Thank you for coming, Frau Bauck," I say softly. Her confidence makes me feel a little better.

"Of course, of course," she says, all business.

Papa and Mademoiselle LeClair bring basins of steaming water, putting them on the table near Frau Bauck. They back away to make room for all the activity. I catch Anna Lise's eye and reach my hand to her. She takes it, her face clouded.

"Anna Lise, wet some cloths in the hot water," Frau Bauck commands. "Herr Rapp, help me sit Jean-Luc up so we can remove his bandages."

"Ach," I grimace as they start to unwrap the swaths of cloth. The last layer is crusted into my wound. Frau Bauck takes hot, wet cloths from Anna Lise and lays them across the stuck bandage. Then, with slow determination, she gently pulls. I twitch with pain and close my eyes tightly. Sweat drips down my face. Anna Lise puts a wet, cool cloth against my brow.

After a moment, Frau Bauck says, "There, I have it off. I don't see or smell anything wrong, but one never knows with infection. It can be deeper inside. Anna Lise, get me more hot cloths so I can dab out the wound and get a better look. Herr Rapp, hold Jean-Luc. This will hurt." He stands above my head, pinning my arms down.

My mind flashes back to the battlefield when Baron Larrey was dressing my wound. What was it he poured onto the wound to help fight infection? ... Vodka! Yes, it was vodka.

"Frau Bauck," I stammer. "Vodka. Pour some vodka on the wound after you clean it. They did that at Austerlitz to help stop infection."

She looks at me quizzically, but doesn't question my request. "Herr Calliet, do you have vodka?"

"Yes." He rushes from the room, returning quickly.

Frau Bauck begins to dab at my injury. I try to resist, recoiling against the searing pain.

"This doesn't look good," she whispers to herself. She probes more deeply into the wound.

I never knew pain could be so intense. I try desperately to escape Papa's grasp, my vision blurring.

* * *

Opening my eyes, I find the room empty and silent. Out my window, snow falls gently in slow motion. The sky is light, and I guess it must be about midday. A fire crackles in the nearby hearth.

A rustling sound. I look to my left, and there is Anna Lise, turning a page of a book.

"Where is everyone?" I croak. "Am I all right?"

"Jean-Luc! You're finally awake!"

I look at her, overjoyed to see her smiling face.

"It's been four days. You've been in and out of delirium all this time." She places her hand on my brow. "It's cool. The fever has broken. Let me get your papa."

"Wait. Not yet," I say. "Tell me more. Tell me what happened. Did I say anything?"

Anna Lise sits on the edge of the bed, holding my hand. "When *Mutti* started cleaning your wound, she found a dark spot and feared it was infection. You passed out as she cut it out. She poured vodka on the wound as you told her, and restitched it. All we could do was pray that you would pull through."

"Have you been sitting with me this entire time?"

"I didn't want to miss your waking up."

"Did I say anything in my delirium?"

"A few things I could understand." She looks around, appearing unsure how to explain. "Sometimes you called out to someone whose name I couldn't understand, telling him to look out. Another time to a Madame Kintelberger, saying you will be able to help her soon. You kept saying, 'so many dead, so many dead.' Tears came down your cheeks." Anna Lise pauses and leans toward me. "I am sorry that you saw such horrible things, Jean-Luc."

I look at Anna Lise, who does not seem so young at the moment.

"Yes, many terrible things. Things that I hoped to keep to myself. You are too young to hear them." I turn away, knowing tears are welling.

"No, Jean-Luc. We are together. Always together."

Anna Lise takes my hand in hers and kisses it. Her tears trickle down to my fingers.

"You called out to my brother once. You said, 'Adrien, killing is madness, madness. Don't be proud of it ...'"

She presses my hand tightly and looks me in the eye. "Is my brother all right?"

Before I can answer, Papa pokes his head into the room. "Ah! I thought I heard voices. Jean-Luc, you're awake. How are you feeling?"

I give my eyes a quick rub with my sleeve and smile weakly.

He comes up to me, first with a look of concern, then of relief.

Anna Lise wipes a tear from her eyes and smiles. "His fever is broken! See the good color in his cheeks?"

Papa's face beams with joy. "I thought I had lost you, my son. The sound of your voice gladdens my heart."

"Anna Lise tells me I've sometimes called out in my sleep these past four days. I've been trying to learn from her if I said anything foolish."

"I heard nothing," Papa says, "but I only stayed with you for short periods. Anna Lise hardly left your side."

I smile at her. "I'm most grateful for all her attention."

Monsieur Rapp and Mademoiselle LeClair come into my room. At once, she checks my forehead and smiles. "Your fever is gone, thank God."

Monsieur Rapp smiles widely with relief and takes my hand.

After fussing over me for several minutes, Mademoiselle LeClair says, "Are you feeling hungry yet?"

"Very much."

"I have a pot of sausage stew warming in the kitchen that I've prepared for the guests. I'll bring you a bowl with a slice of warm bread." She disappears to fetch the food.

Anna Lise smiles. "Don't forget, you haven't eaten in four days. Eat slowly."

In a few minutes, Mademoiselle LeClair returns with a steaming bowl and a plate of bread.

It smells wonderful. I start to wolf down the stew, sopping up its gravy with my bread, but remember Anna Lise's advice and slow down. "A wonderful stew, Mademoiselle LeClair. Thank you."

The mood in the room is festive. Everyone is talking happily among themselves, leaving me to my meal. I smile. It's like we just suffered through a great storm that has now passed. A warm sunshine bathes our spirits.

The remainder of the afternoon is spent in lively chatter. I recount some of my lighter moments of being a soldier while Anna Lise fills me in on her family and friends, and the others about happenings around the village and inn. I probe a little bit about the Mayer family and their daughter. Anna Lise gives me a sideways glance.

I don't want the afternoon to end, but fatigue is catching up with me. Papa looks at me. "We have kept Jean-Luc up far too long. He still needs rest. We can see him again tomorrow."

They each give me a kiss and squeeze my hand. Anna Lise is the last, and after her kiss, she returns to her chair.

"Anna Lise, please, you have been too kind already. Go home. You need your rest as well."

Anna Lise gives me the look of a stern mother. "All right. I will return in the morning. But you must promise to finish telling me about Adrien."

"Of course," I reply, feeling uneasy about what I may say.

She gives me a final kiss on the forehead. A look of concern etches her brow. "I fear for you, Jean-Luc, as I fear for my brother."

* * *

The next morning, I awake and find Anna Lise already sitting by me. She is by a table holding a platter of pastries, cheese, sliced sausage, and bread. She hands me a steaming cup. "Mademoiselle LeClair boiled some ground beans in a silk bag, saying you might enjoy this beverage. She called it coffee and said you likely drank it in the army. I took a taste—it's terrible. So bitter."

I sip the coffee and devour much of the food. "Coffee is an acquired taste, and I didn't like it at first. But one grows to enjoy the flavor and yearn for more."

Anna Lise settles back in her chair, smiling as I enjoy my meal.

"This was delicious. Thank Mademoiselle LeClair for me."

Anna Lise takes away the tray, puts it on the bedside table, and settles back into her chair. "Yesterday, before your papa came in, I was asking about Adrien." She leans forward. "What did you mean when you called to him? You were very upset."

I look hard at Anna Lise. *Do I really want to talk about this with such a young girl?* I fight back tears.

I reach my hand out to hers and hold it tightly. "What Adrien and I did in Austria was honorable. We stopped the Austrians and Russians from invading France. It's a fine line between being proud of doing one's duty and reveling in killing your enemy. I don't believe Adrien reveled in the carnage. I think he was more concerned about pleasing your *vati*."

Anna Lise ponders my words for a few moments. "If *Vati* accepts him back into the family, do you think it will help?" Her face looks strained. "What will happen if he doesn't take him back? Can you help him?"

"I will talk with your *vati*. I'll always be Adrien's closest friend."

Her chin trembles. "*Vati* says he wants to talk with you about Adrien when you're strong enough."

"Have him come tomorrow."

"One other thing about your delirium. You cried out for Hervé. Is he still back in Austria?"

A flush of sorrow overwhelms me. "Anna Lise, could you get my sabre with its leather sheath from my gear stacked in the corner? It's lying on top."

She brings it to me, eyeing what is on it. "What is this design?"

"Do you remember I mentioned the Mamelukes when I first arrived? Their homeland is across the inland sea. They worship a different form of god. The crescent moon and star represent their religion. My Mameluke friend made this for me as a remembrance." I finger the design, longing to see Hervé once again. "Do you see this horse tail hair? It's from Hervé. He died at Austerlitz when I was wounded."

She bows her head. "I feared as much. He was a fine stallion, and I knew you would not come home without him."

Looking up, she adds, "You need a Shagya. You must go to Ostheim and find a new companion. I cannot imagine you not riding a Shagya."

I sigh, holding onto Hervé's tail hair. "Yes, you're right. I should go to Ostheim and see the Shagyas."

I don't mention that only soldiers can have a Shagya, and I may not be one much longer.

Thirteen

Herr Bauck – Winter, 1805 to 1806

I am roused from sleep as Anna Lise and her mother come into my room. Anna Lise is carrying a basin of hot water and her mother some cloths, new bandages, and a bottle of vodka. Frau Bauck puts her hand on my forehead. "Good! Still cool." She examines my bandages. "Some blood showing, but not much. Changing your bandage shouldn't hurt too much this time." She smiles, then hands Anna Lise a cloth. "Dab hot water where the blood shows through."

Anna Lise presses a soaking cloth over my wound. I suppress a wince and watch Frau Bauck cut away the bandages. "It looks good," she says. "I'll pour more vodka on it and wrap it again."

She fusses over the bandages. Glancing up, she hesitates, then asks, *"Mein Sohn,* he is well?" There is a look of sadness in her eyes.

"Yes, Adrien is well. He fought heroically at Austerlitz and was at my side when I was wounded. I don't know how he found me among all those fallen men. I just know how glad I was to see his face."

Frau Bauck smiles with the reassurance. *"Mein Mann,* he wants to talk with you."

"Vati says he'll come after he closes the shop tonight," Anna Lise says.

* * *

I'm strong enough by late afternoon to come downstairs and sit in my favorite armchair near the parlor fire. Papa is pouring me a cognac when a cold gust of wind sweeps across the room from the inn's front door. "I'll go take care of that," he says.

The taste of the cognac is soothing, and I lean back, content.

"Jean-Luc," Papa says. "You have a visitor."

I stand and see Adrien's father. "Herr Bauck, please, sit with me. I've been hoping you would come."

Herr Bauck glances down, looking uncomfortable. "I intended to come just after you came home, but then your infection set in and I didn't know if you would live. I feared I missed asking about *mein Sohn.*"

"Come, sit with me by the fire. Papa has just poured me a cognac. I will pour you one." I tip the decanter and fill a glass. "Here," I say, handing him the glass. "I know you have many questions."

I settle into the warm comfort of my armchair, sinking into the soft leather. The case clock ticks loudly in the silence. What will Herr Bauck ask? He lifts his glass. We both sip without speaking. I see him staring into the flames.

After some moments, Herr Bauck begins. "I have not seen you since you and *mein Sohn* joined the Hussars over a year ago. I didn't think I would ever see Adrien again and am still uncertain I ever will. I'm sure you know how upset I was."

Herr Bauck glances toward me, pausing before starting again. "I felt betrayed, and I was angry he had succumbed to thinking he is French and forgetting his Prussian roots. He dismissed his duties to his family and especially to me."

Now he looks straight at me. "I also put blame on you, Jean-Luc. You are his best friend, and you are French. You did not discourage him from joining the army. But I now realize I was wrong. You were being a friend. You were just being French."

I bite my tongue. *But isn't Adrien French as well? He was born here! His parents just happen to be Prussian.*

The clock's ticking is resonating in my head. *He thought I was partially to blame for Adrien joining the army? Perhaps he's right. I never thought of Adrien as either French or Prussian, just as my friend whom I wanted to share experiences with.*

Herr Bauck continues, and I sense his heart is heavy. "What's done is done. Decisions can't be changed. You say he fought bravely? That's good to hear. Do you think he will ever leave the army and return home?" Herr Bauck's eyes seem to glimmer with a ray of hope.

I sip carefully while framing my response. Setting down my glass, I say, "The one thing driving Adrien is his wish for you to be proud of him. All of his actions are directed toward pleasing you. I don't know if he will leave the army. Army life actually seems to suit him. But he will not be happy until you accept him back into your family."

I pause before going on. "Your anger with him not only affects him, but also Frau Bauck and Anna Lise. Remember, Anna Lise and Adrien have always been close. If not for Adrien's sake, then at least for Anna Lise's, talk to him. She is heartbroken not being able to see her brother."

Herr Bauck drains his glass and pours himself more cognac. He lifts the decanter toward me in a gesture, asking if I want more. My glass is still half full, but I accept his offer.

"I know *mien Frau* and Anna Lise worry about him. I know ... yet I don't know what to think of my son. Would Adrien fight with the French if war broke out with Prussia?"

His eyes narrow. His forehead tenses.

"I would never be able to forgive him. Do you remember Monsieur Renard? The one who supported putting our priest to the guillotine back when you were a child? He's been quiet for many years, but recently, with the rumor that Prussia might join the Austrians and Russians against France, Renard has been denouncing us Prussians in Colmar as spies.

"The Mayer family—you remember the Mayers and their pretty daughter? They will soon be leaving Colmar and returning to Prussia. If the situation worsens, we may have to leave as well. The tsar is still offering bonus money for Germans to migrate. I've heard there is a thriving German community in Moscow. A good butcher is always wanted." Herr Bauck lowers his head, looking like weights have been placed on his shoulders. "We may have no choice but to leave ... no choice."

My eyes widen in surprise. I know Adrien believes in the military life, and I'm confident that if he were told to fight Prussians, he would, but I avoid this issue. "You may leave Colmar? That would crush Adrien and Anna Lise! This is their home."

I lean toward Herr Bauck. "I think our rout of the Austrians and Russians at Austerlitz must give the Prussians pause. I'm confident such a war will never happen, but if it takes place, you can only wait to see what Adrien does. You can't assume you know."

Herr Bauck looks at me, considering my response as he continues to sip his cognac. The fire is beginning to burn low, and he gets up, stoking it with another log.

Returning, he says, "You're right, Jean-Luc. One can't damn someone based on speculation of events that may never happen. I miss my son. I miss him deeply. Please send word that he is welcome to return home."

The sound of the clock chiming five sounds like a celebration. Adrien is welcome to come home to his family. I feel myself beaming as I wrestle my way out of my chair to embrace Herr Bauck warmly.

"I must return to my shop. Thank you, Jean-Luc, for talking with me. Seeing *mein Sohn* again would be a most joyous occasion." He smiles—a hopeful smile.

Herr Bauck leaves, giving me a nod. Within minutes, Anna Lise flies through the door and into the inn. "Is it true? *Vati* wants you to send word to Adrien asking him to come home?" she says breathlessly. "I don't remember being so happy! I'm going to see my brother again!"

She gives me a tight squeeze of appreciation. "Not too hard, Anna Lise," I say, grinning, trying not to wince.

* * *

Several weeks later, a letter arrives from Adrien.

> *Our unit has been moved from Paris to an encampment in Bavaria. Despite the peace and our convincing victory at Austerlitz, the emperor does not trust the Prussians and wants his army stationed near their border to discourage any action by them. But I'm not thinking about that right now.*
>
> *Father wants to see me? I can't believe it! I'm not sure when I can get leave—most likely not until spring, as many others are away. I will write again when I know more. Give Anna Lise my love. I'm going home? I still can't believe it!*

I go to the Bauck butcher shop to give them the news about Adrien. As I approach, the shop door opens and Herr and Frau Mayer and their daughter emerge. "Good day," I say, nodding in acknowledgement and giving their daughter a smile, remembering my daydreams of her.

"Jean-Luc, so good to see you," Herr Mayer says. "We heard of your injury and are pleased to see you are much better. You and your father must come for dinner—perhaps soon after Twelfth Night? I will send him a note." The girl beams a warm smile my way.

"I look forward to it," I say, returning her smile.

Remembering why I came to the butcher shop, I go inside. Spotting Herr Bauck, I raise the letter from Adrien. "Good news," I say. "Adrien expects he will be able to take leave sometime this spring!"

* * *

The new year is quickly upon us. The inn is very busy, and I spend New Year's Eve helping father with chores. Celebratory gunfire erupts at midnight. Looking out the window, I see a bright glow near the edge of town. Going outside, I see flames spiking up within the glow.

"Fire!" I yell, alarmed. "Fire!" Father and Herr Bauck rush out, and we speed toward the shed where Colmar's one fire engine is stored. By the time we reach the shed, the horse team is already pulling the pumper toward the flames.

"It's the Mayers' barn!" shouts Herr Bauck.

When we reach the barn, I see Frau Mayer and her daughter huddled near the home. Herr Mayer joins us as we get the suction line into the stream that runs through his property.

"Put water on the house," says the captain of the fire brigade. "We don't want it to catch fire." A few embers have reached the roof, but are quickly extinguished.

After soaking the house's roof, the captain shouts, "Now, water on the barn." The barn is fully engulfed, and all we can do is keep it under control while it burns to the ground.

I'm working one end of the pumper and look around to see if there are any embers that need to be extinguished. We're fortunate to have a layer of snow on the ground and no other structures near the barn besides the house. In the distance, I see what looks like a man with a torch running away through the Mayers' vineyard.

"Over there," I yell, pointing to the retreating person. Herr Mayer notes the diminishing figure. A look of disgust crosses his sweat-lined face.

By sunrise, the flames have subsided. The remains of the barn are a smoldering heap. Our work is done. Fortunately, only the barn was lost.

During the ordeal, Frau Bauck came to provide comfort to the Mayer family. She takes them into their home. I join my father, Herr Bauck, and Herr Mayer on the porch as the fire engine leaves the site.

"Jean-Luc, did you get a good look at the person with the torch?" asks Papa.

"No, he was too far away."

"I'm sure it was Renard or one of his compatriots," Herr Mayer fumes. "But what can we do? Life has become unbearable for us here!"

We try to comfort Herr Mayer, but in my heart, I know he's right.

A few days later, we receive a note from Herr Mayer, thanking us for our help in containing the fire and sending his regrets that at this time, he cannot have us over for dinner.

Just after Twelfth Night, Herr Bauck comes into our inn. "The Mayer family has packed their wagon and is leaving

Colmar," he says. "They've gotten more anonymous threats that say their home will be the next to burn." He looks worried. "Do you think we will be targeted next?"

"How can they?" I say. "Adrien is a hero of Austerlitz, and they dare not say anything against your family."

Herr Bauck puts his hand on my shoulder, looking pensive. "I hope you are right, Jean-Luc. Colmar is our home, and I don't wish to leave."

Fourteen

Bayard – Spring, 1806

A few months have passed since Twelfth Night. The weather is finally warming, and buds appear on the trees and grape vines. I am finally recovered and itching for an adventure.

"Do you remember you said you were going to Ostheim to see the Shagyas?" Anna Lise reminds me.

"You're right. This would be a good time to go. Adrien will be coming home soon, and then I may not have much time to myself."

The next day, I'm off to Ostheim on one of Papa's horses. There's not a cloud in the sky, and a warm breeze comes from the south. I'm dressed in my sergeant's uniform, the first time I've worn it since coming home. My sabre is sheathed and secured to my saddle. Touching the emblem of the star and crescent moon with Hervé's hair attached makes me think of him wistfully.

Old friend, I'm finally going to pay you homage at the place we first met.

I reach Ostheim before dark and report to the quartermaster. To my surprise, it's the same man who was here when I first trained Hervé. He squints at me with a flicker of recognition. "Welcome back. Calliet, isn't it? Now a sergeant? Congratulations. What brings you back to Ostheim?" He looks at my horse. "Where is your Shagya? Hervé, wasn't it?"

I reach down to my sabre sheath and touch Hervé's tail hair.

The quartermaster notes the sadness in my expression. "Were you at Austerlitz? Did you lose Hervé there? I heard many Shagyas were killed in the battle."

"Yes, Hervé fell to a Russian lance."

The quartermaster's face drops. "He was a fine horse," he says. "Such a beauty." He pauses. "You've come to see if you can get another Shagya? That will be up to our commandant, but come back in the morning and I'll show you some of our two-year-olds. We have one horse from the same broodmare as Hervé. He's called Bayard. A fine, spirited stallion."

I thank the quartermaster and proceed to the same barracks where I once stayed. It's empty, and I put my gear down near my old bunk. So odd to be here again. The dank smell of old bedding fills my nostrils.

Glancing about, I can visualize Bernard and Henri harassing Adrien and me, calling us "Rapp boys." Part of me misses those times in the army, even the threatening presence of Bernard and Henri. Reality is so different. Bernard is dead, and Henri is now a close comrade.

If war comes, and there is talk it may be with Prussia, I can't see how I can honorably leave behind my comrades-at-arms. I am troubled as I think of these things.

From the nearby mess hall, I hear soldiers' voices as they prepare to eat dinner. Anna Lise has packed me a meal, and not wanting to see anyone, I wander down through the nearby meadow to the edge of the River Ill to eat.

It's a warm afternoon, but the snowy peaks of the nearby Vosges Mountains glisten in the setting sun, reminding me it's still early spring. I head for a large river rock, one I've sat on many times in the past. Settling on its smooth surface, I reach into my satchel for the cheese, sausage, bread, and wine Anna Lise has packed. Taking a bite, I look up the river. The banks are shrouded in shadows, but above the water, the sun highlights thousands of tiny insects scurrying along, living their own lives. Single threads of long spider silk flutter in the breeze, trying to snare a meal for their owners. I stay by the river long after I finish eating, listening to the croaking frogs in the deepening dark, soaking up the peace.

The next morning, I rouse in the rose-colored dimness of first light and go to the mess hall for breakfast. Several young privates, I'm sure new recruits, are already there. They make way so that I may go to the head of the line, nodding deferentially as I pass. *What is this? They think I'm important?*

I join the quartermaster at a nearby table. "New recruits?"

"Yes. Since Austerlitz, there's been a surge in the number of men who want to join the army. They sense there will be future glory and want to be part of it."

"Why are they being so respectful to me?"

"They heard that a stranger was visiting and asked me who you were. I told them you were once a green recruit yourself here in Ostheim and that you fought bravely at Austerlitz. They see you as part of the Austerlitz glory."

The quartermaster continues. "I talked with the commandant, Colonel Chantilly, after your arrival yesterday. He's given approval for you to select a new Shagya. Let's finish eating and go to the stables. I'll introduce you to Bayard. He needs to be ridden hard today by someone who knows Shagyas."

For the first time in many months, something in connection with the army excites me. *Hervé, I'll be meeting a brother of yours today!*

I finish eating. "I'll go gather my saddle and riding gear from the barracks and will meet you there shortly."

The quartermaster nods. "I'll be by the south entrance."

With a quickened pace, I head back to the barracks and get my gear. Smiling, I finger Hervé's tail hair and am soon at the stables. The quartermaster is not there yet, but a stallion whinnies in the nearest stall. *That sounds like Hervé!*

Putting down my saddle and gear, I head toward the sound. *This must be Bayard.* The stallion snorts and nods his head. I put my hand on his muzzle, rubbing it. He acknowledges with another snort, then nuzzles his snout against my chest, seeming to breathe me in.

"I see you have met Bayard," the quartermaster says as he walks up. "I've never seen him this friendly with anyone before. He nips most of those who come to ride him."

"He acts as though he knows me," I say, rubbing my hand down his sides while smiling broadly. "A beautiful horse, and so much like Hervé. I'll take him to the upper pastures and go through some riding drills and return by last light."

The quartermaster fastens the bridle while I secure my saddle and gear to Bayard's back. He blows a few quick, impatient breaths, waiting while we finish preparing him for the ride.

My scabbard is the last piece of gear I'll be fixing to my saddle, but before doing so, I take it up to Bayard. I stroke Hervé's tail hair by Bayard's nose. "This is from your brother, my closest and most trusted friend."

Bayard nickers and presses his nostrils to it. He seems to acknowledge my gesture and nods.

Smiling, I pat his flank and climb up onto my saddle. Turning him toward a familiar trail, I give a light kick. Soon we are at a canter, heading north along the river.

It's a glorious spring day, and hawks circle above us, searching for rabbits and field mice we scare out of the brush and grass.

Bayard feels powerful, so different from Papa's horse and so much like Hervé. We slow to a walking gait as we approach the road that leads up into the Vosges. It's the same road I took with the army when we marched toward Boulogne last summer. Not really that long ago, though it seems like a lifetime has passed.

Turning from the road, I pat Bayard's side and point to a small hill topped by a grove of oaks. 'See that hill, Bayard? We're going to attack it, then wheel back to face an enemy who may be chasing us." Bayard snorts.

We start our drill with a trot, then gradually gain speed into a canter and then a full gallop. I reach for my sabre, hold it high, and give a yell as we attack. We are flying across the field, rapidly approaching the hill. Reaching the oaks, I pull up on Bayard and try to pivot him backward to face anyone chasing us.

The charge goes well, but we have trouble with the pivot. We practice the pivot and other maneuvers for a few hours. By midday, I'm ready to have Bayard try again.

Satisfied with his progress, I return to Ostheim, exhilarated. The power and fervor one feels when horse and rider act as one is overwhelming.

At the stable, I remove my gear and saddle, give Bayard some feed, and begin brushing him down.

Two figures approach from the camp's headquarters. I continue to brush Bayard, thinking it's the quartermaster and perhaps one of the recruits. Looking up when they arrive, I find that it is indeed the quartermaster, but with him is the camp commandant.

I snap to attention and give a salute.

'At ease, Sergeant. I wanted to meet you and to pass on a message from General Rapp. He came by to inspect our new recruits. The general told me about you and the injuries you suffered at Austerlitz. About the loss of your Shagya. He was certain you would come to Ostheim to see the Shagyas and perhaps seek a new one for yourself."

Hearing the general's name jolts me. "The general was here? He has a message for me?"

A tinge of panic runs down my spine. It appears that my long-awaited talk with Uncle Jean will happen soon.

"Yes. He wanted me to tell you that he will be in Colmar toward the end of the month."

That's only a week away, I think, trying to quell the knot in my stomach.

Colonel Chantilly pats Bayard's flank. Bayard snorts and takes a few quick shuffle-steps away. "How is this Shagya?" asks the commandant. "He's yours to take."

"Thank you, sir!" I exclaim, even though my thoughts are still half on the general's coming visit. "He is much like Hervé, my Shagya killed at Austerlitz. I will be honored to have him as my new companion."

"Then it is done," Colonel Chantilly replies. "How long will you be staying?"

I regain my composure. "Another day or two. I want Bayard to be fully comfortable with me before I take him to new surroundings."

Then the commandant surprises me. "Come dine with me tomorrow before returning to Colmar. I've never been there but have heard it's beautiful. You can tell me about it."

My remaining time in Ostheim is spent riding Bayard on the trails. With each ride, we form more of a partnership. The two of us practice the drills, but mostly we trot and walk along the paths hugging the River Ill.

Uncle Jean is coming! What is he going to say? What am I going to do? Will I be able to see and talk to Adrien before he comes? A quiver runs down my spine.

My last night in Ostheim comes quickly. I brush my uniform and polish my boots, then head to Colonel Chantilly's quarters for dinner. A recruit greets me at the door and leads me to the dining room. The hallway walls are lined with mementos from the colonel's life: a picture of an aristocratic home that looks to be in Paris, a portrait of Napoleon, an Austrian battle banner, framed documents proclaiming his promotions, and a uniform set that includes the puffed red trousers, green shirt, and blue vest of a Mameluke warrior. There is dried blood on the green shirt. Is this someone the colonel has killed?

We reach the dining room. "The commandant will join you soon," the recruit says.

The recruit takes up a position near the doorway, standing at attention. I walk to the window. Outside is the parade ground, and beyond it, the trees lining the River Ill. The sun is setting, and shadows stretch across the parade ground from the trees. The sound of boots thumping along the hallway draws my attention.

"Ah, Jean-Luc, welcome," says Colonel Chantilly as he enters. "Do you care for some cognac?"

I nod, and he directs the recruit to pour us each a glass.

"Please, let's sit," the colonel says. "Dinner will come shortly."

"I was admiring your mementos in the hallway," I say, "especially the Mameluke uniform. Were you in the Egyptian campaign?"

The commandant smiles broadly. "Yes, yes I was. I took that off one of the infidels after the Battle of Acre. I received my promotion to colonel in Egypt. A most invigorating campaign."

And no promotions since!

"I served with the Mamelukes under General Rapp's command at Austerlitz," I say. "I know of no finer soldiers. They must have been a formidable enemy at Acre."

The commandant hesitates for a moment before replying. "Yes, most formidable, but our emperor defeated them. Now, tell me about Colmar. Is it true that many of your avenues are canals?"

I describe the canals and the German-style homes that line the waterways, but soon the conversation turns back to the military, with most of our talk now dominated by the commandant. Colonel Chantilly tells me he has many friends in high position who come and visit the Ostheim stud farm in hopes of securing new Shagyas.

The commandant offers me another glass of cognac, which I accept.

He shares with me the stories he's been told about Prussia. According to his sources, the Prussians are upset with the formation of the pro-French Confederation of the Rhine and the disputes over the city of Hanover. Queen Louise of Prussia is especially anti-French and advocates war.

I shift uneasily in my chair, knowing I shouldn't be hearing this.

"I've heard the Prussian army is mobilizing secretly in Saxony," says the commandant. "I expect King Frederick William to declare war before the end of the summer. The Prussians haven't engaged in an armed conflict since 1795, while our forces are battle hardened. It will be a quick and decisive victory, I assure you," he says with a smug expression.

This popinjay may be right. We did just defeat the Austrians and Russians at Ulm and Austerlitz, and the Prussians would be hard pressed to fight us.

Our dinner conversation doesn't lessen the qualms I feel about seeing both Adrien and Uncle Jean. Adrien fighting in a war with Prussia would destroy all bonds with his father. He would need to lean on me even more. I'm sure Uncle Jean will ask me how I would feel about such a situation, as well as about my army comrades who may be fighting another war soon.

Fortunately, the emperor's field generals and commanders are accomplished warriors, unlike this buffoon of a colonel. Yet if we must fight, I'll need to confront the terrors of battle. Will I be able to kill again? See my comrades die as well? I try to shut out these fears.

* * *

The next morning, I awaken as the sun, dulled by layers of clouds, crests the eastern horizon. As I saddle Bayard, the unsettled weather matches my spirit. Maybe seeing Colmar again will revive it. I also retrieve Papa's horse.

Off and on, squalls pelt rain and hail on Bayard and me, slowing our progress. The sun is low by the time we reach Colmar. The wind howls, and the sky erupts into a downpour. Drenched, I take Bayard and Papa's mare to the stables. After securing his horse and giving her feed, I remove my gear and saddle from Bayard and brush the wetness from his coat. Bayard seems content, eating the hay in the nearby rick. Satisfied he is comfortable in his new surroundings, I pat his side and leave the stable.

The street is muddy, and the rain continues to fall heavily. I race to the inn's porch and rub the mud off my boots with the boot brush. The bell rings when I open the door, and a far-off voice says he will be there shortly. No one is in sight. I remove my cloak and hang it on a nearby hook. The light is dim, with the roaring fire providing most of the illumination. I light the lamp on the desk, then move toward the fire to warm myself.

'Hello, is someone here?" Papa's familiar voice says.

'Yes, it's me. I'm back."

Papa comes and embraces me.

'Adrien arrived while you were gone."

"Is he talking with his father?

"Yes, and it appears their rift has diminished. The situation looks good. Adrien is anxious to see you. Will you be going to the Baucks' tonight?"

"I'm tired and hungry and not ready to face him tonight. I'll go in the morning."

"Go, change from your wet clothes. I'll have Mademoiselle LeClair bring you food."

"Thank you. Could you pour me a brandy while I change? It will help warm me up."

When I return, a glass of brandy awaits me by my chair. Papa is sitting in the other armchair, already taking a sip from his glass. "How was Ostheim and the Shagyas?"

I smile. "I have a new Shagya named Bayard. He's Hervé's younger brother. A most beautiful stallion."

"A new Shagya?" Papa's eyes rise in surprise. "Have you decided to stay in the army?"

"I'm not sure. I still need to talk with Uncle Jean and see how Adrien is doing. By the way, the commandant of Ostheim told me Uncle Jean will be visiting Colmar soon."

Mademoiselle LeClair brings my food. As I eat and have another glass of brandy, I tell Papa about my dinner with the Ostheim commandant.

"War with Prussia?" Papa says, shaking his head. "What will Adrien do? What will Herr Bauck do? Are you going to tell Adrien about this?"

"Yes, but I need to talk with Uncle Jean. The Ostheim commandant is a peacock, and he may not know the full story or may be embellishing the facts. Uncle Jean will know."

"It's late, and you need your sleep. Rest well, my son." I hear the anxiousness in Papa's voice.

Fifteen

The Decision – Spring, 1806

I rise early, anticipating a full day. Yesterday's storm has passed, promising pleasant weather. The rising sun sends rays of light reflecting from the street puddles into my room. I look from my window to see that the village is just beginning to awaken. There are people going in and out of the bakery, but other than that, the streets are empty.

I'll tend to Bayard before the others rise.

I head toward the barn, where Bayard greets me with a nicker and happily accepts a bucket of oats. I brush his back and girth, cleaning off the dried mud I missed last night.

"Good boy. I'll be bringing round my friend Adrien later this morning to meet you. He has a Shagya too. We'll go riding together."

Gathering last night's gear from the barn, I head back toward the inn. Anna Lise is sweeping the front porch of the butcher shop. She looks up, gives a quick wave, then rushes to open the butcher shop door. Poking her head inside, she shouts, "Adrien, he's back! Jean-Luc is back!"

Adrien is soon upon me. I drop my gear as he wraps his arms tightly around me. He pushes me back to get a good look, flushed with a boyish grin. "Jean-Luc! How good to see you again, my friend."

I clasp him again. "I've missed you too. How long have you been home?"

"Since the night before last."

I give Adrien a quizzical look, hesitating to ask. "... What of your father?"

Adrien laughs. "We're talking. He says he's proud of my part at Austerlitz. But he still asks when I will be leaving the army. I'll tell you more when we have time alone."

He glances at me with concern. "Anna Lise told me you nearly died from infection. Have you recovered?"

"I have, but only because your mother and Monsieur Rapp were able to clean out the wound."

Adrien studies me closely. "Why don't we get away from here? We could go to the river, fish, and catch up."

"Yes, let's do that. I'll get my gear and meet you at the stable. I'll show you my new Shagya."

"A new Shagya? Excellent! So, you'll be coming back to the regiment? I must admit, you've been gone so long I feared you would leave the army."

* * *

Adrien is already at the stable rubbing down Basile's flanks when I arrive. "Basile has caught scent of your new Shagya and is eager to meet him. What is his name?"

I open the stable door to find an equally excited stallion greeting me.

"His name is Bayard."

"*Courage and honor*, a good choice. He looks so much like Hervé."

"He had the same broodmare as Hervé," I say as I lead Bayard from the stable. The two horses touch noses, sharing a gentle exchange of breath. Their ears perk, and both let out a soft snort.

"Good, they approve of each other," I say. "Shall we go fish at the bridge?"

"Of course. Who can forget that time we hid there when the guillotine wagon drove by? When was that ... eleven, twelve years ago?"

"Nearly twelve. That was your birthday and the day Anna Lise was born."

At the bridge, we find a good spot with green grass near the water for Bayard and Basile. We unsaddle the stallions and grab our fishing gear. It's been a few years, and the fishing spot looks smaller now. There's a deep pool under an overhang of fallen trees and brush on the far bank near the bridge. The water is churning with rapids both above and below the pool. The edge of the pool is a perfect spot to catch crayfish for bait.

After baiting our hooks and throwing the lines in the water, Adrien retrieves a bottle of wine and two cups, and we relax on the riverbank, reminiscing about our boyhoods. The branches of the tall trees sway in the warm breeze, causing the light from the midday sun to split and intertwine with the shadows like dancers moving across the water.

There is no action on our rods, but that doesn't matter. We are two friends enjoying the moment.

"Tell me, Jean-Luc, do you really intend to return to the army?"

I stiffen.

"I know Ulm and Austerlitz troubled you greatly. You are much like Captain Bouchet, a reluctant warrior. As for myself, I'm finding I enjoy the military life."

I take a long drink of wine and look over to our fishing poles. Still no action. I can't avoid responding any longer.

"You are right. I find the horrors of combat difficult to endure. I admit, I'm considering leaving the army, but my desire to leave has been wavering. My time in Ostheim last week and my fear that war may once again be upon us have me thinking of returning."

Adrien drains the remainder of the bottle into his cup.

"Did you bring another?" I ask.

"Yes, two more. I thought we might be having a long talk."

Adrien opens the second bottle and fills my cup.

Again, we settle back on the grass, appreciating the warming sun and the accompanying breeze. Casually I ask, "What did your father say to you? When I talked with him, he hoped you would leave the service soon and return to the butcher shop. But this possible war with Prussia complicates everything."

There's a long pause before Adrien replies. "You, my family, and the army are all I have in the world. I didn't have the heart to tell *Vati* I want to make the army my career. How could I destroy his dream of having me take over the shop?"

Adrien shifts his body and stares across the river.

"When we talked about a possible Prussian war, his neck muscles tightened and his eyes burned bright. He said, 'killing your own people could never be forgiven!' Again, I couldn't be truthful. I've just gotten my *Vati* back. How could I lose him again? I told him I didn't think war with Prussia was coming, but if it came, I would seriously consider his words before taking any action. He accepted this answer."

Adrien shakes his head. He holds up the wine bottle, gesturing toward my cup. I shove my cup over and he fills it, spilling some in the process.

"Jean-Luc, you are my only real friend. You, me, and Anna Lise, the three of us have an unbreakable bond. We were together the night she was born, that day with the guillotine in the town square. We were together to help raise her when my mother was ill. Our lives are intertwined. I cannot bear thinking of my life without you or Anna Lise, but I may have no choice. I'm committed to the military, even if it means I must fight the Prussians. I can only hope *Vati* accepts this, and I fervently hope you will be with me."

I reach over to cover his hand with my own. "Adrien, you and Anna Lise are precious to me. A war with Prussia could destroy your relationship with your father, and he may try to keep you away from your mother and Anna Lise." Looking into his eyes, I continue. "But no matter what, I will stand by you. Uncle Jean will be here any day. Let's find out from him what he thinks the future holds. Perhaps there's no need to worry about Prussia."

Adrien gives me a hopeful smile. "Thank you, my friend. We will wait for Uncle Jean."

* * *

By mid-afternoon, Adrien and I are home. We caught no fish, but that was not our goal. The two of us walk arm in arm toward the butcher shop, laughing and joking, buoyed by all the wine we've drunk.

A growing sound like rumbling thunder captures our attention. In the distance, I see the bobbing plumes of approaching soldiers. The rumbling is replaced by the cacophonous sound of clattering hooves on cobblestones. Adrien and I stand on the butcher shop porch, watching a long column of paired Hussars ride by, coming from the direction of Mühlhausen and heading toward Ostheim.

Leading the column is Uncle Jean, who breaks away and stops at the inn. His father is there to greet him as he dismounts. They embrace heartily as the column rides on.

"I know these men," Adrien says. "There is Private Durand, Sergeant Petit, Corporal Laurent! Many from our regiment." Adrien gives me an excited glance. "Something is going on."

I, too, recognize several of the faces. With each passing horseman, an unease knots my stomach. It appears that the army is mobilizing.

Looking over toward Uncle Jean, I see Monsieur Rapp pointing in our direction. Uncle Jean waves for us to come over.

* * *

"Jean-Luc, you look well," Uncle Jean exclaims, clasping my arm. "Your wound is fully healed?"

"Yes. Are you staying long?"

"Unfortunately, I only have a few minutes." He takes hold of Adrien. "My boy, it's good to see you in Colmar. You and your father have come to terms?"

"We have. I'll be returning to the battalion soon. Will you be in Ostheim?"

"For a couple of days. Adrien, would you excuse Jean-Luc and me? I need a moment with him."

"Of course."

Uncle Jean examines my face. "Let's walk," he says.

We move away from the crowds onto the back streets. Nearly the whole town is lined along the road watching the soldiers, and no one gives us any notice. All the excitement has riled the crows, who are cawing madly, following the Hussars.

After a few paces, Uncle Jean says, "Jean-Luc, I need to say more about our last conversation at the hospital in Austerlitz when I told you about my decision to stay in the army. Back then, I thought it would be an easy decision, as I wondered why anyone would ever choose this kind of life. What could possess them to want to face such dangers and kill so many people? But as I convalesced, I thought of my comrades and how we had grown to need and depend on each other. Sharing a battlefield creates bonds that cannot be broken. I began to feel I would be betraying them if I left."

The company of Hussars passes, and the crowd begins to disperse. Uncle Jean and I walk into the town square.

"I feel the same as you in many ways," I say. "What weighs on my heart the most is Adrien. You've seen him in battle. So reckless and always trying to prove himself. I don't understand him. He seems to relish it. Fortunately, he and his father are speaking, but if Adrien fights the Prussians, they will never talk again. I can't abandon him."

I look to the sky, hoping to find strength. "Are we going to war, Uncle Jean? When I was at Ostheim, I had dinner with the commandant. It's hard to know what to believe, but he is confident we will be at war with the Prussians before fall arrives."

Uncle Jean's lips tighten when I mention the commandant. "The emperor has no intention of starting a war with King Frederick William," he says. "The reason the emperor placed a regiment in Bavaria is to quell the king's notion for war. The battalion I'm leading will join our Bavarian regiment for an additional show of power." We are now on the far end of the town square. "Come, let's return. I need to rejoin my troops."

As we turn around, Uncle Jean looks at me. "The Ostheim commandant was out of place to provide such speculation. I should say no more than what I have, but you are facing a grave decision. My own gut says we will have war by the fall. King Frederick William is as much a fool as the Ostheim commandant."

We walk a while longer in silence. A squirrel starts to scramble across our path but stops and looks confused, as squirrels often do. It starts to go across again, then changes its mind and scrambles back. I've often felt this way these past months.

Everything Uncle Jean has told me about his decision to remain in the army, as well as his confirmation of a likely war with Prussia, makes my own decision clear.

"Adrien is returning to the regiment tomorrow," I say, finally. "I will be with him."

Uncle Jean gives me a sad smile. "Perhaps we will have peace, even with the English, in the not-too-distant future. They must be getting as tired of war as we are." He gazes back at the town he has known all his life. "I must go and say goodbye to my father. I will see the two of you soon."

Monsieur Rapp sees our approach and prepares his son's horse for departure.

"Father, I'm sorry I can't stay longer. I'll be back as soon as I can."

He salutes me. "Jean-Luc, we'll see each other again soon."

Uncle Jean gives his father a last embrace, then mounts his Shagya, waves, and rides to join his men.

I see Adrien approaching and go to meet him. "I'll be returning to the regiment with you. When do you want to leave?"

Sixteen

Return to the Army – Summer, 1806

Adrien and I are on a reconnaissance mission, crossing from Bavaria into Saxony on this stormy, rainswept July day. Scouting parties have reported movement by the Prussian army toward the Bavarian border. We are to find out how close they are and in what numbers.

The low clouds hanging over the hills make it difficult to see. A gust of wind slaps rain across my face and nearly whips off my Shako cap. "Let's ride to the top of that far hill," I say, pointing toward some unwooded high ground across the hollow. "It looks like there's a clearing that might give us a good view of the valley."

We follow a thin trace into the forest. "Careful," I call out to Adrien behind me. "This game trail is treacherous." The trees sway heavily, but we keep our destination in sight through occasional gaps in the trees, the swirling clouds, and sheets of rain.

Soon we find a road, but we skirt it, not wanting to be seen. We speak in whispers. I constantly try to hear anything beyond the sounds of the storm. A creaking noise comes nearer from the direction of the road. We both freeze, straining to see and hear. The sound of wheels sloshing through mud grows. Dismounting, we move farther back into the trees. A farm wagon loaded with supplies comes into view with two peasant men sitting atop the wagon bench.

"Are the supplies for them or the Prussian army?" Adrien whispers.

The wagon groans as it passes, and I listen closely for any further sounds. "That's the only one," I say to Adrien, "so no need to follow."

After the wagon is out of sight, we begin stumbling up the slippery hillside toward the clearing. The storm begins to wane as we near the forest opening. Moving ahead, we come to the fringe of a meadow. Securing our horses, we inch our way toward the crest of the hill, crawling on our bellies in the high grass.

At the summit, we peek over the ridge. In the valley below lies a bivouac with thousands of soldiers, all in Prussian blue.

"My God, it's the whole Prussian army!" I whisper to Adrien, astonished by the numbers.

"Why don't they have lookouts up here? They must know scouts could be coming." Adrien and I carefully peer around, staying low in the grass.

"There!" Adrien says in a low voice, pointing to the far side of the wide meadow. "Two Prussian soldiers sitting by a campfire ... They don't see us."

"Let's get out of here!" I say, my heart pounding.

We quietly back our way down the meadow toward our horses.

Untying our stallions, we lead them a safe distance into the woods before climbing on. We dare not talk, but Adrien's face shows he is as shocked as I am by what we have seen.

Without a word, we retreat back the way we came, cross the road, and finally ascend the hills we came through earlier in the day. The sun is setting and the rain has stopped. We don't start a fire, but instead huddle under our blankets on the damp ground.

"It looked like at least a division, if not a full corps," Adrien says in a low voice. "Captain Bouchet will be pleased we found their army!" He pauses, then says uneasily, "I wonder if any of my cousins are down there. *Vati* says I have many."

"You can't worry about that, Adrien. Let's try and get some sleep. We've had a long day."

I hunker down under my blanket, turning onto my back, unsettled by what we witnessed. The sky clears, and the light of a half-moon shines above us. There is a squawk, and I see an owl in the moonlight lifting off the ground with a small body clenched in its talons. My hands tighten into fists, then unclench. I toss about for a long while before sleep finally comes. It's sporadic, filled with dreams of battle and blood.

* * *

Captain Bouchet is indeed happy with our report and orders us to go to General Rapp with the information.

"I feared as much," Uncle Jean says, "though they are closer to the border than I thought. Good work. We will be doubling our battle exercises. Hopefully, the Prussians will have scouts watching so they can report our strength and preparedness to their generals. We may still be able to prevent this war."

I hope so. The thought of fighting more battles makes my stomach twist.

* * *

As July fades into August, and August into September, our tensions ease. It gives me time to catch up with my journal. I'm happy there is still no war. Adrien and I thought we'd be in battle immediately after we sighted the enemy, but the armies have been posturing for three months—first the emperor showing his strength, then the Prussian king countering.

September comes with news of more Prussian troops pouring into Saxony. The emperor orders additional soldiers into Bavaria and masses his Grande Armée along the banks of the Haslach River, which borders Saxony. Our battalion is assigned to the Hussars under Marshal Murat.

After many long days of maneuvers, a messenger arrives at our campfire. "Sergeants Bauck and Calliet, you are to gather your gear and report to Captain Bouchet."

We leap up to follow the orders. "Do you think the war is about to begin?" I ask Adrien.

"That's all it could be," he replies.

Captain Bouchet's campfire is not far from ours. He's busily engaged talking to Henri and another soldier from our battalion when we arrive. Before long, they salute the captain and move toward their horses. Henri sees me and gives a wide grin, his eyes gleaming with excitement.

"Ah, Calliet, Bauck, good to see you." The captain is animated, clearly excited. "Please, sit. I have an urgent assignment for you. We've received word that the Russians are sending their forces to Prussia, intending to join with the Prussians and invade France. Our army is about to cross the Haslach River and attack the Prussians before that can happen. We need eyes ahead of our troops. The two of you are to scout the middle pass through the Thüringerwald Hills and report back what you find. Return before dawn, as the Grande Armée crosses the river tomorrow."

Adrien and I both give the captain a snappy salute. Adrien smiles broadly, and despite my contempt for war, the excitement of the mission makes my adrenaline spike.

We rush to our horses and depart, heading toward the river ford. The fall rains have not begun, so the water is low and we cross easily. The sun is just rising over the hilltops as we make our way toward the middle pass. The road is not much more than a wide path, stretching ahead, ever rising. We enter a forest of oaks first, which soon turn to elms, then to pines as we climb higher. The weather is splendid.

Reaching the crest, Adrien stops. 'Let's think how to proceed. Prussians may be near." We dismount and gaze down the hillside. The road stays narrow and twists through the forest.

'It's safer to proceed at a walk," Adrien says. 'Let's split up. You go walk on the right side of the road, and I'll take the left. At each curve, whoever has the outside bend can go first and look around the corner. The other advances if he is signaled all is clear. Hopefully we won't encounter any surprises, but if we do, at least one of us should be able to get away."

I agree, and we start our descent. The going is slow, but by mid-afternoon, we reach the bottom of the hill. The road becomes wider and not as curvy. The trees bordering the road thin.

At the end of a long straightaway, we come to a large bend. It turns to the right, so Adrien takes the lead on the left side. He signals all clear, but as I move up to join him, four Prussians charge from the trees. We are surrounded without even having a chance to draw our sabres.

I look at Adrien in complete dismay as we're disarmed. My chest is tight, making it hard to breathe. Adrien looks back at me, his face ashen.

In accented French, one of the Prussians says, "What have we here? A scouting party? But scouting for what?"

In German, Adrien responds, trying to be casual. "We mean no harm. Our emperor has no desire to fight Prussia. We are a hunting party looking for deer."

The Prussians look at Adrien in surprise. One rides around him. Ignoring Adrien's use of German, he taunts him in French. "You are Prussian! By your accent, I'd say from Pomerania. I have family in Pomerania. Are you a traitor?" He comes up to Adrien, shoving him off his horse. Adrien starts to get up, but the drawn blades of the other Prussians warn him to stay down.

The Prussian turns toward me. "You don't look Prussian. You are thin and weak and hairy, like a Frenchman. Are you willing to die for your emperor?"

I glare back, saying nothing.

With the Prussian blades threatening, Adrien slowly rises to his feet. Their sergeant circles him, the tip of his sabre inches from his throat. A sneer creases his face as he stares at Adrien.

Still speaking in French, he says, "We need to find out why you are here. We should put our Frenchie Prussian to the test. Don't all of you think so?" he says to his companions. They give each other troubled looks. "A true Prussian would die before breaking, but a Frenchie Prussian? We'll have no trouble."

The Prussian sergeant gives me a hard shove, knocking me off my horse as well. "Bind them, and bring them with us." He examines our horses. "Some fine steeds you have. Are these Shagyas that the French stole from our Austrian friends? They will serve our cavalry well."

At their camp, I'm pushed against a tree while Adrien is forced to sit by the fire. The four Prussians are arguing among themselves, but my German is not good enough to know what they're saying.

"Adrien, what's going on?"

"They're arguing about torturing me. The sergeant doesn't like that I'm Prussian."

"Torture?" I say as their sergeant comes up to me.

"Frenchman, we will not be harming you. Our king, in his wisdom, has banned torture. I won't be torturing your Frenchie Prussian friend either, but I want to test him. I want to see if he is still Prussian or if he has become a soft Frenchman. Corporal Adler, keep watch over the Frenchman. Private Gass, expose the Frenchie Prussian's chest."

Looking hesitant, Private Gass glances toward his companions. The sergeant bellows angrily at him. Private Gass gazes at the sergeant, then slowly unbuttons Adrien's jacket and removes his tunic.

Poking the metal tip of a spear into the campfire and heating it to a glowing red, the sergeant holds it up, smirks, and says, "Gut."

The private struggles to lift Adrien's arm. Another Prussian comes to help, holding Adrien down.

I rip at my bindings, feeling them cut into my wrists, but I can't get free.

The sergeant pokes the hot red tip into Adrien's armpit. Screams of pain echo across the landscape.

The sergeant reaches over and pushes Adrien's arm down against his body, the burning tip still in his armpit.

Crying out again, Adrien collapses to the ground.

"Are you ready to talk now?" the sergeant says in French.

Adrien stares at him, his eyes glazed.

"Not bad, Frenchie," the sergeant taunts. "I'm sure your friend over there would have told me everything by now."

I glare back at him with hate. His companions are muttering among themselves and say something to the sergeant. He shouts back at them and puts the spear tip back into the fire. While they are occupied, I work on loosening the knots around my wrists.

The sergeant says something, pointing to the private, who then pushes Adrien down onto his back. The private takes off Adrien's boots and exposes his feet, pressing them together.

The sergeant takes the spear from the fire and slowly moves the glowing tip onto the arches of both feet. Adrien tries to kick free, but the private holds him tightly. The sergeant gives the weapon one last push into the flesh, then pulls it away.

Adrien bellows in pain.

"Are you ready to talk now?" the sergeant asks.

No response. Adrien can't speak. He groans in pain.

I've worked the knots apart. My hands are free. I must wait for an opening, but I can barely hold myself back.

"I'm impressed, Frenchie. You apparently still have much Prussian blood and mettle. But this concerns me. We can't have Prussian fortitude in the French army. I must do something about that. Private Gass, remove his britches."

Adrien struggles as the private pulls down his pants. Once again, the sergeant returns the spear tip to the fire.

"One last thing to do, Frenchie. Then I'll take you to our headquarters."

"*Arschloch!*" I shout, spitting at him.

The sergeant pushes the spear deep into the fire. Adrien struggles, but his burns have weakened him. The sergeant smiles broadly as he lifts the glowing tip from the flames.

Clenching my hands behind me, I wait, holding back my desire to charge now. Sweat pours down Adrien's face. Panic shines in his eyes.

The private holds Adrien down while the other two spread open his legs. The sergeant spits on the glowing tip, smiling at the sizzling sound. He waves the tip in front of Adrien's face, then moves toward Adrien's groin. Suddenly, one of the Prussians holding a leg grabs the spear and struggles with the sergeant.

I rush and grab a sheathed sabre hanging from a nearby horse. Drawing its blade, I run my sword through the sergeant's back. He gasps and tries to turn toward me, but slumps to the ground. My sabre pulls free as he falls, just in time to slash at the oncoming private. With a swift slice, I lop off his head; it falls to the ground, rolling up to the dead sergeant's body.

My rage is overwhelming as I face the remaining two Prussians. They stand motionless, staring at me. I can't stop myself, and they join their comrades on the ground, lifeless in a growing pool of blood.

Gasping for breath, I stare, horrified, at the bodies and what I've done. I toss the sabre into the fire.

Adrien. I must help Adrien.

Rushing to his side, I bandage the burns as best I can.

"Adrien, can you hear me? I need to get you to a hospital wagon."

He opens his eyes and gives a weak smile.

With difficulty, I pull up his breeches, but leave his boots, tunic, and jacket off. I put these in his saddlebags. "Let's try and get you on Basile and return to camp."

I try to help Adrien stand, but he collapses, crying out in pain. I carry him to his horse. "Can you grab hold of the saddle horn?"

He grunts and grabs it with his one good arm. I push him up and get his leg over the saddle. We succeed, but the effort seems to drain all his remaining energy. He slumps over his saddle horn, groaning. "Do you feel strong enough to hold on?"

Adrien nods.

At a walk, we slowly make our way along the road leading back to Bavaria. A nearly full moon lights our way.

I just killed four Prussian soldiers. How could I have done that?

The image of those four dead men causes me to lean over and retch.

Near the top of the hill, we encounter a platoon of Marshal Murat's Hussars. Their captain barks as the platoon encircles us. "Sergeant, you were among the advance scouting groups? What is your report, and what happened to your comrade?"

I tell of our encounter with the four Prussians. The captain listens as his horse snorts and jostles impatiently.

"Good that they are all dead! You saw nothing else?"

"No, sir."

The captain goes over to Adrien to look at his wounds. Adrien is too weak to talk; he's using all of his strength to remain mounted on Basile. "Your comrade's burns need attending immediately. Take him to the hospital wagons back at the river."

"Yes, sir," I reply, giving him a salute. With that, he and his platoon leave us while we head back to the Haslach River.

It takes the remainder of the night to reach the river. Up and down the water as far as the eye can see, soldiers are crossing, beginning their move against the Prussians. I sight a hospital wagon on the Bavarian shore. Adrien and I make our way through the water to the wagon.

"Please, help my friend—he's been badly burned," I tell the hospital attendants, my voice urgent and tense.

As they treat Adrien's wounds, they ask how this happened. I explain quickly.

"His burns are deep, and he will need to stay with us until a field hospital is established," an attendant tells me. "We'll keep him in this wagon bunk for now and care for him. He may not be able to walk again for some time."

"They'll take good care of you," I tell Adrien. "I'm going to find Captain Bouchet and give him our report." He gives me a weak nod and reaches out with his good arm. I clasp his hand.

"I'll be back to see you," I assure him. "I don't know when or where, but I will."

Turning toward the troops, I scan the different battalion colors, trying to find our green and red. I spot them on the other side of the river and catch sight of Henri, who sees me and waves.

"Where is Adrien?" Henri asks as I ride up. "Wasn't he on the scouting patrol with you?"

"The bastard Prussians took us prisoner and tortured him. We escaped, but he's badly burned. I took him to a hospital wagon."

"Burned? How?"

"By a red-hot spear point," I say as I scan the soldiers nearby. "Right now, I need to find Captain Bouchet. I must give my report."

"Over there," Henri says, pointing to the far side of the battalion.

"I'll tell you more later," I say, making my way toward the captain.

The captain is putting a saddle on his horse as I ride up and dismount. "Sir. My report."

I recount all that happened as the captain listens closely.

"You saw no others?"

"No one else."

"And you killed all four of the Prussians?"

"Yes, sir," I reply, looking away.

"I will inform Marshal Bernadotte. Go back to Henri and our squad. We are preparing to move out, and I'll join you soon." The captain gazes at me. "Killing can't be helped ... I'm sorry to hear about Sergeant Bauck."

The Prussian Campaign – 1806-1807

Seventeen

Prussia – Summer and Fall, 1806

Our squad advances down the road where yesterday, Adrien and I were ambushed. Riding toward us is the platoon captain I met last night with his men. "Captain Bouchet, you're just in time!" he shouts. "There's a bridge ahead with a contingent of Prussians defending it. We must take it before the main army arrives."

His horse is skittish and dances beneath him. He glances over our squad and catches my eye. "Sergeant! You're the one who came in with a wounded comrade last night. Welcome back."

He quickly turns from me to Bouchet. "Captain, are you ready?" Without waiting for a response, he spurs his stallion and leads his platoon at full gallop toward the bridge. Our squad immediately follows.

We draw our sabres and bellow as we approach the Prussian cavalry on the bridge. I hear the familiar zip of bullets flying by. About a hundred infantry with muskets are arrayed behind the cavalry, outnumbering us at least two to one.

Straight onto the bridge we fly, fending off blows from their sabres and slashing with ours. Horsemen clash in a tangled mass, choking any movement in either direction. The Prussian infantry dare not shoot into this indistinguishable swarm of soldiers.

I don't think. I just fend and slash. Either I die or they do. I cut down three of my attackers so fast there is no time to see their faces or hear their last screams. Blood runs down my sabre, making it slippery to hold. To my left, the platoon captain is in danger. Two Prussians are pressing down on him. I don't think he will last much longer. Frantically, I make my way toward him.

Catching sight of me, he yells, "To your right!"

I turn and duck under a Prussian blade, then shove my sabre high, striking my attacker in the neck. Blood sprays as he falls. I rush toward one of the Prussians engaging the platoon captain. We parry violently before I'm able to dispatch him. The captain delivers a final blow to his second attacker, glancing my way with the briefest look of gratitude.

Riderless horses fly from the bridge with bloody saddles, leaving many lifeless and badly injured soldiers from both sides heaped on the roadway. Bayard slips in the blood pooling on the stones. He regains his balance, and several of us break through their cavalry, making headway toward the Prussian infantry and their waiting guns. They dispatch a volley, striking several of our men, but have no time to reload. Pressing forward, I smell their breath and sense their terror.

'Don't let them form a square," Captain Bouchet shouts, but it's too late. The surviving Prussians form a tight square with bayonets bristling from each side. They start backing away. No one wants to charge into their curtain of steel. We let them retreat, having secured the bridge.

After our victory, we treat the wounded, both French and Prussian, telling them hospital wagons will be coming by as our army crosses the bridge. The platoon captain approaches. "Sergeant, I'm Captain Foulon. Tell me your name!" he demands. "I have my life, thanks to you."

Captain Bouchet answers for me. "He is Sergeant Calliet from Alsace, now just returning to service after being wounded at Austerlitz."

Foulon's eyes lock on me. "A hero of Austerlitz as well! I will be talking about you to Marshal Murat. He is a close friend and comrade."

"And Sergeant Calliet is a close friend and comrade to General Rapp," Captain Bouchet adds. "They both hail from Colmar."

Captain Foulon nods.

Captain Bouchet pulls out his maps to find the name of the bridge we just secured. "We must send word to Marshal Bernadotte that we have engaged the enemy and secured this crossing." The captain studies his map. "It's the bridge at Saalburg-Ebersdorf. The enemy appears to be retreating toward the town of Gefell. Sergeant Allard, go and relay this information to the marshal. Hurry!"

Henri gives Captain Bouchet a salute, turns his horse, and begins galloping back toward Bavaria.

Sunlight is waning, and we prepare to camp for the night. Captain Foulon selects a site on the west side of the bridge, away from the dead. "Help bring the wounded to this spot," he says, pointing to an area under some trees near the road. "The hospital wagons and a burial detail will be here tomorrow, at the rear of Marshal Bernadotte's corps."

"Does that include Prussian wounded, sir?" someone shouts.

"What about scavenging the dead?" another adds.

"All wounded are to be cared for!" Captain Bouchet says, grimly staring at the men. "Rummage through the bodies as you see fit after the wounded are attended to."

I help with the injured. Many have deep cuts and we try to stem the bleeding, but I know most won't live through the night.

I have no stomach for scavenging the dead and instead settle on the ground, sitting on my blanket. I'm exhausted, not having slept for two days. Our rations are slim without our *cantiniéres*.

Captain Bouchet comes to join me. "Madame Colette gave me some extra sausages yesterday. Here, have some. She knew we wouldn't see her for several days."

I accept the sausages, devouring them.

"Sergeant, you have performed admirably since your return to the army. Captain Foulon was especially impressed with your actions at the bridge. He tells me he is recommending that you be promoted to sous-lieutenant."

"Sous-lieutenant?" I shake my head. "I only do what is needed to survive and to help my comrades. I don't think I should be given any kind of promotion. You know I still hate war."

"Yes," Captain Bouchet says without hesitation. "Do you think I love war? War is not something to enjoy; it's what we must endure. What more can be asked of a man but to survive and help his comrades survive? What you did at Austerlitz, how you helped Sergeant Bauck last night, and your actions at the bridge today are what the army needs. I would want no one else serving next to me. I trust you with my life."

Captain Bouchet grasps my shoulder, giving it a reassuring squeeze. "Sleep well tonight, Sergeant. Who knows when we will be able to again?"

I'm left with my thoughts. *He says I am what a good soldier should be. Can that be true? What of those two defenseless Prussians I killed yesterday? I hate the killing. What a dismal thing to be a good soldier.*

I shiver, pull my blanket about me, and fall into exhausted asleep.

Captain Bouchet rouses me in the morning. The sun is just rising.

"We must be off. Marshal Bernadotte marched his corps most of the night. They are nearby. We are to ride ahead and determine where the enemy has gone while the marshal rests his troops, waiting for our report."

Looking around, I see that our numbers have fallen from about fifty men to forty. Many good comrades died taking that bridge.

Captain Bouchet and Captain Foulon mount their steeds, and Captain Bouchet turns to address us.

"Captain Foulon and I are uncertain where the main Prussian army is. The unit we defeated at the bridge appeared to be retreating toward Gefell to the south, but our suspicion is that they may be concentrating near Schleiz, not far north of here. My squad will head toward Gefell, while Captain Foulon will lead his platoon toward Schleiz."

"Our purpose today is only to find the enemy, not attack them," Captain Foulon adds. "Find them without being seen. Marshal Bernadotte will engage them with full force and hopefully surprise them with his cannon."

We all mount our horses, ready to proceed. The two captains draw their sabres, lifting them high, and shout, "For the emperor!"

"For the emperor!" we all reply as we gallop off.

* * *

As we approach Gefell, the forest closes around us and we slow to a trot. I take the point position, about ten horse-lengths in front of the squad, keeping my eyes focused as far ahead as I can see. My scalp prickles as I strain to hear any unusual noise. The enemy is close, but are they straight ahead, to the north, to the south, or all three? My whole being focuses on trying to discern any possible danger. My comrades depend on me to give first warning.

The air holds a fall chill, though the sun shines brilliantly overhead. All I can hear is the clip-clop of our horses.

Hours pass with no sign of the Prussians.

Boom ... Boom! The unmistakable sound of cannon fire. It is distant and to our north. We halt and listen intently.

"Captain Foulon's platoon evidently found Prussian troops!" Captain Bouchet exclaims. "Those cannon must be Marshal Bernadotte's."

"Are we going to go north and join the battle?" I ask.

"No. The emperor, Marshal Soult, and Marshal Ney are to our south. We must report Marshal Bernadotte's engagement to them, as well as provide reconnaissance."

Still hearing the cannon, we ride on toward Gefell.

* * *

The next few days are filled with uncertainty as we try to locate the main Prussian forces. We continue scouting missions along the Saale River valley. On our fourth day, we camp by the town of Jena.

As darkness settles into the valley, I notice something strange. "Look up there, across the river."

From horizon to horizon, campfires stretch, lighting up the eastern sky.

"There are thousands of them!" Captain Bouchet exclaims. "Sergeant Calliet, mount up immediately and report this to the emperor. Tell him the Prussian army is near Jena!"

I thank God the night is clear and the moon nearly full. I ride as fast as I dare, reaching the emperor's encampment just before dawn.

The emperor's tent is not hard to find, centered within a square of soldiers with the imperial standard mounted by its opening. A candle glows brightly inside. Silhouetted behind a desk is a man who appears to be writing with a quill pen.

Approaching the tent, I'm immediately challenged by one of the guards.

"Please tell the emperor I have reconnaissance information regarding the location of the Prussian army. I am one of Marshal Murat's scouts."

The guard enters the tent, and I watch the two silhouettes. The man at the desk jerks his head up and motions the other to leave. The guard opens the tent flap. "The emperor will see you."

The realization that I'm about to talk with the emperor is overwhelming, but there, staring at me with anticipation, is none other than my emperor, Napoleon Bonaparte.

His hair and uniform look disheveled, as though he's been up most of the night. He looks fit and not much shorter than myself. Those who say he is small must not have seen him up close. I start to speak, but my throat goes dry. *How do I address an emperor?*

Impatiently, the emperor motions for me to come forward. "Sergeant, the guard tells me you bring important news. What is it?"

Snapping back to reality, I give a quick salute. "Sire, I come from near the town of Jena. We saw their campfires. Thousands and thousands lighting up the sky on the plateau above the town."

A smile creases the emperor's face. "At last!" he exclaims. "Finally, we have them. Thank you, Sergeant. I've been praying for such news."

Turning to his guards, he commands, "Have Marshals Soult and Ney come to me at once! Tell them the enemy has been found!"

* * *

The following day, the emperor and his armies arrive near the town of Jena and take positions on the heights above the Saale River valley. As the sun goes down, fog begins to roll in.

'Sergeant Calliet, take some men and help the artillerymen push the cannon up to the top of that plateau," Captain Bouchet orders, pointing to a rise with a commanding view of the valley. A narrow path winds steeply up to the summit, but it is already disappearing in the fog.

'I can't see a damn thing, can you, Jean-Luc?" Henri says as we push one of the gun carriages.

'No, but be careful. We can't run into the cannon in front of us or roll back onto the one behind."

For hours, we push and inch our way up the hill, finally reaching the top in the middle of the night. 'Line the gun up over here," a gunnery sergeant says.

Henri and I rest against a cannon for another hour, waiting for the last one to come up the hill before moving back down. We still can't see, and we stumble into others. Finally, the muted glow from our campfires leads us the remainder of the way. 'I have some coffee brewing," Captain Bouchet says as we find our encampment. 'Sit and rest."

'Thank you, sir," I say, pouring myself a cup and squatting down by the fire. All around, I hear the sounds of clinking metal, men talking, riders mounting their steeds, and the impatient chuff of horses.

The sky lightens, and before long the fog around us thins. I look toward where Jena should be, but the valley below is still shrouded.

'How far away do you think the Prussians are?" Henri asks.

Even as he says this, the distant, muffled sound of cannon comes from the northwest. 'Those must be Prussian," I say. 'I don't think we have troops that far to the north."

I look where the emperor should be and see his figure through the breaking fog. He's peering through his spyglass at the battle, panning the battlefront from right to left. Reaching the left, he quickly lowers his glass and talks to the general near his side. His arms gesticulate toward the left flank. Emerging through the fog is the corps of Marshal Ney, colors flying. They engage the enemy, but the Prussians seem to be pivoting, trying to surround them.

Seeing this, my comrades mount their steeds. *Are we about to engage?* I climb onto my saddle and try to calm Bayard. He snorts and sidesteps nervously. "It's all right, Bayard. I'm with you." With sweaty hands, I clench and unclench my fingers around my reins. Marshal Ney looks trapped.

Then out of the fog come our soldiers, rallying around the marshal and his men. The Prussians are beaten back. We maintain our position on the heights, ready to attack, but the battle comes to a pause. Strangely, fog again rolls across the battlefield, and the cannon go quiet. My comrades and I dismount, taking this opportunity to eat a little food and drink some water.

I can't settle down. I fidget with my gear and check for the tenth time whether my pistol is loaded. "Bayard, would you like a brushing while we wait?" Blustering, he seems to answer yes. I take out my brush and stroke his flanks. Bayard nickers his approval.

"When do you think the battle will begin again?" I ask my steed as I continue brushing. "The emperor is waiting for the fog to lift, don't you think?"

An hour passes, maybe two, and the sun is now overhead. The fog thins, and breezes tear apart the remaining wisps. There is movement near the emperor's headquarters, and I see three soldiers waving battle flags toward each corps, signaling them to attack.

The nearby cannon erupt to life. The ground trembles, and my eardrums scream in pain. Bayard kicks, needing to be restrained.

He still dances nervously as I try to calm him. All the horses are reacting skittishly to the thunderous noise.

Captain Bouchet mounts his stallion and circles around to face us. "Mount up."

Clouds of smoke drift across the battlefield under a sky that is now clear and sunny. I can see the enemy lines collapsing, holes ripped through them by the cannon fire.

Marshal Murat takes the lead position in front of our cavalry. "Be ready, men! Their left flank is crumbling. We'll be attacking there."

We wait for the signal from the emperor to strike. Nervously, I look toward him. He has his spyglass fixed on the Prussian left flank. Lowering his scope, he motions to a flagman, who waves his flag in our direction.

We thunder toward the now fleeing Prussians. I'm sure they see us coming and are desperately thinking about how to escape what appears to be certain death. With our sabres drawn, we whip past our right flank with our soldiers cheering us on. We spread across the battlefield, each of us taking sight of particular groups of fleeing Prussians. I try to avoid trampling on the mangled bodies strewn across the meadow.

A group of three Prussians turn toward me with bayonets fixed. Instinctively, I hack at them. Two are struck down by my initial slashes. The third stands his ground, his bayonet at the ready, his eyes round with fear. Just as I am making my cut, he drops his musket, raises his hands and shouts, *"Faire Quartier."* It's too late. My sabre is already plunging into him. He falls to the ground. His face stares at me, stunned and horrified.

"I'm sorry, my friend," I whisper as I charge toward the next running Prussian. This one is alone, and he too turns to face me. He is terrified, eyes wide and mouth open. He throws down his gun and raises his hands up halfway, but is unable to speak. I pull Bayard up and yell repeatedly for him to lie flat on the ground: *"Legen flach! Legen flach!"* He looks at me now with a faint flash of hope. He nods and falls flat on his belly. I press my sabre tip to his back and say *"Stehen!"* He nods again, and I ride on.

I encounter thirty, maybe forty more Prussians, and I yell at each of them as I approach, *"Legen flach!"* Most throw away their muskets and fall to their stomachs. Some do not, and they are quickly dispatched.

Finally, there are no more fleeing Prussians, and with my comrades, I turn back toward the way we came. There must have been many who feigned death, as there are several hundred waiting for us with arms raised high. We herd them toward our waiting infantry, who will take custody of them. I come across several of the men who took my advice and fell to the ground. They come up to me, tapping fists against their hearts, tears running down their faces. In the midst of this chaos, I am amazed at this show of gratitude.

Captain Bouchet has apparently been watching. He rides over to me. "You've saved these men from needless death. I commend you. Not many of your comrades were so generous." He pats my shoulder and rides off.

Henri comes up to me. "Why didn't you kill these men, Jean-Luc? They are the enemy, and they were trying to kill us."

I give Henri a sad smile. "They weren't trying to kill me when they were fleeing."

* * *

"Berlin is not as grand a city as Vienna," I say to Henri as we ride down Charlottenburg Avenue looking at all the fine buildings. "It's impressive, but Vienna is a marvel."

Marshal Murat's Hussars have been assigned to secure the boulevard leading to the center of Berlin and the now deserted royal palace. We take our assigned positions and wait for the emperor's entrance.

"Sergeant Calliet, you and Sergeant Allard post yourself here," says Captain Bouchet. "The grand parade will be arriving soon."

I look about and wonder at the success of our armies. Has it only been two weeks since we fought the battles at Jena and Auerstedt? What a victory Auerstedt was! While we were fighting at Jena, Marshal Davout's corps defeated the main Prussian army, even though he was outnumbered two to one. After those two battles, we faced little resistance in our march to Berlin.

It's a fine, warm autumn afternoon, but the city seems gloomy—all the shops closed, no one at the windows, very few people in the streets, and no carriages on the roads.

We hear drums beating, becoming increasingly louder. "There," shouts Henri, pointing up the boulevard. "They are coming." Marshal Lefebvre leads the march with the Imperial Guard. Marshal Davout rides in a place of honor beside the emperor. The sparse crowd cheers "Vive l'empereur," though it doesn't sound heartfelt. The emperor is wearing a simple colonel's uniform, while his marshals are resplendent.

They pass us, and next comes each corps of infantry. Thousands of soldiers march along the boulevard. At the end of the parade are the hospital wagons, making their way to the Berlin hospitals.

Does one of those carry Adrien?

Napoleon Entering Berlin

Eighteen

Berlin – Fall, 1806

Our squad is quartered at an inn near the Prussian king's palace. "My papa's inn is but a rooming house compared to this," I exclaim to Henri. "Have you seen your room yet? In mine, I have a large bed, a sitting area with a fireplace, and a grand view of the imperial palace. And this pub! Marvelous food and drink, with so many tables. I think half the town of Colmar could stay here."

There's a commotion at a nearby table. "Why don't you have Bordeaux?" an obviously drunken soldier shouts at his table server. "I've had enough of your shit beer. I want some decent French wine!"

The table server draws back, frightened by the soldier's anger. Captain Bouchet comes to the server's aid. "Come now, Corporal, it's plain to see you like German beer. Have some more, or try some of the Riesling. It's much like our Alsatian wine."

The corporal starts to rise in challenge, but then sees that it is a captain rebuking him. Lowering his eyes, he sits back down. "Yes, sir," he says in a chastened voice. "The beer is good and I'll have more."

"Please bring the corporal another stein," Captain Bouchet tells the server. "While you're at it, bring me one too."

I look over toward the owners, standing near the door to the kitchen, their arms crossed and looks of disgust on their faces. They whisper to each other while eyeing the crowd of soldiers who are taking advantage of their position as conquerors.

I shake my head. Who can blame them? They're required to provide food and lodging, as well as a bottle of wine each day for our soldiers. If the Prussians occupied Colmar and quartered at my father's inn, it would destroy our business. But it's the way of war.

Captain Bouchet returns to our table as though nothing happened. We continue joking with each other about some of the adventures we had during our march to Berlin. As part of Marshal Murat's Hussars, we were always at the front.

Henri laughs. "Do you remember those peasants outside the gates of the Wittenberg Citadel? I thought they were going to soil themselves when they saw us riding up. They threw tools at us and ran for the gates. That old woman was cursing and shaking her fist all the while." More men laugh as Henri continues. "Then, once they closed the citadel's gates, down came the Prussian flag and up went a white one." A roar of laughter follows. "I saw her when we marched in to take their surrender, still cursing and shaking her fist."

"How about that squad of Prussians camped along the river near Leipzig," I say. "They were no better, throwing away their guns and flopping on their bellies, arms in the air. I wish all wars could be so easy."

A soldier carrying a satchel walks into the tavern. From the look of his clean, crisp uniform, I suspect he is on someone's command staff. Spotting us, he comes over. "Is one of you Sergeant Calliet?"

"That's me," I say.

He hands me a sealed document. "Sergeant Calliet, you are to report to Marshal Murat's headquarters at Charlottenburg Palace at noon tomorrow."

"Can you tell me what for?"

"I don't know," the soldier replies tersely. He turns and abruptly leaves.

"The marshal himself is summoning you? Did you do something wrong?" my comrades ask.

Captain Bouchet smiles knowingly.

"What is it Captain?" I ask. "Do you know?"

"I do. It's something good, but I'll let you find out tomorrow."

I give him a quizzical look. *Is it about Adrien and where I can find him? But a marshal wouldn't summon me about that. Maybe it's that promotion Captain Foulon talked about. I've put that out of my mind, figuring he would forget.*

Finishing my meal and taking one last swig of wine, I excuse myself from my comrades. "I must get ready if I'm to see a marshal tomorrow."

"Better shine your boots well," one of the men says with a laugh.

"I'll let all of you know what happens."

A little shaky from perhaps too much wine, I make my way to my room and turn up the wick in my table lamp for more light. I retrieve my boot black, some cloth, and a stiff brush from my gear before taking off my boots and uniform.

These boots will take some work, I think as I examine the scuff marks. Brushing off some dried mud, I dip my cloth into the boot black. My head is woozy from the wine, and the pungent smell of the polish jolts me back, clearing my head. I take extra time to ensure the boots gleam.

My uniform is in good shape, and the stiff brush removes the dirt that has accumulated. My mind wanders to tomorrow's meeting, and I can't help but speculate. *It must be the promotion. Captain Foulon said he was a friend of the marshal. If so, it would probably be to one of the adjutant levels. Not all the way to sous-lieutenant, like Captain Bouchet said. Regardless, any promotion should make it easier for me to find Adrien.*

It's been over two weeks since I put Adrien in the hospital wagon. I must try to find him before we deploy to the east to fight the Russians.

I'm too excited to sleep very long. Before dawn, I'm brushing my uniform again and adding more spit and polish to my boots. The sun creeps into my room, expanding its presence as the new day dawns.

After dressing, I lean on the windowsill, peering outside. Though it's still early, the street is beginning to bustle with activity.

Ach! My stomach turns. Is it the wine or my nerves?

I decide to take a short walk. Maybe eating breakfast would be a good idea, but I'm not sure I could hold it down. The inn's courtyard is around the corner, and I make my way toward it.

It's the perfect spot to calm my nerves. Several birdfeeders are scattered about the courtyard, and each is swarming with small birds feeding voraciously. Other birds fill the trees, chirping and singing melodies. I sit on one of the many benches, grateful to find this respite.

Regaining control of my jitters, I head toward Charlottenburg Palace. It's only a few blocks away, and I go early in the hope of seeing some of the inside. Maybe Uncle Jean has his quarters and office there. I can talk to him about locating Adrien.

Going inside, I'm amazed. So much grandeur! The hallways are a beehive of activity, filled with many soldiers wearing impeccable uniforms. They walk straight and tall with chests puffed as if it is their duty to look important. Glancing at my uniform, I see my boots are not as shiny as theirs and my uniform, even though it is brushed, looks scruffy by comparison.

Gilded ornaments and frescoes decorate the ceiling and walls. Great chandeliers, looking like small suns, are lit with hundreds of candles, repeating themselves every twenty feet or so and illuminating everything.

"Where is Marshal Murat's headquarters?" I ask one of the soldiers carrying documents.

"Down this corridor to the Oak Gallery. Take a right, and it's at the end of the hall."

Reaching the Oak Gallery, I turn into the adjoining hall. Overcome by its splendor, I turn in circles to take it all in. The walls, lined with oak paneling, have many doors, and in between them are oval family portraits. The floor is beautifully patterned wood. At the end of this hall, there is a grand door with the flag of France on one side and Marshal Murat's colors on the other.

I straighten my uniform and enter. There are about ten other soldiers with hats in hand, waiting. At the desk, the secretary, a bright young lad in a smart-looking uniform, asks, "Are you Sergeant Calliet or Sergeant Duval?"

"Calliet."

"Please, take a seat with the others. The marshal will call for you soon."

I find an empty chair among the other waiting soldiers. We exchange nervous smiles. One by one, names are called and soldiers are led through a heavy door near the secretary's desk.

It is not long before the secretary calls my name. "Sergeant Calliet?"

I nod.

"The marshal will see you now." He nods toward the heavy door. Wiping my clammy palms on my pants, I clear my throat and go through the entrance.

The chamber is large, with expansive windows overlooking a wooded park. The walls are a polished, dark wood with portraits of people whom I assume are the king and queen of Prussia on the wall facing the windows, as if they are gazing out over the garden. A large chandelier glows brightly in the middle of the room, and a smaller one is above an immense desk at the far end. Marshal Murat sits there, his arms resting on the desk as he smiles at me. There are others in the room, standing on either side of the desk, but my eyes are focused on the marshal as I march up to his desk and give him a salute.

"Welcome, Sergeant Calliet. It's a pleasure to meet you. I'm sure you remember Captain Foulon, and I've invited your Captain Bouchet here as well." He indicates them with a nod to his right. *So, it is the promotion.*

"I've also invited General Rapp to attend, as I've learned he is an old family friend of yours." He gestures to his left.

I turn and salute the captains, then pivot and salute Uncle Jean. Seeing him steadies my nerves a bit.

"Captain Foulon has written a glowing recommendation for your promotion after your actions at the clash on the Saalburg-Ebersdorf Bridge. He says you were instrumental in winning that assault as well as saving his life. Captain Foulon is an old family friend. I'm most grateful he's still alive."

Marshal Murat's eyes go from me to Captain Foulon as he smiles. "Captain Foulon recommends that you be not only promoted, but promoted to an officer position: sous-lieutenant to be exact. An unusually high promotion for a sergeant. I've talked in detail about your service with both Captain Foulon and Captain Bouchet. A most impressive record for your short time in the field. I've also consulted with General Rapp, whose word on a man's character has never failed."

Marshal Murat stands and extends his hand. "Congratulations, Lieutenant Calliet." He hands me a document with his signature and seal. "Here is your promotion declaration. Take it to the tailor and have your new uniform fitted."

I shake Marshal Murat's hand, hoping mine isn't trembling. Excitedly, I accept the promotion declaration. *They are actually making me an officer? How can that be? I've only done what a good soldier would do.*

Coming to full attention, I salute the marshal. He sits back down and rubs his hands together, looking at me intently.

"General Rapp has also told me your childhood friend, Sergeant Bauck, was tortured by the Prussians and received severe burns when the two of you were captured. He's a patient at the Charité hospital, just outside the walls of the city. It's the finest hospital in Berlin."

My eyes widen in surprise at this news, and I look from Marshal Murat to Uncle Jean. A feeling of hope surges through me.

"The general suggests I assign you to be the administrator of the Charité hospital. You will certainly be missed in our campaign to defeat the remnants of the Prussian army and their Russian allies, but this job is important too. Once your friend Sergeant Bauck recovers, you will both join us at the front."

Uncle Jean smiles, knowing my promise to look after Adrien is why I came back to the army.

"I would be honored to take this position, sir."

"Good," Marshal Murat replies. "Your office will be at the Charité. Meet with the general, and he will provide details."

Captains Foulon and Bouchet, as well as Uncle Jean, come over to congratulate me. I beam with excitement. The promotion is good, but finding where Adrien is and being able to stay with him is even better. We all salute Marshal Murat. Outside, I thank the two captains before we part.

"Jean-Luc, come with me to my office," says Uncle Jean.

His office is but a few steps away, with a sign on the door proclaiming *Military Governor*. Inside, Uncle Jean points to a chair near his desk, indicating I should sit.

"Jean-Luc, I was most impressed by Captain Foulon's recommendation letter, and I had a chance to talk with my old friend Captain Bouchet. It was only by reading the letter and talking with Captain Bouchet that I learned of Adrien's torture and your escape from your captors. I had records checked for all the hospital wagons and was able to track Adrien down.

Uncle Jean pauses. "Jean-Luc, Adrien is not doing well. The burns on his feet are healing, but those in his armpit are infected. Baron Larrey is in charge of the medical staff at the Charité. He has examined Adrien and is concerned his recovery will be difficult. Your presence may buoy his spirits and give him a chance. The Charité is an efficient, well-run hospital, which will give you time to perform your administrative duties and also attend to the care of the patients, including Adrien."

Adrien can't die! I promised Anna Lise I would watch over him. He is why I rejoined the army. I jump to my feet, feeling as much dread as I would before going into battle. "When can I go to the hospital? I must see him."

"As soon as you change into your new uniform," says Uncle Jean. "I've taken the liberty of having your new one tailored." He nods toward a crisp, new uniform hanging nearby. "You can change in the next room when you leave. Go back to the tailor in a few days and have him adjust it."

Uncle Jean's brow wrinkles, a serious expression on his face as he continues talking.

"It's important you assume your duties in the proper attire, ready to shoulder your new responsibilities. I've assigned Corporal Laurent to be your assistant. He is waiting at the hospital. Before seeing Adrien, you must meet with Baron Larrey and the corporal.

They will identify your duties and responsibilities. Baron Larrey will update you on Adrien's condition and take you on a tour of the hospital ward."

I struggle to take in all that Uncle Jean is telling me, but it's clear that my concern and fears for Adrien can't interfere with my duties. "Thank you, Uncle Jean, for this opportunity. I fully appreciate that my duties come first."

I stand, salute Uncle Jean, and take my uniform.

Nineteen

The Charité - Fall, 1806

After gathering my gear and saying goodbye to my squadron comrades, I mount Bayard and make my way to the Charité. Along Charlottenburg Avenue, I come to an area bustling with activity. Hospital attendants wearing white jackets unload wagons filled with wounded soldiers. In front of me stands a splendid building that looks more like a palace than a hospital. I make my way toward the front entrance and am met by a young private, who gives me a salute. It takes a moment before I remember to return the greeting.

"Are you Lieutenant Calliet?" he asks.

"Yes. This must be the Charité?"

The private smiles. "Yes, sir. Baron Larrey is expecting you. Please, follow me. Your gear will be taken to your room."

I dismount, handing Bayard's reins to another private stationed by the entrance. Climbing the front steps, I can't help but marvel at the building; it's a far cry from my field hospital at Austerlitz. My boots thump on the polished wood floors and echo down the hallway. The walls are lined with pastoral paintings of gardens, mountains, and forests.

"Here you are, sir, Baron Larrey's office," the private tells me as he opens the door to an expansive room. He snaps another salute, turns, and walks back down the hallway.

At the far end of the room, standing by a desk, is Baron Larrey in deep conversation with two hospital attendants. He glances my way, raises a finger, and gives me a quick smile, but turns back to the aides.

The office looks much like Uncle Jean's—large and comfortable, but in more disarray. There are stacks of books on the floor, and a pile of medical equipment takes up a far corner. A large window looks out over a country garden filled with footways and benches. Several people in patients' gowns are slowly walking the paths.

"Lieutenant Calliet, it's so good to see you," says Baron Larrey as he crosses the room to shake my hand. He regards me from head to toe. "You look much better than when I last saw you in the hospital at Austerlitz. Congratulations on your promotion."

"Thank you. Except for a bout of infection, my recovery at home went well."

"Please, have a seat," Baron Larrey says as he moves to sit at his desk. "Infection is an unpredictable menace. Just when you think it has passed, it creeps up again. You are lucky. Many men don't survive."

"I remembered you poured vodka on the wound back at Austerlitz and told those attending me to do the same. It helped save my life."

The baron smiles. "I've found it to be effective."

I want to ask about Adrien but am unsure how to start, afraid of what I will learn. The baron breaks the pause. "I know your first question is about your friend, Sergeant Bauck. He's resting. His feet are improving, and we're attending his underarm burn."

Baron Larrey folds his arms across his chest. "The burn was deep, and when he arrived yesterday, the wound was infected. I excised all the infection I found and rinsed the site with vodka. At this point, we can only hope." I can't keep my lips from pressing together in concern.

The baron gets up. "Let me show you around the ward and then take you to your friend. Afterward, we'll go to your office. Your assistant, Corporal Laurent, will be there."

We walk into the hallway, and the baron leads me to a set of stairs. "The Prussians are cared for on the second floor." Climbing, we pass armed guards and then enter a large room filled with the wounded and sick. Groans echo across the chamber, then a scream of pain from the far end of the ward. Despite the open windows and clean conditions, the stench of infection, medicine, and urine permeates the air. We walk among the beds. "Most are wounded but many have typhus, the camp fever," the baron says.

There must be nearly two hundred Prussians. Several of the men peer up at us with empty eyes. Others blankly stare with trembling lips and chins. It seems nearly half are missing limbs. One man grabs for my uniform, pleading. *"Hilfe."*

The baron gently pulls his hand away. "We can't help him any more than we have, no matter how much he beseeches us," the baron says. We walk across the ward to another door that leads to stairs going down.

"You are a noble man, Baron, enduring all of this to save what lives you can."

We enter the ward for the French soldiers. The fetid smells are the same. Several of the patients see us enter and try to stand or sit up. "Bless you, your honor," several say to the baron as we walk by. Some do not speak but try to reach out to touch the doctor. The contrast between the Prussian ward and ours is the hope that fills our soldiers' eyes. Among our troops, Baron Larrey's reputation is renowned.

"Here he is," the baron says after we have passed through nearly the whole ward.

"Adrien." Tears well as I grasp Adrien's hand, searching his face. There is no movement. His hands feel clammy and cold.

"This morning's procedure required cutting deeply. He is heavily sedated with laudanum. I don't expect him to be conscious until this evening."

"Is he dying?"

It takes a moment before the baron replies. "I honestly don't know." He shakes his head. "If I didn't get all the infection, he won't live." The baron's expression tells me the odds are not favorable. "Come. Sergeant Bauck will be asleep for some time. Corporal Laurent is expecting us in your office."

Leaving the ward, I look back to Adrien for what may be the last time I see him alive. My heart floods with sorrow. I cannot think of losing him.

The baron opens a door. "This is your office. You're next door to me."

Inside, a young man leaps to his feet and gives a crisp salute.

"At ease, Corporal Laurent," I say. "I am Lieutenant Calliet, the new administrator for the Charité. Please, sit back down."

As with the baron's office, the room is spacious. The corporal's desk is kitty-corner to mine. I walk around my desk and sit, running my fingers across the smooth walnut of the chair arms. The baron pulls up a seat facing both me and the corporal. Much like the baron, I have a window overlooking the courtyard. The sun shines in, illuminating the room so completely there is no need to light our lamps.

We spend the remainder of the day going over what I need to do to keep the Charité running smoothly. Baron Larrey shows me the forms he uses to request new supplies. Corporal Laurent goes over similar forms that come from housekeeping and the kitchen.

"Your responsibility is to review all requests," says the baron. "Check them against the records the corporal maintains of the supplies we have in stock, sign the orders authorizing any purchases, and ensure the materials we order are properly delivered. You are to address any problems we have with suppliers. You must keep the hospital running smoothly."

I nod.

"I know you will have many questions," the baron tells me. "My door is always open."

A tall case clock in the corner chimes six o'clock.

"Have we covered everything, Corporal?" the baron asks.

"Yes, sir."

Baron Larrey turns toward me. "Lieutenant, I know you want to be with your friend. I'll arrange for a plate of food to be waiting for you in your quarters, which, by the way, are directly across the hall. Here are the keys. I'll see you in the morning."

On the way to the patient ward, my thoughts race. *Maybe Adrien will be too delirious to recognize me.* I shudder at the thought of possibly losing my closest friend.

Adrien's eyes are still closed when I reach his bed. I sit in the chair beside him. His breathing seems thankfully steady, but he is very pale.

An attendant stops by a few minutes later and examines him. "He appears to be doing well. His bandages look good, and there is no smell." Holding Adrien's wrist, he adds, "His pulse is strong."

"Did you assist with the operation?"

"Yes ... we nearly lost him. He stopped breathing in the middle of the procedure. Baron Larrey had me use a bellows to inflate his lungs and help him start to breathe again."

"Bellows? That kept him alive? My God." In shock, I ask, "When do you think he will wake?"

"I don't think he'll sleep much longer. The effects of the laudanum should be wearing away soon."

He moves on to check other patients, leaving me feeling helpless.

About an hour later, Adrien's head moves. He coughs feebly and hoarsely asks for water. I lift his head and put a glass to his lips. He sips gratefully, then pulls away. I lower his head and wait.

Minutes pass ... then he opens his eyes. "Is that you, Jean-Luc? Can it be you?" His trembling left hand reaches out. "My friend."

He raises his head and tries to move, but grimaces in pain. A brace is keeping his right upper arm away from his body.

"Am I in Berlin? I remember the hospital wagon coming into the city. Basile was tied to the back. When I looked out, I thought I saw you."

"You may have seen me. I was stationed along the parade route, and several hospital wagons drove by. My thoughts were of you as they passed."

Adrien pauses, catching his breath and resting his head back onto his pillow. He glances at the brace on his right side. "My arm was infected, wasn't it? Did they get it all?"

"We don't know. You were lucky. Baron Larrey performed the surgery, and there is no one better than he."

"I doubt I'll survive if the infection returns," Adrien whispers, worry etched on his face.

"That won't happen." But in my heart, I know it is likely. I force a smile. "I'll write to your family and tell them you are recovering here in Berlin. Isn't the town where your parents were born near here?"

"Yes, just to the northeast." He forces a weary smile.

"What is it?"

"The irony."

"I don't understand."

"To die here. At the hands of fellow countrymen."

Adrien looks weary. I don't see a fear of death in his eyes, but rather an acceptance of what may come.

"You need to rest. I'll come back in the morning."

"No, you must stay. I'm tired, but I think the effect of the laudanum is nearly gone." Adrien's head falls back onto his pillow. He twists to look at me. His eyes are tearing. "I may not live through the night, and there is much I need to say to you."

He eyes me from head to foot. "A lieutenant's uniform?"

"Yes, I was promoted today. It's a long story."

"Congratulations. Are you deploying to the east to fight the Russians?"

"Not until you recover. They made me administrator of this hospital. Uncle Jean assigned me here. He is the military governor of Berlin."

Adrien manages a thin smile. "Nothing but paperwork ... and babysitting me."

"Just for a short time. It took only a month or so for me to recover from my infection. We'll still be fighting on the eastern front by this spring. The Russians never seem to give up."

"Or sooner if I die," Adrien chuckles grimly.

For the remainder of the evening, despite all he has been through, Adrien urgently outlines various things he wishes to say. He tells me what he wants me to write in a letter to his parents, and we talk about where he would like to be buried. "I don't wish to be laid in the church cemetery, but my parents will object. They will say I need to be buried in consecrated ground. Fine. Let the priest consecrate that land on the hill above the river by Ostheim. That's where I want to be."

Adrien rests for a few moments, then we reminisce about our childhood, recalling, among many other things, the day of the guillotine. Adrien goes silent for a few moments, as if trying to find a way to say something important.

"Jean-Luc," he says with a solemn voice, "I want to talk about Anna Lise."

"Anna Lise?" I ask. "Don't worry, I will always be there for her. I will take care of her if you can't."

Adrien searches for his words. "If she will have you ... I want the two of you to be together. She is still young, but in a few years, she will be a woman. We will only be in our twenties by that time. I know in my heart it would be the right thing, and I can't think of two people who would be happier. Anna Lise loves you, and you love her."

"Yes, of course I love her ... as a sister," I say, incredulous. "Are you talking about marriage? I promise to watch over her, but marriage can't be something planned and agreed to by others."

"Your hearts have already arranged it."

I shake my head. "Adrien, what are you, some kind of deathbed matchmaker?"

"What will come will come, Jean-Luc. I just want you to know how I feel and remember it when the time is right."

Finally, Adrien's exhaustion wins. "It's getting late and we both need sleep," he says. Gripping my arm, he gives me a warm smile. "It's so good to see you. I felt so alone in that hospital wagon. Now I'm with you, and my comrades are near."

I nod. "I'll be seeing them before they deploy to the east. I'll tell them I've found you. They've missed you."

I get up to leave and see that Adrien has already closed his eyes. His face is calm. I kiss my fingers and pat his forehead. Gazing at all the injured and dying men, I wonder how many will make it through the night. Will Adrien make it?

Twenty

Recovery – Spring and Summer, 1807

Except for some minor flare-ups, Adrien has been recovering strongly. It's now late March, and he's itching to return to our squad. I dare not tell him I much prefer the paperwork needed to run this hospital. In fact, I don't tell anyone this—certainly not Baron Larrey, and especially not Uncle Jean. They all must think I, too, want to be a good soldier and return to our unit.

Adrien bursts into my office and comes to hover over me like a housebound child who wants to go outside and play. "Jean-Luc," he implores, "let's ride the trails along the River Spree. I need to get out of this hospital before I go mad."

Corporal Laurent glances up from his work, looking annoyed, but says, "It's fine to break for the day, sir. You've signed all of today's purchase orders. Besides," he says, eyeing Adrien, "It would be excellent patient therapy."

"Well said, Corporal," Adrien concurs enthusiastically. "Yes, excellent therapy. I need to be fit enough to be discharged, and then we can be off to the eastern front. We're needed, Jean-Luc. The new patients who came in from the battle at Eylau say the Russians are proving difficult. The army needs our prowess!"

I reply with exaggerated sarcasm. "Of course, Adrien, our not being at the front must be the reason the emperor, with his 150,000 men, is having trouble with the Russians. We must get you well so we can bring the emperor victory."

Adrien grins and slaps me on the back. "No doubt, Jean-Luc. No doubt. Let's not waste any more time."

Looking at my paperwork, I see only one small matter needing my immediate attention. "All right, let's make an afternoon of it. I have just a little more work to do."

"I'll get my gear and meet you at the stables," Adrien replies.

Finishing up, I turn to Corporal Laurent. "Corporal, you should take some time off as well. The weather is beautiful."

"And do what, sir? Attending to details like this is what I like to do. Enjoy your ride."

I smile at the corporal, whose nose is already back in his paperwork. I too have come to love this assignment. Running the hospital is like running a great machine. It's an exciting challenge to keep all the wheels greased and rolling. But always, I remember that my goal is to see Adrien well again.

"Hurry up, Mr. Lieutenant, sir," Adrien says as he saddles up Basile. Bayard snorts in anticipation.

As we ride along the river trail, I look at Adrien. "Do you feel any pain?"

"None that I can't live with. I'll probably always have soreness in my right arm, but it's getting stronger. I'm sure I can handle my sabre."

We ride silently, enjoying the sounds of the gurgling river and the muffled hooves against the snow.

After a long while, Adrien speaks. "I got a letter from *Vati* yesterday. He and the family send their best wishes. Anna Lise sends you her love."

Adrien pauses, but he appears to want to continue talking. I glance over. "Did he say more?"

A few more moments pass. "*Vati* says there has been trouble for them in Colmar. Anti-Prussian sentiment is high. Fewer people come to our butcher shop. Out of fear, Anna Lise no longer goes to school."

Adrien keeps looking straight ahead as we ride, but his shoulders droop.

"There's nothing you can do," I reply. "This war will end, and then there will be another war with a new enemies to hate."

Adrien jerks his head to look at me. "I can't just keep sitting in a hospital, Jean-Luc. I must feel like I'm helping to end this war. What else can I do to get out of here? Do you think we could drill with our sabres? Maybe Baron Larrey knows of other ways to strengthen my arm."

"I'll talk with him tomorrow. I'm sure he can recommend several good exercises. That's also a good idea you have about practicing with our sabres. But for now, let's head back to the hospital. It's getting late."

* * *

Swish. Adrien deftly undercuts my swing, and I miss my mark. His sabre strikes mine in a powerful uppercut. We circle each other on our horses, looking for openings. Our swords crash one against the other, over and over again. I feel sweat streaming down, but I won't let Adrien best me.

"That's good. I've seen enough. You've been parrying for nearly an hour," Baron Larrey says. "General Rapp, I think

Sergeant Bauck is ready to join his comrades on the eastern front, don't you?"

My eyes turn to Uncle Jean. He's smiling broadly. "Yes. Most impressive. No Cossack will be able to get the better of either of you. Congratulations, Sergeant Bauck. You are now cleared to return to duty, and just in time. A detachment of reinforcements is preparing to join the emperor near Osterode. Your old squad is near there.

Looking toward me, he adds, "Baron Larrey reports on the excellent job you are doing here at the Charité. You may stay here if you wish, or join Sergeant Bauck."

A choice? No, I have no choice.

"I've learned much and enjoyed my work at the hospital, but it is time to return to the life of a soldier. When does the detachment leave?"

"Not until next week," Uncle Jean says. "That will give you time to train your replacement."

* * *

Adrien and I report to the colonel commanding the reinforcement detachment. He reads our orders. "Too bad you can't stay with these young lads once we get to Osterode. Nearly all of them are green recruits who could use your guidance. I fear their training is woefully inadequate."

Glancing at the column of troops, I see why the colonel is concerned. They look young and exceedingly nervous. Several are fidgeting in their saddles, and others try to appear aloof, sitting erect and attempting to look stoic. It's easy to see it's an act.

"How far is Osterode, sir?" I ask.

"Ten to twelve days, I suspect. We're bringing supplies as well as these reinforcements. The wagons will slow us down."

Adrien and I salute and take our place toward the front of the column.

"Twelve days," Adrien snorts. "On our own, we would be there in half that time. It's already late May. The fighting may be done by the time we join our comrades."

I shrug. "We have our assignment. Besides, it will give you a chance to see the Prussian countryside. I'm sure you didn't see much from the back of that hospital wagon."

Adrien shoots me a glare. "I will take my time to sightsee after we are victorious."

The cold winter and gloomy spring have finally broken into warm days. The countryside is made up of low, rolling hills, much it heavily forested. The smell and taste of pollen fills the air, burning my eyes. The trees seem to press down, making me uneasy. Maybe it's the memory of the day Adrien and I were ambushed and captured that's putting me on edge. I keep feeling the enemy is going to charge out from these trees.

One young recruit rides up next to me. "Lieutenant, sir," he says, "This is my first time away from my family in Normandy. Are the stories we hear about the Cossacks true? Does blood flow from their eyes, and do they look like bears coming at you?"

Several other recruits ride up a little closer, wanting to hear my answer. I chuckle. "I've never seen blood flowing from their eyes, but they are relentless and fierce. Just the sight of them will send a chill down your spine. Their dark woolen hats merge with their mustaches and full beards to make them look like bears on horseback. You must watch out for their favorite weapon, the spear. A very important thing to remember about the Cossacks: they like to attack troops who are not in formation. Unless you stay close and support your comrades, they will pick you off one by one."

While talking to the private, I look down at his saddle and see many items out of place. "Private, look how far forward your sabre sheath is. You will have trouble drawing that sword, and those lost seconds could mean your life. And look at your sleeping roll. It's pressed up against your back. Sure, that makes riding easier, but your mobility is limited. How much training have you had?"

"A few days," he answers sheepishly as he adjusts his gear.

Looking at several of his companions, I see that many have misplaced gear as well.

"Sergeant Bauck," I say, "why don't we pass our time these next few days talking to each of these recruits and giving them pointers. God knows, it may save many of their lives."

The colonel overhears me and turns in his saddle to give a nod of approval. But as I look at this colonel's new uniform and highly polished boots, I judge he too has not seen much action. This worries me. Untrained leaders leading untrained troops into situations that require knowledge and quick action spells forthcoming disaster.

The days pass as Adrien and I go from soldier to soldier. "Lieutenant," says one of them. "Thank you for your help. Please, you must come visit my family when this war is over." His is one of many invitations. If Adrien and I wanted, we could visit every part of France over many years.

* * *

"When do you think we'll get to the front, sir?" a recruit asks. Holding his chest high, he adds smugly, "I've come to fight, not to sightsee." Many of his comrades nod in agreement. Adrien too nods his support and impatience.

The lane we're traveling is now running along the edge of a lake. Carts loaded with goods pull off the road to let us by. The peasants driving them bow their heads in deference with fear in their eyes, likely thinking that we, like most invading armies, are going to plunder their cargos. But this is their lucky day. These recruits have not yet learned the art of plundering and simply ride past.

'What's that ahead?" someone cries as we round a corner. I lean forward. The structure is massive, with a town surrounding it.

'Osterode Castle," shouts the colonel.

This is where the emperor wintered. But now it's June, and I'm sure he and the army are gone, searching for the enemy.

'Private Pettit, ride to the castle and find out where the army is," the colonel commands.

Within an hour, the private returns. The colonel motions me to join him to hear his report.

"There is only a small detachment at the castle, sir," the private states. "The emperor and the army have moved northwest to the Alle River. There are reports the Russians are massing near there. The river is not far, maybe ten to twenty leagues away."

Very faintly, I hear what sounds like thunder rumbling, but it can't be thunder, as the sky is clear. 'Colonel, do you hear that?" I ask. 'It sounds like cannon fire. The battle has started."

It's only about midday, and the colonel commands his attachment to ride toward the rumbling. We'll likely be able to join our comrades tomorrow.

The recruits are becoming excited with the prospect of battle. 'Do you think we'll meet Cossacks, or just their infantry?" asks one. 'I do so want to meet a Cossack and match my skills against his."

'Hope to God you don't," I say.

The next morning, we are already riding as the sun crowns the nearby hill. A cool morning breeze brushes my face, and all is quiet save the clip-clop of our horses. Suddenly, there is a cacophony of screeching overhead. A conspiracy of ravens thunders past, heading north toward where the cannon fire had been. Adrien looks knowingly at me, but I don't think our companions grasp the meaning of their presence. They stare into the sky, gaping at the massive number of them.

"We should reach our armies today," the colonel shouts. "Move out."

We reach the Alle River and follow the road along its banks toward the town of Launau. Again, we hear the rumble from the artillery, and the sound is much closer now.

Coming around a bend in the road, we hear the growing sound of ravens cawing. The entire detachment freezes at the landscape of death and destruction before us. Scanning the field, the only living things I see are the birds. The colonel waves for us to proceed slowly. We move toward the smoking remnants of the village of Launau. The bodies, many only in fragments, lie scattered on both sides of the road. Ravens flock on these remains, plucking away pieces of flesh and strips of skin. Our troops breathe in the scent of war: burnt flesh and burning houses. Many lean to the side of their horses, spewing vomit.

A hog grunts nearby, and I'm horrified to see it gorging on what's left of a soldier's mangled leg. I draw my sabre and charge the beast, severing its head. Several ravens quickly descend on this new corpse, happy to have another meal.

Looking around, I see the dazed, ashen faces of several recruits surrounding me. Not knowing why I was charging, they followed me on my attack of the hog. "Keep your eyes sharp," I say. "Cossacks may be nearby."

This command brings them back to focus. "Sir, should we look for survivors?" a few of them ask.

I know from experience, or maybe callousness, that if there are any survivors, they will soon be dead. "The hospital wagons have already searched this field," I say grimly. "There is nothing more we can do here."

The field of destruction is relatively small, indicating this was not a major engagement, but the consequences are the same for the broken and mangled bodies we pass. Moving through the village, I see the furtive movements of townspeople hiding among the ruins.

As we leave the town, the colonel takes us to a gallop. We pass through several more villages, each with their own areas of devastation and fallen soldiers. By mid-afternoon, we come across the remains of another, larger battle near the village of Langweise. This field is strewn not only with soldiers, but many horses as well, including Shagyas.

Adrien rides up alongside me. "Jean-Luc, do you think our comrades were part of this?"

I eye the Shagyas. "It's likely. Marshal Murat's cavalry is always at the forefront."

Nearby, the colonel is talking with his aides. The rumbling from the cannonade is but a league or two away. He appears undecided about what to do.

"Stay here," I say to Adrien, "and keep these recruits calm. I'm going to talk to the colonel."

"Good that you're here," the colonel says as I ride up. "The battle is near, and these men are not prepared to meet the enemy on their own."

"We may have no choice, sir. I'll ride to that hospital wagon and see what they know."

"Very well," he replies.

As I come up to the wagon, a musket fires. One of the medical attendants stands over a fallen horse with the musket still aimed at its head. He looks up. "Were you part of this engagement, sir?"

"No. We are a detachment of reinforcements. Can you tell me about the situation and where our army is?"

"I can, Lieutenant," a voice says from within the wagon.

I dismount and approach the back of the vehicle. Sitting on a bench with a heavily bandaged thigh is a young corporal.

"We had a terrible struggle here, sir. The Cossacks came from nowhere and nearly surrounded us. Neither side would relent until darkness fell. I guess I'm one of the lucky ones," he says, looking down at his leg.

"Are you with Marshal Murat? Are they nearby?"

"Yes, I was with the marshal. We were heading toward Heilsberg. That cannon we hear is probably the battle there. Sir, be careful of the Cossacks. They are everywhere."

"I will, and thank you."

I look down at his wound. "When they clean your cut, be sure they pour vodka into it. It helped me recover from a wound last year."

The corporal looks up. "Yes, sir, and good luck."

Returning to the colonel, I lay out the situation. "Sir, we likely have no choice but to engage the Cossacks. The corporal in the hospital wagon says they are everywhere. I suggest we divide into three groups. I will lead the first group at the front of the column, you the next, and Sergeant Bauck the third in the rear. By breaking into three, we will each command about a hundred soldiers. If attacked, we can support each other."

"It seems we have no choice," the colonel says with some exasperation.

We gather the men, and I explain our strategy. I look out across the sea of earnest faces. They listen intently, eyes focused on me.

We move out, following the road to Heilsberg. With each corner we round, the sound of the cannonade intensifies. We come to a point where the forest crowds the road's edge. I look around nervously.

Suddenly, from both sides of the road, bands of Cossacks attack. A sea of furry-headed monsters with flaming red pantaloons descends on the colonel and his forces in the middle. One charges the colonel, pushing his spear through him. Many of his troops look befuddled and are quickly dispatched.

Desperately, I try to spot Adrien. We have only one chance, and it will only work if he understands what I want him to do.

Frantically, I wave my sabre to the west, hoping he sees me and understands he needs to go in that direction.

Concentrating now on my own men, I motion for them to follow me to the east to cut off and trap the Cossacks between my forces and what remains of the colonel's. My hope is that Adrien is doing the same.

Blood gushes from men on both sides, but we make progress, pushing our way toward where I hope to find Adrien.

The struggle is intense. The Cossacks are becoming frantic, seeming to know they are now trapped. The quarters are too close for their spears to be effective. In desperation, they drop their spears and reach for their sabres. This opening is all that's needed to strike them fatally.

Finally, emerging through the mass of horses and men, are Adrien and his forces. Some Cossacks escape, but most fall to our sabres. The green recruits have fought and won their first battle ... but at a high cost.

They nervously glance around, surprised grins crossing many of their faces. "We've won!" they shout incredulously. They congratulate each other and slap each other on the back. Then they start looking for particular comrades and find many of them lying on the ground, dead.

The colonel is dead, as are over a third of our forces. This battle of little consequence has cost good men's lives. But perhaps in the long run, this experience will save many who survived today. They are no longer green recruits, but have begun to become hardened soldiers who have proved their mettle.

Although I'm not a religious man, I gather together our surviving troops and say a prayer commemorating those who have died. The men are somber and exhausted, but join me in praying.

The day is late, and the sound of cannon has gone silent. Moans of pain resound from the battle's survivors. I send a messenger back to Langweise to tell the hospital wagon its services are required.

"Adrien, take your men and comb the battlefield to the west for survivors. I'll take mine to the east. Bring those who can be moved back here to the road."

Only a few of those we find still alive can be moved and hopefully saved. For the most part, the wounds are deep and blood loss severe. We make them as comfortable as possible before moving on. They and I know that death is near.

"Lieutenant," one gasps. "Do you remember me? I'm from Normandy. We talked earlier." He struggles to catch his breath. I kneel at his side, clutching his hand.

"I remember. You invited me to visit your family farm."

His tear-stained face looks up anxiously. "Please, you must promise you will visit my family. Our farm is just outside the village of Bayeux." He struggles for every word. "My family name is Devall, and I am known as Renaud."

He strains to remove something from around his neck and holds it tightly in his hands. Using what little strength remains, he squeezes the object into mine. "My mother gave me this rosary to protect my soul from the evils of war. Tell her my soul is at peace. Give my little sister a kiss, and say I hold dear my memories of playing together as children. Let my father know I died bravely and will miss our times working together in the fields." He chokes for breath.

"Of course," I say. A look of relief crosses his face. He closes his eyes and lets go of my hand, slumping back and exhaling a few last breaths.

Finally, all the wounded have been attended to, and we light our campfires. Sentries are posted on all sides. Thankfully, night has fallen before the ravens have found their new feasting grounds.

The sky is clear, and the light of a waxing moon bathes the battlefield with a cold shimmer. The sounds of crickets and frogs fill the night, mingling with the groans of the dying and wounded.

Adrien has brought some coffee with him from Berlin, and the two of us sit beside our campfire, sipping a cup. "I can see why they made you a lieutenant, Jean-Luc. What you did today brought us victory. We would have been lambs for the slaughter without your quick thinking."

"We would have still been lambs for slaughter if you hadn't understood the plan instantly," I reply somberly. "The men fought well."

Adrien pours me more coffee.

"What do you think tomorrow will bring?" I ask. "The cannon have gone silent, but to whose advantage? Will we find Russians waiting for us when we enter Heilsberg, or will we finally see our comrades again?"

Twenty-One

Heilsberg – Summer, 1807

A light fog swirls over our encampment, adding to the gloominess of my mood. Suddenly, my ears perk at a far-off noise.

"What's that creaking sound?" I say to Adrien. We both jump up and peer into the darkness.

I grab my musket while Adrien unsheathes his sabre. The rattling becomes louder, rousing the rest of the men. I raise my hand for quiet, and they too take up their muskets or swords. The sound comes closer, but we still can't make out anything through the fog. Tension rises. Just as the noise seems to be on top of us, I call out, "Who goes there!" We each have our weapon at the ready.

"Medical help," a voice in the darkness says as two hospital wagons emerge. "We received news there was a battle up this way today. Was it here?"

"Yes," I say. I lower my musket, and the men follow suit. "We have many wounded. I'm grateful you have come so quickly."

"We can start attending to them as soon as we unload our equipment," the driver replies. He rapidly jumps down and begins giving orders to his fellow attendants.

I go to each of my wounded men briefly, letting them know medical help has arrived. An owl hoots from a nearby tree, reflecting our melancholy.

"Sir, thank you for saving us," says one, his voice weak. "The Cossacks ... they were horrible."

The young soldier shifts his weight away from his shattered left arm, grimacing, but wants to say more. "I froze. They came at me and I just stared." He hangs his head. "A comrade yelled my name and I got my sabre up in time to hit his spear, but it still ripped into me. I fell, and the Cossack still came. A comrade cut into his neck, but another Cossack killed him. They both fell on top of me."

He looks up in despair. "My comrade died because of me. How can I live with this?"

"Your comrade was doing his duty," I say gently. "He was looking after you. The memory ... the pain will always be there, but time will ease the burden. For now, you can only grieve."

The soldier buries his head into his one good arm, sobbing. I put my hand on his shoulder, giving what little comfort I can. "The hospital attendants are here to attend to your arm," I say, giving his shoulder one last squeeze.

* * *

The attendants save the men they can, working through the night. We break camp and leave before dawn. I don't want my young recruits to see our fallen friends scattered across the field in the morning light.

"Move out," I command, and we slowly make our way north. Only a gentle, ghostly breeze breaks the silence, swirling the fog as it hovers over the field of combat. I thank God the ravens haven't come yet.

With the waxing half-moon coming in and out of view in the fog, the moonlight highlights the lush grass along the road's edge. Our troop strength is now about two hundred. I lead our paired columns of riders at a canter. Adrien rides ahead as our scout. My skin prickles, and I think I see Cossack eyes everywhere.

"Who goes there!" a voice shouts from the darkness ahead of Adrien.

"Halt," I command. I see several soldiers emerge from the darkness, surrounding Adrien.

I can't make out what they are saying, but soon a full contingent of soldiers is rushing toward us. I keep my arm up to indicate no one should move. There is a scraping of metal as sabres are partially drawn. Soon, a sergeant dressed in a French uniform is directly in front of me, his musket pointed at my head.

"Identify yourself," he demands.

"I'm Lieutenant Calliet, leading a detachment of reinforcements. Can't you see by our uniforms we are not the enemy?" I say with agitation.

Not yet lowering his weapon, the sergeant barks, "Show me your orders."

"I don't have them. Our command colonel was killed by Cossacks yesterday. They must be on the colonel's body. I am to report to Captain Bouchet."

The sergeant looks up from his musket. "Captain Bouchet? I've heard of him." Finally, he lowers his gun.

"Sir, Marshal Murat's cavalry is bivouacked ahead. There's a captain and a squadron with a *cantiniére* wagon encamped at its edge. It might be your Captain Bouchet. You can report to him."

"Thank you, Sergeant."

I turn to Adrien, who has joined me. "It would be good luck to find Captain Bouchet so quickly," I say.

Our detachment moves forward, and within a short time, we arrive at a field covered in a sea of campfires. Just ahead is a camp with a wagon. I motion for everyone to stop and dismount. "Men, stay here with the horses while the sergeant and I see if this is where we report."

I glance at Adrien. "That looks like Madame Colette's wagon, don't you think?" We approach the vehicle, hoping to see our old comrades again. A man sits alone, slumped forward with his elbows on his knees, staring into the flames. He turns, and I see Captain Bouchet's face illuminated by the campfire.

"Who comes to bother me so early this morning?" a halting, dejected voice says.

"Captain Bouchet, it's us, Lieutenant Calliet and Sergeant Bauck. We bring reinforcements from Berlin."

He stares at us for a few moments. "Calliet? Bauck? Can it really be you? I thought all my close comrades were now dead." He stands up and shakily embraces us. His voice breaks. "Thank God you weren't in today's battle. Join me by the fire. We can have a few moments of sanity before this new day begins."

"Sir, before we sit, can I tell my detachment where to camp?"

The captain looks over my shoulder at the soldiers awaiting my orders. "They look so young," he says softly. "Have they seen combat?"

"Their first was yesterday. We lost about a third of our men to a Cossack attack. They are good soldiers, ready for battle."

"I lost more than half my men yesterday," the captain says, lowering his head, looking away. "Tell them to make themselves comfortable in that empty patch over there. They won't be staying long."

Adrien and I go over to our detachment and tell them where to settle. We return and see the captain has gone back to his campfire and is standing over it, still with drooped shoulders.

Madame Colette comes from her wagon, carrying a bottle with two glasses. 'Calliet, Bauck, I'm so happy to see you. The captain needs your comradery. He has drunk too much already, but here, have one more with him and make him feel needed."

We join the captain by the fire, filling his glass with more brandy. His uniform is stained and crusted with blood. 'What happened, sir? How did the battle go yesterday?"

'At first, our attack was successful," he says, nearly in a whisper. 'But then their artillery opened up, catching us naked on the battlefield. White smoke clouded our vision, making the oncoming enemy hard to see."

The captain hesitates, tossing some wood into the fire. 'The cannonballs threw up chunks of soil and splinters of iron. One took off the head of a comrade in front of me, continued through the chest of the rider by my side, then blew through the soldier behind him." He pauses, looking at his blood-smeared hands, then his jacket. 'My uniform is still encrusted with their blood."

The captain takes a deep swallow of his brandy, then throws his glass into the fire with disgust, shattering it. Flames flare from the remaining alcohol.

'The cannonade stopped, and then came the onslaught of Russian cavalry. It was fierce hand-to-hand fighting. I saw the marshal try to rally us against the Russians. He was nearly captured when one horse and then another were shot from underneath him."

He pauses, wiping sweat from his forehead. 'All order disintegrated in a wild, frenzied fight. Muzzle flashes from pistols, sabres clashing. We were being routed, and they began to overwhelm us. We fell back. Fortunately, our artillery came into play and covered our retreat. Each side attacked and counterattacked the remainder of the day. Neither could deliver the winning blow. It was nearly midnight before the last shots were fired. I think both sides were too exhausted to carry on."

The captain gazes intently at Adrien and me. "So much carnage, and for no gain. What will this new day bring? All night, I heard the groans and cries of the wounded, but no one dared enter the battlefield for fear of the Russian guns. Our cavalry is spent. We have nothing left."

The light of day swims over the ridges to the east. "Come," says Captain Bouchet. "We can see the battlefield from the top of that hill. The marshal has his tent there so he can view the combat area." As we crest the hilltop, the magnitude of the destruction becomes clear. For as far as the eye can see, there are dead soldiers and horses. Several stallions limp aimlessly amid the ruin, stumbling on the corpses.

"This is a nightmare," Adrien mutters. "What honor can there be in this?"

"Look—over there, on the far side of the field," says someone near the marshal's tent. "The Russians are coming out to retrieve their wounded."

Marshal Murat emerges from his tent and takes up his spyglass. After scanning the Russian side of the battlefield, he lowers his glass and gathers his aides. After a few words, the aides are sent out, scattering in different directions around the encampment. One comes up to Captain Bouchet. "Sir, the Russians appear to be making a truce to take care of their wounded. We are going to do the same. Send some of your men out to help."

Captain Bouchet looks weary. "Lieutenant Calliet, you and Sergeant Bauck take your detachment and tend to the wounded. I can't bring myself to send my men out there."

Adrien and I salute and leave the captain on the hilltop.

"This task will be worse than battle," says Adrien.

I nod, dreading what the next few hours will bring.

Adrien and I pair our men and send them into the destruction to retrieve the wounded. The two of us form a pair and head out in the early morning light.

The task seems impossible. Before us lie hundreds of men. We pick our way through the bodies. Many have already been stripped of their clothes and belongings by the local peasants. There are bodies without heads, without legs. A few are still alive. We carefully carry them back toward our encampment. We have no time to deal with the dead.

"Lieutenant, sir," a man from my detachment calls out. "What about this Russian? What should we do with him?"

Adrien and I come over and find a man barely alive, gasping for breath. His face is partially gone, scarred with burns. His head has lost most of its skin, and he has no eyes, nose, or even a jaw.

"We must put him out of his misery," Adrien says as he looks at me with anguish. "No man need suffer like this."

Adrien pulls his pistol from his vest. I stop him. "It's my responsibility. I will take care of it." I draw my pistol and fire a shot into what remains of the soldier's head.

We work the rest of the morning clearing the battlefield of our wounded. We mingle with the Russian soldiers, sometimes helping one another with wounded men trapped among the debris. My men look grim, but determined.

By late morning, the wounded have been cleared. The day turns hot, and the odor of the corpses festering in the sun begins to grow. The ravens have now discovered this new feeding ground.

Now that the wounded have been retrieved, the Russian guns, from their many redoubts, explode into life. Our cannon return fire, but no cavalry charges or infantry movements take place. Each side seems to be licking its wounds.

My men and I stagger back to the bivouac, overwhelmed by what we have done the past few hours. I can't shake the sight of the Russian soldier with no face and the memory of pulling the trigger to end his life.

Captain Bouchet meets us. He seems to have regained his composure, while we have lost ours. "Thank you and your men for doing that," he says. "We will be moving out in a few hours. I've talked to our regimental colonel regarding your recruits. He wants to merge them into my command. I want you to be their direct officer in charge and have Sergeant Bauck assist you. Gather them up and I'll let them know."

Despite the horrors of the day, I can't help but smile. I've come to consider these young men my comrades. I would trust them with my life and am glad they are staying with me. "Thank you, sir."

Upon hearing about their assignment, the men clasp each other's forearms, grateful to be staying together. It reminds me that the bonds forged in battle are strong.

With cannon booming in the background, we give our horses feed. I take off my jacket and move Bayard to the shade. Needing time to be alone, I begin brushing and talking softly to him. He nickers. I notice others in my company watching me. Nearly all of them retrieve their brushes and begin stroking down their steeds as well. The booming of the cannon is actually a godsend, muffling out the sounds of ravens cawing in delight.

"Prepare to move out," a soldier on horseback commands as he rides down the line of troops.

Napoleon and Tsar Alexander Meeting on
a Raft in the Neiman River at Tilset

Cantiniéres

Twenty-Two

Tilset – Summer, 1807

I slept poorly, remembering all the battle field dead, wondering if our fate will be the same today. "Adrien, do you think we are about to attack?" I ask.

"I don't know," he replies nervously. "If we do, we need to try something new. The frontal attack used yesterday was almost a complete failure. The Russian cannon have the approach to Heilsberg sealed."

Putting my jacket back on, I saddle Bayard and mount up. All of my men are ready, looking at me for my next command. Our squadron is near the back of the corps, and we wait until it is our turn to go forward.

As we finally move ahead, I realize we're moving away from Heilsberg, and relief washes over me.

The troops are taking a road leading to the northwest, away from yesterday's battlefield and the town. From our high ground, the village appears serene, nestled in a hollow on the banks of the Alle River. The scars of battle are muted by the distance.

We ride until dusk. The distant sound of cannon ceases. We set up camp on the hills overlooking the right bank of the river. Word goes down the line that we cannot have any fires. The moon is but a waning crescent, providing little light to pierce the darkness. The stars dazzle overhead; Mars is near Venus, making a vivid pinpoint of light. Perhaps their close alignment is a sign this war will soon be over. Flashes from meteorites streak by. I lie on my back, staring at the sky while reflecting on the past two days. Adrien sits nearby.

"Look! Over there, on the hills above the river on the other side," Adrien says. "There's a whole parade of torches moving north. The Russians must be abandoning Heilsberg! Maybe they think our corps is trying to cut them off from Königsberg."

I stand and see, emerging from the darkness to the south, an ever-growing string of lights.

"What town is north of here?" Adrien asks.

"Friedland. Maybe the Russians are moving toward there. But our mission is to prevent them from getting to Königsberg, not Friedland."

A horseman rides down the road, shouting, "Prepare to move out."

"Whatever our mission, we must stay ahead of those lights," I say.

"Mount up!" Captain Bouchet orders.

I ride up to the captain. "Sir, do you know where we're heading?"

"Halfway between Friedland and Königsberg," he replies. "We are to stop the enemy there."

"Very good, sir." I ride back to my unit to tell them we'll be riding most of the night.

The next order comes. "Forward!"

* * *

After a hard night's ride and just as the sun begins to slip up into the eastern sky, we reach an intersection with a road running north toward Königsberg. Our soldiers are spreading out across the fields on all sides, trampling down the emerging crop of wheat. There is orderly confusion everywhere. Soldiers are dismounting and unloading their gear. Some of those who first arrived have already unsaddled their mounts and are eating rations. Their horses munch on any remaining untrampled wheat shoots. The countryside is mostly low, rolling hills planted with crops. Small stands of trees are scattered about. Only our army is in sight.

The marshal's tent is on the edge of the intersection and is surrounded by a flurry of activity, with aides coming and going in all directions. The marshal leans over a table in front of his tent, intently studying his maps, gesturing both north and south.

"We stop over there," Captain Bouchet says, pointing toward a spot of unoccupied ground. We are among the last squadrons to arrive and are close to the marshal's headquarters.

As our squad dismounts, one of the marshal's aides rushes over to Captain Bouchet. Speaking to the captain, he points to the south, and the captain nods. After a salute, the aide turns to go back.

"Lieutenant Calliet," the captain commands. "Come."

Patting Bayard on the nose, I murmur that I'll return shortly and unburden him of my gear. He snorts and munches on the tender new shoots.

While I approach, the captain dismounts. "Lieutenant," he says, "I want you to take five of your most experienced men and set up a watch point about two or three leagues down this road. The moment you see any Russians, send a messenger back to the marshal. Here, take this spyglass. It may help."

"May I take Sergeant Bauck?"

"No. I've seen how your men look to the two of you for leadership. One of you must stay with them."

"Yes, sir," I say, giving a salute.

Striding back to the squad, I yell, "Bonnet, Perrin, Fontaine, Girard, and Vincent, mount up."

I return to Bayard. "Sorry old friend, we can't rest yet."

Speaking so all can hear, I say, "The six of us are going to establish a watch post down the road. The remainder of you are in luck. You get to rest. Sergeant Bauck, they are in your charge."

I note a look of disappointment from Adrien. "Keep the men sharp, Sergeant," I add. "Cossacks can appear from anywhere."

Riding south, we don't find a suitable observation point until we come upon a bridge over a stream. I bring my patrol to a halt and scan the area. Trees line the creek, and there is a long view of the road to the south. No signs of activity yet.

"Perfect," I say. "Let's set up on the north side of this bridge, back among these trees. There's shade, good grass, water, and an ideal view of the road."

I look up into the clear sky. The sun already promises a hot day.

"Water your horses, men, and drink plenty yourself. It could be a long wait."

The rest is welcome after riding all night, but there are clouds of biting black gnats. I protect my head by draping my jacket over it, leaving an opening for my eyes. The hours pass. Fortunately, the shade and the cool breeze off the stream give us merciful relief from the hot sun.

"Riders approaching," one of my comrades whispers.

"Russian or French?" I ask as I take up my spyglass for a better look.

Private Girard squints. "They look French."

"Yes, they do appear to be French," I say. "But we must make sure it's not a ruse. We'll rush them after they cross the bridge."

The horsemen are at full gallop, seemingly intent on getting somewhere quickly. They cross the bridge and we bolt out, surrounding them with our sabres drawn.

"Where are you going in such a hurry?" I ask.

A sergeant who seems to be in command scans all of us, assuring himself that we, too, are French. "We've come from the emperor with a message for Marshal Murat."

"What message?" I demand.

"It's for the marshal's ears only," he replies. "Is he nearby?"

Scrutinizing these men again, I cannot see anything out of place.

Satisfied, I answer. "Yes, about three leagues away. Private Girard, escort them to the marshal's headquarters."

They charge off toward the marshal's encampment.

The remaining members of my squad give me puzzled looks. "What does this mean?" several ask. "Are the Russians approaching? Is the marshal's corps needed for an attack?"

Equally puzzled, I shake my head. "We need to be patient and see what will come."

Within a couple of hours, the ground begins to rumble, and the low din of horse hooves pounding the earth grows to a roar. Soon, a bedecked Marshal Murat rides past, leading columns of thousands of cavalrymen. *What a terrifying, marvelous sight.* Seeing the power of an entire corps moving as one is breathtaking. Thirty or forty minutes pass before we see Captain Bouchet and our squadron. We join them in the ride.

"What's happening? Where are we going?" I ask Adrien.

"A great battle is taking place in Friedland," he says. "We are to provide the reserve force, but the battle may be finished before we arrive."

"I hope it's not like Heilsberg." The thought chills me. Visions of the gruesome battlefield are hard to dispel.

We ride into the evening. The cannonade we first heard in the distance now seems as though it should be around the next corner. Still, we ride on.

Finally, we reach a ridge overlooking the river valley and come to a halt. The last puffs of smoke from our cannon erupt from a redoubt overlooking the village. The cannon go silent, and the town, nestled along the western shore of the Alle River, is in flames. I take out my spyglass and steady it as best I can. Though the view is wobbly, there is no mistaking the French uniforms pouring into the village and the desperate Russians trying to fend them off, their backs to the burning town and the river. Moving my glass to the river, I see bridges on fire with the Russians scrambling through the flames or trying to swim. Few are making it to the other side. Hundreds of bodies slide away with the river current. All seems lost for them.

A rider gallops up the road from the town. "Where do I find the marshal?" he asks. Several soldiers point to the imposing figure of Marshal Murat, who is with his entourage at a high point to the east of the road. The messenger rides off.

"Adrien, have a look through the spyglass," I say as I hand it to him.

He carefully twists the scope into focus as he surveys the town.

"Jean-Luc," he cries. "The battle is ours. The Russians are routed."

I nod. Elation overwhelms me, not so much for our victory as for the knowledge that I won't be leading men into battle this day. Maybe this even signals that the end of the war is near. Maybe the close alignment of Mars and Venus is fortuitous after all.

Standing up high in my stirrups, I shout, "Comrades, it appears the battle is won. Victory is ours." Soldiers draw their weapons and whip them in circles above their heads while boisterously erupting into cheers and song.

In the midst of our squadron, I see a reserved Captain Bouchet, barely smiling. He's not cheering. Is he thinking back to the death and ruin of the Heilsberg battlefield? He lost so many comrades there.

A rider moves along the road, relaying orders. "Make camp here tonight. Officers are to report to Marshal Murat's headquarters by nine o'clock this evening."

"Probably our orders for tomorrow," I tell Adrien. "But hopefully news about what has happened here today."

We make our camp and eat our meager rations, wishing Madame Colette and her wagon were here.

By ten o'clock, Captain Bouchet and I are back from Marshal Murat's briefing. All in our squadron are anxiously awaiting our report.

"Comrades," the captain says. "The Russians have been routed. Our orders are to sweep the countryside between here and Königsberg for any Russians escaping from Friedland. The emperor expects the war to end soon. The last remnants of resistance are in Königsberg. Sleep well tonight and know our struggles will soon be over."

* * *

We spend the next several days sweeping the countryside between Friedland and Königsberg, finding many Russian soldiers eager to surrender. On the fourth day, a rider approaches Captain Bouchet, then rides on after a few moments of conversation.

Captain Bouchet signals for his squadron to draw near.

We all approach the captain, surrounding him close enough to hear. He is smiling broadly. "Good news! Königsberg has fallen, and the tsar wishes to meet with our emperor to discuss peace! This bloodshed appears to be over. We are to proceed to Tilset and occupy the town in preparation for the peace talks."

Cheers echo across the squadron. Even our prisoners smile, as they know they will likely be released soon. "Onward to Tilset," Captain Bouchet commands.

There is no resistance as we enter Tilset, a small town nestled along the banks of the River Nieman. We set up camp near the bridge. "Let's hurry and join the celebrations," Adrien says. "We need our share of good food and drink."

We hear a *Kaboom!* Then another. "Look, Adrien, fireworks by the river." More explosions are now coming from the Russian side. It's a dazzling display.

"The Russians are as happy as we are," Adrien says. "Isn't the Prussian bivouac in that direction?" He points to the east. "They don't seem to be in the mood to celebrate."

Troops from many different corps fill the village and surrounding countryside. Days pass as we all wait for the peace treaty to be finalized. The two emperors are on a raft in the middle of the river discussing the terms. Feasting, drinking, and fireworks are ongoing.

"Is that Uncle Jean?" Adrien says as a fine carriage drives by, carrying a general.

"Yes, I believe so. It's stopping by the inn. Let's go see."

As we approach, General Rapp is climbing out of the carriage. "Uncle Jean," I call out, forgetting that in public I should refer to him as General Rapp.

He looks around, appearing to have heard my call. I call out again. "Uncle Jean. Over here. It's Adrien and Jean-Luc."

He spots us and turns to one of his aides, pointing over in our direction. The aide makes his way to us. "The general wishes you to join him."

Again ignoring formalities, Uncle Jean embraces both Adrien and me. "It's so good to see the two of you. Come, it is nearly time for dinner. Please join me."

Uncle Jean orders a feast for us all, and his aide brings him several bottles of Alsatian wine. He pours us each a glass and toasts. "To peace, and may it finally last."

After a few more toasts, he says, "I have wonderful news. Do you remember Madame Kintelberger, the *cantiniére*? Her husband died at Austerlitz trying to save her and his children. She was pregnant and injured, but fought off the Cossacks while protecting her family. The Cossacks finally captured her and the children, and apparently they've been living in a Russian prison since."

I look at Uncle Jean with astonishment. "She's alive? And her children as well? How can that be? I could never forget Madame Kintelberger," I say with emotion. "I struggled mightily to reach her at Austerlitz and nearly died in the attempt."

I pause, shaking my head in disbelief. *She's actually alive.*

"They all are alive, including the twins, born while in prison," Uncle Jean replies. "As a gesture of peace, Tsar Alexander is releasing them. The Cossacks hold her in high esteem, and they're escorting her from Moscow. I am to meet them at the river bridge tomorrow and take them to Paris. The emperor himself will be there to greet her and her family."

Adrien looks at me with a joyful grin. "Madame Colette will be most happy to hear this news."

I turn to Uncle Jean. "Can our *cantiniére* meet her at the bridge as well? Madame Kintelberger is a long-time friend of hers."

"Of course, as well as all the *cantiniéres* here in Tilsit," he replies. "You are still with Captain Bouchet, right? I will write orders that you are to assist me in the celebration for Madame Kintelberger. Would you like to escort me and her family to Paris as well? Now that we have peace, there will be extended leave, and you will be able to go home to Colmar after we reach Paris."

More excellent news. Adrien and I both quickly accept. Then I feel a pang of regret. I'll have to leave my men.

Uncle Jean dashes off some orders for Adrien and me to give Captain Bouchet.

"Meet me early in the morning near the bridge over the Nieman," he says. "Bring Madame Colette, and tell the other *cantiniéres* to gather there. Madame Kintelberger and her family are scheduled to cross the river at ten o'clock."

Uncle Jean hands us our orders. We salute, then are off to see our squadron and Captain Bouchet.

"Our comrades will be disappointed that we're leaving," says Adrien.

"It will be hard," I reply, "but we'll be back together again after our leave. It's only temporary."

We ride through the streets of Tilset, weaving our way through the throngs of people.

"Home," says Adrien. "It's been so long. I hope my family has been able to endure this war. Who knows what Monsieur Renard and his gang have done to them? Just think," he adds. "I went through this entire war without killing a single Prussian. *Vati* should be pleased with that, at least."

* * *

The next morning, Adrien and I lead our horses through the throngs as we accompany Madame Colette toward the bridge. "Have you ever seen so many *cantiniére* wagons?" Adrien marvels. "There's hardly any room for us to pass between them, and so many soldiers too. Looks like the legend of Madame Kintelberger's survival has inspired many people."

Madame Colette busily greets all her *cantiniére* friends as we move through the crowds. "Can you believe she and her whole family are alive?" one of them remarks. "Her grit must have impressed the Cossacks!"

A cannon booms, then another on the Russian side of the river. Fireworks follow. "General Rapp said these explosions would be signs Madame Kintelberger's entourage is near," I explain to Madame Colette.

Soon thereafter, a volley of musket fire erupts on the street running along the river, north of the bridge. Uncle Jean stands by a fine carriage at the foot of the crossing. "Come on, we must hurry," I say to Adrien and Madame Colette. "The emperor is approaching, and soon, Madame Kintelberger will be as well."

The crowd roars as Marshalls Ney, Davout, and Lefebvre lead the march down the street hugging the river. Then come the Imperial Guard. More fireworks flare into the sky. We now hear the resounding cry of "Vive l'empereur!" coming from down the street and growing louder.

"There you are," says Uncle Jean. "I was afraid this crowd would slow you down. You must be Madame Colette," he says as he bows toward our *cantiniére*. "It is a proud day for all of you and for all of the army."

Finally, we see the emperor coming up the street, accompanied by Marshal Murat. They take up a position at the foot of the bridge, facing the river. As always, the emperor is dressed in a simple, unadorned uniform, while Marshal Murat is resplendent with his plumed hat, gold braided jacket, and polished Moroccan red leather boots.

Another cannon erupts along with more fireworks as two columns of Cossacks, lances erect, trot down the road toward the bridge. Between the columns comes a magnificent carriage. "That must be one of the tsar's carriages," I remark. "Look there, Madame Kintelberger is sitting with her family."

The Cossack columns stop in the middle of the bridge as the carriage rolls on. They dip their lances in respect.

The carriage rolls up to the emperor and stops. A doorman assists the family from the vehicle, and the emperor doffs his hat, makes a deep bow, then kisses Madame Kintelberger's hand on her one remaining arm. He raises her hand in the air, facing the crowd. "Welcome home to the bravest of all the *cantiniéres*. Our armies would be humbled without your services."

He escorts her to our carriage, a low slung vis-à-vis painted a dark red with its black top folded down. Uncle Jean acts as the doorman, helping her and her children inside. The emperor kisses each of the children, including the toddler twins, on each cheek as they climb in. Madame Kintelberger boards, giving her old friend Madame Colette a warm embrace before they both climb in. The fervently screaming crowd throws kisses. Uncle Jean boards and joins the two ladies in the forward-facing seat of the carriage. The children settle into the rear-facing seat.

Remounting his horse, the emperor leads his entourage, followed by the carriage with the Kintelberger family, Madame Colette, and Uncle Jean, back up the street along the river. Adrien and I are mounted as escorts on each side of the carriage. Madame Kintelberger looks overwhelmed by the situation, holding Madame Colette closely as she looks around in wonder. Uncle Jean is talking to the children. The oldest boy, who must be about ten, leans over the carriage side by me and says, "Lieutenant, sir, did you know my father?"

I look down at his face, looking sad despite all the festivities. "I met him," I say. "I saw what happened to your family at Austerlitz, and I tried to come help. I'm sorry I couldn't reach you. I'm sorry he died."

He stays quiet for a few moments, seeming to ponder what to say next. "The Cossacks were good to us and became our friends, and our prison guards let their children play with us. Where are we going now? Will I have friends to play with?"

I glance over to Adrien, who has heard our conversation. "Son," he says, "we are going to Paris, the most beautiful city in the world. The emperor has arranged a fine home for your family, and I'm sure there will be many boys to play with. My name is Adrien, and this lieutenant is Jean-Luc. We grew up together and are close friends. You too will find a close friend. The trip to Paris is long. Would you like to hear about what we did at your age? What is your name? Is it the same as your father's?"

The boy smiles. "My name is Laurent. My father's was Joseph."

Paris

Twenty-Three

Paris – Summer, 1807

The children are restless after spending two weeks cooped up in a carriage. We all want to get to Paris as soon as possible.

"Sergeant Adrien, what are those buildings ahead?" asks Laurent. He has come to idolize Adrien and has been at his side for the whole trip. He strains to get a better view by standing and pulling himself up against the driver's bench.

"It should be Paris. Do you want to stand on my horse and hold onto my shoulders for a better look?"

"Yes, please," Laurent replies, his eyes wide with excitement.

Adrien glances toward Madame Kintelberger, whom he now calls Maddie. "Maddie, is it all right?"

"You be careful, Laurent, and hold on tight," she says, uncertain this is a good idea.

Laurent crouches on the front seat, holding onto the open carriage's side as he waits for Adrien to bring his horse over.

"Alphonse, I'm moving toward the coach," Adrien warns our driver.

Adrien sidles up to the carriage, and the boy stands on the handrail as he grabs ahold of Adrien's shoulders and jumps over.

Looking anxious, Madame Kintelberger says, "Don't stay long. The sergeant has his duties."

Adrien gives her a warm smile. "He's no trouble."

The boy wraps his arms around Adrien's shoulders. "Hold tight, Laurent," Adrien says. "Let's move farther ahead of the carriage for a better look."

The other children scurry across the front seat over toward me. "Please, Lieutenant sir," they all cry. "Let us ride like Laurent. We want to see too."

I grin at them all, but look over to their mother. She is reluctant, but relents a little. "Aurélia, if the lieutenant doesn't mind, you can join him. The rest of you are too small," she says sternly.

I laugh. "It's no trouble."

Aurélia's eyes light up with excitement. "Let me get a little closer to you before you come grab me," I tell her.

Aurélia cautiously holds the carriage's handrail and gets into a crouching position, waiting for me to tell her what to do next. She makes the move.

"I did it, Mama," she says excitedly. "I'm standing on the horse, just like Laurent."

Madame Kintelberger gives a sigh of relief. "Not too long, Aurélia. I don't want you to get tired and slip off."

Aurélia is a sweet girl. She reminds me of Anna Lise, though she is much younger. She stands tall on my saddle, her arms now around my neck, squeezing me tightly. We ride up to be alongside Adrien and Laurent. Looking ahead, she asks, "What are those spires over there?"

"They look to be from a large church," I say, "but I've never been to Paris. They remind me of the spires I saw on the great cathedral at Rheims."

The younger children clamber around Uncle Jean, who is sitting in the carriage opposite Madame Kintelberger. Each wants to jump on his shoulders for the view. "Take your turns, children," their mother says. "Careful with the general." Uncle Jean laughs and banters with them all, letting one and then another climb up his back onto his shoulders. He holds their legs tightly so they don't fall.

I feel a stab of regret. We've been on the road for nearly two weeks, and we have all become close. Now we've reached Paris, and our brief, idyllic escape from the military will soon end.

I look at Adrien, who is smiling broadly while chatting with Laurent. "Look, Laurent, there goes a rabbit. Let's fall back and point it out to your brothers and sisters."

The other children delight in seeing the animal. They crowd the carriage sides for a better view. "Look, there's another one, and over there, another," they say gleefully. Several more appear alongside the road as we drive along. The children pretend they are shooting at them, squealing, "I got one," with each simulated shot. Aurélia and I have also fallen back alongside the carriage. She, too, wants to hunt the rabbits.

Adrien and Madame Kintelberger exchange discreet but noticeably admiring glances. "The children are such a delight," I say loudly above the din of laughter. They both smile.

Earlier in the trip, Adrien asked me, "What do you think of Maddie? She has gone through so much. All the dangers of being a *cantiniére*, then Austerlitz. Her arm ripped off by a cannonball. Her husband's body lying before her in pieces, all the while continuing to fight off the Cossacks to protect her children." Adrien shakes his head. "I admire her. She is everything a man, especially a soldier, could want."

"Along with all those children?" I ask.

"Yes. The children are wonderful too, especially Laurent. He wants me to teach him how to use a sabre and care for a Shagya. He tells me he wants to be a soldier like his father."

Though we are approaching Paris and the spires of the churches are coming into view, we are still in the country. On the right side of the road is a meadow filled with grazing cows. The milking barn is in the distance. It's old but appears well maintained, with wooden walls painted silver and a roof topped with aging thatch.

To the left are vineyards with a few scattered workers trimming the vines. They all notice our fine carriage, lower their tools, and wave.

"Look! There are statues of stallions rearing up on both sides of the road," Aurélia says. "And the road is getting wider."

We are coming upon a broad avenue flanked on each side by these equestrian statues. The fields and vineyards are giving way to estates and homes, many still under construction. The sounds of hammers and saws fill the air. The boulevard is now lined with soaring elm trees on each side.

"This is the Champs-Élysées, the grand avenue leading into Paris," Uncle Jean says.

"Time to return to the carriage," I say to Aurélia. "You too, Laurent. There are people ahead."

Before us, groups of them are scattered along the sides of the avenue. Apparently, word of our coming has reached the Parisians. Shouts of "Vive Madeleine" echo as we pass. Madame Kintelberger, unsure what to do, smiles and waves at those who cheer her.

"Your new home is coming up soon," says Uncle Jean. "It's near the Park Monceau. Driver, turn left at the street up ahead."

"What a lovely day, and such a beautiful city," says Madame Kintelberger. "We are actually going to live here?" She looks about in wonder.

"There it is, up ahead on the right," Uncle Jean says. He points to an expansive home set back from the road and surrounded by well-maintained gardens.

We come to a stop directly in front of her new home.

"This is mine?" Madame Kintelberger says, her eyes wide. "The emperor has given this to me? It's so large ... and the grounds so extensive. How can I take care of it?"

Uncle Jean smiles. "You will have servants and gardeners to help you. You needn't worry. The emperor has granted you a pension to fund all this."

Adrien points toward the back of the home. "Look, see how your home backs up to the park? There's a lake for fishing and plenty of room for children to explore. You should be very comfortable."

"Much more so than in a prison or camping beneath a wagon in all sorts of weather," she says as she tries to take it all in, her face radiant with excitement.

A group of women come from the home. They stand in a line, waiting patiently. Two men also appear, coming from the stable.

Adrien and I dismount and are about to take Bayard and Basile to the stable when one of these men rushes forward to help. "Excuse me, sirs. I am Emile, the house groom. Let me take your horses for you."

He gives our steeds an admiring look. "These are splendid animals, but I'm not familiar with this breed."

"They are Shagyas," I say, rubbing Bayard's neck. "A breed of Arabian and Hungarian stock. They come from the Ostheim stud farm in Alsace."

"Magnificent!" he says as he pats Basile. "I'll return for the carriage after giving these two some oats and water."

"I'll get the carriage," the other man says, stepping forward. Giving us a quick bow, he introduces himself. "I am the gardener, Monsieur Roche."

"That won't be necessary, Monsieur Roche," Uncle Jean says from the carriage. "I'll be leaving shortly."

"Yes, sir," he replies, then goes to open the carriage door for the Kintelberger family and Uncle Jean, helping them down. The children are as overwhelmed as their mother.

Madame Kintelberger steps away from the carriage, staring in disbelief at the house and gardens while straightening her dress with her one remaining arm. She moves toward an older woman, perhaps in her fifties, standing at the end of the line of servants. "Are you the housekeeper?" she asks.

"Yes, Madame. It's an honor to be in the service of such a great war hero. I am Madame Roche. The gardener, Monsieur Roche, is my husband."

Madame Roche gives a quick glance toward the pinned-up sleeve of the missing arm before she turns to introduce the other women. "Mademoiselle Caron is your lady's maid, Madame Dumont your cook, and Mademoiselle Paget the kitchen maid."

Uncle Jean joins me and Adrien while Madame Kintelberger introduces her children to the staff and they all make their way inside.

"Are the two of you leaving for Colmar tomorrow?" Uncle Jean asks. "I'm going to spend a few days at the headquarters here in Paris, then pass through Colmar on my way back to Berlin. Duty calls."

I look at Adrien, not sure how to answer. It seemed like this trip would go on forever, and we haven't talked about our plans.

"I'm planning on going to Bayeux and visiting Renaud Devall's family. Do you remember him, Adrien? He was one of the green recruits who died in the Cossack attack, and I promised him I would visit his family. I fear they may not know he has died. You're welcome to come with me if you like. I'll probably be in Colmar within two or three weeks."

Adrien looks down with an embarrassed smile on his face and rubs his hands together. "These past few days, Maddie and I have been talking. She's going to need help getting that house organized, even with all the servants. I'd hate to leave her alone with strangers. After she is settled, I'll come home. Perhaps in a few weeks."

I'm only mildly surprised. "A good idea," I say. "Madame Kintelberger will welcome such help, and the children will be most pleased. It sounds like we will both be back in Colmar at about the same time."

Uncle Jean gives Adrien a slap on the shoulder. "That's a lot of children to deal with, my boy. What should I tell your father when I see him? It's likely I will make it to Colmar and be gone before either of you get there."

"Just that I have some business to attend to and will be home soon."

The three of us walk toward the house. "Uncle Jean," I say, "I'll leave with you and stay in the officers' barracks tonight. I hope to have an early start for Normandy. Monsieur Roche, will you have the groomsman prepare my horse?"

"Of course, sir," he replies. He leaves for the stable.

We walk into the main entry, finding Madame Kintelberger conversing with Madame Roche in the study to our right. A chandelier hangs from the high ceiling just in front of a curving staircase leading to the upper floor. The sun plays with the cut crystal, reflecting patterns of light across the walls and floor. The squeals of children exploring echo from the rooms above.

"Gentlemen, excuse my inattention," Madame Kintelberger says. "There is so much to learn. I couldn't help but pepper Madame Roche with all sorts of questions about what goes on in a great house." Her eyes wander about the room with its high ceiling and expansive windows. "Beautiful, isn't it?" she adds as light, reflecting from the crystals, dances across her face. "Will you stay for dinner? Madame Roche tells me the larder is full and the cook superb."

"It's getting late and I need to report to headquarters," Uncle Jean says.

"I'll be leaving as well," I add. "But Sergeant Bauck will be staying to help you adjust to your new life."

She smiles. "It will be wonderful having you here, Adrien," she says, her eyes alight. "Your help will be so appreciated. I'm sorry the two of you must leave. The past few weeks have transformed my life, and the trip from Tilset with you was most memorable. I didn't think I'd ever see France again. Please inform the emperor of my undying gratitude for what he's done."

Both Uncle Jean and I bow and kiss Madame Kintelberger's hand.

"Children, come down and say goodbye. The general and Lieutenant Calliet are leaving."

The children thunder down the stairs and clamber to hug both me and Uncle Jean. "Can't you stay for a few days?" they all echo. "Is Sergeant Adrien leaving as well?"

I rub the heads of the two toddlers, who are clinging to my boots. "Adrien is staying for a while to help all of you."

Embracing Adrien, I hold him close for a moment. "See you in Colmar."

Laurent moves to face me and gives a salute. "Thank you, sir, for all your stories. I hope to find a friend someday as good as Sergeant Adrien is for you." He turns to salutes Uncle Jean. "Thank you, sir, for your kindness and for bringing us to Paris."

With our last goodbyes, Uncle Jean and I walk away from the happy home. He smiles as he climbs into his carriage and I mount Bayard. "Dinner tonight?" he asks.

"Of course."

Twenty-Four

Normandy – Summer, 1807

Patting Bayard's neck, I say, "Will we ever see another person? This forest seems never-ending. Let's take a break by that stream ahead."

I remove Bayard's saddle and let him munch on the tender grasses growing along the creek. The warm sun filters through the branches above, making me sleepy as I rest my head on the saddle. Bayard and I have been following a thin, threading path through this dense forest for several days, ever since leaving a small village along the River Seine on our journey to Normandy.

I've been dozing for about an hour when the tree branches begin clattering above me. Squinting, I look up into the canopy of tall oaks and beech trees, surprised to see the weather changing so quickly. Black, angry-looking clouds are encroaching from the west, and a strong wind is sweeping away the calm afternoon. Clumps of leaves, torn from the branches, shower down as the beech trees sway mightily. Even the limbs of the sturdy oaks grudgingly bend to the will of the growing wind. Our warm sunshine is suddenly fading into stormy darkness.

Bayard snorts and whinnies loudly several times at this new disturbance. "It's all right, boy." I stand and reassuringly stroke his flanks. "Let me saddle you up and find a more protected spot."

I lead Bayard on foot along the path as we dodge the small branches falling around us. The wind whistles deafeningly. Large rain drops splash down intermittently, splattering water in all directions. A flash of lightning, followed quickly by a crack of thunder, heralds the arrival of a downpour. There's a loud pop to my right as a nearby beech tree crashes to the earth.

"There!" I say, partly to myself and partly to Bayard. "It looks like a clearing."

As I strain to look into the meadow through the now driving rain, the outline of some type of structure comes into view.

Lightning strikes a nearby tree, sending sparks exploding from the fractured trunk and causing the scorched treetop to fall. Bayard emits a loud whinny, rising up on his hind legs. Trees all around groan from the strain of the heavy wind. I know going into this clearing is dangerous, but we can't stay here. I keep our profile low by not riding Bayard.

"All right, boy, let's make a run toward whatever that is out there." We rush forward to cross the vast clearing, the structure looming ever larger with each step.

Another flash with an immediate crack of thunder. Its pungent smell fills my nostrils. *That was too close.*

Sheets of rain drench us. The wind swirls heavily against our bodies, making movement difficult. An opening! We push into its protective womb. The structure we've been running toward is a cluster of large stones with enough space to shelter both of us.

Looking around, I don't believe our luck. The storm rages, but we're able to settle and remain protected. "What strange place is this?" I say as I take in the shelter's features. Several immense boulders are holding up a massive, flat stone above our heads.

The tempest intensifies, and the wind whistles eerily through the cracks between the rocks. The forest is some distance away, but we can hear trees bending and snapping in every direction. Despite the surrounding violence, calmness comes over me as the stones provide solace.

"What do you think, boy?" I say to Bayard as I unsaddle him. He nickers and settles on the ground, seemingly unmoved by the storm around us. "You feel it too, don't you? Something odd, but comforting."

Lightning flashes pierce the sky, followed almost immediately by deafening claps of thunder. "Not much we can do but wait this storm out."

Lying down, I use my blanket for a pillow and stare at the covering stone above me. With the next lightning flash, spiral-shaped engravings are illuminated in vivid detail across the ceiling's expanse. *What is that?* I wonder, but my eyelids are heavy and close even though I'm wet and cold.

* * *

I'm awakened by streams of light flowing between the stones, caressing my face with warmth.

Bayard has moved outside to enjoy a breakfast of newly washed grass.

Putting my hands behind my head, I recall the night's unsettling dreams, though they are only hazy remembrances. I concentrate, trying to recall why they bothered me.

It's cold, the snow so deep I can barely stand. A woman clutches my arm tightly. I look at her face, but can't see it clearly. I only see wisps of blonde hair. That noise. It's cannon fire. Cannonballs are cratering in the snow nearby.

"Captain, sir!" I hear a voice say. "You must cross the bridge. The enemy is nearly upon us."

The enemy? Who is the enemy? Is it that bridge just ahead that we must cross? How can we? It's rickety and packed with soldiers, looking like it will collapse at any moment. Ice floes strike the bridge supports, making the bridge tremble. It's so cold.

Shaking my head, I get up, not wanting to remember any more of this dream. I reach Bayard and stroke his neck. "Were you with me in this vision, old friend?" He snorts and continues eating.

The rain has freshened the air and cooled the summer heat I've endured since Tislet. The meadow is littered with debris. Torn-away clumps of leaves are scattered among tree limbs, large and small. At the clearing's edge, the remains of several substantial oaks and beeches, like fallen soldiers, lie broken and still, never to rise again.

"So, what are you?" I say, inspecting my shelter from last night. "What purpose did you serve?"

The standing stones holding the capstone are taller than me. Returning to the interior to retrieve my saddle, I put my hand on one of the boulders. It feels warm to the touch.

After mounting Bayard, I give the structure one last look, grateful for its protection, and admire its majesty and great age. I turn and ride toward the trail. "We should be in Normandy soon," I tell Bayard.

* * *

The woodland thins, and by the next day we find ourselves in a land of pastures with grazing cows and horses and farms bordered by thick hedgerows. The forest path widens into a country lane, and by nightfall, we come to the small village of

Flers. To my surprise, many of the villagers see my uniform and look away. In all other villages, I've been greeted as a hero.

We near a small inn that looks much like my papa's, and I stop to inquire about accommodations. The bell on the door rings as I enter, and from a back room, I hear a man call out in a language I don't understand.

An older man bustles into the room, muttering to himself. He looks up and gasps when he sees me in my uniform. "Pardon my surprise, sir," he says. "We have few Frenchmen and still fewer soldiers coming to Flers. What brings you here?"

"I'm on my way to Bayeux and need a room for the night and a stable for my horse."

He nervously fidgets over his guest book, glancing around. "Of course, you are most welcome. I have a stable in the back for your horse. Please forgive me for calling you a Frenchman. We Normands sometimes forget we are part of France. How goes the war with Prussia?"

I smile. "The Prussians and Russians have both been defeated. We are at peace."

His eyebrows rise in surprise. "That is good news. I thought this war would last for many more years. Perhaps now our local sons can return home."

"It is my hope as well. Do you serve food and wine?"

"Yes, some simple fare. Are you staying only tonight?" His eyes hint that he is hopeful I will answer in the affirmative.

"Yes, I'll be leaving in the morning. Can you tell me how far Bayeux is from here?"

A relieved smile crosses the innkeeper's face. "About a day's ride on the road that leads to the northwest." He turns and shouts toward the back room. "William, please come here and help our guest stable his horse."

A boy of about fifteen rushes in. He, too, gives a start at the sight of my uniform. "My son will take you to the stable and provide feed for your horse," the innkeeper says. "I'll prepare you some food. Would you like a bottle of our local cider, made with apples and pears? We have both a dry and a sweet version."

"The dry cider, please."

I follow William out the door and take Bayard to the stable. "Your father, he seems anxious. Is there anything wrong?"

"A fine horse you have," he replies as he begins to brush Bayard's flanks. His brow wrinkles, and his strokes slow. Finally, he says, "Our village has many people who still believe in the monarchy. We are not among them, but father is fearful your stay at our inn may cause trouble."

Uncle Jean warned me Normandy had strong royalist leanings. It took part in the counter-revolution that was finally quelled in 1800.

"Please tell your father I don't intend to cause problems. I'll be leaving early in the morning, before anyone else in the inn rises."

"Thank you. He will be relieved."

When I return to the inn, the proprietor leads me to a table with a meal of what appears to be lamb accompanied by a bowl of rice pudding and greens. A glass of cider has been poured, and the bottle stands on the table.

"I hope you enjoy the lamb," the innkeeper says. "It's a Normandy specialty. The lambs are raised near the sea in the salt marshes so the meat has a distinctive, salty taste. Please, try the cider. If it is not to your liking, we do have some wines to select from."

The meal looks superb, much finer than the simple fare I was expecting. I sip the cider and am impressed with its wonderful flavor. It bubbles like champagne, but the smell and taste are difficult to describe. Cooked apples, cinnamon, lemons, spices, and even a hint of leather. It is unlike anything I have tasted.

"This cider is my preferred and has been aged five years," the innkeeper tells me proudly.

"This is delightful. Thank you."

The meal is not Alsatian, but every bit as good. I savor each bite.

The innkeeper stands in the doorway between the dining area and the entrance foyer. I nod toward him with my approval of the meal, and he smiles. Then he glances out the window toward the street. Is he watching for any activity outside, or just standing by to ensure I don't require anything else?

His son William returns from the stables and converses with his father. What William says appears to meet with favor, and he gives me an appreciative nod. They both leave and I quickly finish my meal, as I'm looking forward to sleeping in a bed after so many days camping.

Sleep comes fitfully. Although I expect no trouble, my sabre stays within reach. I feel a strong urge to return home to Colmar.

My eyelids open, reacting to the emerging light of dawn filtering through my window. There's a muffled sound from outside in the hall. I grab my sabre, gripping it tightly, and fix my eyes on the door. I remain perfectly still while straining to hear. More shuffling, then retreating steps.

After waiting a few more agonizing moments and not hearing anything, I jump to my feet, sabre at the ready, and fling open the door. No one is there, or anywhere in sight. Looking to the floor, I see a basket filled with food. An unexpected gift.

* * *

Bayard and I ride hard much of the morning, hoping to speed our journey to Bayeux. "We must be near, my friend," I say to my steed. "We'll rest by this upcoming stream and have a bite to eat."

As I dismount and lead Bayard to the stream and green grass, he nickers in appreciation.

"Let's see what the good innkeeper has provided. Apples, pears, bread, cheeses, and sausage, along with two more bottles of cider. Wonderful!"

Bayard and I each eat our fill and are about ready to depart when a man driving a cart filled with hay comes upon us. He nods to me in acknowledgement and asks if I need help. He looks to be a prosperous farmer or herdsman, wearing only ordinary work clothes, but having an expensive-looking velvet cloak on his shoulders.

"I'm trying to find the Devall family. They have a farm outside of Bayeux."

The man eyes me closely, especially my uniform. "I know the Devalls well. Their farm is next to mine. My son and theirs joined the army together and were fighting in Prussia. I received a message that my son was wounded and is recovering, but the Devall family have heard nothing. Do you bring such word? Did you know the two of them?"

I pause and regard this man, whose son I likely know, uncertain how to respond. "I became their commanding officer during a battle with the Cossacks after their colonel was killed. What was your son's name?"

"Our family name is Fosse. His given name is David."

"I know him," I say. "A Cossack lance caught him in the shoulder in our first engagement, but he should recover fully. He fought very bravely."

"And what of his friend, Renaud? My son and he have been friends since birth."

The Devall family don't know their son has died.

Trying to avoid answering him about Renaud, I ask, 'How far away is the Devall farm?"

Monsieur Fosse stiffens at my non-response. 'About two leagues ahead, off a lane on the right after a hedgerow. You will see my pasture of horses just before then. Won't you tell me about Renaud?"

I have no choice.

'Renaud died after the same battle where your son was wounded. I was the last person he talked to, and I promised to see his family should he die."

Tears spring to Monsieur Fosse's eyes. His shoulders shake. 'They were only eighteen, their whole lives still ahead. Why must we fight war after war? When will the emperor stop? Can't the monarchies just leave us be? Why ..."

He sobs quietly, and I move over to comfort him as best I can.

He looks up to me, his eyes red and his face contorted. 'Go. You must go to his family. Not knowing has driven them mad with worry. Your coming, at least, will salve that uncertainty."

I leave Monsieur Fosse in sorrow and kick Bayard into a canter. We quickly arrive at the lane he described. Stopping, I look down the drive. To the left is an old stone cottage with a soaring, conical slate roof, looking much like a huge mushroom. Tall, pink holly hocks border the wall near the front door. Nearby, several ancient-looking apple and pear trees, grotesquely beautiful and knobby, reach for the sky.

To the right is a neatly maintained field of vegetables. In it, a man and woman are toiling, pulling weeds and harvesting produce. Many of their plants are as tall as they are, and all look lush and green. A girl in her mid-teens is coming from the gardens toward the house, carrying a basket of freshly picked tomatoes and summer squash. I can faintly hear she is singing a melody, one unknown to me.

There the three of them are, etched like a painting of tranquility, living their lives, not knowing the tragic news I bring. I hesitate before making my way toward them. Each minute I delay is one more for them to live with the hope that Renaud is still alive. Is not knowing better than the news I bear? I wonder, though I know they must be told.

Slowly, I make my way up the lane. *I must appear pleasant and not look like the bearer of bad news.* The clip-clop of Bayard's hooves catches the girl's attention. She looks up, gives me a warm smile, and says, "Bonjour! How can I help you?" Then she notices my uniform, and a look of panic fills her eyes. Her basket falls to the ground, scattering the tomatoes and squash about her feet. "Are you here about my brother?"

"You are Mademoiselle Devall, and those are your parents?" I ask, pointing to the two people in the garden.

"Yes, Monsieur. Is Renaud all right?" Her eyes now plead with me to tell her he's alive.

"I am here about your brother, Mademoiselle. Can you have your parents come over so that I can tell all of you?"

Her eyes now reflect the certainty of bad news. She turns and runs toward her parents, shouting, "Papa, Mama, come quick."

The three of them huddle together at the edge of the garden. Then the girl's mother takes her daughter into her arms as the girl's shoulders begin to shake. Her father stands alone, staring at me.

This is more difficult than I could have imagined. I'd gladly be charging into the teeth of attacking Cossacks rather than endure this.

I dismount and lead Bayard to the shade of a nearby apple tree. The Devall family walk slowly toward me. A fly buzzes around my head, but I ignore it. It doesn't seem fitting to brush it away at a time like this.

Monsieur Devall extends his hand in greeting. His face is drawn and his shoulders sag. "Lieutenant, Lisette tells me you have news about my son."

"Yes, sir, I do."

"Please, let's go to the patio and have some cider. Lisette, find some glasses and bring a bottle to the table."

Awkwardly, we find seats around the patio table, and Lisette pours the cider before sitting. Her father takes a long drink, indicating that we all should as well.

Monsieur Devall stares into his now empty glass, lightly tapping it on the tabletop. Like me, he is struggling with what to say next. His wife and daughter look toward him.

After another moment of silence and still peering at his empty glass, he says, "Lieutenant, I believe you are here to tell us Renaud is dead." He looks up at me, his eyes moist. His wife and daughter hold each other's hands and gaze at me with tortured, expectant faces. "Is that right?"

I bow my head, then look around at each of them. "Yes, it's true." I clutch my hands together tightly and rush to say more. "We were outside Heilsberg, on our way to provide reinforcements to the army, when Cossacks swarmed us. It took all our courage to drive them off. I'm sorry, but Renaud was badly wounded by a Cossack lance and didn't survive the night."

Each of the Devalls hang on my every word. "I had come to know him after I joined his detachment in Berlin. He talked warmly of his home in Normandy, imploring that I come visit after the war. This is not how I wanted to make that visit."

"Did you see him before he died?" his mother asks. "Had he any last words?"

Tears now well in my own eyes. "Yes, I was with him at the end." I get up and reach into my vest pocket and retrieve the rosary.

Going to her side, I say, "He wanted me to give you this and to tell you his soul is at peace."

Renaud's mother clasps the rosary tightly to her chest, sobbing. She rocks back and forth in her chair, softly repeating her son's name. Lisette wraps her arm around her mother, giving comfort.

"Lisette," I say, "Renaud asked me to tell you he holds the memory of his childhood with you dear and to give you a kiss goodbye on the forehead." I touch my fingers to my lips, then place them on her forehead. She holds her mother even more tightly, crying softly. Her father wraps his arms around both of them.

"Sir," I say to Renaud's father, "he wanted me to let you know he died bravely and will miss the times the two of you worked together in the fields."

Monsieur Devall nods his head in gratitude.

I feel it best to leave them with their grief. "I must return to my own home in Alsace," I say. "I have not been there for some time, and I know my family misses me."

Lisette looks up and says, "Please, stay for a little while longer. Tell us all you remember about Renaud."

I look to her parents, who both implore me to stay.

Monsieur Devall fills our glasses with more cider, and I proceed to tell them about how Adrien and I became assigned to their detachment in Berlin and how we got to know them and taught them to be soldiers. All of us relax and take comfort in the stories.

"They were very green," I say. "Adrien and I spent the two weeks after leaving Berlin giving them instructions. We all became close comrades."

The Devall family recount stories of Renaud's mischief and his close friendship with the neighbor, David Fosse.

"Do you know how David is?" asks Lisette. "His father got word he was wounded."

266

'He too suffered a lance wound, but it was not severe. I expect he will soon come home."

Lisette's eyes perk at this news.

'I must leave," I say, 'but I can see why Renaud talked so highly of his home. I'm sorry he is gone."

We bid farewell, and I mount Bayard to begin our journey. With a quick kick, Bayard and I are on our way. 'It's time to go home, my friend. We've been away too long."

Twenty-Five

The Journey Home –
Late Summer, 1807

It's early evening by the time I reach a crossroads near the outskirts of Flers. The spires from the town's church pierce the clouds, seeming to hold them in place. "I don't think we want to venture into this town again," I say to Bayard. "A band of royalists might think it good sport to track a lone soldier into the forest—a trophy for their cause. Let's take this other road toward Caen. Maybe we can find a side path around Flers."

Bayard snorts and stares up the Caen road. Two specks emerge from the shadows of the trees lining the way. It's too late to hide. The specks become rapidly approaching horses, and soon two finely dressed young men ride up to me, each wearing plumed hats and velvet jackets—one purple and one blue—along with leather riding pants and fine leather boots.

"Bonjour, Lieutenant," one of them calls out. He looks like a dandy, with long, blond curls that fall to his shoulders. "What brings a soldier of the emperor so deep into the countryside?"

Instinctively, I tap my scabbard.

"Visiting friends. Comrades of mine from Heilsberg."

"They are from Flers?" he asks, eyes narrowing. "I know most everyone in Flers, and I daresay, I know of no veterans from the emperor's army."

The blond man's companion, who has short-cropped brown hair, circles my horse on the pretext of bringing his mount under control. His eyes take in everything, from my saddle and gear up to Bayard's nose.

"Not Flers. Up the road, near Bayeux."

The dandy gives me a long stare, his horse fidgeting, as he considers me. Both he and his companion have sabres within easy reach, but I'm sure they don't want to test their skills on me. Still, the hairs on my arms prickle.

"Yes, I've heard some Bayeux men fight for the emperor. I haven't had the pleasure of knowing them." The dandy smiles now. "You must be heading to Flers. It's less than a league away. Come, have supper with us at the inn. Their fare is quite good."

I do not smile back. "Your offer is most generous, but I must decline. I have business in Caen and still have two good hours of sunlight left for riding."

Both men regard me for a few moments. It appears they are considering what to do with me. Then the blond fop smiles stiffly and glances toward his companion, who gives a grim expression and shakes his head.

"Perhaps another time, Lieutenant," he says. "I'm sure you have fascinating stories about the wars and the emperor. When you visit your comrades again, please stop in Flers and ask for me. I am Comté de Redern." He tips his hat slightly. "Good day to you."

The two riders give me one last look, then depart at a gallop toward Flers.

I watch until they are no longer in sight. "Let's get far away from here, boy," I say, giving Bayard a pat. "Those two are trouble. I'll feel safer once we reach the forest again."

We deviate from the main road, working our way around Flers to our original road leading toward Paris. Darkness is encroaching as we reach the edge of the forest. "Let's camp here," I say, looking at the base of an ancient oak. Its trunk is nearly as wide as Bayard is long, and its branches reach high, forming a protective dome overhead.

The moon is nearly full, casting slivers of light through the many branches. A breeze gently sways the limbs of the nearby elm trees, making the moonlight skip across the landscape. An owl hoots, and shadows of bats flick in and out of the light. Crickets chirp in the background.

Out of habit, I start a fire, but soon realize it needs to be extinguished, considering the two men I encountered earlier. They may be trying to follow me. As I scatter the dying embers, I say to Bayard, "Those two are likely cozy at the inn, having their meal and drinking too much cider or wine. No cause for concern. Still, let's both sleep with an eye open, and I'll have my sabre by my side."

The warm night precludes any need to wrap myself in my blanket. Instead, I use it for my pillow and gaze through the branches at the moon. A few clouds drift by, casting their shadows. I close my eyes, ready for sleep, but then notice that the crickets have stopped chirping. I'm wide awake now with my eyes peering into the darkness.

Snap.

I tense, hearing what may be a footstep. Probably only a deer, but I hold my drawn sabre tightly. Listening intently, I hear nothing else, but remain on edge. My stomach churns with anxiety.

Several minutes pass. Then I hear a crunch, followed by another, much closer now. There's a shadow to my left in the moonlight, and another to my right. I charge the figure to my left. He's unprepared for my assault, and his sword feebly falls to the side as I strike it away, plunging my sabre deep into his chest.

Turning, I see the other attacker, the comté. Moonlight plays off his golden curls.

"Lieutenant," he says. "It's time for you revolutionaries to die. You're not welcome in Normandy." The close-cropped brown-haired man joins him. They both charge, swords held high. The comté strikes toward my chest, but I'm able to deflect it away. His companion sees the opening from my parry and strikes for my side. I deflect this blow, too, but feel a sharp pain. Thinking he has me, the brown-haired man hesitates for a moment—a fatal mistake, as my deflection carries through, striking him in the neck. The blow severs an artery.

The comté, still in his purple coat, takes a few steps back, stunned by the sudden death of his companion. Regaining focus, he recklessly charges, only to find my sabre piercing his chest, near the heart. His eyes widen, staring at me, and his mouth gapes in surprise. Coughing up blood, he gasps his last breaths while falling to the ground.

Anxiously, I glance in all directions, holding my breath and expecting more attackers. Instead, I hear a panicked voice shout out. "Denis, Gaston, and the comté are dead! Fall back! We must save ourselves from this traitorous devil."

I hear two, maybe three men crashing through the underbrush, cursing as they fall and scramble up. After some moments, the sound of horses galloping away echoes through the trees. Then silence. No twigs cracking, no owls hooting, and no men breathing but me. Continuing to listen closely, I check my wound. Only a minor cut on my left forearm, which fortunately is not my sword arm. Reaching into my saddle, I pull out a shirt, tear a strip, and bind my wound. "That should take care of it," I say to myself. "We must leave this place, Bayard. Killing a comté will bring many men after us."

The moon guides our way as we move deeper into the forest. Several hours pass, and the dense woodland allows only minimal light to fall on our path, but I push Bayard to a trot, distancing myself as much as possible from any pursuers.

Up ahead, the moon appears to shine more brightly, and soon we are at the edge of a meadow, painted silver by its glow. In the midst of the field looms the stone monument where Bayard and I took shelter during the storm. It soars like a cathedral rising from a silvery lake. Without prompting, Bayard aims for it. "It looks like this will shelter us again, my friend," I tell him, "but this time from men."

Killing men, even in self-defense, always saps my spirit. I don't feel the horror I experienced when I slew the Austrians in my first campaign, but the regret and guilt remain. Being in the presence of the stone edifice calms my edgy nerves and regret. Dawn is only about an hour away, but I lie down, exhausted, leaving Bayard saddled in the event we need a quick getaway. Any pursuers should be many hours back.

* * *

It's midmorning by the time I wake. Strange dreams visited me again in my slumber. In one, I wasn't cold, nor was the enemy pressing down on me. I was strolling through a park on a warm, idyllic day, arm in arm with a woman, exchanging pleasantries even though smoke was billowing on the horizon. Was it the same woman who was in my previous dream? As with my last vision, I could not see her face, nor did I know her name. I only saw strands of her blonde hair.

What do these dreams mean, and where do they take place? I don't know. All I know is that they make me yearn to be home in Colmar with my family.

Bayard snorts and shuffles about nervously. His actions bring me to my senses, and I realize several hours of daylight have passed. "What is it, boy?" I ask anxiously, but I know he must be hearing my pursuers approaching.

Faintly, I begin to hear the sound of hoofbeats.

"Come on boy, we don't have much time," I say, mounting Bayard and kicking him into a gallop in one smooth move.

As we fly down the forest trail, I can hear my pursuers urging their horses on.

"Their steeds must be nearly spent," I say to Bayard. "The Normandy border is only about two hours away. They wouldn't dare go beyond it."

Still galloping, we leave the forest track and enter open country with fields of golden grain and rows of grape vines. Slowing to a trot, I look back and see no horsemen following us. Up ahead, the tips of two spires emerge, silhouetted against the deep blue of a cloudless sky. "Look, Bayard—the Chartres Cathedral."

* * *

I'm now in my fourth day since leaving my pursuers behind. The urge to get home becomes stronger, and I begin descending from the Vosges Mountains to the Rhine Valley by Ostheim. Colmar is near, and I'm finally back to my beloved Alsace. The coolness of the mountain pass gives way to searing heat. The sky is cloudless, and the sun's fire shimmers in waves on the road ahead.

The Ostheim stud farm and barracks come into view on my right. No one is stirring in this heat. Groups of horses gather in the shade under large oaks, drinking from a nearby stream.

"Let's get some water and shade before we make our last push to Colmar," I say to Bayard. Dismounting near the stream, I lead him to its edge to drink. He lets out a grateful bluster and slurps greedily. I drink deeply as well and fill my canteen.

Taking off my shako, I rest on one knee, splashing cool water on my face. I gaze down the road toward Colmar. "What do you think lies ahead, my friend?"

Twenty-Six

Colmar – Early Fall, 1807

Bayard slowly clip-clops along the road leading past Colmar's central square. It's now dusk, but the heat is still intense. The familiar streets are nearly deserted, probably because everyone is escaping to the cool of their root cellars. Up ahead, the outline of Papa's inn is coming into view. My heart lifts as I come closer. A large wagon, filled with furniture and traveling trunks, sits in front of the inn, but my attention is drawn to the Bauck butcher shop across the street. Something is not right.

As I come nearer with each stride, worry grips me. The butcher shop is in ruins. Nothing is left but broken glass, trampled doors, and streaks of black soot inching up the walls.

I dismount and dash into the ruins. "Anna Lise, Frau Bauck, Herr Bauck, are you here?"

The structure is empty save for the broken display cabinet and piles of splintered wood that were once chairs. Where can they be? Then I remember the wagon.

I charge into the foyer of our inn. "Papa, Anna Lise, anyone?"

The sound of steps comes from the stairway. Anna Lise cries, "Jean-Luc, it's you." Rushing to me, she buries her head into my chest. I feel her trembling.

The Baucks come down the stairs and Papa from the back room.

"My son, he is not with you?" Frau Bauck asks desperately.

Herr Bauck wraps his arm around his wife. The two have the haunting expressions I've seen on many faces in the Prussian towns we marched through—fearful we would stop and do something terrible, but also with a glint of hope that we would just pass through, leaving them to their lives. The Bauck family's glint of hope is for me to tell them any good news about Adrien.

"No, he's not with me. He's still in Paris," I say, wishing with all my heart he was here.

My voice rises. "What happened here? Why is your shop in ruins? Who did this terrible thing?" My nostrils flare.

Papa comes up and gently touches my shoulder. Looking toward the Baucks, he says, "I have a table set up in the cellar. Let's go down, have a glass of wine, and escape this heat. We can talk about all that has happened."

The coolness of the cellar is a great relief. Papa has moved several wine casks to the side to make room for a table and chairs. A lamp in the middle emits a welcoming glow. Papa pours us each a glass, and we try to settle into the spindly chairs around the table. They creak, grudgingly accepting our bodies.

I take a sip and look at the Baucks. Their faces are etched with pain. "What happened to your shop? Are you leaving Colmar?"

Herr Bauck's shoulders slump as he gazes toward me. The lamp illuminates his lined, much older face, and a silhouette of his head flickers off the rough, earthen back wall.

He clears his throat. "Throughout the war, tensions were high for Prussians in Colmar, but with news of the triumph at Friedland, the victory celebration turned violent. A mob of masked men stormed our shop, yelling curses and demanding all Prussians leave town. They threw rocks, smashing the front window, and kicked in the door. Storming into the shop, they shouted, 'Where are the dirty Prussians? Get out! Go home!' It was terrifying."

Anna Lise lowers her head.

'I shouted, 'My son is in the emperor's army.' It didn't matter. They just sneered.

Herr Bauck leans closer over the table and shakes his head. 'I saw only hate in their eyes. They threw chairs into my display cabinet and tossed burning torches into the rubble. We fled to your father's inn. I thought they would kill us."

Herr Bauck can no longer hold back his anguish. "These people were our neighbors. They came to my shop. They bought our meat. They told us stories." He takes several deep breaths to control himself. "When they finished with my shop, they moved to Herr Klingmon's, wrecking it too. Your father and I went back in my shop and put out the fire."

"Who did this?" I demand, my hands clenching into fists. "Was nothing done to arrest the thugs?" A memory from my youth, of when the guillotine had been in town, surges to mind. "Did Monsieur Renard have anything to do with this?"

'I didn't see him. Everyone was masked. When General Rapp was here, he interrogated Monsieur Renard, who said he was at the tavern and brought witnesses to back him up. But he gloated about the destruction and how the Prussians had it coming. General Rapp didn't believe his story and ran him out of town."

'Is Uncle Jean still here?" I ask.

'No, he left a few days ago."

"You could rebuild your shop," I say.

"No. Staying in Colmar is out of the question. The emperor's victories embolden them. I had already contacted my brother in Prussia, who told me we would not be welcomed there. Too many people know Adrien serves the emperor."

"Why can't you stay here?" I demand. "Between Uncle Jean, myself, and Adrien, we can control Monsieur Renard's followers."

"But all of you will be gone soon, off fighting some new war far from Colmar. We have no choice."

"That's not true ..." I begin.

Herr Bauck holds up his hand. "I asked General Rapp if he knew anything about the tsar's old offer of bonus money for Germans to immigrate to Russia. I heard there is a large, thriving German community in Moscow."

"Russia?" I say, flustered. "We've just had two wars with them, and we'll likely have another. How can you go to Russia? Your home is here!"

"We're not French, Jean-Luc, no matter how much Adrien and Anna Lise think we are. We can't stay here and we can't go back to Prussia. Moscow is our only hope."

"Jean-Luc, please, try and change his mind," a frightened Anna Lise pleads. "Our home is here."

"*Tochter*, quiet! I'm looking out for you."

I glance toward Anna Lise, wishing this wasn't happening.

"General Rapp found out that the offer still stands. The bounty the tsar would give is big enough to start a new shop. The general made arrangements for us to travel with a contingent of soldiers passing through Ostheim on their way to Königsberg. They will come through in two days and can provide safe passage through Prussia."

"What about Adrien?" I ask. "You will be gone before he returns. This will devastate him."

Herr Bauck hesitates, looking to the ground, searching for an answer from the wooden floor planks. With a quiver in his voice, he says, "There is no choice. The Ostheim soldiers will protect my family. Adrien has made his choice to be a Frenchman. I am Prussian. Tell him we waited for as long as we could. He will always be in our thoughts."

His words pierce my heart.

He looks to his daughter, trying to find something to blunt the ragged edges of his emotions. "You and Anna Lise should spend tomorrow together. It may be the last you see of each other for some time. I am sorry."

Herr Bauck slowly sips on another glass of wine. "Please, tell me why my son is still in Paris. You are home; why not him? General Rapp only told us he is helping a family that traveled with the group of you from Tilset."

I adjust myself in my chair, its joints protesting with loud groans.

I choose my words carefully. "Yes, he's assisting a family released from a Russian prison, a very brave *cantiniére* and her children. The emperor himself received her in Tilset when she was released. Adrien is helping the family settle into their new Paris home. There is much to do, and I'm afraid he won't be returning to Colmar for at least another week."

"We won't see him before we leave, Papa," a tearful Anna Lise says, holding onto her mother tightly.

A dejected Herr Bauck gets up and gathers his family together. "Come, we still have preparations for the trip."

Anna Lise looks up. "Jean-Luc, tomorrow at dawn. Meet me in the inn's dining area. We will plan our day." She turns away, her mother holding her closely as she quietly weeps.

Astonished, I watch the Baucks retreat from the cellar to their rooms. Then I look to Papa. He opens his arms for me and brings me close. "Times have been difficult, son. Let's have some cognac on the porch."

After several glasses and hours of talking about this tragedy and all that has happened in the war, I rise and give Papa a kiss. "It's late, and I must meet Anna Lise at dawn. Despite all this bad news, it's good to be home."

Twenty-Seven

Anna Lise – Early Fall, 1807

The smell of frying sausage rouses me from my sleep. Traces of morning's first light illuminate my room. Dressing quickly in my uniform, I hasten to the dining room and find a sumptuous breakfast of eggs, sausages, and bread. "I've brewed coffee too," says Anna Lise in a surprisingly bright voice. "Adrien left some for *Vati* last time he was here, but *Vati* doesn't care for it."

We both indulge in the feast, joking and laughing as we've always done, forgetting, at least for the moment, that the next two days may be the last we ever see of each other.

"What should we do?" Anna Lise asks, sounding pensive. Her eyes look past me as if to a future she cannot see. "Just for today, I want to try and forget about leaving. Let's do some of the things you and Adrien used to do," she says hopefully. "I don't think he'll get here before we leave tomorrow. Maybe doing some of the things he did with you can at least give me new memories of both of you."

I ponder, trying to think what would be memorable and what she would want to do if Adrien were here as well.

"Have you ever visited the stud farm at Ostheim and seen the herd of Shagyas?" I ask. "They're amazing, and Adrien and I fell in love the first time we laid eyes on them."

Anna Lise's eyes light up. "No, I've never been there. That would be wonderful! Do you think I could ride one?"

"Perhaps. It would be up to the quartermaster. For your first time on a Shagya, we would need to find one with a gentle disposition. They can be spirited."

"Yes, let's go to Ostheim. And after that?"

"The one thing Adrien and I enjoyed most was fishing by the bridge along the Ostheim road. The salmon aren't running, but there should be plenty of trout. We can escape the heat there as well."

She smiles. "It will be a good day, Jean-Luc. One we will always remember. I'll gather some food. You can get the fishing equipment."

"Yes. I'll meet you by the horses."

I come to the stable and find Anna Lise wearing an old pair of Adrien's pants and one of his shirts from when he was a boy. "Do you think these are all right?" she asks. "I want to ride astride, especially if I'm able to ride a Shagya. Riding sidesaddle on one of them would be silly, wouldn't it?"

"I can't imagine you riding any other way but astride," I chuckle.

"What about my hair? Should I hide it? I have Adrien's cap. It's large and can cover my head. Some people don't approve of women riding astride."

"Hiding your pretty blonde hair seems criminal," I say, smiling. Even though she's wearing Adrien's clothes, I'm startled by how much she has grown. She's changing from the little girl I've always known. Her hair is bundled into a French braid, and the excitement of riding to Ostheim makes her sky-blue eyes sparkle.

'It shouldn't be a problem, but it might be best to wear the hat until we leave Colmar and also put it on if we see anyone approaching on the road. At Ostheim, the quartermaster will need to know you are a girl, but if we are near any of the soldiers, wear the hat."

'A girl!" she huffs in feigned indignation. 'I'm a little bit more than just a girl. Did you forget I'll be thirteen soon?"

'Well, my grown-up companion, shall we be on our way?"

Anna Lise mounts her family's old mare. As she climbs on, a chain slips out from her shirt. The sun reflects off my mother's gold necklace and cross that I gave her when she was born. I smile, remembering that day so many years ago. We trot through Colmar on the Ostheim road. No one is on the streets yet, and the only activity is in the bakery. The smell of freshly baked bread wafts through the air. Leaving town, Anna Lise breaks into a gallop, whipping off her hat and urging me to hurry. 'Let's not waste this coolness, Jean-Luc. I want to ride the Shagya before it turns hot."

It takes Bayard little effort to catch the old mare. 'Easy, Anna Lise, your father's horse has seen better days. We don't want her to collapse."

We slow to a walk, and I tell her about the celebrations in Tilset and our travel to Paris with Madame Kintelberger. 'Your brother is quite fond of her," I say. 'She's a few years older and only has one arm, but that does not detract from her beauty."

'Only one arm? How did she lose it?"

'When she fought the Cossacks at Austerlitz. For Adrien, it adds to her allure. He is drawn by her fearlessness against all odds and the love she gives her children. Did I mention she has six children?"

'Six! I know he loves family, but six all at once? Is he serious about her? Does she like him?"

"The feelings seem mutual. Adrien acts like a little boy around her—showing off, teasing, giving her secret looks. She seems to be enjoying the attention, and her children love him—especially the oldest boy, Laurent. The timing is unfortunate, but I'm happy for him."

Anna Lise ponders this for several moments. "I fear for Adrien. He's always trying to impress *Vati*, and sometimes he's reckless. I worry it could lead to his death in battle." Her lips tremble. "Jean-Luc, I know you are the reason he is still alive. I may never see him again, but I'm consoled that you are with him. It sounds like this woman and her family will help him too. I pray for both of you every night."

The shadow of a large bird crosses over us and up the road toward Ostheim, seemingly guiding our way. We both look up. "An eagle. Surely a good omen," I say. Seeing the mighty bird cheers both of us, and a smile crosses Anna Lise's face.

"Is that the barracks?" she asks as a low-hung building comes into view.

"Yes, and to the left are the stables. Look over there—see the horses in the field? The Shagyas. Time to put your hat back on."

Anna Lise glances toward me, her eyes now dancing with excitement. "I hope I can ride one. Is the quartermaster a friend?"

"He's an old friend. He was quartermaster when Adrien and I first came here to train the Shagyas several years ago."

We quicken our pace and steer clear of the barracks.

Quartermaster Beaulac comes out of the barn as we ride up. He squints up at me. "Jean-Luc! So good to see you again. Now you are a lieutenant? And who is this with you? He looks a little young to be a new recruit."

Dismounting, I give Quartermaster Beaulac an embrace. "I'm happy to see you again, my friend!" Turning toward Anna Lise, I say, "This is not a new recruit. You remember Adrien? This is his sister, Anna Lise. She wants to see the Shagyas and is hoping to ride one."

Anna Lise dismounts and removes her hat, revealing her honey-colored hair. She curtsies. "I'm so happy to meet you, Monsieur. My brother always talked highly of you."

The quartermaster's jaw slackens as he stares at the girl before him. "You are Adrien's sister?" He examines Anna Lise's face closely. "Yes, I can see some of his features in you." He glances toward me with a look of concern. "And you want her to ride a Shagya?" he asks, shaking his head in disbelief.

"Yes, Monsieur, most definitely. Perhaps you have a gentle one?"

I can see that the quartermaster is about to refuse. "Anna Lise, stay here. The quartermaster and I will look in the stables to see if there is a suitable horse." He starts to protest, but I put my arm around his shoulder. "Come, old friend. Let's see what you have in the stable."

Once out of earshot of Anna Lise, I explain the situation of how Adrien's family were attacked in Colmar and that they are leaving for Moscow tomorrow. He looks uncertain, but then says, "I've been grooming that mare over there this morning. She's getting old, but perhaps the girl could ride her."

I grab the old quartermaster and give him kisses on both cheeks. "Thank you, my friend. This will mean the world to her."

"But," he adds, "she needs to wear the hat. The commandant would be most displeased if he knew. Let me saddle the horse up."

The quartermaster leads the saddled mare out to Anna Lise. She presses her fingers to her lips, glancing from me to the quartermaster. She curtsies. "How can I thank you, sir? This is wonderful! I will be very careful."

The quartermaster grunts. "Keep that hat on and don't get hurt." He turns to me. "Take the trails to the west, up into the hills. Men are training horses in the north pasture. Be back within a couple of hours, before the men return."

He offers Anna Lise the reins, which she takes, nodding thanks. Her eyes are glowing with excitement. She mounts the mare, looking a little unsure. The Shagya is much larger than any horse she's ever ridden. She straightens, tucks her hair under her hat, and says, "I'm ready, Jean-Luc. Lead the way."

I mount Bayard and give the quartermaster assurances we will not be gone long. "We'll go to the overlook, up the hill on the far west trail." He still looks worried, not sure he should be allowing this.

Leaving the stables, we are soon on the narrow trail going up to the overlook. We wind our way between oak trees as we ascend. A golden eagle, perhaps the same one we saw earlier, circles high above, watching to see if we scare up any potential game. Clouds are cresting over the mountains, promising a cool day. I look back toward Anna Lise. She appears a little nervous, but determined. Catching me watching, she gives a quick smile, though her forehead is wrinkled.

"About fifteen more minutes to the top, Anna Lise."

A large boulder sits at the peak of the hill, providing an expansive view of the valley below. We dismount and climb up to the smooth surface at its top and sit, taking in the panorama below. The Rhine River curves like a mighty snake bloated by its last meal. The barracks are hidden by the trees, but in the distance, we can see Colmar.

"Did you and Adrien come here often during training?" Anna Lise asks. "It's so peaceful, and the valley is magnificent."

"Yes, many times, especially when we were homesick for Colmar."

"Was Adrien homesick often? It seemed like he always wanted to get away, embarrassed by his Prussian parents."

"We both love Colmar, but it seemed our future was cast if we stayed. For me, the inn, and for Adrien, the butcher shop. The army gave us a chance to put off these decisions."

I look down to the valley, feeling my life spinning. "What I didn't bargain for was the terror of war and the regret for so many deaths. I should have stayed in Colmar."

Anna Lise scoots closer, putting an arm around me.

"What will our lives bring, Jean-Luc? The war is over. Will you be able to come home, or will another war start? And what of me? *Vati* is taking us to a city in a strange new land. I'm so scared, Jean-Luc. I can't think of a future away from Colmar."

I put my arm around her, and we stare down into the valley in silence. Our eagle is still with us, circling high overhead. It gives a low *kuk-kuk* call, perhaps reminding us it's time to go.

Anna Lise takes the lead back down the trail to the barracks, riding more confidently now. As we reach the meadow and are within sight of the stables, she gives me a sly smile, then kicks her mare into a gallop, taking off in a race just like her brother would. I let her have some room, then urge Bayard into a gallop. We both fly across the field, Bayard gaining with each stride. We reach the stables side by side as Quartermaster Beaulac comes out to meet us.

He gives Anna Lise a surprised but approving look. "You had no trouble. Adrien would be proud."

Beaming, she climbs off her horse, patting the mare lovingly on the neck. "That was the most fun I've had in a long time. Thank you so much for letting me ride. I gave Jean-Luc a good run at the end," she adds, grinning at me.

* * *

The clouds are thickening as we arrive at the bridge where Adrien and I once fished. The breeze is picking up, and looking into the mountains, I see thunderheads forming. "A storm is coming," I say. "But we should have enough time to fish. I'll prepare the fishing kits, and you can catch some grasshoppers for bait."

Setting up our fishing poles takes me back to the many times Adrien and I came here.

Our lines cast, we settle back to wait. "Fishing," I say philosophically, "is the opposite of riding. With fishing, we are unhurried. Our prey has their own schedules, and maybe they'll let us catch one of them. It's a time to reflect and to nap."

We settle for a while, and then I hear Anna Lise fidgeting. "Doesn't this get boring?" she says. "All we're doing is sitting with a piece of string in the water. I don't understand how you can enjoy this."

"Give it some time. Did you know Adrien and I were at this very spot fishing the day you were born? We caught three salmon and saw the guillotine wagon go by."

Anna Lise cries out excitedly. "Jean-Luc, my pole jerked. There's another. What am I supposed to do?"

"All right, Anna Lise, pull hard when you feel the next tug."

She jerks the line, and now it's dancing back and forth in the water, pulling strongly on her pole. "Now what?"

"I've got a net. Start backing up the bank while I get in position. That's it, keep going ... another few steps ... got him! It's a fine trout."

"Let me see," she cries excitedly. "My first fish! What do we do with it?"

"I say we cook it right now for dinner. It's big enough for both of us. Here, take my pole and see if you can get another while I clean this one. Fishing isn't so boring now, is it?"

She glares at me for a moment, then smiles. "It's a lot more fun if you catch something."

I finish cleaning the fish and start a fire while Anna Lise holds my rod tightly, staring with anticipation at the line dangling in the water.

"Looks like this is the only one we're catching," I tell her. She looks over to me, disappointment on her face.

The wind is picking up, and the clouds are now thick. "We may have only an hour before the rain comes," I say. "Can you finish cooking the fish while I put away the fishing gear?"

I saddle up both our horses and pack away my equipment. Retrieving the satchel from Anna Lise's horse, I pull out a bottle of wine, a pair of plates, glasses, and some bread.

We attack our meal ravenously when the fish is cooked, realizing we haven't eaten since morning. "This is the most delicious fish I've ever eaten," Anna Lise remarks between bites.

A drop of rain spits into vapor on hitting our fire, then another. "It won't be long until it's pouring. We better get moving."

"One more sip, Jean-Luc ... to a wonderful day."

We clink our glasses. "To a wonderful day," I reply.

The rain picks up, and we scurry to put out the fire and gather our utensils, then mount and race for home.

Galloping down the road, we can't outrun the rain. It pours from the heavens, drenching us to the bone. The sky has gone dark, and mud flies from the pounding hooves. Colmar is in sight, with the light from Papa's inn guiding our way.

At the doorway, the Baucks, Monsieur Rapp, and Papa welcome us. Monsieur Rapp takes the reins and leads the two animals to the stables. Frau Bauck takes Anna Lise into her arms, thankful for her daughter's return.

"We had the most wonderful day," Anna Lise exclaims. "I rode a Shagya and we went fishing down by the bridge."

Both her parents shoot me a look. "You rode a Shagya?" her mother says. "You are only twelve. Wasn't that dangerous?"

"It was a mare, not a stallion," I say. "Anna Lise handled her well."

Frau Bauck undoes her daughter's hair and begins drying it with a towel. The blonde locks fall halfway down her back. Her eyes shine as she relates the day to her parents.

I find myself wishing we could have more time together and, to my surprise, thinking she is very pretty. She is still Adrien's little sister, but she has captivated me today.

"We must get you out of these wet clothes," Frau Bauck instructs her daughter. "Thank you, Jean-Luc," she adds, glancing toward me with a smile.

I'm sitting on a bench, pulling off my boots, when Anna Lise charges across the room and kisses me on the cheek. "I will always remember this day," she says happily.

Herr Bauck comes and shakes my hand. "I know my son relies on you, and that means very much to me. You have been like a brother to him, and also to Anna Lise. I will miss you." The Baucks head up the stairs to retire for their last night in Colmar.

"Come, son," Papa says. "Let's have a cognac, and you can tell me about your day."

* * *

The next morning, near daybreak, the Bauck family is ready to leave. "Won't you stay for breakfast?" Papa asks. "Mademoiselle LeClair is ready to cook your meal."

"Thank you for the offer, but we can't chance missing the soldiers at Ostheim. *Mein frau* has put together food for us."

In tears, we all embrace and wish the Baucks well in Moscow. Anna Lise again kisses me on the cheek and whispers, "Remember what my brother told you at the Charité. He told me as well."

I rub my thumb across her cheek, wiping away a tear. I say quietly, "You are young and will have a new life in Moscow. I'll remember what Adrien said, but your life will change. We can talk when we meet again."

* * *

It's been a week since the Baucks left Colmar, and still no sign of Adrien. I've been fishing at the bridge each day, hoping to intercept him before he reaches Colmar and sees the destruction of his family's shop. Today, many riders pass, and I watch closely for my friend. Finally, I see him riding across the bridge.

"Adrien," I yell, standing and waving my arms. "Adrien, it's me."

He stops, looks around, then spots me along the shoreline. "Jean-Luc, what are you doing here?"

"Fishing, and waiting for you."

He dismounts and we embrace warmly. "Let's go," he says, beaming. "I'm most anxious to see my family again. I delayed too long in Paris, though I don't regret it."

"Adrien, sit down. We must talk."

He peers at me. "What is it, my friend? You seem strange, just like you do after a battle. Sad and torn. Is my family all right?"

I look at my friend, pained by what I must tell him. His expression shows he understands that what I am about to say is difficult.

"Your family left for Moscow a week ago. They're not returning."

"What?" he gasps, jumping to his feet. "They are gone? They didn't wait for my return?"

I stand and clasp his shoulder.

He finally stops to breathe. "Did you see them?"

"Yes."

I am uncertain how to console my dearest friend. We spend several minutes together along the river's edge as I tell him what happened.

He shakes his head in anger. "All the townspeople, they either drove my family out or did nothing to help them? How can I call Colmar home when they did this? You say Uncle Jean drove Monsieur Renard from town? Unfortunate. I would have taken my revenge on him."

We ride into town and immediately go to his family's shop. "It's in ruins," he says in despair. "All of my parents' hard work destroyed, and for what? Because they are Prussians?"

Adrien's anger is barely held in check. It's fortunate Monsieur Renard is not in town.

He walks through the shop, sifting through the pieces of broken furniture and debris. Something catches his eye, and he leans down to examine it. Lifting a small object, he brushes it with his hand and blows off the dust. It's a small porcelain figurine of a shepherd boy, bent on one knee.

"From my mother's nativity scene that she always kept on the counter. She was so proud of it and left it on display year-round. She told me her mother had given the set to her when she left Prussia for Colmar."

Adrien caresses the small figure, then places it into his vest pocket. "This may be all I ever have from my family."

He pauses, gently rubbing his vest. Turning to me, he says, "You spent a day with Anna Lise? How was she? Will she be all right?"

"Yes. She's remarkably strong and should be fine in Moscow."

Adrien's eyes are filled with anger and sorrow. His shoulders sag, as if carrying the weight of the world. "You do remember what I told you about Anna Lise. I told her as well. Don't forget it."

'I won't, my friend, but you must remember she has a mind of her own."

Tears are now running down his cheeks. 'I can't stay here, Jean-Luc, and I will never return. Colmar does not exist anymore for me. I must go to the Ostheim barracks and wait for my next assignment. I'm sorry, but this is too much for me to bear. We'll meet up again there."

'Yes, my friend. I will come tomorrow. We can ride up to the promontory overlooking the Rhine. Anna Lise and I were there last week."

With that, Adrien gives me a long embrace, mounts his horse, and rides away.

Gascony Stilt Walkers

Twenty-Eight

The Pyrenees – Winter, 1808

I am completely puzzled by the tall men who have come alongside our column of troops. "Who are these people?" I ask,

Adrien stares at the men on stilts. "They must be the Gascony shepherds Captain Bouchet told us about last night, the ones who will guide us to the Pyrenees and Spain." He watches them for a few more moments. "Amazing, aren't they?"

"Completely," I say, shaking my head in wonder. "They must be five feet off the ground! How do they stay up? Look how fast they're moving!" Remarkably, we are riding at full trot and they're keeping pace.

I'm happy to see the start of this new campaign has invigorated Adrien, who was sullen and disagreeable in the months after learning his family had left for Moscow. He spent time in Paris visiting Madame Kintelberger, but even that did not seem to help. His mood finally improved when we received orders to join Marshal Murat and his corps to reinforce General Junot in his occupation of Portugal. Now, seeing the stilt men and entering the Pyrenees foothills, he is cheered even more.

One of the stilt men comes close to me, nodding and smiling. He is clad in a coat made from black sheepskin and wears a bright red beret. Looking closely, I see his wooden stilts have a platform for standing on about five feet above the ground, with a strap wrapped around his foot for support. The base of the stilt is enlarged to provide more traction. Along the man's lower leg, the stilt is flat and secured by several other tight-fitting straps.

I nod to the man. "Those stilts are amazing. Why do you have them?"

"See how flat the terrain is? Covered with stunted bushes of dry heath and mounds of grass? After the slightest rain, it turns mushy. Without these stilts, we couldn't navigate the soggy land. Grazing sheep is about all this countryside is good for, and our flocks roam over a large expanse."

Looking out across the empty landscape, I understand what he means. In the far distance, I see a few scattered huts, but no villages or even roads in sight. The closer we come to the towering mountains, the more remote and sparsely populated the land becomes.

The shepherd salutes me and moves away.

Captain Bouchet drops back in the column to talk with us. "What do you think of our friends?" he asks. "Without the stilt men, we would have no idea where to go. They don't tire easily. And look over there—see how that man has stopped, leaning on his walking stick like the third leg of a tripod? There is also a seat attached to the pole that he can lean into. That's what they do when they want to rest or just stop to watch their sheep."

We must be a strange sight: our massive column of cavalry accompanied on each side by these gangly, long-legged men. The normal clip-clop of our horses' iron-shod hooves does not resound here. We are like a ghost army making our way into the unsuspecting Spanish domain.

Using their walking sticks, the stilt men point to a dip in the mountainous horizon to indicate which way we should go. We're past the low lands, and their job is done. We wave our shakos in farewell and continue to move toward the ominous, snow-capped peaks.

The flat, barren terrain of Gascony yields to hills with forests of pine and cork oaks. We cross the Bidasoa River and enter the Spanish village of Berrizaun. Our reception is completely different than it was in the villages of France and Northern Europe. As soon as they see us, the inhabitants greet us with disdain, no matter their class. Priests and monks point their crosses toward us with heads bowed, mumbling some chant as if trying to drive Satan and his followers away. The grated windows and doors are tightly shut as we trot along the narrow, crooked streets.

"Adrien, what's going on?" I ask. "Does everyone hate us? I thought Spain was our ally."

"It's the Church, Jean-Luc. You're not Catholic and don't understand how strong the Church can be. Our revolution in France fought not only the nobility, but also the Church, reducing its influence by seizing its lands. In Colmar, our priests accepted the decrees from Paris and relinquished the parish lands. But that was not enough for some of the revolutionary extremists. You remember Monsieur Renard and Father Benedict, don't you?"

How could I forget Father Benedict being guillotined in the town square?

"The Spanish Catholic Church is powerful," Adrien continues. "The Inquisition still takes place here, and the people both revere and fear their priests. We are seen as threatening their way of life, and they consider us as nothing more than blasphemers and heretics." He shakes his head. "Our alliance with Spain is only a convenience to curtail Portugal, their long-time enemy, and Portugal is our enemy because it supports England. The Church, and the people it influences, still fear and hate us."

At the edge of the village, several men extend their right hands balled into a fist, but with their index and little fingers pointing up, like horns, in what appears to be an obscene gesture. They spit on the ground when we pass. As we leave the town and enter the wilderness of the Pyrenees, I don't look back, glad to leave such hatred behind me.

* * *

Although I'm sure Marshal Murat and even Captain Bouchet were aware of the difficulties in moving such a large troop of men over these mountains, I had no idea how the narrow tracks and the snow in the Pyrenees would slow us down.

Three weeks have passed since we left the stilt walkers and entered the Pyrenees. The wind is howling, and snow is beginning to fall—at first lightly, then so thick I can barely see Bayard's nose in front of me. I pull my cape around me tightly, trying to seal in some warmth. Faintly, the command to set up camp echoes down the ranks.

"Quickly, men, set your tents close together," Captain Bouchet orders. "We may be staying here for some time."

Captain Bouchet and I scratch out an area for a central fire in the frozen ground, then direct our squad members to pitch their tents, circling around this firepit like spokes in a wheel.

The snow continues to fall heavily, but our tents provide some relief from the wind.

"Wood! We need lots of wood," I shout, and we all scatter into the surrounding forest, bringing back all we can carry. While we are gathering the wood, Captain Bouchet lights the fire. Soon, the blaze is roaring, and we each retreat into our tents to arrange our gear. The warmth from the fire penetrates the opening of my tent, warming it all the way through. Bayard is near the back flap of my tent. I give him some feed, though he is already pawing at the snow to uncover the grasses below.

Nearly a week passes before the storm begins to abate. The sky lightens and the wind calms. The snow is only lightly falling. "Jean-Luc, do you have any coffee left?" Adrien asks from the opening of his tent. "I've used all mine."

"I still have my full ration," says Private Fosse from across the firepit. "I don't care for it. Do you have any extra hardtack?"

"A little," Adrien says. "Do you have any extra, Jean-Luc? We can share the coffee."

We complete the deal and boil some fresh coffee just as the sun cracks through the clouds. The snow is melted near the fire, but the backs of our tents and the surrounding countryside are buried under over two feet.

Just as we are finishing the coffee, the command to break camp resounds down the line.

I pack my gear onto Bayard and give him a pat on the neck. "It's good to see the sun again, isn't it, my friend?" Despite the joy in seeing the sun, the going is slow as a procession of soldiers and horsemen trample down the snow. It is hard work, and we rotate squads to the forward position as we press ahead.

In mid-March, we reach the city of Burgos, a sprawling town that once served as the capital of Castile. As our horsemen proceed through the expanse of buildings at the edge of town, an imposing castle towers above us, seeming to watch our every step. Church bells begin to peal from every direction, echoing against the maze of stucco buildings that branch away from the main road. Moving deeper into the city, we come to an open square dominated by a massive cathedral. There are hardly any people in the square, just as the avenue we followed to reach this spot was nearly empty. Those I see are scurrying away quickly, giving us furtive glances. The bells must be announcing our presence, warning everyone to stay inside. Our reception is as cold here as our treatment in Berrizaun when we first entered Spain.

Clouds of vapor puff from each of us and our horses as we come to a stop. There's no snow on the ground, but the cold grip of winter still holds. Looking around, it appears that the city is folding up around us, telling us to move on. All the windows are shuttered, nearly everyone has escaped inside, and the din of the bells seems to be saying *leave ... leave ... leave.*

Up ahead, Marshal Murat is gesturing toward one road while his lieutenants point at another. After a few moments of discussion, our column turns toward the road indicated by the marshal. Instead of continuing southwest toward Portugal, Marshal Murat has us turn south in the direction of Madrid.

"What do you think the marshal has in mind?" Adrien asks as we begin our journey toward the Spanish capital. "I thought our orders were to reinforce General Junot and his occupation of Portugal."

I shrug. "The emperor must have other ideas."

While I don't know the emperor's plans, I'm happy to move on, distressed by how unwelcome we are here.

* * *

After several days, we reach Madrid. To my amazement, cheering crowds greet us.

Instead of camping with the troops, I am billeted in the home of a prosperous shopkeeper, one of the advantages of being an officer. The proprietor knows some French and receives me heartily into his home. "Thank the saints you are here. Your emperor will talk sense into our monarchy and stop their squabbling."

Is that why we are here, or is something else in play?

Madrid Massacre - Goya

Twenty-Nine

Madrid – Spring, 1808

I am quickly putting on my boots. "Manuel, wait," I call out to my host's eldest son.

I arrived at his family's home three days ago, and during this time I've become friends with all of the Arroyos, especially Manuel, who is a few years younger and several inches shorter than me. He asks many questions about France, the revolution, and the emperor. Though the Catholic Church condemns the revolution, many of the educated Spaniards are curious about it and sympathetic to its ideals.

"You must hurry," Manuel replies. "The muezzin is making the call for Fajr from the mosque. The market springs to life once the prayer is complete. You don't want to miss it. I'm sure you don't have this in France."

I straighten my uniform as I run, trying to keep up with the lean, olive-skinned, dark-haired boy who is making a path for me through the crowds. As we move along, he tells me, "We are a Christian country, but many Muslims live in Madrid. Most are merchants."

The light of day is growing stronger, and sunrise is not far away. We continue to hustle our way from inside the walled city toward the imposing city gate. "The marketplace is just ahead," he calls over his shoulder. We are headed to the Puerta de Alcalá, the main portal into the city and the location of the market.

Nearing the gateway, Manuel stops and waits for me. Market stands line both sides of the boulevard. Some merchants are straightening their stalls, while other stands appear unattended. "Look toward the back," Manuel says, pointing toward some unmanned booths.

I spot several men in the shadows splashing water on themselves. "What are they doing?" I ask.

"They are finishing the Wudu cleansing ceremony of washing their hands, mouth, nostrils, arms, head, and feet before prayer."

Going farther into the market, I see several men in the back corners of their stands, stooped over and kneeling on small rugs, bending and chanting quietly. I know enough about Muslims to know this is the first of five times they will pray today.

The first rays of morning sunshine strike the nearby church steeple. I'm blinded by the reflection from the copper-clad spire. Shielding my eyes, I peer up and gasp. The sun must be playing tricks; the gargoyles carved into the spire seem to dance as light passes from one to the next. In moments, the whispering quiet of the prayers is shattered by the cries of the merchants peddling their wares. The rising sun officially opens the market. I look toward Manuel, who's watching my reactions.

"See?" he says with a smile. "I'm sure your marketplaces are nothing like this."

"No," I reply as I gaze about at the bustling mass of people. "Nothing at all."

We snake our way through the stalls, my eyes darting from one wonder to the next. A slight breeze touches my face, filling my nose with the smells of cooking meats. Manuel purchases some meats skewered with sticks and hands me two. "What kind of meat is this?" I ask.

"Mostly goat or lamb, but sometimes it's best not to ask or think about it."

He takes a bite, and I follow suit. I've never tasted such flavors and quickly devour all of it. "What spices were those?"

"Many kinds. See that stand over there?"

I look where he's pointing and see a table with platters of different colored powders, seeds, and what appear to be dried threads, sprigs, and leaves.

He points. "That red spice is paprika. Yellow is turmeric, and the brown is cinnamon, my favorite. That is saffron," he says, pointing to dried, reddish threads. "A most treasured spice." His voice is almost reverent. "It comes from the center of the crocus flower."

"We don't have such spices in Colmar."

The crowd is a mix of many kinds of people. We pass several men wearing robes with heavy folds, like pictures I've seen of Roman senators in their togas. There are goat drovers clad in kilts of hide that look like short tunics. Up ahead are men with their hair bound in silken scarves, their skin and eyes darker than most of the Spanish people I've seen. "Who are they?" I say, pointing.

"They are Moors, who originally came from Africa and ruled Andalusia for centuries. We defeated them, but they are not treated as enemies."

Despite my French uniform, no one gives me any heed, except when I take interest in their goods. I sample various wines and liquors and, with Manuel's help, purchase several to give to his father as gifts.

Even though I am far from home, I feel happy, delighted to be in this exotic place.

Several days pass, and I'm treated as an honored guest by Señor Arroyo and his family. We don't eat dinner until late in the evening, but the wait is well worth it. One night, we eat a stew made of vegetables, chickpeas, sausage, and pork. The broth from this stew serves as our first course, followed by a course of the chickpeas and vegetables, and ending with the meat. At night, I write in my journal: *Indescribable!*

Another night we have seared pig ears with mushrooms. Very strange, but delicious. All our meals are washed down with bottles of fine red Spanish wine.

We enjoy lively dinner conversation, as the family all know at least some French. Most of the talk is about our home cities and countries, but each meal includes an update of news about the royal family, courtesy of their parish priest. My hosts attend church each morning, and part of the priest's sermon includes news of what is happening in the city. The presence and activities of the French army is a prime topic.

About two weeks into my stay, as I'm enjoying one of the pigs' ears, Señor Arroyo says, "Our padre told us this morning that our king, Charles, and his son, Ferdinand, who wants his father to abdicate, have been invited by your emperor to come to Bayonne near the Spanish border. Maybe a solution to our royal family squabbles can be conciliated there?" Señor Arroyo smiles, but I see uncertainty in his eyes.

"I'm sure that will be the goal," I respond. "The emperor is a very difficult person to ignore, and Spain is an important ally."

He brightens with my answer.

For several days the padre has no news regarding the royal family. In the marketplace, vendors begin to look at me suspiciously, and my bargaining for their wares is cut short with little movement on price. The Arroyo family remains friendly, though now we spend more time speculating about what may be happening in Bayonne. In Manuel's free time, we wander the streets of Madrid as he tells me the history of the city.

On the first of May, I'm welcomed as usual when I come to dinner, but Señor Arroyo appears uncomfortable. His smile is strained, and our conversation steers clear of talk about the royal family. Unlike previous evenings, we talk about my life as a soldier.

"How can you go into battle, knowing you may die or be wounded?" Señor Arroyo asks. "What of those you fight? Those men are like you, only trying to survive. What of your family?"

I pause, looking at each of their faces as they wait for my response. They don't look condemning or angry, but instead curious, genuinely not understanding the reasons I would choose to be a soldier.

"When you're young, the military offers honor and glory."

I stop, weighing what to say next.

"But I've learned these are just concepts to justify killing and destruction. It's important to defend your country, but at what cost? I know I'm here today because I killed and maimed so many. My actions haunt me."

I cannot bear to look at them. My voice tightens, and I speak just above a whisper. "This is not what I thought honor and glory would be like. I miss my home in Colmar and the time I spent helping my father run our inn." I pause. "Knowing what I do now, I would not have chosen this path."

Silence fills the room for several moments. "Thank you, my friend," Señor Arroyo says at last. "Fighting to save one's way of life is important. I know we Spanish would do the same."

I am surprised by my emotional response to Señor Arroyo's question, and so is the family. Many, with tears in their eyes, walk around the table to embrace me. Señor Arroyo announces, "It's time for us to eat our flan. Then, I have news from our padre."

The delicious custard lightens the mood. As we finish, Señor Arroyo says, "The padre tells us that a messenger has arrived from Bayonne. The remaining members of the royal family are being summoned to join the king." Looking at me, he adds, "This seems most unusual, don't you think?"

I try to hide my surprise. "Perhaps the emperor is planning a feast to celebrate a conciliation and thinks the entire royal family should attend."

Señor Arroyo looks skeptical. "Perhaps you are right. The padre will know more by tomorrow. He is expecting a church messenger tonight."

My night is restless, and I sleep little. I wonder what the emperor is planning.

The next morning, I am about to leave for the market when I see Señor Arroyo rushing down the street toward me.

"My friend, you must leave quickly. The padre tells us the king and his son have renounced the crown and are being sent into exile. Your emperor has named his brother as our new king. All the priests are instructing their parishioners to rise up against the French. You have little time."

"Señor?" I say, though I see he is frantic.

"Go! You must go! A mob is growing. They want to kill Frenchmen."

I embrace him briefly, then rush home to throw together my gear and retrieve Bayard from the stable. We make our way through the Puerta de Alcalá toward the outskirts of Madrid. Near the gate, I recognize the faces of several vendors who now have hate in their eyes.

The crowd grows, jeering and throwing rocks.

"Quickly, Bayard!" I yell as I give him a kick.

As we gallop away, we are joined by other comrades who were also billeted in town. We reach our encampment, finding it roiling with turmoil. "Did you see Pierre? André? Gaston?" I hear comrades asking about their friends. As we try to make sense of what is happening, riderless horses begin thundering into camp, many dragging the mutilated bodies of friends. Men mount their horses, shocked and angered, drawing their sabres.

"All officers report to Marshal Murat's headquarters immediately," a corporal shouts as he gallops along the encampment's edge.

The sun is edging toward setting as we gather around the marshal's tent. I see him silhouetted inside, pounding the table. He storms through his tent flap to address us, eyes burning with rage.

He glares across the assemblage. "Men, as you've seen, many of our comrades have been brutally killed. The people are in revolt, butchering any soldier they find. They are furious at our emperor for putting his brother on the throne of Spain."

Voices buzz. The crowd is ablaze with fury. Fists are raised. "Revenge! We must have revenge!" they shout.

Marshal Murat holds up his arms to quiet everyone. "This uprising will not be tolerated. We march within the hour. Round up those who oppose us and bring them to the central square." Staring at all of us, he clenches a hand into a fist. "Kill whoever resists. Dismissed!"

I return to where I left Bayard, my path illuminated by the light of the moon, tinged orange from the fires set in the city. I can't believe what I've heard. Few Spanish soldiers are in Madrid. I look to our captain. "Sir, are you going to order us to attack civilians?"

He is as shocked as I am, his face strained, his eyes sad. "No, I will order our men to ride toward the central plaza and nothing more unless we are attacked. We are soldiers, not demons."

I nod, relieved.

But not all of our men feel like the captain. Most are bent on revenge. Thousands of us converge on the city, splitting up among the alleys and byways, bullying our way into the surging masses. Bloodshed and chaos ensue.

Our squadron follows an alley lined with angry people. They throw sticks and rocks, but the sight of our drawn sabres seems to keep them from trying to overwhelm us. Up ahead, I see the alley is blocked. A priest, holding his crucifix high, stands in our way. A crowd of Spaniards fill the alley behind him. Captain Bouchet raises his arm for us to halt.

Eyeing the priest, he says, *"Padre, podemos hablar?"*

One of our corporals leans in. "The captain is saying, 'Father, can we talk?'"

The captain adds, *"Mis hombres y yo debemos llegar a la plaza."*

"My men and I must get to the square," the corporal whispers.

The priest looks like he is in a trance. He clutches his crucifix tightly, beads of sweat dripping from his brow.

Again, Captain Bouchet addresses the priest. *"Padre, quiere usted morir?"*

The corporal translates. "Father, do you want to die?"

I can now hear the priest muttering. His hands holding the crucifix are shaking. Opening his eyes, he looks at our mounted men, then to his angry but terrified parishioners.

Finally, he replies, *"No quiero morir en vano. Lideraré el camino."* He lowers his crucifix.

The corporal says, "I do not want to die in vain. I will lead the way."

Our captain looks at all of us sternly, then dismounts and approaches the padre. My spine tingles as I clutch my sabre tightly.

In the windows above, people hold rocks and sticks. They stare past us toward their priest, awaiting his word.

Captain Bouchet and the padre talk tensely while we fidget in our saddles. We are now surrounded by hundreds of angry Spanish civilians. It will be a bloodbath if we need to break out.

"What are they saying?" Adrien asks, peering around nervously.

"I don't know," I say tensely.

They are speaking too low for any of us to hear.

Bayard shuffles impatiently. I pat his neck to calm him, wishing I could calm myself.

With tension mounting, Captain Bouchet gives a short bow to the priest, then saddles up. The padre starts to walk forward, his crucifix held high.

"Follow the priest," our captain shouts, "and avoid conflict."

We slowly move forward, surrounded by the masses, all of them armed with makeshift weapons.

"The padre is leading us to the central square," Captain Bouchet tells us. "He does not wish for his parishioners to die."

We pass throngs of angry people who step away as the padre passes.

The plaza comes into view. It's large, able to hold several thousand people. At every entrance, people are shouting and screaming and pushing to enter, but our horsemen are holding them back. The padre goes into the square, then steps aside, and we gain entrance. Horsemen are herding together the civilians in the square, pushing them to the north, near the church. They are creating two perimeters: an inner one around the prisoners and an outer one around the edge of the plaza. The prisoners are panicked. Many plead to be freed and some try to break through, but cannot. Sabres are brandished and pistols fired to keep them secured and to hold back the throngs frantically trying to get to these captured civilians. Sporadic shrieks of pain erupt along the edges of the plaza.

Our squadron is in the mayhem between the two perimeters. Bayard rises up onto his hind legs and whinnies loudly.

"Jean-Luc," Adrien shouts, pointing. "They've split off about half the prisoners and are lining them up against the side of the church."

The hair on my neck prickles.

A column of soldiers holding muskets quickly marches into a line parallel to the people positioned on the wall. They stop, then turn toward the frightened men and women. Ten feet separate them. The captives appear to know what is about to take place. Many press their backs into the building, seemingly hoping to melt through. Some run toward the soldiers but are roughly struck back with a quick snap from a musket butt.

I look toward Adrien. He stares at the scene, his mouth agape.

A young woman extends her arms wide, showing her enlarged belly. The soldiers ignore her. My stomach turns, but I can't look away.

The soldiers prepare their muskets and point them at the civilians. A few throw their muskets to the ground. Their superiors, riding behind them, jab them with their sabres, demanding they pick up their guns. Those who still refuse are pushed in with the Spaniards in the firing line.

Marshal Murat rides behind the line of soldiers, waving his sword.

"No, this can't be," I shout to no one.

Reaching the end of the line, Marshal Murat turns and bellows. "Ready ... Fire!"

Smoke rises from the musket fire, and most of the prisoners drop, mortally wounded.

I can't breathe.

Some, still alive, are shot by soldiers walking the line. When they're finished, they raise their muskets, shouting, "Vive la France, Vive l'empereur!" Many soldiers in the crowded square return their chant.

I look for Captain Bouchet. *What just happened?* I want to scream. He is nearby, his head bent in shock.

The remaining half of the prisoners struggle to get free but are pushed back into an even tighter circle, then kicked and shoved by hostile soldiers yelling insults and jeers.

I can't stop staring at the crumpled line of dead or the mayhem among the remaining prisoners. A voice breaks through my numbed senses. "Follow me," it commands. Looking toward the sound, I see Captain Bouchet leading our squad away from this massacre site. "Dismount," he commands, his voice strained. "I'm going to the marshal's headquarters."

* * *

Dawn is only a few hours away. Neither Adrien nor I can sleep. I'm haunted by the memory of seeing so many unarmed people slain, the bodies of our mutilated comrades, and the hatred in the Spaniards' eyes.

"What kind of people are these?" Adrien asks. "Nowhere have we been treated like this. Maybe they needed to be put in their place."

"What? Those people deserved to be lined up and shot? When have we ever massacred civilians?"

"They attacked us! If they act like an enemy, shouldn't we treat them like one? If we didn't strike back, wouldn't we all be dead?"

I look at Adrien in disbelief. "Our sabres and guns against their stones and sticks?"

We glare at each other and say nothing more.

The night is warm, and the sky lightens as it nears dawn. In the square, the prisoners are wailing. From the edge of the square, voices call out. I can't understand the words, but I feel the emotion and fear.

Captain Bouchet returns and takes several things into his tent. After a few moments, he calls out, his voice leaden. 'Lieutenant Calliet, come join me."

Inside the captain's tent, I see fifteen muskets lying at his feet. He doesn't look up. 'I've just returned from Marshal Murat's." His voice quivers. 'Fifteen of our men are to participate in the firing squad at dawn. The prisoners are all to be shot. 'A lesson for the Spanish not to interfere with the French army,'" the marshal says. 'We have no choice."

Captain Bouchet nudges the butt of one of the muskets with his foot.

"Three of the guns have only a powder charge, no ball. Those who shoot will not know if their musket provides one of the deadly shots."

"They all are to die? Just to provide an example?" I cry out. 'I joined the army to defend France against its enemies. Spain is no enemy, and these people have no arms."

Captain Bouchet looks up at me, stains on his cheeks from tears already shed. 'I know. You and I will each take a musket. Go back to your comrades and send to me the first thirteen men you meet. Don't try to think who should or who should not bear this burden."

I'm stunned, but I salute and return to our squad. The first person I meet is Adrien, and I tell him to go see the captain. As instructed, the remaining twelve are the first ones I encounter.

The captain explains our orders and the fact that three of the muskets don't have a killing ball. We make our way toward where the prisoners are being held. They are now arrayed along the church wall, where the bloodstains from the night before are still evident on the stones.

Men from other detachments join us, and we make a firing line, three hundred or more soldiers long, shoulder to shoulder, facing about two hundred and fifty prisoners. Only a few yards separate us. I glance down the row, feeling their terror and their awareness of impending death.

To my shock, standing in front of me is the padre who led us to safety. His eyes are closed, and his crucifix is held tightly to his heart. His lips move in a final prayer.

The marshal, dressed in his finery and mounted on his stallion, rides behind us. "Men, prepare your weapons." Once he's satisfied everyone is aiming toward the prisoners, he shouts, "Fire!"

I look directly at the priest, knowing no matter what I do, he will die. I can only try to make his death a quick one.

A musket ball takes the padre down. Blood spurts from his chest as he crumples to his knees, then into a heap on the ground. His crucifix falls, clattering across the stone pavement. I know how a musket feels when firing a full load of powder with shot.

The ball that killed the padre was mine.

The sound from hundreds of guns echoes across the square. Bodies fall. Screams of anguish erupt from the crowds watching. Our horsemen keep them from entering, using their sabres to strike those who try to push through.

The image of the padre joins the wall of faces of those I've killed, each etched into my memory like portraits in a gallery, his more than any of the others.

Down the line from me, a fallen man moves slightly. He seems familiar. The soldier in front of him is reloading his musket. I move closer. The soldier raises his weapon. The man's face lifts up, staring at the gun. "Manuel!" I shout, as I race to try to stop the shooting. Manuel hears my voice and looks toward me, terror in his eyes, just as the musket fires.

The gentle breeze of my youthful soul has now turned into a tempest, roiling with self-recrimination. Will I ever be able to calm this storm, or will my soul be lost?

I turn away, trying to escape this macabre theater, but there is no escape.

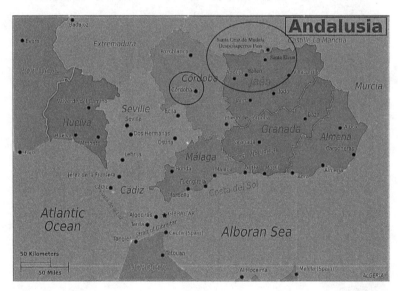

Andalusia

Thirty

Andalusia – Summer, 1808

I feel my thought drifting. "Jean-Luc! Pay attention. You need to be sharp. It's getting rocky and narrow, with many places for the enemy to hide." A voice shouts crossly.

Who's talking to me? Do I care?

"Jean-Luc! Snap out of it. Do you want to get killed?"

Maybe that's not such a bad thought. That would end the nightmares. Manuel, I'm so sorry. Padre, I can't shake the vision of my musket ball shattering your chest.

I look toward the voice. "Adrien, why are you yelling?"

"Because you're not paying attention! You drank too much again last night. Guerrilla fighters could spring from behind any of these boulders, and we've fallen behind our comrades. You know how they love to pick off stragglers."

Something zips by my head. Then another. Atop a boulder near Adrien, two peasants kneel, desperately trying to reload their muskets. Three others jump at Adrien, trying to pull him from his horse. My mind clears instantly. Drawing my sabre, I strike at the men attacking my friend. One is beheaded in a moment, and his head rolls across the dirt as I sever another's arm. Adrien finishes off the third, and we swing our horses around to confront the two with muskets. They're still trying to reload, but seeing us bearing down, they turn to run, only to face our fast-approaching comrades. Soon, these two also lie dead.

Captain Bouchet wipes his bloody sabre clean, glaring at us. "You know the dangers of straggling," he snaps. "You're lucky to be alive!"

"The fault is mine. It won't happen again," I reply.

"Lieutenant, I've overlooked your drunkenness and dispiritedness in the weeks since Madrid. I understand how you feel, but I expect a return to professionalism now that we have been ordered into action. You nearly cost your best friend's life just now, not to mention your own. I won't tolerate this again."

Captain Bouchet turns his horse away, returning to the lead of our squad. "We will be in Andalusia soon. Keep a sharp eye. Guerillas may attack from anywhere."

Sobered, I ride to Adrien's side. "I'm sorry, my friend. You saved my life."

Adrien nods and touches his lips, and I know I'm forgiven.

"You must shake this off, Jean-Luc. Madrid was a tragedy, but Spaniards are the enemy, and we have our duty."

These words pierce my heart. *The padre was an enemy? Manuel? Adrien, my friend, where is your soul?*

I only nod miserably, knowing it's pointless to argue.

"Let's join our comrades." I give Bayard a kick so we can catch up.

The clarity that came only moments ago when we were attacked is now replaced by the purgatory—no, hell—from my drinking. My uniform is nearly soaked, despite the day's cloud cover and cool temperatures. Sweat covers my brow. Has someone stuffed cotton in my mouth? My head is a giant, pulsing nerve, hurting with each jostle of Bayard's gait.

"Here, have some water," Adrien says irritably as he hands me his canteen. "You look awful. Keep a clear head and scan the rocks and crevices carefully. We can't take the chance of being ambushed again."

I nearly drain the canteen. The water makes me feel somewhat better.

We left Santa Cruz de Mudela early this morning, and the road is now leading us into the heights of the Sierra Morena. The clouds now burn away, allowing the sun to blaze down upon the stark, rugged countryside.

We approach a ravine with a small river when I spot a group of men coming toward us. Drawing my sabre, I cry, "To the left!"

Expecting battle, I'm surprised to see them waving their arms in apparent greeting. Our squad soon surrounds them, sabres drawn. I look at Adrien, puzzled. "That sounds like German."

"That is German. They're welcoming us."

"Who are you people?" Captain Bouchet asks.

The men explain they are colonists invited to live in these mountains by the Spanish royal family.

"Are any Spanish nearby?"

Their apparent leader shakes his head. "You are safe. It's so wonderful to speak with strangers in German. We were over by that far hill when we saw the long trail of dust. We got here just as you came. Do you have time to stay a while? We have some food we can share. Can you tell us what you know of our homeland?"

Captain Bouchet stands up in his stirrups and scans the surrounding landscape. "We can stop for a few moments to have some water. Anton and Gaston, take watch positions." Turning back toward the German leader, he asks, "How much farther to the top of Despeñaperros Pass?"

"The mountain crest is but one or two leagues away. Our village, Santa Elena, is just beyond the pass."

Two men approach Adrien and me. They are pleased to learn we are from Alsace. "Our village is not far from there, near Stuttgart. We've heard your country had a revolution and you no longer have a king. You now have an emperor who was a commoner and have fought many wars?"

Adrien and I tell the Germans the highlights of events since the revolution.

One of them eyes me. "You look pale, sir, much like my brother after he has had too much to drink. See those prickly plants growing along the road? Eating their knobby fruit is a sure cure."

He uses his staff to knock off some of the fruit from the spiny plant. The spines come off as he rolls the fruit in the dirt with his sandal. "Here," he says as he hands me three of them. "Use your knife to peel away the skin."

As I take the fruit, one of the remaining spines pricks my hand. A tiny drop of blood seeps out. "Careful, sir. I probably didn't get all the spines."

I suck the blood from my hand and give Adrien a questioning look.

"It's worth a try," he says, shrugging his shoulders.

I take my dagger and peel off the skin to expose a pinkish-orange pulp, which I pop into my mouth. "This tastes good. Very sweet. Thank you. Adrien, you'd like this."

After about fifteen minutes, we leave the Germans. Meeting them was a welcome respite, reminding us of home. The remainder of our ride to the summit is uneventful. My mind is occupied with scanning the countryside, but my thoughts still flash back to that firing squad in Madrid. With each passing hour I begin to physically feel better—thanks to the strange fruit, I assume—but the depression still bears down.

A warm breeze brushes my face as we drop over the summit. "Smell that air, Jean-Luc," Adrien says. "It smells sweet, like home when we harvest the grapes."

Inhaling deeply takes me back to Alsace. The scent does not have quite the same sweetness as our grapes, but something is definitely being harvested.

Dropping over the pass gives a panoramic view of the Andalusian countryside. Our troops extend far into the distance, strung out along this rocky track, as we bring up the rear.

The ravine we are following begins to widen into a valley, and we soon find ourselves surrounded on both sides by orchards of olive trees. Peasants are working in the groves, gathering the olives. They pay us no attention. Melons and squash grow beneath the canopy of trees, scattered between rows of corn. Rising above the groves like a mighty crown are the distant, snow-capped peaks of the Sierra Nevada, which, along with the Sierra Morena, separates Andalusia from the rest of Spain.

We ride into this rich landscape, feeling the strain of marching through enemy territory lighten. Rosettes of tall, thick, fleshy spikes that reach to the height of the trees, along with tall bushes with pink flowers, divide the olive groves into a patchwork. We pass many homes, all deserted, their occupants probably working the harvest. The homes are of a different design than those we have seen so far. Each has a central courtyard paved with flagstones. In the center of most is a gurgling fountain, shaded by cypress and citrus trees, with chairs and tables scattered around its perimeter. These homes look so inviting.

We join several other squadrons and stop along the banks of the Guadalquivir River, near the village of Bailén, to rest and water and feed our horses after the arduous descent from the Despeñaperros Pass. Though nearly recovered now from my hangover, I'm happy to take this break. Two boys from the village come visit us. They indicate with hand motions that they have food and drink for us in some of the nearby cottages. Wary after our experiences in Madrid, we refuse. They move to the next squad and make the same hand gestures. Two members of this squad follow them toward the houses.

"They'll likely get poisoned," Adrien chuckles as he takes a drink from his canteen. "Have you noticed their uniforms? So crisp and new. I'm sure this is the closest any of them have gotten to battle."

Some time passes as I rest on the ground with my head propped by my sleeping roll. "Adrien, aren't those the same children who led those soldiers away a while back, now talking to that other squad?"

Adrien looks over. "They are. I recognize that one boy's shirt. Something is not right. Let's check it out."

As Adrien and I move toward the cottages, I call to the squad, asking if any of them has seen their comrades.

"No," they reply, and several join us. Adrien and I draw our sabres as we come closer.

"Do you hear that?" Adrien asks as we come to the door. We stop, stand frozen, and listen.

I hear a weak, muffled cry for help and crash into the door, breaking it down.

"It's Anton," a man from the other squad cries. "What have they done to him? Where is Louis?"

Hanging with arms outstretched from a roof beam is the naked, bloody body of Anton. Cuts run from head to toe, and his face is smashed from being beaten. His comrades hold him as I slice my blade through the ropes. On the other side of the room, another body hangs from the rafters, motionless. Adrien rushes toward what must be Louis's body and holds him as I cut his ropes.

"This one is dead," Adrien says.

We rush back to Anton, who is near motionless.

Whispering, he says, "The boys ... led us into a trap."

He gasps for breath.

"Inside, men grabbed hold of us. Stuffed rags in our mouths."

Another struggle for breath.

"They held me down, making me watch while they stripped off Louis's uniform ... They strung him up and beat him. Cut him."

"Here, have some water," a comrade offers.

He gratefully accepts, then rests for a few more moments. His eyes are puffed closed, and his wounds are too extensive for us to stop the bleeding.

"I couldn't understand them," Anton says, his voice barely audible. "Each time they punched him, they shouted in anger."

He strains to suck in another breath, but is soon still.

Anton's and Louis's comrades look stunned. Gathering up the two bodies, they emerge from the cottage and find men from many squads gathered round. Several turn away from the brutal, bloody scene and retch.

"Anton and Louis have been butchered! We must have revenge!"

"Here are the children that brought them here," a soldier says as he shoves two young boys onto the ground before the bodies. Many of the men start kicking them.

"Kill them," they say.

I step in, pushing the frightened boys behind me, toward Adrien.

"We don't kill children," I shout, but several soldiers start pressing toward me, hate in their eyes.

A pistol shot splits the air, stopping everyone in their tracks. Captain Bouchet steps forward, his other pistol in his hand, pointed at the crowd.

"There will be no more killing here. Return to your camp and bury your comrades."

He waves his hand for everyone to leave, then turns toward Adrien and me. "Lieutenant Calliet and Sergeant Bauck, take charge of these two and go back to our camp. I will go and meet with the general."

Grumbling meets the captain's words, but the soldiers disperse.

Sensing they will be safe with Adrien and me, the boys huddle up close to us. We move cautiously away, keeping one eye on our comrades and the other toward the deserted village. No peasants are in sight anywhere.

* * *

Not long after, Captain Bouchet returns. I see messengers going to each squad, ordering them to mount up.

"We are attacking Córdoba tonight instead of tomorrow. The men are riled and ready for action, and the general wants to take advantage of their anger."

He pauses and looks at the two boys. They must be no older than eight. "He wants them killed. As we leave, I want you and Sergeant Bauck to stay behind." Looking directly at me, then Adrien, he says, "You know what to do."

The army soon moves out while Adrien and I sit with the children, our muskets at ready. Captain Bouchet turns to us, giving a salute.

As the last soldier disappears from view, Adrien and I raise our muskets, pointing them toward the terrified boys. Looking toward Adrien, I raise my musket skyward. He follows suit. "Now," I command, and our muskets fire.

"For Manuel," I say, giving a sad sigh.

The boys jump at the sound of the muskets. They look at each other with tear-stained faces, then back toward me with expressions of uncertainty and fear. "Go," I say, as I motion for them to leave.

Their eyes widen in surprise. "*Gracias, señors,*" they both say, and dash toward their homes.

In the nearby trees, a branch cracks and leaves rustle, but no one appears.

Thirty-One

Bailén – Summer, 1808

As dusk overtakes daylight, we come upon the Spanish army at the bridge near Alcolea. Córdoba is but two leagues away. Perhaps the Spanish hope to stop us here.

Adrien glances at our troops, his eyes sparkling with anticipation. "Jean-Luc, look at them. They can barely hold back their excitement. So young, so confident."

"And so foolish. Look at their gear. They're just like those young recruits we marched with from Berlin. See that one? His sabre sheath is too far forward. By the time he reaches for it, he'll be dead. And over there. That one's saddle will probably slide to the side when he attacks. It needs to be cinched up."

Adrien looks back at me, his excitement dampened. "They'll be all right after a few battles."

The roar from our cannon splits the air. The ground quakes, and nearby trees tremble. As always, their thunder strikes fear in my heart, taking me back to Ulm where a cannonball nearly took my life. Through the twilight and smoke, eruptions of dirt surge high, sometimes carrying the body of an unlucky soul. Terror-stricken Spanish soldiers run in all directions, many throwing down their weapons.

Our battalion of cavalry lines the ridge, awaiting orders. Nearby, General Dupont gestures toward several men holding staffs with flags.

Adrien is surveying the activity below us. "They're not holding their formation," he yells over to me. "Once they see us, they will definitely go into full panic. We should ride straight across the bridge and not worry about those on this side."

"Look over there," I shout. "The general's flagmen are signaling for us to attack."

We draw our sabres and, with piercing howls, fly down the hill toward the Spanish troops.

Adrien takes the lead position, advancing us straight toward the bridge. "Ignore those running," he shouts. "Attack those making a stand on the far side."

Our horses' hooves clatter on the bridge's cobblestones. Clouds of smoke drift across the landscape. No one has challenged us yet, but ahead, through the smoke and increasingly darkening skies, there are shadowy images of soldiers holding their ground. Several are frantically trying to reload as our horses slam into them, causing chaos. Many die under the sharp hooves. Sabres slash. Blood spurts. In less than an hour, the battle is over. We suffer few casualties and quickly continue our march toward Córdoba, hoping to arrive before the middle of night.

Adrien beams victoriously.

I look over the field of dead, and my chest aches.

The white-washed walls of Córdoba come into view, reflecting the dim light of the waning moon. They rise silently like a massive stone mountain from the banks of the Guadalquivir River. The general orders us to halt.

The city gate is open, and civilians are waiting for our approach.

"What do you think is going on?" Adrien asks as he points toward a messenger talking with Captain Bouchet. We have the answer quickly, as the captain joins us when the man leaves.

"We are one of the few experienced squadrons in the general's forces, and our orders are to determine if the city is undefended. The main army will enter after we confirm."

Fresh from their first victory, our army appears anxious to claim their reward: plunder from the city of Córdoba.

We make our way to the open city gate, where we're received by what appear to be some of the city's leading citizens. They are richly dressed, but their chins are low to their chest and their eyes are downcast. One of their leaders steps forward, speaking French. "Our soldiers have moved to the east, and our town is undefended. Please, we have gathered gold and silver for your taking. We only beg you not to sack our city."

Torches light our way through the gate and city walls. Several wagons filled with treasure line the avenue. We pay them little heed and proceed into the town.

We come upon the Guadalquivir River and the ancient stone bridge that crosses it. Silence prevails, save for the clatter from our horses' hooves. Looming in front of us is a massive structure. "That looks like it might be a mosque," I say to Adrien. "I saw one in Madrid."

Coming closer, we see lights in a spire rising above one side of the building. "Jean-Luc, there's a cross at the top. It's a church now."

Riding nearer, I see the exterior walls of the church covered in patterns of black on white with interwoven vines, tendrils, and flowers. Strange-looking calligraphy designs cover other walls, and horseshoe-shaped arches open up into interior gardens. "What an exquisite place this is," I say to Adrien as we move forward. "Unlike anything I've seen."

"Keep your focus, Jean-Luc," Adrien says gruffly. "We're not here to sightsee!"

Captain Bouchet split us into pairs to penetrate deeply into the city. The pastel blues and stark whites of the homes and the intricate, patterned detail carved into the columns and doorways keep my eyes darting from one building to the next. "We can't destroy this," I say in awe.

Finding no military presence, we return to where the general awaits our report. "We found no signs of any Spanish soldiers or resistance," Captain Bouchet tells him. "The townspeople have gathered several wagons full of gold and silver as a bounty to save their city from destruction."

The general nods. "Unfortunately, a few wagons of booty will not appease our soldiers' lust for revenge or their expectation for plunder." He looks sad, but resigned. "You veterans of Austerlitz and Prussia may not approve. Keep your men by the city gate and ensure the Spanish army does not try to trap us."

Believing they are entitled, our young French comrades proceed to loot and burn parts of the city. I can only watch in sorrow, mourning the beauty being destroyed.

* * *

The sack of Córdoba lasts four days, and our comrades' greed is shocking. The looting only stops when a horseman rides hard into the city, shouting, "The Despeñaperros Pass has been taken by the Spanish!"

Immediately, squadron leaders are summoned to the general's tent. After a brief meeting, the general says, "The Spanish have us trapped. They control the pass. We must retreat back toward the Sierra Morena to wait for reinforcements."

We retreat erratically in the sweltering heat, going back up the Guadalquivir River to the village of Andújar, not far from

Bailén. Burdened by five hundred wagons of loot, our progress is slow. The creaking wagons, loaded with plunder, stretch back as far as I can see. They continually break down. The young soldiers frantically make repairs, fearful of Spanish retribution but not wanting to leave anything behind. "Do they think they can actually get all of this back to France?" I ask Adrien, incredulous.

"Their officers are at fault, and the general should have stopped it. The only booty we've ever taken is food and drink and whatever we could carry on our horses." Adrien shakes his head in disgust.

* * *

The sun begins cresting the ridge of the Sierra Morena. Through the dusky light, I look around at the soldiers preparing the tools they will need for today's work. We've been mired for over four weeks in Andújar, waiting for reinforcements. I'm sure the Spanish are taking this time to build up their strength and train their soldiers. We've had no time for training. We spend all our time foraging for food.

The air is cool at this early hour, but the clear sky promises another day of intense heat. Before me is a large field of wheat, ready to harvest. "Too bad our comrades didn't pillage some food when they sacked Córdoba," I say to Adrien as he sharpens his weapon of the day, the scythe, in preparation for a long morning of mowing.

"I'd trade a bag of gold for a sack of grain," he replies as he stands up. "I guess we are lucky these fields are here, but it's hard to believe we are having to harvest the fields, grind the grain, and bake our own bread."

Whisk, whisk, come the sounds from Adrien's scythe as he moves into the wall of wheat, cutting the stalks with wide swings from right to left. I follow behind him with my sickle, not cutting the wheat, but using the sickle bow to gather bundles of the cut stems and laying them on the ground, ready to be secured. Corporal Charron follows me, pulling three to four stems of wheat from each bundle and using them to wrap around and tie the sheaf tightly.

"Do you think reinforcements will ever reach us?" the corporal asks me. "It's been over four weeks. Scouts report Spanish troops massed near Córdoba. We must do something soon!"

"Yes, Corporal. I'm sure the general has options he's considering."

In reality, I don't believe the general has any idea what to do.

Hours pass, and as the sun rises higher in the sky, the heat intensifies. I discarded my jacket hours ago and curse my woolen breeches.

"Time to rest," Captain Bouchet calls.

With the hot weather, we've adopted the Spanish custom of siesta. The hot sun will dry the sheaves of grain, making them ready to move to the threshing floor tonight.

Our squad settles at the river's edge, washing down and cooling off. "I never thought I'd turn to farming as a soldier," I say ruefully. "When we leave the army, I'm going back to work in my father's inn. No more farming!"

Corporal Charron calls out in a voice laced with panic. "Horses!"

I quickly grab my sabre and pistols, which are never far from me. Others along the river hear the rumbling hooves as well and retrieve their weapons, preparing for battle.

The rumble turns into a roar as we brace for the worst. We're an easy target, unprepared for an attack. If it's the Spanish, we are dead.

My heart beats madly as the first riders come into view. To my great relief, they are wearing French blue. "It's the reinforcements," I cry out. Cheers and shouts of joy erupt from our ranks, up and down the river.

* * *

In spite of our excitement, the reinforcements only add a few thousand men to our army and bring limited food, keeping our position in Andújar perilous. "At least the mountain pass is secure and we are no longer trapped," Adrien says. "I hope we can attack soon. All this waiting seems pointless."

"If we were smart, we'd retreat back to Madrid and organize a better invasion force. The uprising has spread everywhere, making the guerrillas and peasants as much a danger as the Spanish army."

We've been on patrol for several hours when a movement across the Guadalquivir River catches my eye. "Look up onto that ridge. There must be thousands of Spanish troops."

Captain Bouchet takes up his spyglass and regards the soldiers on the far hill. "We must immediately report back to General Dupont."

The captain and I report to General Dupont's encampment. The general paces as we make our report. "How many did you think there were again?"

"As large as a division, and there may be other armies out there as well," Captain Bouchet replies.

The general walks to his desk and begins to write furiously. Folding the page, he dabs hot wax on the crease and seals it with his signet ring.

"Take this to General Vedel. He's camped near the river. Tell him what you saw and relay the urgency of this order. He must march to Bailén immediately and shore up our line of defense along the river, as well as protecting the mountain pass. You and your men accompany him. Show him where you spotted the Spanish."

"Yes, sir." We salute and quickly mount our horses.

* * *

General Vedel's encampment is on the far side of Andújar. We wind our way through many companies of soldiers, each encircling their own set of plunder wagons. They eye us with suspicion.

We reach the general's command tent, and Captain Bouchet hands him the communiqué. Reading it quickly, he glances toward our captain. "You think maybe a division or more?"

"I do, sir."

The general again reads the note. Looking up, he says, "I agree with General Dupont. We must reinforce Bailén." He puts down the message. "The general also wishes your squad to accompany us."

"Yes, sir. I believe he feels our military experience will be helpful."

He eyes our uniforms. "Gentlemen, I see from your campaign ribbons that you have fought in the emperor's army for many years. Most of my men have only fought in the battle for the Alcolea Bridge. Hardly a great test of mettle. Yes, your experience will be most useful."

"Sir, if I may add, your men cannot take along their loot. I fear many of them will be reluctant to leave it behind."

The general's eyes narrow. "They will be told we will come back for it. If any refuse my order to march, they will be shot. You are dismissed, Captain."

He turns toward his aides. "Notify the men we move out within the hour. Only combat gear is to be taken. We march to Bailén."

On the far side of the encampment, a shot is fired. Then a little closer, another. *We are actually shooting our own men,* I think with revulsion.

* * *

Captain Bouchet is pointing to the ridge where we saw the Spanish army when a messenger comes riding at full gallop. "General Vedel," the messenger blurts out, "the Spanish have defeated us at Mengibar and taken the village. I fear they will attack Bailén next!"

"How many troops?"

"At least a division, sir."

The general wastes no time, ordering his aides to inform his company commanders of the situation. After dispatching his aides, he looks toward Captain Bouchet. "To Bailén!"

As Bailén comes into view, it appears deserted.

"Sir, with your permission, I will take my squadron and enter the village first," Captain Bouchet says.

The general nods.

Cautiously we enter, the captain dividing us into pairs to search different parts of the village. It's empty. Reporting back, Captain Bouchet tells the general, "There is no one in the village, not even our own troops."

"The Spanish must be trying to retake the pass," the general says. "We must follow and engage."

We march under darkening skies, making our way up the mountain road. The full moon reflects off the lightly colored boulders and outcroppings lining the road. We reach the summit by morning, but we don't find the Spanish army, only a scattering of lightly armed peasants.

The soldiers are weary from their night-long march. Not having an enemy to fight is a blessing. They collapse in place and drink thirstily from their canteens. The rising sun promises another blazing day.

Our squad dismounts near the general. There is panic in his face. Frantically, he meets with his aides and calls Captain

Bouchet over. His loud, rattled voice carries to me. 'I've made a grave error! The Spanish army must be moving on General Dupont. I don't know if we have enough time, but we must go back down into the valley and help them."

Bone-weary, the men grudgingly turn and head back down the mountain road. The troops stumble on the downhill grade, exhausted. Nearing Bailén, they cannot go farther, and the general orders a rest. We've been marching continuously since yesterday afternoon.

As his men crumple to the ground, General Vedel approaches our squad. Eyeing us all, he asks Captain Bouchet, 'Do your men have enough strength to scout ahead and see what is happening?"

The captain looks toward me. My shoulders droop with fatigue and my muscles ache, but I nod.

'If we can give our horses some feed and a quick drink, of course, sir," Captain Bouchet replies.

Bayard nuzzles up to me, appreciating the food, water, and short rest. 'Ready to go?" I ask him, patting his flanks.

After about a league, we begin hearing the sound of gunfire. The echo of a great battle funnels up the canyon. Captain Bouchet signals us to stop. 'Sergeant Bauck, ride back and inform General Vedel a battle is taking place in Bailén. The rest of you, follow me."

The captain leads us toward a protected area within a field of boulders. 'Lieutenant Calliet, come with me," he says as we dismount. 'Everyone else, remain with the horses. Return back up the pass if anything happens to us."

Captain Bouchet takes his looking glass from his saddle pouch. 'We need to see what's happening."

As we near the top, the din from the battle becomes deafening. Buzzards and ravens are already circling overhead. Puffs of cannon smoke come from the hills surrounding the village. Forces on all sides are converging on the town, but with the naked eye, I cannot tell who is Spanish and who is French. Captain Bouchet hands me the looking glass, deep concern lining his face.

I peer through the glass. A full division of French troops appear trapped. A white flag begins to wave within the French ranks. The sounds of battle slowly fade.

I hand the looking glass back to the captain. "It appears we are surrendering."

He takes the glass and looks through it intently. "Yes. Spanish generals are moving through the barricades and approaching General Dupont ... He is handing them his sword. It is over!"

We climb back down the ridge to our comrades just as General Vedel and his troops arrive. "Captain Bouchet, what have you learned?"

"Sir, General Dupont has surrendered."

Bailén Surrender

Thirty-Two

The Escape – Summer, 1808

Appearing stunned by this news, General Vedel says nothing for a few moments, staring at Captain Bouchet. 'Surrendered? How can this be? No army of the emperor has ever lost a battle. Are you certain, Captain?"

'Sir, I saw the white flag through my looking glass and saw General Dupont presenting his sword to the Spanish general."

The shocking news sweeps through the ranks, disturbing the deep confidence of the French army. 'They can't have surrendered," a few men shout in dismay. Other voices, now frightened, ring out everywhere.

'What will become of us?"

'What about our loot?"

'Will we be trapped in this wretched land forever?"

A few stand fast. 'We must fight on!"

'Silence!" the general bellows. 'We must see firsthand what is happening. We march to Bailén!"

'A rider from the valley!" a soldier calls.

A lone rider in a captain's uniform gallops up the road. His uniform is splattered with blood, and his face covered with black soot. Sweat streaks down his brow, cutting rivulets through the grime.

"Sir! I have a dispatch from General Dupont!"

General Vedel takes the message, turning it over as he examines it, noting the imprint in the wax seal. He hesitates, seeming reluctant to read its contents.

Looking over to the disheveled captain, he breaks the seal, then looks down to read.

Several moments pass as the general stares at the note.

"This was given to you directly by General Dupont?" he asks.

"Yes, sir."

"The general has surrendered?"

"Yes, sir."

General Vedel again stares at the note as a hush rolls along the line of soldiers.

"Dismount!" he orders. "All company commanders are to meet with me immediately." He points to a spot shaded by an immense boulder. "Over there."

A messenger mounts up to deliver the general's order, galloping alongside the long line of soldiers that stretches far into the mountain pass. Nervous murmuring becomes louder as it spreads among the thousands of soldiers along the road.

The general glances around, seemingly trying to organize his thoughts. He catches sight of Captain Bouchet. "Captain, I know you and your men are not assigned to my division, but please, join us. You must hear this news too."

General Vedel hands his reins to one of his attachés and slowly makes his way toward a high point within the shade. His walk is heavy.

"I think the general has orders to surrender," I whisper to Adrien.

Adrien's eyes blaze. "I'll never surrender as long as I have a sturdy horse and a sharp sabre!"

My stomach churns, hoping my speculation is wrong.

Within an hour, all the company commanders are gathered near General Vedel. He clutches the communiqué tightly. No sound can be heard as he stares out over the soldiers gathered to hear his commands, their expressions pained and their arms crossed.

Adrien and I are too far away to hear what the general says, but as he speaks, I see most of his commanders bowing their heads. Some go to a knee, holding their foreheads in cupped hands.

The general ends his speech by lifting his fist and shouting, "Vive la France, Vive l'empereur!" The commanders return the chant, but their voices are subdued.

"It can't be," Adrien whispers in disbelief. "We're going to be told to surrender and we haven't even fought yet!"

I press a hand on my friend's shoulder, glad to at least be with him at this dreaded moment. The thought of being a prisoner sickens me. I'd rather take my chances in the countryside trying to escape and die fighting than endure that humiliation. All these years fighting Austrians, Prussians, and Russians, and now this? Why are we even here? Spain was our ally.

Slowly, the general's company commanders disperse, going back to their troops. Only Captain Bouchet remains, talking earnestly with the general.

Word spreads quickly throughout the ranks that General Dupont has indeed surrendered, and that he has ordered General Vedel to do the same. Shouts of protest erupt, but they don't sound heartfelt. Each of us knows down deep that we can do nothing but follow the orders.

Our squad of fourteen is huddled near another boulder, keeping the sun's hot rays away as best we can. Captain Bouchet returns and calls us around.

"I'm sure you all have heard that General Vedel has been ordered to surrender his division to the Spanish," he says. "The terms of the surrender are generous. We are to give up our arms and then be taken to Cadiz. If we swear not to oppose the Spanish any further, we will be put on ships and returned home to France."

Captain Bouchet pauses and looks each of us in the eye. "The general is going to obey his orders, but he pointed out to me that our squad is not attached to his division. It will be our choice to surrender or not."

Nervous talk breaks out among us. "What does this mean? How would we survive? Where would we go?"

The captain holds up his arm to quiet us. "I told the general we would stay here while all the troops pass, then cover the rear flank from possible attack. After ensuring their safety, we would either join them or disappear into the mountains."

We wait silently for the captain to say more.

"Each of you will make your own decision. The odds of surviving while trying to escape over the mountains are slim. Surrendering may mean going home, or it could lead to years of confinement within a prison hulk in the Bay of Cadiz."

Again, the captain pauses and watches our faces closely.

"I intend to test my luck in the mountains," he says finally.

One of the young privates speaks up. "Sir, wouldn't we be captured by the peasants, and wouldn't they do to us what they did to Anton and Louis?" Others nod in agreement.

"That is a likely outcome."

The private's head drops.

"I will be joining the captain," I say firmly.

"As will I," Adrien adds emphatically.

"You needn't make your decision now," Captain Bouchet says. "It will take several hours before all our troops go by. Stand at attention to honor them. Once they pass, those who want to surrender can join the rear flank, and those who want to try and escape can stay. There is no loss of honor with either decision."

Our squad stands off to the side next to our horses. Heavy-footed soldiers pass, their faces frozen into distant stares. Bayard munches contently on scattered bunches of grass. The sun burns overhead, adding to everyone's misery.

As it sinks into the western horizon, the last of the troops ride by. "Mount up!" Captain Bouchet orders. Adrien and I position ourselves on each side of him. From the end of our line, the young private who spoke up earlier rides up before us, gives the captain and me a salute and Adrien a nod of his head, then joins the rear ranks of the army. One by one, members of our squad ride forward, give their salutes, then join the retreating line of soldiers. Corporal Charron is the last to ride forward. He gives his salutes, but doesn't join the others. "Sir, I would be honored to join you." He takes a place next to me.

As I watch the last of the soldiers disappear, panic grips me.

"What do we do now, sir?" I ask Captain Bouchet. "The enemy could be anywhere."

Captain Bouchet points up the hill. "Up there, just before the ridgetop by that cliff face, it looks like there is an opening. That could be a good spot for us to hide and watch for a while. We can't risk moving around until we have a sense of where people are."

Adrien is scanning the countryside as we dismount, preparing to lead our horses up the hill. "No sign of life right now, sir—but they could be anywhere."

"Keep a sharp eye," the captain says. "I fear guerrillas might be watching."

The last breath from today's sun is extinguished as it sinks beneath the horizon. We proceed up the hillside toward the cliff opening, praying we will find a cave. The going is rocky and steep. Heat still radiates from the ground. My brow drips with sweat, but I wonder, is it from the heat or my frayed nerves?

The captain points to a bush. "Corporal Charron, cut a branch from that bush and use it to brush out our tracks."

"Here, let me take your horse," I say. "You can't do both."

He nods appreciatively as he hands me his reins.

The last remnants of light show us the inside of an opening. "It's a cave!" Adrien whispers. He scrambles down to investigate. "It's not deep ... perhaps big enough to hide the horses, but not all of us. We'll need to stay low outside of the cave behind these rocks."

"Not ideal," the captain says, "but it will work. Let's quickly settle in as best we can."

I take my gear from Bayard and pour some water for him into a tin bowl. "Perhaps this will be our greatest adventure yet, my friend," I say as I pat his flanks, trying to see something good in our situation. "I'll get you some grass to eat."

Stepping a few feet away from the cave, I cut some grass with my sabre for my close companion and friend, reflecting back to my first horse, my beloved Hervé. *Austerlitz! It feels like a different lifetime since that fateful battle that cost Hervé his life and nearly cost mine. We fought with purpose then—to save France. What are we fighting for now?*

In the distance, I see the glow from thousands of campfires cutting pulses of light into the pitch black of the night. The stars form a welcome canopy with no moonlight to diminish their glow. Though exhausted, I'm calmer, feeling somewhat secure in our newfound hideaway.

A tiny light catches my eye far up the road toward the pass. Then there is another, and a third and fourth. I drop to my chest, though I know there is no way they could see me, and drop my voice to a loud whisper. "Lights! There are lights coming down from the pass."

I run to my companions near the cave opening. Captain Bouchet is scanning the lights through his looking glass. "What are they?" I ask.

The captain adjusts the glass's focus. "It's a group of about ten men—perhaps peasants, maybe guerrilla fighters. They seem to be checking the sides of the road, possibly looking for stragglers. They'll soon come up to where we went up the hill."

Adrien clasps my shoulder. We wait. I try desperately to see through the darkness. We hold our breath, waiting for the captain's next update.

"Nearly there ..." he says. "They've stopped. It looks like they have found our tracks! They're looking around, spreading out with their torches."

The three of us gasp as one. "*Scheiße*," Adrien mutters softly.

"They're going up the hillside ... Now they have stopped, flashing their torches around ... They're now moving back toward the road. They couldn't follow our tracks!"

Captain Bouchet lowers his looking glass. "Excellent job, Corporal Charron. You swept away our tracks well."

We shake each other's shoulders in triumph and relief. We have passed our first challenge.

"We need to stay here until our water runs out," Captain Bouchet says. "It will be dangerous to go down to the stream, but we'll soon have no choice, as our supply is short. Until then, let's keep close watch. Corporal Charron and I will take the first shift. Corporal, you watch the downhill and I'll watch the uphill. Lieutenant, Sergeant, get some sleep. I'll wake you in a few hours."

Bayard snorts as I make a sleeping spot for myself near him just outside of the cave. Adrien makes his next to mine. "Sleep well, my friend," I say. "I hope we made the right decision."

'It was the only decision we could make. Get some sleep, Jean-Luc."

Soon, I hear Adrien's heavy, rhythmic breathing. Sleep? How can I doze in our situation? I lie back, resting my head on my saddle. The stars are bright. Above me is the summer triangle. Piercing between Deneb and Altair and streaking toward Vega is a shooting star. Around my neck I find the locket that Anna Lise gave me so many years ago. I hold it in my palm.

* * *

'Lieutenant Calliet, Sergeant Bauck, it's nearly morning," Captain Bouchet says as he nudges us. I'm awake in an instant. Corporal Charron is still peering down the hillside toward the road coming up from the valley. Adrien takes a drink of water, offering me some as well.

"Thanks."

'No signs of life, sir?" I ask.

'No lights, but I swear there is some muffled rustling down by the road. I can't see anything in this dark."

I sit forward, straining to hear. 'Yes, I hear it too. Maybe our tracks were spotted after all and they're waiting until there is light before they come after us."

Suddenly Captain Bouchet orders, 'Quick! Pack up. We must leave now!"

A rock rolls behind me and another in front.

A hood slips over my head, and I'm pinned to the ground. 'Adrien, I can't see!" I cry out in panic. In an instant, my hands are bound, and I'm roughly pulled up to my feet.

"Captain, Adrien, are you there?"

A fist smashes into my stomach, and I double over in pain. Someone yells in Spanish. I'm jerked up again, then given a push to move down the hill. Stumbling, I do my best to move forward, but apparently not as fast as my captors wish. They give me a hard shove, throwing me into a tumble down the hillside. My head cracks against a rock, and blood runs down the side of my face.

All around me are angry voices and the grunts of my companions, who are also hurtling down the hillside. Up toward the cave, Bayard is whinnying loudly.

Finally, I am on level ground and sense the presence of many people. Male and female voices are murmuring indecipherably. Feet are shuffling.

"Señores, you thought you could get away from us? Just slip into the night without our knowing?" someone nearby says in broken French. "We've been watching all the while. The cave you were in. We know it well. You could never escape. How foolish of you to think so."

I take a deep breath, summoning the courage to face certain death. My back is straight, my head erect.

"Before you die, I want you to see the faces of the people whose farms you destroyed. Whose fathers, brothers, sisters, and children you killed."

Someone rips the hood from my head, and I see before me a gathering of families: men, women, and children. They stare at us. Most of their eyes are not filled with hate, but instead with sadness from the needless suffering they endured in this pointless war.

Men with machetes in hand pace back and forth in front of us, their eyes full of rage. I look toward Captain Bouchet, a man I've admired through all my years in the army. He has been my guiding light, and without him I would not have survived this long. I nod goodbye to him. He stands stoically, waiting to accept whatever is to become of him. He nods in return.

Corporal Charron stands next to the captain. Fear shines in his eyes, and tears run down his face. He is so young, still in his teens. I give him a nod too. He nods back weakly.

Adrien is by my side, as he's always been since we were young boys. "This must be our fate, my dearest friend," I say to him. "I'm glad we are meeting it together."

Tears come to his eyes, and with a trembling voice, he says, "Jean-Luc, I will see you again very soon."

I turn to face forward, expecting a machete blow at any moment.

There is some rustling in the crowd, and a peasant with a girl and two little boys pushes forward. He approaches the man who appears to be the leader of the execution squad.

I look at the two boys. *Are these the two we let live back when Anton and Louis were killed?* Looking over to Adrien, I see that he too seems to recognize them.

The peasant points in our direction as he talks. The head man stares over toward us with a look of disbelief on his face. He bends over and talks to the boys directly. The boys point to me, Adrien, and the captain as they answer the man's questions. With his machete, the man points toward Corporal Charron. The boys shake their heads no.

The men with machetes come together, and heated voices erupt. Several wave their blades toward Adrien and me, arguing loudly with their leader. He shakes his head.

The men look disgusted and turn their attention toward Captain Bouchet. The voices become even more heated, and some of them are pleading with open hands and knives held high. Again, he shakes his head.

Their leader points his machete toward Corporal Charron. The others talk among themselves, then nod in agreement.

The head man barks what sound like orders, and four of them take positions directly in front of each of us, their blades at the ready. Their leader raises his arm, and as he swings it down, I close my eyes, thinking this is the end.

A thick liquid splatters my cheek, but to my amazement, I'm still alive. Opening my eyes, I find the ropes binding my hands are being cut. Adrien and Captain Bouchet are being freed as well. Both look shocked that they are still alive. Then, I look toward where Corporal Charron stood. He is not there. Looking down, I see his decapitated body lying at my feet.

A man with a bloody machete holds up the corporal's head in triumph, displaying it to the assembled peasants. He smiles broadly, likely expecting cheers, but there are none. Instead, the families turn away and start down the road toward what remains of their farms. He shrugs his shoulders and spikes Corporal Charron's head onto a long staff, which he props up against a boulder.

The leader comes before us, shaking his head. 'Señores, you are very lucky to be alive. You won't be so fortunate next time. Your French army is far from here, and we are everywhere. This family can't protect you forever. Adiós!" He and his men head back up the road toward the pass.

'Jean-Luc, your face," says Adrien, concern lacing his voice. "You're bleeding badly!"

I try to step forward, but stumble and fall. A hand takes hold of my shoulder, and something wet is placed on my face. Steadying myself, I look up, and through a blur, I see the peasant girl. She is saying something, but all I make out is her young voice through the ringing in my ears. More voices—men's voices—off to the side. They must be the captain and Adrien, but I can't understand what they are saying. My mind is becoming fuzzy. *Yes, now I hear you, Adrien. We can't go fishing now. A girl's voice—is that you, Anna Lise?*

* * *

The smell of spices wakens me. The peasant girl is stirring a pot over a fire. Her two brothers are next to her; one clutches a pail of water, and the other is holding two small bowls. From one of them, she spoons a deeply colored yellow powder, dumping several scoops into the kettle. From the other, she fingers up a few delicate yellow sprigs, rubbing them into dust over the pot.

Jerking up in alarm, I look for Adrien and the captain. The girl sees my panic and points toward a shady area. My companions are with the girl's father, filling in a freshly dug hole. It must be Corporal Charron's grave.

Relieved, I settle back down, leaning into my saddle, still feeling weak and sick.

Looking skyward, I see that the sun is low in the west.

The girl brings over a cup of steaming liquid and hands it to me. She indicates I need to drink the potion. Taking a sniff of the pungent concoction, I hesitate. The girl mimes raising a cup to her lips and nods. Her two brothers are now with Bayard, staring at me with anticipation.

I take another sniff. The odor is disagreeable, but I take a sip.

Gulping, I nearly spit it out; the bitterness is overwhelming. She smiles, and the boys laugh. Again, she signals I need to drink it all. I grudgingly finish the cup, and then she gives me another. I look at her incredulously, but she nods, and I force down the second cup.

Finally, she gives me some water, and again I lean back into my saddle. My head still aches, but not as badly as before. The ringing in my ears is gone.

Bayard is nickering contently. The two boys are rubbing his neck and giving him handfuls of grass.

The weather is not as hot as it has been, with scattered clouds and a cool breeze coming up from the valley. The girl is laying out some bread, cheeses, dried meats, and fruit on a blanket. She must be nearly the same age as Anna Lise but is as dark-haired and brown-skinned as Anna Lise is blonde and fair.

The captain, Adrien, and the girl's father are heaping the last few shovelfuls of earth onto the grave. *I must pay my respects,* I think as I slowly get up. My walk is unsteady, and the girl rushes over to help. I point to show that I want to go to the grave, then put one arm around her shoulder and start to stagger toward the site. Adrien and Captain Bouchet see me coming and rush to help. They take over from the girl, saying, "Thank you, Aniceta."

As I stand by the corporal's grave, a wave of guilt overwhelms me. *I should have told him to surrender. He was so young and couldn't know the dangers of trying to escape.* Several moments pass in silence, then Adrien and the captain help me back toward where the peasant family wait for our return. How odd this is. Everything seems so peaceful.

We eat our meal as Captain Bouchet tells me what he has learned from the boy's father. "Do you remember the Germans we met near the summit of the pass?" he says. "There is a church with a large courtyard and stables in their village of Santa Elena. If we can get inside, we will be protected by church sanctuary. Then we can hope for a rescue party." The captain's eyes burn with hope.

"We have a chance, Jean-Luc, if we can get to Santa Elena," Adrien adds excitedly.

I look at my two eager friends. Their belief that we can escape is contagious. "How can we get there? We know the guerrillas are watching the pass road."

Captain Bouchet smiles as he unwraps a roll of paper.

"Señor Campo," he says, indicating the peasant who saved us, "has helped me draw a map of goat trails that go along the ridge to the north and drop down to Santa Elena just before the steep rise of the pass." The captain fervidly punches his finger to the map, then points up the hill. "We should leave as soon as you are up to it, Jean-Luc."

"I do feel better. The rest, food, and whatever Aniceta gave me have helped. I should be strong enough by tomorrow."

Señor Campo leans in and says something to Captain Bouchet. The captain responds in a questioning way, sweeping his hand from Señor Campo to his children.

Señor Campo nods and says something else to the captain.

Wide-eyed, the captain says, "Señor Campo has made a most generous offer. He says we should leave when it is dusk, but the trails are hard to see in the best of light, much less at dusk. He will lead us up onto the ridge tomorrow, then point out the trails we need to follow when the sun rises. The boys will take Bayard, and Aniceta will stay with you, Jean-Luc, helping when you need it. He says it's the least he could do after we saved his sons."

I clutch Adrien, a broad grin on my face. "We will see Colmar again, my friend."

"First, we must change into these peasant clothes that Señor Campo has brought us," Captain Bouchet says. "He said the people of his village found us clothes to wear that would fit us, again in thanks for saving the two boys."

The next afternoon, we change into the peasant clothes. The Campo family is ready to leave. "Let's go!" Captain Bouchet says, looking at Adrien and me excitedly.

The sun has set, and the slow progression from dusk to dark begins. We all peer nervously into the fading light, reassuring ourselves we are alone, but fearing guerrillas are watching.

Thirty-Three

Hiding – Fall, 1808

My head throbs and I'm having torouble keeping my blance. "Captain ... Adrien ... I must rest. You go ahead with the horses. Aniceta can stay with me. I'll be along shortly."

Captain Bouchet stops, and through the thickening darkness, I feel his eyes on me. "We can't leave you here, Lieutenant."

"You must! We are exposed on this hillside, and the horses are easy to see."

"I'll stay with Jean-Luc, Captain," Adrien whispers.

"No!" I say hoarsely. "The fewer of us, the better. Aniceta will help me once I catch my breath."

Señor Campo whispers something to his daughter, and she replies, "*Sí.*"

"Very well, Lieutenant. Once we are in a secure spot, Sergeant Bauck will come back for you."

Adrien and the captain continue up the hill. I raise my arm in their direction, signaling that I will be all right. Once they are out of sight, I lean over, putting my hand to my head.

Damn, this hurts. The gash in my forehead is throbbing so hard it feels like my heart will pound right through it.

Gentle hands grasp my shoulders and arms, helping me to the ground. A girl's voice says something unintelligible, and a canteen touches my lips. I'm too weak to drink but am so grateful for the water that trickles down my throat.

Anna Lise? Is that you? Are you taking care of me again?

Briefly opening my eyes, I realize I'm not home and this girl is not Anna Lise.

Aniceta helps me lie back against the hillside, pushing away some rocks near my head. As I sit with my hands clutching my forehead, the sounds of men and horses are fading away.

When I open my eyes again, my breathing is steady and the throbbing not as intense. It's now very dark. Aniceta's silhouette, illuminated by the light of the half-moon, stands near me. She touches my arm, and I nod to indicate it's better. A breeze flows up the hill, rustling a nearby bush, somehow warming and comforting. Blackness covers the valley below. Scattered on the distant hillsides are isolated campfires—likely those of goat herders, but maybe guerillas out looking for us. Bats flicker by, and only the muted sounds of their beating wings give them away.

After taking a few deep breaths, I stand. Aniceta wraps her arm around my waist, and we begin moving up the hill. I must stop after twenty or thirty steps. Another deep breath and another twenty or thirty steps. We repeat this process for about two hours, slowly making our way up the steep hillside.

Finally, we reach the ridgetop and a discernable trail. A branch cracks nearby. Aniceta and I freeze in our tracks. I pull out my sabre, and she reaches down for a rock.

Through the darkness, I hear a whisper. "Jean-Luc, is that you?"

"Adrien, thank God!" I breathe, sheathing my sword. Aniceta drops her stone. He comes forward, wrapping his arm around my other side.

"My friends, we've been so worried. The others are less than a league away, up this trail. Sunrise will be in a few hours. We must hurry. We can't be caught out in the open."

I nod, too weak to speak. Even with them supporting me, I must stop a few more times, but in about an hour, we join our companions. The first thing I hear is Bayard nickering his welcome. Then the captain greets me. Señor Campo and his sons rush to Aniceta, and the two boys hug her.

Sunrise is less than two hours away. Grimly, Captain Bouchet says, "We must try to reach a spring that Señor Campo says is not frequented often. He and his family must leave and try to return to the valley floor before sunrise so they are not seen on the hillside. Jean-Luc, can you ride?"

"Of course," I say weakly, not really knowing if I can.

Señor Campo and his family gather to say goodbye and wish us luck. We bow in thanks, and I take Aniceta's hand and kiss it, tears welling. Without her family, but especially without her and her brothers, I would not be alive.

The four of them disappear into the darkness, and the three of us are once again alone in enemy country.

"Mount up," the captain commands. "Sergeant Bauck, cut some branches to drag behind your horse. We must cover our tracks."

With Adrien's help, I climb onto Bayard. "You will do fine, my friend," he says. "Just stay close to Captain Bouchet." Soon we are going as fast as we dare on the dark, narrow goat trail.

Captain Bouchet comes to a stop as the first traces of morning light filter around us. He points to a tiny stream. "This rivulet must come from the spring Señor Campo told me about. He says it's about half a league up this ravine. Pray no one is there."

We make our way up the barely discernable trail along the stream. After we've ridden for a few minutes, Captain Bouchet holds up his hand to stop. We strain to hear any sounds beyond the trickle of the stream, but there is only silence. We start riding again, then stop once more to listen. Hearing nothing, the captain whispers, "The spring must be around that upcoming bend. I'll go ahead. Wait for my signal." Captain Bouchet disappears around a large boulder. Several moments pass before he reappears, motioning us to come up.

The spring gurgles up, forming a small pool of water, green grass lining its edges. We dismount and let our horses take a drink while Adrien and the captain scout the area. I sit near the water and splash some onto my head. The hike up the hill and the ride have exhausted me, and my head is pounding fiercely. The gash under my bandages throbs as I lie back on the soft grass. It's difficult staying awake while I wait for my friends.

* * *

Water splatters across my face. *What's going on?* I feel so hot and dizzy.

"Jean-Luc! Wake up!"

Looking up, I see Adrien leaning over me, lines of concern crossing his face. Captain Bouchet is there as well, his face looking equally distressed.

"I'm sorry. I dozed off. I was feeling so tired, and I needed to close my eyes."

Trying to stand, I'm so dizzy I nearly fall.

"Sit back down and let me check you over," Captain Bouchet says. His hand covers my forehead. "You have a fever, Lieutenant. We need to check your wound."

I close my eyes as Adrien pours water on my bandages. Someone is unwrapping them. The stench of rotting flesh floods over me as the last of the bindings are removed.

"There is infection," the captain says. "You need proper treatment."

Opening my eyes, I see the captain and Adrien exchanging worried glances.

"What can you do?" I ask, my words slurring.

"We need to cut away the worst of the infection, then cauterize the wound with a hot blade," the captain says. "It will be very painful, Lieutenant, but there is no choice."

I nod, hoping I will quickly pass out from the pain. "Get on with it," I say shakily.

Adrien builds a fire and places his dagger within the flames. Captain Bouchet sharpens his own knife.

"Ready, Jean-Luc?" the captain asks.

"Yes."

Adrien places a small branch between my teeth, telling me to bite hard. I can taste the bitter bark. Adrien holds my head between his knees and grabs my arms. Captain Bouchet straddles my body, his dagger at the ready. Adrien's knees tighten, my fingers dig into the soil, and I close my eyes just as the captain's dagger moves toward my wound. The blade touches my skin. Then comes the first cut. Piercing pain explodes, forcing my teeth to grind deeply into the wood. Tears run from my eyes, but I don't cry out. More cutting and more clenching on the branch. My arms shake, but Adrien holds tight.

"That's all the infection I can see. Adrien, hand me your dagger."

Briefly opening my eyes, I see the white-hot blade inching toward me. When I try to twist away, Adrien clenches his knees more tightly and grabs each end of the stick to keep me secure. I scream in agony, nearly biting through the branch as the sound of sizzling flesh intertwines with the smell of burning skin.

* * *

The sounds of nearby muffled voices stir me awake. *Have they finished cleaning out the infection? How long have I been out?* Touching my face, I feel fresh bandages, but quickly draw my fingers away, as the slightest touch sends searing pain roaring through me.

"Adrien, is that you? Captain Bouchet?" I say, my voice weak and rasping.

Footsteps move toward me, and soon both are kneeling by my side.

"Jean-Luc!" Adrien says. "You've been out for over a day. How does your forehead feel?"

"The two of you are no doctors," I say, managing a weak smile. "It hurts, but I don't feel feverish."

"That's good news, my friend," Adrien says. He eyes the captain. "As you said, we aren't doctors, and we're worried we didn't get all the infection. You are too weak to travel, and the nearest French presence is likely way back in Santa Cruz."

"I'll be strong again in a few days. We can travel toward Santa Cruz then."

"No, Lieutenant. Even if you were well, Santa Cruz is too far away, and we don't know if our army is still there. The sergeant and I have been talking. The German community is not far from here, and Señor Campo said they have a church with an interior courtyard and stables. We need to get to that church."

"Then we travel toward the Germans?"

"Not we. Sergeant Bauck is going to the Germans. They acted friendly when we met them before, and since the sergeant is Prussian, they may help us figure out how to get out of here. If we can get to the church, we can claim sanctuary and wait until our troops are nearby. The German village may not have a doctor, but they likely have someone more skilled in medical care than me or the sergeant."

"We are splitting up?" I say, looking at them both. "Is that wise?"

"Unless the French army sweeps across the pass, it's our only chance," Adrien says. "I'll need to leave Basile with the two of you. He would attract attention."

"What is your plan?"

"No plan at the moment. First, I need to see if the Germans will help, then I'll find a way to get back to the two of you. It may take some time. Fortunately, these clothes Señor Campo gave us will help me fit in. We still have some bread. Let's eat, and then I'll be on my way."

Our meal is exceptionally quiet—somber, really. This may be the last time I ever see my friend.

"We'll see you soon, Adrien. The captain and I will take care of Basile."

With tears in my eyes, I hug my friend and watch as he follows the spring's trail back to the main goat track. He stops and waves before he disappears.

* * *

It's been nearly two weeks since Adrien left for the German enclave, and I'm feeling much better. We moved and made our camp up the ravine from the spring, out of sight of any goat herder who might come by, being careful to minimize any disturbance to the ground around the pool.

I'm skinning and cleaning our catch of rabbits when Captain Bouchet returns quickly from one of our viewpoints. "A herder and his goats are coming toward the spring," he says in alarm. Clutching our sabres, we hide among the rocks.

The goats attack the pool of water as if they haven't drunk in some time. The herder walks around the pool, slowing in the areas most disturbed by our use, and I instinctively stiffen.

I look toward Captain Bouchet. *Should we attack?*

He's watching the goat herder closely. We see him hold a bag in the air and then put it down by the edge of the pool before herding his goats back down the trail.

The captain and I wait for several minutes after the herder and his goats have disappeared and then go to investigate the bag. Captain Bouchet opens it and finds a note on top of a supply of carrots, bread, cheese, and wine. "It's from Adrien!" he says excitedly.

Adrien! Thank God! He's alive!

Captain Bouchet scans the note, then looks up to me. "Good news. Adrien has found sympathizers among the Germans. They've hatched a plan to rescue us. I'll open a bottle of wine while you read."

I hold the note with trembling hands.

I'm at the church in the German village of Santa Elena and have learned our plight is well known. The guerillas search for us, but the Spanish peasants and those in the German community support our efforts to escape. Unfortunately, the Spanish have driven away our forces from Santa Cruz, and the closest are in Madrid. There is a rumor the emperor himself is coming to Spain with his most elite divisions. Maybe then we can escape. In the meantime, we need to get you to Santa Elena. The church is about to make its annual purchase of wine from the merchants in Bailén. A convoy of wagons is now leaving and should be returning up the pass road in the next few days. Make your way down to the road and wait in cover until they come. Be careful; guerillas still patrol the road.

Captain Bouchet hands me a glass of wine and a chunk of cheese. "Wonderful news. Tomorrow, we'll descend to a viewpoint overlooking the road and wait for them to go by on their way to Bailén. Once they pass, we'll move closer to the road and await their return."

We cook our rabbits on skewers over our campfire and drink wine. "Here's to Adrien," the captain toasts. "Our lives depend on his success!"

I know much danger is still ahead of us, but we have a real chance to survive. Our spirits are light, and the wine goes down easily. As the sun sets, I take water and feed to Bayard and the other horses. Finding my brush, I stroke Bayard, telling him we will be going home soon, though I know for Bayard, being with me is his home.

Returning to our fire, I find Captain Bouchet sipping his wine, deep in thought. He motions for me to sit, then fills my cup. "Lieutenant, I've known you and Sergeant Bauck for years—since Ulm and Austerlitz. I've come to trust and respect both of you and think you are my closest friends. It's hard to express friendship across the ranks, so I need to bluntly say it. I thought we were going to die when the guerillas captured us, and your nod of friendship at that moment meant everything to me."

I gaze over to the captain. I respect him more than anyone in the army, and lift my cup to him.

He continues. "Spain is a strange place, and for the first time, I question what our purpose is. Spain lost her fleet at Trafalgar, supporting us, and then we turned around and deposed their king. Why wouldn't they hate us? Then there was Madrid."

Captain Bouchet looks down into the fire, turning silent.

"Sir, Madrid was horrific," I say.

I poke a stick into the fire, sending hot embers into the sky as I weigh my next words.

"I considered desertion, or even letting myself die in battle."

The captain eyes me. "Such thoughts are understandable after what we did."

"You helped me regain my focus when Adrien and I were ambushed. Now I only hope the three of us escape this hell and return to France."

Again, I poke the fire, then look at Captain Bouchet. "Yes, I too consider you among my closest friends. I am honored to know you."

We both fall silent and stare into the flames. Bats flick by, devouring insects attracted by the light.

"Let's get some sleep, Lieutenant. We'll see if we are falling into a Spanish trap or if indeed Sergeant Bauck has found a way out for us."

* * *

The next morning, in the filtered light before dawn, the captain and I make our way down the hill. We find a spot high above the pass road with an expansive view both up and down the rutted lane. By midday, we spot a caravan of three empty wagons coming, making their way toward Bailén. Through his spyglass, the captain examines the entourage. "It's the Germans. Sergeant Bauck is with them. He's seated in the second wagon."

He hands me his spyglass and, to my joy, I see Adrien.

"We'll work our way down near the road," the captain says. "They'll likely be coming back by midday tomorrow."

Now close to the road and flush with excitement, we settle down for the remainder of the day among a field of boulders.

* * *

The sun is nearly overhead when the sound of creaking wheels comes up the pass. Captain Bouchet and I look at each other anxiously, then turn to see who is approaching. The first wagon comes into view. From his perch, the driver whips the straining horses while his passenger casually peers around. The second rounds the bend and appears the same. Still no sign of Adrien. The third comes by, and finally, there he is, sitting on the wagon's bench.

Captain Bouchet motions me not to move, and he peers down the road to see if there is anyone else coming. Satisfied that all is clear, he calls out, "Sergeant, we're over here."

The caravan stops and Adrien jumps out, running toward us. He embraces us both. "Come, we must hurry and hide you."

The others in the caravan act as though they are checking on their wagons as Captain Bouchet and I approach. Adrien takes our horses and ties them up at the end of the last wagon. He stores our saddles and gear in an opening under the cases of wine, blocked off at the end with more boxes.

He leads us to the second wagon. "Captain, quick, crawl into this hidden space. Jean-Luc, come with me to the first wagon and I'll show you where to hide."

I look at the space he wants me to go into, and panic overwhelms me.

"In there?"

"Yes, quickly, Jean-Luc," Adrien says, not noticing my disquiet. He looks around to see if anyone is watching.

I swallow hard and squeeze into the tight space between cases of wine. It's barely enough room to be on my knees and be able to lean forward onto my elbows. My sheathed sabre is by my side. Planks are layered above me, then more boxes of wine on top of them. My hands clench, and I concentrate on my breathing— one breath, then another, ensuring it stays in control.

"Are you set?" Adrien asks.

"Yes," I barely manage to say.

"Good! We travel on to Santa Elena. We should be at the church in two to three hours."

The wagons lurch forward.

Suppressing my anxiety is difficult. The space is becoming hot under the afternoon sun, and I can't see out. The boxes of wine shift in and out with the bouncing of the wagon, pressing me even more tightly into this nightmare. I try to concentrate on happy memories: fishing with Adrien when we were boys; eating Mademoiselle LeClair's salmon fillets on a bed of sauerkraut, smothered with my father's Riesling white sauce; riding on Shagyas with Anna Lise in the hills above Ostheim.

After a few hours, I hear shouting. The sound makes my heart race, distracting me from my fear of this entombment but bringing the new fear of being discovered. The wagons grind to a halt. One of our party asks if there is any trouble. In broken German, a voice says loudly, "We are looking for some renegade French soldiers. They were last seen in this area."

Guerrillas!

Several horses walk around the wagon, and I reach for my sabre, wishing there was enough room to draw it.

Something smashes into the crates, breaking several bottles.

"You Germans are much like the French, aren't you? Thinking you are superior to our people."

Another crash rocks the wagon. Wine now pours into my enclosure.

"What do you carry? Your friends the French?"

Another crunch, and more bottles are breaking.

In German-accented Spanish, a man says, "My family settled here over thirty years ago at the request of your king. We have seen no French soldiers and only carry our annual supply of wine for our church."

Now there is rattling among the wine bottles above my head. I clutch my sabre tightly, peering up through the emerging shafts of light to see if the guerrillas find my hideaway. Wine drips down onto my face.

"I'm sure you won't mind our taking some bottles of your wine. We get thirsty under this hot sun."

From farther back of our caravan, another voice calls out. "What of these horses? They look like they are from the French cavalry."

"I believe they are," a voice responds. "We purchased them in Bailén from the many they have there. They are strong and well cared for and will help with our farming."

More shuffling of horses around my wagon. Several voices are speaking excitedly in Spanish.

After several moments, the man speaking in broken German says, "Go ... but be warned ... we will kill anyone helping the French."

I breathe a sigh of relief as my wagon lurches forward.

After another hour, I hear voices and the creaking of gates as our caravan comes to a halt. We then move forward before quickly stopping again.

"You've returned with our wine," an older man's voice calls out in German. "Very good! Did you have any trouble on the road?"

"All went as planned, Father," Adrien replies. "We were able to secure all the wine. A band of guerillas searched us, breaking several bottles, but our cargo is secure."

The gates creak again, and soon the rack of wine bottles above my head is removed. The sun shines brightly in the late afternoon, and I shield my eyes as I climb from my shelter, stiff and sore but overjoyed to be free from this prison.

"Welcome to Santa Elena," the older voice says. "I am Father Schmidt. I believe this will be your home for some time."

Thirty-Four

Going Home –
Winter and Spring, 1809

We finally reach the ridgetop high above the mountain pass road. "This trail doesn't get any easier, does it, Bayard," I say. We stop to rest and gaze out over the valley, seeing the village of Santa Elena as a small speck in the distance. We're both hot and sweaty and thankful to escape the valley. "This cool breeze seems heaven-sent."

Bayard lets out a snort. He, too, appreciates the rest and the coolness.

'Look at the way those thunderheads are billowing high in the sky. I hope the goat herders are near so we can deliver their supplies and return to the church before the storm breaks."

These weekly trips into the mountains to deliver supplies have saved my sanity. During the first few weeks of our stay in Santa Elena, we never left the church grounds. Then we heard the guerrillas who normally patrolled the pass road had left to join their comrades near Ronda. Apparently, they hope to drive the French from there as well.

The welcome sound of bleating goats flows up the ridgetop trail toward us. Soon, the goat herder appears. "Herr Lieutenant, I saw you coming up the hill. Thank you for the supplies." He turns to look down the valley. "You need to return quickly to Santa Elena. That looks like a bad storm coming."

Hastily, we unload the supplies and say our farewells. Bayard and I turn to head back down the hill. After a short distance, a reflection from far up the pass catches my eye.

"What can that be, boy?" I say, reaching for Captain Bouchet's spyglass. Focusing, I see five mounted men coming down the pass toward Santa Elena. They look like guerrillas! I close the spyglass and return it to my satchel. "We must get down quickly to warn Adrien and the captain."

The hillside is too steep to ride, so I lead Bayard down as quickly as I can. Gusts of wind try to hold us back. The temperature is dropping, and sheets of hail begin pelting us. The sky turns dark, illuminated by streaks of lightning and accompanied by a chorus of resounding thunder.

"Let's take cover behind those boulders until the worst passes," I yell to Bayard.

We find shelter from the wind, but the hailstones pound us. The rumbling thunder now booms at nearly the same time as the lightning. Flashes are everywhere, lighting up the sky like a roaring campfire. I clutch Bayard, pressing him into the protecting stone. The storm's intensity seems to send a message: *Begone!*

Finally, the intensity of the storm subsides as it moves farther up the mountain, leaving the ground covered with a heavy layer of hail. The wind still howls, trying to push us back, but we have no choice except to continue our descent, despite the treacherous footing. I slip several times, falling to the ground. Bayard nearly loses his footing, but stays upright.

Reaching the bottom of the hill, I mount Bayard and we charge at full gallop toward Santa Elena. Sunbeams break through the clouds, leading our way. I ride up to the butcher shop, where Adrien has been helping, then jump from Bayard and slam open the shop door. Adrien is grinding meat for sausage and looks up in alarm at my sudden appearance.

"Guerrillas are coming! We must go to the church and find Captain Bouchet."

Adrien rips off his apron, and we dash out the door.

"Are they in the village?" Adrien asks as we hurry toward the church.

"Not yet. I saw them through the captain's spyglass. They were far up the road, and I'm sure this storm slowed them down."

The church's courtyard gate is open, and we rush in, finding Captain Bouchet talking with Father Schmidt.

"Captain, guerrillas are coming. We must close up the church grounds."

"Are you certain?" Father Schmidt asks.

"Yes, I saw five of them coming down from the pass."

"I hope they are not Muslim guerrillas who do not observe church sanctuary," Father Schmidt says. "Just closing the church grounds won't be enough. We must hide you just in case."

The priest thinks for several moments while the three of us wait anxiously.

"We will need to put your horses in harness and have them pull a wagon to the wheat fields. As for you three," the priest says, hesitating, "there is a secret chamber beneath the altar, only known to the priests." He waves over a novice and instructs him to deal with our horses. He then walks toward the church, all of us in tow.

"This place we're going is there to hide the body of Christ if we come under attack. It's large enough to hold a few men and has a shaft leading to the outside for light and air, but it's small. There isn't any other choice." We follow the priest, our sabres in hand.

Father Schmidt points toward the stone floor behind the altar. "It's there."

I see no evidence of an opening.

"See those carvings on the floor butting up to the altar? Those are the handles for lifting the slab covering the entrance."

We lift the stone and slide it back, revealing the chamber.

Sweat beads on my forehead. *Another entombment!* I survived the wagon; I can survive this.

"With this storm, they likely won't be here until tomorrow," Father Schmidt says. "Stay here, close to the altar. I will climb the steeple and watch for their approach. Once they are spotted, I will seal you in."

The night passes slowly. None of us can sleep. "Why do they come now?" Adrien asks. "Is something happening?"

"Maybe our army is on the move," Captain Bouchet says. "Maybe the emperor has come to Spain."

A few hours after dawn, Father Schmidt breathlessly rushes into the church. "They are here! Quickly, climb into the chamber."

A dim ray of light from the air shaft provides us a shadowy greeting as we lower ourselves into the enclosure. Blood surges to my head as I concentrate on breathing evenly. The effort makes the scar on my forehead pound. I shut my eyes tightly, and my hands clench and unclench. *I can do this.*

"Captain," Adrien says. "You once told us you met our Uncle Jean at Marengo, during the battle. To help us pass the time, could you tell us that story again? Jean-Luc, wouldn't you like to hear it?"

I open my eyes. *Does Adrien know of my fear of confined spaces? Does the captain? Are they trying to help?* "Yes, I would," I say, relieved by this distraction. "Uncle Jean was most grateful to you. You saved his life."

Captain Bouchet begins recounting in whispers about when he first met Uncle Jean. His storytelling helps. I still feel anxious, but I'm in control. Time passes, but there are no sounds from the outside. The captain finishes his story, and Adrien immediately starts speaking, seemingly wanting to ensure that I stay focused. "Isn't it ironic that I'm helping in the butcher shop? I remember the old sausage recipes like it was only yesterday. *Vati* would be proud."

Suddenly, we hear the church door crash open, followed by the thumping of many heavy boots on the stone floor. Instinctively, we all hold our breath and listen. The clatter from men walking above now seems to be everywhere, accompanied by the sound of tables being turned over, votive lamps shattered, and objects smashed.

"Where are they, priest?" a voice shouts in broken German. "We know they are here."

"Yes, they were, but they left when word came of your approach. They are likely high up in the mountains by now."

I hear the sound of a slap and someone falling to the ground. "You admit you hid them! We warned you anyone helping them would die! Lucky for you our orders say we can't kill priests."

A single set of boots clumps on the stone floor above us. "Priest, I was told the one with blonde hair helped in the butcher shop. We go there now."

He tells the others, "Destroy all the idolatry." I hear more crashing, then a rush of pounding feet as the men leave the church.

"They're going to kill Herr Timmerman! We must stop them," Adrien cries.

"Help me with the slab," Captain Bouchet orders.

We push away the lid and scramble out. With sabres drawn, we rush from the church. The butcher shop is close, and we come upon the guerrillas pulling Herr Timmerman from it. One guerrilla has a machete in hand, and the weeping butcher is thrown on the ground at his feet. The crowd of villagers see us coming and open a path for us. Adrien charges the man with the machete, quickly severing his head.

Within minutes, only one guerrilla is left, and his skills as a swordsman are impressive. His back against the shop wall, he continues to defy us, parrying away our thrusts. Then he stops, holding his sword high. "This village will be leveled once our fate is known!" He then storms at Adrien, who buries his sabre in the guerrilla's chest.

Herr Timmerman scrambles to his feet.

Father Schmidt crosses himself as he comes up to us. "He's right," the priest says. "If it becomes known they were slain here, we will all be killed and the village destroyed."

Fear etches his face and the faces of all the villagers.

Captain Bouchet looks over those gathered round. "We will take their bodies and horses with us and make it look like we attacked and killed them far up the road. Clean up the church and replace its statues. When their comrades come, say you saw us riding on the ridgetop above your village, heading for the pass summit, just before the storm hit."

The three of us pack the bodies onto the guerilla's horses while ours are retrieved from the field. The villagers stay gathered around us, unsure what to do next. Some have brought us bread, and Herr Timmerman gives each of us a satchel filled with dried sausages.

We mount our horses and nod thanks to all the villagers. "Viel glück," they say—good luck. Father Schmidt blesses each of us, then asks Captain Bouchet, "What will you do? Where will you go? Once the bodies are found, guerrillas will mass and search everywhere for you."

"We will have to ride hard and fast for Madrid and hope your blessing will protect us. With luck, we will be there in two to three days." Captain Bouchet looks up into the sky. "The weather is turning. I hope it's not snowing at the summit. Farewell, my friends."

Our fate is now cast. I estimate it's sixty leagues to Madrid. A lot of enemy ground to cover. We can only hope we'll get lucky and come across a French patrol.

The going is slow as we look to see where the guerrillas camped during the storm. We want to leave their bodies at this spot so that it looks like we ambushed them there. A cold wind rushes up the narrowing canyon. Dark clouds thicken above us.

"Over there, under those boulders. That looks like the spot," Adrien says as he points toward the remnants of a recent campfire.

We take the bodies and arrange them strategically in defensive positions, placing their swords in their hands. Adrien pulls the decapitated guerrilla's head from a sack and places it just downhill of the body. We tie up their horses to the nearby trees, then shuffle our feet around the location to give it the look of a struggle.

"That should be good," says Captain Bouchet. "Let's get going."

The grade is becoming steeper as we approach the summit, and we can go no faster than a walk. Snow begins to fall—lightly at first, but becoming increasingly heavy.

"Let me ride ahead of the two of you so that if we come upon a guerrilla outpost, they will only see me," the captain says. He disappears into the falling snow, and we follow his tracks. The wind is howling, and the captain's tracks are quickly disappearing. Finally, the ground levels and begins to drop. We've reached the summit!

A shadowy figure appears ahead of us. Both Adrien and I draw our sabres. The form turns toward us with its hand raised.

'It's the captain," I whisper. We sheath our swords and come up next to him.

'See over to the right?" The captain says softly. 'A campfire. It must be an outpost. This snow and wind are our first blessings. The snow will keep us hidden and soften the sound of the hooves. The wind will quickly erase our tracks."

In single file, we slowly ride past the unsuspecting guerrillas. Down the mountainside we go, gaining speed as the snow lightens and the temperature rises. Elation overcomes me. We've passed our first trial!

It's now dark, and we slow our pace to a walk. Light rain is falling, and we can barely see the road. 'I'm hoping we can get past Santa Cruz de Mudela before dawn," says the captain. 'We can hide and rest then."

The excitement of finally attempting our escape keeps me wide awake. We slide by the edges of the small village of Almuradiel and can now see the fires from Santa Cruz. The air smells newly washed, and stars peek through the diminishing clouds. We follow a road that leads around Santa Cruz in the grayness of predawn.

Captain Bouchet points to a ruin near the edge of the road. "There's an abandoned building. Let's shelter there and get some rest."

We find that the ruin has only a front façade. The side walls have crumbled, and the rear wall is completely collapsed.

'It looks like others have used this spot for shelter as well," I say, seeing an area cleared of rubble and a spot where fires have burned.

'I'll keep first watch," the captain says. 'You two get some sleep before we move on. We need to stay ahead of any news regarding the guerrillas we killed."

Despite the pounding of my scar, exhaustion pulls me into deep sleep.

Someone shakes my shoulder to wake me, and I see Captain Bouchet's face. Outside, the midmorning sun peeks through the clouds. Adrien is awake now too, and the captain holds his finger to his lips. "Something is happening," he whispers. "Many horsemen just galloped by—heading east, away from Madrid."

I look through an opening just as a peasant family guiding a mule-drawn cart creaks by. Nearby are two horsemen who appear to be guerrillas. A boy in the cart sees me and starts pointing and yelling. The two horsemen take note, draw their swords, and move to see inside. Adrien and the captain hide behind some rubble, and I raise my hands as the guerrillas come around and see me. They dismount and move forward, appearing wary of the situation. Adrien and the captain leap from their positions and quickly dispatch the two intruders.

"We must leave now!" Captain Bouchet commands.

We ride north furiously toward Madrid.

For nearly a league, we see no one. Then, up ahead, we see several riders in the uniform of the Spanish army who signal for us to stop. "Ride through them in attack formation," the captain shouts.

We charge, felling many but not all. The survivors are quick to pursue. Our horses have superior speed, and we soon distance ourselves from all except one rider, mounted on a fine, black stallion. As he closes in, Captain Bouchet wheels to the left and confronts him. The rider is an exceptional swordsman, and he gains an advantage over the captain. He is nearly ready for his final thrust when an explosion rips the air. The Spaniard's eyes widen in surprise as he drops his sword and falls to the ground, dead. I stash my pistol, and we are off again just as the other Spaniards begin closing in.

Realizing they cannot catch up to us, they break off their pursuit. We slow our horses to a walk as we continue in the direction of Madrid. We no longer come across able-bodied enemy soldiers, but rather the rag-tag remnants of a defeated army. They pay no attention to us, but focus only on moving forward, one step at a time.

The sound of cannon reverberates through the air, at first distant but now closer. "It must be our army!" Adrien exclaims. "We made it!"

Coming to a ridgetop, we see the carnage of battle below. The cannon go silent, and our cavalry is charging through the fleeing Spanish soldiers, mowing them down like a scythe through wheat. No prisoners are being taken.

"We are not in uniform!" Adrien says. "Will they know we are not an enemy?" A patrol surges toward us, their sabres held high.

We sheath our swords and raise our hands, yelling, "We are French! We are French!"

The lieutenant leading their charge comes to an abrupt halt, just feet from us. The others circle around, their swords ready.

"You are French?" the lieutenant asks. "Where did you come from, and why are you dressed like Spanish peasants?"

The captain quickly sums up our past few months.

"You escaped from the disgrace of Bailén? Or are you deserters? Come, we will have General Saint-Cyr deal with you."

We are led away as prisoners and presented to the general at his field headquarters. Captain Bouchet details our months in hiding, starting from when General Vedel said our squad could attempt an escape. He describes our time in Santa Elena and finally our dash for freedom over the pass and to this battle site, where we were taken into custody. The general listens without asking questions.

At the end, he says, "A remarkable story, Captain. After the Bailén surrender, the Spanish returned Generals Dupont and Vedel to France, and they were immediately court martialed. The emperor provided copies of their court martial statements to all of his commanding officers as a warning about the results of incompetence. In his statement, General Vedel noted that he gave your squad the option of surrendering. It is fortunate you didn't join the others, as nearly all your comrades were slaughtered."

The general spits in disgust onto the ground. "The Spanish call themselves Christian, but they are nothing but barbarians."

Picking up his quill, the general begins to write something. "The emperor is in Madrid, preparing to return to France. He will be most interested in your eyewitness account of what happened." He finishes two notes and impresses his seal on each.

Handing us the first, he says, "This will ensure your safe passage to Madrid and must be presented to one of the emperor's attachés. He will set up the appointment to see the emperor."

He reaches for the other note. "Once you have seen the emperor's attaché, present this to the quartermaster. You need to be properly dressed in new uniforms for your meeting."

The general rises and gives us each a salute. "Welcome home, and congratulations on your remarkable escape."

* * *

We enter Madrid through the Puerta de Alcalá. Sorrow cascades over me at the sight of the gate and the bustling marketplace nearby. I can't bear to see this spot with its many memories of Manuel and the Arroyo family. I keep my eyes lowered, not wanting to see anyone along the avenue. What would I do if Señor Arroyo saw me?

We slowly make our way along the Calle de Alcalá, which ends at the palace where the emperor resides. The image of the dead padre seems to accompany us. The guards at the palace give challenge, but after reading our papers, direct us toward where we must go.

"Welcome. We've been expecting you," the attaché says. "General Saint-Cyr included news about meeting you in his daily dispatch, which arrived a short time ago. The emperor is most anxious to meet with you. Come this way."

"Shouldn't we report to the quartermaster first so as to be properly dressed?" Captain Bouchet asks.

"No, the emperor made it clear that he is to be informed immediately upon your arrival. Uniforms can wait."

We are ushered into an ornate waiting room. The room is filled with many officers dressed in their finery, waiting their turn to speak with the emperor. All eyes turn to stare at us as we enter. They whisper among themselves as they look us up and down. Some hold their noses at the odor emanating from our old and tattered clothes. We stand in a parade rest stance, ignoring them as best we can.

"Captain Bouchet, Lieutenant Calliet, and Sergeant Bauck? This way, please."

The whispers become more intense as we are ushered in before any of them.

As we enter the room, a stout man of about medium height, dressed in a dust-gray cloak, white breeches, and top boots, greets us. One would never know he is the most powerful man on Earth.

As we formally salute and bow, he says, "Enough of that. Please, sit here close to me. I understand you are good friends of General Rapp, a particular favorite of mine. It seems he is always victorious, but always wounded, no matter the campaign."

We talk for several minutes as though we are old acquaintances catching each other up on our lives, but then his eyes turn serious. "The three of you are fortunate to have survived so long, hiding from the enemy deep in their territory. You are also lucky you did not surrender. Bailén is a stain on our empire, and it cannot happen again. I believe General Saint-Cyr has told you most of the men who surrendered are now dead. General Dupont and General Vedel have both been repatriated and court-martialed. I've read their statements, but I would like to hear your observations of the campaign." The emperor stands and moves to look out the window.

"Your majesty," Captain Bouchet says. "I find it difficult to say anything against my superiors."

"But I am your emperor, and I need to know." Napoleon turns and looks at each of us. "Please, start with the sacking of Córdoba."

Captain Bouchet leads our side of the conversation, but both Adrien and I join in. We tell him about the five hundred wagons of loot taken from Córdoba despite the city opening its gates to us, as well as the number of poorly trained troops and lack of discipline.

"Your majesty, the bottom line is that General Dupont and General Vedel had never led men into a major engagement and were ill-equipped to lead this campaign, much less men unprepared to be soldiers," Captain Bouchet says.

The emperor paces as he listens to us. "Perhaps the ultimate blame is mine," he says.

"Placing blame is a game of hindsight, often misplayed," says Captain Bouchet. "There were poor decisions made in the field and lessons to be learned from Bailén, but I would not be able to place blame on anyone."

The emperor cocks his head at this comment but does not reply to it directly. "One consequence of Bailén is that our enemies are emboldened. I've received word Austria plans to attack us, thinking we are now weak. I'm leaving soon for Paris to prepare for war."

Still pacing, he adds, "I have sent orders to General Rapp inviting him to join me in this new Austrian campaign. I hope the three of you can join us as well with your new ranks of major, captain, and lieutenant."

We look at each other in astonishment. "Of course, your majesty. We are honored," Captain Bouchet—now Major Bouchet—says.

Sitting down, the emperor writes several notes, impresses them with his seal, and hands them to us. "These are your orders and my proclamations of your promotions. General Rapp will be most pleased to see you."

We salute and make our way to the quartermaster station.

"Home! We are going home!" Adrien exclaims, forgetting that he vowed never to return to Colmar.

Major Bouchet smiles and slaps each of us on the back.

I smile as well, relieved to finally be leaving this cursed country.

Thirty-Five

Ostheim - Late Fall, 1811

I sit at my desk, a candle in a holder burning at each end, buried deep in paperwork. There is a knock on my door. "Yes?"

"Captain, an officer on horseback is approaching," my assistant says.

"Alone?"

"Yes, sir. He's coming down the Strasbourg road."

I get up and walk to the porch. A cool November breeze stirs up a pile of leaves, and they swirl up several feet before darting across the road. Another rises up. Ominous clouds hang low over the nearby Vosges. The clouds move to obscure the sun, giving an eerie duskiness to the landscape despite the midday hour.

Have I held this post for nearly two years now? I look toward the advancing lone horseman as my thoughts stray to how I got here.

It was Uncle Jean's idea to have me posted as the commander of the Ostheim barracks to replace the buffoon colonel who was forced to resign. "You need to recover from your head injury," he said. "It's the perfect posting for you. You loved the administrative details of running the Charité in Berlin. Adrien and Major Bouchet will fight this Austrian war with me."

The horseman draws nearer. "It's Adrien!" I say in disbelief, recognizing Basile's unmistakable gait. I haven't seen my friend since the end of the Austrian war, almost a year ago. He's been assisting Uncle Jean, who has become governor-general of Danzig.

My dearest friend dismounts and we embrace, slapping each other on the back.

"It's been too long," I say. "What a joy to see you again!"

"Jean-Luc, I've missed you so much. You look well!" Peering about the grounds, Adrien adds, "The old barracks look the same as they did when we helped train the Shagyas years ago. Is Quartermaster Beaulac still here?"

"Yes, he is, and still as ornery as ever. Let's go to the stables and see him—but first, what brings you to Ostheim?"

"I have news and a proposition Uncle Jean and I want you to consider." Adrien's words tumble out. "It appears war with Russia is coming, and we want you to be with us for the fight. We can find my family and rescue Anna Lise from Moscow ..." His voice trails off. "That is, if you are well, if your headaches have eased."

"My headaches rarely occur anymore." I push hair back from my forehead. "I'll always have this scar, but it doesn't ache like before. Having this assignment made my recovery easier. Dealing with paperwork and caring for Shagyas is much easier than fighting Austrians or escaping guerrillas. But you say war with Russia?" My stomach tightens.

Up ahead, Quartermaster Beaulac is stepping out of the stables. He spots us and gives a wave of recognition. "We will talk about this later, Adrien."

"Lieutenant Bauck, is that you?" the quartermaster says as he embraces Adrien. "What brings you to this backwater? Just stopping by to chat?" The quartermaster looks both of us over, grinning, as happy to see Adrien as I am.

"It's midday," I say. "The three of us can have some food and talk." I wave over my assistant, who has been trailing behind. "Have the cook prepare us a meal. We'll eat in my office."

He salutes and dashes toward the kitchen. Adrien asks the quartermaster about the Shagyas as I ponder what Adrien said. *War with Russia? I've grown accustomed to not fighting. Will we find Anna Lise?* A smile crosses my face, then a deep fear rises. *I'm not sure I could face her after what I did in Spain.*

Over lunch, Adrien tells us of his duties in Danzig. "The work with Uncle Jean is fascinating. We have intelligence networks in Prussia, Sweden, and Russia. Our sources are telling us the tsar is becoming dissatisfied with the embargo against trade with the British. Many in his royal family are losing money and have begun smuggling to avoid the trade barrier. I'm on my way to Paris to report these findings."

"So, there is only the possibility of war?" I ask. "The emperor has not yet learned of this smuggling? Surely he must know."

"Yes, he has gotten previous reports about some smuggling, but now it's widespread. I'm sure he won't stand for it."

"For once I'm glad I'm getting old," Quartermaster Beaulac chuckles. "I don't need to worry about marching into battle anymore, unless someone attacks Ostheim."

Adrien does not mention his proposition for me to join him and Uncle Jean in battle if we go to war with Russia.

We finish our meal and walk out onto the porch. "How long are you here?"

"I must leave for Paris in the morning. This intelligence can't wait."

I pause, thinking about how to continue.

"Why don't the two of us camp tonight on the promontory overlooking the Rhine," I say. "We always enjoyed going there."

"Great idea, Jean-Luc, if the weather holds." He looks up to the sky. "It looks like the clouds are moving on. We can talk, have some wine, stare at the stars, and remember the old days. Sounds perfect."

"Good! Let's meet at the stables an hour before sundown. I'll have my assistant gather some food and wine. You and Quartermaster Beaulac go check out the new colts. Basile will be ready to retire to pasture before too long. One of the new colts might catch your eye. I need to finish up some paperwork before we leave."

Adrien laughs. "I can't imagine life without Basile, but you are right. He has earned a rest. Perhaps after our next campaign."

Adrien and Quartermaster Beaulac move toward the stable while I settle at my desk. The remaining work is cursory and takes little time. I pour myself a glass of cognac and open a locked drawer in my desk. The compartment holds a handful of letters, and I pull out the top one, the most recent from Anna Lise and the one that touches my heart the most. How many times have I read and reread these words and the other letters from her? Why did it take me so many months to finally write back? I treasure them all. Taking a sip, I read:

My dearest Jean-Luc,

How much I miss the warm summers and mild winters of Colmar. Moscow becomes frightfully cold in the winter—unbearable, really.

I was very happy to learn in your last letter of your appointment to commander of the Ostheim barracks. You always loved the Shagyas so much. Do you ever ride up to the overlook where you and I rode the day before I left for Moscow? Such a beautiful place! I remember the eagle overhead, watching over us. Do you think we are still being watched over? That day, riding the Shagyas and then fishing for trout, was the most perfect day of my life. How I dream there will be more days such as that.

Adrien hasn't written. How did he take the news of Madame Kintelberger getting married? He seemed very fond of her. I was glad to hear he is now a lieutenant and that he fought bravely against the Austrians. I'm thankful you did not fight in that war.

You wrote little of your time in Spain. The stilt-walkers sound amazing, but what of your time in Madrid and Andalusia? You say you met the emperor and he personally promoted you to captain. You must tell me more. I want to hear everything.

It's unfortunate that letters take so long to be delivered. Your last one took six months. I cherish each of them.

I'm sorry for sounding so homesick, but Colmar is my home and I dearly wish we would return. Unfortunately, Vati is doing well here and likes being part of the German community. There is little chance he will want to return to Colmar. Remember that promise Adrien made both of us take? That we are to meet again? Probably only a wistful thought, but one I hope can come true.

Write to me soon.
My love,

Anna Lise.

I fold the letter, bowing my head in thought. *She wants to know everything about Madrid and Andalusia. She would reel in horror if she knew the full story.*

* * *

Adrien and I meet at the stables and soon are on the trail leading to the overlook. The path snakes among ancient oak trees as we ascend. Their branches are haunting in the growing dusk. Cold gusts of wind remind me that it is nearly winter, but the clouds have cleared. We make good time and soon reach our destination. I look around, searching for the golden eagle that accompanied Anna Lise and me to this same spot, but he is nowhere to be seen.

After tying our horses to a nearby tree, I take the satchel my assistant gave me and look inside. Bread, cheese, sausage, and several bottles of wine.

I point toward a large boulder nearby. "We've always watched the river from up there. Let's go up."

We climb to the smooth surface at its top and sit. Darkness creeps in. Above me are the stars, the half-moon reflecting off the trees, and, in the distance, the many fires along the river. I open a bottle for each of us.

I take a bite of food and a gulp of wine. "Tell me how you think we can possibly find Anna Lise and the rest of your family."

Excitement fills Adrien's voice. "Taking Moscow will likely be one of our main objectives. It's an opportunity to bring my family home. They need to be in Colmar, not Moscow, and of course you know Anna Lise needs to be with you."

"She might not think so."

"She will. I'm certain!"

I take another long drink from my bottle and lay my head back, staring into the sky. *Adrien is right. Anna Lise shouldn't be in Moscow, but would she want to be with me? That is her choice. If it was mine, we would be together, forever ...*

"Adrien, look over there to the south. This is the first time I've seen Orion's belt this season. My father always told me that its three mighty stars are the great teachers of the night sky. Gaze at them, and your mind clears." I take another drink. "Perhaps their appearance tonight is an omen. Maybe you are right. Maybe we can find your family."

"Of course I'm right! Our army will subdue the Russians and we will be able to rescue them!"

"Moscow is a big place. We might not be able to locate them. But what if we find them? Do you think your parents want to leave Moscow? Do you think Anna Lise will want anything to do with us after I tell her about Madrid? We murdered those people."

Adrien glares at me. "We only followed orders. We had no choice! You needn't tell her about the massacre."

"You know I must. I could never hide that from her."

"Why not? I don't intend to tell her or my parents. Some things need to remain unspoken."

"We are different people, Adrien. I still have nightmares. Seeing the padre, his head bowed in prayer, waiting to be shot. Being unable to stop Manuel from being killed. The visions from that day send chills up my spine."

Adrien eyes me, contemplating.

"You're right, Jean-Luc. We are different. I know you will feel compelled to tell her, but you must also tell her we saved those boys in Andalusia."

"Those boys? They were innocents. No one would have killed them."

"Don't you remember? We were ordered to kill them. Only by the grace of God did they survive. Only because we let them free." He pauses. "I know that you and Anna Lise are meant to be together, no matter what we have done. I feel it in my bones."

We don't talk for several minutes as we both swig our wine reflectively.

Finally, I say, "We should have disobeyed orders and refused to shoot those people."

"And to what end? They would have died regardless of what you or I did, and a refusal would have led to our own deaths. We needed to follow the only alternative given, and we did that. She will understand. She has always understood you, Jean-Luc."

A long silence ensues. "All right, Adrien," I say. "If war with Russia comes, I will join you and Uncle Jean. We will find your parents and Anna Lise."

"Excellent!" Adrien cries, embracing me tightly. "We will do our best to find them!"

My chest tightens with apprehension.

* * *

Winter has turned into spring, and the rumors of war grow fervent. I've resigned myself to the inevitability of fighting Russia. I fear it will become nothing more than another Spanish campaign, but my happiness at the thought of seeing Anna Lise overcomes that dread. She is a touchstone to my past and, perhaps, my future.

Looking out my window, I notice the new leaves on the trees that shade my office. They catch the breeze, and the branches sway rhythmically. Beyond the trees, I see two riders approaching. With the talk of war, we've had many visitors from officers requisitioning young Shagyas for the cavalry. These riders are probably doing the same. I return to my desk to attack the never-ending paperwork.

Minutes later, I hear boots clomp on my porch, and my front door opens. A voice addresses my assistant. "I am Major DeLong to see Captain Calliet. It's most urgent."

The major is ushered into my office, and the young corporal who accompanied him is out in the foyer. After a salute, Major

DeLong hands me a sealed document bearing Uncle Jean's distinctive stamp. I break the seal and read it twice.

"War is imminent?" I say sharply.

"Yes, Captain. General Rapp wants you to quickly wrap up your duties here and ride to Danzig to join his forces. Our troops are massing there, preparing to cross the Nieman River. I am your Ostheim relief."

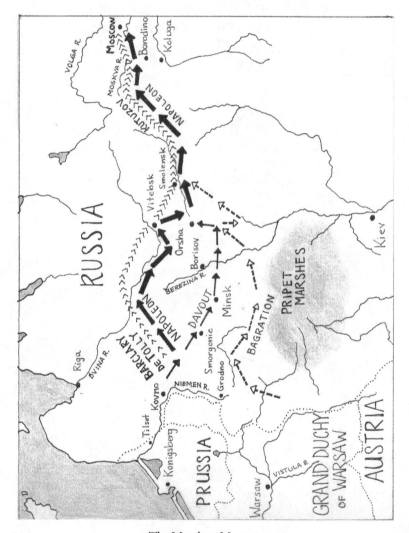

The March to Moscow

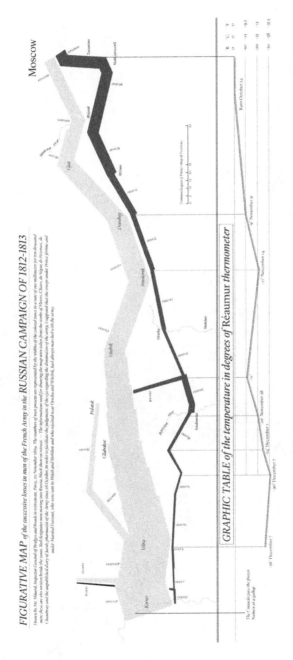

Illustration of French Losses in the Russian Campaign

393

Thirty-Six

Crossing the Nieman – June 1812

Sappers crowd the riverbank, cutting trees and laying out their ropes and tools, preparing to build three pontoon bridges across the Nieman. "We ford the river over there!" Major Bouchet shouts to his company of about one hundred Hussars, pointing to a calm stretch of the river. I gaze out over the water. I have crossed many rivers while in the army, and though this one is very wide, the section we are about to cross appears manageable. But I know I need to be cautious, as rivers are always dangerous. I have never been a strong swimmer.

I look at Adrien, hardly believing we are actually going to cross over into the Russian province of Lithuania. "To Moscow," I say, forcing a smile.

"To Moscow!" Adrien replies, his eyes wide and his face flush with excitement.

We splash into the cold water, pressing our horses forward into the river's increasing depth. As we enter the main channel, our forces drift apart. The current is strong. "Keep swimming, Bayard," I say, more for my own benefit than his. "The other bank is not far." We strain as the current stretches its fingers to pull us downriver. Bayard begins to struggle, his breathing becoming strained. Giving a hard kick, I feel him lean forward, extending his legs ever farther. "Keep pushing. We're almost there!"

Thoughts of drowning flash across my mind. If I slip off Bayard, will I be pulled under by the weight of my uniform? My breathing is as labored as Bayard's. Finally, his legs scrape the river's bottom. I sag forward, clutching his neck in relief.

Reaching shore, I look around and see Adrien and Basile scrambling up the riverbank. Adrien's face is ashen and his eyes wide. He shakes his head, looking as thankful as I am to be on dry land.

"Calliet. Bauck!" Major Bouchet shouts from the top of the riverbank.

"Yes, sir?"

He points downriver. "Those four are having difficulty. Take some men and throw ropes to them before they drift away. Quickly!"

We throw the ropes several times, but our efforts fail. Exhaustion overcomes our comrades as they flail for the ropes but drift farther downstream. "Into the river!" I cry. "We must get closer."

Urgency keeps my fears of drowning at bay as we throw and rethrow the ropes. Finally, lines reach all four. Each of them ties the line to his saddle pommel, and we do the same. We begin to pull them in as our horses scramble back onto the riverbank. I am pulling the fourth man in when he is suddenly swept into a stronger current where a creek joins the Nieman.

"Hold him, Bayard," I shout, but the rope is jerked off my saddle pommel. It burns into my gloves, and I'm unable to keep it from slipping. The man panics and jumps from his horse, clutching onto the line. His head bobs, then disappears, despite my effort. The line slackens, and I see him float to the surface, face down. His body rushes downriver, following the corpse of his abandoned horse.

My shoulders sag, staring at the body as it drifts from sight. Adrien comes up to me. "You could do no more, Jean-Luc."

We rejoin Major Bouchet. The major looks us over. "Where is Private Joubert?"

"Lost in the current, sir," I say, my voice dead. "We could not save him."

Major Bouchet lowers his head and sighs. "I know his father." He looks away. "He petitioned to have his son be part of our company, thinking he would be safe with me. Now, he is the first to die."

A moment of silence follows as the major gazes over the water. "There will be other losses in this war," he says, turning away. "Captain Calliet, take Lieutenant Bauck and a squadron of men to the north and see if there are any signs of the Russians. Then, ride inland on any trails you come across. Set up camp to the north and send a messenger to me with your findings."

We ride out, looking for any tracks or campsites that may indicate the Russian army is nearby. A cool breeze blows off the river, giving relief from the intense June heat. Dense forests envelop both sides of the waterway, and biting bugs swarm around us whenever we stop.

The sun will set in a few hours, and I know the sappers are anxiously awaiting our signal so that they can begin building the pontoon bridges. The woodlands and meadows behind them are filled to overflowing with masses of troops waiting to cross the Nieman.

A young corporal rides up. "Sir, no signs of the enemy yet. There is a trail leading into the forest just ahead with a single set of fresh hoofprints."

"Good work, Corporal. Lieutenant Bauck, take half the men and continue to search the shoreline. I will take the other half and ride up that trail."

We cautiously ride deep into the forest, following the tracks of the single horseman. The trail widens and we join a small road. The tracks lead to the north, but there are no signs of additional hoofprints. I point to a corporal and two privates. "You three remain here and stay until morning, unless you spot something."

The rest of us return to the Nieman and find Adrien and his men waiting for us. He tells me they have seen nothing.

"Sergeant," I say to one of my men. "Report to Major Bouchet that we found one set of tracks, but nothing more. We will remain on our guard." I turn to the others. "Men, we camp here tonight."

The biting gnats are everywhere, and we make smoky campfires to drive them away. Apparently Major Bouchet has given the signal to the sappers to begin work, as the air is now filled with the sounds of hammers pounding and men shouting.

The forest on the other side of the river glows from thousands of campfires. A half-million men crowd the Neiman's west bank, waiting to pour into Russia. A breeze sways the trees, making the glow pulse and shift like a living creature. The sounds of crickets chirping and frogs croaking drift upstream, giving a voice to this glowing beast.

"This should be a short war," Adrien says. "Think how quickly we defeated the Austrians and the Prussians, and our army is now twice as large. No one can stop us! Not even the mighty tsar."

"I hope you are right, my friend, but there is no expanse like Russia. No army has been able to conquer it since the Mongols. The king of Sweden tried one hundred years ago, and he failed. No one has dared since."

"You worry too much, Jean-Luc. We'll be in Moscow before the summer ends."

We say little more. I brush Bayard and check my pistols and sabre before lying back and listening to the night sounds. The sappers are hard at work.

I roll over onto my side, thinking back to all my campaigns and to the safety I've had the past two years in Ostheim. Whatever lies ahead, I am here with Major Bouchet and Adrien, and we will find Anna Lise.

By midnight, the sounds of construction end, and I doze. Before first light I'm awakened by a commotion filtering through the trees on the far bank.

Adrien is already up. "How could you sleep with all that is about to happen? I don't think I slept a wink. We still have time to see the first troops cross the bridges if we hurry."

It only takes moments to break camp and mount up. Riding south, we catch glimpses of the three bridges through the trees, illuminated by bonfires on each shore. "There's Marshal Murat with the main cavalry," Adrien says, pointing to the imposing, flamboyantly dressed horseman leading his men with sabre drawn across the middle river span. His gold-embroidered red vest matches his Moroccan leather boots. The morning light glints splendidly from his brocade, sabre, and chest full of medals.

"Now that the emperor has crowned him king of Naples, his uniform has become even more majestic," I say, amused in spite of myself.

"But his men love him," Adrien notes. "No one can match his bravery in battle. How he dresses is of no consequence to them."

The king of Naples lets his horse prance across the bridge. He looks as excited as Adrien is. Waiting for the marshal on the Russian side of the Nieman are Major Bouchet and the other company commanders serving under him.

Once the cavalry has crossed, the masses of infantry begin marching onto the pontoon bridges, their lines stretching as far as the eye can see.

"It will take days for the full army to cross," I remark. "Do you think we will be going north or south of the Pripet Marshes?"

"I hope north, as that will take us closer to Moscow."

Again, the intense heat of the day is settling in, even though it's early. I keep brushing away mosquitos and gnats but know they will be a continual nuisance no matter which side of the marshes we travel.

Our company of Hussars does not have long to wait before Major Bouchet joins us.

"The army is heading toward Vilna," he says. "That will lead us north of the Pripet Marshes and allow us to put pressure on both St. Petersburg and Moscow. Russian General Barclay de Tolly has made Vilna his headquarters. I think the emperor believes we will engage the general and his army very soon. Our orders are to search for Russian outposts and determine exactly where their main army is."

We ride for several days but see no signs at all of the enemy, only an occasional serf's hut. Our food supply has dwindled much more than we expected, and our focus turns sharply toward securing provisions.

Finally, on the fifth morning since crossing the Nieman, a corporal shouts, "Over there—some farm buildings."

We gallop up and surround the hut and animal shed. The hut looks dilapidated, with a sagging thatch roof, but the shed is large and well maintained.

A visibly shaken, fearful family emerges from both buildings with their hands held high, speaking a language we do not understand. Some fall to their knees, their hands stretched before them, open with the palms up. Our force of nearly a hundred horsemen must appear like the coming of the apocalypse to them.

Several of our men ride up to them, sabres drawn.

'Sheath those swords!' Major Bouchet says, dismounting before the man who appears to be the head of the family. He uses his fingers to indicate eating, then dispatches men to search their home and shed.

'Here's hay,' one of our privates calls from the shed.

'Good, bring some out for our horses,' the major says.

'Bread! There's bread,' another private shouts from the house.

'And they have hogs and chickens. Lots of them!'

'Slaughter half the chickens and rope up half the hogs,' Major Bouchet says.

The family headman clutches Major Bouchet's arm, appearing to plead for mercy. Other household members watch in horror as chickens are slaughtered, hogs taken away, and bread loaded into sacks. It only takes about an hour to secure all the provisions we are taking.

Once the final chicken is slaughtered and the final hog secured, Major Bouchet reaches into his saddlebag for some coins. He hands the family headman a fistful of francs. "This should pay for what we are taking."

The serf looks at the coins. Disgust lines his face, but he forces a small smile. He wraps his fingers around the coins and bows.

A gust of wind sweeps across the flat farmland, stirring up clouds of dust. In our hurry to gather the provisions, I hadn't noted the darkening sky to our north. I look up and see that a storm is close. All of us are suddenly aware of the approaching squall.

The major's face clouds. 'Where did that come from?' he gasps. 'Quickly, we need to shelter in that shed. Tie the horses to its protected side and get inside. There should be just enough room for all of us."

The serfs are also alarmed by the dark clouds and hurry into their hut with their surviving chickens and hogs.

It seems we can't get the horses tied fast enough. This storm is approaching more quickly than any I have ever seen. Huge drops of rain begin pelting us before we've gotten half the horses secured. Their eyes are wide and frightened, and they fight our attempts to tie them off.

Roiling black thunderheads surge above us with brilliant white veins of lightning bulging and pulsating across their faces. The storm's booming voice bellows its fury. Rain comes in torrents, then turns to hail.

Getting inside, I huddle with my comrades. The building shakes, and I fear the wind and pounding hail will actually pulverize the roof and walls, sending them down to crush us. Through the shed walls, I hear Bayard and the other horses frantically whinnying. The wall where they are tethered creaks as they pull against it. How I wish Bayard was next to me so I could calm him.

The tempest is unrelenting, and the temperature drops to near freezing. What was once a hot day, causing sweat to stream down our faces, now has us shivering with cold.

"What is this, Jean-Luc?" Adrien asks, his voice trembling. "Is God angry with us? I've never seen such a storm."

The shed shudders. I, too, am dumbfounded. "Perhaps he is," I say. We all huddle together, waiting—cold, dismayed, disbelieving, but thinking it must soon end.

It doesn't.

Hours pass, and the rain and hail are incessant. Finally, in the dark of night, the storm subsides. Hesitantly, I try to open the shed doors, but they barely budge. Several men move to help, putting their weight to the door until finally we push it open. The entry had been sealed with hail nearly a foot deep. We all walk onto the piles of ice, taking in the landscape now illuminated by a nearly full moon. Its light, reflecting off the ice, is an eerie blue. The shadows play tricks on our eyes. Are those Cossacks watching us or just trees swaying?

We check our horses, and I'm relieved to find Bayard alive and well, snorting and stamping at the hail, seemingly as confused by this storm as I am.

Adrien shouts, pointing toward where the serf's hut should be. "What happened to the hut? It's in ruins." We slog through the ice toward the house, its roof gone and jagged edges of its walls sticking up here and there.

We find the family huddled among the ruins, dazed. Their eyes are as hollow as ours. The chickens and hogs that survived press themselves into the nooks and corners of the rubble.

"Scrape away the hail and build fires," Major Bouchet commands. We settle the family of serfs around one fire, and the rest of us warm ourselves around other fires.

* * *

The sun rises with the promise of a clear sky. There is grumbling among the men, now that their terror has subsided. "That storm was a warning from God! We must leave this place. This spot! This land! This war! They are all evil!"

"Quiet!" Major Bouchet orders. "It was just a storm, and the serfs are alive. No one was hurt. We will eat, then continue our mission. Nothing has changed."

By midmorning, the sun is hot, and much of the hail has melted, leaving the ground muddy. We break camp and follow our road to the Vilia River, whose raging waters are now overflowing its banks. The remains of a bridge lie at the river's edge.

"We'll follow the river until we find a safe ford or another bridge," the major commands.

The mud, now everywhere and deeper, sucks at our horses' feet, slowing our progress to a near crawl.

I have taken the point position and see forms emerging on the horizon. "There are wagons and caissons ahead," I shout.

Coming up on them, we find several dozen supply wagons and gun carriages abandoned, entrapped in the mire. Horses lie dead, still harnessed, and we see the frozen bodies of a dozen soldiers slumped against the wagons or caissons they were trying to push, their legs stuck in mud up to their knees.

"They are French," I say as we ride around each of the wagons, checking for survivors.

"Dismount!" The major commands. "We will bury these comrades."

Under the hot sun, the mud is beginning to harden, making it difficult to retrieve the bodies. The major points to a small hill nearby. "We will bury them near that lone tree." He rides up to the spot, pulls out a small shovel from his gear, and begins to dig. It's a desolate but perfect place with a view to the south, toward our homeland across the hard scrubland of Lithuania.

We bring up the bodies, and all of us join him in digging. We work in silence, each with our own thoughts.

After burying these unfortunates, we gather around the graves and Major Bouchet says a few words, his head bowed. The men observe him and nod, moved by the respect he shows these unknown comrades.

After some moments of silence, the major looks up. "Mount up. Check the wagons for any supplies we can carry."

We ride on for several hours, following the scattering of abandoned equipment along a narrow road that twists along the edge of the river.

The summer days are long in these northern lands. There are only three or four hours of darkness each night, and darkness is closing in. "We will camp on that hill," the major says, pointing to a rise overlooking the river.

* * *

The next morning, we continue to ride along the banks of the Vilia River. The mud has hardened, but the road is filled with deep ruts, no doubt left by the forces that abandoned the wagons and cannon we found yesterday. The fields of grain on each side of the road have been flattened for as far as the eye can see. "We must be following a full regiment," I say to Adrien. "We should be catching up to them soon."

"Up ahead—smoke," the corporal who is riding point shouts back to us.

We come upon the remains of a small village of five homes and a church nestled in a bend of the river. All of the buildings have been torched and still smolder. The bodies of the village's inhabitants are scattered in all directions—men, women, and children, all cut down by a sabre or shot. There are no signs of livestock or food. We search for any survivors and find the village priest by his church. He has a deep cut to his leg, but is still alive.

"We cannot leave these people unattended," Major Bouchet says. "There is a graveyard behind what remains of the church. We will bury them there."

Collecting the bodies of these innocents is gut-wrenching. I lift a young girl and carry her to the graveyard, tears streaming down my cheeks. My comrades, too, have difficulty. Many have never been to war, and I'm sure the sight of these massacred villagers reminds them painfully of their own families. I'm filled with thoughts of Spain.

Adrien attends to the priest, binding his wounds.

We lay out the bodies at the edge of the cemetery, unsure where to dig or who should be buried near each other as families.

The priest hobbles over with Adrien's assistance. He looks at all of us and nods in thanks, then goes body to body, laying his hands on each face and saying a prayer. I stare down at the bodies as the priest walks among them. A breeze, hot and humid, carries the dust of the burned village to my face and into my lips. I want to spit it out. There is no honor in this. It tastes of war and death.

Finishing, the priest points to certain bodies, indicating they should be buried near each other, and then indicates the spot where their graves should be dug.

We break into groups, gently lifting his former parishioners and moving them to their final resting places. The only sound is the shovels striking the earth.

Once finished, we move to the side, and the priest walks from grave to grave, giving the sign of the cross. He then turns to us, says something in Russian, and blesses us all.

The major nods toward the priest. With a quiet voice, he says, "Mount up."

We turn to continue our journey, many of us crossing ourselves as we climb onto our horses.

I'm filled with sorrow. This must have been done by the army we are following. Russia is already becoming like Spain. Images from Madrid wash over me.

There is none of the usual banter among us as we ride. Everyone stares straight ahead, expressions blank. I catch Adrien's eye and he shakes his head, looking grim.

After a few more hours, we come upon the troops we've been following, a regiment of several thousand soldiers scattered on the hillsides above the riverbank. They appear exhausted.

Working in the river below are pontoniers, feverishly creating a new bridge.

Finally, we see their commander, a colonel sitting astride his mud-encrusted horse, overseeing the bridge construction. Major Bouchet and I ride up to him. The major salutes. "Sir, we are of the Seventh Hussars, scouting for the enemy."

The colonel returns the salute. "You've found no signs either, have you? Are they running from us?"

His horse is skittish and dances restlessly. Surveying our company, the colonel says, "It appears you weathered the storm. We were not so lucky. The road became a quagmire. It was all we could do to push forward to here."

He looks back at his men. "I've lost nearly half my cannon and supply wagons. The horses could go no farther. Many of my men are straggling or have deserted. My Hussars are scouring the countryside, rounding them up as well as scavenging for food."

He gazes at the nearly completed bridge. "Vilna is less than ten leagues from here. The emperor hopes to engage the Russian forces under General Barclay near there. I need to create a forward line close to the city, but I must know if Barclay has retreated." He looks disgusted. "My Hussars are not at hand."

The pontoniers signal that the bridge is now safe to cross.

"Major, I know you are not part of my command, but I need Hussars to reconnoiter the city. Can I rely on your company to do so?"

"Of course, sir," Major Bouchet replies. "My orders are to find the enemy."

"Good! Very good! Report back to me what you find. I am going to rest and regroup my troops until your return."

Major Bouchet hesitates before speaking again. "Colonel, we came across a razed village a few hours ago. Were your men responsible?"

The colonel's shoulders droop, and he looks away. "That was dreadful. It happened sometime before my troops arrived. I suspect it may have been my Hussars. They are an undisciplined group with no regard for the local people."

"We buried them," Major Bouchet says, giving the colonel a cold look.

"Thank you," the colonel replies.

* * *

The sun is rising high, and already the heat is shimmering up from the ground, drying out the mud. The humidity is nearly unbearable. It takes us less than two hours to reach the walls of the city. I take about half of the company and ride to the left, paralleling the wall, while Major Bouchet takes the remaining soldiers to the right. We meet near the city's north gate with neither of us finding any signs of Russian troops.

A man on horseback, holding a white flag, comes through the gate and rides up to the major. "The Russians have gone, and Vilna welcomes the emperor and his soldiers," he says in French. "Please, let me show you the way to our central square."

At the words *central square,* the hairs on my arm prickle.

We ride through the city gate and are greeted by throngs of cheering people, some waving crude replicas of our flag. "Perhaps they think we will liberate Lithuania, much like the Poles think we will give them their own country again," I say to Adrien.

"Perhaps ... or else it's a ruse to entrap and kill us," an ever-suspicious Adrien replies, riding with one hand on the hilt of his sabre.

The town mayor and other dignitaries flourish their hats and bow as we approach.

"Captain Calliet, take a squad of men and ride through the western streets," the major commands as he dismounts before the Vilna welcoming committee. "Lieutenant Bauck, you take another squad and go through the eastern sector."

My men and I gallop through the streets, but only find people cheering our presence. Returning to the square, I give my report to Major Bouchet, and Adrien soon joins us with a similar account.

The major turns to a nearby soldier. "Corporal, ride back to the colonel. Tell him the Russians have retreated and we have taken command of Vilna."

Thirty-Seven

Vitebsk - July 1812

My eyes sting from the sweat oozing from my soaked shako. The sun beats down mercilessly, slowing the squad's progress to a slow walk. I take a swig from the nearly empty canteen and gaze across the featureless landscape, my mind numb. Heat waves rise from fields of ripening grain, distorting the view ahead.

Thump.

I turn back. Private Segal is splayed on the ground. We quickly dismount and gather around him.

"Here, take a drink," I say, giving him the little water I have left.

He takes a sip but coughs it up and begins to flail, uttering nonsense.

"Take it easy, Private," Sergeant Lebeau says. He pours a little water onto a rag and presses it to Segal's forehead. "Try another drink." Lebeau holds a canteen to the private's lips. He takes another sip and begins to calm.

"Our maps say there should be a stream nearby," I say. "We need to find it quickly, or we will all be like Private Segal. Look after him while I ride ahead."

Almost immediately, Bayard snorts and his ears perk. "What is it, my friend? Do you smell something?" Then, in the distance, I begin to see a curving green line. "Water!" I shout. "There's a stream ahead!"

The men are still in sight, and I shout and wave to them. They catch up with me quickly. Sergeant Lebeau is holding Private Segal in front of his saddle, while another private holds onto the reins of Segal's horse.

"Up ahead," I say, pointing. The squad breaks into cheers and laughter.

Bayard needs little encouragement to break into a full gallop. For several moments, the thought of cool, fresh water becomes my all-consuming passion, but military discipline returns and I motion my men to slow and approach cautiously. "There may be Cossacks," I tell them, and all eleven ease their horses to a walk.

I send some of my men upstream and others down as I approach straight ahead with Sergeant Lebeau and Private Segal. Across the ford, I see the remnants of a campsite with equipment scattered—indications of a struggle.

I dismount and help Sergeant Lebeau lift the private from his horse and set him by the creek.

Segal gratefully dunks his head into the water while the sergeant and I stay cautious, hands on our sabre hilts, waiting to hear word from our comrades.

"Up here, sir," a squad member calls. The sergeant and I walk upstream and come upon a grisly scene. Three dead French soldiers are stripped naked and tied to tree trunks, their uniforms torn apart and strewn across the ground. They've been beaten savagely, and knife wounds stretch down their torsos.

"Did Cossacks do this?" a private asks me quietly, his face pale with shock.

"I don't believe so. Soldiers don't do this to soldiers. It may be peasants, seeking revenge."

"Peasants?" another private echoes in disbelief. "They would do something like this?"

"Yes, it's possible. Peasants in Spain did similar things to our soldiers."

A collective gasp comes from most of my men. For many, this is their first campaign, and the idea that they must fight not only enemy soldiers but civilians as well leaves them shaken.

"Let the horses have water while we bury them." Digging the graves in this heat saps our energy. Finishing, we collapse along the sides of the stream, but I can see everyone is anxious to leave.

Finding the water and cool shade should have been a welcome diversion from patrolling under the blazing sun. But here, all we want to do is drink our fill, replenish our canteens, and move on. This place is disquieting, making us all anxious.

The refreshment from the water does not last long. Within a few hours, the sun seems to burn straight into my soul. We slowly follow the lane toward the village of Krivino, where we expect to rejoin Adrien, Major Bouchet, and our comrades. It's been almost a week since we split from them, with their patrol going to the south. We are all bone-weary, worn down by the constant heat and meager meals.

Two more days drag on, but we never see the enemy, except for occasional Cossack patrols, who scatter when they see us. Our discouragement is palpable.

Finally, our lane merges with another that is full of hoofprints. "Maybe they're from Major Bouchet and our comrades," Sergeant Lebeau says, allowing a little hope in his voice.

"Perhaps, or more Cossacks."

I dismount and examine the tracks, fingering the imprints. "These horses are wearing horseshoes. They must be French, as Cossacks generally don't shoe their horses."

We pick up our pace, hoping to catch up to these riders. Movement ahead catches my eye. "Sergeant, does it look like horsemen by that stream ahead?" I say as I bring us all to a halt and reach to retrieve my spyglass.

"Yes," the sergeant says as he stands high in his stirrups. "I'd say thirty or more."

I focus my glass and see a French platoon surrounding a group of about twenty French infantry. The infantrymen are cowering in fright.

Several are separated and lined up along the creek. A dozen horsemen dismount and retrieve their guns.

This can't be!

"Quick, to the stream," I order.

As we near, one of the soldiers facing the guns looks up and catches my eye. He stares at me with a pleading look.

Shots ring out. The soldier's body jerks back. His expression turns to one of horror and disbelief. His eyes never leave me as he begins to crumple, only closing after his knees hit the ground. In an instant, all of them have been shot. One is still moving, but another musket ball to the head ends his struggle.

We are too late.

The horsemen along the creek draw their sabres, ready to fend off our charge, then see our French uniforms and let us through. Riding up to the major who appears to be in command, I give a clipped salute. With an edge to my voice, I say, "Sir, I'm Captain Calliet of the Seventh Hussars. What is happening? Why have those men been shot?"

Bayard dances nervously, unable to settle down, reflecting the same agitation I feel.

The major returns my salute, looking unconcerned by what just happened, and seems unaware of my anger. "The Seventh Hussars? Ah, you must be with Major Bouchet. A fine soldier. We served together in Austria," he says, as if we are socializing at a banquet.

He turns toward the bodies; their graves are being dug nearby. "This?" he asks. "These are deserters we came across camping by the stream. I could have shot them all, but spared most. We need soldiers, and seeing their comrades shot should keep them in line, don't you think?"

I stare at the major in disbelief.

"Where are you headed, Captain?" the major asks.

"To Krivino."

"We're going north, across the Dvina River. Perhaps we'll meet again," the major curtly replies, having finally noticing my look of disdain.

"Very good, sir," I spit out as I salute.

With my face set grimly, I turn toward my men. "We continue to Krivino."

* * *

Soon after we leave the other soldiers, one of my squad members asks quietly, "Sir, why were those soldiers shot? They appeared to be only camping."

Others echo this question, all very troubled.

I bring the squad to a halt and turn toward my men. "The major called them deserters, but I don't know how he could have known that. Many men lag behind because of this heat and constant marching. The major was wrong. They should not have been shot. I will be reporting this to Major Bouchet."

On the day after we witnessed the executions, we come across a small band of stragglers. They, like the others, are huddled along a creek.

"Thank God you have found us!" one says. "Serfs attacked us at night. We were barely able to drive them off."

They join us as we continue toward the village. After more days of struggling in the heat, Krivino finally comes into sight. I note a large number of infantrymen, camped in whatever shade they can find. They are among the many battalions scattered across the landscape in advance of the emperor and the main army.

"Perhaps those are your comrades," I say to our stragglers.

"Yes, they are! There are our battalion colors."

They join their compatriots, who greet them with enthusiasm, as we ride toward the river, searching for Adrien and Captain Bouchet.

Soon, the Dvina River comes into view. Movement on the other side draws my attention. It looks like ants are swarming the hillside.

"Halt!" I command.

I reach for my spyglass and peer toward the moving specks, not believing my eyes.

I hand the glass to Sergeant Lebeau. "Sergeant, look at the far ridge. What do you see?"

He twists the scope into focus. "Sir, it's an army ... It's the Russians!"

He hands back the glass, looking stunned. I look again, sweeping up and down the far ridge. "It appears to be at least a division, if not a full corps. I wonder if Marshal Murat knows about them."

"Captain, over there!" an agitated Sergeant Lebeau shouts as he points down the hill. "Cossacks!"

Coming up from the river are about twenty Cossacks, unmistakable with their tall fleece hats and long spears in the attack position. Our twelve men would have no chance against them.

"Fire your pistols! Then ride hard!" I bellow, hoping someone will hear the gunfire.

The Cossacks are within a thousand yards and closing quickly, but their steppe ponies are no match for our horses in speed. We begin to pull away, but then, in the confusion, the horses of two of my privates collide, knocking them both to the ground.

"Cover them!" I order as I whirl Bayard around, coming to a defensive stance. They scramble to their feet and retrieve their horses. As soon as they are ready, we again try to escape. The Cossacks are now within a hundred yards, bellowing blood-curdling screams.

They close in as we try to regain our speed. A spear comes within inches of me before I smack it away with my sabre. One, then two of our horses fall. The Cossacks press in. I turn my head and see one bearing down on me, his spear pointed at Bayard's flank. I swerve and buy more time, but now two have me in their sights. "Faster, Bayard!" I yell as I give him a hard kick, hoping for a burst of speed.

Sergeant Lebeau is riding just ahead when suddenly he wheels his horse around, sabre drawn, and dashes back past me. I turn and see him attack the two Cossacks pursuing me. They fall, but soon he does too.

His sacrifice gives us time to regain full speed, and the Cossacks are no longer closing in. Unexpectedly, they stop their attack and turn to retreat toward the river.

Whoosh.

One horseman and then another fly by me, pursuing the Cossacks. I look and see that it is Major Bouchet and the remainder of our company. How grateful I am to see them! They overwhelm the enemy, and within minutes, none are left alive.

I turn and rush to Sergeant Lebeau, who, amazingly, is still alive. One spear runs through his shoulder, and the other is embedded in his thigh. I hack off the spear ends, but leave the shafts in his wounds to minimize the bleeding.

"Thank you for my life, my friend," I whisper, giving him water.

He gratefully accepts. "No thanks needed, sir," he gasps. "I was doing my duty."

Adrien gallops up and jumps from his horse. "Jean-Luc, are you all right? Are you wounded?"

I manage a small smile as he hovers over me like a mother hen. How good it is to see him again after so many days apart. "I'm fine, thanks to Sergeant Lebeau."

Major Bouchet rides up, a look of relief on his face. "A narrow escape, Captain. We heard gunshots and got here as quickly as possible."

He dismounts and comes over to examine the sergeant. "The wounds can be mended, but you need a surgeon. There is a hospital wagon in Krivino."

He turns to a nearby corporal. "Ride to the village and have the hospital wagon come here. Tell them the sergeant has two spear shafts lodged in his body."

Thinking of the two horses I saw go down, I look that way and am relieved to see my two fallen comrades walking toward us. Unfortunately, their steeds remain down, shuddering as their lives end. I give Bayard a stroke on his neck, thankful this was not his fate.

I turn toward Major Bouchet. "Did you see the Russian army on the other side of the river? It looks like the main force we've been seeking for more than a month. They are moving quickly toward Vitebsk."

"Yes, their position had been reported. Marshal Murat is preparing to attack tomorrow. Our company will be part of it."

* * *

Since dawn, we've been riding with Marshal Murat's forces toward Vitebsk, chasing the Russians we saw yesterday across the river and hoping to reach this Russian stronghold by mid-afternoon. The sun is still low in the morning sky when our scouts report that the Russians have taken a position just ahead, near the village of Ostrovno.

Coming over a rise, I find the battle is already engaged. The Russian front is protected by a wide ravine. Their right flank stretches along the banks of the Dvina and their left against a thick forest.

Russian soldiers pour from the forest, overwhelming our forces and driving them back.

Marshal Murat is on the ridgetop, looking down at the Russian advance. He leans forward, and I can see the muscles in his jaw ripple with tension. "Damn it!" he shouts and gives his horse a kick.

Galloping back and forth in front of us, he shakes his sabre, slicing the air above his head. Making his horse rear dramatically, he rouses us all to follow as he charges down the hill into the thick of battle.

The Russian infantry can do little to stop our charge, and we cut through them mercilessly. The tide of battle turns, and the Russians fall back into the depths of the forest.

Reaching the edge of the trees, Adrien turns to me, panting. "Do you think we should go in after them?"

The woodland is dense and would be an easy place for the Russians to set up ambushes.

"Only if the marshal orders us to do so."

Marshal Murat examines the forest. He appears satisfied that the left flank is secure and makes no attempt to enter it. Turning from the woods, he scans the other fronts. Despite our success on the left, the Russians hold their ground on the others and appear content with stopping our march to Vitebsk. Their positions are heavily armed and would be difficult for us to penetrate.

Marshal Murat decides to wait for expected reinforcements.

By evening, the reinforcements reach us, but the marshal decides to delay our attack until the next morning, as little daylight remains. The emperor and the main army are also close at hand and expected to arrive tomorrow.

* * *

Sunrise comes, and we find the positions held by the Russians abandoned.

"They dodge direct engagement again!" a disgusted Adrien says. "Perhaps at Vitebsk they will make a stand."

"Perhaps," I say, though in truth, I don't mind their refusal to have a decisive battle. Moscow is almost within reach, and we are still alive!

The emperor and his Old Guard come into view. The marshal rides up to him, pointing toward the abandoned Russian posts. The emperor waves his arms, appearing agitated, but signals for everyone to continue the advance toward Vitebsk.

Nightfall edges toward us as we near the plain at the foot of the city. The Dvina River comes into view, and beyond it, the town's church steeples. A multitude of Russian campfires surround the town up and down the river valley, making it look like an impenetrable bastion. The emperor sets his tent on high ground, overlooking what will likely be tomorrow's battlefield.

Before daybreak, Major Bouchet awakens me and the others in our company. "Prepare to mount up. We are to accompany the emperor as he reconnoiters the enemy's positions."

The first rays of the sun reveal the whole of General Barclay's Russian forces encamped on elevated positions, commanding all the avenues into Vitebsk. The Dvina River marks the foot of his position, with what looks like over ten thousand cavalry along its banks on one side and a large body of infantry on the other.

"Over this way," an aide to the emperor orders. Napoleon takes his station on a high hill, overlooking the positions of both armies. The position gives me a panoramic view of what is to come.

"Look," says Adrien as he points to our infantry. "They are advancing."

Couriers dart back and forth between the emperor and his commanders as he gives orders for the troop movements. A regiment of over five thousand French infantry advances toward the Dvina, moving directly in front of the Russian cavalry. They are backed by Marshal Murat with his Hussars and cannon.

"Why don't the Russians attack?" Adrien asks.

"It's to our benefit they don't. It gives us time to position our cannon."

Then there is sudden, unexpected movement in front of the Hussars.

"What is Marshal Murat doing?" I gasp.

"He's leading the Hussars in a frontal attack against the Russian cavalry!" Adrien cries. "He's outnumbered! He'll never succeed!"

I glance up the hill toward the emperor. He's pacing back and forth, pointing his arm down the hill repeatedly. The Russian cavalry is decimating our Hussars.

I retrieve my spyglass and stare down at the carnage. The Hussars in the front are being cut to pieces. The others are fleeing. Marshal Murat is fighting for his life. A small band of Hussars surround him as they back away.

"Jean-Luc," Adrien cries as he mounts Basile. "Look over there! Their cavalry is coming this way. Are they moving to capture the emperor?"

"Mount up!" Major Bouchet commands.

The Russian cavalry surges across the Vitebsk plain, appearing intent on taking this hill. The infantry surrounding the emperor open fire with their carbines, shooting round after round into the advancing Russian horsemen.

"Attack!" Major Bouchet bellows, and we plunge into the Russian front line, our sabres slashing. I take down one, two, and keep hacking. Everything around me is a blur. I can think of nothing but swinging my sword and surviving. The tip of one enemy's blade nicks my thigh, but I barely notice.

Gradually, the Russian attack slackens and they begin to retreat. We push them back until we hold a line at the hill's base, ensuring there are no openings for any Russian counterattack. To my right and left, French reinforcements come streaming onto the field, slowly pushing the Russians back across the Dvina.

* * *

The day comes to a close with neither side making permanent gains. Our men bivouac where they stand. We ride back up the hill, close to the emperor's tent. Adrien and I feed our horses and brush them down before collapsing, exhausted, onto the ground to eat.

"The Russians fight bravely," I say. "They nearly killed Marshal Murat."

"They are fierce fighters, and I think their plan all along has been to avoid fighting us until we were deep within their country and weakened by the long march," Adrien says solemnly, his usual bravado subdued.

Across the Dvina, the Russian campfires are as extensive as they were last night. I can see the shadows of Vitebsk in the light cast by the many fires.

"With the reinforcements we now have, I'm sure we are going to push across the river in the morning," I say.

Adrien stares into the sky. "Sunrise is only about three hours away. Let's try and get some sleep."

* * *

I'm awakened at first light by loud voices coming from the emperor's tent. The emperor is shouting, enraged. "They're gone? How can they be gone? What of the campfires?"

"A ruse, sire," an aide responds. "There are no Russians. Vitebsk is deserted."

More angry shouting. "Tell my commanders we move to Vitebsk. We will send pursuit and scout parties. They could not have gotten far!"

Our company stays with the emperor. We ford the Dvina and enter the town, finding it empty save for the French soldiers securing it. We pass through one section with fine homes and a large synagogue and continue until we reach the town square. On one side is a great cathedral with spires topped by onion domes. Directly across the square is the town hall. The emperor and his staff occupy the town hall, making it his headquarters.

Scouts are dispatched, as well as a company of Hussars to locate the enemy.

Hours pass before the Hussars return.

"Those Hussars appear to have been in battle," Adrien notes. "Look, they're attending to several wounded."

"The other scouts are arriving now as well," I say.

The scouts, along with Major Bouchet and other senior officers, enter the town hall to participate in a war council.

Adrien and I are stationed along the street in front of the headquarters, providing security. We are both near the building's doorway, and from inside, I recognize Marshal Murat's voice, speaking in a heated tone. Soon after, he storms from the building. The other officers file out and return to their commands, most smiling.

Major Bouchet comes out and motions for our company to come close and listen. "The emperor is tired of this cat-and-mouse game with the Russians. Our supplies are low and our troops worn out from the constant heat and long marches. We've had great success liberating Lithuania and Poland from their Russian yoke. We will winter here, regain our strength, and prepare for continued war next spring." The major cannot suppress a small smile. He looks across our stunned faces. "Dismissed."

The news about wintering in Vitebsk spreads quickly, and a palpable sense of relief comes over the troops.

"Astounding news!" I say as I look toward Adrien, expecting him to be unhappy with the decision. Moscow is his goal, and it is only about a hundred leagues away. We could be there in two or three weeks. But he's smiling.

"The emperor has made a wise decision. By next spring, we will be strong again and nothing will stop us from conquering Russia. After we get off duty, we can open one of the bottles of wine I've brought from Alsace. I'll save the other to share with you and Anna Lise in Moscow."

"You brought Alsatian wine?" I am incredulous. How did Adrien keep this secret for so long?

Adrien opens the precious bottle. I find some bread and cheese, and we retire to an open balcony of one of the deserted houses. We sip our wine, wanting it to last as long as possible, reliving memories of home with each delicious mouthful. The air is still warm, but a cool breeze sweeps over us from the nearby Dvina. As with the past two nights, campfires blaze across the ridges hugging the river, but now they are ours.

"I wonder what my parents and Anna Lise think of our invasion," Adrien says. "They must know we are part of the army, with Moscow in our sights."

"The Russians may be giving them trouble, especially if they learn their son is part of the French army," I respond. "For their sake, maybe it would be best if we push through to Moscow now and not in the spring."

Adrien glances over to me, his face turning pale. "You may be right. Perhaps we should keep going, but we have no control."

* * *

The next day, Marshal Murat comes and goes several times from the emperor's headquarters. Why was he so upset yesterday? No one else was.

In late afternoon, all senior officers are summoned again to a meeting. Adrien and I are back at duty, stationed near the town hall's front entrance. Unlike yesterday, there are several loud voices.

Marshal Murat is the first to leave, and today, he is the one smiling.

Major Bouchet comes out with a grim look and calls us over.

He scans our faces, hesitating to speak. Finally, he says, "Men, the emperor has changed his plans. We are to stay and recuperate in Vitebsk, but only for two more weeks. After that, we march to Moscow."

Smolensk

Thirty-Eight

Smolensk – Mid-August 1812

Our stay in Vitebsk over the past two weeks has been a welcome change from the endless patrols in the sweltering heat, the scattered clashes between the armies, and the tragedy of our relations with the peasants. Our encampment is within the courtyard of the cathedral, not far from the river. The tall steeples shade us during the hot afternoons, and the river provides cool breezes. The priests come outside and visit with us, even talking Adrien into attending mass once they learn he is Catholic.

Many of the town's residents have returned, trying to reestablish their lives. To my surprise, much of the population is Jewish. I've encountered Jews in the past, but never a full community. They are segregated in their own quarter, but inside the Vitebsk marketplace, Christians and Jews conduct their business without regard to religion. It reminds me of the Christians and Muslims in the Madrid marketplace.

"Jakub has the finest provisions," one of the priests tell us, "but he is a sharp negotiator and often doesn't display his best goods, keeping them for his favored customers. Tell him Father Malak recommends you. It may help."

"You buy from Jews? Doesn't your congregation expect you to buy from Christians?"

"They expect me to spend the church money wisely," the priest replies with a sly smile.

Following his advice, I buy dried sausages from Jakub to take with me when we finally move out. His prices are reasonable, and the quality is indeed good.

I've also purchased a few bottles of vodka, having developed a taste for it, but I only have one glassful each night as I watch the sun set and stars emerge. I keep reflecting on where life has taken me and what is about to unfold. In my heart, I'm uncertain if I will ever return to Colmar, though I want desperately to go home, have a family, grow old, and run our family's inn. It's hard to think about the distant future knowing we will soon be in battle.

Today is especially hot, and our squadron rests under the shade of an ancient oak. I sit on some steps, updating my journal, and Adrien is nearby, sharpening his sabre yet again. With the wisps of cool air coming off the river, I momentarily forget we are in the midst of a war, hundreds of leagues from home.

"Will you come join me at mass tomorrow, Jean-Luc?" Adrien asks. "It will do you good."

"I went once with you already. That's all the spirituality I need for quite a long time."

Adrien gives me a contemplative look. "I'm not sure why I've been going. I've never felt a need before, but it seems like I have one now. Listening to the priests chant is calming," he says as he slides the sharpening stone down the blade of his sabre. "Peaceful."

"Lieutenant, may I join you at mass?" Corporal Coulane asks. "I haven't been to church since joining the army. My priest wouldn't be happy if he knew."

"Of course! I'd like some company," Adrien replies, giving me a smug look.

The corporal recently joined our squad after everyone in his previous detachment was either killed or seriously wounded in a Cossack attack. Major Bouchet assigned him to our squad, as the corporal is from a town near Colmar.

"The cathedral here is much more imposing than our simple church back home in Riquewihr," he says, gazing up at the towering steeples.

"Yes," I say. "I've seen your church, an easy ride from Ostheim. When Adrien and I were young recruits, the Ostheim commandant would send us to your village to replenish his supply of wine. The peaks of the Vosges Mountains seemed so near that I felt I could reach out and touch them. It was a grander sight to see than this church, despite its splendor."

The sound of an approaching horse interrupts our conversation. Looking up from my writing, I see Major Bouchet rein in his horse next to us. "Captain Calliet, Lieutenant Bauck, prepare the men to move out at dawn tomorrow. We march toward Moscow." Looking at Adrien, he adds, "Maybe we'll find your family yet this summer, Lieutenant."

"Yes, sir. I hope so, sir," Adrien replies as we both salute.

"Our company is part of Marshal Murat's cavalry," the major adds. "In the morning, we will assemble outside Vitebsk along the river. We move first toward Smolensk, then Moscow."

The major rides on.

Adrien grabs my shoulders. "At last, we are moving out to Moscow!"

"Yes, our rest is over." I smile at my friend but feel my stomach tie into knots. "The Russians will not give up their ancient capital without a fight."

"Come now, Jean-Luc, don't be so grim. Remember, the Austrians gave up Vienna and the Prussians Berlin without too much of a fight. The Russian soldiers proved their bravery at Vitebsk, but their generals don't seem to have the stomach for real battle, and St. Petersburg is their capital now, not Moscow. They'll probably put up a good front, then retreat again as soon as they're engaged."

We give our soldiers the news, which they receive with initial enthusiasm, but as they make their preparations, they say little. I see in their eyes their fear that the Russians will no longer flee before us—that their backs will stiffen as we get nearer to the gates of Moscow, their most revered city.

Soon, many of my men will die.

Even Adrien's bravado has dampened. As we gather our belongings, we talk about the likely battles ahead and about finding Anna Lise and her family.

"Do you think they will be happy to see us?" Adrien asks.

"Of course," I assure him. "Especially your sister."

Adrien is quiet as he arranges his gear. He reaches into his saddlebag and retrieves the bottle of Alsatian wine.

"Here, Jean-Luc, you take the bottle and keep it safe. You're the one who needs to share this with Anna Lise, not me. My happiness will be seeing the two of you finally together."

He glances at my journal. "Keep your writings in a safe place as well. She'll want to know about our years away from home."

I wrap my fingers around his hands and the bottle. "No, my friend. We will both be seeing her soon, and you need to finish carrying it."

My words seem to cheer Adrien. He nods, giving me a wistful smile, and returns the wine to his saddlebag.

"And don't worry. I keep my journal well protected."

* * *

The next morning, we leave Vitebsk, heading south toward the Dnieper River and the small village of Rosasna. The emperor is hoping to surprise the Russians by not taking the direct road to Smolensk.

"We're making good time," I say. "Two weeks of food and rest have made us strong again."

"I'm glad we're riding in the front," Adrien says as he gazes back. "Look at the clouds of dust kicked up by the infantry."

I twist around and see that the dust obscures those farthest away. To the tens of thousands of soldiers behind us, breathing the hot dust must be miserable.

As I turn forward, a cool breeze crosses my face. "Do you feel that, Adrien? The Dnieper is close."

The two of us scan the horizon, looking for signs of the river. "Over there!" Adrien says, pointing toward a string of trees meandering across a wheat field. We can see the sun glinting off water through the branches. As we get closer, we see a small church, then a cluster of homes.

"That must be Rosasna," I say.

Major Bouchet orders our company to halt while he pulls his spyglass out and scans the village.

"Horsemen are riding toward us ... Cossacks! ... Wait, they're stopping, and one is pulling out a spyglass ... They are turning back to the village."

Major Bouchet pockets his spyglass. "Quick! We must catch them before they report our position."

We race at full gallop, gaining ground with our faster horses. The Cossacks head through the village and onto a narrow bridge over the Dnieper. Villagers emerge to watch the spectacle.

"We've got them!" shouts Adrien, his sabre held forward, ready to drive it into an enemy.

We rush onto the bridge. The Cossacks are just ahead, coming to the other side.

Abruptly, ten of them turn toward us, while two continue up the road toward Smolensk. They charge with their spears in the attack position.

We collide mid-span.

With a low thrust, I push away a spear with my sword, then pull it up to strike the Cossack in the neck. He topples into the river. I attack another, and he joins his comrade in the water. In minutes, ten Cossacks are floating away down the river. I'm relieved the skirmish ends quickly, but in scanning the water, I sadly see the lifeless bodies of two of our privates among the Russians. The killing has started. Although the clash doesn't last long, it does give the other two Cossacks enough time to escape.

"Corporal Coulane, take two men and retrieve the bodies of Privates Dennel and Garçon," Major Bouchet orders. "We will bury them here by the bridge."

We are just finishing our moments of respect for our two fallen comrades when Marshal Murat's cavalry begins fording the Dnieper. The riders spread north and south, creating a secure zone along the riverbanks, and the sappers immediately begin to build four pontoon bridges. They work through the night, completing the conduits the army will use to travel over by early morning. Despite having four bridges, it takes most of the day for the emperor's army to cross.

The main army travels over the river as Marshal Murat with his cavalry and Marshal Ney with his infantry move north along the road to Smolensk.

"With luck, we can be at Smolensk by the end of the day," Adrien says.

I nod. "Yes, it's possible. But don't forget about those two Cossacks who got away. The Russians may be moving toward us as we speak."

A double row of trees lines each side of the road. It's getting quieter the farther north we move, and I notice everyone slowing down to peer through the trees more closely as if they know something is waiting. Their instincts are correct. We round a bend and find a contingent of Russian infantry, their muskets aimed at us. Marshal Murat orders a charge just as a volley explodes from the enemy's carbines. Several horses fall, but we charge on. The Russian infantry abandon the roadway, retreating into the trees where our horses can't follow. Our cavalry is helpless. We can't get to them through the trees, nor can we get too close for fear of being shot.

General Ney's infantry pursues, and the Russians fall back in what appears to be a strategic retreat. A line of Russian soldiers fires a round, then withdraws behind the next wall of soldiers in wave after wave of firing and retreating. We push the Russians back but can't get the upper hand.

By nightfall, we reach Smolensk, still pursuing the enemy. The retreating Russians seal themselves into the walled city and shut the gates behind.

* * *

The emperor and his main army reach the outskirts of Smolensk the next morning. Upon his arrival, cannon fire in salute. Both Marshal Murat and Marshal Ney ride up to Napoleon, remove their caps, and bow. I'm puzzled by these actions, then remember, *of course, it's the emperor's birthday.* We ready our positions, building redoubts and placing cannon in preparation for the upcoming battle, but much of the day is spent with the emperor reviewing his troops.

We are camped on a hillside in the same area as Marshal Murat's cavalry, with a clear view of the city. The Dnieper River flows through the center of Smolensk. The larger, older portion of the city sits on the south side of the river, encased by a tall wall with many defensive towers. The newer portion is on the north side of the river. A wide bridge connects the two parts of the city.

High on a hill within the old city walls is a massive turquoise church topped with five rounded gold domes, each crested with a golden cross.

"That must be the Assumption Cathedral," Adrien says. "The priests in Vitebsk told me that one of Russia's greatest icons is housed in that church. It shows the Virgin Mary holding the Christ child and was painted by St. Luke hundreds of years ago. They urged me to see it."

Adrien's face seems to glow as he stares transfixed at the church.

* * *

We begin our attack on August 17, two days after the emperor's birthday.

First, there is heavy cannon fire on the old walled city, where most of the Russian forces are ensconced. Our infantry marches up to the wall multiple times throughout the day but can't breach it. The walls withstand our cannon salvos, and we have no scaling ladders.

There is no one for the cavalry to attack, so we wait for the Russians to emerge and confront us.

They don't.

None of the cannonballs fall near the cathedral, apparently at the emperor's direction, but the remainder of Smolensk is pounded with round after round. Fire erupts, and soon most of the old city is engulfed. Thick, black columns of smoke rise in the sky, carrying sparks and burning embers. Pyramids of flame erupt, jumping from building to building, then join together in a great conflagration.

I can hear distant screams of pain and anguish rising from the burning city. *My God, they are being burned alive!*

Adrien stares at the inferno, saying nothing, his eyes unfocused.

Corporal Coulane moves close to me. "Is there nothing we can do?" he says in a pleading tone.

"Nothing can be done," I admit sadly.

For hours, we watch the flames and hear the cries of the dying.

As night falls, an explosion rips through the air, and a fireball roils high above the burning city.

"It must be their ammunition stores," I say. "Do you think they just caught fire, or did the Russians set them off?"

"They're retreating! I'm sure of it," Adrien says. He points toward a far hill. "Let's move over there and check to see if there is any movement on the bridge."

We quickly move to a new vantage point, which has a partial view of the crossing connecting the old city with the new.

Staring intently at the smoke-clouded bridge, I see intermittent glints of firelight reflect off metal. "Do you see the reflections off their guns as they march across?" I ask.

"Yes. They keep going on, line after line of them."

"They must be falling back again," I say. "We must report this to the major!"

* * *

At dawn, we ride into the old city, which is still burning and smoldering but empty. Our infantry marches in, banners flying and military music playing, triumphant over deserted ruins. It's a spectacle without spectators, a hollow victory scarcely better than futile.

"Captain Calliet, take our men and check the area to the east of the church," Major Bouchet says. "Meet me back by the church steps with your report."

The only area of the old city still intact is that surrounding the undamaged cathedral. The turquoise walls gleam through the billows of smoke. At a walking pace, we move from lane to lane. The heat from the smoldering fires is unbearable, but worse is the stench. I've smelled burning flesh on the battlefield, but nothing like this. The odor is so dense that it coats the inside of my mouth. It's almost a taste, nauseating and putrid, yet with a sickly sweetness. Many of my men retch, then cover their mouths and noses with kerchiefs.

There are masses of bodies lying in the streets that we are threading through, and we take care not to step on the corpses. Most of the victims are severely burned, but some have no marks on them. "They must have suffocated," I say.

"Sir, I hear something!" Corporal Coulane cries out.

The corporal is pulling timbers and tossing stones. He stops for a moment when we come near. "Do you hear? It sounds like a child!" The corporal digs with greater vigor, and we all join his efforts.

From a back corner of the building, a woman's hand appears, then more of her body. She is dead, but nestled under her arm, within a protected spot, we find a young girl of four or five years. Corporal Coulane lifts her to safety as she cries and attempts to reach back for her mother. The corporal holds her close, trying to give her comfort.

Tears come to my eyes. I know many other families lie trapped and crushed. "Corporal, take her to the church square. A hospital wagon should be there by now. The rest of you, spread out and listen carefully for any sounds from the rubble."

We spend much of the remainder of the day searching the ruins, finding only a few more survivors. After several hours, we return to the church courtyard and find Major Bouchet in conversation with other senior officers. The emperor is nearby, surrounded by his marshals and generals. I can't hear what he is saying, but from his gestures, he appears upset.

"We found a few injured civilians, sir, but no other signs of life," I say to the major. "There are hundreds of dead in the streets. Nearly all of the buildings have been destroyed."

The major closes his eyes for a moment. "Tell the men to camp here. We move out tomorrow after the main bridge connecting the two parts of Smolensk is reconstructed and new pontoon bridges built across the Dnieper. Moscow is still our goal."

Our company secures a position high within the cathedral's courtyard, exposed to the breezes from the river. The stench is embedded in our nostrils, but the wind gusts help. Adrien and I find hay in the church stables, and each of us takes an armful for Bayard and Basile. They nicker their satisfaction while the two of us give them a thorough brushing.

"We are another step closer to Moscow now, Jean-Luc, but this horrible spot makes me uneasy. Do you want to go into the cathedral with me? Perhaps the sight of the ancient icon will be calming."

"Of course, my friend."

"Corporal Coulane ... Arnaud, would you like to join us?"

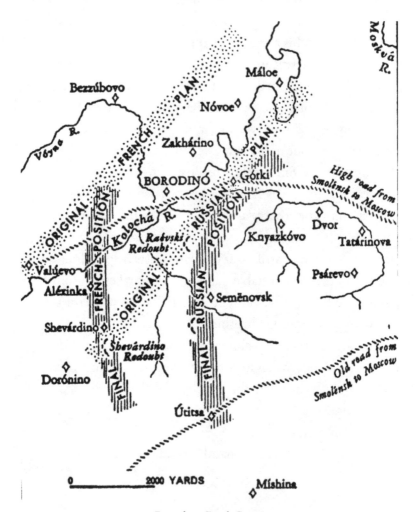

Borodino Battle Lines

Thirty-Nine

Borodino – Early September 1812

All thoughts but survival are drowned by the thunder from thousands of pounding hooves. I rush into the grasping arms of death, ignoring the hissing shrapnel flying past and the bodies of falling comrades ripped asunder by the deadly cannon fire. Sabre drawn, I'm braced for whatever fate awaits as the Russian cavalry surges toward us.

Glancing to my right, I catch Adrien's eye. His face is flushed with intensity as his sabre swirls a halo of steel. *May we both survive this somehow.*

The Russians close in. One thousand yards ... five hundred yards. Smoke swirls everywhere, and they disappear and eerily reappear. We slam together, plunging into a death struggle. The cries of dying horses mix with the constant reverberations of steel striking steel and the screams of men. The Russian army seems endless. I see their faces, lined with fear but with determined eyes, as they see mine before they die. We advance slowly, inching closer to the earthwork redoubt rising above us, built by the Russians to protect their flame-belching cannon.

How we're supposed to breach this obstacle, I can't fathom. Too steep for our horses, the frontal wall is insurmountable. There must be paths near its sides.

The bulwark looms over us. An endless roar comes from the cannon on its upper level, deafening us and filling the air with smoke. I push toward the right, searching desperately for a trail.

"Jean-Luc, this way!" Adrien shouts.

I motion for my men to follow. Adrien has found the path I hoped for, leading up the redoubt's side. Russian infantrymen block our way, but we dispatch most of them quickly and dash between the cannon, cutting down the gunners where they stand. One gunner lets fly his cannon ramrod like a javelin, hitting me square in the chest and throwing me to the ground. Staggering to my feet, I find several Russian infantrymen closing in, swords drawn.

My sabre! Where is my sabre?

It is a few feet in front of me. As I lunge toward it, pain from the ramrod blow takes me to my knees. I look up as one of the Russians charges, his eyes gleaming as brightly as his sword. There's nothing I can do.

A thick splat of liquid hits me in the face, and the Russian attacker's head rolls up to my knees, his eyes still wide with anticipation.

"Captain, get to your horse!" a familiar voice cries. "I will hold them off."

I sweep up my sword. Struggling, I get to Bayard and pull myself onto my saddle. The searing pain in my chest brings tears to my eyes, but I grimace and hold my sword at the ready, looking for the next attacker. Most of the Russians have been pushed off the redoubt, but one cannon continues to fire, its gunners protected by a few of their infantry. They fight with steely determination, swords slashing, but soon this cannon is shutdown as well.

Though the thunder of the mighty guns is silenced, I still hear gunfire and clashing steel nearby.

"Sir, are you able to ride?" Corporal Coulane asks, urgency filling his voice. "The Russians are mounting a counterattack. I don't think we will be able to stop them!"

"I can ride."

He gives me a quick nod, but his attention is focused on the far side of the redoubt.

I look and see the huge surge of Russian infantry pouring into the bulwark.

"Back down the path!" I order, panic gripping me.

The Russians sweep us off the fortification but thankfully don't pursue. They are more intent on retaking their cannon.

With the Russian cannon silenced by our attack, our infantry makes it to the base of the redoubt. Spotting them, Marshal Murat turns to go back up the trail. "Forward, men!" he shouts as he points his sabre ahead with one hand and waves his plumed hat with the other. We rally and retake the redoubt. Smoke filters through the air as our infantry lays down heavy fire on the Russians. They move back toward their even more imposing and towering "Great Redoubt," which lies to the east.

With the fortification secured, I look for Adrien, but don't see him. "Corporal, have you seen Lieutenant Bauck?"

"Yes, sir, before our retreat. He was with Major Bouchet on the far side of the rampart. They were cut off from us."

My heart races.

"Corporal, leave our horses and come with me. We need to see if he is among the dead."

"But sir, your injury. Can you walk?"

The pain is piercing, but I tell the young corporal, "I'll manage."

Grimacing with each step, I examine the faces of dead comrades scattered across the battlefield, not wanting to find what I fear. *Adrien, you can't have died with Moscow so near!*

This fate seems inevitable, as we see no signs of life. The corporal and I continue to walk through the carnage for nearly an hour, and my only relief is that we haven't found him yet.

"Sir, over here!" Corporal Coulane shouts.

He is staring down a hillside speckled with a scattering of bodies.

I feel nauseous.

"Have you found something?"

He points. "Look at the bottom of the hill. There are horsemen coming our way."

Peering closely, I see a few dozen men riding toward us. Instinctively, I think about retrieving my spyglass, but realize we left our horses behind.

"Can you recognize anyone, Corporal?"

"Not yet, sir!"

The riders make their way up the hillside. *Yes! That's Basile and Adrien! Major Bouchet is leading the group!*

"It's them," I cry, my heart wanting to burst.

Adrien spots us and eagerly gallops ahead of the rest. "Jean-Luc! You're alive!" he laughs joyfully as he dismounts. "I was worried—so worried. I kept thinking, 'You can't abandon me now!'"

"I thought the same," I say as we hug like long-lost friends. I ignore the pain in my chest. "You might have been right if not for Corporal Coulane. I was unhorsed by a cannon ramrod, and the corporal fended off those moving to kill me."

Adrien smiles broadly toward Corporal Coulane. "You were a lucky find for us, my friend."

Major Bouchet and the other riders join up with us. His eyes light up at the sight of our reunion. He turns toward the others. "Dismount and prepare your camps."

Looking back at me, he asks, "Is Marshal Murat here in the redoubt? I need to give him my report."

"Yes, his command tent is pitched near the abandoned Russian cannon."

"Let's get your horses," Adrien says as he slaps my shoulder happily.

I wince and buckle over as the pain from the ramrod shoots through me.

"Have you been wounded?" Adrien asks anxiously as he lowers me to the ground.

"I'm just sore where the ramrod hit me. I'll be fine."

"Let me take a look."

My protests are to no avail, and soon Adrien is examining my bare chest.

He lightly touches the huge black and blue swelling on my left side, just below my heart. I flinch, but he continues to press the discoloration all around. Pain flares with each touch.

"Maybe it's only a deep bruise," he says, eyeing my abrasion closely. "But you may have broken some ribs. All we can do is wrap your chest to keep your ribcage from moving."

Looking up, he spots Corporal Coulane. "Corporal, I have a spare shirt in my gear. Get it and cut it into long strips." He turns back to me. "Jean-Luc, this will hurt for several weeks. You need to rest."

I want to laugh at what he says, but it hurts too much. "I'm not going to a hospital wagon or any hospital, even with this pain! I'd be more likely to die there than on the battlefield."

Adrien eyes me, knowing it would be fruitless to argue. "Have it your way, but stay close to me in battle."

"I'll stay close too," Corporal Coulane adds.

* * *

The sun is low, marking the end of a long day. Adrien makes our camp in a spot with a full view of the Russian army. Thousands of enemy campfires come to life in the encroaching twilight. Those near the base of the nearby Great Redoubt are so close we can make out individual soldiers moving about.

The struggle of the battle, my injury, and the continual heat has sapped all my energy. I drain a canteen, trying to slake an unquenchable thirst. The first day of battle is over, but I fear it's just the beginning of a much greater clash. The Russian campfires stretch farther than I can see, many more than we saw in Smolensk or Vitebsk.

With my parched throat finally appeased, I stand with Adrien on the hill's edge, examining the enemy's position in the remaining light. I tug at the wrappings on my chest, easing the soreness as best I can.

"Where do you think we'll fight first?" Adrien asks as he surveys the vast number of enemy troops.

"We'll attack on the right," I say, pointing south. "They have those three small redoubts down there, but the ground provides the Russians no terrain advantages—no forest, no streams, just flatness."

"I don't know, Jean-Luc," Adrien says, shaking his head. "The cannon fire from that huge redoubt straight ahead will be smothering. We have to take it, and the sooner the better."

I study the Great Redoubt. "The rampart looks steep and high, and the nearby river ravines make it even more secure. Taking that fortification will be bloody. Those in the advance will be decimated."

"We'll probably be part of any advance front," Adrien says grimly. "We must watch over each other."

I look to my friend. He's never been this somber before battle.

I glance toward the Great Redoubt, and the sight of it makes my heart race. The hair on my neck seems to rise in protest at the thought of attacking something so formidable.

A large central fire ignites in the midst of the campfires just ahead of us. I find my spyglass and focus on this new activity.

"What do you see, Jean-Luc? It looks like a great commotion."

Twisting my glass brings into focus a procession of priests dressed in their full ceremonial grandeur, led by a boy holding a golden cross and flanked by other boys swinging incense burners.

"It's some kind of religious ceremony."

Coming into view at the end of the procession are two priests, holding a picture high. "It looks like they have the icon of the virgin with child we saw in the cathedral in Smolensk. How did it get here?"

I hand my spyglass to Adrien.

His voice softens, reverent. "Yes! It's the holy icon."

He hands the glass back. I scan the progress of the procession and see they are moving toward a stage and a waiting Russian general. The icon is brought to him and he begins to speak, making great gestures with his arms. Thousands of soldiers are looking on, including many on top of the ramparts. Puffs of smoke from the incense burners waft across the crowd. All of their faces are turned in rapt attention toward the icon.

The general finishes and the priests wade into the crowd, splashing what must be holy water on the heads of those they pass. The icon is taken away as the soldiers genuflect and make the sign of the cross.

I give the glass back to Adrien. The slight fragrance of incense drifts up the hill.

Disquiet overcomes me.

* * *

Fortunately, I can rest the next day while the emperor prepares his battle plans. My chest pain doesn't go away, but it recedes to a bearable level as long as I keep the wrappings in place.

Marshall Murat sends out a few platoons to create limited skirmishes with the Russians to help with the plan for tomorrow's battle. The emperor rides from one side of the front to the other, reconnoitering and pointing out where he wants to build his own redoubts and where to place his cannon.

The air is filled with tension, and chills run down my spine. Adrien checks over and over to ensure his equipment is ready for tomorrow. Corporal Coulane stays close to Adrien and me. Taking the redoubt yesterday was Arnaud's first major action, but it will be dwarfed by what we will experience tomorrow.

Major Bouchet goes soldier to soldier among the six hundred men in his battalion, giving them what assurances he can, comforting them and listening to their fears.

I am catching up with my journal, wanting it to be complete up to this day, wondering if I will be adding to it in the future. The sunflowers in a nearby field point their faces toward the waning sun. I smile at the sight. *How Anna Lise loved the sunflowers her mother grew behind their home in Colmar. In the fall, she would cut them and bring a bouquet of them to Adrien and me, beaming proudly.*

* * *

September 7 dawns with a cloudless sky, and I have the fleeting thought that tomorrow is my birthday. *Not the way I would have chosen to celebrate.* The air is comfortably cool, a relief after weeks of heat, and I'm reminded fall is coming. At home, the grape harvest should be starting. If we were there, Adrien and I would likely be fishing. Thoughts of home flood over me as I saddle up. I give Bayard a tender pat, then shake hands first with Adrien on one side of me and then Arnaud on the other. We nod to each other, and I take a deep breath. Surrounding us are my comrades—six hundred men, all mounted, ready to depart and face their fates. Below, we can see the Russian troops forming their firing lines at the base of their redoubt. We wait for our order to move out, not knowing if we are attacking the Great Redoubt or going to the south.

Marshall Murat is near us, dressed in his customary splendor, though today his uniform looks grander than usual. He wears long boots of bright yellow leather, crimson riding breeches embroidered with gold, a sky-blue tunic covered with gold lace, and a scarlet velvet pelisse lined with fur, all topped by a three-corner hat heavily braided with gold and decorated with white ostrich feathers.

Adrien chuckles despite the tense situation. "The marshal is in exceptional form today. The Russians will be humbled and beg to surrender before all that grandeur!"

The marshal checks his pocket watch. He turns and shouts. "Men, at the sound of cannon, we ride to the south."

He looks at his watch again, then pockets it. Drawing his diamond-hilted sword, he calls out, *"Vive l'empereur! Vive la France!"* Thousands of voices return the chant just as the emperor's cannon open fire.

Even though we are nearly a league from the emperor's guns, the thundering is overwhelming, especially after the Russians begin to return fire. We ride hard to the south, behind the lines of our artillery and infantry, and move east toward what we hope are unsuspecting Russians.

We are wrong.

Ahead, we see a regiment of Russian infantry waiting for us to attack. Infantry are rarely a match for cavalry, and we surge forward confidently. But then we find that the Russian artillery has waited for us to come within range, and they begin barraging our position. It appears the infantry was bait to draw us in.

Our artillery responds, pounding fire into the lines of the Russian infantry, but does not have the range to reach the Russian cannon. Our shells fly overhead, some falling short and landing within our ranks. The Russian cannonade is overwhelming, and our troops begin to panic. Some ride to the right and some to the left, trying to evade the incoming shells. Men and horses are blasted brutally apart into unrecognizable pieces. We have no one to fight, just cannonballs to dodge.

"Fall back!" I command, and we try to extricate ourselves from the massacre. Major Bouchet comes into view, then disappears into a cloud of dirt and debris. I catch sight of him trying to stand, his horse lying in a mangled heap. "Major, grab my hand," I yell, forgetting my injury. He takes hold, but the pain causes me to fall from Bayard. Another ball blasts into the earth near us, again shrouding our view.

"Jean-Luc! Major Bouchet!" Adrien shouts. He dismounts swiftly and helps me back onto Bayard. Arnaud grabs Major Bouchet, pulling him up onto his horse. Another shell blasts nearby, nearly knocking me off Bayard.

Adrien remounts, and I shout, "Ride hard!"

I know my voice is barely audible above the din, but my message is clear. We must retreat immediately! Shells fall all around as we ride, kicking up dirt and sending shrapnel into the air. Only luck saves us from death.

Finally, beyond range of the shelling, we find shelter behind a regiment of infantry.

"Captain Calliet, Lieutenant Bauck, take a count of how many men we lost," Major Bouchet says. "Corporal Coulane, try and find me a new horse."

Adrien and I quickly survey the condition of our battalion and somberly return to make our report. 'Sir, we've lost about a third of our men," I tell him.

Within a half hour, Corporal Coulane returns, leading a horse. "The only fit horse without a rider that I could find is this one. It was wandering alone just behind the battlefield."

'It's Russian," Major Bouchet says, 'but it looks like a fine horse." He inspects the animal closely. 'I've never ridden on a Russian saddle, but I can manage until I can get a new one. Thank you, Corporal."

While we talk, our cannon are repositioned, and the Russian guns are brought into range. Salvo after salvo is fired until their cannon fire subsides. Our infantry attacks, taking the southern strongholds from the Russians, ensuring our control of the southern flank.

* * *

We rest for about an hour, awaiting our next orders. In the distance, the Great Redoubt looms, still in Russian hands. It looks like a volcano, belching smoke and fire while spewing masses of iron and lead. The Russians form a new defensive line, protecting the Great Redoubt. In the plain between us and this fortification, the earth is torn asunder, black from blood and cannon fire. Bodies of men and horses blanket the earth, the remains of earlier attacks and counterattacks.

'Mount up!" Major Bouchet commands. 'We attack the Great Redoubt!"

Our artillery starts an intensive cannonade. The guns pound the Russian infantry and the redoubt rampart, but can't reach the Russian cannon. The Russians return fire. Clouds of dirt and dust are thrown into the air as each cannonball strikes. The dust mixes with the smoke to create a vast, swirling sea, with the battlefield appearing and disappearing as ghostly images of Russian soldiers are tossed about like toys.

The scene before us looks like it came from Dante's *Inferno*.

Marshal Murat rides to the front of our cavalry, waving his ostrich-plumed hat. He yells something that can't be heard above the thunderclaps of cannon fire, but there is no mistaking his intent. He firmly puts his hat back on, draws his sabre, and leads us, galloping, into the fire and brimstone. Bodies are strewn everywhere, as if vomited by a great beast upon the battlefield. We can barely maneuver over the heaps of corpses and masses of wounded. Cannonballs cut into our ranks.

I lose sight of Adrien and Arnaud, but have no choice but to drive on. I reach the base of the Great Redoubt and find a protected haven from the cannon, a zone they can't bombard, as they are unable to point their cannon directly down toward us. Our forces gather strength within this protected zone. Marshal Murat is still among us and exhorts us to charge up the sides of the rampart. The ramparts are steep and difficult to ascend. The Russian infantry fires volley after volley into our ranks. Our numbers thin, but the marshal continues to lead us farther up. We reach the crest of the Great Redoubt and are met by hundreds more of their infantry. They fire a volley, but the quarters are too close for reloading. Determined to stop us, they attack with their bayonets. We falter and begin to fall back, but Marshal Murat, still unscathed, rallies the last of our strength to surge forward and finally overwhelm them.

The Russian cannon are taken.

In that hush, I weep.

Our infantry secures the position and fends off a counterattack. Guns go silent across the battlefield. Today's fighting appears to be over. Riders all around me dismount and collapse with exhaustion.

I look for Adrien, but can't find him. Nor can I find Major Bouchet or Corporal Coulane.

From the top of the rampart, I gaze out over the battlefield. There is some movement from survivors, but even with my spyglass, I can't make out who they might be. The dust and smoke are still too thick.

Feeling dizzy with fear, I lead Bayard down to the field of death. *There are thousands here. How will I ever find them?*

The smell of burned flesh and the beginnings of decay permeate the air. I cover my mouth and nose with a kerchief and begin my journey among the dead and dying, ignoring the pain from my ribs. Hands reach out to me and voices plead for help, but I can't help; I must find Adrien. I slog between the endless dead. Blood and gore cover my boots. I stumble and see that my right foot has become tangled in the crook of a severed arm. I lead Bayard on, passing and stepping around face after face. Some of them I recognize. Their bodies are mangled terribly.

An hour passes, maybe two. Up ahead, I see a horse standing by a soldier on his knees. The horse is Basile! Is that Adrien?

My body prickles, and I become breathless as I scramble as fast as I can toward them. "Adrien! Is that you? You're alive?"

The soldier looks up, and the weight of the world falls on my shoulders.

It's not Adrien. It's Arnaud.

I come closer. Arnaud is crying.

"Jean-Luc! I couldn't save them! There was nothing I could do!"

At his feet is Adrien, missing his left shoulder and arm, taken from him by a cannonball. Nearby is Major Bouchet and his Russian horse, both bodies ripped apart by cannon fire.

"During our charge, I saw Major Bouchet's horse go down. Lieutenant Bauck came to help, but after he dismounted and came to the major's side, they were both hit by a cannonball. I rode over, hoping I could do something."

Arnaud is shaking, weeping uncontrollably, gasping for air. He looks at me as if pleading understanding, forgiveness for not saving them.

"The major's legs were gone ... the lieutenant ... I couldn't help them ... but I couldn't leave." Arnaud drops to his knees.

I kneel next to my dear Adrien, remove my shako, and brush back his blond hair.

Adrien. What has this life brought us? Why did we ever leave Colmar and our families?

His eyes and mouth are open, surprised in death, his face asking, *What has happened?*

I sit on the ground, cradling his head on my lap, and I rock back and forth, unable to stop, tears streaming down my face.

"What am I to do without you?"

I notice his necklace, the same as the one I've worn since we entered the army so long ago. I take it from his neck and open the locket. A snip of blonde hair is secured within. Anna Lise's hair.

I press the necklace to my chest, then place it around my neck and continue to rock, gazing down at my friend.

"Is Major Bouchet here?" I ask in a daze. "He and I can take Adrien to the hospital wagon. I'm sure Baron Larrey can heal him."

Corporal Coulane touches my shoulder. "Sir, the major is gone. He and the lieutenant are dead."

"Dead? They can't be dead! We all have to reach Moscow. We are nearly there!"

My gaze turns toward Corporal Coulane, but I don't see hope in his eyes, only sadness.

"They are gone, sir."

Despair wrenches from the depths of my soul. *My dearest friend, you are truly gone!*

I hold Adrien tightly for what seems both a lifetime and a fleeting moment. Our lives together, always intertwined, are now severed—only a memory, a shadow, of what we had.

Through a fog, I hear Corporal Coulane calling to me. He sounds distant, but his face, looking into mine, becomes clearer. I don't know how much time has passed, but the sun is lower in the sky than I remember.

'Sir, if we are to bury the lieutenant and major, we must do it soon. Scavengers from the nearby villages as well as our camp followers have moved onto the battlefield."

I look up and see the dead bodies being looted without regard for what uniform they wear, their clothes and boots stripped away. The looters move methodically from body to body. Some appear to have pliers, using them to pull teeth from the mouths of the dead.

A few are getting close to us. 'Away!" I cry angrily, waving my sabre. They look at me as a mere annoyance but fall back from us, continuing with other bodies.

I pull a blanket from my gear. 'Arnaud, get Adrien's blanket from Basile!"

We first wrap Adrien and lift him onto Bayard, then place Major Bouchet on Basile.

I touch the major's body, remembering all our years together. 'His first name was Paul," I say softly, 'but we never called him that. He was always captain, or major, but mostly, for me, he was my teacher and friend. His parents were dead and he never talked of his family, but I know he grew up in Strasbourg, not far from Colmar. When we return home, I will find his surviving family and tell them what a great man he was."

I scan our surroundings, hoping to find a spot not covered with death. "Over there," I say, pointing. "Perhaps there is a spot near those woods."

Leaving the battlefield, we come to the trees and find an area on a small rise, nearly pristine, with a view away from the bloodbath and toward a small creek. Arnaud and I dig deeply, not wanting wolves to uncover our friends. I cut a blaze into the bark of the nearest tree to mark the spot, though I know it's unlikely I will ever come this way again.

The sun has set, and the first sliver from a new moon appears over the horizon. Lantern lights dot the battlefield, evidence that the scavengers are still at work. An owl hoots from deep within the woods, away from the trauma of the day. The howls of wolves echo from the heights. I'm sure they are anxious for the looters to leave so they can begin their grim feast.

Arnaud and I have not spoken since we buried our friends. I go to Basile and retrieve the bottle of Alsatian wine from Adrien's saddlebag. I hold it tightly, wondering how I can ever share this with Anna Lise. I promised to protect her brother, but now he's dead.

Still, even with this doubt, I carefully stash the bottle within my own saddlebag. While doing so, I find what remains of my vodka, about half a bottle. I pull it out and retrieve two tin cups.

"Arnaud, would you like a drink?"

"I would," he says simply.

We sit near the graves, sipping the vodka and listening to the babbling from the nearby creek. A soothing sound, incongruous with my grief.

"It must be past midnight now," I say. "It's hard to believe that today is my twenty-sixth birthday. Adrien has been at my side for each of those years. I'm not old, but today I feel I've lived a lifetime and seen things no one should ever have to witness."

'I lost a close friend myself," says Arnaud, 'In the raid by the Cossacks. At this time last year, I was helping my family harvest grapes. I felt trapped in that life and wanted to do and see so much more. My friend, Robert, felt the same, and we thought the army would change our life, so we joined. Now, all I want is to go home. How I wish I was in that old life again."

The sound of soldiers marching disturbs our calm. It comes from down near the river. We are too far away to see, but it is unmistakable. An army is on the move.

'It must be the Russians!" I say. 'Are they moving to attack or retreat?"

We crouch and peer down toward where we hear the disturbance, but the river is too far away and the moon gives little light.

I press my hand on my thigh as I lean forward.

What's this? The trouser over my right thigh is sticky and wet.

Forty

The Gates of Moscow –
Mid-September 1812

*D*amn! *Was I hit?* The wound is oozing, slowly soaking my pants. I pull down my breeches, but it's too dark to see the extent of the wound.

"Here's my canteen," Arnaud says. "I'll find a bandanna to clean off the blood."

I splash water onto the injury, gently rubbing with my fingers, flinching at the pain.

"Take this," Arnaud says. He hands me a bandanna that he has somehow found in the dark.

I dab at the wound, then wrap the bandanna around my thigh and tie it off. "We'll need to wait until morning to see, but it feels like a bullet graze. Not too much of a problem."

"You need to see a doctor!" Arnaud says emphatically.

"No," I reply. "They are overwhelmed with serious wounds. I'd be taking their time from those truly in need. We'll wash and bandage it at first light."

Visions of the carnage, the legs and arms shattered or gone, make my graze seem insignificant. "Right now, let's visit with Adrien and the major until morning."

I settle on the ground next to Adrien's grave, putting my hand on the mounded dirt that covers him. *My friend, do you remember back to when we were but nine and we were out catching salmon, and the guillotine rolled into town? What a day that was, and all capped with Anna Lise's birth. I cherish all the times we had together—taking care of your little sister, fishing, and stealing up to the Ostheim barns to see the Shagyas. I wrote it all down, Adrien, all in my journal. Our time as children, joining the army, and all our campaigns. I wrote my memories for Anna Lise, but also for you, for us to read as we grew old.*

I talk with Adrien for the rest of the night. Arnaud keeps silent company, letting me reminisce with my old friend.

With first light I get to my feet, touching Adrien's grave site one last time and taking a handful of soil from it, which I save in my right pocket.

Turning to Major Bouchet's burial spot, I take some dirt from it as well, putting it in my left pocket. *Goodbye, Major Bouchet. Without you, I would never have survived this military life. I was nearly lost after Madrid, remember? I drank to forget the massacre and nearly let Adrien die in that ambush, but you brought me back. Made me realize there was nothing I could do. The face of the priest, of Manuel, I live with and accept. I know if you were alive, you would counsel me on how to endure the loss of my two closest friends. I hope I can do that on my own, somehow.*

Finally, I turn to Arnaud. "We must go. It's time to join our comrades."

"Not before I attend to your wound," he says sternly. "You and the lieutenant talked endlessly about your mission to reach

Moscow and find this girl, Anna Lise. You must finish this quest and not die of infection with the gates of Moscow so near."

I acquiesce, and he carefully washes and binds the wound. "You were right. A bullet grazed you. Not too deep, but serious enough that it needs to be looked at. You need to see a doctor!"

"If one rides by," I say.

Arnaud eyes me, knowing I have no intent of seeing a doctor. "Time to mount up."

Arnaud looks uncomfortable. "Should I ride the lieutenant's horse?" he says, gazing toward me.

"Arnaud, you need a horse and Basile needs a rider ... please, Adrien would be honored if you took care of him."

A flash of relief crosses Arnaud's face. He knows he must have a horse to be able to fight. He pats Basile and introduces himself. "I hope I can be as good to you as Adrien."

Basile snorts his approval.

Uncertain where to go, I look back toward the battlefield, now filled with ravens feasting and cawing. On the far side of this vision of Hades is a detachment of soldiers performing the grim task of burying the dead.

I have no desire to go in that direction.

Rising above the battlefield, the Great Redoubt still stands, menacing but now silent. There is no sign of life there and no reason to go toward it.

"We'll go down by the river and follow it to the village of Borodino," I tell Arnaud.

Bodies lie for a long stretch from the battlefield, men who died from their wounds as they retreated. The ravens protest as we ride by, not wanting to be interrupted in their gorging. I ignore them, brooding in my sadness over my lost friends.

The village is filled with soldiers, resting and cleaning themselves in the river, thankful they won't be fighting again today.

'Do you see any of our comrades?" I ask Arnaud as I gaze across the expanse of men.

'No, sir," he says. 'They can't all have died. Perhaps they've been assigned to a new battalion."

Eventually, I see a major nearby and ride up to him. 'Sir," I say, saluting. 'We've lost our company commander and cannot find any of our company comrades. Whom should we report to?"

'Who was your commander?" the major asks.

'Major Bouchet."

'I know of him. A good man from Alsace. Are you from there as well?"

'Yes, sir, both the corporal and me. I hail from Colmar."

'Colmar, you say. Then you must know General Rapp."

'Yes, he's an old family friend."

'He was wounded yesterday, but the emperor's physician bandaged him and he remains in command. His regiment is camped on the far side of Borodino. Join them."

Joining Uncle Jean would mean telling him of Adrien and Major Bouchet. Maybe it would be better to attach ourselves to another battalion where I know no one.

"Thank you, sir," I say as I snap a salute.

As the major rides on, I find I can't think. My mind is hazy, frozen.

What should I do?

'Sir, we must join with General Rapp," Corporal Coulane says, eyeing me closely. 'You need to be with old friends!"

I look at him blankly, uncertain what to say.

He takes command. 'The general is this way, sir," he says as he rides away.

I blindly follow.

It doesn't take us long to find Uncle Jean's command tent. An aide to the general has set up a portable desk outside the tent's main entrance. Soldiers are all around, cleaning and maintaining their gear.

I dismount and approach the aide, who jumps to his feet and salutes. "Can I help you, Captain?"

"Yes, would you please tell General Rapp that Captain Calliet wishes to talk with him?"

"Can I tell him what it is about?"

"Tell him ... it's family news."

The attendant disappears into the general's tent. Soon, Uncle Jean is at the flap. He sees my desolation and limps toward me, wrapping his arms around my shoulders, sensing something is seriously wrong.

"Jean-Luc, I'm glad to see you alive, but where is Adrien?" Uncle Jean asks with apprehension. "What has happened? Has he been wounded?"

Gratefully, I let him hug me, tears flooding my eyes.

"Come into my tent and tell me about it," he says, looking as grieved as I feel.

There are two chairs and a table in the tent, along with a bottle of cognac and glasses.

"Please sit," he says as he pours us each a drink and sits next to me.

I take a drink and clutch the glass to my chest, my tears now contained. Looking at Uncle Jean, I can barely get the words out. "Adrien died in our last attack on the Great Redoubt."

I look down at my glass and take another sip. Uncle Jean places his hand on my shoulder.

"He was trying to help Major Bouchet, but he too was killed."

I start sobbing, finding it hard to catch my breath. Pain from my ribs causes me to bend over, pressing my hands to my chest.

I feel Uncle Jean's eyes inspecting me closely. "Have you been wounded, Jean-Luc? Baron Larrey is nearby and could attend to you."

"I only have bruised ribs. No need to take the doctor away from more serious wounds."

The bullet graze seems too minor to bring up. *My pain is in my heart.*

Uncle Jean touches my shoulder lightly, looking at me with gentle eyes. "You must be strong, Jean-Luc. In a few days, we will be in Moscow, and you need to be sturdy for Adrien's parents and Anna Lise. Tell me about Adrien ... and about Paul."

I nod, then recount all that has happened since we arrived at Borodino and the first redoubt. We talk for an hour, maybe two, finishing the cognac. Uncle Jean listens closely, and after a while, tries to lighten the mood by joking about his four wounds. "Nothing serious," he says. "It amuses the emperor that I am wounded in nearly every battle."

The talking helps, but my grief still fills my soul.

The sun is now low in the sky, and I know I've taken more time than I should from Uncle Jean's duties. "Thank you for listening," I say as I get up.

"Have you found your battalion, Jean-Luc?"

"Not yet. So many of them were killed, my battalion may not exist anymore."

Uncle Jean gives me a sad look. "We'll fix that. I'll have you assigned to my command. I'm still recovering, so we are being held in reserve. It will give your ribs a chance to heal before Moscow."

"Thank you, Uncle Jean, I will. I do have a comrade with me—Corporal Coulane. He saved my life during the battle for the first redoubt."

"He will join us too."

We walk to the tent flap and out into a beautiful day. The afternoon sun is shining, and a cool breeze blows. How can there be such a lovely evening just one day after Adrien died?

"Sergeant," the general tells his aide. "Record that Captain Calliet and Corporal Coulane are assigned to my command."

Turning to me, he takes me by the shoulders. "Jean-Luc, come visit with me at any time, especially before we reach Moscow."

"Thank you, sir."

* * *

Six days have passed, and we haven't sighted the Russian army. We should be able to see Moscow soon. My ribs are better, but it seems like I've come down with fever. I feel cold, but I'm sweating. My mind can't focus.

A rider gallops up to Uncle Jean. "Sir, Marshal Murat has entered the city," he says breathlessly. "The Russians are gone. Moscow is deserted, save for some German and French residents. The city is ours."

"What news!" I exclaim to Corporal Coulane, the excitement driving away the effects of my fever. "The war may be won. Surely the Russians will sue for peace, especially now."

Our pace quickens in the hope of seeing Moscow soon. Up ahead is a high hill being overtaken by running infantrymen and galloping horsemen. I can hear thousands cheering. "Moscow! Moscow!" they cry. *"Vive l'empereur!"*

"Quick, Bayard. We must see the city." Bayard and I charge up the hill, accompanied by Uncle Jean and his staff and Corporal Coulane.

As we come to the top, the magnificent spectacle of Moscow is laid out before us. The city stretches as far as I can see, with the afternoon sun glittering off its thousands of domes, spires, and gilded palaces of many colors. The display is magical, an oasis beckoning to us. Not even Vienna can match this splendor.

Sorrow fills me. *Adrien, you should be here.*

I hear a voice. *Adrien, is that you?*

"Of course I'm here, Jean-Luc. Did I hear the messenger say there are Germans still in Moscow?"

I turn to smile at him where he sits beside me, astride his faithful Basile.

"My family must be among them, Jean-Luc. But you are ill. If you don't get treatment, you will die, and our march across Russia will be meaningless."

It's not Adrien, it's Arnaud. His voice is very far away.

* * *

I see a face hovering over me. "You were lucky that Baron Larrey and his hospital wagon were nearby."

Who's talking? I know the voice, but can't place it.

"I sent Corporal Coulane into Moscow to locate the German quarter and find Adrien's family."

I now see that the man whose voice I heard is wearing a general's uniform. "Uncle Jean?" I ask.

Another face comes into view next to Uncle Jean. I remember this face from Austerlitz. "Baron Larrey, is that you?"

"You would have died in another day or two," the baron says sternly. "The bullet graze was infected. You should have sought treatment."

I smile weakly, but don't answer him.

"Uncle Jean, did you say Corporal Coulane is trying to find Anna Lise and her parents? Any word yet?"

"It should be soon. For now, you need to rest."

I close my eyes and drift into a pattern of sleep, dreams, sleep, dreams. I hear voices, but they seem distant, and I don't understand what they say. It feels like I am being lifted and taken away.

Am I dead? Are they taking me to my grave?

More voices, and I feel myself being jostled. Bayard snorts, and I hear the clip-clop of his hooves on cobblestone. I'm being lifted again and am taken to a dark place.

This must be my grave. They're about to shovel the dirt to cover me.

But I don't feel any dirt. I don't hear anything anymore.

I exhale and inhale, convincing myself I'm not dead. I open my eyes and see a small speck of light near me. I move to get a better view. "Is someone there?" I ask.

A feminine gasp fills the air, and suddenly my face is covered with kisses.

"Jean-Luc, you live!"

"... Anna Lise? Is that you? ... Can it truly be you?"

"Yes, I'm here."

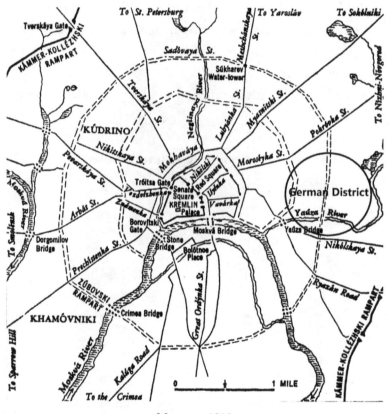

Moscow - 1812

Forty-One

The German Quarter –
Mid-September 1812

I feel hot, yet I'm shivering. My mind jumps from one dream to another until a single vision stands clear.

There she is. Anna Lise insisting she wanted to ride a Shagya. Staring at me with a look I hadn't seen before. Maybe that's when I realized she thought of me as more than just her older brother's closest friend. She had a young girl's crush, and I thought it amusing, but nice. Was it then I started to think of her as a young woman instead of a little girl? She was only twelve, but I remember her beauty that day and how she made me feel.

The journal I've been keeping was a gift from her. "Please, Jean-Luc, write about your times in the army," she said. Did she know that writing in that journal would make me think of her? That I would visualize her growing into womanhood?

She was right.

* * *

Ach, that hurts. What's happening?

The pain pulls me from my dream, and my eyes crack open. Through a haze, I see someone hunched over my leg.

Is that Frau Bauck? How can that be?

Involuntarily, my leg jerks.

Frau Bauck pulls away the knife she's holding. "I think I've cut the last of it out. It was not deep."

She glances up to my face and sees I'm awake, giving me a brief, encouraging smile.

Turning back to my leg, she says, *"Tochter,* pour more vodka along the cut. *Mein Mann,* hold his leg."

Anna Lise? Herr Bauck?

Pain sears through me as the vodka washes over my leg. I groan and close my eyes tightly.

A hand squeezes mine.

* * *

The early morning light rouses me from what seems to have been a very long sleep. Gingerly, I prop myself up, and pain shoots down my leg as I move. The room is small, with a single, curtainless window facing the street. The first rays of sunlight crest the top of the nearby buildings and begin to light the space.

How did I get here? My last clear memory was seeing Moscow from the hilltop. I remember being jostled and lifted, thinking I was about to be buried. It must have been when I was taken here. But where am I?

I can't make anything out in the shadows, and I lie back, my thoughts returning to Anna Lise. Did I dream Anna Lise was kissing me, was it another hallucination, or did it really happen?

As the darkness of the room fades away, I realize someone is near the side of my bed, asleep in a rocking chair. My heart beats faster as a sunbeam illuminates the bowed head of a young woman.

Anna Lise. It's you!

Seeing her leaves me breathless, but my stomach churns, knowing I must tell her and her parents that Adrien is dead.

Anna Lise stirs and opens her eyes. She smiles warmly and presses her hand softly to my forehead. "Your fever has broken. We've been so worried. You've been asleep for nearly two days." She stoops and kisses me on the forehead.

I lower my head, unsure how to say what I must.

When I look up, I see Anna Lise's face, framed by her honey-blonde hair. "Uncle Jean told us about Adrien when he brought you here," she says.

My hands clinch into fists, and there are beads of sweat on my forehead. "I couldn't save him, Anna Lise. I'm so sorry." My words stick in my throat. "I promised you he would be safe ..."

Her guileless, beautiful, sky-colored eyes look so understanding and forgiving. "You couldn't have done more," she says as she wraps her arms around my neck, tears streaming.

"When news of Borodino came to Moscow, everyone was shocked by the accounts of the number of dead on both sides. We didn't know if you and Adrien were in the battle, but I felt in my heart you were. When the young corporal came to our home and told us you were wounded but alive, we were so grateful. *Vati* insisted you be brought here. The corporal wouldn't tell us about Adrien, saying that you or General Rapp needed to tell us. I knew then he had been killed."

* * *

After a knock at the door, Frau Bauck's head pokes around its edge and looks our way. "I've come to give you a clean bandage."

Anna Lise backs away to give her mother room, and soon Frau Bauck's efficient hands remove my bandage and wash my wound. I wince as she wipes away some of the dried blood. She looks up. "Is there much pain?"

"No," I lie. "It's just a little tender."

"I don't smell any infection. Good!" she says as she rewraps my wound. "You can start walking to regain your strength."

I reach for Frau Bauck's hand, holding it. "I'm sorry about Adrien," I say, tears flooding my eyes. "All he could talk about these past months was finding his family in Moscow. He deeply regretted not getting home from Paris in time to see you before you left Colmar."

Frau Bauck presses one hand across her mouth and looks down at me, her eyes veiled with tears. Anna Lise walks up and slips her arm around her *mutti*'s waist.

With a quivering breath, Frau Bauck says, "You are both my sons, Jean-Luc. You and Adrien. I can only thank God I still have one." She bends down and kisses my cheek, her tears mingling with mine.

Frau Bauck holds my hand tightly. Anna Lise extends her embrace to include both her mother and me, holding the two of us close.

When we break apart, I look to Anna Lise and smile, feeling a great burden lifted from my soul. I had dreaded talking to them about Adrien's death even more than I realized.

She kisses the top of her mother's head, then turns to me.

"There's a young corporal who insists on guarding our front door. He came with you and Uncle Jean and says he's sworn to protect us."

I manage a small smile. "That's Corporal Arnaud Coulane. He's also from Alsace, and he's a close friend. He was the last to see Adrien alive and now rides Adrien's horse, Basile. A good man."

Frau Bauck gathers together the supplies she brought in. As she leaves the room, she says, "You must be hungry. You haven't eaten in two, maybe three days. I will send in some food."

After she has gone, I ask Anna Lise, "Can you ever truly forgive me? I anguish over that day." My words rush out. "We charged the Great Redoubt, and I lost track of Adrien in the attack. Should I have gone back and tried to find him? I don't know. I don't know how I could have ever found him."

"Jean-Luc, stop!" She looks at me, her eyes showing her resolution. "I'm thankful you survived. I can't imagine what it is like on a battlefield, but I know it's a terrible place." Anna Lise pauses, turning her gaze to the ceiling. She is trying to hold back her tears. "You could not have changed anything. I'm trying to accept his death." She looks down at me. "You too must accept he's gone. It was his fate in this war."

She takes my face in her hands and kisses my forehead again. "I love you, Jean-Luc. Since the day we rode the Shagyas, I've loved you. I know I was only twelve, but you've owned my heart since then. Every day I've prayed to see you again."

My heart rises to my throat. Only in my daydreams did I think I would ever hear such words. "Anna Lise," I whisper pensively, "you may think differently of me when you learn what I have done in those years since then. Horrible things. Do you remember the journal you gave me just as you and your parents left for Moscow? You wanted me to write about Adrien's and my experiences so you could know and understand what Adrien and I went through. I've written it all down, all the good ... all the evil."

I look around the room and see my saddlebag in the far corner. "The journal is over there," I say, pointing to my gear. "I'll get it for you."

"Jean-Luc," Anna Lise says, alarmed. "I'll get it."

"No, it's time to check how my leg feels. The wound was only an infected bullet graze, not a deep cut. It should be fine."

Getting up, I feel a sharp sting of pain, but I don't let it show. I take a few steps. "See? It will be as good as new in no time." I'm happy for the distraction this short journey provides.

The journal is at the top of the saddlebag. Pulling it out, I see the bottle of Alsatian wine and cover it over.

Gently, I hand the journal to Anna Lise.

There is a knock, and a servant enters pushing a cart holding a bowl of steaming potato, cabbage, and sausage soup with a side dish of bread. "*Fräulein* Bauck?" the servant says. "Here is some food for the captain. Frau Bauck thought he should be hungry."

"Thank you, Vlad. Jean-Luc, you eat while I sit in the rocker and read."

I sit on the edge of the bed, finding myself ravenous, and lift a spoonful of soup to my lips, my eyes on Anna Lise as she opens my journal and begins to read. I fear my words will expose the evil in my heart.

Exhausted after eating the delicious soup, I lie back on the bed and immediately doze off. I wake, and Anna Lise looks up from my journal.

For a while, the room is silent except for her turning the pages of my journal.

"You've written about our childhood!" she says, looking up at me and smiling. "How wonderful! I remember hearing about the guillotine, but didn't realize it all happened the day I was born."

I smile. "Anna Lise, I'd like to take a short walk and test my leg a little more. Is there a place we can go? We can talk about what you have read while we walk."

"A wonderful idea. There is a beautiful park just a few minutes away."

Has she read about the battlefields and death? Austerlitz and the Prussian campaign? My stomach twists as I wonder what she will think of my actions in those wars—and there is still Spain, a thousand times worse. She leaves the room so I may dress.

Frau Bauck has taken the time to clean and repair my uniform. I dress like I am going into battle, though it's only a stroll in the park.

I meet Anna Lise in her parents' sitting room. She comes in, and I try to take in how lovely she looks. She's wearing a fine walking dress, a light blue to go with her eyes. A bonnet covers the top of her head, but does not hide the beauty of her hair flowing down her back in a French braid. She carries a small parasol to protect her from the sun. I'm stunned! Is this the little girl I've known all my life? I feel like a young schoolboy, uncertain what to do.

"You look beautiful, Anna Lise. Are you ready?"

She smiles, and I grin foolishly, my heart melting. "Yes."

We go out to the avenue in front of her parents' home, which is next to their butcher shop. Herr Bauck has done well in Moscow. His shop here is much more impressive than the one in Colmar. As Anna Lise said earlier, Corporal Coulane is stationed at the Baucks' front door.

I embrace him. "Arnaud, I'm so pleased to see you. Anna Lise, did I tell you the corporal saved my life during the first day of battle at Borodino?"

"I didn't know," she says, smiling. "My family is grateful."

Arnaud grins sheepishly, kissing Anna Lise's hand and bowing. "After hearing Jean-Luc and Adrien talk about you so much, I can see why Jean-Luc was so anxious to get to Moscow."

She blushes.

"You needn't stand guard, Arnaud. Where are you billeted? You can go there."

"I'm staying across the street with General Rapp's entourage. I don't know any of them, and standing guard makes me feel useful. Frau Bauck brings me food."

"We're going for a walk in the park and shouldn't be gone for more than an hour or two. It looks like there's a small fire over there." I point to a wisp of smoke to the west. "Keep an eye on it."

All my years commanding men do not help me to start a conversation with Anna Lise. I feel a lump in my throat, worrying I might stutter or mix my words. She takes my arm and leads me to the park. It's a remarkable day—not a cloud in the sky, the air warm and clean. I didn't realize how accustomed I had gotten to the smell of an army and the stench of a battlefield. To the south are the onion domes of the Kremlin, gleaming in the sunlight. I look again at the smoke, feeling some trepidation, but look away. My eyes are on Anna Lise. We enter the park and turn onto a tree-lined path twisting along the Yauza River.

"Jean-Luc, tears came to my eyes as I read your memories of Colmar. We had a blessed childhood—you, me, and Adrien. How I miss the days the three of us spent together. What do you think lies ahead for us?"

I shake my head. "I don't know, and won't until after you read the journal."

"I will read it all soon, Jean-Luc. I know you're concerned about what I may learn, but I am not unaware of the world. I know soldiers are faced with many terrible decisions."

We walk farther along the river's edge. The war, the world, all seem distant.

"How long do you think the emperor will stay in Moscow?" Anna Lise asks.

'It's likely the tsar will negotiate for peace and we'll spend our winter here. I can't imagine we would try to return home in the cold and snow."

We walk a bit, then rest on a bench. Anna Lise tells me about her time in Moscow. 'It's a beautiful city, as you've seen, and the Russians treat us well. *Vati* is very happy here. I've made friends, but no one close. My heart is still in Colmar."

'Yes, a most beautiful city. Grander even than Paris. How could the Russians abandon it?" My leg is beginning to hurt and I'm becoming fatigued, but I ignore this, not wanting to leave Anna Lise's side. Walking back toward home, we stand on a bridge over the Yauza River, and I'm finally brave enough to pull Anna Lise close. My heart quickens, and I kiss her gently.

She leans her head into me. The feel of her body so close is comforting.

'Jean-Luc. We've been gone long enough, and I fear you have tired."

'Yes, I am a little weary, but being with you drives away all thoughts of resting."

'We can come back tomorrow," she whispers.

Going slowly, savoring every moment, we walk back through the park. We come across only a few people, some drunken soldiers who stare at Anna Lise but back away once they see my captain's insignia. Some older German couples are also taking in the park's beauty. They nod, acknowledging us, but their eyes reveal an inner fear as they take in my uniform.

As we leave the park, I finally notice that the wisp of smoke I saw earlier has become a towering black cloud. Anna Lise sees it too and clutches my arm. 'Quick, we must get home."

Corporal Coulane rushes up as we arrive back at the Baucks'. 'Sir, the northwestern corner of Moscow is on fire! The wind may be bringing the flames our way. General Rapp says we must be ready to evacuate."

The tolling of alarm bells splits apart the day's stillness, confirming what Corporal Coulane has just said.

"Are we in danger, Corporal?" Anna Lise asks.

"We may be. The cloud of smoke has gotten much larger over the past thirty minutes."

Herr and Frau Bauck join us as we stare at the smoke to our west. How could we not have seen this from the park?

The black cloud is getting closer, billowing skyward, looking like an angry thunderstorm with spikes of flame dancing in and out of the roiling smoke.

"The fire looks like it's near the Chechera River, about half a league away," Anna Lise says. "Maybe the river will keep it from coming our way."

Others living in the neighborhood have already brought out their wagons and are feverishly loading furnishings, clothing, whatever they can carry.

"I'm riding to the river to see if the flames have jumped over," Arnaud says. He saddles Basile and rides, weaving in and out of the panicked throngs of people.

"*Vati, Mutti,*" Anna Lise commands. "We must pack and be ready to leave. If the fire crosses the river, we'll have little time to escape."

They look toward Anna Lise and nod, accepting her direction, then turn to look helplessly at their beautiful butcher shop and home.

Anna Lise looks at me, panic in her eyes.

"Help your parents," I say. "Food is the most important thing to take, especially cheese and dried sausage. I'm heading to see Uncle Jean."

Rushing across the street into the home where Uncle Jean is billeted, I find his staff quickly packing his belongings. "Where do I find the general?" I shout.

"He's in the study with the homeowners."

I find Uncle Jean in an animated conversation with the couple who own the home. "You must leave! The fire has crossed the river and will be here within the hour."

The couple both look to be in their late sixties, well dressed and surrounded by the finest of furnishings. "No, General, we won't leave. Our entire life is here. We are prepared to accept the inevitable." The couple take each other's hands and sit, holding tightly to each other.

The general sighs and runs a hand over his face before responding. "Very well. I will take my leave. You have been most gracious hosts." He bows to the gentleman and kisses the lady's hand.

Turning, he sees me. "Jean-Luc, the fire has jumped the Chechera, but I've received word that the area around the Kremlin is safe, protected by the Moskva River and the Kremlin's walls. We are going to regroup in Red Square. You and the corporal must bring the Bauck family and come with me. We leave shortly."

"The Baucks are already gathering their things, Uncle Jean. Corporal Coulane has gone to check on the fire. I expect he will soon return."

"We can't wait. The flames are too near. Have the Baucks ready to leave in ten minutes."

"Yes, sir," I say as I rush out the door, ignoring the stabs of pain in my leg.

Anna Lise is helping her parents load boxes of sausages and cheese into the carriage. "Almost packed?" I ask, trying to catch my breath. "Uncle Jean is taking us to the Kremlin, where it's safe."

"Yes, nearly so," Anna Lise says. "What of Arnaud? He hasn't returned yet."

"If he hasn't come back by the time you leave, I will stay and wait. I must go and saddle Bayard."

"You can't stay," Anna Lise pleads. "Can you even ride with your wound?"

"I'll be fine."

Anna Lise rushes into my arms, burying her head deep into my shoulder. "We will all be fine, won't we, Jean-Luc?" she whispers.

"Yes, we will. Uncle Jean knows what to do."

I am saddling Bayard and ensuring I have all my equipment when General Rapp and his entourage ride by, followed by the Baucks in their carriage. Vlad, their servant, is madly dashing to catch up to the carriage. They stop briefly and he climbs in, tossing a knapsack down around his feet. Anna Lise gives me one last fleeting wave. "I'll see you in Red Square!" she says. Then she motions frantically toward me.

"Jean-Luc, your journal, I think it's still in your room."

I look at her in panic, then remember she set it on the table when we left for a walk. I wave back and shout, "I know where it is. I'll see you at the Kremlin."

I rush into the room. *Where is it?* Frantically, I look everywhere. By the table. Under the bed. In the bedding. *It's not here. Did someone else find and take it to safety? I can only hope, and I can't take any more time to find it.* Quickly, I rush back to Bayard.

The smoke is now heaving down the street, warning that flames are not far behind.

Arnaud, where are you?

I kick Bayard, and we head into the oncoming firestorm. Maybe he's injured. We ride, but it's hard to breathe and the heat is overwhelming. There is no one to be seen. Memories of the dead in Smolensk flash through my mind—the smell of burning flesh and the sight of the bodies of those who suffocated. I have no choice but to turn back.

I send Bayard into a full gallop and feel him gasping for breath as we race back the way we came. We reach the Baucks' home, but there's no sign of Arnaud.

No time to think as I look back and see fire devils dancing from roof to roof.

I gallop on, then slow to study the diverging streets. Uncle Jean was headed in this direction, but now I come to a fork in the road. Which way? A glint of light flashes like a beacon to the right. It's a reflection off one of the Kremlin's onion domes. 'Go, Bayard," I shout as I kick him into a gallop. The street is filled with overturned carriages and carts and a throng of panicked people fleeing the oncoming inferno. Some move aside when they hear the clatter of Bayard's hooves, but others jostle into Bayard, unnerving him. He snorts and dances left, then right, trying to clear a way. In frustration, he gives a loud whinny and rises up on his hind legs. People scatter, running in all directions. I draw my sabre, raising it to the attack position in order to strike more fear. The tactic works as those in front of me scramble aside to keep away.

Crossing a bridge over the Moskva River, Bayard and I go through a portal in a red wall and enter a plaza at the foot of a massive, onion-domed cathedral.

Where are Uncle Jean and Anna Lise? They must be nearby.

'Jean-Luc," I hear someone shout. 'Over here."

It's Arnaud! I maneuver my way through the crowd. I reach him, and we lean across our saddles and embrace. 'Have you seen the Baucks or General Rapp? They were headed here."

The press of humanity in the packed square makes it difficult to move. 'Arnaud, you circle to the left and I'll go to the right. They have to be here." Bayard pushes his way through the crowds. I scan the swarm of people, but no luck.

What if one of those carriages I saw tumbled over was theirs? They could be dead or still in that mob trying to escape the flames. Anna Lise, where are you?

Nearly an hour passes, and still no luck. Then, at the far edge of the square, I see soldiers and a carriage. *Maybe it's them?*

I keep pushing Bayard forward, biting my lip with cautious hope. Finally, I'm close enough to see a young woman, her blonde hair blowing as she stands on a carriage seat, peering out over the masses.

Moscow Burning

Forty-Two

The Fire – Mid-September 1812

The sun is beginning to set, and light reflects off the cathedral's domes, casting wavering shadows across Red Square and the landscape. It's hard to make progress in this crowd, but the young woman with blonde hair is getting closer.

"Anna Lise!" I shout, waving wildly and standing in my stirrups. The woman's gaze sweeps over me, but she gives no sign of recognition. She sits down in her carriage. I keep pushing Bayard forward, frantic to confirm it's her. Her carriage is only about ten feet away, and I jump from Bayard, pushing past the last few people in my way.

"Anna Lise?" I cry, taking hold of the carriage. The woman turns, looking surprised that I'm addressing her. The shock fells me. It's not Anna Lise.

I lower my head, sinking to my knees. *Where can she be? Maybe Arnaud has found her ...*

The woman in the carriage reaches down, touching my shoulder. "Are you all right?"

"Yes, thank you," I answer, giving her a weak smile.

With new resolve, I mount Bayard, scanning the crowd while stretching up from my saddle. Nothing.

I keep pushing through the swarm as darkness settles over Red Square. At last, I spot the corporal, who is searching the crowd intently and coming in my direction.

"Arnaud," I shout. He sees me and urges Basile forward through the throng.

"Did you find them?" Arnaud asks me urgently.

"No. I've been praying you had."

"No, I haven't seen Anna Lise or her family, or General Rapp," Arnaud reports with dismay. "Maybe they're in the center of the square where we can't see them."

"I don't think so," I say. "We wouldn't have missed them. She's not here." My hands tremble. "We'll split up again. You search for their carriage in the nearby streets. I'm heading back to the German quarter. If their carriage crashed, they may have had to return to their home."

"No, Jean-Luc. We need to stick together. It's too dangerous."

"The danger will not be lightened with both of us together. Splitting up gives us our best chance."

"But the fire! Where you are going is in flames."

"I'll find a way." I give Arnaud a steely look. "I will not lose Anna Lise now that I've found her. I pray for our success. Keep guard over her if you find her."

Arnaud nods and directs Basile toward the nearest portal through the wall. I move toward the one I first entered.

Fewer people are streaming into Red Square from the north. Some soot-covered soldiers are among those fleeing. "What's happening?" I ask them. "Is the fire nearby?"

"The flames swept through the German quarter, and the wind is pushing them east," a private less bedraggled than the others says. "If the wind shifts, it will come this way and threaten the Kremlin."

"Have you seen a young woman with blonde hair who may be with an older couple?"

"There were many women with blonde hair, some accompanied and some trying to escape by themselves," he says exhaustedly. "Everyone's trying to escape."

He salutes and moves on with his companions.

I continue toward the German quarter. Although the sun has set and night has fallen, the fire lights the sky ahead of me, outlining the homes, palaces, and churches. I fear all will succumb to the flames.

As I ride north, the heat intensifies and sweat beads on my forehead. Smoke hinders my view, and flames lick the walls of buildings ahead, blocking my path. Seeing a crack of an opening to the west, I spur Bayard through the blast furnace to a street spared from the fire. These structures are ghostly silent, in contrast to the howl from the inferno now behind me. No one remains.

I turn down an unburnt avenue that I hope leads to the street where the Baucks lived.

The glow of the moon is blotted out by the smoke, and the blaze is now far to the east, giving me little light. The going is slow, as the street is filled with overturned carts and abandoned wagons. In the dark, it's difficult to know if I'm going in the right direction. Hours pass, and it seems like I'm seeing the same overturned wagons again and again. My leg throbs, telling me I've got to rest, but I drive myself on.

I come across an old man, trudging slowly toward the Kremlin.

"*Parlez-vous Français? Sprechen sie Deutsch?*" I ask.

"*Deutsch,*" He replies.

I try to remember the German name for a butcher shop. "*Ist Fleischerei dort drüben?*"

"*Ja, dort drüben,*" he answers, pointing up a nearby street going north. "*Verbrannt.*"

"*Danke,*" I say, and I make my way in that direction. *"Verbrannt," what does that mean? burned?*

The news that a butcher shop is nearby lifts my spirits, at least for a short while. Pulsing pain throbs up my leg with each step Bayard takes. I droop low in my saddle, holding onto his mane, trying to conserve what energy I have left.

We leave the area of spared buildings and come into the ruins left by the fire. Heat radiates intensely from the burned buildings we pass. Bayard is spooked by the thunder of walls collapsing and the echoing sound of structures crumbling. New flames erupt with each collapse. "Keep going, Bayard," I say, patting his neck. "I'm depending on you."

* * *

Later, Bayard gives a loud snort, and I'm roused from my half slumber to find a new day has arrived. Clouds of smoke drift by, but through the wisps I see we are in the park along the Yauza River where I strolled with Anna Lise what seems like an eternity ago. The trees are nothing but black spikes. By the bridge where I kissed Anna Lise for the first time, a patch of green grass survives. I look in all directions. Everything in view is in ruins. Smoke still rises from the charred buildings, but the fire has moved on. I can't see the Baucks' home, but there seems to be no chance it could have survived.

I dismount and lead Bayard to the river near the unburned grass. He drinks insatiably, and so do I. After washing the soot and grime from my face, I retrieve a few crusts of bread from my saddlebag. Slumping to the ground, I hungrily devour the crusts, feeling as helpless as I did at Borodino when I was trying to find Adrien.

I lay my head back, unable to stay awake. My mind is filled with visions of clutching flames pulling Anna Lise into their fiery embrace.

* * *

Something pushes my shoulder. I hear nickering, then another shove. Opening my eyes, I see Bayard. He gives me yet another push.

"I'm awake, my friend ... where are we?"

My head clears as I look around and remember my quest to find Anna Lise. I cover my face with my hands. *Where is she?*

It's late afternoon, and the sun is beginning to peek through the smoky haze. Getting up, I test my leg. "Damn!" I cry out as I take a few steps. It hurts, but I'm able to walk. Leading Bayard, I walk to where the Baucks' home once stood. The house and all the structures around it are now nothing but burned-out shells. The home where the older couple decided to stay is in complete ruins. I cross myself, hoping their deaths were quick.

Though the building still radiates heat, I walk inside what remains of the home into the remnants of their sitting room. The doorway that Anna Lise entered when she stunned me in her blue dress and bonnet is gone, but the memory still burns, much like the fires across the city.

A set of footprints in the soot and debris follow a path in and out of the room. Holding my breath, I stoop down and examine the prints. *They could be from an older child, or ...*

Rushing out onto the deserted street, I look around and shout, "Anna Lise?"

No sounds. My shoulders drop. Where is she?

I put my foot into my stirrup and swing myself up onto Bayard. "Come, my friend. Let's see if Arnaud has found her."

A few hours of daylight remain, and we make our way through the burned and deserted streets. Billowing smoke is heading toward the Kremlin. A horse and rider fly by, then several more. Civilians driving carts appear, followed by several soldiers lugging bags likely filled with loot.

I grab the collar of a passing private laboring under the weight of his sack. "What is it?" I demand. "Why are all of you fleeing?

He looks at me with panicked eyes. "The fire! The wind has shifted, and it's now moving toward the fortress." He shakes loose from my grip and joins the others fleeing the scene.

The crowd of evacuees is now so dense that Bayard and I scarcely make headway. With my stomach churning, we push aside several people in our way. We come to a cross street and find an opening at the edge of a nearly empty park.

"Bayard, look," I say in a stunned tone. The park is on a hill overlooking the Moskva River with the walls of the Kremlin, the church domes, and Red Square in sight. Flames engulf the buildings around the fortress, blocking all access to the square. The wind pushes the fire up against the fortress walls. It seems inevitable that soon the Kremlin itself will be overwhelmed.

We are about half a league away in an area that was already burned, but the heat from below radiates intensely around us. Despite that, I stay to watch the unfolding tragedy. One wouldn't know that night has fallen with the glow from the fire lighting the sky.

I walk back and forth across the width of the park, looking down at the spectacle. Frustrated and immobilized, I now sit and watch the inferno throughout the night.

An ache pulses in the back of my throat, making it difficult to swallow. I want to scream, but nothing comes out. I cup my face into my hands and cry. Fear overcomes me.

* * *

By morning, the flames have moved away, and remarkably, the Kremlin still stands. My fingers clutch the locket Anna Lise gave me so many years ago. I rub it as I stare over the scene, and the memento gives me resolve to continue. Climbing onto Bayard, I pat his neck. "Come on, boy, we must find Anna Lise."

We thread our way through the debris-laden avenue leading to one of the portals through the Kremlin's walls. Inside, troops are using blankets and buckets of water, trying to stop hot spots from flaring into flames. French soldiers drag two civilians and push them up against the fortress wall. "Fire!" bellows a sergeant, and two bodies slide to the ground, their blood adding a streak of deeper color to the red walls. I think of Madrid, and my heart lurches.

"Why were they shot?" I ask a nearby lieutenant.

"They're arsonists we caught trying to burn the cathedral." The lieutenant spits in disgust. "We've caught many throughout the city and had them shot." He gazes toward the recently burned buildings on the other side of the wall. "With the city almost gone, I don't see how we can winter here."

A horrible possibility. Surely the emperor and the tsar will negotiate a peace.

Why are there arsonists? Do the Russians want to burn their sacred capitol?

I shake away these thoughts. "Did the emperor escape?"

He's not looking at me, but watching his men handle a flare-up. "Lots of water," he tells them. "Remember, the arsenal is nearby."

Satisfied with their efforts, he turns back to me. "Barely," he says. Now pointing, he adds, "He and a number of people broke through the flames on that street over there, then followed the Moskva River to the northwest."

"Do you know if General Rapp was with him?"

487

"Sorry, Captain. Embers were landing everywhere, and I was trying to save the Kremlin. I just know the emperor and others went that way."

"Thank you, Lieutenant."

Bayard and I turn in the direction the lieutenant pointed and head along the river. We travel for another hour or so with no luck. I question passing soldiers and look down each side street we cross. My gaze darts back and forth, trying to see anything. A gunshot in the distance makes me jump in my saddle.

Down one street, I see a carriage, then a familiar form standing stoically, guarding the front door of a home.

Could that be Arnaud?

I kick Bayard into a gallop, dashing toward the man. He turns in my direction, drawing his sabre.

"Arnaud, have you found her?"

He sheaths his sword. "Jean-Luc! Yes, she is here with her family and is safe."

I dismount and embrace him wildly. "You found her!" I gasp breathlessly. "Where is she?"

"She should be in the sitting room. It's down the far end of the hallway."

I look at the door, hesitating. "She is all right?"

"Yes, and most anxious about you."

My heart pounds, and I give Bayard's reins to Arnaud. With tingling hands, I open the door and slowly make my way down the hall. The only sound is the clump of my boots. Three doorways present themselves, but I focus on the door latch at the end of the hallway. I slowly slide the handle. It feels warm to my touch. The door silently swings open, and there is Anna Lise, sitting near a window, reading. Tears well in my eyes at the sight of her. She looks up and gasps, clasping her hands to her chest.

"Jean-Luc."

It's all she can say. As she rises, the book she's reading falls to the floor.

She steps toward me, her eyes wide with disbelief.

We embrace, then I hold her out and examine each feature in her lovely face. Her smiling eyes, wet with tears. Her high cheekbones. Her soft mouth. I stare into those light blue eyes. I cannot believe she is alive. She takes my face in her hands as she presses her lips to mine. I pull her body tightly to me, kissing her over and over. Her heart beats against my chest.

"My love, I thought I lost you."

"Never again," she whispers, kissing me once more.

Forty-Three

The Marriage – Mid-October 1812

With tears sliding down her cheeks, Anna Lise takes my hand and guides me to the nearby sofa. Looking at me intently, her eyes a little wild, she clutches both my hands. "Jean-Luc, the fire—it was so frightening. I thought you were dead. I thought we all would die. Arnaud told me you went back north looking for us, but how? It looked like the whole city was on fire."

She buries her face in my shoulder, continuing to cry.

"It's all right, Anna Lise. We are together again, my love."

I rock her gently.

"I couldn't find you in Red Square. Arnaud and I looked everywhere. Where were you?"

Her shoulders shudder.

"Anna Lise, please."

After a few moments, she sits back and wipes her eyes, not yet ready to smile.

"Jean-Luc, if Arnaud had not been driving the carriage yesterday morning, I don't think we would have made it through that inferno. You and I must keep him close. He's now saved us both."

"Yes. We will keep him with us. The young corporal is a blessing." I kiss her on the forehead. "Can you tell me what happened after you left your parents' home?"

"When we got to Red Square, it was nothing but chaos," she says, her voice barely above a whisper. "We couldn't move. Uncle Jean finally got us out of the citadel to a building that looked safe. Arnaud found us there."

"But how did you get here, to this building so far from Red Square?" I ask.

I can feel Anna Lise's heart pounding, her breath rapid and uneven.

"During the night, the wind changed. Uncle Jean's men hammered on the doors, shouting that we had to go."

Her chin trembles, but she holds back more tears. "We got to our carriage and Arnaud was already in the driver's seat. Smoke was closing in, small fires sparking up all around us. Uncle Jean and his men charged ahead, and we followed."

I give Anna Lise some water and brush back a strand of hair that's slipped into her face, squeezing her hand to encourage her.

She looks into my eyes, more composed. "We got back to Red Square and again found chaos. The emperor and the Old Guard were racing toward the river. We tried to follow, but flames blocked our way. The Old Guard got the emperor through, but then a burning building collapsed on the right, and it seemed our way was completely blocked."

Anna Lise takes a deep breath. Her eyes are filled with fear, and new tears slide down her cheeks.

"Uncle Jean pulled out his sabre like he was going into battle and charged into the inferno. We followed blindly. It was so hard to breathe, and the heat ... the heat was like we were all in an oven. Jean-Luc, I was so frightened."

She rests her head on my shoulder, and I stroke her hair.

After a few moments she continues, wiping away tears again.

"Finally, we broke through the flames onto an avenue along the Moskva. No fires ahead of us. I don't know how long we rode ... we were all dazed by the fire, but finally we came to this house. The owners must have left quickly. You can see it's filled with fine things—art, porcelain china, silverware, and there's a larder full of food."

Frau Bauck knocks and comes through the sitting room door. "I thought I heard voices. Jean-Luc! Again, you have overcome all odds and returned to us."

Anna Lise and I both rise as she rushes over to hug me. Not far behind is Herr Bauck. As Frau Bauck holds me tightly, Herr Bauck says, "My son, I'm overwhelmed to see you again." His voice is filled with anguish.

"Arnaud tells us you tried to make your way back to the German quarter," Frau Bauck says.

"Yes, I got to your home. I'm sorry to say it is gone."

"I expected no less," Herr Bauck says softly, his shoulders slumped.

Frau Bauck takes her husband's hand and holds it tightly, her own face full of grief. "What of Herr and Frau Timmer, the couple from across the street who stayed behind?"

"Their home is burned as well."

Herr Bauck shakes his head as he stares down to the floor. "Why didn't they leave? I know they were old and didn't want to face rebuilding, but we could have all helped. They were such good friends."

There are several moments of quiet as the Baucks take in this information and grieve over the loss of their friends. Then Herr

Bauck looks up at me. "But you are here. Alive. We are all alive, thanks be to St. Christopher. Let's celebrate that."

"Vlad," he calls out to his house servant.

Vlad enters the room and bows. "Go to General Rapp and invite him to dinner," Herr Bauck says. "Tell him Jean-Luc has found his way back to us."

Vlad excuses himself, and Anna Lise says, "I'll help *Mutti* in the kitchen. *Vati*, I saw some cognac in the sitting room. Perhaps you and Jean-Luc would like a glass while we prepare dinner."

She smiles at me and nods slightly. I know what she's expecting me to do.

Herr Bauck and I retire to the sitting room, where I find the bottle of cognac and pour each of us a glass. We raise our cognac to each other, then take a sip. The warm tingle of the fine brandy sliding down my throat is soothing. I pause, trying to find my courage.

"Herr Bauck, may I call you Martin?" I ask.

"Of course," he says.

"Adrien and Anna Lise have been my closest friends all of my life ... I can't tell you the despair I feel over Adrien's death."

I take another sip. Herr Bauck grips his glass with both hands, staring straight ahead.

Feeling like a dam ready to burst open, I blurt out, "Coming to Moscow and finding Anna Lise has overwhelmed me with joy. I know now she is more to me than the young girl I knew growing up. She is everything. The only person I want to be with the rest of my life. I love her and hope you will give me permission to ask her to marry me."

I look desperately toward Herr Bauck to see his reaction. He smiles, and my heart lifts.

"Jean-Luc, when we left Colmar, her *Mutter* and I could not console her. *Mein frau* gave her the blank journal to give you, thinking it would keep your friendship alive and give Anna Lise solace. She has always asked what the emperor was doing and what we thought you and Adrien were going through. She cherished the letters you sent, reading them over and over. I believed she would never see you again, but *mein frau,* she knew you would find her."

Herr Bauck looks pensive. "I'm happy for both of you, but Jean-Luc, you are not Catholic. *Mein frau* cares not about this, but the church means much to me. These are strange times, and I know *mein tochter*'s heart is with you. I will give you my blessing if you marry within the church."

I look at Herr Bauck incredulously. Although I was baptized a Lutheran, my family had little to do with the church. Being Lutheran or being Catholic is just a label to me, but I know Herr Bauck is devout. Even Adrien regained interest in the church as we crossed into Russia. Perhaps it is important to Anna Lise as well. Of course I will do as he asks.

"Sir, I'll marry within the church if that's what is needed to have Anna Lise."

Herr Bauck smiles. "Good! How I wish Adrien could be here. We left each other on such bad terms, and I regret that deeply." His sorrow is plain on his face.

"Adrien and I talked often of his remorse for not seeing his family before you left Colmar. He treasured all of you." I bow my head. "Martin, I miss him terribly. His dream was for our families to be one. I can see him now, standing proudly in a church next to me."

Herr Bauck gives me a wistful smile. "Thank you, Jean-Luc. Your words mean much to me. Now we have this war. It confounds everything. My home and shop are gone. What am I to do? I can rebuild, but will I be welcomed in Moscow again? Much depends on the peace the tsar and emperor can agree to. Maybe *mein Frau* and I need to return to Colmar."

* * *

"Frau Bauck, where did you find the meat to make your sauerbraten?" I ask as I savor another bite. "It's wonderful."

She smiles and looks to Uncle Jean. "The general's staff was able to procure meat from a Jewish merchant," she says. "It is good, isn't it?"

Uncle Jean rises to give a toast. "It's gratifying we are all here together, safe. I think back to the last time I had dinner with all of you—back in Colmar when Jean-Luc was very young and you, Frau Bauck, were about to give birth to Anna Lise. So much has happened since then. Adrien would have wanted so much to be here ... to be with his family. I raise a glass to his memory."

I look at Anna Lise and see her eyes are red. There is a small, sad smile on her lips as we raise our glasses.

We drink our toast, but Uncle Jean does not sit. "Our children are who we ultimately live for. Jean-Luc and Anna Lise are our collective children. May the madness of war soon become but a memory, and may the children after us know only peace."

* * *

The evening is late when Uncle Jean excuses himself from our company.

"Good night, my children," Frau Bauck says as both she and Herr Bauck retire for the night. As Anna Lise and I make our way to the sitting room, the sound of heavy rain reverberates through the house. "That sounds heavenly, doesn't it, Jean-Luc?"

"Yes. Hopefully it will quench the fires."

We enter the room, and I see my journal laying on the table. "You have it," I exclaim. "How did it get here?"

"When we left our home in the German quarter, Vlad made one last check of the house and found it," Anna Lise says. "You were only gone for two days, but I was so afraid for your life, and thought this might be all I would have of you."

I touch my fingers to the leather binding. "Have you read more?"

"Pour us a glass of wine, Jean-Luc, and sit down by me."

I fumble with the bottle and spill a few drops on the tabletop.

"Here, Anna Lise," I say as I hand her a glass, searching her eyes. I settle next to her on the sofa.

"With all the chaos, I've only read through your time in Spain."

I flinch at the word "Spain."

She sets aside her wine and takes my hands. "Madrid was an unspeakable tragedy," she says, looking at me directly. "The priest and Manuel ... I can see why you were afraid of my reading it. What happened was horrifying, but what could you have done? If you had resisted, you would have been killed as well."

"Following orders is an acceptable excuse? Shouldn't I have followed my conscience and refused to follow those orders? Fighting for survival, as we have had to do many times for France, I accept. But that?"

I put my glass aside and bow my head.

"All of you would have needed to resist, or your action would have been futile. The priest would have died with or without you. It sounds cruel, but the priest died quickly and humanely. The blame lies with Marshal Murat."

"The blame lies with all of us who pretend to fight for our country against a false enemy. Spain was not attacking us. We attacked them without provocation. Is Russia much different? The serfs hate us, and the entire population is bent on destroying everything they hold dear in order to keep it from us. Look at Moscow, their most revered city. They have burned it!"

I let out a deep breath, trying to keep my emotions under control. Anna Lise pulls my head to her shoulder and gently strokes my hair.

"Jean-Luc. Don't forget the two boys you helped save in Spain. They would have died if you weren't there."

Her hands feel so gentle, her voice soothing.

"You must forgive yourself. Your journal bares your soul, and I'm thankful you let me read it. I love you, Jean-Luc. Our lives belong to the future."

* * *

Nearly a week has passed since I spoke to Herr Bauck about marriage and talked with Anna Lise about Spain. There is still no word from the tsar regarding the emperor's peace initiatives. On the horizon, wisps of smoke still twine up into the sky, but where we are is untouched by the fire. A marketplace near the river is open, and a surprisingly large number of people are shopping, all foreigners left behind when the Russians fled. What remains of Moscow is tranquil, like there is no war at all.

In this interlude, Anna Lise and I take long strolls along the Moskva River, enjoying the beautiful fall weather and the calm away from fires and battlefields. We talk about what I have written, laughing about the stilt-men and visualizing the beauty of Vienna and Berlin. We talk further about Spain and our war with Russia. The memories of Madrid are horrific, but I am learning to endure them with Anna Lise's help. Does she truly accept what I've done? I need to have no doubt of this before I ask for her hand.

"Let's picnic today, Jean-Luc. The weather is perfect, and that spot along the Moskva near the bridge by the Kremlin walls is so pretty. I'll get some bread and cheese."

"I'll bring the wine," I reply. *It's time for Adrien's Alsatian bottle.*

We spread a blanket on the lawn, and Anna Lise brings out our food while I uncork the bottle and pour us each a glass.

"This is excellent!" Anna Lise exclaims. "It tastes like wine from home. What is it, Jean-Luc?"

I smile. "It is from home. It's Alsatian. Adrien brought it for the three of us to drink once we found you in Moscow. He gave it to me to celebrate our future together. He always wished for us to have that future, and I've come to want it with all my heart."

Taking a deep breath, I fidget with my glass, knowing what I want to say, but not how to speak it.

Anna Lise gazes at me and smiles. She knows I want to say more.

I can wait no longer. Looking into her blue eyes, I take her hands. "Anna Lise, will you be my wife?"

She reaches out, taking my face in her hands, and kisses me. Then she sits back, staring into my eyes. "*Vati* told me you talked to him about this." Her face shows a tinge of exasperation. "What took you so long to ask me? Were you fearful that after I read your journal, I would not love you?" She grasps my hands. "Of course I will marry you. I love you, Jean-Luc. I've wanted this since we rode the Shagyas so many years ago. You needn't worry. You have my love now and forever."

With a sigh of relief, I hold her tightly and gently kiss her, at a loss for words but thankful she is now my life and focus.

"I don't know how or when we can marry. When will this war end?"

"I will go with you, no matter where. I will not lose you," she replies.

We cannot seem to let go of each other, reveling in this moment. Finally I hold her at arm's length, looking at her beautiful face. "I am overwhelmed, my love. Will you be happy helping me run an inn in Colmar?"

"Yes," she says without hesitation. "Yes, very much."

"Adrien would be so glad."

"We can name our first child after him, be it Adrien or Adrianna," she replies.

I smile at the thought.

* * *

I visit Uncle Jean, who is staying in an abandoned home nearby, and tell him the news.

"No surprise, my boy. Will the wedding be here or in Colmar?"

"It depends on what happens with the war. Are we staying the winter in Moscow? Is there peace with the tsar?"

"The emperor has heard nothing from the tsar. Wintering in Moscow will be very difficult without a peace settlement, since so much of the city is destroyed and we'd need to secure enough food for the winter. If the tsar does not negotiate, we will need to retreat to Smolensk or likely as far as Vilna, but the weather must hold if we're to be successful."

The possibility of retreating gives me chills. "Time is running out, isn't it, Uncle Jean? I need to warn Anna Lise and the Baucks."

Excusing myself, I return to the Baucks' home.

I tell Anna Lise and her parents about what Uncle Jean and I discussed, and we talk about wedding plans. "We can marry here if we stay the winter. But God forbid, if we retreat, it would be best for all of you to stay. Traveling with an army is dangerous, and if the weather turns bad ... I wouldn't want to think about that."

"Jean-Luc, we are never separating again," Anna Lise says. "If you leave, I leave. I will follow the army if I must."

Herr Bauck only says, "Let's see what the tsar does. Winter is not far off, and a decision must be made soon."

* * *

A decision does come, much too quickly.

Uncle Jean summons me the next day. "Jean Luc, the tsar has dismissed all of our peace overtures. The emperor is ordering a retreat to begin in two days."

Fear wraps its cold fingers around my throat. Uncle Jean looks at me, lines of worry crossing his face, and quietly says, "I pray to God that this weather holds. Vilna is a long journey from here."

Can winter hold until December? It must, or our chances to survive are small.

I rush to Anna Lise and her parents to give them the news. "The three of you must stay. Vilna is hundreds of leagues away. Only with the grace of God will we make it there before winter sets in."

Anna Lise gives me a determined look. "Jean-Luc, I am going with you."

Herr and Frau Bauck exchange glances.

"We have nothing left here, Jean-Luc," Herr Bauck says. "Our home, my shop, all gone. The Russians may think of us as collaborators and kill us anyway. We must go!"

I look at them all and see their resolve. "Then you must load your carriage with as many provisions as you can carry, and be sure to bring oats for the horses. Hide as much as you can. It's important you stay separate from the camp followers. They will be especially in danger from the Cossacks, who nibble at our weak points. I will talk to Uncle Jean about having you travel with the emperor's support wagons, and I will try to see you as often as I can."

"What of your wedding?" Frau Bauck asks. "You must have it before we leave. I know our priest well. He's a Jesuit and will understand the circumstances."

I look to Anna Lise, who nods encouragement. "Do I tell him I'm Lutheran?" I ask.

"Tell him only what he asks," Frau Bauck says firmly, glancing toward Herr Bauck. "I will talk to him, and he will not inquire. You must marry tomorrow!"

"But Jean-Luc is Lutheran," Herr Bauck protests. "He must become a Catholic before he can marry Anna Lise."

"Shush," Frau Bauck says sternly. "There's no time for formalities, and I don't think God is going to worry if Jean-Luc is Lutheran. Thunderbolts won't erupt from the sky."

Herr Bauck lowers his head, pressing his lips together tightly. After a few moments, he turns toward me and says, "Mein frau is right. There's no time for you to learn the needed catechism lessons. Do you promise to take them and become Catholic when we return to Colmar? I don't want my grandchildren born into sin."

I know how important this is to him.

"Yes, I promise."

Heaving a sigh of relief, he smiles and clasps both mine and Anna Lise's hands. "Good! I give you both my blessing."

Turning toward his wife, he asks, "Have you seen Father Mathew since the fire? And where can we hold the wedding? I'm sure our church is gone."

"I will find him," Frau Bauck says determinedly. "There's a small Russian Orthodox chapel nearby we can likely use. I will go there and see if the chapel's priest knows where Father Mathew is."

Frau Bauck bustles from the room and out the front door.

* * *

I straighten my uniform, trying to smooth out the wrinkles. I had no chance to properly clean it.

"Come Jean-Luc, it's time," Uncle Jean says.

"You look excellent, sir," Arnaud adds.

It's midmorning, and a warm sun greets us as the three of us walk the short distance from Uncle Jean's billet to the chapel. I'm numb. Was it only five weeks ago I was brought into Moscow, near death, and miraculously found Anna Lise? So much has happened. All I feel is disbelief and joy.

Ahead is the small Russian Orthodox chapel where the ceremony will be held. Like St. Basil's in Red Square, the church is topped by golden onion domes, but on a smaller scale. Entering, I see a small group of people gathered in the pews, friends of the Baucks. A priest stands beside Frau Bauck by the altar. I suck in my breath and glance toward Uncle Jean, who gives me a smile of support, then go and join the priest and Frau Bauck.

"Jean-Luc," the priest says. "I'm honored to meet you. Frau Bauck holds you in the highest esteem."

I shake the priest's hand firmly. "Thank you, Father."

The front doors of the chapel swing open. My breath catches as Anna Lise and her father enter. She is radiant, wearing the same blue dress she wore when we walked along the Yauza River. The sight of her gown brings me back to that first kiss on the bridge. She could not have chosen a more perfect dress.

Despite all of his misgivings that I am Lutheran, Herr Bauck is beaming as he stands next to his daughter. The two walk up the aisle to meet us. Anna Lise takes my hand, staring softly into my eyes. We turn to face the priest, who gives us the rite of the marriage sacrament, then asks if we have wedding bands to exchange. Embarrassed, I say no, then see Frau and Herr Bauck remove their wedding bands. They hand their rings to us.

With the exchange of rings, we are sealed. We both smile broadly, but barely have time for a gentle kiss before the chapel doors crash open. I turn to see four soldiers march in. "We've come for General Rapp," a captain among the four announces loudly.

"Here," Uncle Jean shouts as he makes his way toward the interlopers. An animated discussion ensues, then the soldiers salute and take their leave.

Uncle Jean turns toward me, clearly distressed by their news. He addresses us all. "Marshall Murat's army has been attacked by the Russians. The emperor has ordered us to evacuate Moscow. Pack now ... hurry. We leave today."

Gasps of disbelief come from the attendees. They murmur among themselves, unsure what to do. Anna Lise and I rush down the aisle, barely noticing wishes of congratulations. My stomach is in knots as we near Uncle Jean. "It's true?" I ask.

"Yes. I must go and prepare to leave." Uncle Jean quickly embraces me and kisses Anna Lise on both cheeks. "It will take me a couple of hours to notify my troops and get them ready to march. Anna Lise, I hope you and your parents have changed your minds about going with us. I implore you. Stay in Moscow. We will be in grave danger."

"No, we are coming. My parents have nothing left here and face retribution from the Russians as collaborators, and I must go with Jean-Luc."

His face reddening in frustration, Uncle Jean looks at me. "Talk sense into them, Jean-Luc. I leave at one o'clock." He turns and walks from the chapel.

Arnaud joins us, along with Herr and Frau Bauck.

"*Mutti, Vati*, Uncle Jean wants us to stay."

Forty-Four

Escape from Moscow – Late October 1812

I shout, "Stay close to me, Vlad," as he tries to control the horses pulling the carriage holding Anna Lise and her parents. He looks at me in panic, obviously uncertain he can take charge of his two steeds. "The Kaluga Gate is near," I tell him. "Once we pass it, we'll be in the countryside with more room." He nods, then stares straight ahead, clenching the reins tightly.

Bayard snorts, sounding unhappy. The air is filled with the sounds of hundreds of horses whinnying, the grinding of wheels on stone pavers, and the pounding beat of uncountable marching infantrymen. The faces of the Grande Armée soldiers look grim. Besides their backpacks, many lug large sacks over their shoulders. Loot, no doubt. *What wasted effort.*

I glance toward Anna Lise. She's twisting her wedding band as she looks out over the mass of soldiers, her brow furrowed. She catches my glance and smiles tightly.

Our progress is painfully slow, like molasses seeping from a spilled jar. It's early afternoon with a brilliant sun moving toward the west, beckoning us to follow. Better weather could not exist. The air is comfortably warm, and the clear blue sky is like a brilliant sapphire, extending forever.

I've been given command of a squadron within Uncle Jean's division. It includes only a sparse fifty horsemen, a far cry from my squadron of two hundred soldiers at Borodino. Fortunately, Arnaud is part of my command.

We round a corner, and the Kaluga Gate comes into view. We pass through and emerge into the countryside, finally free from the confines of the city. As we look back toward Moscow, the domes of St. Basil's gleam in the sun. Traces of smoke still drift from several areas. The masses of people and wagons coming through the gate look like bees escaping their hive.

I move closer to Vlad and the Bauck family. "General Rapp has arranged for you to travel with his supply wagons. Thankfully, since he's the emperor's aide-de-camp, his wagons will be with the emperor's." Peering back toward the portal, I add, "Those must be their wagons coming through now. Corporal Coulane, have our men dismount while we wait."

Anna Lise gazes over the men and wagons filling the road and nearby fields. "The army is immense," she says, her eyes round. "We should be able to keep the Russians away with so many of us. Jean-Luc, we'll be fine now, won't we?"

I smile, but think back to when we crossed the Neiman with six hundred thousand men just a few months back. Our losses have been staggering, and now the Russians outnumber us.

"Jean-Luc, look at all those cabbages," Anna Lise cries as she points to a field to our north. "There must be a million of them! Can we pick some?" Her eyes shine at finding an unexpected surprise as we begin our journey.

I glance at the approaching line of wagons, knowing it will take them nearly an hour to reach us. "I'll ride over and get you one or two."

"Wonderful. I'll chop some to cook with our sausages tonight."

It takes me only a few minutes to reach the field. Dismounting, I look out over the endless sea of cabbages, amazed by their size—at least three times larger than what we grow in Colmar. I cut off a cabbage head with my sabre. It's so big, I have trouble mounting Bayard with it.

As I return to give Anna Lise the cabbage, a messenger arrives with orders: "We ride toward Kaluga with the emperor," he says. "Prepare to leave."

Kaluga! A much better way to get to Smolensk. It hasn't been devastated by either army as yet.

Herr Bauck has joined Vlad on the driver's bench. "I must leave," I say. "Join the caravan near the wagons bearing the imperial standards. I'll join you whenever I can."

My squadron is mounting up. I take Anna Lise's hands in mine. *"Mon amour,* I'll soon see you again, but no matter what happens, stay close to the emperor's wagons. They will be well protected, and the Cossacks would not dare attack them." I hold her close for a long moment, knowing that every separation is a time of danger. Then I mount Bayard and ride.

They shouldn't have come.

* * *

Several days have passed. The heavy rain that began last night eases, and only a light sprinkle adds to the mud already covering the ground. My squadron guards the emperor and his generals while they inspect the death and destruction of yesterday's battlefield. "My stepson has won a great battle," I hear the emperor say, "but where are General Kutuzov and his Russian army? They slip away again!"

"Cossacks, sirs!" I yell as a handful of them come out of the woods on the far side of the battle site. They quickly disperse after seeing our numbers.

The emperor gives my warning little notice as he continues to talk to his generals. "We must find Kutuzov. We cannot let him stop us from getting to Kaluga."

I reflect on Napoleon's comment about his stepson as I look at the field littered with thousands of dead French and Russian soldiers. *General de Beauharnais won, but the cost was so high.*

"It's late, sire," Uncle Jean says. "We'll dispatch scouts at first light."

The emperor shrugs, disgruntled, as they walk away and return to our encampment.

I sleep fitfully, wondering what is happening with Anna Lise. The emperor's tent is nearby, and people are coming and going throughout the night. In the distance, the Russian campfires come in and out of view as a thin fog drifts in, chilling the air.

Suddenly, before first light, the emperor comes out of his tent and orders his horse saddled. "I must know where Kutuzov is," he shouts. "Let's go!"

"Sire, this is foolishness," Uncle Jean tells him. "The fog is thickening, and the sun has yet to rise. You won't be able to see anything."

"We must see if those campfires are his or a ruse," he shouts back. In a few minutes he is racing to the east, his generals at his side.

Uncle Jean yells to me in exasperation. "Captain Calliet, awaken your men and follow us, quickly." He sends a messenger to rouse more troops to be at the ready.

My squadron quickly gathers its gear and moves toward where the emperor went. Dawn is hardly showing, but soon, through the fog and thin light, I see Cossacks charging toward Napoleon and his generals. *The emperor!* My men draw their sabres and fling themselves into battle. With the fog, I can't see anyone else, and the clash of steel and the shouts of the men are the only signs of where they are fighting.

I fend off a Cossack's lance and plunge my sabre through his chest. Turning, I catch a fleeting glimpse of Uncle Jean. Several Cossacks converge and overwhelm him. He and his horse are knocked to the ground, in danger of being trampled by the attacking enemy. Suddenly, more squads of our men burst through the fog, beating back the attack. Another enemy lunges toward me, but he leaves as the Cossacks begin to retreat. Uncle Jean is on his feet by the time I reach his side. He appears unhurt, but his horse lies dead, pierced by a lance. On the rise above us, the emperor is surrounded by cavalry.

After securing our position against the Cossacks, the emperor rides back to camp, sending my squadron on reconnaissance patrol to determine the position of General Kutuzov's army. Their campfires apparently were a ruse, as we find him several leagues away, preparing a line of defense just outside Kaluga on favorable ground. My heart sinks at the thought of possibly fighting another battle. Reporting this to Uncle Jean, I say, "It would likely take another effort like Borodino to dislodge him."

New orders come in the morning. We are turning away from Kaluga and instead retreating along the same road we used coming to Moscow, the Old Smolensk Road—the road that runs through Borodino. My stomach clenches at this realization. We will have no new supplies until we reach our stores in Smolensk.

I'm given leave by Uncle Jean to find Anna Lise and her parents. Picking my way through the crowd of troops, wagons, and carriages, I pass body after body of men who died during our approach to Moscow, their rotting corpses filling the air with the stench of death. I'm sure Anna Lise and her parents saw this too. I hope they have not reached Borodino yet, the place of so much horror. The place where Adrien lies.

Forty-Five

Return to Borodino –
Late October 1812

The fighting near Kaluga has kept me from seeing Anna Lise for nearly a week. With that battle finished and none expected in the near future, Uncle Jean has given me temporary leave to rejoin Anna Lise and her family.

My face reddens in frustration as I struggle along the Old Smolensk Road. The line of wagons and carriages stretches far into the horizon. The emperor's wagons must be near the front, and I pray that Anna Lise's carriage will still be traveling with them.

I'm caught in the mass of civilians following the army. Heavy rains have mired some of the wagons, their wheels sunken up to their hubs, too heavy with loot to move forward. Desperate men are tossing fine furniture, goblets, candelabras, leather-bound books—anything to lighten their load and free their wagons from the mud. I cannot help but think back to the sacking and looting of Córdoba and how those overloaded wagons slowed the army and led to doom for most of them.

The road is traversing an extensive marshland, the roadway barely a foot higher than the treeless, waterlogged expanse surrounding us. Tufts of grass poke up through the murky water as far as I can see. Two wagons are stuck in the mud side by side, blocking the roadway, and another one attempts to go around by moving off the road. The moment it leaves the track, the muck and water cover the wheels and begin to fill the wagon bed. The man and woman driving the wagon jump for their lives, barely able to wade back to firmer ground.

Their horse screams in panic and rage, thrashing violently, as it sinks up to its haunches. The wagon leans heavily to one side, knocking the horse over, and its screams intensify. I can't bear the cries from the doomed animal, so I take out my pistol, aim it carefully with both hands, and shoot. The shot momentarily freezes everyone in place. Faces look from me to the now silent, sinking horse. The wagon owners, covered in mud, look at me with anguished understanding, then drop to the ground to watch their possessions sink from sight.

I stay close to the side of the stuck wagon as I go around it, avoiding the marsh and wanting to leave the experience of what just happened as quickly as I can. The way continues to be littered with disabled vehicles and crowded with civilians. Some are rummaging through discarded loot. "Move aside!" I order. They pay me little heed until I reach for my sabre.

I give Bayard a kick, trying to rush through a momentary opening. It closes as a wagon lurches into my path. "Aside!" I shout, glaring at those in my way. Seeing that I don't intend to stop, those pushing the disabled wagon jump away, waving angry fists.

I keep pushing ahead and receive more curses. The sun is getting low, and the line of vehicles now stretches into a forest that rises above the marshland. Many wagons have moved off the road to make camp among the trees.

I know this place! Borodino is nearby. I must find them before they reach that horrific scene.

The road is now clear enough for me to send Bayard into a gallop. The sun-dappled leaves create flickering shadows across the track, becoming dimmer as the sun nears setting. My chest tightens around my racing heart. Grotesque piles of bones, stripped bare by crows and wolves, lie in piles along the roadside. Mercifully, there's no smell of rotting flesh.

A berline comes into view. *I found them!* But then I find it occupied by several young women. Coming to a stop, I ask, "Mademoiselles, have you seen another berline?"

One of them raises her skirt to her knee. "No, but you can stay with us, Captain," she says provocatively. "We are in need of protection."

"Thank you, Mademoiselle," I say as I tip my hat. "I'm sure you'll find another more than willing to help you. I must move on."

The last quarter of the sinking sun slides under the horizon just as a woman's voice—Anna Lise's voice—shouts, "Jean-Luc! Here we are!" My hands shake as I grip my reins. She's there, just ahead, waving her arms.

* * *

I kiss Anna Lise as the morning sun peeks through the nearby trees. We have our own fire for warmth, away from Vlad and her parents, farther in the trees. The shrubs and grass sparkle in the sunlight. Our first frost.

Cuddled under a blanket, Anna Lise rests her head on my chest. She's smiling. "Jean-Luc," she says, "I think we will be having a baby."

My eyes widen and my muscles tense. Looking down at her upturned, smiling face, I say, "How can that be? It's only been a week since we had an hour alone after the wedding."

"I know it's too soon to be sure," she says, then softly kisses my cheek. "But I feel different. In my heart, I'm certain I am pregnant. And I believe it's a girl."

I look away for a moment. *If Anna Lise is truly with child, her pregnancy will make this journey even more perilous.*

"Jean-Luc, are you not happy?"

She is staring at me uncertainly. I smile and kiss her. "Yes! Yes, of course I am happy! A girl will be wonderful, and so would a boy." I lay my head back and stare up into the trees. I want to feel truly happy, but the dangers are so great. The early morning sunlight sifts through the trees, making it easier to see the clouds of our breaths in the cold. "Adrianna will be a fine name. Thank God she'll be born in the warmth of a Colmar summer."

"Yes, near the time of your birthday."

Snuggling close, I feel her heart beating. A slow, contented rhythm. She squeezes my hand and looks into my eyes. "Jean-Luc, let's keep this possibility to ourselves. I don't want *Mutti* and *Vati* to fret."

"Of course, my love," I say quietly.

I hear someone shuffling, walking through the dead leaves. Out of habit, I reach for my sabre. As I'm drawing my sword and beginning to stand, I see it is Frau Bauck.

"I'm sorry to disturb you," she says, apologetically, glancing at my sabre. "We have food ready, and Vlad is harnessing the horses. We don't want to lose our place in the procession."

Knowing what today will bring snaps me back to reality. "Thank you, Frau Bauck—*Mutti*—and please excuse my sword. It's an army habit. We must talk while we eat. You need to know what you will see today. We are coming to Borodino."

I take a few quick bites of the fried sausage and cabbage, then put my food aside, dreading what I must do next. I take Anna Lise's hand and squeeze it tightly. "My *Familie*, today will be one of profound sadness. We will be passing through the Borodino battlefield ... I know the horror of battlefields, but this surpasses them all. Seeing it again will be most difficult for me and overwhelming for you."

They are all watching me, waiting for my next words.

"The carnage that took place here is incalculable, made worse by the passage of nearly two months' time. You have seen the bones of soldiers along the road, but here you will see bones covering corpses piled on top of more corpses. Some were buried, but not all, and the heavy rains may have disinterred a great number. Many of the dead were piled high in ravines. The crows and wolves have feasted on them, but there will still be rotting flesh. The smell will be overwhelming."

Frau Bauck puts trembling hands to her lips.

The thought of seeing this all again brings me to tears. Anna Lise presses my hand, giving me comfort.

"We will find where I buried Adrien and Major Bouchet. I've missed them both dearly since the day they died. Arnaud and I buried them away from the other dead, on a rise overlooking the river. It is a quiet place."

I stand, rubbing away my tears. Creaking wagons start to move, telling me we must leave. Taking Anna Lise's hand, I lead her to the carriage door. Her parents and Vlad follow.

"Are we ready?" I ask as I mount Bayard. They all nod apprehensively.

* * *

Our somber group joins the procession of wagons and carriages making their way toward Borodino. I look at all the people moving toward this ghastliness, knowing most have no idea what they are about to see.

The day is cool, though still clear. Gray clouds are on the horizon. We come upon a river whose freezing waters roll over a ford; it's the river that runs near the graves of Adrien and Major Bouchet.

Cannon carriages, stuck in the muddy riverbed, block much of the ford, but there is enough room for us to get past. Moving up the embankment, we find buckled trees, mutilated from the battle's shelling. As we reach the top, we see the expanse of the battlefield. Before us are the flat-topped rises, the redoubts so many men died capturing or defending. Some of the palisades and parapets have collapsed on the dead or dying, their bones sticking through the mud and rocks. Dry creek hollows are filled with layers of bones sinking into the decaying bodies below them. Clouds of fattened crows still feast on the exposed remains. The smell of death is everywhere.

The battlefield below the Great Redoubt, the field where Adrien and Major Bouchet died, is now sprouted green with new grass, fertilized by the blood and bodies of the fallen.

I turn toward Anna Lise and her parents. Frau and Herr Bauck look away, covering their faces. Anna Lise is dazed, her eyes drifting from the feasting crows in the hollows filled with the dead to the Great Redoubt. She turns to me. "Jean-Luc, I could never have imagined such depravation, even after reading your journal. No words can describe this. I don't know how you lived through this ... is Adrien's grave near here?"

"Yes, not far. Vlad, follow me this way."

The rains have disinterred thousands of bodies. Thousands more appear never to have been buried and are nearly bereft of flesh. We skirt the edges where the bodies are exposed, the dead hardly retaining a resemblance of humanity. The wheels of our carriage make crunching, moaning sounds as we move forward, bones popping up as we go.

"By that tree over there," I say, pointing. My mind floods with the memories of Arnaud and me carrying Adrien's and Major Bouchet's bodies away from the battlefield and the body scavengers.

I hadn't noticed someone sitting near the graves. He stands up. It's Corporal Coulane. "Arnaud," I cry. "How did you get here?"

I gallop ahead to meet him, dismount, and embrace him tightly. We are both without words, overcome by memories of this spot.

Finally, Arnaud says, "General Rapp sought me out and ordered me to find you. He knew Borodino would be difficult. I thought my best chance of finding you was to come to this grave site. How are you, my friend, and how are Anna Lise and her parents?"

"As well as can be expected. What an awful place this is."

"Arnaud, how good it is to see you," Anna Lise says quietly as the carriage comes up. Her smile is forced, but I know her words are heartfelt.

I help Anna Lise from the carriage while Arnaud assists Frau Bauck. Taking Anna Lise's hand, I lead her to the two mounded coverings of earth. I look toward Herr and Frau Bauck. "Adrien lies here, in this grave to the left. To the right is Major Bouchet."

Herr Bauck falls to his knees next to Adrien's grave and begins to sob. Frau Bauck holds his shoulders. "My son," he cries, "I was wrong to drive you away. Please forgive me."

Anna Lise joins her parents as she grieves over her brother. After a few moments, she looks up to me. "And this is Major

Bouchet? I feel I know him after reading your journal. Do you still have the handful of dirt from his grave?"

"Yes, both his and Adrien's. I am taking Major Bouchet's to Strasbourg and Adrien's to Colmar."

Anna Lise gazes out over the battlefield and its sprouting greenery. "How long will it be before nature reclaims this spot, this horror?" Her eyes turn up toward the Great Redoubt. "Is that where you looked down trying to see Adrien?"

"Yes."

"Would you take me up there? I would like to see where you and Adrien fought."

"You want to go through all those corpses?"

"I will never be here again. I want to see what Adrien gave his life for and try to understand how he died ... Arnaud, could I borrow your horse?"

Arnaud looks toward me with confusion.

"Anna Lise, I don't understand why Adrien died, or even why I fight. Duty to country? Duty to comrades? I may never know."

I look at her sternly as I wave my arm toward the field of dead. "It's too dangerous to venture out there. Basile was Adrien's horse, but Basile is not like the Shagya you rode with me at Ostheim."

"And I'm not twelve anymore," she states firmly.

I look to Frau and Herr Bauck for support. They give me none.

Resigned, I turn to Arnaud. "Can Anna Lise ride Basile?"

He looks at Anna Lise with uncertainty, then turns to me. "Of course."

She approaches Basile and calmly rubs his nose. "I'm Adrien's sister. Can you take me to that high ground?"

Basile snorts and shakes his head, then lightly nudges her.

"It seems he knows you are part of Adrien's family. Perhaps a familiar scent."

We find a path for our horses through the carnage, one likely made by the body scavengers, and make our way toward the Great Redoubt.

"My squadron attacked along this path," I tell Anna Lise. "Cannon shells exploded all around. The sound was deafening. I could hardly see through the smoke and flying dirt, but I saw many of my men blown apart. Adrien and Major Bouchet were still nearby."

Basile follows Bayard as we wind our way through the bodies. Crows caw loudly, not wanting to be interrupted. The stench is nearly unbearable. I take out two handkerchiefs. "Anna Lise, wear this. It will help with the smell." She takes one from me, and we secure them over our noses.

"I lost sight of Adrien and the major about here—halfway toward the Great Redoubt. The cannonade was increasing in intensity, and all I could do was charge forward."

Anna Lise is silent. She is staring out over the battlefield from left to right, taking it in.

Arriving at the base of the Great Redoubt, we dismount and walk our horses up the steep trail to the top as I describe our final push up the slope. I move aside skulls and other bones from our path as we go. Reaching the summit, we have a panoramic view of the folly of this war. There is death on all sides of the Great Redoubt. The sight is grotesquely overpowering. Anna Lise stoically surveys the scene.

Both Anna Lise and I are silent in this landscape of enormous devastation. Even after two months, I still feel the reverberation of the cannon.

"Why do men do this to each other?" she whispers to herself.

Then she points to a rampart. "Were you scanning the battlefield from there when you were trying to find Adrien?"

We walk to the rampart and look over its edge. "Yes, this is the spot, but on that day, smoke and dust blurred everything."

We stare across the expanse, saying nothing for several minutes. She presses into me, tears running down her face, pooling at the tip of her chin before falling to the earth. "Jean-Luc. How could you and Adrien survive for so many years enduring such as this? I can't put words together to describe my anguish and pain at what the two of you suffered."

She takes my hands, her blue eyes staring resolutely into mine. Firmly, she says, "We will go home to Colmar and move beyond these scenes of horror. You'll still have your memories, but they will be of your comradery with my brother, Major Bouchet, Uncle Jean, and now Arnaud. Your journal also has many good memories. And we will have our daughter."

Tears well in my eyes as I smile at her sadly and kiss her forehead. We turn and look again across the field of death. Above, gray clouds have thickened, and a cold breeze lightly stirs. Soft flakes of snow begin to fall gently.

Forty-Six

Return to Smolensk –
Early November 1812

Anna Lise and I return from the Great Redoubt to find Herr and Frau Bauck on their knees, digging small holes near the tops of Adrien's and Major Bouchet's graves. Arnaud is carving something onto a board he holds on his lap, and Vlad is whittling the end of another board down to a point. All four are wearing bandannas over their mouths and noses, trying to filter out some of the overpowering smell.

They stand to welcome us back. "We are making grave markers," Herr Bauck says. "I wish a priest could be here."

A bandanna covers most of Herr Bauck's face, but I can see his tears.

"I found some planks for making crosses from that overturned cart over there," Arnaud says, pointing. "I'm just finishing carving their names. Major Bouchet's name was Paul, wasn't it?"

"Yes ... yes it was," I say, my mind still distracted by the images I've been reliving from the battle.

Anna Lise and I dismount and let Bayard and Basile munch on the tender, green grasses growing nearby.

Anna Lise takes the board carved with *Lieutenant Adrien Bauck* and one of the longer, pointed boards, holding the two into the shape of a cross. "Do we have anything to secure this?"

"No nails, but there was a leather knapsack in the cart that I cut into strips," Arnaud says.

Anna Lise and her parents work on creating a cross for Adrien, and Arnaud, Vlad, and I put together one for Major Bouchet. *Major Paul Bouchet*, I read, and I wonder why he never talked about his family. *Surely there is someone who would want to know he died.*

We plant the crosses, then solemnly form a circle around the two graves. We bow our heads, and Herr Bauck talks for several minutes in German. I'm uncertain what he says, but it brings Anna Lise and Frau Bauck to tears.

When he finishes, Frau Bauck takes his hand and turns to the four of us. "*Mein Mann* and I would like to camp here tonight. The air *ist gestank,* but we will never be by our son again." Both she and Herr Bauck look imploringly toward me.

"Of course," I say. Light snow continues to fall, and the air is getting colder. "This snow and cold may help dampen the smell. Arnaud, this will give us a chance to unshoe the horses. They'll slip and fall on any ice if we don't, and we have no frost nails to pound into their hooves."

"I'll get the tools," he replies.

* * *

A blanket of white greets us the next morning. The snow has stopped, but to our north, there are swelling, dark clouds coming our way, promising much more treacherous weather.

"The battlefield doesn't look so appalling now, does it, Jean-Luc?" Anna Lise says. "The whiteness has cleansed away much of what we saw yesterday. The bones and corpses are nearly hidden." Her eyes move up toward the imposing structure across the field. "But the Great Redoubt still looks as sinister as ever."

Frau Bauck is preparing to fry some sausages for breakfast. "*Mutter!* Not so much food," Anna Lise scolds.

Frau Bauck is taken aback. "We must eat," she says. "This is no more than our usual."

I glance at how much food she has brought out. Enough for a sumptuous meal. "We must eat only half that amount, or less. I'm sorry I haven't communicated the gravity of our situation."

I glance over to the carriage. "Herr Bauck. How much food is left in those chests on top of the berline? Enough for another month? How about for the horses? I know the chest in the back has oats. Have you used any?"

"We haven't used the oats, but we have only enough sausage and cheese for another two weeks. Won't we be getting more food in Smolensk? Doesn't the emperor have stores there?"

"Yes, Smolensk is a supply depot, but we have the weather, the peasants, and the Cossacks to slow us down, and it may not be enough. We must ration our food, scavenge wherever we can, and be prepared for the worst."

After a meager breakfast, we leave Adrien and Major Bouchet for the last time.

We wind our way back the same way we came in, trying to stay clear of the now snow-covered bodies. The crunching of bones under our wheels tells us we are on the right path.

Reaching the Smolensk Road, we find ourselves mixed in with the camp followers and other civilians. "Arnaud, come with me and we'll try and make a way around these wagons. I fear that Cossacks and Russian peasant patrols will be attacking these people. Vlad, follow us."

We struggle to make headway. No one wants to be passed, even when threatened with drawn sabres.

"There's only two of you," one of them hisses back at me. "Do anything to us, and I can assure you that your carriage will be lost and those inside killed."

To our rear, bugles sound. Then horsemen approach, telling everyone to move aside, as the emperor's berline is nearing. The emperor, coming from the Kaluga battle site, sweeps by with additional imperial wagons and berlines following. More horsemen approach, and I see Uncle Jean, along with my squadron.

"Corporal Coulane, you and I must make an opening in the emperor's entourage for the carriage. Vlad, start moving into the flow as we make room for you."

Vlad nods and gets the carriage into position. A gap begins to form as the men in my squadron recognize us and clear a space. Vlad begins to move the carriage into the gap, but a horse bumps it on the left, then another on the right. The carriage is knocked off balance and nearly tips onto its side. One of the trunks holding food is knocked off the roof, splitting open and scattering a hoard of cheese and sausage.

Vlad pulls on the reins, but his team kicks out in protest. A wagon knocks hard into the carriage. Vlad loses his balance and nearly falls off just as I leap from Bayard to the driver's seat. As I take the reins, Vlad hangs off the side, clutching the end of the driver's seat. I reach out my hand. He grabs it desperately and pulls himself back up onto the seat. Wide-eyed, he nods thanks to me and holds on tightly.

Now in the flow with the cavalry, I push the carriage horses forward. "Is everyone all right?" I yell.

"Yes, Jean-Luc," a shaky-voiced Anna Lise answers.

"Arnaud, grab Bayard and bring him along."

* * *

We ride for several more hours before the column stops to rest. Now near the front of the procession, we are ahead of the camp followers and among the imperial wagons and carriages. It's becoming colder, and thick snowflakes drift lazily down from the leaden sky. I know I should be reporting to Uncle Jean, but I don't want to abandon my family.

"I'll get some oats for the horses," Herr Bauck says.

"No, not the oats. There's still green grass poking through the snow," I say, wanting to keep the oats untouched for as long as possible. "Food will be tight with the loss of the trunk. We have to hope we will be able to get more rations in Smolensk."

"Jean-Luc, those wagons off to the side by themselves, what are they?" Anna Lise asks.

I look over through the falling snow and see they are hospital wagons. "Those hold the wounded. I traveled in one at Austerlitz and in another coming into Moscow."

I pause, knowing most if not all of their occupants will die before seeing France again. One wagon carries the imperial standard. "Baron Larrey, the emperor's physician, should be with that one at the front," I say, pointing. "Anna Lise, you must meet the baron, the finest physician in all Europe. He saved my life twice and Adrien's once. It's a short walk, and we likely will be here about another hour."

The snow is gently falling as Anna Lise and I stride over the fresh blanket of white toward the imperial hospital wagon. Several men are gathered around a large fire, some standing and others stooped on their haunches, warming themselves. The wagon is close to the fire, with its canvas side lifted so that the warmth can reach those inside.

Anna Lise and I stop. No one has seen us yet. I scan the faces. Most look empty.

"Do you think it is all right for us to go to them?" Anna Lise asks, hesitating.

I'm uncertain myself, but a tall man in civilian clothes sees us and calls out, "Mademoiselle, Monsieur, can we be of assistance?"

The voice. There is no mistaking Baron Larrey. "Baron, I'm sorry to trouble you, but I saw the imperial standard and thought you might be here. I'm Jean-Luc Calliet. You saved my life at Austerlitz and again just outside of Moscow. This is my wife, Anna Lise. You saved her brother's life as well. I wanted her to meet you."

The baron regards me closely. "Yes ... you are General Rapp's friend, right? I've lost count of the number of times I've attended the general." He regards Anna Lise and smiles warmly. "This is your wife? I'm pleased to meet you. How did you come to be here?"

Anna Lise curtsies and smiles back. "I grew up with Jean-Luc. He was my brother's best friend, but my parents moved to Moscow. Jean-Luc found me there."

"Your brother has died?"

"At Borodino."

Baron Larrey gives Anna Lise a slight nod. "I'm so sorry, Mademoiselle." He sweeps his hand toward his wagon. "Please, come and warm yourself."

We make our way to the fire. The sight of Anna Lise brings smiles to almost everyone, except for a few of the injured who continue to stare blankly into space. One patient in particular can't take his eyes off Anna Lise. He has no legs, and his face is etched with profound sorrow.

One of Baron Larrey's staff brings up a saddle for Anna Lise to sit on. I briefly recount the story of the Bauck family and how they arrived in Moscow, as well as Adrien's death and my reunion with Anna Lise.

"Was Adrien the friend I treated at the Charité in Berlin?" Baron Larrey asks.

"Yes, it was him," I reply, thinking back to those happier times when I managed the affairs of the Charité, far from any battlefield.

Anna Lise rises. "I know we need to get back to the carriage," she says, "but I want to meet each of these men before we go."

"Thank you, Mademoiselle. It would mean a great deal to them."

She goes man to man, holding their hands and wishing them the best. The last is the soldier with no legs. He takes her hands and squeezes them tightly, staring at her with sad eyes, tears streaming down his face, mumbling something unintelligible. Anna Lise kisses him on the forehead. He loosens his grip and cries silently.

"Let me walk with you as you go back," Baron Larrey says.

After a few moments, he says, "Mademoiselle, that last man—the man with no legs. I believe you granted his last wishes."

He glances toward Anna Lise. "I think he saw family in you, perhaps his wife. Thank you for talking to him. You were most kind."

"If only I could do more. Do you know how he lost his legs?"

"No. He was found while we were crossing through the Borodino battlefield. He emerged from the open belly of a horse, where apparently he had kept shelter for fifty-two days. The cavity gave him warmth, and he must have gnawed sustenance from the meat inside and drunk rainwater. It's a wonder he's alive. We don't even know if he is French or Russian, as his clothes were gone and he has not spoken."

Anna Lise puts her arm around my waist and leans into my shoulder. "That man could have been you, Jean-Luc, or Adrien. Please, let's get home to Colmar."

Baron Larrey stops, bows, and kisses Anna Lise's hand. "I must go back. I'm happy to have seen you again, Jean-Luc, and to meet your lovely bride. Perhaps we will meet again in happier times."

"I hope so, Monsieur," Anna Lise replies.

I wonder if there will ever be happier times again.

* * *

A week has gone by since we left Borodino. Smolensk is still about a week away. Uncle Jean has assigned me and my squadron to guard the imperial supply wagons. He confided to me that the Baucks were as much family to him as my father and is allowing me and my men to stay near the imperial wagons so they can be protected.

The weather has been hovering around freezing, yet we've struggled in muddy roads for several days. But today, there is a fearfully cold wind. The snow begins falling heavily, and the temperature drops sharply. My hands turn numb, and I fear for my toes and feet. With bent heads, we trudge forward, following the tracks of those in front even as the blowing snow tries to cover them.

It's midmorning when the Bauck carriage begins to weave and I see Herr Bauck slumped forward, the reins dangling loose by his feet. I grab the carriage harness and bring the berline to a stop. Climbing up onto the driver's bench, I give him a shake. "*Vati!* Can you hear me?" He starts to move and mumbles something about the cold. I take him down and put him into the berline, where Anna Lise and her mother wrap him with blankets and furs.

"Arnaud, tie Basile to the back of the carriage and take over driving until Herr Bauck recovers."

At midday we stop to rest, but no one in the Bauck carriage dares leave what little warmth there is in the cab. "Jean-Luc,

Arnaud, come inside and get warm," Anna Lise pleads. "We can squeeze together."

"We must feed the horses and stay on patrol," I say. "How is your *vati?*"

"Much better. He will be able to drive the carriage when we're ready to leave."

"Arnaud, start a fire so that we can melt snow for the horses to drink. I'll get them some oats." Our four horses eagerly eat their oats and drink the thawed snow. *I hope there's feed in Smolensk. The oats will only last another week or two.* Bayard nuzzles me in thanks. "We'll get through this, my friend. We always do," I tell him, patting his neck. But I feel pain in my chest as I survey our surroundings.

The line of vehicles and men begin to go forward, but I notice several wagons not moving. Going up to the one directly in front of us, I find two men huddling together. "Get going!" I order, but they don't stir. I come closer and see their faces are blue, frozen.

I'm stunned, but I know this is only the beginning.

I look back toward the Baucks' carriage. "*Vati*, move around them." From his perch on the driver's bench, he nods.

We pass more unmoving wagons, then come across a horse that has just died. On all sides of this poor animal, men are attacking the carcass with their daggers and swords, cutting away chunks of meat. Many of the men are eating the meat raw. Back in Moscow, while the Baucks loaded their berline with food, these men loaded their wagons with loot.

We come up on another dead horse, this time with no one swarming over it. "*Vati*, can you butcher it into chunks? We can store the meat on top of the berline."

He nods and moves the carriage to the side of the road. Men are trying to move in on the dead horse, but Arnaud and I keep them at bay with the threat of our drawn sabres. Herr Bauck brings out his butchering knives and begins his work. Deftly, he skins part of the animal and slices out chunks of flesh. Frau Bauck and Anna Lise have emptied the remaining chest of sausage and cheese into the cab of the berline. They lay out the chunks so they will freeze and then load them into the chest.

As Herr Bauck is working, several men gather round, pleading for some meat.

"We have all we can carry," I tell him. Herr Bauck looks up at the pleading men and continues to cut, throwing chunks of meat to the starving onlookers. Finishing, he cleans his knives in the snow, drying them on his pants, and puts them away. Arnaud, Herr Bauck, and I hoist the chest onto the berline as many men jump onto the carcass. Much of what remains is frozen, but they gnaw on the bones, hoping to chunk some meat off in their mouths. Others gather the blood-soaked snow into pots, presumably to warm it over a fire and eat the coagulated blood.

"Cossacks!" someone shouts. I look up and see about twenty of them emerge from the forest behind us. I quickly mount Bayard and draw my sabre. My squadron, which has been strung out among the vehicles, joins me. The Cossacks don't move. Then another twenty appear from the trees in front of us. Cries of panic sound from members of our procession as I survey the situation, seeing if any more of them appear.

"Corporal Coulane, take twenty men and challenge those in the front. Sergeant Perrot and Private Dupont, stay here. The rest of you, follow me."

As my men approach the Cossacks, they fade back into the forest. Stopping, we hold our position to see if they return ...

Nothing.

"Back to our march," I order, feeling uneasy for those far to our rear. The Cossacks are likely picking apart these stragglers.

The sight of the Cossacks has given our column new life and a desire to move more quickly. Throughout the day, they appear, then disappear. By late afternoon, dense fog envelops us and the snow is still falling. The cold is nearly unbearable. I've kerchiefed my face to protect my nose from freezing and falling off. My mustache and beard are frosted and nearly solid with ice, and my brain is numb.

"Jean-Luc, the sky is gone," Herr Bauck shouts in panic. "The fog ... the snow ... I can see nothing in front of me, not even the tracks of the wagon I'm following."

"Halt!" I command, the order echoing up and down my squadron. "We camp here."

I ride to the Baucks' carriage. "Herr Bauck, go into the cab and warm yourself. Arnaud and I will take care of the horses once we start a fire."

Herr Bauck nods and stomps his feet before climbing into the cab.

"Anna Lise, Frau Bauck, stay inside until we build a fire."

"I've been warmed by my fur and blankets," Anna Lise replies. "I will unharness the horses and get some oats."

Herr Bauck, barely able to move, climbs into the carriage.

I nod at Anna Lise and turn to Arnaud. Pointing into the oblivion, I say, "There must be an abandoned cart or wagon nearby that we can break up into firewood. You go that way, and I'll look over there."

I inch away, and soon I can see nothing. *I can follow my tracks back once I find wood,* I think, and I continue my search. I stumble and fall over something lying in the snow. It's a soldier who could go no farther. I rise, then stumble over another frozen body. Falling forward, I find myself next to a wagon.

"Arnaud," I shout, "over here, I've found a wagon." No one answers. The wind howls. "Arnaud? Anna Lise? Can anyone hear me?" Still nothing. My heart begins to race. "Arnaud? Anna Lise?"

Grabbing the wagon, I pull off some boards with more strength than I knew I had. "I'll get these back to Anna Lise, start a fire, then come back for more," I say to myself.

Carrying two planks, I start to retrace my steps. I rush ahead, panting for breath as the traces of my path begin to disappear. Then there is nothing but the white, virgin snow. I stop and shout. "Arnaud? Anna Lise?" Again, no answer.

I plant the ends of my boards into the snow and lean against them, feeling dizzy. My first impulse is to rush ahead and hope I'm going the right way, but I dismiss that idea. *Be patient, Jean-Luc. Someone will come looking for you.* I stay standing, leaning against the planks, trying to see through the whiteness. Every few minutes, I shout again, "Arnaud? Anna Lise?"

It's dark now, but the snow has stopped and the fog is thinning. The cold is unbearable. "Arnaud? Anna Lise?" I rasp with all the strength I have left.

Gazing around, I wonder how much longer I can last. Then I see it. A dull glow of light.

A campfire? With renewed energy, I move toward the light, using the planks like crutches. As I get closer, Anna Lise and several other voices shout, "Jean-Luc?"

"Here," I cry, but my voice has no strength to carry. I keep moving, and finally, the fire is near and people are discernable. "I'm here!" Relief floods over me as arms take hold of me. It's Anna Lise.

"Jean-Luc," Anna Lise cries, kissing me with tears running down her cheeks. "Come to the fire and warm yourself. We have food." She leads me slowly to the fire. "Sit on these planks while I get you something to eat. You were missing for so long. We looked for you, but the snow and fog did not allow us to venture too far."

I plant myself down on one of my boards near the fire, the warmth seeping into my frozen body. I can't talk, too relieved to be with them all again. "Here is some meat, Jean-Luc," Anna Lise says as she settles down on the plank next to me. "We've roasted several chunks of the horse we butchered. I'll cut it into bites for you."

* * *

I sleep fitfully that night, dreaming I am still lost in the snowstorm, but am comforted by my full stomach and the warmth of Anna Lise's embrace.

As we hitch the two horses to the carriage in the morning, Arnaud calls out. "Jean-Luc, come look. Someone snuck in last night and bled one of the horses." I come over and inspect the animal.

"He looks weak. They must have taken a full pot," I say as I examine the wound. "We'll need to be more careful guarding our horses each night. Everyone's hunger is growing. We can hitch up one horse and tie this one to the back of the carriage. Hopefully, he can recover."

The sky clears, as Mother Nature has seemingly tired after brutalizing us for so many hours. Anna Lise joins her father on the driver's bench, appreciating this respite. Frau Bauck is content to stay in the warmth of the cab.

We pass several unmoving carts and wagons and see many snow-covered mounds near the vehicles, likely the remains of the drivers. Many horses lie frozen as well. Several soldiers are trying to cut meat from one of them, but it is too frozen for their knives to penetrate. They eye our horses hungrily. I loosen my sabre as they watch.

The column has spread out, and I fear it is now more susceptible to Cossack attacks. I send word up my column of squad members to stop until we are all close again. Most of the imperial wagons and carriages are no longer in sight, and we are now among the vulnerable stragglers. Small groups of Cossacks appear all along our way to Smolensk, but they don't attack. My squadron of about forty men is too strong for them, considering there are likely many other, weaker groups they can find.

* * *

As we come over a rise, the Dnieper River valley appears below us. "Smolensk!" I announce. Sprawled ahead is the sacred city, its fortress walls still intact, but much of the old city is still a blackened ruin. "What's that marvelous building on the hilltop?" Anna Lise asks, pointing toward the massive turquoise building that survived the burning of the old city.

"The Assumption Cathedral. It held one of Russia's greatest icons—a painting by St. Luke of the Virgin Mary holding the Christ child. Adrien was quite taken by it. The Russians took the icon to Borodino to inspire their soldiers to be brave. I don't know where it is now, since we've occupied Smolensk ever since."

The air is very cold, but fortunately, the wind is no longer raging as it did yesterday and the snow has stopped falling.

"The hill down to the bridge over the Dnieper is very steep and covered in snow and ice," Herr Bauck says uneasily. "Do you think one horse pulling the carriage can make it?"

No one in our column has yet attempted to go down the incline. They've all gathered at the top, assessing their chances for success. Most of the horses are shod, which will make their hooves slip on any ice. Finally, one moves forward, a wagon with two shod horses in relatively good health. The wagon successfully navigates the upper part of the hill, and a second wagon begins to follow. This one is heavily loaded and has only a single horse. It starts down the hill, but the weight of the wagon causes the horse to dig for footholds. It hits a patch of ice, and the metal horseshoes can't hold. The horse falls and the wagon careens down the hill, hitting the first wagon. Both then slide down the rest of the hill and crash onto the river ice, breaking through and submerging. One driver is able to jump to safety at the last moment.

Panic ensues among the drivers, many cursing and shouting that it isn't possible to go down.

"Quiet, everyone," I shout. "The horse pulling this berline is unshod and should not slip. I will drive it down the hill."

I look toward Anna Lise and her parents. "Herr Bauck, after I start, bring your family down by foot."

"But Jean-Luc," Anna Lise says, "you could be killed."

"What choice do we have?"

I hand Bayard's reins to Arnaud. "Corporal Coulane, if I'm successful, have every horse unshod, then follow me down."

Looking at everyone else, I add, "The only other option is to abandon the vehicles."

I climb onto the driver's bench and proceed to move down the hill, avoiding icy patches as best I can. Partway down, I lurch to the left on my seat as a carriage wheel slides on a patch of ice. The carriage rocks, nearly turning over, but catches on rocks and steadies. Finally, I come to the bridge and take the carriage through the gate into Smolensk. Soldiers stationed at the gate give me handshakes to congratulate me. Anna Lise and her parents navigate the hill on foot without incident.

All our attention is now turned to the top of the hill. The first wagon begins its descent, moving very slowly. It makes it to the gate and comes into the city. Arnaud wisely only allows one vehicle at a time on the hill. The second reaches the bottom without incident. The third starts down the hill but quickly has problems. The driver jumps free, but his wagon and horse skid the rest of the way down and, like the first two, slide into the river. Luckily, the remaining thirty or so wagons come down without incident.

* * *

Aside from the Assumption Cathedral and a few buildings near it, Smolensk exists in name only. Most buildings are ashen ruins with a few stone walls standing here and there. We find where General Rapp and his army are bivouacked, and my column of men and wagons camp nearby. I report in to Uncle Jean. "You're alive, my boy," he says with relief, clasping my shoulders. "How are the Baucks and Anna Lise and your friend Corporal Coulane?"

I assure him they are fine, then detail the condition of my squadron. "I lost fifteen of my men to cold. There are thirty-five of us left. We probably lost over half of the wagons and carts we were escorting. I've never seen such terrible conditions."

"Any trouble with Cossacks?"

"They let us know we were being watched, but they never attacked. They went after easier prey."

"I have bad news," Uncle Jean says, glancing down to the floor before looking back at me. "There were supposed to be enough stores in Smolensk to give us the option of wintering here. But the soldiers defending the supplies heavily depleted the stocks, and looting has taken more. We cannot stay, and what supplies are left will be distributed. It won't be much. The next supply depot is a few days away in Minsk."

"We have no supplies now, Uncle Jean. My men are starving. When can we get them?"

"Now, Jean-Luc. You can get them now." He sits at his desk, writes an order, impresses his signet ring in some hot wax, and hands me the paper. "Here, take this to the supply officer at the warehouse near the cathedral. It authorizes a draw of thirty-eight shares of food along with thirty-six shares of oats. Do it quickly before more looting occurs."

"Thank you, Uncle Jean. We'll have a proper reunion and meal at my father's inn this spring."

"Good luck, my boy," he says, embracing me. There's a hint of tears in his eyes.

He too is wondering if we will survive this retreat.

Forty-Seven

Orsha – Early November 1812

The disappointment of Smolensk is now but a faded memory as we cling to ever-thinning threads of life. Food is scarce and the weather unbearable. Our lamp of hope shines toward Minsk with its vast store of supplies, but the city is a week, maybe two weeks away. Beyond Minsk is the safety of Vilnius. One natural barrier exists between us and safety: the Berezina River.

The weather is fiercely cold with heavy snow, making the road nearly impassable. The sound of wagon wheels crunching into snow and ice fills the air. The long column of vehicles and troops stretches apart, then breaks into separate groups. Through the blowing snow, I'm uncertain how large our group is, but it can be no more than ten wagons with fifteen horsemen besides myself and Arnaud—the last remnants of my squadron. Vlad and Herr Bauck take turns, one driving the carriage while the other warms inside the cab. The road winds through a dense forest, the trees pressing in close. My eyes scan the thick timber, looking for signs of Cossacks.

"Captain, look back—our trailing wagon has stopped," one of my men shouts.

Squinting through the snow, I see that the wagon's back wheel has slipped into a rut and can't move. My eyes sweep across the trees again for Cossacks. Seeing no sign, I order Privates Aveline and DeRose to go back and see if they can help.

The wagon is only about a hundred yards back, and I call for our column to stop and wait. Just as the two privates dismount, six Cossacks sweep in, impaling my men with their lances before they can reach for their sabres. The wagon driver and his horse are also speared. The Cossacks grab the reins of my soldiers' horses and disappear in an instant back into the forest.

I'm stunned. It happened so fast I couldn't react. Fearing an all-out attack, I draw my sabre and twist my head around in all directions, looking for more Cossacks.

"Sir, should we go back and retrieve the bodies?" one of my soldiers asks.

Bayard jostles as I stare back at the tragedy. I sheath my sabre. "No. There is nothing we can do for them, and going back will only endanger the rest of us."

"Can't we bury them, Jean-Luc?" I look over toward the carriage and see Anna Lise leaning out from an open door, looking at me with pleading eyes.

"I can't," I say forcefully. "The ground is frozen. Please, get back in the carriage. The Cossacks are watching through the trees as we speak, waiting for us to make a mistake."

"Sir, what of the meat from the wagon horse?" a soldier asks. "Our rations are very low."

"No, the horse must stay," I reply, though I myself am feeling a strong urge to secure more meat. "Danger from the Cossacks is too great. Orsha is only a day, maybe two away, and there is a small cache of supplies there. We have enough food to reach the village."

The soldier looks longingly at the horse, but salutes.

"Move the vehicles closer together," I order. "We continue the march."

Anna Lise is still looking back at the dead soldiers.

"Anna Lise, please, we must go."

She looks at me sadly and nods, then closes the berline's door.

The remainder of my men gather together near me and encircle our vehicles.

Just as we start to move, a young private, no more than seventeen, stares past me with maniacal eyes. "I need that meat!" he shouts, and gallops back toward the dead animal. Before he can even dismount, a lance flies through the air, striking him in the chest. His lifeless body slides to the ground, and a lone Cossack rides out to take the private's horse. I take my pistol and fire. This Cossack, too, slumps dead onto the red-stained snow. About ten Cossacks emerge, silently staring, challenging us to attack.

"Hold your position," I order. I wait to see the Cossacks' next move. One of them shouts in imperfect French, "Give us the woman and we'll let you go."

I draw my second pistol, take aim at the insolent Russian, and shoot again. The bullet hits a tree branch just above his head.

He brings his steed a few steps forward. "Maybe you won't give her up now, my friend, but I assure you, she will be mine." They then slip back into the forest.

Looking toward the carriage and through the frost-encrusted circle of clear glass, I see Anna Lise staring at where the Cossack had been. Her face is drained of blood. She turns toward me, panicked.

I give her a tight smile as dread overwhelms me.

"Forward!" I command.

* * *

The sky is becoming murky, threatening to storm, and darkening with the coming end of the day. Farms have begun to appear, making me believe Orsha is near.

I catch a glimpse of a small house and stable to my right, just off the road.

"Halt!" I yell. "Private Camus, come with me. Corporal Coulane, take command until I return."

Private Camus and I ride slowly toward the structures, looking for any signs of habitation. The snow is nearly two feet deep. We see no tracks, but with the wind, any tracks would be erased in only a few minutes. We each have our sabres drawn, wary of Cossacks.

"Private Camus, take that position over there," I whisper as I point to a spot near the stable's entrance.

Bayard snorts. There's no light coming from the house, but at the far end of the stables, the dying embers of a campfire glow. I dismount, not wanting to be hampered by the low roof of the stable. I signal for Private Camus to do the same and point toward the stable's interior.

Leading our horses, we slowly inch our way in. Snow has blown onto the stable's dirt floor, helping to muffle our footsteps. Something large is lying on the ground ahead of us. In the increasing darkness I see it's a horse, partially butchered and now solidly frozen.

We continue to move warily, going past the horse. I strain to keep my breath controlled, but it's difficult, and the hairs on the back of my neck prickle. Only the muffled sounds of our movement can be heard.

Suddenly, five men jump from the shadows. One grabs for Bayard's reins, but his severed arm slides off my blade. The man howls in pain, falling back, but his comrades keep us surrounded. They have taken Private Camus' horse, but he remains at my side, his sword still drawn. He moves his feet nervously, trying to keep an eye on all of our attackers.

To my surprise, I hear them speaking German. "Captain, *sprechen sie Deutsch?*" one of them asks.

"*Etwas,*" I say.

"*Gut,*" he replies in German. "My French is terrible. We were part of the Württemberg Corps, but now we are on our own, seeking to escape this madness. The French have lost. We must go home."

The soldier speaking is a corporal, about my age. The others are very young, all privates. They look uncertain, waiting for the corporal to give guidance. The private with the severed arm is on his knees, sobbing, knowing he will soon die from the loss of blood and deep cold.

"We have no wish to kill you, nor do we want your skilled swords to slay any of us. We just want your horses. We need food."

"Corporal, you can't take our horses. Attack us if you want to die. The remainder of my squadron is nearby, waiting for Private Camus and me to return. Come join us. Our food is limited, but we will share what we have. Orsha is close, and a supply depot is there."

The corporal scoffs. "That supply depot has been stripped bare, and the great supply warehouses in Minsk are now in the enemy's hands." He eyes me closely. "We are all trapped. If your squadron joins us, perhaps we can make an escape to the south. As a group, we would be strong enough to fend off Cossack patrols."

There is a glimmer of hope in his eyes.

A splat of blood hits my cheek as the Württemberg corporal falls dead at my feet. It's my men attacking, and Private Camus and I join in. Our skills with a sword are far superior to the abilities of these infantrymen, and soon, they too are slain.

I look at the bodies with regret. *We now kill our own soldiers ... was their decision to desert so wrong?*

"Captain, we heard a scream," Corporal Coulane says. "I know we shouldn't leave the wagons and carriage, but I knew there was trouble, so I ordered everyone to come. I heard voices in the stable, and we moved in."

Arnaud's look of happiness fades as he looks down at the men we just killed. "Those are the colors of the Württemberg Corps, not Cossacks. We killed our own men?"

"Deserters wanting our horses for food," I say with a heavy heart. "Most of them were so young."

I hear the clank of vehicles as they come into the field in front of the house.

The news from the deserters about Orsha and Minsk is devastating. Our supplies are very low, and now we are nearly trapped by the Berezina River. I know of only one remaining bridge not in Russian hands: the bridge at the village of Borisov, a difficult thirty leagues from Orsha.

"Private Camus, could you understand what the Württemberg soldiers were saying?" I ask.

"No sir, I don't understand German. You were talking to them, weren't you?"

I contemplate my answer. The news of Minsk being captured will devastate everyone. For now, I will keep it to myself and let everyone have one more day of hope.

"I only understood bits, Private. Nothing of importance."

I look down at the dead Württemberg soldiers. "Men, we will move their bodies to the back corner of the stable. We can't bury them in this cold, but at least we can lay them out honorably. They've fought valiantly as comrades since our campaign began."

Arnaud and I begin to move one of the bodies. I look at Arnaud and know he has become an important friend to both me and Anna Lise. If he were Adrien, I would tell him all about the fall of Minsk, but I can't bring myself to do that. He's not Adrien.

As we place the body, I hear a horse snort from the darkness. "Let's see what we have," I cautiously say to Arnaud. With sabres drawn, we slowly make our way into the blackness. There is another snort, very close now. I inch my way toward the sound, putting my hand forward to feel but fearing someone could attack at any moment. My hand finds the coat of a horse. "There, boy, take it easy," I say as I take his reins and lead him outside. "Arnaud, I found a horse."

The steed is a fine French cavalry horse. "It appears we are not the first to encounter the Württemberg deserters. They must have killed the owner to have this steed for future food. We may need this horse to serve the same purpose. Bring him along."

As we come back to the entrance of the stable, I see there is enough hay to feed all our horses tonight. Perhaps the last time we will be so fortunate.

The last of the wagons and the Baucks' carriage roll into the area in front of the house.

"Private Camus, gather some wood and make a fire in the cabin. Corporal Coulane, have our men and the wagoners unbridle their horses and put them into the stable. Then create a three-man watch rotation to protect the house and our horses. Put me in the second cycle near the home."

The fear that the Cossack will try to carry out his threat and take Anna Lise chills me. I don't want to be far from her. I'll be with her during the first cycle while she is still awake, then watch over her during the second cycle while she sleeps.

I smile, trying to appear in good spirits. "We will all stay in the warmth of the house tonight and share the last of Herr Bauck's horsemeat."

The thought of a warm place to sleep and food to eat brightens everyone's face. They move quickly to put away the wagons and horses, bantering a bit among themselves.

The Baucks' carriage comes to a stop. I rush to help Anna Lise from the cab, then immediately take her into my arms, pulling her in tighter, not wanting to let her go.

"Jean-Luc, is everything all right? Did you run into trouble?"

"I'm fine now that I know you are safe. We will talk later, after everyone is settled."

She looks quizzically at me, her eyes searching my face for signs of what I've left unsaid.

"Please, go to the house now," I say beseechingly. "I will be there shortly. First, I need to talk to *Vati*."

"Of course," she answers, but she knows something is wrong. "*Mutti,* come with me while they talk."

I nod to Frau Bauck, then take Herr Bauck aside. "*Vati,* how much of the sausages and cheese do you still have?"

"Enough for a few days, if we eat sparingly," he replies. "I've hidden it in the compartments under our seats so no one is tempted to steal it."

"And oats?"

"About the same, a few days' worth."

"Good," I reply. "We may not have new supplies for some time. I found a horse in the stables that I will make part of your carriage team. But in truth, we will need to bleed him for a while, then butcher him. Keep tight rein on what food you have left."

"But didn't you tell the men that tonight we will eat the remainder of our horsemeat?"

"Yes, I did say that. We lost three men today, and their spirits are low. They have little food among themselves, and with a warm house and some horsemeat, we can momentarily forget what we are facing."

Herr Bauck looks at me. "What more do you know, *mein Sohn?*"

I take a moment to answer. "Private Camus and I came upon deserters in the stables. Before they died, their leader told me that the supplies in Orsha have already been ravaged, and even worse, the great supply warehouses in Minsk are now in the enemy's hands.

"Minsk is gone? That was our shining Christmas star, Jean-Luc." Herr Bauck seems staggered by this news. "What will we eat? Our remaining supplies and the horse won't be enough to reach Vilnius."

"Please, keep this to yourself. I want the men to have a night of quiet before learning of this news tomorrow. I will talk to Anna Lise tonight about this."

I give Herr Bauck an embrace. "We will scrounge for whatever we find, *Vati*. Let's take the meat to the house. It looks like a fire is started."

"Do you think it wise to tell Anna Lise this?" he asks.

I don't answer, but I know I will never keep anything from Anna Lise.

Forty-Eight

Borisov – Mid to Late November 1812

After eating the last of the horsemeat, Anna Lise and I sit on the far side of the fire, away from the others, wrapped together with a blanket. She drinks from a cup of melted snow. "What are we going to do with the supplies in Minsk gone?" she asks, staring into the flames. "We'll likely need to kill the horse you found in the next day or two. He didn't look well."

"We'll need to scavenge through every abandoned vehicle we pass," I reply. "Perhaps we'll get lucky and find another horse."

She turns to me with steely eyes. In a steady, low-pitched voice, she says, "That Cossack today, the one who wanted to bargain for me. You won't let him take me, will you, Jean-Luc?"

The thought of Cossacks pulling her away from my dead body fills me with dread.

She takes my hands and stares at me intently. "If he should ever get hold of me, I will know it will mean you are dead. I won't want to live ... not like that. I must have your dagger. I must be able to fight or die on my terms."

"Anna Lise!" My voice is a harsh whisper. "If I'm dead and you fight, you will likely die, but even if I'm dead, you could live, and there's at least a chance you would see Colmar again."

Her face reddens angrily as she continues. "You must give it to me, Jean-Luc! If you won't, I'll ask Arnaud, or maybe Uncle Jean ... I will get a knife."

Her eyes burn into my soul.

Though I feel ill thinking of her fighting someone off, I retrieve my sheathed dagger. Fingering the leather, I can't help but visualize it being pushed into the chest of a Cossack, then retrieved by Anna Lise to use on herself.

"Make sure to keep the blade close by," I whisper.

She takes the sheathed weapon and slides it under her coat.

"Thank you, Jean-Luc." She smiles at me, grateful for an honorable way to die. It sends shivers down my spine.

After a moment, she turns to me, her face still flush, and pulls my hands to her stomach. Her look of determination is now replaced by a soft smile. "I've missed my monthly bleed. I really am pregnant. Adrianna is here, growing." She gently moves my hand across her abdomen.

My mind reels from fearing for Anna Lise's life to understanding what she has just said. "My love, is it true? With every ounce of strength we have, we will make it safely home!"

As I hold her tightly, a soldier makes his way to me. "Captain, it's time for your watch shift."

I nod, then kiss Anna Lise tenderly. "My watch station is just outside the house. I won't be far."

* * *

We reach Orsha by midday, finding the town in turmoil. The emperor and his entourage take up the center of the village, with the encampments of regimental generals encircling his position. Couriers dash madly between the generals and the emperor's staff.

"Captain, there must be something wrong," Arnaud says. "The couriers all have fear in their eyes."

I'm sure the fear is over the loss of Minsk. I should have told him last night. He's my right hand now, not Adrien.

"There's General Rapp's colors. He can tell us. Corporal, have our group make camp here while I speak with him."

The general's attaché recognizes me and says he will let the general know I want to see him. Moments later, he returns and leads me into a building.

I find Uncle Jean writing dispatches and handing them to couriers. He glances up. "Jean-Luc, please sit." Looking down again, he frenetically scribbles another dispatch.

When he has finished, he focuses on me. "I'm so relieved to see you. We are losing so many men between the cold and the Cossacks. Are you ... are all of you well?"

"Yes, we are well, but I have less than fifteen men left in my squadron, and we escort only nine wagons and the Baucks' carriage. I encountered some deserters last night. They told me Minsk has fallen. Can this be true?"

Uncle Jean winces. "Then you know our current position is dire. We are trapped by the River Berezina with few supplies. Desertion is widespread, which adds to the chaos, and this bitter cold won't relent." He looks at me intently. "Jean-Luc, keep Anna Lise very, very close."

"She's pregnant, Uncle Jean."

The general looks up, his eyes widening. "Pregnant?" he says, allowing himself a small smile. "Congratulations! But your timing couldn't be worse. Is she able to get along?"

"Yes, she's fine. It's very early in the pregnancy." I take a deep breath. "I'm happy, but now I fear even more for her life. A Cossack caught sight of her yesterday and vowed to take her. I have trouble sleeping, always wanting to be on guard."

"Is Corporal Coulane still with you? He seems to be good luck for you and Anna Lise."

"Yes, Arnaud is still with us."

"Good! With God's mercy, he'll continue to protect you and Anna Lise. You need whatever protection God wills to give."

Uncle Jean pulls out his maps and points to a spot along the Berezina River. "This is Borisov, where the last remaining bridge stands." He uses his fingers to measure the distance. "It's about thirty leagues from here." He points to another spot on the map. "Here's Minsk, where the Russians are. It's only about fifteen leagues from Borisov on the other side of the Berezina."

He looks up at me grimly. "We control Borisov, but the question is, can we hold it until we can get across?"

I examine the map, feeling dread in the pit of my stomach. "Is there any other way across?"

"If the weather stays this cold, the river might be frozen hard enough to get over," Uncle Jean replies. "Maybe there is a fording area, but that would have the danger of ice floes. I just don't know," he says wearily. "Regardless, we must get there quickly.

"Another thing—the emperor is ordering we leave behind half of our wagons so we can quicken our pace. The horses can be used to help pull the remaining wagons or be kept for butchering. What do your wagons carry?"

"Mostly pontoons and pontoniers' equipment, along with loot from Moscow."

"The emperor has ordered we leave behind the pontoons, but I fear we will need them." Uncle Jean stares at me, knowing what he says, rightly or wrongly, will be obeyed. "Leave the pontoons, but make sure all the sapper tools and equipment are kept and brought to Borisov."

Uncle Jean feverishly begins writing again. "I want you and your men, along with the sapper gear, to join General Jean-Baptiste Eblé's contingent and make haste to Borisov. He leaves at dawn tomorrow. Give him these orders."

* * *

Herr Bauck examines the horse we got from the deserters. "He's been bled many times," he says. "He won't last a day of marching."

I pat his flanks and examine him closely, hoping to see any sign of good health.

"You're right, *Vati*. We must put him down and butcher him." Retrieving one of my pistols, I pat the horse's neck and talk soothingly. He nickers contently. With a single shot to his head, he falls to the ground. I look over at Bayard. *Could I ever say that about him?*

Herr Bauck prepares his knives and butchers the horse that evening, giving each person within our group an equal share.

While we're gathered for the meat distribution, I tell everyone that we are going to leave behind four wagons. Panic ensues. The wagons mostly hold the pontoons and sapper equipment, but also loot taken from Moscow—much of it the booty of my soldiers and the wagoners. How much will they protest leaving booty behind?

"Which wagons? What cargo? Who decides?" they shout.

"Silence!" I command. "We are leaving behind the two wagons with pontoons but keeping the sapper tools, forging equipment, and coal."

There is a murmur of satisfaction from the soldiers.

"Take everything out of the remaining wagons and identify what you want to keep. Since Corporal Coulane has nothing in the wagons, he will make the determination about what is to be kept. Be quick. We move at first light. We will be joining up with General Eblé's contingent of four hundred Dutch sappers."

"What about the carriage?" one of the wagoners cries.

Angrily, I say, "The carriage has no plunder, only a supply of food and Herr Bauck's butchering knifes. Should we leave food behind? Or the butchering knives? What is in the carriage is none of your concern!"

"And the extra horses?"

"Each vehicle will have one of the horses secured to it. I'll determine when we bleed and when we butcher. This may be the only food we have for many days."

There is more grumbling, but everyone goes about unloading the wagons under the watchful eyes of Corporal Coulane. The process is slow and painful. The temperature is well below freezing, and snow continues to fall heavily. It is dark by the time the wagons are reloaded.

In addition to needing to leave behind booty, the fall of Minsk with its stores of supplies disheartens everyone. As we settle down to sleep, some of the men are whispering among themselves.

Dawn arrives, and I find half of my squadron and wagoners gone. Also missing are two of our loaded wagons and two of our extra five horses.

"Shall I go after them?" Arnaud asks.

"It would be useless, and we need to join General Eblé immediately. If we found them, there would be little recourse but to fight. I don't wish to have French blood on my hands."

* * *

General Eblé is happy that we bring extra sapper tools along with foundry equipment and the coal to fire it.

"I argued with the emperor about leaving the pontoons, but to no effect," he says. "Fortunately, he never mentioned our tools or foundry equipment, and I didn't bring it up. I feared he would leave those behind as well."

The general inspects our wagons, looking pleased with what we carry. "Who rides in the carriage?" he asks.

"My wife and her parents."

"Wife?" The general pauses. "May I meet them?"

"Yes, of course, sir."

We slowly walk toward the carriage. "If you don't mind, sir, could my wife remain in the cab?" I ask.

The general looks at me questionably.

"A couple of days ago, we were attacked by Cossacks. My wife, Anna Lise, opened the carriage door and was seen by them. Their commander has vowed to take her."

"I understand. Perhaps it's best my men don't see her either," he says.

As we approach the carriage, I see Anna Lise through the cab window. Looking excited, she begins to open the door and step out. I block the door, keeping her from exiting.

"I'm sorry, but Cossack eyes are watching."

She glares, but retreats to her seat.

"Anna Lise, Herr and Frau Bauck, this is General Eblé. We will be traveling with him and his sappers."

The general edges close to the door opening. "Please forgive all this intrigue. Captain Calliet told me about your encounter with the Cossacks. They watch us constantly, but dare not attack my four hundred men."

"A pleasure, General Eblé," Anna Lise responds as the general kisses her hand and then Frau Bauck's. "Perhaps after we cross the Berezina, we will be in safer surroundings."

"That is our hope," the general replies.

The general looks at me, glances at my men, then says, "Madame Calliet, I want to make a request of your husband that I hope you approve. Captain, you and your men are the only cavalrymen we have. I want you and your men to ride to Borisov and let me know about conditions there. My men and I should be there in about three days."

"Yes, sir. If I could be so bold, can Corporal Coulane stay with the carriage?"

The general glances toward Anna Lise, then back to me. "Of course. Let me assure you Madame Calliet will be safe. The wagons and the carriage will be flanked on each side by my sappers."

* * *

My three men and I ride hard toward Borisov, by nightfall reaching a hill overlooking the Berezina River valley and the village. The sky is clear, and the weather has warmed considerably. Melting snow drops from the trees around us. We see campfires coming to life not far down the hill from us, clustered about a league east of the river and Borisov.

I take out my spyglass to examine these men when Private Camus touches my shoulder and points toward the village. "Sir, are those flames coming from near the river?"

I turn toward the fire and focus my glass. "The bridge! They're burning the bridge." The flames are growing, now engulfing the entire structure. I can't take my eyes off the water as it reflects the flames dancing from one end to the other.

"My God," I say to no one. "We're trapped!"

"The Russians have taken Borisov, sir?" Private Camus asks.

Stunned, I take a moment to regain my train of thought. "It appears so, Private. That must mean these campfires below us are French."

Focusing my glass on the encampment, I see they are a Polish contingent of our army, a regiment of about two thousand men, the ones who had been defending Borisov. Some of them are wrapping their comrades' injuries, while others sit by their fires, looking dejected.

Suddenly, a growing thunder of horses comes toward us from behind.

"It must be Cossacks coming to finish off the survivors. Quick, hide in the trees."

The full moon lights the scene, reflecting off the edges of the snow-covered road and causing the riders' uniform buttons to glitter.

"They are French," Private Camus says.

"Stay hidden. We are on reconnaissance for General Eblé," I remind them. "We'll watch what happens from this hill."

The galloping army takes nearly a half hour to pass; there are perhaps as many as ten thousand men. The ground shakes from the pounding hooves. They move down the hill toward the encampment. I pull out my spyglass again and stare into the mayhem of horses and men.

"What's happening, sir?" one of my men asks anxiously.

"No one is dismounting, and the encampment seems to be packing up."

I scan the mass of horsemen, looking for whoever appears to be in charge.

"It's Marshal Oudinot and his men. They must be coming to reinforce Borisov."

I close my glass. "Now that they know the bridge has fallen into enemy hands, it looks like they plan on retaking the bridge and Borisov tonight. Maybe they hope the bridge can be salvaged."

We watch the ghostly line of shadows snaking its way toward the village. I keep my spyglass pocketed, as its focus is too narrow. I need to watch the entire scene develop.

Distant gunfire erupts, and the shadows of Marshal Oudinot's forces balloon like the flow of water hitting a dam. They must have encountered Russian resistance. The surge swells for several hours, enveloping the blockage, then overwhelming it and rushing through, pulsing forward into a new, narrow stream of ethereal shadows as soldiers flood toward the bridge and village. The gunfire goes silent until this new rush of men reaches the Berezina.

Fire spreads, illuminating the battle scene. Again, I take out my glass, watching for many minutes.

My men move closer to me. Looking over, I see their anxious faces.

"Did we drive off the Russians? Is the bridge still standing?" Private Camus asks.

"The Russians are on the run. Mount up. We're going to the village to see about the bridge's condition."

We reach the river just after dawn, the sun peeking through scattered clouds. The warm temperatures are quickly thawing the frozen ground, turning it to mud. The Berezina is no longer frozen solid, but now flowing swiftly, with dangerous chunks of ice swirling by and rough water frothing and crashing. An ice dam has formed at a river bend upstream, sending frigid waters over its banks, flooding the fields next to the road. *A poor time to warm up, just as we need a frozen river for our army to cross.*

Marshal Oudinot's troops are everywhere, setting up encampments on the higher ground above the flooding river.

"There's the bridge," Private de la Rue says, pointing to the remaining charred timbers and piers of the crossing, pieces breaking off as the flowing ice crunches into them.

I spot the marshal inspecting the wreckage and talking to his senior staff. Dismounting, I approach. "Captain, do you need something?" the marshal's aide asks.

"General Eblé has sent me and my men to check the condition of the bridge," I say, saluting. I look over at the wreckage. "Do you think it's salvageable?"

The marshal glances my way. "Captain. You're with General Eblé and his sappers?"

"Yes, sir."

The marshal glances toward the bridge ruins. "It could be repaired, but the Russian army is massed on the other side of the river, waiting to see what we will do. I'm sending scouts downstream to look for a ford, but this peasant here has given us information on a ford he uses upstream, near Studenka. He says that yesterday, it appeared to be about waist high."

I examine the peasant, who is busily talking to another of the marshal's aides using an interpreter. *Peasants have proved to be as much an enemy as the Russian army.*

"Do you trust him, sir?"

"He's Lithuanian and has no love for the Russians, but no one can be trusted. You and your men ride with him and see about this ford. General Eblé and his men should be here by the time you return."

"Yes, sir," I reply, looking toward my men, who I know were hoping to catch some sleep.

"Sir, may I send Private de la Rue back to General Eblé to report on the destruction of the bridge?"

"Of course, Captain." The marshal looks at the peasant and the interpreter. "Take the interpreter with you as well. You will need his skills to communicate."

I salute, and the marshal turns away to talk with his aides.

"Private de la Rue, go to General Eblé and tell him the bridge has been burned and that I am going north to see about a possible ford."

"Yes, sir," the private says. He snaps a salute and turns to ride back to the general and his sappers.

"Corporal," I say to the interpreter, "you and the peasant will be traveling with us to Studenka. I am Captain Calliet, and these are Private Camus and Private Remy."

"Yes, Captain, I am happy to go," the interpreter says. He wears a corporal's uniform in the colors of the Polish contingent. "I am Tomasz, and the peasant is Petras."

Petras climbs onto his pony and leads the way north.

"Studenka is about four leagues away," Tomasz says. "Lithuanian peasants live there, and I fear they will become caught between two great armies with little chance to survive unless they flee." Looking at me intently, he says, "We must warn them that they need to leave. They are innocents, unintentionally caught in this madness."

I look away, contemplating what he asks. I know all rules of war argue against this, but needless killing must end somewhere. However, if they flee, the Russians may learn our plans, and more French soldiers would die.

"I'll consider it, Corporal, if it does not endanger our men's lives. Right now, we are to see if there is a usable ford at Studenka."

A narrow trace skirting intermittent marshlands leads to the village. The warmer temperatures of the past few days have melted some of the marshland ice, allowing noxious gasses that stink of rotting eggs to escape. Trees line the east side of the track. A cold wind begins to stir, and gray clouds slowly slide in from the north, blotting out the sun.

My shoulders tighten as I crane my neck and peer into the dense cover of larch and fir trees. "Corporal, has your Lithuanian seen any Cossacks in this area?"

The corporal speaks to the peasant, who looks toward me and says something while shaking his head.

"They've seen no Cossacks, but he fears they may be coming as they follow the French army."

Shortly, the trees change to groves of white birch, looking like ghosts waiting to add more dead souls to their ranks.

"Studenka!" The peasant shouts, pointing to about ten cabins along with a small church and what appears to be a community stable. Two young children rush from a cottage, joyfully greeting our peasant as he dismounts. A woman, holding a baby, is framed by the cabin entryway. Others in the village warily come out from the other homes, keeping their distance.

The peasant shouts happily, picking up the children and carrying them toward the woman and baby, calling out their names.

"This is Petras's family," Tomasz says. "His wife Adele with the baby Zita, his son Tadas, and his other daughter Katre."

Petras shouts something to the others in the village, who grumble and return to their homes.

I look around, knowing that if our army comes this way, this village will be destroyed. Snow flurries are starting, and the temperature has dropped. Only about another hour of sunlight remains.

"While there is still light, Petras will show us the ford," Tomasz says. "We can sleep in the stable, and his wife will prepare a meal to eat after we return."

I smile and tip my shako toward Petras and his family, and we proceed a few hundred yards to the Berezina. The waterway looks rough and uncrossable, with chunks of ice slamming into each other and whitecaps forming with the increasing wind. The riverbank is soft, and the hooves of our horses sink into it.

I've seen this before. Cannonballs are cratering all around. A woman is clutching my arm, telling me we have to cross the bridge. I see wisps of her blonde hair. She turns, looking at me wildly. "We must go now, Jean-Luc!" Her face is coming into focus. Anne Lise?

The impression vanishes. Cold fingers seem to stroke my cheek. I force myself to look back across the river, but I want to flee.

Petras talks and points out into the river. Tomasz interprets. "The river has risen a great deal since Petras saw it a few days ago. Then, it only looked to be waist high at its deepest, but now, it must be nearly twice that."

"Sir, we could never cross this ford," Private Camus says.

I gaze over the turbulent waters. "You're right, Private. Let's hope the Borisov bridge can be repaired. I've seen enough."

We return to the village and bed down our horses in the stable. Bayard knickers with satisfaction at having plenty of hay to eat.

I try to look as presentable as possible before going to Petras's home. We make our way to his cabin through the blowing snow. *"Sveiki atvyke!"* Petras says as he welcomes us into his home.

"Welcome," Tomasz translates.

Adele hands us bowls and ladles bubbling borscht from a large kettle over a fire. As our bowls are filled, we join the family at a long table. Several loaves of brown bread are arranged down the middle of the table, along with tankards of ale. Petras and Adele smile, so willing to offer their hospitality. Their children gaze up at us, wide-eyed.

"After the French army swept through this region last summer, the Russians abandoned the area, no longer demanding tribute for the tsar," Tomasz says.

"Tell us, Captain," Petras says through Tomasz, "how is your life in France, and what wondrous things have you seen while in the army?"

As we eat our borscht and drink our ale, they seem mesmerized by what I and my comrades tell them regarding our home lives and time in the army.

"Vienna and Paris," Adele says through Tomasz. "They sound magical. Our life here is simple, but comfortable." She pauses for a few moments. "Forgive me, Captain, but there is sadness in your eyes as you tell your stories. I fear you have lost close friends."

"Yes," I say simply. "I've lost many close friends."

I can't bring myself to talk about Adrien, nor am I able to tell them about Anna Lise. It's painful thinking of her, not knowing if she is safe, and I want to keep her presence a secret from everyone.

What Tomasz said earlier to me, about warning this family and the others in this village, must be addressed. I wouldn't be able to bear the guilt should any harm come to them.

"Petras, Adele, I must tell you about what might happen if the army comes to Studenka."

They both look toward me.

"The ford here at Studenka is not usable with the high water, and I expect that we will try and repair the bridge at Borisov," I tell them. "But there is a chance the Russians won't allow us to repair that bridge, which would likely mean the army would come here and build a new one."

I can see them pondering my words as Tomasz translates.

"You would need wood to build your bridges, right?" Petras asks.

"Yes," I reply.

I look into their faces as they begin to realize what the source of that wood would be.

"I'm sorry, but the buildings of your village would be that wood."

Petras's chin lowers to his chest, and he takes his wife's hand.

'If we don't build a bridge somewhere, the Russians will defeat us, and thousands more people will die. Myself, Tomasz, and my men would all die."

Petras and Adele talk quietly among themselves, and Adele's voice sounds particularly urgent.

"Captain," Petras says through Tomasz, 'I now realize I've put my family and all the villagers in grave danger."

Adele says something more to Petras. 'My wife reminds me that we, and most of the people in this village, have relatives in Zembin, less than three leagues to the north."

Again, Adele speaks urgently to Petras. "We are grateful you told us these things," he says, 'but I know the villagers will be angry when I tell them this news tomorrow. It would be best if you retire to the stable and get some sleep, but leave before dawn and have me take the brunt of their anger. We will pack for Zembin tomorrow."

Building the Berezina Bridges

Crossing the Berizina

Forty-Nine

Crossing the Berezina –
Late November 1812

My men and I get a few hours of fitful sleep before leaving Studenka in the semi-darkness of predawn. The groves of white birch trees seem to be escorting us away from this spot, a place I pray I will never see again. Snow is now spilling from the sky, but the temperature is not cold enough to ice over the Berezina or the marshlands.

I hear movement coming from the forest. It must be Cossacks.

"To arms!" I shout as I unsheathe my sabre. A dozen or so armed horsemen pour from the trees onto the narrow track in front of us. The snow is too thick to see who they are, but I know we're outnumbered and must initiate the attack if we are to survive.

"Charge!" I command, pointing my sabre toward our unknown assailants, urging Bayard into a gallop.

The falling snow stings my eyes and blurs my vision, but as we close in, the shapes of shakos and the blue color of their uniforms emerge. *They are French!*

"Halt!" I order. I pull Bayard up short harshly, and he whinnies in protest. Plumes of mist pour from his nose as he paws the ground. I hear the troops behind me slide to a stop.

A young lieutenant rides up. "I was thinking we were going to have to kill you," he says wryly as he gives me a salute. "Are you Captain Calliet?"

"Yes, and you are?"

"Forgive me. I am Lieutenant Bret, attaché to General Eblé. He is most anxious to hear your report about the ford. He sent us up here to wait and escort you to his camp."

"Is everything all right? You made it to Borisov safely?" I ask.

"I believe you want to know about your wife and her parents," the lieutenant says. "They are fine. She is helping cook for the general's sappers and pontoniers." The lieutenant chuckles. "I've never seen such a lot of lovelorn Dutchmen."

Damn, I told her to stay out of sight. Why didn't Arnaud stop her? He's probably as besotted over her as the Dutchmen ... or that Cossack.

The lieutenant and his men escort us for about a league to General Eblé's tent. "He wants to see you immediately." Pointing down the hill, he adds, "You'll find your wife and family in that direction when you are done."

I'm ushered into the general's tent and am surprised to also see Marshal Oudinot. Both men are studying a map laid out on a table. Hearing me enter, they look up.

"Ah, Captain Calliet!" General Eblé says. "We've been most eager for your return. Please, give us good news about the ford."

I look at the guarded faces of the marshal and general and feel pained about the news I carry. "I'm sorry to report that it is too treacherous to use at this time. According to the peasant who took me there, the water was only about waist high a few days ago." I shake my head. "But with the warmer temperatures, the snowmelt has turned the Berezina into a raging torrent. By his guess, the depth is now about twice what it was. Too high and too swift for infantry or wagons."

Marshal Oudinot lowers his head and leans against the table in despair. "Damn, why did the emperor have us destroy the pontoons?"

General Eblé stares straight ahead, looking deep in thought.

"Can't the Borisov bridge be repaired?" I ask.

"It could be if there wasn't a large Russian army on the other side of the river, sitting on higher ground," the general replies.

"The emperor will be here soon," Marshal Oudinot says. "We must give him some reasonable options!"

"Captain Calliet," the general says, "describe the riverbanks on both sides of the Berezina at Studenka."

"It's a straight stretch of the river with sloping banks on each side that rise a few feet above the current water level. The west bank is low, with extensive marshes. There's a village on the east bank on higher ground, with marshlands to the south along the river. Just north of the town, there is a low, rising bluff."

"How wide is the channel?"

"About two hundred feet."

"Would there be room for two or three bridges?"

Incredulously, I look at the general. "Bridges?" I ask.

Marshal Oudinot listens intently, a glimmer of hope crossing his face.

"Yes, possibly two wider bridges for artillery, wagons, and horsemen and a narrower one for foot soldiers."

"There is room, but the waters are violent and filled with swirling slabs of ice."

"It would be dangerous, and many men would likely die," the general says. "But there is no other option. You say there's a village near the river?"

"Only about a hundred and fifty paces away."

"Good. The buildings could serve as our source of wood."

My heart sinks thinking of the villagers and their kindness. Petras and his family will have no village to return to, but it can't be helped.

Marshal Oudinot nods his agreement, but adds, "This plan must be kept secret from the Russians."

The general's aide interrupts. 'Sir, the emperor is nearing our camp and wants to meet immediately with both of you. Shall I escort him here?"

"Yes, please do," the general replies.

"Marshal Oudinot, I suggest that some of your men stay here in Borisov and that I leave about fifty sappers to work on building pontoons and trestles," General Eblé says, his eyes gleaming. "Hopefully, the Russians will think we are going to repair the Borisov bridge and stay where they are."

"Captain," Marshal Oudinot says. "You've seen the Berezina at Studenka. Can this work?"

"Yes, sir. It could work."

"Good! We will present this plan to the emperor," Marshal Oudinot says. "Captain, remain with us when we speak to the emperor. You'll be better able to answer any questions he may have about the Studenka area."

* * *

Two hours later, after the emperor agrees with General Eblé's plan, I take my leave. The snow has stopped falling, and a half-moon lights my way as I look for Anna Lise.

A large campfire comes into view, and I see Anna Lise, her parents, Arnaud, Vlad, and even the Polish corporal Tomasz sitting around one side of the fire with several of the Dutch pontoniers and sappers on the other. Some are roasting chunks of meat, skewered on the ends of their sabres.

I gaze down on the scene. Looking at their camaraderie, a momentary warmth fills me. They are talking quietly together, sometimes laughing, distracted from our situation. 'Look, Bayard,' I say, patting him. 'See how beautiful Anna Lise has grown to be. Do you remember riding with her at Ostheim? How young she was then.'

The sight of her comforts me as much as the dangers of our situation give me knots of fear. Will the Berezina be the final noose around our necks?

My eyes moisten as I wonder how I will ever get her home to Colmar. Building a bridge at Studenka seems impossible, much less three of them.

'Anna Lise!' I shout. Her face turns up immediately, and her smile can't be contained.

'Jean-Luc!'

I rush toward her as she comes up to meet me, struggling through the deep snow.

'Come, meet our new friends,' she says, leading me by the hand toward the campfire.

'Captain, your family has been most gracious to us, sharing their food and campfire,' one of the Dutch soldiers says. 'Corporal Tomasz tells us the ford at Studenka is impassable. Is there a plan on what to do?'

I look at their eager faces but know they must wait for the news from their own officers.

'I can only say a plan has been agreed to. You will be hearing soon from your general.'

I stare into the fire, not wanting to know these men, knowing most will die trying to build a bridge for the emperor.

* * *

General Eblé and all but fifty of his men leave before dawn for Studenka. We follow close behind with our wagons holding sapper tools of all types, including axes, saws, clamps, rope, chisels, and sledgehammers, along with two forges.

Over the last few days, the snow has melted and turned to slush. We slip and slide our way along until finally the inevitable occurs, and the Baucks' carriage skids into the marsh. The wetlands are still soft, and the muck grabs our wheels, stopping our progress.

"Corporal Coulane, ride ahead and report our problem to General Eblé."

Vlad whips his horse to no avail, trying to get the carriage back onto the track. Anna Lise looks through her window, and I signal for her to stay put. I can see no way out of our difficulty without help.

Arnaud returns with a hundred sappers. "The lane becomes stable about two hundred yards ahead," he says. "The sappers are going to cut down trees and make a log road up to that point."

Within a couple of hours, the roadway is built. They help push the carriage and wagons onto the logs, and we are underway again. The snowfall lightens, but the temperature continues to fall. As the freezing temperature firms the mud, the lane becomes coated with a glaze of water that hardens into a sheet of ice. Our horses gingerly move forward, and the wheels of our vehicles slip with each rut we encounter.

The groves of ghost trees now line the east side of the track, letting me know Studenka is close. We round a bend and the village comes into view. Much of what I saw just two days ago has already changed. Many of the buildings have been disassembled and nearby birch trees cut down. The wood is being hauled into a ravine near the river to hide the activity from the Russians, who have troops stationed on the west side of the river.

"Captain, we're glad to see you," a Dutch lieutenant says. "We desperately need the tools and forges you've brought." He turns to a fellow sapper. "Corporal, unpack their supplies and fire up the forges quickly. We will need dozens of angle irons, straps, and nails."

Looking back at me, he says, "General Eblé would like you and your companions to camp by our bivouac. We are tucked in a gully between two cabins and have a large fire for warmth."

The idea of a fire is most welcome, as the temperature continues to fall and frigid gusts of wind begin sweeping down the river. Daylight is fading when we arrive. Herr and Frau Bauck prepare a sleeping area with our blankets and furs.

"Jean-Luc," Anna Lise asks, "will you take me to see the river?"

"Is that wise? Cossacks may be watching."

"It's near, isn't it? I can hear it, and there are many soldiers around us."

"Yes, it's less than two hundred yards away. Arnaud, will you come with us? I would feel better with another sabre nearby."

"Of course. I'm anxious to see what the river looks like as well."

We bundle tightly in our coats and walk to the river's edge. "It's higher than it was two days ago," I say. In the dwindling light, snow-dusted chunks of ice appear, barreling straight for us before careening off the bank. I can't imagine trying to build a bridge with these monstrous ice floes crashing down upon us.

"Those poor men are going to build bridges across this?" Anna Lise says. "How can they?"

I look across the darkening water, wondering why fate has brought us to this last, seemingly impossible barrier.

"I don't know, Anna Lise. We must have faith in General Eblé. He has built pontoon bridges over many rivers."

Word spreads among the pontoniers and sappers that Madame Calliet is encamped by their main fire. Many bring her letters to send to their loved ones back home. Their eyes look haunted and fearful, reflecting their acceptance that building the bridges will depend on them dying in the frigid waters.

Anna Lise takes every letter as each man bows and kisses her hand. I see her holding back tears while she tries to assure them all that she'll be giving the letters back once they cross the Berezina.

* * *

Marshal Oudinot and most of his men arrive as night falls. Along with his cavalry and infantrymen, he brings forty pieces of heavy artillery. Despite the darkness, he orders the artillery to be taken up the bluff near the village and placed in positions to protect the construction area and provide cover across the far side of the river. The light from about a thousand Russian campfires on the west bank provides guidance for the gun placements.

His other men waste little time joining General Eblé's in deconstructing homes and building pontoon boats and bridge trestles in the hidden ravine. My men and I join the work, sawing planks for the roadbed and preparing circular bundles of branches called fascines to cover the mud in front of each bridge entrance and protect the pilings from the ice floes.

We work throughout the night, and by morning the bridge pieces are ready to be moved to the river and assembled. The emperor arrives from Borisov as dawn breaks and immediately consults with General Eblé and Marshal Oudinot and inspects our work.

I'm standing not far from the emperor and his senior staff, able to overhear what they are saying.

"Is everything ready?" the emperor asks General Eblé.

"Yes, sire, but we have only enough wood for two bridges."

The emperor grimaces, then turns abruptly toward the river, where General Rapp is calling out excitedly. 'Sire! The Russians have been taken in by your ruse. Their soldiers across the river are moving south toward Borisov."

'Our fortunes are finally changing?" the emperor says, his eyes lighting up.

Many of us edge toward the top of the ravine, careful not to be noticed, and, yes, the trailing end of a line of soldiers can be seen heading south. Only a handful of men have been left behind.

'Marshal, send a squadron of cavalry to ford the river and secure the bridgehead on the west side," the emperor commands. 'General Eblé, start construction."

The cavalry enters the river, mixing with the ice floes in the strong current. Near midstream, the horses are forced to swim, and the river pulls them downstream until they can find footing again. Some of the horses are unable to secure a foothold, and their riders are swept away with the frigid waters, the torrent and ice floes pulling them under.

I watch helplessly and can only hope that most of the cavalry will make the crossing.

Turning back to our work, we hoist the pontoon boats, trestles, and other bridge material to the river's edge where the start of each bridge will be. On the Berezina's west side, tall poles are placed into the ground, providing a line of sight for where the bridges will end. We work feverishly for several hours getting all the materials in place.

While we're moving the wood from the ravine to the river, a line of tattered soldiers comes up the road from Borisov. Arnaud and I stop to watch as they come near. They carry the eagles of Marshal Ney's III Corps, who were among the last to leave Smolensk. I look down the track toward where it disappears into the forest, and I see more and more men emerge. It is an unending line of shuffling, ragged ghosts.

Arnaud and I stare in shock as these walking skeletons go by, their gaunt, gray faces covered with ragged beards, many without weapons. This army does not march, but stumbles forward, their eyes fixed on the ground, each following the man in front of him. This is the fate of those who could not find food, could not find shelter. These soldiers came after the leading armies, finding a land already scavenged of all supplies.

General Eblé stands nearby, and I can see his grim face as he watches these soldiers shamble by. He lowers his head for a few moments, then looks up and commands: "Into the river."

The first pontoon boat is launched. Men at each end of the boat hold up cross-tied trestles that look like giant sawhorses. They use the trestles as guiding poles as they inch the boat into place. An engineer with a Jacob's staff uses the instrument to steer the boat to its proper position. Once in place, men sledgehammer the trestles deeply into the river bottom. The river current tries to push the boat out of position, forcing several pontoniers to jump into the frigid water to push against the structure while the trestles are further sledgehammered. On the downriver side, additional log supports are leaned into place from the river bottom to the trestles at about a forty-five-degree angle.

Logs, fifteen to sixteen feet long, are laid across from the shore to the boat, which is now nestled between the legs of the trestles. Icy waters splash over the logs and the men as they lash and nail logs and trestles to the boat frames. The process is repeated with the next pontoon and the next. Twenty pontoons will be needed for each bridge. Men on the boats use poles to provide more support and to divert the chunks of ice away. The emperor's army has used this technique many times in the past, and I've seen it before, but each time I am impressed by its ingenuity.

But here the danger is high. "Ice!" one of the men shouts as a large chunk crashes into his pole and he is unable to guide it away. Free from his pole, it catches two of the pontoniers in the water, knocking them off their feet. They flail their arms helplessly before disappearing beneath the surface of the freezing river. Other pontoniers and sappers momentarily look up, eyes wide, but see there is nothing they can do and return to hammering and pounding as they struggle to build a bridge.

At midstream, the water is nearly six feet deep, and only the tallest pontoniers endure jumping into the river, where the water reaches up to their chins. To reach the upper parts of the trestles, pontoniers are forced to climb on each other's shoulders to provide the needed push of support. They hold the trestles in place with all their strength, but too many lose the battle against the frigid Berezina and slip from sight.

The contingent of Russians on the west side of the river has placed four small-caliber artillery pieces on one of the few spots of high ground. Now that we are nearly halfway across, they fire their cannon, but the balls fall short. Immediately, our heavy artillery opens fire. In a few seconds, the Russian guns are obliterated.

Work on the bridge continues into midday. My duty is to help secure fascines onto the upstream trestles to protect them from the ice that continually slams into them. Arnaud assists by holding onto my legs as I lean over to nail fascines into place.

"Jean-Luc!" Arnaud cries, but it's too late, as a large chunk of ice slams into the trestle I'm working on. Stunned, I hit the icy waters headfirst. My muscles violently cramp as I struggle to reach the surface. It seems a lifetime before I bob up. "Arnaud!" I gasp, my lungs burning. I reach up and feel a hand, then another, grab onto mine. I'm pulled onto the pontoon bridge, coughing and gasping. I can already feel the water in my hair crusting into ice.

"We must get you to a fire," Arnaud shouts as he pulls me up and puts one of my arms across his shoulder. I stumble along, my muscles almost useless. Arnaud hefts me onto his back and trots toward the sappers' main fire.

My mind goes numb, but I'm sure I hear Anna Lise's voice calling my name. I feel my uniform being stripped off. Someone wraps a fur about me, and I'm laid back onto the ground. I see Anna Lise's blonde hair as she places my head into her lap and begins to gently rock me back and forth. I close my eyes, comforted by this gentle swaying.

* * *

I wake from what seems like a long sleep and hear familiar voices and feel the warmth of someone holding me close. "Anna Lise?" I ask as I open my eyes.

I look up and see her shining blue eyes, filled with both relief and fear. "Yes, my love," she whispers. "The Berezina nearly took you."

Remembering where I am, I sit up. "The bridges. Are they complete?"

"Yes," Anna Lise says. "They are finished, and almost all of our soldiers have crossed, including the emperor and those poor souls we saw earlier today. But the bridges keep breaking down. At least half of the pontoniers and sappers have died repairing them."

It's dark, and many campfires blaze across the field where the town of Studenka once stood.

"What are all of those fires?" I ask.

"It's the stragglers and civilians. The bridges are just now clearing of soldiers, but none of these people have moved to cross. I've seen soldiers going from camp to camp and heard them pleading for them to go, but they don't want to leave their warm campfires."

Anna Lise looks at me, her expression serious. "Jean-Luc, we must cross now. Uncle Jean came by earlier. He told us the Russians are closing in from both the east and south, trying to trap us against the river."

"How long before daybreak?" I ask as I put on my now dry clothes.

"It will soon be dawn."

"Where is Arnaud?"

"I sent him to the bridge head to ensure it would be clear. I also told him to take Bayard."

"You sent Arnaud?"

"Yes. He didn't want to leave you unconscious, so I had to insist."

"Good! That was the right thing to do." I glance over toward Anna Lise's parents. They are fast asleep.

"The carriage is packed, save for these blankets and furs," Anna Lise says. "I'll wake my parents."

We move toward the larger bridge just as the light of predawn spreads across the landscape. Arnaud is waiting for us.

"Is the bridge in good shape?" I ask.

"Yes, sir, it is for now. The remainder of the army had no difficulties hauling their heavy guns across."

Scattered groups of people are crossing. It is still bitterly cold, but the sky is clear with no wind. In the distance, far to the east, line after line of Russian campfires burn. Flashes of light begin bursting from among these distant camps, followed by eruptions of earth and the flying bodies of stragglers, and finally the sounds of the cannon fire.

"They're coming, Jean-Luc," a fearful Anna Lise says. She turns back to look as the cannonade explodes again.

I grasp her hand as we walk onto the slippery roadway. The river roils beneath us, and floes of ice slam into the trestles. The Berezina wants to devour us, but we keep pushing ahead.

Anna Lise stumbles. "Jean-Luc!" she cries, and I pull her sharply up to her feet. She leans momentarily on one of the trestles, gathering her courage.

The two-hundred-foot span seems to never end. Ice floes strike the trestles, and the bridge shudders beneath us with each step we take.

We finally make it across the bridge just as a massive explosion erupts behind us. A munitions wagon abandoned by the army has been hit, and debris showers down on us.

"Over there, Jean-Luc," Anna Lise shouts, pointing to a small hillock overlooking the Berezina. "We should camp there."

Assessing the terrain as quickly as I can, I agree. Much of the area away from the river is crowded with troops. On this hillock we'll be momentarily safe, and we might be able to help the pontoniers and sappers, or any other survivor who needs assistance.

"Vlad, take the carriage to that knoll over there and set up camp," I shout.

Soon, Herr Bauck takes down a large cauldron from the carriage's roof and starts a fire around it. I give the cauldron a questioning look.

"We spent yesterday warming and feeding the pontoniers and sappers after their stints in the river," Anna Lise says. "We made them horsemeat soup. Those making repairs will still need to be warmed and fed."

I smile to myself, warmed by her kindness.

More of our rear-guard infantry arrive and cross the footbridge. The mass of stragglers is panicked, pushing and shoving, pressing toward the wagon bridge and overwhelming its capacity. Part of the left side collapses, throwing people, horses, and vehicles into the river. Many try to swim, but the cold overtakes them and they sink from view.

"Can't we do anything, Jean-Luc?" Anna Lise cries.

"Only for those who reach the west bank and need to be warmed. General Eblé's men are the only ones who can repair the bridges."

For a while, the horde of people on the east bank continues to push ahead, unaware that the bridge is impassable. Those near the crossing are shoved forward into the water, the Berezina sucking them down like a mythical monster. The water is littered with bodies, broken wagons, and dead horses, floating away downstream.

The cannon fire continues, hour after hour, devastating the tightly packed crowd. The bridges collapse, are repaired, and collapse again throughout the day. Fortunately, we are too busy helping survivors, sappers, and pontoniers to watch this horror unfold, but we hear the cannonade and the screams.

I hand a bowl of food to an exhausted, shivering pontonier. "You survived, Captain," he says to me. "I helped your corporal pull you from the river. Few people, even among our pontoniers, survive being fully submerged like you were."

"Thank you, Sergeant. You and your comrades saved us all. I'm sorry so many of your lives were lost."

The sergeant bows his head. "We would do anything for General Eblé, but the toll is very heavy. I've lost most of my friends and comrades. There are only a handful of us left."

At dark, the cannonade stops, and the panic subsides. Unfortunately, the bridges are both impassable. The remaining pontoniers and sappers work to repair them. We can see the stragglers' campfires come to life. By midnight, both bridges have been repaired, but only a few people come over. Like the night before, they foolishly stay by their campfires rather than cross the river, apparently lulled into thinking the Russians have been beaten back.

In the morning, Anna Lise stirs life into the fire while I scoop buckets of snow into the cauldron and add the last of the horsemeat Herr Bauck butchered yesterday from one of the horses that floated to shore.

The last of our rear-guard infantry is crossing the foot bridge when the Russian cannon open fire. This time, swarms of Cossacks can be seen charging toward Studenka. Their battle shrieks fill the air. Like yesterday, panic ensues, and the throngs again press onto the bridges.

Looking back to the river, I see a man being passed across the bridge over the heads of those in the crowd. I move closer, and then, as the body gets nearer, I realize that it's Baron Larrey. The revered doctor is rescued by the men who love him.

The bridges fail again, but now, instead of repairing them, our soldiers set them on fire. The Russians are closing in, and we can take no chances of having them repaired and used by our enemy. With the bridges burning, dozens of people jump into the water, hoping to swim through the floating chunks of ice. No one reaches the western shore.

No more of General Eblé's men come to our fire, and I fear most have died. As we wait, Anna Lise and I watch in horror as the stragglers and civilians try to escape the Cossacks on the opposite shore. The Cossacks hunt them down, spearing any who try to escape.

A large group of people who didn't run are now huddled together, surrounded by Cossacks with their lances at ready. One horseman comes up to a man and, using the tip of his lance, pokes at his clothing, indicating he wants it removed. With no other choice, the man complies. The other Cossacks start to close the circle, also making motions for clothes to be taken off. Again, with no choice, the group complies, leaving their clothes in piles for the Cossacks to rummage through in search of any hidden loot. The temperature is well below freezing as these poor people are marched away.

"This is too much," Anna Lise says, turning her head away. "How can there be such brutality?"

I gaze out over the mass of people being killed or rounded up by the Cossacks, knowing we could have been among them. The thought sickens me.

"We'll never be able to forget this, Anna Lise," I say. "It will be much like my memory of Madrid. Always there and always haunting."

She presses her head into my chest.

"Come," I say. "It's time to go."

Anna Lise and I move toward the carriage. Vlad and the Baucks have ensconced themselves inside the cab, not wanting to witness the carnage. Arnaud has been loading what few supplies we have left and is harnessing the horse.

"Is that cannon fire coming from downriver?" Anna Lise asks fearfully. "Will we now be captured too?"

"It's Marshal Oudinot and his forces. The emperor ordered him to go toward Borisov and protect our southern flank."

I listen more closely. "Damn! There's musket fire as well, and it's not far away. We must move quickly!"

Nearby, masses of our troops are marching toward a corduroy road stretching across the marshlands to the west toward Vilna. At the water's edge, a rear guard is now in place to stop any Cossacks who try to ford the river.

"Anna Lise, into the cab. Vlad, have the carriage join in with those troops. Quickly!"

Anna Lise's face is ashen as she climbs inside. I feel a tingle of fear and anticipation as I mount Bayard and reach for the handle of my sabre, ensuring it's ready for battle. Arnaud joins me as we make room in the troop column for the carriage.

Fifty

Smorgoni – Early December 1812

It has been nearly a week since we crossed the Berezina. The cold is fierce and unrelenting. I can only hope the Russians and Cossacks are as affected as we are. Our group hasn't seen any, and only scattered encounters with them have been reported.

The road today first meandered through wooded hillocks, but the landscape has now changed to a vast marshland. We traverse pinewood bridges and corduroy roads. These log roads are difficult for our horses, as their hooves slip on the rounded tops of the wood. There is no wind, and we travel under cloudy skies. The weather is so cold that there is little new snow, and when it does fall, the flakes are scattered, silently floating down as tiny crystals, not much larger than a pinhead.

The army plods forward at a steady pace, clumped into a series of small groups for as far as I can see. We march steadily, knowing that stopping means freezing to death. The sides of the road resemble a battlefield, with countless frozen corpses strewn along them. Many soldiers use the bodies like logs to build protected spots for the night. We've passed some of these gruesome shelters where men are roasting meat. I turn away from the sight, knowing there can only be one source of meat with so few horses remaining.

Arnaud and I walk alongside our horses to keep our circulation going. Vlad leads the carriage horse on foot. We all wear thick scarves around our faces, leaving only a slit for our eyes. The cab of the berline is kept tightly shut to conserve Anna Lise's and her parents' body heat, and they are all wrapped in furs and blankets. When we stop to dump chamber pots, I've found the cab interior smelling of sweat and urine. I'm not sure which is worse, the cold outside or that intense odor inside.

At night, we build our fire near the carriage. Arnaud, Vlad, and I keep the flames going through the night and rotate sleeping in half-hour shifts. When we're awake, we march in circles around the camp with the horses to keep our blood moving and to guard them against blood gleaners. On our last night before arriving in Smorgoni, I give our horses the end of our feed, hoping we'll find more tomorrow when we reach the village. For ourselves, we have no more horsemeat, and our cache of sausage and cheese is nearly depleted.

Throughout the night, we heat stones in the fire for warming the interior of the carriage. While I'm placing one of these stones in the cab, Anna Lise clasps my hand. "Jean-Luc, you, Vlad, and Arnaud must join us here in the cab—at least for a little while."

"No, my love. The fire must be kept going and our horses protected. We will try and find a cabin to stay in when we near Smorgoni." I lower my scarf and gently kiss her on the cheek, keeping my ice-crusted beard away as much as possible. "This cold will break soon, I'm sure," I say, trying to believe my own words.

I close the door to stop any more heat escaping.

* * *

By midday on what I believe is December 5, we pass through farmland on the outskirts of Smorgoni. It's difficult to tell one day from another. The sun has emerged, providing a bit of warmth, though it is still intensely cold. I now feel safe riding Bayard again, no longer worrying about freezing.

Horsemen approach from the direction of the village. I recognize one of the riders as Lieutenant Bret, attaché to General Eblé. I signal to Vlad to stop the berline.

Anna Lise flies out of the carriage as soon as it stops. She bends over, holding her stomach, and retches. I dismount and rush to her side. "Anna Lise, it's not the camp fever, is it?"

As I anxiously feel her forehead, she looks up at me wanly. "It's not the camp fever. It's from being with child. The nausea will pass, and I will be all right." Her temple is cool, which greatly relieves me.

"Captain!" Lieutenant Bret says as he catches sight of me. "Madame," he adds, giving Anna Lise a bow from his saddle.

Anna Lise straightens up and forces a smile.

The lieutenant continues. "I'm relieved to see that you and your family appear well. General Eblé would like you to join him and other officers at General Rapp's headquarters in Smorgoni at sunset tonight."

"Of course, I'll be there. How are General Eblé and his men?"

A shadow passes over Lieutenant Bret's face. He hesitates for a moment. "Only forty of our pontoniers and sappers survived the Berezina." Lieutenant Bret looks around at the frozen countryside. His eyes are hard. "Now, half of those have died in this damnable cold. The general worked nonstop on that crossing for days. He collapsed from exhaustion after it was over and hasn't been well since. He is under Baron Larrey's care."

"I'm sorry. They were brave men, and none of us would be here without them."

The lieutenant turns to Anna Lise. "Madame, I saw you and your parents feeding and helping our men on both sides of the river. Thank you."

She nods.

I look toward her, worry clouding my thoughts, and I feel my throat tighten. She's not feeling well, and I don't like the way some of the soldiers watch her as they march by.

I turn back to the lieutenant. "Why are we meeting?"

"I only know it concerns news about the emperor." Giving me a salute and Anna Lise a bow, he says, "I must be off to find General Rapp's other officers."

I help Anna Lise back into the berline. "What is happening?" she asks. "I don't understand. What news could there be about the emperor?"

"I don't know. Perhaps there is a cease-fire agreement."

"Must you go?" she asks, and I can see that she is fighting to be brave.

My mind fills with dread. "I have no choice but to go, my love, but I promise I will return as quickly as possible."

Closing up the cab, I scan the passing groups of soldiers. Some of their eyes still linger on the carriage door.

I remount Bayard and turn toward Arnaud. "We should find somewhere to stay tonight. A place away from all these soldiers and out of the cold. Have you seen anything?"

"No, sir. Not yet."

We ride farther along, and after a sharp bend in the road, Smorgoni comes into sight.

"Over there," Arnaud says, pointing toward a building far off the road. "I don't think it's visible to those walking, and I don't see any horses or men around it."

"Good. That should be a safe spot away from everyone but still close enough to the village that we shouldn't have to worry about Cossacks." Even so, I feel a sense of foreboding. "Let's wait for these men to pass. There is a long gap between them and the next group. Perhaps no one will see us heading over there."

Slowly, the men trudge by and the gap appears.

"Let's go," I say, and we wind our way over the frozen field to the building. We position the berline behind the stable, out of sight. Going inside, we find it is a peasant family's home. No one is there, as I'm sure the sight of the army passing so close drove the owners away.

A small stable is attached to one side, with a doorway between the house and shed.

"Look," Anna Lise says in wonder. "There's food on the shelves and wood by the hearth."

"They must have left in a hurry. Maybe they also left feed in the stable."

I turn toward Vlad. "Take the horses to the stable and find them something to eat. I'll be in soon to brush down Bayard."

Herr and Frau Bauck take out the blankets and furs from the carriage, laying them out to air in the stable. The pungent smell from days of accumulated sweat fills the air. Thoughts of a bath and clean clothing briefly enter my head, but these luxuries are still far away. Anna Lise lights the fire, and the cabin slowly warms. We leave the doorway between the stable and home open to give heat to the horses.

Arnaud joins me in brushing down our horses. The peasants have left feed, and soon, Bayard and Basile are slowly chewing on hay, looking exhausted. I take my brush and start to stroke Bayard's neck. He knickers appreciatively. "Rest, my friend," I say. "The end of our journey is coming into sight."

Finishing, I tell Arnaud to keep watch over them, and I return to the cabin.

I sit by Anna Lise near the comforting fire. My arm around her shoulder, we gaze into the flames. An unexpected calm comes over me, and I kiss her cheek.

"This is the closest I've felt to being home since the fires in Moscow," she says.

"And for me, since leaving Ostheim," I reply. "Are you feeling better? How is little Adrianna?"

"I'm fine now, Jean-Luc, and I think Adrianna is hoping we'll be home soon to the warmth of a Colmar summer."

"We're close to Vilna now, where there should be food and reinforcements. Perhaps the worst is over."

I give her a gentle kiss and get to my feet. Suddenly my sense of calm evaporates and the hairs on the back of my neck begin to bristle. What is this apprehension?

"I must be off to my meeting with General Eblé and Uncle Jean. I'll leave as quickly as possible. Arnaud, Vlad, keep watch over everyone and our horses."

Walking outside, I scan the landscape. No signs of anyone. Still, I am not comfortable leaving them. Anna Lise comes up to me, taking my hand. "We are safe here," she says with a note of worry in her voice. "But be quick. I feel so much better when you are by my side."

* * *

I find Uncle Jean's colors outside a building filling with officers. Dismounting and going inside, I see the two generals on a platform near the back of the room. General Eblé looks frail, and he sits while Uncle Jean stands, casting his eyes across the many men. There are perhaps fifty officers assembled.

"Attention!" Uncle Jean's attaché calls out, and the crowd goes silent, all eyes fixed on Uncle Jean.

"I'll make this brief," Uncle Jean says. "At this moment, the emperor is preparing his sledge to leave for Paris tonight."

Murmurings erupt across the room.

"Attention!" the attaché shouts.

Uncle Jean starts again. "As many of you have heard, there has been an attempted coup in Paris. The rebel leader is now dead, but the emperor feels compelled to return to calm the people and to begin raising a new army. He is not deserting us."

Again, murmuring erupts, and once more the room is called to attention.

"The king of Naples, Marshal Murat, is in command of the army," Uncle Jean says. "In a few days, we expect to reach Vilna, where there is food and also reinforcements. After that, we go back over the Nieman River to Prussia and then home to France!"

Despite all the earlier murmurings, the thought of heading home to France evokes cries of *"Vive l'empereur! Vive la France!"* from the assemblage.

I push my way forward so that I can say a few words to the generals before leaving. First is General Eblé, who looks at me weakly. "Captain Calliet, isn't it?" he asks.

"Yes, sir, it is."

"You survived the Berezina. Such a terrible place. So many lives lost."

The general gazes around the room, clearly in pain.

Looking back at me, he says, "You had your wife with you. My men were quite taken with her. Did she survive as well?"

"Yes, sir. She and her parents are here with me in Smorgoni."

The general leans toward me. "Don't believe that this war is over," he whispers. "The Cossacks are massing to attack Vilna, and the Russian army is marching from St. Petersburg. We are far from safe."

He collapses back into his chair, his energy spent.

Leaving the general, I turn quickly to Uncle Jean.

"Is it true? About the Cossacks?"

Uncle Jean looks toward General Eblé with a frown.

"Perhaps ... some of our scouts have reported a Cossack buildup, but the emperor has dismissed these reports, believing they would never attack Vilna with the reinforcements we have there." Uncle Jean glances at General Eblé. "However, I'm not so sure. I, too, think they might attack. We only have a few thousand fresh troops in Vilna."

The mere mention of Cossacks so near unsettles me greatly. "I need to go, Uncle Jean. I must be with Anna Lise."

"Of course. Is she close?"

"At the edge of the village."

Uncle Jean smiles. "She should be safe. Stay a while longer and have a cognac with me."

"Please excuse me, Uncle Jean, but I must go."

* * *

The sky is clear as I race Bayard toward the cottage. The moon is full, its light reflecting off the snow, but the cold is biting, stinging my eyes and making it difficult to find my way.

I find our carriage tracks ... and new footprints leading toward the cabin.

My heart hammers in my chest and I kick Bayard into a gallop.

The home comes into view, and my mouth goes dry. Firelight is flowing through the open door, illuminating a body blocking the entrance. In the shadows near the doorway, there are one ... no, three more bodies in the blood-soaked snow covering the ground.

I leap from Bayard with my sabre drawn. Three of the dead are wearing tattered French infantry uniforms, and the fourth, I realize with shock, is Arnaud. His still body is the one blocking the doorway.

Climbing over my friend, I shout, "Anna Lise!"

Inside are the bodies of two more intruders in French uniforms. My dagger is protruding from the back of one of them.

"Anna Lise," I cry out again.

I hear quiet weeping from the far side of the room. Anna Lise is there, kneeling next to her parents, holding her mother's hand. Vlad is there as well. He nods and steps out of the way.

"Anna Lise ... Anna Lise," I whisper, kneeling down and wrapping my arm around her heaving shoulders, noticing that her dress is ripped.

She falls into my arms, sobbing. "Dead! My *Mutti* and *Vati* are dead."

We sit, holding each other for a very long time, her body shuddering with sobs. Finally, I ask her to tell me what happened.

Trembling, she begins to speak. Her voice is flat, her sentences rushed and broken.

"We were preparing food when I heard loud voices outside. I opened the door. Arnaud was fending off attackers. He shoved me away and kept swinging his sabre. But he couldn't hold them off, and two of them overwhelmed him. *Mutti* and *Vati* and I were frozen in fear."

She leans her face into my shoulder, momentarily unable to continue.

Fury builds inside me. *Our final enemy is our own men?*

Anna Lise looks up; her terrified eyes hold mine. "Vlad tried to stop them, but they hit him hard and he fell to the floor. *Vati* pushed *Mutti* behind him and leapt at the assailants. With one slash, he was gone. *Mutti* shrieked and I rushed to her side, but they shoved me away." She turns her gaze toward one body and points. "That one, with red hair, plunged his sabre into her chest. Then he turned toward me."

Anna Lise stops talking again, her breaths ragged, her face as white as ashes.

My chest is so tight I can barely breathe as I wait for her to continue.

"I backed up into a corner, trying desperately to find the dagger you gave me." She looks at the dead soldier's body. "He said he had seen me outside the carriage."

I hold her tightly.

"I got the dagger from the sheath I had strapped to my leg. Clutching it, I kept it hidden in the folds of my dress. He kept coming toward me. He started to touch my hair. He was so close. I could smell his foul breath."

She shudders.

"I fixed my eyes on his chest. I was flat against the wall, as if I had become part of it. I was so afraid ... frozen.

"He stepped back and pulled off his pants.

"Coming at me again, he stumbled and fell against me, tearing at my dress. I dropped the dagger but kicked my knee hard into his *hodensack*. He howled and fell to the floor, and I found the blade.

"He swiped at me but missed, and I used both hands to shove the dagger into his chest as hard as I could. Then I pulled it out."

She stops again, breathing hard. I wait.

"The other soldier started toward me. I held my dagger at ready, waiting for an opening, when suddenly Vlad appeared. He clubbed him on the head, giving me my opening."

She stares at the dagger still protruding from the intruder's back.

"The attacker turned and went at Vlad. I rushed him, driving the knife into his back. Vlad took another swing of his stick, crashing it into his skull."

Anna Lise's eyes fill with tears as she remembers the moment. "Vlad saved me."

We sit together for a long time as she sobs quietly, looking at her parents' bodies. I look at Vlad, giving him a nod of thanks, but his eyes are on the Baucks.

"What are we to do?" she asks.

"I only know I need to get you and Adrianna back home to Colmar."

I look around at the room and the dead bodies, thinking about what to do. From the stable, both Bayard and Basile whinny. My pulse races as I reach for my sabre. "Anna Lise!" I whisper tensely. "Get your dagger." I motion to Vlad to grab a sabre from one of the dead attackers.

Her eyes fill with fear as she dashes toward the knife. With shaking hands, she pulls the dagger from the dead attacker's back.

I motion for her to stay put as I move quietly toward the stable door.

Stepping inside the shed, I hear rustling sounds and labored breath in the darkness.

A voice calls out—a young voice. "Please, sir, don't kill me," it pleads.

A private, no more than a lad, stumbles out of the dark, his hands held high.

The tip of my sabre is but an inch from his throat.

"How many more of you are there?" I demand.

"There's no one else, sir," the terrified youngster answers. "My sergeant ordered me to bleed the horses. I didn't know he and the others were going to attack. I heard the fighting and hid in the dark."

"Come with me, boy," I say as I push him toward the cabin.

He stops when confronted by Anna Lise, her dagger raised. "He's just a scared boy," she says. She slowly drops her arm.

I give him a shove with my boot, and he falls through the doorway onto the floor.

The private rises to his knees, his hands held high. Speechless, he surveys the room.

"What do we do with him?" Anna Lise asks.

"He seems innocent enough," I say. Dropping the point of my sword, I glance over at Arnaud's body. "He's even younger looking than Arnaud."

"Private, did anyone else see you come toward this cabin?"

"No, sir. We waited until it was dark and the road was empty." His voice is high and fearful.

The boy tentatively lowers his arms, looking from me to Anna Lise.

"Please, sir, I only want to get home to Normandy."

The mention of Normandy brings back the memory of Renaud, the young recruit who died in my arms so long ago. But this boy is not Renaud and can't be trusted.

"Private, check the pockets of your comrades for loot."

He starts to go toward one of the bodies, but suddenly pulls a dagger from his coat and rushes to grab Anna Lise. He holds his blade to her throat. "Drop your sword, Captain. I'm sure you don't want me to kill her." He looks toward Vlad. "You too. Drop your weapon."

What stupidity! We were all fooled just because he looked so innocent.

We both comply and drop our weapons. I look at Anna Lise. She appears unafraid, her face steely and her blue eyes on fire.

"You, servant, go through the pockets of my friends. You'll find some loot. Put it in a sack."

Obediently, Vlad rifles through their pockets and puts coins, jewelry, and gemstones into a bag.

"Good! Now we go to the stable. Saddle up that horse nearest the door and load the sack of loot into a saddlebag."

"Servant, you go first, and Captain, get your sword and go next. I want you to slit the throats of the other two horses."

I pick up my sabre, plotting how I can overcome the boy without hurting Anna Lise. Vlad begins saddling Bayard as I go through the narrow doorway. I stay close, seeing that it will be difficult for the boy to get both himself and Anna Lise through the doorway at the same time.

He starts to push Anna Lise through, loosening his grip on the blade at her throat. She begins to stumble, but instead of falling, she whips around and slashes her dagger across his face. He shrieks in pain, bringing his hands up to the cut. I push past Anna Lise and plunge my sabre into his heart.

As the boy falls, Vlad grabs hold of him and pulls his body into the stable. I grasp Anna Lise. She is panting, breathless.

"It's over?" she gasps.

Taking her into the cabin, I sit her at the table and check to see if she is wounded. There is a trickle of blood on her neck, but the wound isn't deep. I dab the blood away with my scarf.

"Jean-Luc, do you think there are more of them?" she asks, raw fear in her voice.

"I don't know, but we must get away from here quickly."

"What about *Mutti* and *Vati*? And Arnaud? Just leave them here?"

I glance at their bodies, my heart aching. "We must. Anna Lise, listen to me carefully. I want you to wear Arnaud's uniform and ride Basile."

Anna Lise stares at me incredulously.

"Arnaud was not a large man, and his uniform will not be too big for you, especially since you'll be wearing a greatcoat over it. The shako can cover your hair, and the length of it will be hidden by the greatcoat. You've already ridden Basile, so that won't be an issue."

"I would become Arnaud," she says with a slight nod.

"Yes. Arnaud would still be protecting us from his grave. But I have another idea, which may be even crazier."

Anna Lise looks at me, her eyes questioning.

"Last night, when I was meeting with Uncle Jean and General Eblé, the general said scouts have reported a massing of Cossacks. He thinks they will attack Vilna."

"But Vilna should have reinforcements and supplies for us. It's supposed to be where we are finally safe, isn't it?" Anna Lise asks. Her voice is flat, her state of high energy draining away.

"If the general is right, we don't want to be in Vilna." I hesitate to say what I must. "I think we should leave the army and head south toward Warsaw and then to your uncle's farm in Prussia."

She gasps. "No, Jean-Luc. Even if you're right, you cannot become a deserter!"

"But it might be our only chance to get home."

"No! You can't desert." Anna Lise's eyes are again steely and filled with determination. "We must talk to Uncle Jean. He may have some ideas. You say he is in Smorgoni? We must go see him!"

She is right.

"All right, we will go and see Uncle Jean. I'll take care of Arnaud and retrieve his uniform. You and Vlad attend to your parents. Wrap their bodies in the blankets we took out of the carriage. We can lay them by the berline when we leave. I'm sorry that we must do this so quickly, Anna Lise, without the ceremony they deserve."

I place Arnaud's body on a blanket and pull it to a spot near the carriage.

Thank you, my dear friend. Without you, Anna Lise would have been raped and likely killed.

I take off his uniform and boots and finish wrapping him in the blanket.

Returning inside with the uniform and boots, I see that Anna Lise and Vlad have finished wrapping Frau and Herr Bauck in the blankets.

Anna Lise is kneeling next to her parents. She looks up at me. "Jean-Luc, how can they be dead?"

I take her hand. "Come, it's time to go ... Vlad and I will carry them out by the carriage."

When her parents' bodies are lying next to Arnaud, Anna Lise lays a crucifix on their remains. I look disdainfully at this symbol of God. We stand in silence for a few moments, Anna Lise holding onto me. The wind kicks up, blasting snow into our faces. "Goodbye," Anna Lise whispers. We turn and go back to the cabin.

"I will help you with Arnaud's uniform," I tell Anna Lise. "Vlad, you will need to ride the carriage horse. Did you see an extra saddle in the stable?"

"No sir, but I saw a length of rope. I'll fashion a rope bridle and put a blanket on the horse's back."

"Good. Perhaps we can buy one in Smorgoni with the loot from the attackers. Once you are done with the carriage horse, start saddling Bayard and Basile. Anna Lise and I will be out shortly. Oh, and also get Herr Bauck's butchering knives from the carriage."

Anna Lise ties her hair into a bun and discards the torn and bloodstained dress she's been wearing. "Help me with the boots," she says. When she puts on the shako, her hair is covered, and her young face looks not much different from that of a young recruit.

We walk through the door to the stable. Anna Lise takes one last look back inside the cabin, the site of so much horror for her these past few hours.

Fifty-One

Wolves – Mid December 1812

The sun is rising as we enter Smorgoni. Another clear and frigid day. We ride up to the building displaying Uncle Jean's colors and dismount. 'Sir, this horse has been bled,' Vlad says. 'He won't last but a few days, especially if I am riding him.'

Vlad glances toward Anna Lise, who nods that he should continue. 'Sir, I'm a Jew. We passed by several Jewish homes coming here. If I may, while you are meeting with General Rapp, I would like to talk to some of them about buying a saddle and another horse.'

Anna Lise quickly jumps in. '*Mutti* and *Vati* retained Vlad because he is Jewish. Many Jews are traders, and they give their best prices and goods to fellow Jews. He's given my family years of service.'

I look at the two of them, then pull out the bag with loot and toss it to Vlad. 'Don't take long!'

'Yes, sir, I will be quick.'

'Stay close to me, Anna Lise, and don't make eye contact or speak. Don't forget, I'll be calling you Corporal Coulane."

We walk inside, and the room is in a flurry of activity, everyone preparing to depart. 'General Rapp," I cry as I see Uncle Jean across the room, giving instructions to his staff. He hears me and beckons me over.

Anna Lise and I reach him, and I snap a salute. 'Sir, may Corporal Coulane and I see you in private?"

Uncle Jean looks at me, then to Anna Lise. A stunned expression crosses his face. 'Of course, Captain, follow me."

We go to a nearby room with a desk and several chairs. He dismisses the men inside and closes the door.

'Please, sit," he says, unable to keep his eyes off Anna Lise as he takes a seat at his desk. 'Jean-Luc, what happened?"

I recount the events, and Uncle Jean doesn't say a word. He looks from me to Anna Lise, his eyes welling. 'Corporal Coulane, I'm so sorry." Turning back to me, he says, 'Do you plan to travel with the army like this? Your ruse would not last long."

'I know, but after last night, I've realized our army is as dangerous to us as the Cossacks. I have a plan, but I don't want to be a deserter."

'What would that be? You want to follow the emperor's route toward Warsaw, then France?"

'Basically, yes ... I want to take the corporal to Prussia and the safety of an uncle's farm."

Uncle Jean's finger taps his desk as he looks blankly across the room. He gets up and starts pacing. 'You would be in great danger, traveling on your own. You would be no match for the Cossacks."

'True, but the Cossacks will be at Vilna," I reply.

'Please, Uncle Jean, there must be something," Anna Lise says in a whisper.

Uncle Jean looks at her, pressing a finger to his lips to warn her not to speak.

"Does the corporal agree with you, Jean-Luc?"

"Yes, sir."

Uncle Jean continues to pace, his fingers cupping his chin.

"How far is this uncle's farm from Berlin?"

"Within a few leagues," I reply.

"Very well. I'll cut you orders to go to the Charité in Berlin. Baron Larrey intends to take his hospital wagons to the Charité once we cross the Nieman River. You will inform the administrators of this so they can prepare. Also, your orders will release you to go home afterward."

He sits at his desk and writes the order, imprinting his seal on the document. I look at Anna Lise and nod slightly.

She gives me a small smile and nods in return.

Uncle Jean furrows his brow. "Here are your orders. I can only wish you godspeed!"

He turns to Anna Lise. "Corporal, I hope we meet again in happier times."

Unable to further restrain himself, he embraces both of us, kissing our cheeks. "Good luck, Captain, Corporal," he says, giving us a salute.

We turn and rejoin Vlad by our horses. He still has only the carriage horse with its handmade rope bridle.

"There are no extra horses," Vlad says. "But the man I talked to has an uncle with a farm on the road toward Grodno. He may be able to sell us one."

"How far away is the farm?" I ask.

"Two or three days out."

* * *

The land we've entered is a wilderness with league upon league of dense forest. Fortunately, we've so far avoided seeing any Cossacks. As General Eblé told me, they must all be massed near Vilna to attack the remnants of the army. We have come upon groups of frozen corpses, most likely deserters. We scavenge what food we can from these poor souls.

On the third day, we slow to a walk, as Vlad can no longer ride the carriage horse. He leads it along, though the poor horse seems ready to collapse. I try to hurry Vlad along, as I fear for our lives. We've garnered the attention of wolves, and the howls that have followed us the past two days seem to be getting closer. Last night, we barely slept, our senses on edge.

Darkness is coming when I hear rustling in the trees. "Have your sabres in reach," I say, trying to see through the cover of trees. "The wolves are here."

The shadows part, and a massive, tawny wolf emerges from the trees. It stands squarely in the middle of the road, challenging us to pass. Light from the setting sun reflects off its golden eyes. It snarls, revealing sharp teeth and long fangs, dripping with saliva. "Close up!" I command. "Vlad, take my hand and climb up with me on Bayard."

Our horses are rearing and skittering in panic, and Anna Lise nearly falls from Basile. More wolves appear from behind and start nipping at the now panicked carriage horse. He kicks and circles as each wolf approaches, trying to keep their hungry fangs from his flanks.

Basile moves ahead of Bayard, getting away from the wolves attacking the rear. Vlad holds onto me tightly. I look toward Anna Lise, who is still trying to control Basile when the wolf in front of us breaks into a full run, heading for her.

Giving Bayard a hard kick, I move to block the attack. Just as the animal goes airborne, I swing my sabre, catching the wolf on its neck. Basile is knocked to his knees by the weight of the wolf colliding into him, sending Anna Lise violently to the ground. Vlad leaps off Bayard to help Anna Lise while I snatch Basile's bridle. The pack snarls as they rip into the carriage horse, too lost in their hunger to pay attention to us.

Anna Lise holds onto one of her shoulders. "Vlad!" I yell. "Help her onto my horse. Anna Lise, take my hand." I hold her uninjured arm and pull her up. She yelps in pain but is able to swing her leg over Bayard and sit behind me.

"Can you hold tight while we ride?"

"Yes," she says in a pained whisper.

Vlad mounts Basile. I quickly scan the forest and road ahead and see no more wolves. I glance back to where the predators continue to tear into their prey, then give Bayard a kick. We ride hard, distancing ourselves from the wolves. Anna Lise's arm grips me tightly.

After about a league, I spot a barn in a clearing next to the road. We ride to it. "Vlad, come quickly."

I gently lower Anna Lise into Vlad's arms. Once she's down, I jump from Bayard and hold her. She turns toward me, pain etching her face. "My shoulder," she says, grimacing. "It might be broken."

I carry her into the barn. "Vlad, bring the horses inside. Those wolves will be after us again soon."

I lay Anna Lise down on a bed of hay. "This will hurt, but I need to take your jacket off."

I gingerly begin removing the jacket. Anna Lise flinches with each pull of the sleeve.

Once the jacket is off, I see that the shoulder is misshapen, bulging out to the side.

"Your arm has popped out of its shoulder socket," I tell her as I examine the shoulder closely. "I don't think its broken, but I need to pull your arm back into place ... this will hurt."

"Do it quickly, Jean-Luc," she groans. "The pain is getting worse."

"Vlad, come here and help me. Hold her tight while I pull." Anna Lise's face is white with pain, but she gives me a pained, determined frown. I yank her arm forward sharply.

She screeches in agony, but her arm is back in place. After breathing heavily for several minutes, she rubs her shoulder. "That feels better."

"We need to get this jacket back on you for warmth, then put your arm in a sling."

"What about the wolves?" she asks. "Won't they track us down?"

"I fear they will, but probably not till morning after they finish their current kill."

Vlad gets blankets from our gear and covers Anna Lise.

"Get some rest, *ma chérie*," I tell her. "Vlad and I will make a fire and think about how to fight the wolves." Exhaustion overtakes Anna Lise, and she is soon fast asleep.

I retrieve my pistols, as well as Arnaud's, from our gear. I hand Arnaud's set to Vlad. "Do you know how to use these?"

"Yes."

"Good. Let's lay out our gunpowder flasks and pistol shot. The pistols may be our only chance."

We take turns sleeping while keeping the fire going and listening for the wolves.

Vlad shakes me awake. "Sir, the wolves are here."

Howling and yips can be heard from all sides. Anna Lise awakens, sitting up to listen. She clutches my arm with her good hand.

"Is your shoulder less painful?" I ask.

"Yes. How do we fight the wolves?"

I hand her a loaded pistol. "If a wolf gets past Vlad or me, use this on it."

She holds the pistol, practicing pointing it with her uninjured arm. "How much gunpowder do we have, and how many more balls for shot?"

"Not much of either. We can afford no misses. Don't shoot until the wolf is nearly on you."

I start moving toward the barn door. "Where are you going?" Anna Lise asks.

"I want to see how far away the wolves are."

She looks panicked. "Is that wise?"

"I'll be quick. I want to know where they'll be coming from."

I peek through the cracks in the barn wall but see only trees and the snow-covered field. I turn the door handle tentatively. "Vlad, cover me."

I take just one step outside the door when, without warning, a wolf bolts for me from the side. Before I can turn, a shot rings out from Vlad's pistol behind me, echoing against the trees.

There's a yelp, and the wolf retreats, apparently only grazed by the shot. The other four scatter into the trees across the clearing.

We huddle inside while waiting for the next move by the wolves. I try to plan our response.

Before long, we hear the patter of wolves walking, just feet away. They start scratching and pulling on the walls. One sticks its snout through an opening in the boards near me. I jam my pistol's barrel into its mouth and shoot. That should leave four.

Another lull, then one after another, the wolves claw and jump against the closed barn door. I brace my feet against the door, pistols at ready. One finds a weak spot in the wall near Anna Lise, pushing aside a board just enough to squeeze in. Snarling, it moves toward her. I fire, but am too far away for an accurate shot, and miss. Anna Lise fires, and the animal drops at her feet. Vlad rushes to the opening, pushes the loose board back into place, and moves the dead wolf against it.

They continue to claw at the barn door. "I can't move my feet, or they'll break through," I say. "Vlad, reload Anna Lise's pistol, then mine."

Vlad reloads the two pistols. "That's the last of our black powder," he says. "We have only three shots left."

Suddenly, the wolves stop attacking, and I hear the pounding of several horses approaching.

"It must be Cossacks," Anna Lise cries. "They must have heard the gunfire."

We exchange wary glances as we strain to hear. The horses stop, and the riders begin to talk. I can't make out the language, but Vlad's face lights up into a broad smile. "It's Yiddish!" he says. "It must be the family of the Jews I talked to in Smorgoni."

"A gutn tog!" Vlad yells out, saying hello in Yiddish.

"A gutn tog!" they shout back. I can hear surprise in their voices.

Amazed at our good fortune, I help Anna Lise to the barn door while Vlad rushes to talk to our saviors. After several minutes, he returns.

"The man I talked to in Smorgoni—this is his uncle's farm," Vlad says, his words rushing out. "The uncle's name is Abraham Efram, and we are welcome to stay with his family for as long as we need. His farm is just down the road."

"Vlad, you ride Basile—but first, help Anna Lise up onto Bayard after I mount up."

We arrive at the Efram household and are met by Abraham's wife. She looks us over carefully and says something in Yiddish to Abraham. Abraham replies. She goes to Anna Lise and helps her off Bayard. Vlad tells her something more in Yiddish, which causes her to look at Anna Lise more carefully. Like a mother, she takes Anna Lise under her wing and leads her to the kitchen, where she gives her food and inspects her shoulder.

Using Vlad as an interpreter, Abraham says, "My wife says the girl mustn't travel for several days. She also wants to know how long she has been with child."

"About two months," I say.

"My wife says she must get stronger before you continue ... Vlad is her servant, and you are the father?"

"Yes."

Abraham and his wife begin arguing. Then he says, "We have room for only two extra people in our home. Vlad can stay here with the girl so that he can translate. You can sleep in our stable." Abraham's wife gives me an accusing look, clearly wondering why I would have a wife with child in this wilderness.

"Of course. Thank you. I'm so grateful."

* * *

The next few days we stay with the Efram family are a luxury. We enjoy baths and good meals, recuperating a little from the trauma of the last few months. Anna Lise's shoulder becomes stronger, allowing limited movement.

"Are you able to ride?" I ask her.

"Yes, so long as we don't encounter wolves again," she says with a smile.

"Your uncle's farm is at least another week away. Your shoulder will get sore."

"No matter. We need to go."

Grodno is only a day away, and it has a bridge over the Neiman River, the boundary between the Russian and French empires. We purchase a horse and gear for Vlad and begin our journey anew. We know we'll never see the Efram family again, and we try our best to tell them how grateful we are. Abraham accompanies us to the bridge, saying he wants to ensure we have no problems crossing.

My orders to report to the Charité are reviewed at a station blocking the bridge. The guard eyes Anna Lise suspiciously and begins to approach her. My hand finds the hilt of my sabre. Abraham comes forward, slipping the guard some of the jewels we gave him. The guard gives Anna Lise another look, then lifts the gate. We proceed across the span. I look down on the ice-bound river, remembering back to that warm, late June day when half a million men crossed this river to subjugate the Russian empire. *How many survived?* I wonder. *Maybe ten thousand?*

We are now in Poland, and Prussia is only a few days away.

Fifty-Two

Prussia – Late December 1812

Thanks to Vlad, the week it took to travel through Poland was remarkably uneventful. The Poles generally gave us no heed, and Vlad negotiated with the Jews we encountered for food and places to sleep. Though he didn't don the yarmulke in Moscow, he has worn it since being in Smorgoni, and this has allowed us entry into their community.

But now we are in Prussia, and the deeper we ride into this country, the more hostility we find toward anyone in a French uniform. Fortunately, the cold keeps most people off the roads.

"Schweinehunds!" an older man hisses as we pass him on the road. He spits toward our feet in disgust. The Jews we encounter here are more reluctant to help us, as they don't want to antagonize the Prussians. Our supplies are running low, but I'm uneasy about approaching anyone to purchase more.

'Sir," Vlad says, 'let me go alone into that upcoming village. They'll curse me for being a Jew, but they won't attack me for being French. I'll be able to buy food."

Just then, a horseman comes toward us. He starts to approach, but as he comes near, I see a look of disdain cross his face. He brings his horse to an abrupt halt, turns away, and gallops off toward the village. "He wanted no part of us once he saw our uniforms," I say. I look at Vlad, reluctant to send him to the town alone.

"It's our only choice, Jean-Luc," Anna Lise says. "We have very little food left, but we shouldn't need to buy any more after this. My uncle's farm is only a day or two away."

Apprehensive, I finally nod in agreement.

Turning to Vlad, I say, "We'll make camp over by that large oak and await your return. Don't take long. That horseman might be going to tell his friends we are here."

An hour passes, and Vlad has not returned. Dusk is seeping into the landscape as my apprehension rises. I pace back and forth, staring down the road.

Anna Lise gets up from the fire and also looks toward the village. "Something must be wrong. We must go find Vlad!"

Agreeing, I rush to load our gear and go.

Mounting our horses, I scan our surroundings and see no one, but my worry deepens. "Keep your sabre close, Anna Lise."

Approaching the edge of the village, I see there is a commotion with four men holding torches as they surround someone on horseback. Because of the deepening dusk, they have not seen us, and I signal Anna Lise to stop. We're close enough to see the men and hear what they are saying.

"This stinking Jew!" one of the torch men says. "I saw him buy supplies with gemstones. Where did you get them, Jew?" He pokes his torch toward Vlad threateningly.

"They've got Vlad," Anna Lise whispers in alarm.

Another, whom I recognize as the horseman who approached us previously, says, "I saw him earlier with some Frenchies I passed when riding into town. Did you buy that food for them, Jew?" he demands.

They all begin waving their torches threateningly at Vlad. His horse is skittish, rearing up and snorting loudly.

I draw my sabre and motion to Anna Lise to draw hers. "Stay behind me," I tell her.

I give my sabre a twist in the air, then point it forward as we charge at full gallop toward the assemblage. I bellow a war cry at the top of my lungs.

The men with torches turn toward us. "Frenchies!" they shout. Three of the men drop their torches and run in panic, but one is determined to take me on. He swings at my sabre and I strike his torch, sliding my blade down to his hand.

He screams in pain as Anna Lise and I sweep past. Instantly, Vlad and his mount join us and we race through the village, following the road into the nearby forest, riding hard in the moonlit night. After nearly an hour, we slow to a walk.

"Are you all right, Vlad?" Anna Lise pants, out of breath from the hard ride.

"Yes, Frau Calliet. Those men wanted me to toss the food and the rest of my jewels to them, but I wouldn't," Vlad says with a slight smile. "I knew you would come. I kept stalling."

I look back toward the village but don't see anyone following us. "We need to ride all night. I fear they will come after us. Anna Lise, you think your uncle's farm is only a day or two away?"

"Do you know the name of that last village, Vlad?" Anna Lise asks.

"It was Rauen," Vlad replies. "I asked the name of the next village, and they said it will be Wildau—around eight leagues away, off a side road to the right."

Anna Lise brightens. "That's the village near my uncle's farm! We might get there by tonight."

Encouraged, we move on for another hour or two. Venus makes its appearance near the horizon as dawn approaches. Vlad and I are tired, but I see that Anna Lise is exhausted. "We'll have some food and rest for an hour or so behind those trees," I say, pointing to an opening in the forest. "Any riders should be far behind."

We dare not build a fire, though the temperature is near freezing. I cut some boughs for us to rest on, and we sit, eating chunks of bread and slices of sausage. Anna Lise falls asleep, leaning into my chest.

The new dawn begins to break when I hear the pounding of hooves coming down the road. Anna Lise awakens with a start.

"Pull the horses back into the trees," I say. We hold our steeds firmly as ten horsemen fly by.

"They must be after us," I say. "We'll follow behind them."

A cold wind kicks up, swaying the trees and knocking off small branches. Clouds soon follow, blotting out the rising sun. Within an hour, light snow begins to fall.

"I hope they think we are going to Berlin. They may not find us after we turn off the road toward Wildau."

By midday the snowfall becomes heavy, but it turns again to flurries as the day progresses. Judging from the tracks, the horsemen are less than an hour ahead of us.

"A side road to the right ahead, sir," Vlad says.

Coming to the side road, we find no signs to help us. "It must be the road to Wildau," Anna Lise says.

I dismount and inspect the hoofprints closely. "Most of the horsemen appear to be continuing toward Berlin, but it looks like two split off and went down this side road. Do you recollect anything about the roads by your uncle's farm?" I ask Anna Lise.

She shakes her head. "It's been several years now, and I didn't pay much attention. I was too distraught about leaving Colmar."

"I hope it's the road to Wildau. We'll chance it."

After about a league, darkness is beginning to set in as we break out of the forest onto the edge of a large, snow-covered field. The snow is still falling lightly, and the tracks we've been following lead off the road toward a cabin with smoke curling above it and candlelight glowing from within. I look toward Anna Lise.

"Yes, I think that's my uncle's cottage," she says. "I remember those deer antlers hanging over the doorway. What do we do about these tracks? It looks like the men we're following are taking shelter at my uncle's home."

"We will need to hide in the forest until they leave," I say, frustrated and angry at encountering yet another barrier to our getting home. "Let's go into these trees across the road and keep watch." I dismount and hand Bayard's reins to Vlad. "I'll join you shortly after I brush away our tracks."

Anna Lise and Vlad have moved into the trees just as a crack of light beams from an opening door. The ground near the cabin is illuminated, but I'm still hidden in the shadows. Two men step out. One walks to the stable where their horses must be, and the other takes a few steps toward the road. I can feel his eyes trying to pierce the darkness. It seems he is staring right at me. I hold my breath, thinking that will somehow help. After a few moments of gazing my way, he turns around and joins his companion, saying something to him in German. I relax as the door closes, then quickly finish brushing away our tracks and rejoin Anna Lise and Vlad.

"What happened?" Anna Lise asks.

"We must have unsettled their horses," I reply. "You and Vlad get some sleep. I will keep watch."

Taking my sabre and pistols, I move to a hidden spot closer to the cabin and wait. The notion crosses my mind to go inside and kill the two, but thankfully, reason prevails. They don't pose an immediate danger, and their comrades would come looking for them if they came up missing. Most importantly, I couldn't put Anna Lise's family in danger.

* * *

The snow ends during the night, and the dawning rays of sunlight crack through the trees, creating shafts of brilliance across the field. One seems to illuminate the front door as the two men again come from the house and go toward the stable. The double of Anna Lise's father stands in the doorway, saying something to them. Then he turns and stares intently into the forest.

He sees me! Will he tell those two? I grip my sabre tightly.

The men ride out of the stable past the man in the doorway. What sound like pleasantries are exchanged and they ride back the way they came. There is no indication they see us or the tracks that I covered over. The man in the doorway watches until the two men are out of sight, then stares one last time into the trees before returning indoors.

I make my way back to Vlad and Anna Lise.

"I'd forgotten how much my uncle looks like *Vati*," Anna Lise says. "He seems to sense we are here."

"I think so too. We'll wait a while longer before going up."

A man and a boy of about fifteen emerge from the cabin, holding axes. They begin splitting wood.

"That's my cousin Franz," Anna Lise says. "Let's go."

I nod, and we make our way out to the road. The man and boy stop working and stare toward us.

"Let me go first," Anna Lise says as she takes off her shako, revealing her long blonde hair. "*Guten Morgen, Onkel Alik und Cousin Franz. Es ist Anna Lise.*"

"*Anna Lise? Ist mein Bruder und seine Frau bei dir?*"

"No, my husband and servant are with me. My parents were killed."

The man's shoulders sag as he learns of his brother's and sister-in-law's deaths. A woman emerges from the cabin and takes the man's arm.

"Anna Lise? Bitte, sie und die anderen kommen in die Hütte und werden warm."

"Jawoll, Tante Astrid."

Anna Lise rushes into her aunt's waiting arms. "Aunt Astrid, I can't tell you how overjoyed I am to be here." She wraps her arms tightly around her aunt and buries her head into her bosom, trembling. Aunt Astrid kisses the top of her head and murmurs something comforting.

I make my way to Uncle Alik and shake his hand. As I start to say something in broken German, he reassures me, "We all speak French here. You needn't struggle with your German." Eyeing me, he adds, "You must be Jean-Luc. Anna Lise could not stop talking about you or Adrien when she was here last. How is the boy?"

I lower my eyes. I haven't thought of Adrien for several weeks. Is my memory of him already turning to dust? I can't let that happen. "I'm sorry, but Adrien died at Borodino."

Uncle Alik's face saddens. "I'm surprised any of you are alive. I am glad to see my niece again, and you and your servant are most welcome to stay here for a while. Come inside and get warm."

"Only for a short time, sir," I say. "I must report to the Charité hospital in Berlin. Once I give them the orders from General Rapp, I will no longer be in the army. Then, I will return and take Anna Lise back to Colmar."

Uncle Alik looks at me skeptically. "The two men who stayed here last night are looking for you. The French are not liked around here, and now that your great emperor has been beaten,

France will soon be our enemy again. Berlin is a very dangerous place for a French soldier."

We enter the cabin, and Uncle Alik says, "Astrid, don't we have some coffee hidden away for special occasions? Seeing Anna Lise and her husband is a most special event. Jean-Luc, you must tell us how you found Anna Lise, how the two of you survived, and what happened to my brother and his wife."

Aunt Astrid brews fresh coffee and pours me a cup, which I drink gratefully.

"Thank you. It's been a long time since I've had real coffee."

After we finish the coffee, I rise from the table. "I apologize for needing to leave so quickly, but I must be off to Berlin to deliver General Rapp's orders. I will return in a couple of days."

Uncle Alik puts his hand on my shoulder. "Do you know what today is, Jean-Luc? It's Christmas Eve. No one in authority will be at the Charité. Stay a few days, then go if you must."

"Christmas Eve?" I say in disbelief. I sit back down. "You are right. I can't go today. I will stay a day or two, then go."

* * *

Anna Lise and I sadly recount our experiences since finding each other in Moscow. The Bauck family remains silent as we tell of each ordeal, their faces lowered and their shoulders drooping. After our descriptions of the Berezina River crossing, Uncle Alik looks up. "How did my brother Martin and his wife Willa die?" he asks softly.

Tears come to Anna Lise's eyes. "It was French soldiers." She looks at me, her eyes pleading for me not to say anything else. "They were after our food."

"Your own soldiers? Not the Russians?" Uncle Alik says with disgust. "I'm sorry, Jean-Luc, my regard for the French sinks further. But no more of this. It's Christmas Eve, a time to rejoice in the birth of our savior, and now we also celebrate the safe return of my brother's daughter and her husband. Let me get each of us a mug of *glühwein*, then we'll make our Christmas preparations." Disappearing into the kitchen, he returns with mugs for Anna Lise and me.

"Thank you, Uncle Alik," I say. The hot red wine is infused with cinnamon, cloves, sugar, and brandy. It tingles my throat and warms me to the bottom of my belly. "How can we help?"

"The *linsensuppe und bauernbrot*, lentil soup and brown bread, are ready for tonight, but we must kill two geese for tomorrow's feast and go into the forest to cut a Christmas tree," Uncle Alik says. "Franz, go kill the geese and pluck them. Anna Lise, you can help Astrid prepare the geese, red cabbage, and dumplings. Vlad, perhaps you can help Astrid as well?"

"I'd be most happy to," Vlad says with a smile. "I helped Frau Willa many times preparing the Christmas feast."

Uncle Alik nods toward Vlad, then turns to me. "Jean-Luc, let's go to the forest and cut the Christmas tree."

I take a last swig of my *glühwein*, savoring its taste and warmth. I haven't had this treat since I was in Colmar, and I am taken back to my boyhood. Adrien and I would sneak cupfuls when our parents weren't looking.

Herr Bauck and I trudge through the snow toward the forest where we hid last night. "You were easy to spot," he says. "Those two men did not have the eyes to see the signs: the unevenness of the snow on the ground, the lack of snow on the branches above where you hid. Just as well. You would have likely killed them, and then I would have the blood of two Prussians on my hands."

I hold back a branch for Uncle Alik. As he passes, he says, "Promise me you will kill no Prussians while you are here."

"I don't take lives unless it's needed," I reply.

"Of course," he says. "The two men here last night told me you sliced off the fingers of one of their comrades. They also told me about the Jew and said that the third person appeared to be a woman in a soldier's uniform ... I don't know why, but it crossed my mind it might be Anna Lise."

"It couldn't be helped. He came at me with his torch, and I had to block it. Those men, they clearly intended to harm us."

"Here's a good tree," Uncle Alik says. "I'll pull it back while you cut it down."

With a few swings of my hatchet, the small tree is felled.

"Yes, this tree will do us well," he says. "I know you plan to ride to the Charité the day after Christmas. My advice to you is not to wear your uniform or ride your battle horse. Patriotic hotheads are filling the capital, and many Prussian troops have ridden by over the past several days. I'm sure you would be arrested. Your message is to have the Charité prepare for French survivors, but now it seems unlikely that the French will be allowed to enter Berlin. But if you must go, wear some of my clothes and ride one of my horses."

"Thank you, sir. I'll consider your words."

"I may not like the French, but you are all Anna Lise has left of her life, and I couldn't bear to see more tragedy come her way."

I stop and stare at Herr Bauck. "Sir, promise that if anything happens to me, you'll make sure Anna Lise gets to Colmar. My father and Vlad can care for her. She is with child, and we both desperately want the birth to be there."

Herr Bauck's eyes widen and his face softens. "With child ... yes, that complicates the situation. I promise."

* * *

"Jean-Luc, the tree is crooked," Anna Lise says, looking at me with a smile I haven't seen so bright since Moscow. "Push the top away from you ... That's it, Franz, pound the nails into the stand."

"Perfect!" Uncle Alik says. "I'll put on the candles. Franz, you and Jean-Luc put on the decorations."

There's a rap on the door, and we all freeze.

"Act naturally," Uncle Alik says. "I'll take care of it."

Uncle Alik opens the door. Before him stands a stout man with a round, red face. "Herr Münster! What brings you by? Come in, come in. Do you remember my niece, Anna Lise?" he says with a wide grin. "And over there hanging candles is her brother, Adrien. He wasn't at the house the last time they were here."

"*Guten tag,*" I say.

"Please, Herr Münster, come in. We are about to have another mug of *glühwein,*" Herr Bauck says.

"No, I can't. I wanted to check on you since I saw the extra horses." Herr Münster focuses on Vlad, his gaze cold. "Who is that?"

Anna Lise speaks up quickly. "This is my servant, Vlad."

"*Guten tag,*" Vlad says.

Herr Münster nods toward Vlad, then says, "Didn't your brother's family move to Moscow, and wasn't your nephew in the French army?"

"Yes, we moved to Moscow," Anna Lise answers smoothly. "But the climate was too cold, and we returned to Colmar. Adrien retired from the service with an injury after his last campaign against Spain. My parents hired Vlad while in Moscow, and he came back with us to Colmar."

I am impressed with her quick thinking, knowing I couldn't speak because of my bad German.

"Very good," Herr Münster says. "Sorry to trouble you, Herr Bauck. I will see you tonight at church?"

"Yes, at midnight mass. Thank you so much for checking on us," Uncle Alik says as he closes the door. We all let out our breaths slowly.

"He suspects something," Anna Lise says.

"He does," her uncle agrees. "But he won't do anything about it until after Christmas. Jean-Luc, your trip to the Charité must be quick. I'll gather together some supplies for you to take. You need to have a sledge. You would call too much attention if Anna Lise were riding on horseback, and with all this snow, you'll get back to France much faster by sleigh."

"Do any Jews live nearby?" Vlad asks boldly.

Herr Bauck eyes Vlad in surprise, then looks back at me. "Do you have funds to buy a sledge?"

"We do. Vlad could buy the sledge early Christmas Day. No one will be out."

Herr Bauck hesitates. "Yes, there is a Jewish family just outside of Wildau. They are prosperous and may have a sledge to sell."

"Good. I'll leave at first light," Vlad says.

We put aside the threat of Herr Münster and return to preparing the food and decorating the tree.

"The tree is beautiful!" Anna Lise exclaims. The fir tree is filled with hanging apples, bread wafers, dried roses, candies, and of course candles.

"We can light the candles soon," Aunt Astrid says. "It's getting dark, but first we'll have our traditional Christmas Eve dinner … the lentil soup and brown bread."

I am like a small boy, filled with the magic of Christmas and the anticipation of the tree lighting as we get ready to eat.

We sit at the table in the darkening room, lit only by the glow from the fireplace. "This soup and bread are outstanding," I say as I dip a piece of my brown bread, slathered in butter, into the soup. We eat quietly together, grateful for one another's company.

Aunt Astrid smiles as we finish the meal. "I'll clear away the bowls," she says. "Alik, light the candles."

Franz adds more *glühwein* to our cups, then we sit and gaze in wonder at the tree. The candles flicker. "Magnificent," Anna Lise says. "It's like looking up to the twinkling stars. One can imagine the Christ child looking up from his manger."

Aunt Astrid gets up and goes to a small bookshelf. She brings back the bible and a lantern to the table. She goes back again to the bookshelf and returns holding three small objects. Opening her hands, she reveals porcelain figurines of Joseph, Mary, and the Christ child. "Anna Lise, I know how your mother loved figurines. Please, take these with you to Colmar as our gift to your parents' memory."

Tears spill down Anna Lise's cheeks as she embraces her aunt. "I don't know what to say but thank you. We will treasure them always."

"You are most welcome, my love," Aunt Astrid says. She lights the lantern and hands the bible to Uncle Alik.

"Let me read from Luke and Matthew," he says. *"About that time Emperor Augustus gave orders for the names of all the people to be listed in record books. These first records were made when Quirinius was governor of Syria. Everyone had to go to their own hometown ..."*

We settle into the glow of the evening, mesmerized by the tree lights and the reading.

* * *

Dawn comes, and the final preparations for the Christmas feast are underway. The geese are roasting in the oven, and the red cabbage is simmering on the stovetop.

"How far is Wildau?" Vlad asks Uncle Alik.

"About half a league."

"How will I recognize the house of the Jewish family?"

Uncle Alik laughs. "It will be the house with no Christmas decorations." Then in a more serious tone, he adds, "Once the village comes into sight, it will be the first house on the right." Herr Bauck considers Vlad. He appears uncertain what to think of him. "Good luck, Vlad," he adds.

As the day goes by, the cabin is filled with the smell of cooking geese along with the tart scent of red cabbage. Anna Lise sets the table while Aunt Astrid makes the dumplings. She opens the oven door, and a cloud of heated mist surges out, filled with the smells of the geese and stuffing. "The geese are ready to carve, Alik," she says, pulling out the roasted birds and placing them on the counter.

"Franz, it's time you learn how to carve," Uncle Alik says. "You take this bird while I carve the other. Follow what I do."

"Yes, *Vati*," Franz replies, excited to be trusted with carving a goose.

I hear the creak of an approaching vehicle. "It must be Vlad," I say, but uncertainty makes me grab my sabre. Putting on my coat, I walk outside and see that it is Vlad riding a sledge toward the barn. I join him. "Vlad, this looks like the perfect sledge. Room for a driver and two passengers, with the harnessing to be a troika if we want to travel quickly. Did it take much of our remaining funds?"

"Nearly half, but we should have enough to get to Colmar." Vlad smiles, pleased with his bargaining.

"Let's hope so. If Prussia joins the Russians in the war against us, it will be hard to cross the border."

"Yes, it could be difficult. We need to leave as soon as you return from the Charité."

"Come Vlad, it's time for the feast. We can worry later about tomorrow."

Back in the cabin, we find a sumptuous spread of food on the table, a carved goose at each end with large bowls of red cabbage and dumplings, and a huge platter holding the stuffing from the geese, rich with apples, dates, chestnuts, onions, and prunes.

"Please, everyone, sit," Uncle Alik says. Vlad looks toward me, his eyes questioning whether he should join us at the table. Uncle Alik catches the look. "Vlad, sit here by me."

Vlad smiles widely. "Thank you, sir," he says, bowing. "Everything looks delicious."

We sit and take one another's hands. Uncle Alik bows his head. "Thank you, Lord, for this feast, but even more for the coming of Anna Lise, Jean-Luc, and Vlad to join in this celebration." He looks up and gazes into each of our faces with a tinge of sadness. Lowering his head even farther, he adds, "Lord, wrap to your bosom the souls of my dear brother Martin, his loving wife Willa, and their only son Adrien ... their lives cut short by useless warfare."

Fifty-Three

Berlin – January 1813

The dim light of predawn filters through the window. Anna Lise is nestled into my shoulder, her eyes still closed, with a small smile blessing her lips. I kiss her forehead, and she opens her eyes. "It's time," I say.

"Must you go? As Uncle Alik says, it may not be necessary anymore."

"We don't know that for sure, and I have my orders. Remember, once I'm done with the Charité, we can begin a new life."

"Yes," she replies, smiling broadly. "We will be free."

I start to put on my uniform. "Please, Jean-Luc, wear my uncle's clothes," Anna Lise says. "Your uniform will draw too much attention. The Prussians may arrest you."

I touch Uncle Alik's clothes. "You must know, my love, if I'm caught wearing these, I could be shot as a spy."

"Which offers the greater danger?" Anna Lise asks.

I weigh my two options. Wearing the uniform nearly guarantees my arrest, while the risk is low if I look like a civilian. I put my uniform aside and begin dressing in Uncle Alik's garments.

Anna Lise comes over to help. "I know you will return. Home is so close now."

Uncle Alik is stirring the fire as we come to the table. He glances at my attire. "Good, you are not wearing your uniform. Remember, you need to ride my horse as well. Yours looks like a cavalry horse."

Vlad stands next to me. "Sir, I'm coming with you. I'll ride behind, keeping you in sight, and will be able to help if you're stopped."

I hesitate, not wanting to endanger Vlad.

Anna Lise steps forward and grasps my forearm. "You must have him go with you."

I look into her pleading eyes, then turn to Vlad. "All right, Vlad. You can trail behind me, but don't get too close."

"Jean-Luc, here is some food," Aunt Astrid says as she hands me a satchel. "Vlad, I'll put together a satchel of food for you as well."

I gaze at Anna Lise, the mother of my unborn child. "It's only about seven leagues to Berlin. I hope to be back by dark or soon after. Ready, Vlad?"

"Yes, sir."

"Wait until I'm nearly out of sight, then come."

"Very good, sir."

"Until tonight," I say as I give Anna Lise another kiss and mount my horse. I give a last wave, then kick the horse into a gallop. I reach the forest's edge and look back. The sun shines down, illuminating them all.

My heart pounds as I enter the forest. *I must do this. I owe this last obligation to Uncle Jean.* A cold gust of wind pushes me along, sending a chill down my spine.

I have only gone about a league, just to the junction of the road to Berlin, when ten Prussian soldiers charge out of the trees, surrounding me immediately. Even if I could get to my sabre, I would have no chance against so many. My heart sinks.

A lieutenant addresses me in French. "This man," pointing to a civilian among them, "says you are a French soldier."

I look over and see Herr Münster grinning at me.

"He says you were keeping his neighbor's family captive. Is this true?"

I look back down the road and catch sight of Vlad disappearing into the forest. I must do nothing to endanger Anna Lise and her family. "Yes, they were my captives," I reply.

"Search him," the lieutenant says.

His soldiers pull me from the horse and rifle through my pockets and gear. They find my sabre as well as my sealed orders from Uncle Jean and hand them to the lieutenant.

Opening them, he says, "You are going to the Charité? What, as a spy? Tie his hands and put him back on his horse."

He tips his shako to Herr Münster. *"Danke, mein Herr."*

"I'm no spy, sir. I'm Captain Calliet, assigned to General Rapp."

"Then why the civilian clothes, Captain?" the lieutenant snaps.

"I thought I would be stopped and arrested if I wore my uniform into Berlin."

"You'd rather be shot as a spy? That is your fate now."

"Zurück nach Berlin!" the lieutenant orders, and we begin to gallop toward the Prussian capital.

* * *

I'm taken to a jail not far from the Charité and roughly shoved into the office of the jail's commandant. With my hands tied behind my back, I'm unable to keep my balance and slam face first onto the floor. 'Stand to attention!" the lieutenant who captured me shouts, giving me a sharp kick to my side.

'Sir, we caught this French captain dressed as a civilian," the lieutenant says. 'He was carrying these orders."

I struggle to my feet and come to attention as the lieutenant hands over my orders. The commandant reads the paperwork, then eyes me closely. 'Are these a French ruse to gather information on activity in Berlin? Why would you be sent to the Charité by this General Rapp?"

'Sir, we have thousands of sick and wounded needing treatment. The general wants the Charité to be prepared to handle them."

'Why send you?"

'I was the Charité administrator after the Prussian War."

'Maybe yes, or maybe you are a spy who should be shot. I'll forward these orders to Colonel Reiseweber, the current administrator, and see what he says."

The commandant examines the orders further. 'These also say you are to be discharged from the army after delivering the orders. Too bad ... unless Colonel Reiseweber comes to your aid, you will be shot. Take him away."

The lieutenant leads me to a cell. It's cold and damp, and the winter wind is heaving through the barred, open window. The stench of human waste nearly overwhelms me. He unties my hands and shoves me in. 'Enjoy your last few days of living, Frenchie. The firing squad is not a bad way to die. Better than camp fever."

I rub my wrists, trying to regain the circulation from the tight ropes. A small cot with a blanket sits in one corner of the cell. In the opposite corner is another cot, occupied by someone clutching tightly to the blanket enveloping him. The man coughs, then turns his weathered face toward me. 'Are you here to be shot in the morning too?" he rasps.

I shake my head. "Perhaps in a few days. Why are you to be shot?"

The man shifts into a sitting position, the blanket wrapped around his head and body. His face is emaciated. I can't tell if he's twenty or fifty. "I am Sergeant Russo and was in the army of the king of Naples. When he deserted us in Russia to go home to Naples, I decided to desert as well."

The man hacks many more times, finding it difficult to catch his breath. "My uniform was in tatters, and I wrapped my feet with rags. I still had a little loot and bought clothes and boots from a Prussian farmer. He turned me in to the Prussian army. Said I was a spy."

He coughs again, and I see it wracks his body. "Being shot may be better than this." He turns away, leaving me to my thoughts.

My mouth tastes like soured milk. I climb onto my cot, thankful I still have my greatcoat, and wrap my blanket over my head and around my shoulders. The day comes to an end as blackness fills my cell. There are a number of short squeaks and rustling sounds, and I pull the blankets more tightly around me. I curse Herr Münster but am thankful he believed I was holding the family captive.

Reaching into the bottoms of my greatcoat pockets, I'm strangely comforted to feel the small bags of dirt I have from Adrien's and Major Bouchet's grave sites. *My old friends. Will I be joining you soon?*

* * *

The shuffling of boots awakens me. A guard opens my cell door and carelessly puts a bowl of food on the floor, spilling out much of it. He looks at me. "Your gruel." Then he looks at where my cellmate lies. "You! Russo! Get up, it's time for your execution."

Russo doesn't move, and the jailer comes over and kicks out the legs of the cot, tumbling Russo to the floor. He lies there, not moving, his face frozen with his mouth open, seemingly crying out for someone in his last moments of life.

"The rotter," the guard says. He turns and leaves me alone with Sergeant Russo. I go and cover his head with a blanket. *Instead of a musket ball, will this be my fate?*

Days pass before Sergeant Russo's body is finally dragged away. I get only one bowl of thin gruel each morning and begin to struggle with my efforts to stay fit by pacing.

I find it difficult to focus. My mind wanders, but always comes back to Anna Lise. Did Vlad see me being arrested and tell the others? Has he come to Berlin trying to learn my fate? Do they think I'm dead and are already on their way to Colmar?

I pray that is the case. Anna Lise will be better off if she forgets me and somehow reaches Colmar. I spend hours in the dank cell thinking of this and daydreaming of Anna Lise playing with our daughter in the sunlight by the river. The thought warms me.

Almost two weeks pass before I'm summoned into the commandant's office.

"Sit down, Captain Calliet," the commandant says.

"I prefer to stand if it is allowed."

"Very well, it makes no difference. I'm sure you have not heard, but we have a cease-fire with the Russians and are in talks with the British, Russians, Swedes, and Austrians about defeating your emperor once and for all. His voice softens. "You survived the Russian invasion?"

"Yes, sir, I did. I was to deliver my orders from General Rapp to the Charité, then be discharged from the army."

He examines me. "You were at the Berezina crossing?"

"Yes, sir."

'Most unfortunate to survive the Berezina and now die in Berlin. I sent the orders we found on you to the Charité administrator, but have heard nothing. I must assume they mean little to him."

The commandant gets up and paces around the room. 'I have no choice but to sentence you to be executed as a spy. You and some other spies will be taken to the jail courtyard and shot tomorrow at sunrise."

Though shaken by this pronouncement, I stand perfectly still, staring straight ahead. 'May I send a note to my family in Colmar?"

'No. We offer no quarter to spies," he says, averting his eyes. 'I'll send one more message to the Charité, but if I were you, I'd make peace with God. Dismissed!"

I'm returned to my cell, overcome with anguish, knowing I will never see Anna Lise again, never rest my eyes on my daughter. I pace my cell throughout the night, going over my life, remembering my regrets as well as my joys. Will my greatest regret be following Uncle Jean's final order? *Adrien, Major Bouchet, it appears that I will indeed be joining you.*

It is nearly dawn when the jailer comes for me. I'm taken to the courtyard.

'Stand against that wall, next to the others," the jailer orders.

I go to the wall and press my back against its cold stones. Some of the others with me along the wall plead for mercy, falling to their knees. Prussian soldiers roughly pull them up and shove them back against the stones. A mere fifteen feet away from us is a squad of soldiers with muskets, standing at attention. All is lost. This is what Miguel and the padre felt in Madrid those many years ago. Staring at the soldiers in front of me, I don't see them. I see the people of Madrid.

The commandant enters the courtyard, taking a position near his line of executioners. "Your sentences will be carried out as the sunlight breaks over that far wall," he says.

My eyes become fixed on the wall, and I estimate the sun will crest it in about three minutes. The commandant raises his arm. The soldiers bring their muskets up and point them toward us. I wait for the first ray of the sun to slice across me.

Anna Lise, I love you.

Fifty-Four

Return to Colmar – January to February 1813

There's a commotion by the door leading into the courtyard. 'Let me in! I demand to be let in," a voice bellows.

A man in full uniform shoves his way into the courtyard. 'Stop the execution," he demands. 'I'm Colonel Reiseweber, administrator of the Charité."

The commandant stares at the man for a moment before recognizing him. 'Stand down," he orders.

My mind is in a fog. Did I actually hear, *Stop the execution?*

The soldier aiming at me lowers his musket. In relief, he puts a trembling hand over his mouth.

'Is one of these men Captain Calliet?"

'Yes, the one at the end. Calliet, come here."

I'm too stunned to move. I gaze toward where the voices are coming from, bringing the speakers into focus.

'Calliet!" the commandant shouts.

"Yes, sir," I say. I stagger my way up to the two men, my knees shaking uncontrollably. The colonel examines my face closely. "When you were a lieutenant, were you the administrator of the Charité?"

I look at the colonel, but don't recognize him. "Yes, sir, in 1806," I reply, my voice sounding distant to me.

"Well." He throws his hands up. "Thank God I finally saw your orders this morning. Commandant, this man and Baron Larrey saved hundreds of lives, including mine, at the Charité after our war with the French. Release him to my custody."

"Yes, sir, as you please."

"What of these others?" I ask, my senses returning to me. "Do they need to die?"

The colonel looks down the line of the frightened men. "Commandant, the sun has already risen. Their appointed time to die has passed. Commute their death sentences and send them to prison."

"Yes, sir," the commandant replies.

Many of the men along the wall fall to their knees, sobbing. Others stand, but wobble in disbelief.

"Come with me, Calliet," Colonel Reiseweber says.

"Yes, sir."

I stumble along after him, having difficulty walking.

The colonel stops. "How long since you've had a good meal?"

"I think two weeks."

The colonel shakes his head. "We'll have you cleaned up and get you some food. Private, go to the Charité and find clothes for this man. Also, get us both some potato pancakes, eggs, and sausage and bring it to my office."

I hadn't noticed the private standing near the colonel. "Thank you, sir," I say.

The realization that I am going to live finally sinks in. "Will I be sent to prison, sir?"

"You are not a soldier anymore. The orders from General Rapp said you were to be discharged once his orders were delivered. They were delivered."

My head spins as I gasp for breath. "No longer a soldier? But you are Prussian. How can you discharge me?"

"The orders only said you are considered discharged after delivery. General Rapp has given you the discharge."

We walk to the Charité and enter the colonel's office—my old office. The private is preparing two place settings at a table near a window overlooking a courtyard. "The food will be here soon," he says, "and a bath is being drawn and new clothes laid out in a room down the hall."

"Calliet," the colonel says, "get cleaned up and come back when you're ready. The food can wait."

Still stunned, I nod and am led to an adjoining room. New clothes are laid out on the table. I strip off the ones I'm wearing, which are quickly taken away, and slip into the warm bathwater. It's heaven. I lie in the water, motionless, savoring the heat and steam. An attendant pours water over my head and scrubs my hair.

Refreshed and grateful to be clean, I return to Colonel Reiseweber's office. "Have a seat, Calliet, and eat," the colonel says. "I'm having my assistant, Private Bruno, find you a horse."

My stomach growls at the sight, and with as much decorum as I can manage, I ravenously devour my food. The colonel nibbles on his, pushing his unfinished plates to me.

I finish, feeling guilty. "Sorry, sir, it's been so long since I've had anything but watery gruel. Forgive my manners."

The colonel smiles. "What plans do you have now that you are discharged?"

"I need to find my wife."

"Your wife?"

"Yes, her family had moved from our home city of Colmar to Moscow, and I found her there. She is now at her uncle's farm, not far away."

"You wish to go to Colmar?"

"Yes, most desperately."

"Crossing the border could be quite difficult, especially if a new war breaks out. I will write you and your wife notes of passage under my seal."

"We have her servant, Vlad, with us as well."

"I'll also write him one. What is your wife's name?"

"Anna Lise. Anna Lise Calliet, and her servant is Vlad Steinman."

I stand and walk around the room as the colonel writes our notes of passage. I gaze at the clock, the desk, the courtyard where I spent so many days over six years ago. It seems like it was in a different lifetime.

The colonel drips wax on the documents and presses his signet ring into each.

"There," he says as he hands me the papers. "I know you are anxious to leave. Let's see if Private Bruno has that horse."

We walk outside just as Bruno brings up a horse. "Sir, this one is the best I could find."

The animal is an elegant Arabian, much finer than Uncle Alik's horse.

"Monsieur, be assured we will treat all French soldiers who come here the same way you and Baron Larrey treated our Prussian soldiers. Good luck getting home to Colmar."

I start to shake the colonel's hand, then impulsively embrace him tightly instead. "Thank you, sir! Thank you for my life."

I mount the Arabian and begin winding my way through the streets of Berlin to the road that leads to Anna Lise. If stopped,

I should hope no one would question releases signed by the administrator of the great Charité hospital, but scoundrels are everywhere.

"Move aside," I shout as I try to make my way through the crowds.

Anna Lise must believe I'm dead ... She and Vlad surely must be heading for Colmar. I must get to the Baucks' home.

Leaving the city provides little help speeding up my travel. Snow is falling thickly, making it difficult to see the road. Much snow already covers the lane, but it's becoming deeper and deeper, making it almost impossible for my horse to pass. I keep pushing until I'm near collapse, and so is the horse. We find shelter in the trees on the side of the road, and I scrape away enough snow to expose some grass for him to eat.

With the snow-laden skies, it's difficult to know the time of day. Is it midafternoon, or is the sun about to set? To my dismay, the sky darkens further, making any more travel today impossible. Frustrated, I cut some boughs, retrieve my blanket, and sit on the branches, wrapping the blanket around my greatcoat. All my muscles cry out in pain. They got so little use while I was in the jail cell. I cough and feel light-headed.

I try to rest but can't stop wondering if Vlad came to Berlin to find out my fate. What of Herr Münster? Regardless, I need to get to Uncle Alik's cabin. If Anna Lise is gone, he will know what direction they went.

In the morning, snow is still falling heavily and the wind is howling, creating nearly impassable drifts. This Arabian horse is handsome, but doesn't have the strength of Bayard, and I lead him on foot. Thankfully it's clear, and I know we are still on the road since the forest is heavy on both sides, but our pace is very slow. The wind whips down from the north, directly into my face. I tuck my chin into my coat, blocking the tearing fingers of each gust. We press forward. After several hours, the storm's rage wanes. The clouds break, letting the sun pour across the landscape. No one is in sight, and the snow on the road is pristine. I keep trudging forward.

Finally, we reach the side road to Wildau. Fresh tracks from a sleigh come from the north and turn down the road toward the Baucks' cabin. I mount the Arabian, and we thread our way down the road, following the trail of the sleigh's runner. I haven't eaten since my meal with Colonel Reiseweber and feel woozy. My energy is fully sapped. Only the vision of Anna Lise keeps me moving. I give the Arabian a kick, trying to speed our progress.

Up ahead, like a vision from God, the lowering sun casts waves of shimmering light across a field of snow. "We've made it!" I tell my horse. The curl of smoke rising from a cabin comes into view. With all my remaining strength, I guide the Arabian up the path toward the cabin. I give the horse one last kick. He whinnies in protest, but we near the cabin door.

The door swings open. Is it Anna Lise? I can't see the face as I slide off my horse and fall into the snow. Hands take hold of my arms and legs. "His forehead is hot," a woman's voice says. "Camp fever," a male voice adds. "He must be isolated." I'm taken to somewhere in the cabin and feel my clothes being stripped away. "I don't see any lice," a young woman's voice says, "but we can't take chances. Burn his clothes. I'll cover him with blankets." Something warm slides down my throat and warms my belly. I open my eyes and see Anna Lise giving me spoonfuls of warm soup.

Shivering overtakes me. I occasionally hear distant voices, but don't know what they say as I drift in and out of consciousness.

For what seems a lifetime, my mind wanders in and out of the spirit world. Adrien is there, guiding me.

"Do you remember that guillotine, Jean-Luc, and poor Father Benedict's head rolling into a basket?" Adrien asks. "How about the first enemy you killed in the Austrian war? You tried to save him, but it was no use."

I see that first soldier, then find myself on the Austerlitz battlefield. The charging Mamelukes, then the sight of Madame Kintelberger holding off the Cossacks. *I must try to help her!* But a Cossack lance kills Hervé and another impales my chest.

"You lived, Jean-Luc, then we left for Spain."

"Are there no good memories?" I cry.

Adrien studies me. "Yes, even Spain has good memories. The stilt men were wondrous, and don't forget those two boys we saved from execution near Bailén."

"I remember," I say, but crowding into those memories are the haunting faces of the priest and especially Manuel, their backs against the courtyard wall in Madrid. The shots I fired.

"You killed the padre mercifully, Jean-Luc. Remember that. Then there were all the Prussian soldiers you saved at the Charité."

Adrien leads me through battle after battle, one dead enemy soldier after another, until we reach Borodino. "The end of our time together," Adrien says, "and the end of your time with Major Bouchet. The two of us have kept watch over you and Anna Lise, trying to help you get home to Colmar. You are nearly there!"

Adrien, am I dying? Don't let me die! Anna Lise?

I hear myself crying out Anna Lise's name. I inch myself up onto my elbows to see.

"Jean-Luc, I'm here," Anna Lise cries out as she rushes to my side. She feels my forehead. "Your fever has broken. Thank God!"

The Bauck family stands nearby, expectant and hopeful. "You've been delirious for nearly a week," Uncle Alik says. "We weren't sure you would make it."

Feeling weak, I collapse back onto my bed.

"I'll get you some soup," Aunt Astrid says.

Anna Lise presses a cold, wet towel to my forehead. I smile up at her weakly. "I'll be strong again soon."

* * *

Two days later, I am wel enough to walk around the cabin, though I have a persistent cough.

"You're still too weak to travel, Jean-Luc," Aunt Astrid says.

"I agree," Uncle Alik says. "I've been thinking you should stay until after the baby is born. Franz and I could use the help, and perhaps the talk of war will cool."

"And Herr Münster and others like him? What of them?" I reply. "No, we must leave. War is imminent, and we need to cross into Westphalia while there is time. Then, it's not far to Wiesbaden and the crossing of the Rhine into France. I'm certain the Rhineland Confederation will stay loyal to the emperor."

"Jean-Luc is right," Anna Lise says. "If we use the sledge as a troika, we can travel quickly. We could reach the border with Westphalia in less than a day, the Rhine crossing within three, and then Colmar in just two more days." Her eyes blaze with excitement. "Vlad has much experience driving troikas in Moscow."

Colmar in less than a week! My heart pounds with this realization. I turn to Vlad. "Can Bayard, Basile, and the horse you rode be used to pull a sledge? They aren't trained to do so."

"I believe they can. They'll object at first, but will grow used to the harness after a league or so."

"And you can rest in the sledge, Jean-Luc," Anna Lise adds. "Riding Bayard would sap what little strength has returned to you."

I look around at everyone's faces. Their eyes gleam with excitement, knowing Colmar is within our grasp. "Tomorrow, then. We leave at first light."

* * *

My cough keeps me awake through most of the night, but I give it little thought, thinking it's caused by the excitement of the upcoming trip and my recent illness. Vlad opens the door, and a brisk gush of cold air sweeps in. "The weather is good!" he says. "Sunshine, little wind, and still cold. I'll go and set up the troika."

"I'll come with you. I will need to settle Bayard and Basile down."

"And I will help pack some feed for the horses on the back end of the sledge," Franz adds.

The three of us crunch our way through the snow up to the stable. I find even this short walk tiring, and I cough several times, but the thought of seeing my father, warming myself before the inn's fireplace, and having a brandy with him brings a smile to my face.

Vlad harnesses his horse into the central spot, and I move Bayard to the outside left position. Bayard protests having the harness placed over him, but I pat his neck and coo into his ear, settling him down. Basile is a little more difficult, but soon is harnessed into the right-side position.

Franz and I climb into the open cab of the sledge and Vlad onto the driver's bench. He gives the reins a snap, and awkwardly we move down to the cabin. There is much snorting from each horse. When we reach the cabin, I climb out and try to calm them by stroking their necks.

Anna Lise fills the cab with supplies and a number of blankets. "Can I get to my journal and a pen easily?" I ask. "I need to catch up with my writing."

"Yes, it's in your saddlebag at the top of our supplies," she says. "You can write tonight once we cross the Elbe River into Westphalia."

We all exchange warm embraces with the Bauck family and are soon on our way. Exhilaration overwhelms me as I pull Anna

Lise close and wrap the blankets tightly around us. If I limit how much I move, my cough subsides.

It doesn't take Vlad long to get the three horses to act as a team. We slide quickly through Berlin and race down the wide road at full trot toward Magdeburg and the bridge over the Elbe River.

Nearing the bridge, we come to a backup of soldiers and people trying to cross into Westphalia. In front of us is a squadron of Westphalian cavalry. Their uniforms are tattered and their horses downtrodden, but their spirits are high.

"Do you come from the emperor's retreat?" I ask.

"Yes, we've been discharged and are trying to get home," their captain tells me. "The damn Prussians want to fight the emperor and don't trust us. They are checking everyone's paperwork carefully before allowing them to cross."

The captain eyes us. "You are French. They will give you even more trouble. Do you have papers?"

"Yes. I am Captain Calliet. I was part of General Rapp's regiment and got my discharge in Berlin. We have papers from the Prussian Charité administrator."

"Ah, General Rapp. A most brave commander, loved by all. Stay with us until we cross."

We reach the bridge, and the Westphalians are questioned by Prussian soldiers. There are maybe forty of them guarding the bridge's entrance.

"Your papers are good. Move on," a Prussian lieutenant tells the Westphalians.

"We will wait for our friends," the Westphalian captain says.

"Suit yourself." He turns to me. "Your papers?"

I hand him all of our papers. He inspects them closely. "You are a French captain?"

"I was, but I received my discharge. You can see the signature and seal of Colonel Reiseweber, administrator of the Charité."

The Prussian continues to stare at our papers and then goes to confer with another Prussian officer.

"We need more time to examine these," the Prussian says on returning to us. "Move your sledge to the side and let those behind you pass."

"Is there a problem?" the Westphalian captain asks.

"That's none of your concern, Captain. Move on."

"We will move with our friends," the Westphalian captain replies. Then, without further word, all of his squadron draw their sabres.

The Prussian lieutenant and Westphalian captain coldly stare at each other. Horses snort in the cold, crisp air. The Prussians soldiers unshoulder their muskets, looking to their lieutenant to see what he orders. Moments pass. The Prussian lieutenant glances around, appraising the situation, and curses quietly. He hands me back our papers. "Very well. You are free to cross."

We traverse the Elbe, another step closer to home. "Thank you, Captain, and all your men," I say to the Westphalians. "We will always be comrades and are deeply grateful."

"We wish you the best in your journey," the captain replies. "Your emperor has been kind to the Rhine states, and we won't forget."

It's been enough for the day. We stay at an inn not far from the Elbe. "Anna Lise, can you get me my journal and a pen?" I ask. "I have much to write."

* * *

For the next two days, our troika flies down the road toward the Rhine crossing. We pass into the Rhine state of Nassau without issue, approaching the City of Wiesbaden and their bridge over the Rhine. The city comes into view, along with the far banks of the river. France!

"Jean-Luc! Home is so close," Anna Lise cries as she holds me tightly. "France is right there!"

I, too, am overwhelmed, but I'm having trouble stopping my cough and my fever is back.

"We must hurry, my love. I fear my fever has returned."

She presses her hand to my forehead. "It's hot," she says. "We will push hard to reach Colmar." Her voice is edged with worry. "Vlad, Jean-Luc's fever is returning. We need all the speed you can muster."

We cross the Rhine into the city of Mainz. "We are in France, Jean-Luc," Anna Lise says, holding me tight. "See to the south? The Vosges Mountains. Your father's inn is only a day or two away."

The Vosges! So many memories. Adrien and I crossed them near Ostheim in our first campaign. I lean back into the sledge, feeling flushed, and close my eyes to rest. *Adrien, we are nearly home again.*

Fifty-Five

Home – Summer, 1829

I wait nervously as my tutor reads the final section of the story I've taken from my father's journal.

"This is good, Adrianna," she says, looking up from her reading. She taps her finger on a page. "But I would reword this part here to show action. Just telling about the event is not as exciting." She smiles. "An easy fix."

"I wish Papa were alive to read it. Mama helped me understand many of his notes, but she was so young herself when he wrote much of it. I fear I may not have gotten all of it right."

"You've done well, my dear. This rendition is a remarkable achievement. Jean-Luc would be proud of how well it's written and the years of commitment it took to finish. What you and your father have done is put some humanity into those awful, devastating years."

"I'll make the changes you've suggested, then give it to Mama for her birthday tomorrow."

"It will bring tears to Anna Lise's eyes. Does she know you're so close to finishing?"

"No. We are riding up to Papa's grave. I will give it to her there. To think she was just seventeen when she married Papa in Moscow, almost the same age as I am now." I laugh. "But I'm nowhere near ready to be married."

"What about that man who has a vineyard in Riquewihr, Yves Coulane?" my tutor asks, smiling. "He seems to come by often, and his visits have gotten more frequent."

"Yves? No, not Yves. He's been coming to visit since Papa was alive. You remember reading about his older brother, Corporal Coulane, a very dear friend of father's. He died trying to save Mama and my grandparents. He checks up on Mama, not me."

My tutor smiles, a twinkle in her eyes. "Don't be so sure."

"Adrianna," I hear my mother call. "Vlad needs help at the inn. Several people are arriving, and he will need assistance with their luggage."

My tutor comes and kisses my forehead. "Congratulations, my dear. I'll go with you to help Vlad as well."

* * *

"Adrianna," Mama says the next morning, "go saddle Hervé and Biyou while I finish packing us some food and wine. Be sure and take extra blankets with our sleeping rolls. It will get cold in the mountains tonight."

I go to the stables, and both horses nod their heads at me in greeting. "Good morning Hervé, Biyou," I say as I take them out of the stable. "We'll be riding near Ostheim today, where your papa's pasture is."

Hervé snorts, sounding like he doesn't care. I pat his neck. "Well, you may not be excited to see Bayard, but I am. He must be close to thirty years old by now." Giving him a firm look, I add, "You should hope to live that long, especially considering everything Bayard went through with Papa."

Biyou nickers, much more excited about a ride than Hervé.

"I'm glad at least one of you want to see your papa today," I tease, rubbing down both their necks and saddling them up.

Mama and Vlad come from the inn carrying saddlebags of food and drink. "Happy birthday, Mama," I say.

"Thank you, my love. A beautiful day for visiting your papa."

She and Vlad load the supplies. Mama looks lovely with her long blonde hair arranged into a French braid, topped with a colorful sun bonnet.

A soft, warm breeze caresses my cheeks under a cloudless, deep blue sky. The Vosges Mountains tower high to our north, their tallest peaks still crowned with snow.

As we make our way toward Ostheim, we cross the bridge where my father and uncle often fished when they were children. I smile, remembering the story of how the two of them hid in the bushes when the guillotine wagon passed. Mama sees my look and smiles as well. She's probably remembering that this is also the spot where Papa took her fishing just before she left for Moscow. "Did you bring your writings from your papa's journal?"

"Yes, and you will be proud to know I finished the last section yesterday. I can't believe I'm finally finished after working on it for over three years."

Mama smiles and touches my arm gently. "Oh, my dear. I can hardly wait to read it."

We ride toward the mountains, coming into the west pasture. "Is that Bayard up there?" I ask, pointing to an imposing stallion coming into view.

"Yes, that's him," my mother says fondly.

Bayard nods and nickers as we approach him. Still looking fit, he comes up and nudges Mama, giving a snort of recognition. She pats his flanks. "Hello, old friend, it's good to see you. Adrianna and I are going to visit Jean-Luc up on the overlook."

"I miss Basile," Adrianna says. "It was very sad when he died last winter, but he had a full life."

We bid Bayard farewell and begin winding our way up the narrow, tree-lined trail. We scare up some rodents that catch the attention of an eagle looking for an easy meal. He soars over us as we make our way along. "It seems like every time we come here, an eagle appears," Mama says. "Even the first time your papa brought me here."

The horses clamber up the last portion of the steep trail, finally arriving at the top. A panoramic view of the Rhine Valley presents itself in all its grandeur. Near the large boulder at the crest of the hill are three long, mounded sets of rocks. We dismount, and Mama walks over to them. "Hello, Jean-Luc. I see that you and Adrien and Major Bouchet have given us a beautiful day."

She sits quietly near Papa's grave and the two memorials to Adrien and Major Bouchet, each holding the dirt Papa gathered from their graves at Borodino. I walk around the meadow collecting wildflowers and quickly have a large bouquet. "Mama, is the vase still here from our last visit?"

"Yes, it has toppled down off the rocks." She gets up and cleans off the vase with the hem of her skirt. "I'll get some water."

I sit with Mama as she arranges the flowers, careful to ensure that each is placed perfectly. "Jean-Luc," she says. "Adrianna has finished her rendition of your journal. I haven't read the last section yet; we can read it together tonight before the sun fades. First, we'll finish setting up our camp and we'll eat. Then we will read." Mama gazes around. Softly, she adds, "Such a beautiful place, Jean-Luc. Someday, I'll join you here for eternity."

* * *

Another hour or two remain before sunset. There's already a slight chill in the air, and Mama and I huddle next to each other. Hervé and Biyou graze on the sweet, early summer grass nearby. I take my whole document from my satchel. It's several hundred pages, and I've a marker inserted where the last section begins. I take out the last section and solemnly hand it to her. "Here, Mama. Happy birthday."

She smiles and takes this section like a precious gift. She sips her wine and reads silently. I watch her reactions, nervously drinking my own wine. She slowly turns the pages, smiling at some passages and anguishing over others. She reaches the last page, then looks up to me with tears in her eyes. "This is magnificent, my sweet. Please, read it to your father."

She hands me the stack of pages. I glance from her to Papa's grave, then begin reading his words.

I open my eyes, and my surroundings seem familiar. I'm home! I'm in my own room at my father's inn. I'm alive! A flush of joy comes over me, then panic. "Anna Lise," I cry out. "Where are you?" Then I see her sitting next to me. Watching over me.

"I'm here, my love." She puts her hand to my forehead. "It feels cool. The fever is gone." Relief washes over her face. She lies down beside me, wrapping me in her arms. Never have I felt such comfort. We lie together for a long time, wordlessly grateful to be together.

Finally, I try to get up, but fall back into my bed. Anna Lise rises, smoothing back my hair. "Rest, my love," she says. "Camp fever makes your joints ache and your muscles weak. It will take a long time to recover." She gazes back down to me. "Thank God you are alive! I must go tell your father now."

She starts to leave, but I touch her arm. "Are we really here? In Colmar?"

Anna Lise smiles. "Yes, we made it home. We are actually here."

She opens the door and calls out. "Monsieur Calliet, Jean-Luc is awake."

My father hobbles into the room, looking much older than I remember. Seeing me awake sends tears down his face. I manage to get to my feet, and we embrace for a long moment. Being in Colmar, seeing Anna Lise and Papa, seems surreal. My relief is overwhelming.

"The last thought I remember in the sledge was of having a cognac with you by the fire in our drawing room. Perhaps we can go and do that?"

"I'll get Vlad to help you, Jean-Luc," Anna Lise says. With Vlad's help, we get to the drawing room, where we're greeted with the warmth of a roaring fire.

"I haven't had any cognac in years, only cheap brandy," Papa says. "But I know I have hidden a bottle somewhere in the cupboard." He rummages around. "Yes, here it is, and it's a good vintage." He pours us each a glass, then stands near the fire. His voice breaks as he declares, "To the safe return of my son, his wife Anna Lise, and my new friend, Vlad. Santé!"

* * *

Winter finally fades, and the sweet smell of spring fills my lungs. I still have soreness in my joints and am continually fatigued. "It will get better, Jean-Luc," Anna Lise assures me each day. I spend much of my time keeping the records for the inn. Vlad helps my father with the inn's upkeep and taking care of the guests. I'm happy to find Mademoiselle LeClair still in charge of the inn's kitchen.

I smile watching Anna Lise. She has become beautifully pregnant. But as I watch, she suddenly bends over, crying out a little. Straightening, she is pale, but her voice is strong. "Jean-Luc, get the midwife." Again, holding her stomach. "Adrianna wants to be born!"

I race to the kitchen. "Mademoiselle LeClair, Anna Lise is ready! Help her while I fetch the midwife."

I run as fast as I can to summon the midwife. It's still Mademoiselle Bosch, the same one who delivered Anna Lise.

"The baby is coming," I gasp. Mademoiselle Bosch grabs her birthing stool and rushes to the inn. I'm out of breath and must pause for several minutes before returning.

Coming back to the inn's drawing room, I find Vlad and my father. They look as nervous as I feel. "Any word?" I ask.

"None yet," Papa says. We pace, then sit, then pace again, sometimes running into each other.

Four hours pass. I look at Papa. "Do you think everything is all right? It's been so long."

He smiles. "You took nearly ten hours to be born. I'm sure everything is fine."

Finally, the squall of a newborn baby fills the room. Papa and Vlad and I pump exultant handshakes. "She's here! She's finally here!" The hours of waiting slip away from my memory.

The bedroom door opens, and a beaming Mademoiselle Bosch bustles out, wiping her hands. "A girl," she proclaims loudly.

I go to Anna Lise, who is exhausted but beaming and holding a tiny blonde-haired infant. "Adrianna, here is your papa, Jean-Luc." I bend down and kiss Anna Lise on her forehead. Anna Lise extends the baby toward me. "Take her, Jean-Luc. Didn't I always say our baby would be a girl?"

* * *

It's now over three years since my return to Colmar. The emperor was beaten at Waterloo and is in exile, and the monarchy is restored. Like in the days of the Jacobins, who came with their traveling guillotine and sought revolutionary purity from everyone, we now have bands of royalists going village to village seeking revenge against Bonapartists.

Though I'm still weak, I go to my neighbors and organize a militia to stand ready should these royalists come to Colmar. We must protect our families and businesses.

A scout I sent to Mulhouse barges through the inn door. "Captain Calliet, the royalists are rioting and looting in Mulhouse, and many buildings are burning. Their leader is telling them it's time to teach the Colmar Bonapartists a lesson as well. They're on their way."

"Let them come," I say as I grab a musket and sabre. "Go, tell the militia to gather in the town square."

Anna Lise grabs my arm. "Jean-Luc, you're too weak to fight."

"I'll fight if I must, my love." I kiss her and rush out, heading for the town square, Vlad by my side.

"It seems there's always an enemy no matter where I am," I say to Vlad.

About two hundred men with weapons gather around me. I climb onto a park bench to address them. Excitement and energy surge through me, just as they did before going into combat in the wars. "Men, we have no fight with royalists unless they threaten us with harm. In Colmar there are those who believe in the monarchy, and many of us who agree with the ideals of the revolution. King Louis has said the new French monarchy won't return to its old ways. He will uphold the rights we won. I will accept that, and I think all of you will as well. The great leader of Colmar, General Rapp, accepts this."

I gaze across the gathered men, each of them listening intently. "Take positions on each side of the Mulhouse road, up and down the square. Let them ride in, then we will surround them."

We take our positions and wait. An hour passes before we see a line of advancing torches moving quickly our way. "Have arms ready!" I command, and our muskets are raised to the firing position. The torch men gallop into town and immediately find themselves surrounded.

I step out onto the road. "Why are you men here?"

Their leader looks around, taking courage from his group of about a hundred men, but is clearly taken aback by our show of force. "We come for the Bonapartists. We've heard Colmar is filled with them."

I look at their leader. "Do you think all of these men surrounding you are Bonapartists? We think of ourselves as Frenchmen, determined to protect what is ours, and are prepared to fight if you so wish."

The royalist leader appraises the situation and confers with his lieutenants, then addresses me. He has found a way out of the situation. "Perhaps we are mistaken. Perhaps the Bonapartists are in Strasbourg."

"I think you will only find Frenchmen there as well, but you're free to go and find out. We'll let them know you are coming. You will also find the road to Paris up in that direction. Taking it may be more to your liking."

I have my men who are blocking the road toward Strasbourg move aside. "Please, have a safe journey and give my regards to the king."

"And who, sir, may you be?"

"I am Jean-Luc Calliet, formerly a captain under General Rapp's command. It is my understanding that the general is currently in Paris to receive a citation from our new king. Please give him my regards should you see him."

The royalist leader looks at me insolently but motions for his men to follow him away from Colmar. After they ride out, cheers erupt from the militia and are taken up by those who'd stayed hidden in their homes.

My rush of energy has sapped me, and I collapse to my knees, dropping my musket and sabre.

"Jean-Luc," Anna Lise cries as she runs to me, quickly helping me up. "Vlad, help me get him inside." Others join to help Anna Lise and Vlad, and I'm soon back in my armchair.

"Congratulations, sir! Well done," they say on their way out.

I smile weakly. "Thank you."

"Here is some soup, Jean-Luc," Anna Lise says as she gives me several spoonfuls. "You were wonderful, my love."

I gratefully accept the soup, but am troubled by my collapse. "Anna Lise, am I getting worse? I should not have been so affected."

"No, Jean-Luc, you are getting stronger." she says. "The situation was very stressful, and you handled it splendidly. Give it time. You'll get even stronger."

"But it's been three years!"

"And during the first two years you could hardly cross a room. You are improving!"

* * *

I spend my days helping run the inn and taking pleasure playing with Adrianna, who is nearly three now. She has so many questions and is constantly on the move.

"My sweet, would you like to visit the horses?" I ask her. "I'll introduce you to one of my dearest friends."

"Yes, Papa. Who?"

"Come, I'll show you." I lift her into my arms and take her to our stable to meet Bayard.

"So big, Papa," she says, leaning back into me and clutching my neck, her eyes round with wonder. She ventures to put out her hand and pat his nose. Bayard nickers from the attention, and soon the two are best friends.

* * *

I've neglected writing in my journal for several years, content to be with Anna Lise and Adrianna. Adrianna is now eight, and we're returning home from a cool November day of fishing to find Anna Lise waiting for us, her face telling me something is wrong. With her is Uncle Jean's father. I hand Adrianna our fish. "Go to the kitchen and clean these, my sweet. Tell Mademoiselle LeClair we can eat them for dinner. I'm going to talk to Mama."

Adrianna dashes away, and I turn to Anna Lise, waiting for the news.

"Jean-Luc, Uncle Jean is dead."

I'm stunned. Uncle Jean was such a constant in my life.

We go into the inn's lobby and find a frail Monsieur Rapp holding a note, which I'm sure tells of his son's death.

"I am so sorry, Monsieur Rapp. When, where did he die?" I choke on my words.

"Yesterday, from stomach cancer—not far away, across the Rhine at his estate," Uncle Jean's father says. "He left his will with me. Come and sit. You and your family are mentioned in it."

How can he be dead? My mind races through the many years I have known and fought next to him.

"He is to be buried here in Colmar and his heart taken and enshrined in Saint Mathew's Church," Uncle Jean's father says. "He wishes for you to bring his body home to Colmar, and he has set aside money to hire a tutor for Adrianna."

Anna Lise is pouring us some water. "A tutor?" she says with surprise.

"Yes. The last time all of you visited him back in April for his birthday, he saw how much Adrianna was drawn to his library."

"I remember. His wife took Adrianna and their young son to play, and Adrianna asked if they could go to the library. As we were getting ready to leave, Uncle Jean found Adrianna and his son

sprawled on the floor going through a book filled with illustrations. She was turning the pages and pointing out the pictures to the boy."

Early the next morning, Vlad and I prepare a wagon to leave for the Rapp estate. Adrianna runs up. "May I go with you, Papa?"

"No, my sweet," I reply. "Look at those gray clouds. It looks like it might snow." I hold her tightly, giving her a kiss, and hand her to Anna Lise. "We should be back before dark."

Anna Lise gives me a guarded smile. She worries about me every day. "Be careful, Jean-Luc. Don't let yourself get too tired."

By midday, we reach the Rapp estate and are met by his wife, Albertine. Vlad and I and one of Uncle Jean's servants place the coffin in the wagon bed. Albertine clutches a bronze box. "His heart," she says. "I will bring it with me when we come to Colmar tomorrow."

"There will be rooms at the inn for you and your children to stay."

"That is most kind."

We leave the Rapp estate, heading back to Colmar. A cold wind sweeps down the Rhine, chilling me to the bone. The cold compounds the weariness I have felt all day. Uncle Jean's death has left me deeply sad.

"Here, sir," Vlad says. "Wrap this blanket around you." A light snow swirls in the wind. "Winter comes early. I'll get you home to the warm fire soon."

We reach the inn as darkness sweeps over Colmar. Vlad helps me to the door, where Anna Lise meets us. Her face turns ashen when she sees me. She puts her hand on my forehead. "Jean-Luc, you are warm."

"I'll be fine. I just need to sit by the fire for a moment."

"Papa!" Adrianna says with a pained gaze as I settle into my armchair. She too sees that the trip and the cold have exhausted *me. My face must look drawn and pale. She snuggles up in my lap, holding my neck. Anna Lise brings me coffee.*

"I'll be much better after drinking this," I assure her.

Before long, the fire and the coffee revive me a bit, but Anna Lise sees that I still feel weak. "Let me bring your supper to you here by the fire," she says.

After we eat, Anna Lise checks my forehead again. "It's still warm."

Adrianna climbs into my lap with a book. When I finish and close the cover, Anna Lise says, "It's time for sleep, Adrianna. Give your father a kiss."

I kiss Adrianna goodnight and move to my writing desk. "Anna Lise, would you bring me my journal? I want to write about Uncle Jean."

"Yes, but don't take too long. I don't want that fever getting worse."

"I only need to write a few pages. It won't take much time."

She hands me my journal and settles into her armchair.

I'm finishing the entry when my heart seizes in pain. Bending over and clutching my chest, I knock over my inkwell.

"Anna Lise!"

I close the journal and look over at Mama.

"That was wonderful, my sweet. I'm glad you finished his story where he could not." Her eyes are red, and she brushes away a few tears with the cuff of her shirt. "When we get home, I want you to add more to this section, about how you wrote this rendition and about our trip today."

Mama bends her head forward and unlatches her necklace from around her neck. She cups it in the palm of her hand and then, with reverence, hands it to me. The small gold cross twinkles in the remaining sunlight as I hold it up. "Mama, you can't give this to me. It's the first thing Papa gave you, and you've worn it all these years."

"It was his mother's, and it's time to pass it to you. Here, let me help." Gently, she wraps it around my neck, fastening it in place. She holds me at arm's length. "It's beautiful, don't you think, Jean-Luc?" she says, glancing toward Papa's grave. She hugs me tightly. "Now, my love, with the remaining light, I'd like you to read Papa's journal from the beginning, just a few pages. When I hear the story you've created from your father's journal, I feel the wind of his soul embracing me. We are children again in Colmar with Adrien. We find each other in Moscow. We make our way home."

My eyes well.

"Yes Mama." I turn to the first section, and begin reciting.

A hard tug on my fishing pole jolts me from my slumber. Another tug. "Adrien, wake up," I whisper as I tense, waiting to jerk the pole with the next tug. But there's no need, as the pole nearly flies from my hands. I give Adrien a kick and ...

About the Author

A. G. (Gary) Cullen was born in St. Louis, Missouri. Moving frequently as a child, he grew up in Alexandria, Virginia, Billings, Montana, Portland, Oregon, and finally graduated from high school in Waldport, Oregon (where his family moved after his father retired). He began college at Oregon State University, but his education was interrupted by a two-year stint in the US Navy on a refueling ship off the coast of Vietnam. His experience in the navy gave him a strong appreciation for education and shortly after his discharge, he received his bachelor's degree from the University of Oregon and his master's degree from the University of Missouri-Columbia.

His entire professional career has been in the promotion of energy conservation, helping utilities and government organizations design programs for their customers. While raising his two children with his wife, Kathleen, he gained an appreciation and love for soccer, coaching youth teams for nearly two decades.

He has always loved history and particularly enjoys reading and writing historical fiction. He currently lives in both Vancouver, Washington and Waldport, Oregon.

Bibliography

Image 1: Europe 1812- Napoleon's Power. Public domain.

Image 2: Alsace region map. Public domain.

Image 3: Battle of Austerlitz, Situation at 1800, 1 December 1805; Source:http://www.dean.usma.edu/history/ The Department of History, United States Military Academy]. Public domain.

Image 4: Map of Prussia. Public domain.

Image 5: Entry of Napoleon I into Berlin, 27th October 1806 Source: Painting by Charles Meynier. Museum of the History of France. Public domain.

Image 6: Treaty of Tilsit. Source: Painting by Adolphe Roehn. Museum of the History of France. Public domain.

Image 7: Soldaten bei einer jungen Markthändlerin auf der Rast. Öl auf Leinwand. Source: Painting by Andrien Moreau. https://www.hampel-auctions.com/. Public domain.

Image 8: Notre Dame of Paris Source: Armand Guillaumin. Museu Nacional de Belas Artes. Public domain.

Image 9: Alamy liscensing purchased July 2021. Image ID: F1KY8A

Image 10: The Third of May Source: Painting by Francisco Goya. Museo del Prado, Madrid. Public domain.

Image 11: Map of Andalusia. Public domain.

Image 12: The Surrender of Bailén. Source: Painting by José Casado Del Alisal. Museo del Prado, Madrid. Public domain.

Image 13: March to Moscow drawn by LJMBastida. All permissions given.

Image 14: Napoleon 1812 Russian campaign drawn by Charles Minard- modified by Lopez. Licensed under the Creative Commons Attribution-Share Alike 4.0 International.

Image 15: Battle of Smolensk on 18 August 1812. Source: Painting by Albrecht Adam. http://album.foto.ru/photo/197510/ Public domain.

Image 16: Map of Borodino, from book *War and Peace* by Leo Tolstoy, on page 698 in the translation by Louise and Aylmer Maude. Public domain.

Image 17: Map of Moscow from book *War and Peace* by Leo Tolstoy, on page 698 in the translation by Louise and Aylmer Maude. Public domain.

Image 18: Fire of Moscow in 15-18 September, 1812, after Napoleon takes the city Source: Painting by Aleksêi Smirnov. Public domain.

Image 19: The Crossing of the River Berizina - 1812. Source: Painting by Lawrence Alma-Tadema. Amsterdam Museum. Public domain.

Image 20: Napoléon traversant la Bérézina. Source: Painting by January Suchodolski. National Museum in Poznan. http://www.napoleon-empire.net/tableaux/berezina.php Public domain.

Cover image: Berezina Crossing Source: unknown artist. Alamy liscensing purchased July 2021.

HOME (773) 685-4400

Privately owned and operated
Kenneth C. Halter, Director
www.tohlefuneralhome.com

it : $250 - $500 Discount on pre-arranged services.